To
Jordan Ayley

My young friend, former student, and fellow teacher, with the hope that you will enjoy this book on the Canadian Army, one of the best in the world, and one in which you so ably served.

I can only wish you the very best in all your future endeavors, and look forward in having a long and successful friendship with you.

Affectionately!

The Long War

By
Paul Desautels

1663 LIBERTY DRIVE, SUITE 200
BLOOMINGTON, INDIANA 47403
(800) 839-8640
WWW.AUTHORHOUSE.COM

© 2006 Paul Desautels. All rights reserved.

No part of this book may be reproduced, stored in a retrieval system, or transmitted by any means without the written permission of the author.

First published by AuthorHouse 4/10/2006

ISBN: 1-4208-6251-0 (e)
ISBN: 1-4208-4092-4 (dj)
ISBN: 1-4208-4093-2 (sc)

Library of Congress Control Number: 2005902545

Printed in the United States of America
Bloomington, Indiana

This book is printed on acid-free paper.

To My Country

NOTE

This is a work of fiction. While it is true that no single Regiment could have been involved in all the actions described in this book, and while certain facts, processes and events have been altered to fit the story line, this, in no way, lessens the truth, validity and integrity of those events.

ACKNOWLEDGMENT

This is an historical novel dealing with a war that occurred more than 60 years ago. As a result, the following works have been consulted in order to ensure the accuracy and authenticity of the actions shown: Enzo Angelucci and Paolo Matricardi, *World War Two Airplanes*, New York, Rand McNally and Company, 1978; Ron Baybutt, Colditz, Boston, Little Brown and Company, 1982; Ken Bell, *Not In Vain*, Toronto, University of Toronto Press, 1973; Pierre Berton, *The Great Depression*, Toronto, Mclelland and Stewart Inc., 1990; Daniel G. Dancocks, *The D-Day Dodgers*, Toronto, Mclelland and Stewart Inc., 1991; Norman Davies, A *History of Poland*, Oxford, Oxford University Press, 1981; Jacques Delarue, *The Gestapo*, New York, Dell Publishing Co., Inc., 1964; Hans Dollinger, *The Decline and Fall of Nazi Germany and Imperial Japan*, New York, Gramercy Books, 1995; Dwight D. Eisenhower, *Crusade in Europe*, New York, Doubleday, 1948; Norman Gelb, *Desperate Venture*, New York, William Morrow, Inc., 1992; Dominick Graham, *The Price of Command*, Toronto, Stoddart Publishing Co., Limited, 1993; J. L. Granatstein, *The Generals*, Toronto, Stoddart Publishing Co. Limited, 1993; *The Hachette Guide to France*, New York, Pantheon Books, 1985; Terence Macartney-Filgate and William Whitehead, *Dieppe 1942*, Toronto, Personal Library Publishers, 1979; Ross Munro, *Gauntlet to Overlord*, Edmonton, Hurtig Publishers, 1972; Airey Naeve, *Little Cyclone*, London, Hodder and Stoughton, 1954; G. W. L. Nicholson, *The Canadians in Italy, 1943-1945*, Ottawa, The Queen's Printer, 1956; P. R. Reid, *Escape from Colditz*, J. B. Lippincott, 1952; Warren Shaw and James Taylor, *The third Reich Almanac*, New York, Almanac, 1978; C. P. Stacey, *The Canadian Army, 1939-1945*, Ottawa, The King's Printer, 1948; John Swettenham, *McNaughton*, Toronto, Ryerson Press, 1968; Richard M. Watt, *Bitter Glory*, New York, Simon and Schuster, 1979; W. Dennis Whittaker and Shelagh Whittaker, *Tug of War*, New York, Beaufort Books, 1984; W. Dennis Whittaker and Shelagh Whittaker, *Rhineland*, Toronto, Stoddart Publishing Co., Limited, 1989; W. Dennis Whittaker and Shelagh Whittaker, *Victory at Falaise*, Toronto, Harper Collins Publishers Ltd., 2000; Jeffery Williams, *The Long Left Flank*, Toronto, Stoddart Publishing Co., Limited, 1988; and Mark Zuehlke, *Ortona*, Toronto, Stoddart Publishing Co., Limited, 1999.

CONTENTS

1	In The Beginning	1
2	Training	57
3	Aldershot	111
4	Brest	131
5	England	181
6	Across The Channel	255
7	Escape	305
8	Over the Pyrenees	341
9	Freedom	361
10	North Africa	387
11	Sicily	431
12	Italy	477
13	Waiting	519
14	France	549
15	Ostend	569
16	Germany	589
17	At The End	623

BOOK ONE

IN THE BEGINNING

CHAPTER 1

When he reached the bank David Lindsay slowed down and stopped near it. He got out of his Ford on the driver's side and closed the door behind him. He made sure he took his briefcase with him and began walking toward the bank. Dave had parked on the right side of it and when he reached the front door, he stopped and looked at it. Then he opened the door and went in. There were quite a few people inside the bank and Dave made for the manager's office. The office stood to the right of the bank and was half way between the front door, the three wickets and the large marble counter at the other end. As he walked there Dave could see the manager through the open door.

The manager was a tall, slim and gray-haired man who was in his early fifties. He was wearing a dark-gray pinstripe suit with shirt, tie and shoes to match. Right now he was sitting behind his large mahogany desk and going through some papers. When Dave reached his office and knocked on the door, he looked up from his papers and said: "Yes?" "I was wondering if I might see you for a moment?" Dave said. "By all means," the manager said. He pushed back his big leather armchair and motioned for Dave to come and sit in the one facing him from across his desk. Dave walked in the office and sat down. He made sure he put his briefcase down on the right side of his chair and leaned forward a little.

Dave then put his arms on the manager's large mahogany desk and said: "First I would like to thank you for seeing me like this."

"No problem. It's my pleasure."

"I really appreciate it."

"No problem."

"If you don't mind I would like you to help me."

"Certainly."
"I would like to make a withdrawal."
"By all means. Do you have an account here?"
"I do."
"What kind of an account? Current or Savings?"
"Current."
"That's no problem. You can go through one of our wickets."
"No. I would like to go through you."
"That won't be necessary. One of our tellers will be more than happy to take care of this matter."
"No. I would like to go through you specifically."
"Why? One of our tellers will be very happy to take care of this."
"No. I'd prefer to go through you specifically."
"Why?"
"It's a special kind of withdrawal."
"What kind of withdrawal?"
"A highly unique and personalized one."
"What kind of unique and personalized one?"
"One on one."
"One on one?"
"That's right. Swift and discreet. Between you and me."

Now the manager got it. His face flushed suddenly and angrily and he said: "What are you talking about? This is ridiculous."
"Oh no it isn't."
"You won't get away with this. What the hell do you think you're doing?"
"I'm making a withdrawal."
"I've been a bank manager for over 20 years and nothing like that ever happened. I won't stand for it!"
"Sure you will. There's always a first time."
"Oh no I won't! I won't have it!"
"Believe me you will."
"Oh no I won't! I won't stand for it!" the manager came to get up.
"Sit down! Settle down!" Dave snapped and opened his jacket and showed him what was inside. "You see this gun? It's a 9 mm Parabellum Luger. Very deadly. Very accurate. Don't be stupid and force me to use it. I don't think you'd like it."
"But—"
"No buts, ifs or maybes!"
"But—"

"No buts, ifs or maybes I said! Or I'm going to blow your goddam head off! You got that!"

"I got it."

"All right then."

CHAPTER 2

Now that the manager knew what was going on he suddenly slumped in his armchair. The pleasant and confident manner with which he had greeted Dave began to crumble and his face became pale and strained. He began sweating a little and his hands shook slightly. He kept on looking at the gun in Dave's belt and sneaking a glance at the right-hand corner of his desk. Dave followed his glance to his gun and to the right-hand corner of the desk and said: "I wouldn't try that if I were you. Unless you want to end up as a dead hero. Or a very dead bank manager." The manager swallowed hard and sat up a little straighter. His face was still pale and strained. He was still sweating a little and his hands were still shaking slightly. Then he sighed suddenly and said: "All right. What do you want me to do?"

"It's simple. I want you to take one of the cloth bags you use and put money in it."

"And then?"

"Then I want you to go to the three wickets and withdraw specific sums of money like $300.00 dollars for instance. Or $500.00. Or $700.00. Make sure those sums are not too large to create suspicion but big enough to make it worthwhile. And then I want you to come back here."

"I hope you realize this is highly unusual. What if one of the tellers gets suspicious?"

"It won't happen."

"What if it does?"

"Just say it's for one of your clients. And that you're handling the transaction yourself."

"It is very unusual. What if it creates suspicion?"

In The Beginning

"It won't."
"What if it does?"
"I'm telling you. It won't."
"And if I don't do this?"
"Don't even think about it."
"But if I don't?"
"Listen. You don't think I'm pulling this off alone, do you? You don't think this is a spur-of-the-moment thing, do you? Believe me everything has been thought out extremely carefully. I've got people in the bank who are watching us now and who'll follow every move you make. So, unless you want to start something you'll be truly sorry for, I'd suggest you do exactly as I say. Do you follow me?"

The manager nodded. He wiped a few beads of sweat from his forehead and Dave went on: "Now then. I want you to be at ease and natural with the tellers. I want you to smile a lot. Even joke. But don't let on anything unusual is going on. Because if you do—"

"Because if I do—"

Dave grinned.

"You live in a big house in Westlynn. You have a nice wife and two lovely daughters. I wouldn't want anything to happen to them."

"Do you have my wife and daughters!"

"That's none of your business!"

"Do you really!"

"Enough! Enough on this!"

The manager swallowed hard and Dave said: "So, unless you want something really unfortunate to happen to them, do exactly as I say. Do you understand?"

"I understand."

"Do you?"

"I do indeed."

"All right. Move."

CHAPTER 3

The manager got up slowly and used a second door behind his desk that led to the employees' space behind the counter. Through the open door of his office Dave could see him after a moment. He was carrying a cloth bag in his right hand and heading toward the first wicket. On the way there he greeted a few elderly customers absent-mindedly and when he got to the first teller, he took a few stacks of bills from her cash. He put those stacks of bills in his cloth bag and moved on to the next wicket. The girl there was quite good-looking. She was a young slim blonde and had a cheerful and friendly manner. When he came to her wicket the girl smiled at him and they spoke for a little while. She also handed him some stacks of bills and must have joked with him for he smiled.

But there was nothing easy about the manager's smile, however. It was stiff, strained and frozen and all the time they were together, his eyes kept on glancing sneakily at a spot to the right-hand side of her wicket underneath the counter, at the people on the floor, at the counter itself and at the front door. That silly stupid sonofabitch! Dave thought. He's checking out the place and wants to see where my people are. Well, my friend, he thought, you better not get smart and try and stop this thing. You don't know where I've been. You don't know where I am. And you sure don't know where I'm going. So you better wise up and go along with me, he thought. Believe me. No funny stuff. No surprises. No crazy moves. Or else you're not going to like what you'll see. You better believe it you're not going to like what you'll see.

The manager was now at the third wicket. He spoke to the teller there and took some more stacks of bills from her. When his bag was full he turned and began walking back toward his office. He walked slowly and carefully and when he got there, he handed the cloth bag to Dave who put it swiftly into his briefcase on the right side of his armchair. As soon as he put the cloth bag in his briefcase Dave motioned for the manager to come and sit down in his big office armchair. The manager nodded and came and let himself in this chair. When he sat down Dave saw he was still sweating slightly and his face was still pale and strained. Now that the manager was back in his office Dave gave him enough time to sit down properly and catch his breath and then said: "You did well. You did very well. Now here is what I want you to do next.

"You're going to get up and walk with me to the door of your office. At the door you're going to smile and shake hands with me in front of everybody and wish me a good day."

"And then?"

"Then you're going to walk back to your desk and go back to your papers as if nothing had happened. You got that?"

The manager nodded and Dave went on: "All right. One word of warning, however. When we get to the door of your office and shake hands, I don't want you to get cute and try and take me on. My people are standing nearby and they'll shoot you at point-blank range. Is that clear?"

The manager nodded and Dave went on: "All right. Now. What time do you have?"

"A quarter to three."

"Okay. For the next 30 minutes, that is until 3.15, I want you to do one thing and one thing only. I want you to go and sit at your desk and look at your papers. Is that understood?"

"Yes."

"Just that. And nothing else."

The manager nodded and Dave went on: "Okay. One last thing. While you're in your office I don't want you to talk to your staff. I don't want you to call the police. I don't want you to call your wife. I have to get out of here and make a coded call to your place. If I don't make that call you can kiss them all goodbye. Do you understand?"

"I do."

"Do you really?"

"I do."

"All right. Let's go."

CHAPTER 4

Dave got up with the manager and began walking to the door of his office. He had shifted his briefcase to his left hand and when they reached it, the manager gave Dave a polite if somewhat strained smile. He shook hands with him and wished him a good day. Dave smiled back at him and wished him the same. He left his office and began walking toward the front door. The distance from the manager's office to the front door was only about 65 feet. And yet as he walked there Dave could feel quite a few people were staring at him. He could feel their stares burn right through his back and when he reached the front door, he opened it and left swiftly. Dave walked toward his Ford and when he got to it, he opened the door on the driver's side.

    Dave threw the briefcase on the front seat and some of the bills spilled on it. He slid in and closed the door behind him. He reached for his keys and turned on the ignition. The car didn't start. He turned on the ignition again. Once more the car didn't start. Come on! Come on! Let's go! Dave thought. Let's get the hell out of here! On the third try the motor finally caught on and Dave eased the clutch and let the car out of its parking space. He began driving west on Marine Drive and away from North Vancouver. At the corner of Lonsdale Avenue Dave slowed down and let a tall long-legged blonde-haired girl cross the Drive. The girl smiled at him as she ran by. Her shoulder-length silky hair blew back in the early September wind and when she was gone, he stepped on the gas and headed west.

    It was a bright, clear and sunny afternoon and as Dave kept on driving west, the sun shone warmly on the emerald-green Coast Mountains on his right, on the salmon-gold waters of the Narrows on his left and on the achingly-white city of Vancouver in the distance. Dave kept on driving west and when he reached the Lions Gate Bridge, he got on it and headed south. Then, when he finally came into Vancouver proper, he turned left and headed east. He kept on driving carefully and steadily and found himself passing through streets like Pender, Skeena and Sperling and when he pulled into Ardingley, he slowed down as the Municipal Park loomed straight ahead. At the Park Dave rode over the railroad tracks running alongside it and came and stopped at a small and deserted parking lot next to those tracks. As he stopped there he turned off the ignition and sat in his car with his hands on the steering wheel.

Man! I did it! I did it! Dave thought. He bought it! He bought it all! The story of my people in the bank and of men being with his wife and two daughters and of my having to make a coded phone call to his place. How about that! Hey! How about that! But pipe down! Settle down! he thought. It's no use going on like this and cheering and celebrating too quickly. You've got an awful lot of work to do and you're not out of the woods yet. So let's cut all this going on like this and cheering and celebrating and let's get down to it, shall we? Dave took his hands off the steering wheel and looked around the parking lot. There was no one there. In fact the lot was empty except for an old Chrysler and a rusty Chevrolet. He looked around the parking lot once more and opened his briefcase.

Dave brought out two big brown shopping bags. In the first one he put all the bills that had spilled on the front seat as well as those in the cloth bag. In the second one he placed his briefcase containing the cloth bag, his car keys and the Luger. He took out his large white handkerchief and made sure he wiped his keys, the briefcase, the Luger and the steering wheel clean of all fingerprints. Then he paused and looked at himself in the rearview mirror. With his matted, curly, blond hair parted on the side and his thick, bristly, walrus mustache he had a bushy, friendly, outgoing look. This look changed a great deal, however, when he removed the fake thick mustache and curly blond wig he was wearing. It gave way to a face that was lean and clean and framed, as it were, by clean, well-trimmed, pale-brown hair and clear, piercing, pale-brown eyes.

As he took off his curly blond wig Dave ran a hand through his hair and proceeded to put the blond wig and fake mustache in the briefcase in the second brown bag. Then he took off his shoes, socks, tie and pale-brown suit he was wearing and put them in the briefcase. He reached for a pair of black shoes and some dark-blue slacks and socks from under the driver's seat and slipped into them. With the white shirt he had on Dave now looked completely different from the man who had been at the bank. He looked at himself for a last time in the rearview mirror and picked up the two big brown shopping bags. He stepped out of the Ford and outside put the two bags down and closed the door on the driver's side. He removed all traces of fingerprints on the door handle with his handkerchief and looked at his reflection in the polished shiny door.

The reflection showed him as he really was: tall, slim, muscular, with the sharp well-defined wiriness and swift powerful stance of a well-built 22 year-old. Dave turned away from his reflection and looked around once more. Then he picked up his two bags again and began walking out of the parking lot. On Sperling Avenue Dave hailed a cab and told the driver to take him to Renfrew Heights. He sat in the back of the taxi and watched the driver take him there and when they got to Rupert and 20th Avenue, Dave told the driver to stop and paid him. He stepped out and waited until the taxi was gone. Then he began walking south on Rupert and when he reached 25th Avenue, he saw what he was looking for. This was a house being demolished at the south-west corner of Rupert and that had a large industrial container next to it.

As Dave reached the industrial container he turned and looked around him quickly. At the same time he slowed down and in one swift motion reared back. He threw in the brown shopping bag containing his briefcase and walked on.

CHAPTER 5

Near Wellington Avenue Dave flagged down one more taxi and told the driver to take him to Fairview. He told him he wanted to go to 12th Avenue and Burrard. They left Wellington Avenue and in this now late and sun-filled afternoon, the traffic became bigger and heavier the closer they got to downtown. It was now close to 5.00 o'clock in the afternoon and when they got near Burrard, they were hardly moving. Dave sat in the back of the taxi and watched the heavy traffic and when they finally reached the corner of 12th Avenue and Burrard, he stepped out and paid the driver. He began walking east along 12th Avenue and turned north on Bedford Street toward the large two-story white clapboard house where he lived. This house, which looked pretty much like the other houses on the street, was near the middle of it.

Like most houses in that area it was small, modest and slightly rundown. As a matter of fact it perfectly reflected the plainness and ordinariness of the whole neighborhood and when he reached it, Dave went in and walked past the apartment of his blowzy and floozy landlady on the ground floor. Dave headed for his small and crowded room on the second floor and when he reached it, he went in and saw how his room also reflected the very plainness and ordinariness of the whole neighborhood. There was nothing special about it except for the overly big brass bed standing right in the middle of it, the scratched, second-hand, five-string guitar on the bed, the old chair, waste basket and dresser next to the bed on the right side, and the many books piled high on all walls—novels, histories, biographies as well as books of all kinds on war, science, philosophy, psychology and especially languages.

The Long War

    Once he had come into his room Dave locked the door behind him and put on the light. He stepped to his bed and opened the other big brown shopping bag he was carrying. He spilled the bills on the bed and began counting them. This didn't take too long and when he was finished, Dave shook his head and stared at the bed incredulously. There was over $2,000.00 dollars on the bed. This was no illusion. There was, in fact, when he had counted it all, $2,143.00 dollars to be exact. What do you know? Dave thought. It's not bad. It's not bad at all for an afternoon's work. You should do that more often. You see what happens when you don't give a damn about the world or about yourself or about anything even. But it's a good thing you're getting out of Vancouver and going east though, he thought. Very far east. With all this money you can bet they'll be looking for you. You bet, my friend, they'll be looking for you.

    Dave bent and gathered the bills on the bed. He put them in his big brown shopping bag and looked for his suitcase. It was a large dark-brown one made of leather and scuffed and scratched from the places it had been on trains and trucks and buses all over the country. The suitcase was standing in front of his clothes' closet and facing the bed. Dave stepped away from the bed and went and picked it up. He brought it back to the bed and opened it and began to pack. He didn't have many clothes: a couple pairs of slacks, a few shirts, ties, a windbreaker, some socks and underwear, and a dark-blue suit which he put down on the bed to the right of his suitcase. Then he took out the bills from his big brown shopping bag. He crumpled the bag and put it in the waste basket next to the chair. Then he stuffed the bills in the pockets of his slacks and windbreaker and kept quite a few for himself.

    When he had put away the bills he didn't want to keep for himself Dave took off the dark-blue slacks he was wearing and put them in the suitcase and closed it. He put on his dark-blue suit with a tie to match and went and sat on the chair next to the bed. Dave sat on this chair until it was close to 7.00 o'clock. At that time he got up and picked up his suitcase from the bed. He moved to the door and gave his room a last look. He turned off the light. Then he left and made sure he closed the door behind him.

CHAPTER 6

Dave walked downstairs and left the house. He had already paid his landlady a month's rent and told her hew was leaving. He moved down Bedford Street and when he got on 12th Avenue, he hailed a taxi and told the driver to take him to the CNR station. This wasn't a long ride. With the stop signs and traffic lights it was about 20 minutes from his place. The driver pulled out and headed east on 12th Avenue. Then he headed north on Main Street and when they finally reached the station, Dave went in and saw the policemen, plainclothes men and train officials right away. They were everywhere. Some were walking along the concourse. Others stood at the corners. A few were at the gates. But all of them were walking or standing. They must have been told about the money and were really working out there.

Dave tightened the grip on his suitcase and walked by a policeman who was talking to a big burly blond-haired man with a thick bristling mustache. The man was taking out some papers and showing them to the policeman. Dave walked past them both and headed for one of the wickets. He bought a ticket for the train he wanted and got a large current-news magazine from one of the newsstands. He went and sat down on one of the long wooden benches on the concourse and buried his head in his magazine. Not long after he heard the announcement for his train. Dave got up and began moving toward the gate from which it was leaving. He walked past the cold hard stares of a couple of policemen and at the gate, he showed his ticket to the railway official. The official waved him through.

Dave walked toward his traveling coach and climbed in. He went and sat in one of the seats by the window. The seat was on the right side of the coach and he put his suitcase in the baggage rack above him. By then there were so many policemen, plainclothes men and train officials moving around on the platform Dave found himself looking at his watch and watching the door of his coach. He kept on watching the door and breathed deeply when he heard the all aboard call. There was a lurch followed by another lurch. A few more people rushed to get on board and there was one more lurch. Then slowly and imperceptibly the train began pulling out of the station. In no time they hit the purple and crimson twilight outside and the downtown buildings and houses were all bathed in a last lingering gold.

As they left the station the train picked up speed and began moving past the sun-swept streets and avenues. After a while it left Vancouver behind and then Burnaby and finally New Westminster. As Dave was watching the train wind its way from the coast and leave behind all those dark, bluish and amber-hued mountains and as he kept on looking at his large current-news magazine from time to time, the darkness came on and fell across the landscape. Soon it blanketed everything and as they kept on heading east, Dave began relaxing a little until he became aware of a boy who was watching him from across the aisle. The boy was sitting in a swungover seat and facing him. He was 19 or 20 years old. He was very skinny and wiry and yet, although he only weighed around 120 pounds, had surprisingly strong and powerful shoulders.

The boy was about five feet five or five feet six and was wearing pale-brown slacks and a dark-brown windbreaker. He had a heavily freckled face crowned with a shock of red hair. A few strands were falling over his face and his clear blue eyes and as he kept on watching him, Dave got up and walked over to him. He stopped by his seat and said: "You seem interested in watching me. Is there anything wrong?" "No. Nothing," the boy said and moved to the other seat. As he moved there he motioned for Dave to take his former seat, which Dave did. "It's just you don't seem to like trains very much."

"So what? I don't have to like them, do I?"

"Of course not."

Dave didn't say anything and the boy said: "It's just you looked quite funny staring out the window and reading your magazine. That's all."

"That's my business, isn't it?"

"It sure is."

"If it's my business, why don't you let it go?"

"Sure. I have no problem with that."

"If you have no problem with it, why don't you do that then?"

In The Beginning

"Hey! Hey! Don't get mad. I was only looking at you. What's the big deal?"

"It's no big deal."

"Why are you so mad then?"

"I'm not mad. Who said I was mad?"

"Okay. You're not mad."

"I'm not mad. It's just I don't like being stared at."

"Okay. I won't do it again."

The boy now fell silent and eyed Dave carefully. After a while he leaned forward and put out his hand: "By the way my name's O'Hara. Bill O'Hara. My friends call me Red."

Dave also leaned forward. He shook Red's hand and told him his name.

"Where are you going?"

Dave told him.

"I'm going to Winnipeg."

"Why there?"

"To enlist, no less."

"Why do you want to do that?"

"Good God, man! Don't you know what day it is?

"No."

"It's September 11, 1939."

"So?"

"So, yesterday, Canada declared war on Germany!"

"Ah yes. The war."

"For sure. The war."

"So that's why you're going to Winnipeg?"

"You bet."

"Why do you want to go there? Wouldn't it have been simpler to enlist in Vancouver?"

"Sure. But I didn't want to do that."

"Why not?"

"I didn't want to end up in the Pacific."

"Why would you end up there?"

"Vancouver's close to the Pacific. I didn't want to take the chance to end up there."

"If that's the case, then you should go much further east. And join this Regiment," Dave said and went on and gave Red the name of the Regiment.

"Why this Regiment?" Red asked.

"Because they're probably the best and finest Regiment this country has ever had. During the First World War do you know what their motto was? *No Prisoners.* That's how tough they are."

"That sounds like a pretty good Regiment."

"It is."

"How come you know so much about them?"

"Me? I read about them. I read about a lot of things."

"Can't say I do that. But I must say it sounds like a damn good Regiment."

"It is a good one."

"I wouldn't mind going with a Regiment like that. What about my size, though? Wouldn't it affect me?"

"It won't. You want to go, don't you? They'll take you."

"You're sure?"

"Of course I'm sure."

Red didn't say anything and then said: "There's only one problem."

"What problem?"

"I'm all out of money. How will I get there?"

"I have money. I'll pay."

"You will?"

"I'll pay."

"All right! Hey, all right!" Red said and suddenly reached out and slapped Dave's thigh. "Why don't you join with me?"

"I'm sorry. I can't."

"Millions of people are doing it. Why not you and me?"

"I'm sorry. I have other plans."

"Two people are better than one. How about it?"

"I'm sorry. It's not for me."

"Come on. Join!"

"I can't."

"Oh, come on!"

Well, why don't you do it? Dave thought. Why the hell don't you go and join with Red? This should be interesting seeing how you hate the Army and what it stands for and does to people. Also, with a move like this, it'll sure be interesting to see how long you'll last and how far you'll be able to go before you just can't stand it anymore and want out. Not to mention, back at the bank, he thought, you really wanted the way of the gun, didn't you? You really wanted to go down in style, didn't you? So, even though this doesn't quite fit in with your plans and with what you had in mind, what a better way, what a fantastic way, for you to do this now and go and join with Red and realize, in a spectacular way, with hundreds

and thousands and millions, what you've been wanting to do all alone in the first place!
　　Dave looked at Red.
　　"Sure. Why not?"
　　"You mean that?"
　　"Sure. Why not?"
　　"Fantastic! Hey, isn't this absolutely fantastic!"

CHAPTER 7

Dave didn't answer Red. He just leaned back in his seat and stared straight ahead. He kept on staring straight ahead and when he spoke to Red again, he didn't talk about enlisting. He only talked about the train, the weather, the people and the country, and during the next four days and four nights they were on the train it turned out to be quite a journey. Indeed, from the towering might and splendor of the sun-swept Rockies, to the awesome and golden flatlands of the Prairies, to the craggy and barren ground of the Great Lakes, always their train kept on heading east. It kept on moving across this vast and endless land that was the second biggest on earth and almost 4,000 miles wide.

It was a country that had a little over 10 million people and was made up of so many huge and different regions. There was, to begin with, the massive and soaring mountain ranges of the West, followed by the spread-out and sparsely-populated expanses of the Prairies, then the rich and industrial cities of the East, and finally the grim and storm-lashed coast of the Atlantic. And as the train kept on heading east, and as young men kept on getting on it in order to go and enlist, it was as if the war had suddenly caught up with them and was moving and keeping pace with the train. As a matter of fact this feeling the war had suddenly caught up with them and was moving and keeping pace with the train stayed with them throughout their entire journey and when they reached Winnipeg, Dave paid for Red's ticket to go further east, of course.

In Winnipeg they didn't stop long. They only stopped there to take on baggage and add a couple of passenger cars. Then they were on their way again and as they kept on heading east and passing so many towns and villages, Dave went back to sitting on his side of the coach. Red came and sat opposite him on the swungover seat. They sat like this for the rest of the journey and on the morning of the fifth day when he woke up, Dave saw Red was sound asleep opposite him. Dave looked at him for a while and then looked out of the window. He did this for a while and then turned to Red again and said: "We're here."

Red didn't answer.

"I said we're here."

Red still didn't answer.

"Come on. Wake up. We're here."

Red groaned and opened his eyes. He straightened up in his seat and said: "Oh man. I said I liked trains. But this is too much."

"It's one thing to like them. It's another to sit in one for five days, isn't it?"

"It sure is. And I'll tell you something else. This is a big country."

"They don't come any bigger."

"They sure don't."

"I know."

CHAPTER 8

Dave turned and looked out of the window again. It was getting light outside and they were now passing vast and deserted fields. Some of the fields had farmhouses on them. A few had shacks. In some of the fields livestock was grazing. In others horses stood still by the wire or wooden fences. In a few mares ran softly and gracefully with their foals. They were also going by quite a few woods. Some were stiff and isolated. Others were running into fields with farmhouses or barns on them. Then, when they left all those fields behind and got into a long slow turn, the river surged out of nowhere suddenly and Montreal came into view. A proud, vain and imperious city, it loomed darkly against the orange sky.

The mountain towered sharply over the city and the skyscrapers and churches and buildings gleamed in the morning sunlight. Far below in the harbor ocean liners and freighters rode whitely at anchor. In the early light the St. Lawrence ran dark-blue and silver. Its clear and pristine waters took on the fiery blazing colors of sunrise and when they got onto the Victoria Bridge and began making for the other shore, Dave looked at a seagull that soared swiftly past his window. It climbed and climbed until it flew so high over the river it seemed to hang there, so white, stark and magnificent, before it turned swiftly and disappeared in mid-river past the greenery of St. Helen's Island and the majestic rise of the blue-green Jacques Cartier Bridge in the distance.

Three years, Dave thought. Three years I've been away and yet the city hasn't changed. It's still as damn beautiful and fascinating as it ever was. That is, it's beautiful and fascinating if you live in Westmount or in those other rich English or French districts. But it's not so good if you live in the Point or in St. Henri or in the East End though, he thought. There it's not beautiful at all. It's just incredibly bleak and grim with the blood and sweat of the many for all those rich English and French families who own all the plants and factories the people work for. You bet it's not beautiful. Dave turned away from the window for a moment, and in no time they reached the other shore and began moving past the deserted, morning-filled, downtown streets. They slid past those streets slowly and some time later, they slowed down even more as they came and stopped in the deep confines of Bonaventure station.

As soon as they stopped there Dave got up with Red. They both picked up their suitcases and left their coach with the other passengers. They walked along the dark disembarkation platform and in the station, they went and put their suitcases in large metal lockers. Then they walked outside and near the curb, Dave raised his hand and hailed a taxi. He took it with Red and told the driver where he wanted to go. They left and soon found themselves on Sherbrooke Street west. They drove past tall apartment houses, stately mansions, elegant boutiques, small art galleries, first-rate hotels and fashionable rooming-houses. Close to Atwater Avenue the driver got on Ste. Catherine Street and drove west toward Westmount.

Near Greene Avenue Dave told him to stop and stepped out with Red. He paid him and began walking with Red along Ste. Catherine Street. Dave headed west and when he reached Hallowell Street where he had once lived, he saw it too hadn't changed very much. It was still the same small neat dead-end street that ran onto the railway tracks and faced the extensive, sumptuous and well-kept grounds of the Montreal Amateur Athletic Association. Dave passed it and kept on heading west and when he reached Kensington Avenue, he turned and suddenly saw them.

CHAPTER 9

There were three of them. All of them were wearing smart and expensive sports jackets, shirts and slacks and were coming down Kensington Avenue. They were moving with the cocky and arrogant confidence of people of means and affluence and the first boy on the left was tall, slim and good-looking. He had neat, clean, blond hair and was walking briskly with the easy and effortless stride of someone used to being in the lead. Slightly behind him stood a boy who was nearly as tall though slightly thinner. His hair was a pale and almost sandy shade of brown and he had a wild and unruly tuft of hair that was sticking out at the back of his head. On the right was a boy who looked quite different from the other two.

This boy was shorter and smaller than them and didn't have a strand of his jet-black hair out of place. He had a thin straight nose and a narrow thrusting chin. He was also wearing an expensive gold watch on his left wrist and clothes of a far more severe and conservative nature. The three of them were coming down fast and heading toward Dave. They were three deadly serious and intense young men on a big mission and when they finally got to Ste. Catherine Street, they also saw Dave as well as Red. As they turned right on Ste. Catherine Street and then headed west a little behind Dave and Red, the first boy on the left called out to them: "Hey guys. Where are you going?"

Dave didn't answer and kept on walking ahead with Red.

"Hey guys. Where are you going?"

Dave slowed down and turned to the boy who had called out to them. Goddamit! he thought. What is this? Why is it you can't ever do anything without other people coming into it?

"What?"

"I was saying. Where are you guys going?"

"Oh, we're heading west."

"Where west?"

"We're going to enlist," Dave said as the three boys finally caught up with them. They walked alongside them and the first boy walked next to Dave on his right.

"Oh man, so are we. We're all going to enlist."

"That's good."

"You're damn right. After all we've all got to do our bit for the country. Right?"

"Sure."

"Just like they're doing." The boy grinned and pointed to some boys ahead of them. They were walking in groups of twos and threes and were also going to enlist.

Dave nodded.

"I tell you though. Is my old man going to be furious! Is he ever going to hate my guts!"

"Why?"

"You see, he wants me to get a commission and go in as an officer. I want to join as a foot soldier in the infantry. I don't think he's going to be too crazy about that."

"To be the toughest of the tough, hey?" Red said.

"That's it," the boy said. "I tell you. There's going to be plenty of wailing and gnashing of teeth and wringing of hands in the old mansion tonight."

"It's always tough going for the big one, isn't it?" Dave said.

"You bet," the boy said. "Oh, you have no idea how I want to see their faces when I tell them what I've done. It's going to be quite something."

"I'm sure."

"It's true. You see, they all want me to go in and join the Glengarry Grenadiers. My father was an officer there. So was my grandfather and my great-grandfather. That's fine for them. But not for me. I don't like the Grenadiers. They're from Toronto and I'm not too crazy about the place."

"I'm not too crazy about it either," Red said.

"That's why I think it's about time I made the decisions for a change and choose what I want to do and not what they want. And that's why I made up my mind to enlist here and not with the Grenadiers or with the Stormont Dundass Dragoons as one of my uncles suggested."

"The Stormont Dundass Dragoons!" Red said. "You mean there's such a Regiment?"

"That's right," the boy said. "They're also from Toronto."

"That sounds like a circus. With a name like that, why not the Stomped on Dumbass Baboons while you're at it!"

"Exactly," the boy said. "That's why I decided to enlist here and not care about what they want. After all a man has to stand on his own two feet. He has to make his own decisions, right?" he turned to Dave.

Dave nodded and the boy said: "Where are you guys going? To Park Place?"

"That's it."

"To the armory?"

"That's the one."

"To enlist there?"

"You got it."

"It's a good Regiment."

"You bet."

"It's the best there is."

"I think so."

"No prisoners," Red said.

"You're not kidding," the boy said.

"It's certainly a well-known and well-publicized fact," the third boy on the right said. "They're the very best there is. They're really in a class by themselves. That's why it's truly well worth joining them."

"That's true," Dave said and thought: Oh my God! Can you believe this? I mean, can you really believe this guy? Of all the things he can say, he has to put it on a class basis!

"That's for sure," the first boy said. "And with all of us joining, you can bet we'll be pretty hard to beat."

"You think so?" Dave said.

"Of course," the boy said. "With all of us in, you can bet old Hitler hasn't got a chance."

Wait till you find out, Dave thought. Then we'll talk about it.

"I'm not so sure. I think the Germans are going to be a lot tougher than you think."

"I don't think so. Not with all of us in, they won't."

"Yes," the second boy said. "Wait till we get in. Then they'll find out what real soldiers are."

Dave looked at him and didn't bother answering.

The first boy looked at Dave and then at his friend. He turned to Dave again and said: "Anyway, whether unbeatable or not, whether the best or not, what are your names, you guys?"

Dave told him.

In The Beginning

"Mine's Jim Higgins," the boy said. "This is Bob Addams," he pointed to the tall sandy-haired boy. "And this is Steve Mitchell," he pointed to the smaller dark-haired one. "Better known as the Three Musketeers. All for one and one for all. In good times and bad times. Richer or poorer. For better and for worse. In sickness and in health. And all that jazz."

Dave nodded and Higgins went on: "Where are you guys from? I don't remember seeing you around here."

"Oh, we're from out West."

"Where from out West?"

"Vancouver."

"Vancouver. Hey. It's a hell of a nice town."

"Have you been there?"

"Sure. Many times. It's quite a place."

"It is."

"As a matter of fact it's one of my favorite cities."

"Really?"

"It sure is. I love the place."

You would, Dave thought. It's funny how guys like that always seem to love the last place they've been to. And they can't wait to tell you about the next great one they're going to go to. I guess they all talk like that.

"What are you guys doing around here?" Higgins asked.

"Oh, we were just coming here for a holiday," Dave said. "And when the war was declared and when we saw everyone was joining, we decided to do the same."

"It's not such a bad idea. I mean. What else is there to do?"

"I agree. And besides I used to live here. What could be a better place to do it?"

"That's it. Especially since you know the place, right?"

"Exactly."

"Well, it's a damn good thing we're all joining," Higgins said. "That way it'll sure save me from having all those terrible fights with my old man and from having to go into the retail business."

Dave looked at him.

"Higgins," Higgins said. "You know. The coast to coast department stores. That's me." He laughed. "I mean. Not me personally. But my family."

"Oh yes. Higgins. I know the stores."

"So do I," Red said. "And I'm also familiar with your catalogue."

"Are you?" Higgins said.

"Sure. It used to be one of the big events from where I come from."

"Where's that?"

"Stattler, Alberta. I used to live there on a farm before I went to Vancouver to become a short order cook."

"Stattler. Hey. I know that place."

"You do?"

"Sure. I drove through it a couple of times on my way to Vancouver. I must say though it's not much of a place."

"It's not."

"That's for sure."

"Anyway, about your catalogue," Red said. "Every Spring and Fall we used to get it and my father would come into the living-room and tell me and my four brothers we could each choose one thing. Then he'd turn to my mother and say the same thing. So I'd look at the catalogue and choose a football or a baseball glove or a pair of skates. My mother would also do this and after she had made her choice, she'd go into the kitchen and talk with my father. At first they would discuss this closely and intently and then heatedly and angrily. Finally my father would come back into the living-room and tell us we couldn't have what we wanted. Instead we always ended up getting what we needed but really didn't want, like a lamp or a carpet or blankets. Believe me. I know that catalogue very well."

"Sorry about that," Higgins said. "It was my father's idea. But it sure made a lot of money."

"It still does," Mitchell said.

"And how," Addams said.

"It certainly does," Higgins said. "But, no matter, it's still not going to change the fact I'm joining and it'll definitely save me from going into the retail business; and him," he turned to Addams, "from becoming a dentist, and him," he turned to Mitchell, "from lawyering."

"It'll save you all from doing a lot of things," Dave said.

"Oh, for sure," Higgins said. "What will it save you from?"

"Me? It'll save me from becoming an undertaker."

"All right," Higgins laughed. "Hey, that's all right."

CHAPTER 10

They were now coming to the armory and when they reached it, Dave looked at it and thought it was quite an impressive place. It was huge, massive and sprawling and covered a whole block from Park Place to Blenheim Place. It towered over the whole area and was a tall red-bricked building that had a sharp-looking high-gabled green-tiled roof, long opaque horizontal windows and enormous spike-studded iron doors. As he looked at it Dave could just imagine what kind of Regiment would use such a building and what kind of soldiers would be found in such a Regiment. At the entrance, above its massive iron doors, stood the name of the Regiment carved in a stone scroll: THE WESTMOUNT FUSILIERS.

Above the name, carved in smaller letters, stood the Regimental motto in Latin: *Perpetua fidelitas. Nullus passus retro.* Below the name, also in smaller letters, stood the motto in English: *Loyalty always. Not a step back.* To the right of the doors, also carved in stone, was the Regimental Patch. This was a black gold-rimmed rifle with a black gold-rimmed bayonet that ran on a slant across a field of red. The same Patch was also to the left of the doors and bore in black the names of three of the places where the Regiment had fought so fiercely and fanatically during the First World War: Arras, Vimy Ridge and Passchendaele. Finally, on each side of the entrance, there was a big poster. The one on the left read: CANADA DECLARES WAR ON GERMANY. The one on the right: HELP YOUR COUNTRY. JOIN THE FUSILIERS.

That morning two gigantic muscular Staff Sergeants stood at the entrance. They had huge rock-hard frames, thick waxy mustaches, smart spotless uniforms and high polished boots, and were saying in loud booming voices to the oncoming recruits: "Come on in, boys! Join the fight! Come on in! Join the fight!" They nodded at Dave, Red and the Musketeers and when they were inside, Dave saw how crowded the armory was. The boys were lined up in the entrance hallway and in the main hall. On the left side of the hall, as you came in, there were quite a few Corporals and Lance Corporals. They were sitting down at a long row of tables and were busy processing them. At the far end, in an area set up with white screens, there were doctors who were having a look at them. On the right side, cordoned off by a rope, there was another area where a great many boys were standing around and waiting.

The sunlight was falling in long, blinding and diffuse slants across the main hall. There were quite a few boys, Lance Corporals, Corporals, Sergeants and officers who were moving in and out of that light and when it came time for him to step to one of the tables alongside the left wall behind Red and the Three Musketeers, Dave handed his birth certificate and driver's license to a tall, thin and bespectacled Corporal. The Corporal took those documents and wrote some details on a form. As soon as he had finished he returned those documents and the form to Dave and asked him to go to the area set off by white screens so he could be seen by one of the doctors. Dave nodded. He left the Corporal and when he got to the area with white screens, he looked in.

The whole area inside the white screens had been broken down into small alcoves. The alcoves had also been partitioned with white screens and contained a table, a chair and a medicine cabinet. All the alcoves had an opening in the middle that led to the third section that was cordoned off by a rope. When Dave looked in the first alcove was free. In it he saw a doctor who was in his late forties and who definitely looked tough enough and fit enough to be on a recruiting poster for the Westmount Fusiliers. The doctor, who was wearing a white smock, was tall, gray-haired and had a crew cut. He had a lean wiriness that belonged more to a youth than to a man of over forty. He also had a tanned healthy face that spoke of plenty of tough outdoor training and hard disciplined conditioning.

Right now he was bending over the alcove table and writing something on a form. When Dave looked in the doctor turned to him and said: "Good morning, son. Coming to do your duty for your country?" "Yes sir," Dave said. "Good," the doctor said. "Take off your clothes and sit on the table. Keep on your shorts though." Dave nodded and began undressing. He put his clothes at the foot of the table and when he was in his shorts, the doctor handed him a small urine bottle in order to get a sample. Dave didn't take too long to give him one and when the doctor had that sample, he sat on the table while the doctor wrote something on a sticker which he put on the small bottle. He sealed the bottle and put it in the medicine cabinet. Then he turned to Dave and began examining him.

The doctor used a small flashlight to look into his eyes. He took another one to check his ears and a small hammer which he tapped on his knees. He wrapped a black armband around his right arm and slipped his stethoscope underneath the armband. He pumped the blood pressure gauge and looked at it. Then he unwrapped the armband and put his stethoscope in his ears. He moved closer to Dave and when he began probing and examining his chest, he said: "Take a deep breath."

Dave did.

"Release."

Dave released.

"Again."

Dave took another deep breath.

"Let go."

Dave let go.

The doctor shifted to his back.

"Cough."

Dave coughed.

"Louder."

Dave coughed louder.

"Again."

Dave coughed louder once more.

"All right. Now lie down on the table and lower your shorts."

CHAPTER 11

Dave brought down his shorts and stretched on his back. He watched the doctor as he put on a surgical glove and began examining his scrotum. Then he made him turn on his stomach and also probed his rectum. The doctor checked him closely and intently and when he was through, he stepped back from the table and removed his surgical glove. He motioned for Dave to sit up and get dressed. The whole examination had taken no more than four or five minutes and Dave said: "Is that it?" "That's it," the doctor said. "You don't have anything else to check?" Dave asked. "No. That's it," the doctor said. My God, Dave thought, as he got off the table and began dressing.

If that's all they check they must be pretty damn eager and taking in anybody! I've heard of fast medical examinations but this is ridiculous! he thought. Bing! bang! boom! In and out and you're gone! If it had gone any faster I wouldn't have been there at all! I know they want to get as many people as possible but this is ridiculous! Dave finished dressing and when he was ready to leave, the doctor asked him to go and wait in the cordoned off area. Dave left the small alcove and began walking toward that area. When he got there Dave saw Red and the Musketeers were already in that area with quite a few other people. Dave joined them and stayed with them. He didn't have to wait long. Soon a young Captain came their way. The Captain was tall, lean and wiry. He moved briskly and crisply and when he reached them, he stopped in front of them and put his hands behind his back.

Then he planted his feet firmly on the ground and said: "Gentlemen. At ease." Everyone stopped talking. They all turned to him and he said: "Thank you for coming to the armory and thinking of the Westmount

In The Beginning

Fusiliers. Your papers are now being processed. In three to ten days if we haven't called you, you can call or come and see us. Everything should be ready by then and it should be okay for you to leave for Ontario and for our training ground in Terreyville. For now though. That's it. You may leave." The Captain then unhooked the front rope of the cordoned off area and motioned for them to file out. They all began heading slowly toward the entrance and as Red was moving with Dave and the Musketeers in the middle of the line, he turned to the Musketeers and said: "How about that? Hey, how about that? We made it! We made it! We're the Westmount Fusiliers! Oh man, we're the bloody Fusiliers!"

Red launched into a wild and excited discussion on this with the Musketeers. Yet, as he walked behind them, Dave didn't join in. He looked at them and at the Captain and at the sun-filled armory and thought: Well, you always wanted to do an absolutely final and irrevocable act, didn't you, my friend? You always wanted to jump the rails and go for the brass ring, didn't you? You always wanted to do something so wild and extraordinary it would go beyond everything, didn't you? Well, how do you like it now? Yes. How do you like it? Dave didn't. At least not at that moment. But for now he knew one thing. One thing for sure. He had to listen to what the Captain had said and follow his instructions.

Dave walked behind Red and the Musketeers and left the armory.

CHAPTER 12

Outside Dave slowed down and stopped behind Red and the Musketeers. As he stood there Higgins looked at him and told him the Musketeers would see him and Red at the training ground. Then he left with the Musketeers and Dave watched them go in the bright dazzling mid-morning sunlight. After a while he turned away from them and when he stared at Red, Red asked him what they were going to do next. Dave told Red to follow him and crossed Ste. Catherine Street with him. On the other side he hailed a taxi and told the driver where he wanted to go. They left Blenheim Place and began heading east past Kensington Avenue where they had first met the Musketeers.

At Atwater they turned left and headed for Sherbrooke Street where they turned right and drove east. Past Guy the street became truly exciting and dynamic. It was lined with smart shops, stylish boutiques, small art galleries, expensive jewelry stores, quaint houses, stately mansions, tall office buildings, secluded Men's Clubs and the Museum of Fine Arts, and when they finally reached Mountain Street they slowed down and stopped in front of the beflagged and brightly-lit entrance of the Ritz Carlton Hotel. A doorman stepped out and opened the door of their taxi. Dave got out with Red and paid the driver. He walked into the hotel and headed for the reception desk on the left side of the lobby. He spoke to a tall, balding, skeletal clerk and told him he wanted a large and luxurious room for three days and that he would let him know if they wanted to stay longer.

Dave paid cash for those three days and gave the clerk a big tip. He signed the registry and followed a young blond bellhop to the tall gleaming bronze elevators opposite the registration desk. Dave got in one of them with Red and the bellhop. They went up and got out on the seventh floor.

In The Beginning

They turned left on that floor and walked down a long hallway until they came to their room near the middle of it. Their room was on the right side of the hallway and when they got to the door, Dave also gave the bellhop a big tip and took the key from him. He opened the door and went in with Red. He closed the door behind him and when he turned and looked at Red, he saw the look of shock and amazement on his face. The room they were in was, no doubt about it, quite impressive.

There was on the right wall, as you came in, a shiny white-pine desk with plush red-upholstered armchairs in front of and on both sides of the desk, an enormous white-tiled bathroom on the opposite wall, and, to the right of the bathroom, two huge single beds separated by a large white-pine night table with a big bedside lamp on it. When Dave saw the look of shock and amazement on Red's face he told him not to worry and that he had the money to pay for this. He told him back in Vancouver he had won a great deal of money by playing and winning 18 consecutive hands of poker. This impressed Red a great deal and he was even more impressed when Dave took out two twenties and a ten and gave them to him so he too could gamble and maybe win some money.

Red took the money and when they had settled in, they both left and went to eat at the hotel restaurant downstairs. After the meal they stepped out and went to see a first-run action movie in one of the theaters on Ste. Catherine Street, and for the next three days and nights they really had a good time staying at the Ritz, sightseeing and going out on the town. As a matter of fact those three days and nights went by very quickly and the following Monday morning, September 18, 1939, on a bright, clear and sunny day, they went and signed their enlistment papers. That morning they both got up early. They had a quick breakfast and went to the Bonaventure station to get their suitcases. Back at the hotel Dave went to a bank nearby to change the whole of his money into bigger and more manageable bills.

Then, around 11.00 a.m., they took a taxi to go and enlist. It was a short and pleasant ride to the armory and when they got there, the first thing they did was sign their overseas duty papers and various other papers. Once those formalities were over they were led by a tall hard-nosed steely-eyed young Captain to the same cordoned off area where they had been before. In this area, along with quite a few other recruits, they were sworn by the young Captain to an oath of allegiance to King, Country and the Regiment. After the swearing-in ceremony they were let go and given a white cardboard card with the numbers III stenciled in black on it. This meant they had been assigned to B for Bravo Company. They had been

The Long War

assigned to the First Section of the First Platoon of the First Battalion, or the Big Three as Red called it.

Dave put the card in his pocket and, near the entrance, stopped and spoke to one of the gigantic and thickly-mustachioed Staff Sergeants. He found out they were lucky. One of the trains heading to Terreyville was scheduled to leave Bonaventure station at 8.00 o'clock that evening. This train gave them plenty of time to rest and take it easy. As a result Dave and Red took a taxi and came back to their hotel and, around 7.00 o'clock, picked up their suitcases and went down to the lobby. Dave settled their bill with the tall, balding, skeletal clerk at the reception desk and then they left and took another taxi to the Bonaventure station.

CHAPTER 13

The ride from the Ritz to the Bonaventure station didn't take very long and when they got there, they went in. They headed for their embarkation platform and when they reached it, Dave saw how crowded it was. Commissioned and non-commissioned officers were standing around and giving instructions. The whole platform was full of recruits. They were hanging about and running around and jumping up and down. They were yelling and waving and rushing in and out of cars and looking for an empty seat, a friend, a girlfriend, a wife, or to get some information from one of the COs or NCOs. As he saw this Dave kept on walking and moving along the platform.

Dave was looking for a car with two empty seats for Red and himself and when he had almost reached the middle of the train, he suddenly heard above the crowd: "Guys! Hey! Guys! This way! Come on! This way!" Dave looked up and saw the Musketeers. They were hanging out of a window in one of the cars a little ahead and motioning for them to come their way. They were in the middle of the car and Dave waved he had seen them. He headed for their car and when he reached it, Dave stepped in with Red. He walked down the aisle and when he came to them, he greeted them. He swung his suitcase in the baggage rack above the two swungover seats they had saved for them as well as for themselves on the right side of the car. Red also swung his suitcase in the baggage rack above the two swungover seats, and Dave sat down against the window and faced Red and Higgins who sat opposite him.

The other two Musketeers stood in the aisle next to two swungover seats they had also saved for themselves on the left side of the aisle. The Musketeers looked at him and Dave turned to Higgins. He leaned a little bit forward in his seat and said: "Tell me. How is The Wailing And Gnashing Of Teeth And Wringing Of Hands In The Old Mansion Saga?"

"Oh, hot. Very hot."

"That good."

"You're damn right. Any hotter and it'll burn the house down."

"What do you know? A tense and exciting Saga."

"You're not kidding. In fact it's so tense it's the first time I've ever seen my old man so mad. For a while there I thought he was going to hit me."

"What was he so mad about?"

"Oh, he thought my enlisting as a foot soldier was stupid and asked me what I was trying to do. Fight him? In fact he got so worked up at one point he threatened to go to General McNaughton if necessary and have my enlistment canceled."

"Could he do that?"

"I don't know. But he's got a lot of connections. That's for sure."

"How about that? A man who loves his own son."

"You can say that again. And that's exactly what I told him. I mean, here is a man who is so obsessed with making money and being with the right people and doing the right thing all the time I rarely saw him except during the summer holidays when we went to Montebello or Cap Rouge or Pointe Au Pic. And even then he only went to those places to be with the right people and do the right thing; not to be with me. And now all of a sudden, just because I want to do something for myself for a change and not for him, he's all over me and yelling and screaming. I'm telling you. I just don't get it."

"That's because he has your best interests at heart."

"Oh, sure. And that's what I told him too. I mean, the man was traveling so damn much all the time, I rarely saw him. And when I did, instead of talking to me and getting to know me, he would pick on me and we would have all those terrible fights. Then, when those fights were over, he would go and buy me expensive gifts. Hell, I didn't need expensive gifts! I needed him to talk to me and get to know me! And now that I don't need him, and don't want to be with him anymore, he's all over me and yelling and screaming. I'm telling you. I just don't get it."

"I guess you got a lot more than what you bargained for."

"You're not kidding. I know I said I was excited and couldn't wait to see his face when I told him I had enlisted. But man, I sure didn't expect this!"

"It's not easy going for the big one, is it?"

In The Beginning

"It sure isn't. And do you know what my father told me before I left? He said that when all is said and done I'd find out three things: one, that, in this best of all possible worlds, going in at the top and doing things first-class is the only way; two, that money is everything, absolutely everything; and three, that everything else, no matter what people say, is just pure and sentimental nonsense. That's what he said."

Dave laughed.

"How about that? Your old man's a cold and hard-nosed realist."

"You're telling me."

"From all that I guess you could say he didn't like the idea of your going in as a foot soldier."

"That's putting it mildly."

"What about you?" Dave turned to Addams. "How did your old man like the idea of your enlisting?"

"Oh, he didn't like it too much. But he didn't say anything."

"Bob's lucky that way," Higgins said. "His old man's a dentist and he's pretty quiet. I wish my old man was like that."

"Don't we all wish," Mitchell said.

"What about you?" Dave turned to Mitchell. "What did your old man say?"

"Oh, he didn't like it. He didn't like it one bit."

"Did he yell and scream?"

"Oh no. You have to remember my father's a corporate lawyer. That's not his style. In his case he just told me in his very cold and chilly way he had always known I was a rebel and on the left of every cause. And he wondered if my joining as a foot soldier wasn't maybe a Bolshevik move on my part."

Dave laughed again.

"How about that? Another man who loves his son."

"It sure is something, isn't it?"

"It sure is. But are you? A Bolshevik, I mean."

"God, no. But, yes, I sympathize with people who have little and who try to do the best they can with what they have."

"And that makes you a Bolshevik?"

"Apparently. In my father's eyes."

"It doesn't take much to frighten him, does it?"

"It doesn't. My father frightens easily."

"How come?"

"I don't know. That's just the way he is."

"Well, from what I can see," Dave said, "there sure are a lot of nice and understanding people in Westmount."

"There sure are," Mitchell said.

"You're not kidding," Higgins said. "And I'll tell you something else. That was a pretty tense and exhausting week-end we just had. So I'm damn glad we're getting the hell out of here and going to Terreyville."

"That makes two of us," Mitchell said.

"Make that three," Addams said.

"People are not that easy to handle, are they," Dave said, "when they want you to do things their way."

"They sure aren't," Higgins said. "And I'm telling you. I knew this thing was going to be tough. But not this tough."

"Well it's over and done with. You did what you wanted. Forget it."

"Sure. But it's not so easy to do."

"Did I say any different?"

"No."

"Well all right then. And besides. What else can you do?"

"I know."

"Also. Look at it this way. It may make your life hard to take for a while. But it sure makes it interesting."

"That's for sure. Although, to tell you the truth, too interesting sometimes."

"Well it's better than not interesting at all."

"That's true."

"And anyway. You wanted to stand up to your old man and did it. That's the main thing. That's all that matters."

"That's true."

"So that's it then."

CHAPTER 14

Higgins nodded and suddenly there was a lurch. There was another lurch. Dave turned away from Higgins and watched as they began moving slowly and sliding past the embarkation platform. In a little while they began making a long extended turn out of the Bonaventure station and into the sudden, heart-stopping and achingly-beautiful light of evening. Now, right on the stroke of 8.00 o'clock, the sun was setting and turning into an ever-deepening gold, orange and purple all over the city. They kept on moving slowly and steadily and when they cleared the last approaches to the station and the marshaling yards, they picked up speed and began heading for the West End and for the Ontario border.

When they left the station Dave, Red and the Musketeers looked out of the windows and watched as the sun began setting over the city. In a little while they reached the city's outskirts and in the distance they could see the mountain and the St. Joseph's Shrine. The mountain and the shrine stood darkly against the blazingly red, orange and purple sky and the shrine was crowned by its shining and brightly-lit cross. Then they began leaving the city behind and they all turned from the windows and began talking about life in general, their training ground in Terreyville and the Regiment. As they talked they made the extremely happy and unexpected discovery the Musketeers had been assigned to the same Section, Platoon and Battalion Dave and Red had been.

They talked about that for a while and Red suggested they play a game of poker at a quarter a hand. Dave didn't feel like it. So Red played with the Musketeers. Dave watched them play for a while and then turned away from them and lay back in his seat. He closed his eyes and fell asleep and was only disturbed twice during their long and endless journey. The first time was around 2.00 o'clock in the morning when they pulled into the bluish glare of Union Station in Toronto and began taking on more recruits. The second time was roughly four hours later when Dave felt a lurch and then another lurch and opened his eyes. He found himself staring at the pale graying light of dawn and saw their train was slowing down. At that moment it was coming out of a long extended turn past some marshaling yards and suddenly the town of Terreyville sprang into view.

It rose darkly and sharply out of the pale graying dawn and stood as a tough and hard-working frontier town of about 10,000 people. It perfectly matched the low rocky barren hills that stretched all around and its harsh and rugged skyline stabbed the sky with its many church steeples and with the stark and stiff outline of its other prominent buildings. It stood at the northernmost point in the line and was extremely close to the bush and the wilderness. It had a raw and savage quality about it that seemed to give an edge to the whole landscape and it loomed over the cold and blue-gray expanse of Lake Wastassini that showed in patches through the white birch and green pine forests on its right and the huge and distant site of the Harrison Nickel Mines on its left.

In the pale graying dawn the town kept on getting closer and closer and soon they began slipping past its many small streets lined with one, two and three-story clapboard and redbrick houses. In a little while the small redbrick station, with its square wooden sign that had the letters TERREYVILLE painted in red on it against a white background, got bigger and bigger and then came and stopped in front of them. As soon as it did Dave got up and reached for his suitcase. He began filing out of his car with Red and the Musketeers. Outside he paused and breathed the cold crisp northern air. That early in the morning the sky was slashed with wild and fiery streaks of gold and as he looked around, Dave saw how big their train was. It sprawled for quite a way past both sides of the railway station. From all the recruits getting out Dave guessed there must be over 500 of them.

They were made to line up alongside the train. Then the COs and NCOs who had been with them during the journey began leading them away from the station and down Main Street. Even though it was early in the morning quite a few people had come out to see them. They lined Main Street and most of them grinned at them. Many waved. Some gave them the thumbs up sign. A few flashed the V-for-Victory sign. Some of the recruits grinned and waved back and when they reached the corner of Main and Nolan, the whole formation was made to stop and stand at ease. Dave was in the middle of the formation with Red and the Musketeers. As he stood there he looked around and saw how this frontier town was like any other frontier town of that size.

It had, on the right, the usual market place, the town hotel, the fire and police departments, various churches, stores, shops and businesses. It had, on the left, the usual garage and gas station, the town restaurant, a hardware store, a furniture store, the Town Hall, the City Arena, and various other stores, shops and businesses. It was just a tough and hard-working frontier town and as Dave looked at it, the formation stayed at ease and didn't move for over an hour. Then it began heading slowly toward the Town Hall and around 10.00 a.m., Dave found out why it was taking them so long to move.

CHAPTER 15

When they got closer to the Town Hall Dave found out they were going in single file. That was the reason why it was taking them so long to move. Dave kept on heading there and when he went in, he saw how the council chamber had been stripped of all furniture and turned into a supply depot for the Regiment. The chamber, Dave saw, was huge and had two enormous oaken doors. These had been pushed open and it had a shiny hardwood floor and a black iron passageway that ran all around the second floor. There were offices to the right of the passageway and black spiral staircases at the four corners of the passageway that led down to the council chamber.

That morning the chamber was filled with Corporals, Lance Corporals, Sergeants and officers who were moving and rushing around the extended rows of tables that had been set up and piled high with equipment. In the chamber some of the NCOs under the watchful eyes of a few COs were giving everyone two of everything: battle-dresses, field fatigues, inspection uniforms, caps, puttees, boots, blankets, combat packs, the big one and the small one, a helmet, a gas mask, webbing and a giant-size duffel bag. It took a while to pick up all those things and when he had his full gear and had put it in his giant-size duffel bag, Dave headed out of the Town Hall with Red and the Musketeers. Outside they fell in line with another group of recruits who had their full gear and who were waiting on Main Street by the side of the road.

Finally, when their line was long enough, a young Lieutenant came out of the Town Hall and began leading them toward their training ground. They marched down Main Street until they reached Lumsden Road. Their training ground was alongside Lumsden Road and faced the end of Main Street. When they reached it Dave saw how it had the same kind of raw and savage quality he had found in the town of Terreyville itself. At the entrance Dave noted it had a six-feet chicken wire fence that ran all around it and was topped by four feet of in-leaning barbed wire. The words DEPARTMENT OF NATIONAL DEFENSE arched over the entrance and on each side of the front gate there was an armed sentry who stood outside his sentry box. Dave walked past the two armed sentries and inside, he saw what a huge and impressive place it was.

To the right, as you came in, stood three tall white flagpoles flying the Red Ensign, the Union Jack and the Regimental Colors, a flag with a black gold-rimmed eagle holding on a slant in its right claw a black gold-rimmed rifle with bayonet against a field of red. About 10 feet in front of those flagpoles there was a lone and solitary megaphone. To the right of the training ground ran six long rows of pale-gray Bell tents and in front of the tents stood the hard and flat dirt of the Parade Ground. At the back of the tents, and right in the middle of the training ground, there was another gate flanked by two armed sentries. Those two armed sentries stood outside of their sentry boxes and those sentry boxes were outside the fence. Further, beyond the gate and the fence, there was a grim and forbidding white birch and green pine forest.

Through a small gap in the trees you could catch a glimpse of the cold blue-gray expanse of Lake Wastassini. At the rear of the training ground there was, on the right, the firing range and, on the left, the artillery range. All in all this made for quite a huge and impressive place and after he had looked at it, Dave followed the young Lieutenant. He took them into the training ground proper and brought them to where the tents were. He stopped in front of them, in the middle of the first row, and told them to go and wait in front of the tents they had been assigned to according to the cards they had been issued. Since Dave, Red and the Musketeers had been issued a white card with the numbers 111 stenciled in black on them, they looked for a tent with the same markings.

In a little while they found it. The tent was in the first row. It was the fourth tent from the left and when they found it, they went and put down their gear about 15 feet in front of it. By that time it was near noon and the sun was shining brightly and warmly on them. As he stood in front of his tent Dave looked around. He saw there was a constant stream of recruits coming into the training ground. They were being taken there by junior officers. Dave looked at the oncoming recruits for a while and when he turned away from them and looked at the training ground again, his eyes came and rested on the most unlikely group of recruits he had ever seen. There were four of them. They were standing between him and the first three tents. Dave looked at them for a while and wondered whether they belonged to their Company, B Company, with its black and white markings, or to A Company, with its black and blue markings.

From where they stood Dave couldn't tell. All of them looked very self-conscious and ill at ease and they were putting on an air of boredom and indifference that was neither credible nor believable. The first of those recruits stood on the right. He was lean and wiry. He was of average height and had wild and unruly black hair. He also had bright and fiery eyes burning with a seething and smoldering impatience and he was walking back and forth in front of the other three and watching and checking everything. Next to him stood a recruit who was of equal height and build but who looked taller and a little bigger somehow. This recruit had neat trim pale-blond hair and clear watchful pale-blue eyes. He just stood next to the first recruit and looked around the training ground carefully and thoughtfully.

Beside him stood a man who was an absolute giant. He was around six feet four and weighed about 240 pounds. He had a huge pale-blond square-jawed head. He also had powerful rock-hard muscles, broad massive shoulders and a narrow tapering waist. As a matter of fact he looked as if he had been carved in stone. The fourth and last recruit was a man who struck Dave as being quite different from the other three. In his case maybe it was his somewhat trim tallness and leaner build; his neat dark hair falling in a long strand over his wide forehead; his bony angular face; or his sharp penetrating eyes. But, whatever it was, there was an awareness in this man that was quite different from the other three. These four recruits stood together and seemed to seek in their collective unease and discomfort a certain amount of relief from the starkness and rawness of the training ground.

This was quite obvious from the looks on their faces, from their gestures and from their moves. In fact they were such an unlikely group of men, and were so different from the other recruits in the training ground, that, with Red and the Musketeers following a little behind him, Dave began walking over to them.

CHAPTER 16

Dave walked toward those recruits and when he reached them, he came and stopped in front of the first one. This was the boy with wild, unruly black hair and bright, fiery eyes. He had been walking back and forth in front of his three companions and when Dave reached him, followed by Red and the Musketeers who stood a little behind both of them, he came and stopped to the right of his companions. When he stopped there Dave walked up to him and said: "This place is quite something, isn't it?"

"It sure is."

"You don't seem to be too happy about it."

"I'm not."

"How come?"

"I mean. Look at it. This place looks like a goddam concentration camp!"

"I have to admit. It doesn't look like a summer camp."

"That's for sure. And mark my words. Nothing easy's going to come out of here."

"I agree."

"As a matter of fact I can just imagine the kind of training we're going to do here."

"So can I."

"Yeah. This place sure looks like a goddam relief camp, doesn't it?" Red said.

"You know about relief camps?" Dave turned to Red.

"Sure. There was one at Brownridge near where I lived. Some of the men who worked there used to come to our place to ask for food.

They called their camp a slave camp. But they said it was run more like a concentration camp, really."

"What exactly were relief camps?" Addams asked.

"Oh, they were camps for guys who didn't have a job," Red said. "The government put them there and made them do stupid work like building roads going nowhere or farming in areas where it couldn't be done. They closed them down a couple of years ago."

"They weren't pleasure resorts. That's for sure," the first recruit, the boy, said.

"You know about the camps too?" Dave turned to the boy.

"Sure. I rode freights for a while and saw quite a few of them. Believe me. They were no picnic."

"Why did you come here then?"

"Who knows? Maybe I'm crazy."

"To be with the toughest of the tough, hey," Red said.

"Yeah. Something like that," the boy said.

"Well, this place certainly looks tough enough and mean enough to make everybody miserable," Dave said.

"That's for sure," the boy said. "What the hell's going on? Why all the sentries and barbed wire? What are they trying to prove?"

"Who knows?" Dave said. "Maybe they're trying to keep this place secret so not too many people know about it."

"What are they afraid of?" the boy said. "That people will steal the guns or the flagpoles?"

"Who knows? Maybe they think this place is so wonderful it has to be guarded."

"Oh sure. We're in the bush, with barbed wire and tent accommodation. What more could anybody want. Right?"

"Exactly. Who could ask for anything more."

"Well, I just don't get it."

"I don't get it either," Dave said. "But, whatever it is, I must say it's quite a place."

"I'll buy that," the boy said as he stepped forward a little and put out his hand to Dave. "My name's Gennaro. Gianni Gennaro. Gino for short."

Dave shook his hand and introduced himself, Red and the Musketeers. Then he turned to the second recruit, the boy with neat trim pale-blond hair and clear watchful pale-blue eyes who stood next to Gennaro, and said: "What about you? Why did you come here?"

The boy pointed to Gennaro.

"Same as him. Maybe I'm crazy too."

In The Beginning

"You don't like this place?"
"Not really."
"Why did you come here then?"
"Who knows? Maybe I had no choice."
"What do you mean?"
"Who knows? Maybe I just had to do it."
"Why?"
"Maybe in order to do the things I want to do later on."
"What things?"
"The things I want to do later on."
"That seems to me like one hell of a choice."
"It is."
"It's certainly one I wouldn't like to make."
"Neither would I. But, who knows, maybe in these things none of us really has a choice."
"Maybe."
"But, I tell you, after I enlisted I really had a bad feeling about this place."
"Why?"
"I don't know. I didn't have it before I enlisted. Then I thought it was a great idea. But after I'd done it, it hit me and I've been feeling bad ever since."
"Why?" Dave said.
"I don't know," the boy said. "Maybe it has something to do with the way I rushed out to do it, with the people, the officers or the armory."
"What armory?"
"The one in Kitchener."
"I hear it's quite an armory."
"It is."
"Are you German?"
"No. But my parents are."
"From where?"
"Kiel."
"The heart of Socialist Germany."
"You got it."
"So you felt bad when you enlisted?"
"I did. And now that I'm here and look at this place and the way it's set up, I feel even worse and say to myself: 'What an idea! What a crazy idea!' And wonder why I've done it in the first place."
"Like you said. Maybe you were crazy too."
"That's what I'm thinking."

The Long War

"But then maybe we all are."

"Maybe."

"So that's why you came here? Because you had to do what you had to do?"

"That's it," the boy said as he also stepped forward a little and put out his hand to Dave. "By the way my name's Eric Lang. Eric will do."

Dave shook his hand and turned to the third recruit, the gigantic blond-haired square-jawed boy who was standing next to Lang, and said: "What about you? Why did you come here?"

"Oh, I just had to."

"What do you mean?"

"Hitler doesn't like Slavs."

"Hitler doesn't like a lot of people."

"True. But he doesn't like Slavs particularly."

"Hitler doesn't like anybody. Period."

"That's true. But he doesn't like Slavs particularly."

"Listen. The Slavs aren't the only people Hitler doesn't like."

"I know that."

"Believe me. He doesn't like Jews, Czechs, Poles, Russians, Frenchmen, Englishmen. Hell, I don't think he even likes himself."

"That's true."

"Who knows, if the sonofabitch had been married, maybe things would have been different, hey?"

"Maybe."

"It's true. If he had been, maybe he would have taken it out on his wife instead of on everybody else, hey?"

"Maybe."

"Anyway, that's why you enlisted?" Dave said. "Because Hitler doesn't like Slavs?"

"That's right," the boy said.

"What else?"

"Because this is a good Regiment. A very good Regiment."

"I'll buy that."

"And because the Germans are strong and won't be that easy to beat."

"I'll buy that too."

"That's why I came here. This is a good camp. A very good camp. And here, I believe, they'll turn us into tough soldiers and teach us how to beat them."

"Maybe," Dave said.

"I believe they will," the boy said and put out a huge bear-like hand which Dave took and which crushed his own, as they shook hands, before the boy let it go. "By the way my name is Michael Slavomir Marchenko. Mikhail, actually."

"Slavomir. What kind of a name is that?"

"It's Polish. On my mother's side. It's the name of my grandfather."

"It's an unusual name. At least for around here. But it's okay."

"It *is* unusual."

"What do we call you then?"

"Slav. You can call me Slav. That's what everyone calls me."

"Okay. That's what we'll call you," Dave said and moved away from Slav. He turned to the fourth recruit, the tall dark-haired angular-faced boy who was standing a little apart from the other three, and said: "What about you? Why did you come here?"

"Maybe I'm crazy too," the boy said in a slightly-accented English.

"Are you really?"

"Sure. Why not?"

"That's good."

"Not really. It's just the way it is."

"Well, whatever."

"And, anyway, maybe I wanted to come here."

"Did you?"

"Maybe I did. After all a training ground's a training ground. We're all going to learn and do the same things. What's the big deal?"

"It's no big deal. But you think this training ground's just like any other training ground and there's no difference?"

"That's right."

"None at all?"

"None."

"And that's why you came here?" Dave said. "Because you wanted to?"

"That's right," the boy said. "And, besides, my family thinks this is just an English and German war. I don't think so."

"I don't think so either."

"And, anyway, in something like this you have to put your money where your mouth is. You just can't talk about it."

"That's true."

"You just can't go on and on and always keep on talking about this."

"That's for sure."

"At least that's what I think."

"That's what I think too. But is that what your family's doing? Just talking about this, I mean?"

The Long War

"They are."
"Well, that's certainly easy to do."
"It is."
"Talk is cheap."
"Talk's always cheap."
"You're not kidding," Dave said. "It's the doing that's tough."
"That's it," the boy said. "It's the old problem of doing as opposed to talking."
"I agree. But I have a feeling there's going to be plenty of doing here and very little talking."
"That's what I think too. And, besides, I think it's about time I found out what kind of a country this is."
"Why? What's wrong with this country?"
"There's nothing wrong with it. I just want to find out how it's going to take what's coming and how I'm going to take it too."
"That's a pretty tall order."
"It certainly is."
"You want to go the distance."
"That's it."
"It's really something."
"It is. And, while I'm at it, I want to see how it's going to treat us French people in it."
"Why? You don't think the country's treating the French right?"
"I don't know. That's what I'm going to find out."
"That should be interesting."
"It should be. And, besides, I also want to see how the French are going to be treated in the whole world even."
"Now that's something."
"It is."
"Well, why not? Why not do that?"
"Sure."
"It's true. What's wrong with that?"
"I agree. By the way my name is Delorme. Pierre Delorme."
The tall dark-haired angular-faced boy put out his hand. Dave shook it and so did Red, the Musketeers and the other three boys. When they had all shaken hands Dave looked at them and then said: "What a bunch."
"I'll buy that," Red said.
"The Big Ten," Dave said.
"We're only nine," Addams said.
"Don't worry. We'll find another one," Dave said.

CHAPTER 17

Dave wanted to go on and say something else on that when his attention was drawn by a non-commissioned officer who was coming into the training ground. This non-commissioned officer was flanked on the left by a short, stocky and overly serious Lance Corporal and on the right by a tall, bony and unsparingly grim Corporal. He marched past the two armed sentries at the gate and stepped into the compound. He walked in the middle of a group of NCOs who were also coming in with their assistants and who were heading toward the various Companies. When he stepped into the compound he began marching toward their own Company and Dave watched him and thought: Oh my God! Who is that? Who the hell is that?

This non-commissioned officer Dave was watching was indeed quite a soldier. He was in his early thirties and stood around five feet ten or eleven. He weighed about 180 pounds and had a big clean-shaven head, a huge bull neck and sharp penetrating eyes that kept on roaming all the time and on checking and never missing anything. He also had a thick handlebar mustache that was waxed crisply and curved up smartly at both ends, broad massive shoulders, trim narrow hips and powerful muscular legs. He was wearing an immaculately-pressed wedge cap and, with the deep tan on his face that was changing every once in a while into a surprising and unmistakable sallowness, with his clear glittering eyes and with the deep strong curl of his mouth that could widen into a snarl or a growl or a grin, he had a baleful, malevolent and Asiatic look that made him appear, at times, brazen and insolent, if not positively chilling and frightening.

At the moment he was carrying a shiny leather swagger stick in his right hand and was marching at a fast pace. He kept on heading toward their own Company and toward the long lines of recruits who were waiting in the Company area in front of their tents. By that time most of the recruits had finally arrived from the supply depot. When they saw him they stepped out a little over 30 feet in front of the tents and formed up in three extended rows on the Parade Ground. As he reached them he slowed down and stopped abruptly in front of them. The Lance Corporal and the Corporal also slowed down and stopped slightly behind him. As he stopped in front of them he planted both feet firmly on the ground and barked: "Attention!"

Everyone snapped to it.

He just stood there and stared at them. Then he began marching back and forth in front of their lines. His dark, swift and penetrating eyes moved and swept slowly over everyone and Dave felt an icy shiver run up and down his spine when he suddenly felt the man's eyes on him. It stripped him down, rolled him inside out and stood him on end. The man's eyes stayed on Dave briefly and then moved on to another recruit. As he kept on marching back and forth in front of them and on eyeing and checking them, a bright sparkling grin broke on his face and showed a flash of white impeccable teeth. Then he stopped marching and came and stood in the middle of their lines. As he stood there he stared at them and then said: "Gentlemen. My name is Harold T. Bostwick. T stands for Terence. But to you I'm Sergeant Major!

"Now. All of you may have joined the Army and come over here to get away from the Depression and the bad times and the bread lines and the food riots and the lack of work. Or you may have done it to have a better life and a roof over your head and a little money in your pockets. Or, God help you, you may have done it because you think this is the best, the one and only, the greatest Regiment there is. Or because there's even a goddam war on! But let me explain something to you and let me be very clear. The Westmount Fusiliers is a Regular Army Infantry Regiment. It's an Elite Assault Unit created by the Federal Government in the First World War in order to give punch and experience to any attack the Canadian Army might make. We may be assigned to any Canadian Division, or Allied Division, to do what we were created to do in the first place: *Taking Care Of Business.* Do you know what that means? Do you understand what I'm talking about?"

Bostwick gave them another bright sparkling grin and another flash of his white impeccable teeth. He began marching back and forth in front of them again and his shiny leather swagger stick rapped stiffly against his right leg. He stared fiercely and ferociously at them and after a while, he came and stopped in the middle of their lines again. As he stood there he stared at them and said: "That's right, gentlemen. This is a Regular Army Regiment. A Rifle Unit. Not the lousy Militia where they spoil you, pamper you, indulge you and want to make a goddam career out of it! Oh no, gentlemen. This is an Elite Assault Unit where every manjack is a sorry-assed, pig-headed, cold-hearted sonofabitch! a hard-case volunteer! This is a place where, as a regular soldier, we'll show you how to fight, where and when.

"This is a place where we'll show you how to take every situation, recognize it for what it is and act on it. As a matter of fact this is a place where we'll show you how to adapt, invent and improvise. Also, since we're a Rifle Regiment, we'll show you how to use your gun and call it your rifle, not your gun. Although, from the looks of all of you, I must say you don't truly know how to use your gun and have used it very little, if at all. But that'll quickly change, gentlemen. Trust me. You don't have to worry on that score!" Bostwick paused and stared at them. By that time most of them had begun listening to him very closely and intently and after a moment, he went on: "Now then. Since you all look so incredibly blissful and happy to be here, so damn keen and eager to get going, so truly moved and impressed by this place, I want to see you on the Parade Ground in your newly-issued field fatigues at 1700 hours sharp.

"At that time we'll get to know each other and have a little workout before we really start training in earnest tomorrow. For the non-educated and non-military among you that means I want to see you on the Parade Ground at 5.00 o'clock this afternoon. That's roughly four hours from now. I'm sure that'll give you enough time to find your assigned tent, settle in and familiarize yourselves with your surroundings. However, during that time, you better enjoy yourselves, gentlemen. You better make good use of it. And you better live it to the full. Because after that, after 1700 hours, you'll have do deal with me and you'll be mine! *Do you hear me*! MINE!"

BOOK TWO

TRAINING

CHAPTER 18

Bostwick then dismissed the men. He turned away sharply and began leaving the training ground with his two assistants. Dave, who was standing in the middle of the first line of recruits with the Big Ten, watched him until he was gone. Then Dave turned and began walking back toward his gear standing about 15 feet away. He picked it up and headed toward their tent. When Dave reached it he went in and took the first bunk from the entrance on the right. Red chose the second one. Higgins, the third. Addams and Mitchell, the fourth and fifth ones. Gennaro took the first bunk on the left side. Lang chose the next one and was followed by Slav and Delorme.

The last bunk was taken by a pleasant, affable, flaxen-haired and frail-looking 19 years-old boy who now came in and introduced himself. His name was Leon Dabrowski and he was a Pole whose friends were all scattered in the Second and Third Platoons. After the introductions with Dabrowski Dave opened his foot locker and, from his suitcase, began stowing his gear as well as his personal effects. While he was doing this the Corporal who had been with Bostwick came into their tent and handed everyone red tags. He told them to put their names and the number of their Section, Platoon and Regiment on them, tie those tags to the handles of their suitcases and bring them to the last tent of the sixth row where they would be picked up in a few days and transferred to the Quartermaster store in the City Arena.

Then the Corporal left and when he had finished stowing his gear in his locker, Dave began putting on his brand-new field fatigues. He slipped first into his khaki T-shirt, then his shorts and socks, and finally his shirt, overalls and boots. When he was dressed Dave picked up his red tag and did what the Corporal had asked them to do. He tied his red tag to the handle of his suitcase and brought the suitcase to the last tent of the sixth row as he had been asked. Then Dave left that tent and began walking back to his own tent. He walked past the mess and shower tents that were right in the middle of all the tents and saw NCOs were patrolling the fences in pairs and not letting anyone near those fences. When he reached his tent Dave went in and put the finishing touches to his foot locker.

Finally Dave sat on his bunk and talked with the Big Ten. Near 5.00 o'clock he left with them and went and lined up in the first of three rows in front of their tents as Bostwick had told them. At 5.00 o'clock sharp Bostwick marched into the compound and headed for the Parade Ground and for their tents with his two assistants. When he reached the Parade Ground he stopped and eyed them sharply and penetratingly. Then he began running them. Bostwick took them slowly around the compound. The compound was two miles long by two miles wide and when he had taken them around once, he made them go around two more times. By the time he had made them go around for a fourth time, Dave saw how incredibly tough and hard-driving Bostwick really was.

As they kept on running, there was Bostwick rushing in and out of the Sections and Platoons. He was yelling and screaming and pushing. But he was always there with the Platoon Sergeants and running the men to the limit of what they could take. He kept on running them like this and on one of the many turns around the site, Dave found out how incredibly tough and hard-driving Bostwick could be. By then Bostwick had made them drop down in front of the tents on the Parade Ground and do push-ups. While he was doing those push-ups Dave suddenly felt Bostwick's hard hobnailed boot in the small of his back. He was pushing him down and forcing him to rise against its pressure while saying in a harsh cutting voice: "Come on! Come on! Pump those arms! Pump those arms, soldier!"

Dave grunted. The sweat was pouring down his eyes and he was gasping for breath. He felt his lungs were going to burst and his arms and legs were shaking. Still he tried to do the push-ups sharply, cleanly and as best he could. Bostwick kept his boot in the small of his back. He kept on pushing him down and forcing him to rise against it. Dave kept on trying to do the push-ups and it took a while before Bostwick eased the pressure on his back and made him stand up and face him. When he did Bostwick glared at Dave and said: "What's your name, soldier?"

"David M. Lindsay, Sir."

"What did you say?"

"David M. Lindsay."

"I didn't hear you."
"David M. Lindsay."
"What does the M stand for?"
"Martin."
"Sergeant Major. You say: 'Sergeant Major.'"
"Sergeant Major."
"I didn't hear you!"
"SERGEANT MAJOR!"
"LOUDER!"
"SERGEANT MAJOR!"
"LOUDER!"
"S-E-R-G-E-A-N-T M-A-J-O-R!"
"OKAY! THAT'S WHAT I WANT TO HEAR! THAT'S WHAT I ALWAYS WANT TO HEAR! DO YOU UNDERSTAND!"
"Y-E-S! S-E-R-G-E-A-N-T M-A-J-O-R!"
"DO YOU!"
"Y-E-S! S-E-R-G-E-A-N-T M-A-J-O-R!"

CHAPTER 19

Bostwick then left Dave and went on to jump on another recruit not too far from him. He made that recruit do the same kind of push-ups Dave had just done and for the next three hours, from 5.00 o'clock in the afternoon until 8.00 o'clock in the evening, he kept on working them out like this. As they kept on running and doing push-ups the temperature dropped a little and a cool wind rose. Bostwick gave them short five-minute breaks every once in a while for them to get their wind back and around 8.30, he made them come and stop in front of their tents on the Parade Ground.

When they stood there Bostwick stepped forward and told them, now that they had worked out with him and found out what it was like to be with the Fusiliers, he wanted to see them on the Parade Ground at 0545 tomorrow morning. Then they'd start training in earnest and find out if they really had the stuff to soldier in an Infantry Regiment and especially in an Elite Assault Unit as tough and mean as the Westmount Fusiliers. At this point Bostwick dismissed them. He turned away sharply and began leaving the training ground with his assistants. Dave watched them go. Then he also turned and began heading back toward his tent with the Big Ten. At the rolled-up flap entrance Dave walked in and went and sat down on his bunk.

As he sat there Dave found out how incredibly hard and demanding his three-hour workout had been. When he took off his shirt and overalls he saw he had sweated salt which had burned itself into two huge white streaks right through his khaki T-shirt. Every bone in his body was aching. There was a strong and persistent shaking all through his thighs and legs. Since the shaking went on even when he was sitting down Dave massaged his thighs and legs for a while. He also stood up and walked around in

Training

order to get rid of the shaking. When he was able to do that and felt better, he put on a clean pair of fatigues. Then he turned and headed for the rolled-up flap entrance of his tent where he looked out. Now, a little after 9.00 o'clock in the evening, the sun was going down in a deep smoldering gold all over the training ground.

It was falling across and sweeping the Parade Ground, the firing range, the artillery range, the three tall white flagpoles, whose flags were flying briskly and stiffly in the cool crisp evening breeze, and the city of Terreyville beyond. Dave just stood at the rolled-up flap entrance and looked at this truly magnificent and extraordinary evening. Then, as he was about to turn away and go back to his bunk, he saw the five-men Bugle Detail. It was made up of a young Captain, three young soldiers and a Bugling Sergeant who appeared to be in his early thirties. Right now the Bugle Detail had reached the front gate and was coming into the training ground. The Detail marched into the compound and came and stopped in front of the three tall white flagpoles. The three young soldiers each stood in front of a flagpole.

The Bugling Sergeant stood behind the solitary pale-brown megaphone. The young Captain stood between the Bugling Sergeant and the three soldiers. At a command from the Captain all of them turned and snapped to attention. The Captain saluted sharply and the three soldiers began lowering the flags. The one on the left lowered the Red Ensign. The one in the center lowered the Union Jack. The one on the right took down the Regimental Colors. All of them folded the flags lengthwise and rolled them from the non-halyard to the halyard side. They tucked the flags neatly under their left arms and turned and stood at attention facing the Captain. As they faced him the Captain finished his salute. He turned with the Bugling Sergeant and both of them stood at attention with the three soldiers as they all faced the training ground.

At that moment the Bugling Sergeant stepped to the megaphone and began playing the Last Post. In that clear and sunny evening he began playing it slowly and powerfully. The full rich throaty notes began rising and falling, climbing and soaring, rolling and echoing across the silent and deserted quadrangle and gave this truly magnificent and extraordinary evening an indescribable note of pride and sadness, of joy and sorrow, of longing and melancholy at martial and military deeds that had been done in the past, that were in fact being done now and that would undoubtedly be done in the future. This Last Post was, in fact, a timeless and immemorial salute to the merciless demands and heroic sacrifices their harsh, hard, hectic, much-maligned, much-ignored and much-misunderstood profession required of them in order to be, first of all, men, certainly, human beings, but, above all, soldiers.

The Bugling Sergeant played it all that way. He played it with a depth and understanding, a power and intensity, a pride and confidence that was both moving and touching since it seemed to match that truly magnificent and extraordinary evening and become part of it and deepen and enhance it even. He played it all slowly and powerfully like this, with a sureness of touch at once swift yet undefinable, knowing yet intuitive, wise yet reckless. He paused over some phrases and hurried over others. He lingered over some and swept over others and when he finally came to the end of his Last Post, he stopped suddenly and let the last lingering notes, that were unbelievably soft and caressing in their fullness, move on and fade across the silent and deserted quadrangle.

As this happened the Bugling Sergeant stepped back from the megaphone. He stood at attention and held the bugle at his right side. At a command from the Captain they all made a half-turn to the right. They began leaving the training ground and the Captain led the Detail. He was followed by the three soldiers and the Bugling Sergeant brought up the rear. Dave stood at the rolled-up flap entrance of his tent and watched them leave. He was in the grip of an extremely powerful and totally unexpected emotion and when they were gone, he left the entrance and went and lay down on his bunk. He lay on his back with his hands behind his head. Right now, after all he had seen, done and lived through today, Dave knew one thing. He had to make a move. No matter what happened, even if at risk to himself, he had to make a move and try and get out of this place.

But now, instead of trying to consider this and analyze it in order to work it out, Dave was too tired and exhausted to do it. Every bone in his body was aching. His thighs and legs were still shaky. He had a dull splitting headache. In fact it was so bad Dave had to lie very still in his bunk and stare at the ceiling. After a while he became aware of his heart skipping every once in a while. He also felt all the back-breaking and bone-crushing fatigue pulsing and throbbing within him and as he lay there, he closed his eyes and heard, saw and listened to absolutely nothing.

CHAPTER 20

"Rise and shine! Rise and shine! Grab your socks and move your butt! Come on! Come on! Let's go! Move!"

Dave opened bleary and exhausted eyes and found himself staring at the huge and towering figure of Bostwick. He had come into their tent and put on their ceiling light. Even when showing up so startlingly and unexpectedly like this Bostwick was dressed in such sharply-pressed and spotlessly-clean field fatigues he looked as if he was going out on an extremely formal and ceremonial Dress Parade. He was moving around and rattling some of their bunks with his leather swagger stick. He was kicking others with his brightly-polished hobnailed boots. But he was telling the men he wanted to see them in half an hour fully washed, shaved and lined up in three rows in front of their tents by height. He wanted the smallest men to stand in the first line and the tallest ones to be in the third one. Then he marched out and disappeared to go and pounce on some other star-crossed and ill-fated tent.

Dave rubbed his eyes and looked at his watch. It was 4.15 a.m. He thought it was typical of Bostwick to tell them he wanted to see them on the Parade Ground at 5.45 a.m. and wake them up at 4.15 a.m. It was probably his way of wanting to teach them never to take anything for granted nor at face value and, in this manner, try and break them the way he wanted. Dave tried not to think about this too much and threw his blanket off. He swung his feet on the circular wooden floor and shivered as he felt the cold dark-filled morning chill in his khaki T-shirt and shorts. He slapped his sides a few times to get his stiff sore muscles working again. Then Dave got up with Higgins and the rest of the Big Ten and dressed quickly. He left his tent with them and walked over to the shower tent in order to wash, shave and comb his hair.

Dave had to hurry. Thirty minutes wasn't very long to do that. When he was finished he rushed with the Big Ten and the other members of the Company to line up in three rows in front of their tents in their Company area. He had no sooner done that than, right on the stroke of 4.45 a.m., Bostwick showed up with his two assistants. He told the men to be at ease and introduced them. The Lance Corporal was called Sam Elliot and the Corporal, Bob Murdoch. Then, once the introductions were over, Bostwick turned to the men and began running them in a single file. He moved them off at a steady pace and had the smallest men at the front of the line and the tallest ones at the rear. Dave was standing at the rear of the line. He saw Bostwick was making them run a little faster than yesterday and made them throw themselves on the ground after a while and do push-ups.

Then Bostwick made them get up and walk and run before he made them throw themselves on the ground again and do leg-ups and sit-ups. He made them do that several times and although it was quite cool and chilly outside, Dave found himself beginning to sweat profusely. The hot salty perspiration was stinging his eyelids and making his field fatigues feel wet and soggy and when he finally reached the six-feet chicken wire fence opposite the tent area, he was made to drop down on the ground with the rest of the Company and do some more sit-ups. Dave grunted and groaned. But he did those sit-ups and after a while his stomach muscles, arms and legs began aching and screaming from the pain. Dave kept on doing those sit-ups and when Bostwick yelled for them to get on their feet and begin moving again, he suddenly flew into a towering rage at the total stupidity and insanity of what he was doing.

As a matter of fact Dave flew into such a towering rage he didn't really notice the sun rising in the east nor the city of Terreyville nor the training ground beginning to stand ever so sharply and starkly against the skyline. He didn't really notice the other two Companies that had also come into the Parade Ground and had started training under the cold and watchful eyes of their Company and Platoon Sergeants nor the five-men Bugle Detail of the previous evening that had turned up to raise Colors and play Reveille. Dave didn't notice any of these things. Instead he kept on moving furiously and savagely in this bright and sunny day a little on the cool and windy side and when noon rolled around, Bostwick brought them to the mess tent to have their first meal since they had gotten to the training ground.

This was a sumptuous meal of chicken, vegetables, french fries, ice cream, apple pie and coffee. However, given the sheer fatigue and exhaustion the men were feeling, it just showed how incredibly shrewd and cunning Bostwick really was. Indeed, in their present state, very few of them could stomach to look at the meal, let alone eat it. Bostwick kept them in the mess tent for what seemed a long time and when they left it, he took them back to march and train on the Parade Ground. Bostwick kept on making them walk, run and throw themselves on the ground to do push-ups, leg-ups and sit-ups. He kept on making them do that for the rest of that day, and in the days that followed they were kept busy from dawn to dusk going through various drills, lectures and exercises in the compound, on the Parade Ground and at the Town Hall.

There were, to begin with, endless drill marches and full-pack hikes in the bush or in the wild beyond the training ground area. They did physical training and bayonet fighting. They practiced weapon handling and infantry tactics. They studied dress codes and military laws. They did all of those things and as the days went on, Dave found they became easier rather than tougher to do. When he discovered this Dave also found all the towering rage he had felt began cooling down and leaving him. He came to the conclusion maybe he was going to survive Basic Training after all and wouldn't have to make a move and try and get out of this place.

And it was at that time, when he had finally come to that conclusion, that there occurred an incident on October 18, 1939, a little over a month after he had come to Terreyville, that, in itself, wasn't much but that, in the overall development of things, was going to have such profound and far-reaching repercussions for his life in the Regiment.

CHAPTER 21

This incident occurred on a cold, brisk and blustery Wednesday afternoon. That morning they had been extremely busy training and exercising in the compound and it occurred right after lunch when they had gone to the Town Hall. That afternoon they had moved into the huge council chamber. The chamber had been turned into an indoor gym for them and had a boxing ring to the left of the entrance as you came in. They had gone there in order to listen to their Platoon Sergeant, Norm Moran. Moran was a tall, lean and dark-haired Noncom who was in his early thirties and he had brought them there so he could teach them how to strip, clean and reassemble the brand-new Lee Enfield .303 MK IV rifle.

A small shipment of this rifle had arrived at the training ground and Moran had brought them to the gym in order to teach them how to take care of such a rifle. One of them was presently lying on a small wooden table in front of the Company near the center of the gym where he had taken them. At the moment Moran was standing in front of the table and was about to turn to it in order to grab the Enfield and show them how to do it. As he came to do this, however, Bostwick came in. He walked over to where Moran was standing and motioned for him to step aside. Moran stepped to the left of the table and Bostwick came and stopped in front of it. He faced the Company and then turned to the table. Bostwick grabbed the Enfield and turned and faced the Company again.

Bostwick held the Enfield high over his head and swung it slowly to the left and to the right for the men to see. Then he lowered it and began showing them how to take care of it. Swiftly, expertly, almost contemptuously, Bostwick lifted the sight, removed the bolt, snapped free the magazine and took out the sling. He flipped it around in order to open the butt, dig up the oil bottle, the pull-through and the four-by-two cleaning patches. In no time, Dave noted grudgingly, yet with a certain amount of admiration, Bostwick showed them how to clean it and reassemble it. He did this with the cool off-hand speed and crisp efficient skill of someone who could only be a highly trained and extremely competent professional; one, in fact, who had done this so many times he could go through this drill with his eyes closed.

Then, once he had put the Enfield back together, Bostwick laid it down on the small wooden table and turned to them all and said: "All right then. Who, among you, will come over here and show me how it's done?" No one moved or said anything. "Come on, gentlemen," Bostwick said. "Who'll come up here and show me how it's done?" Again no one moved or said anything. "Oh come on, gentlemen," Bostwick went on. "Don't be so shy or afraid. Who'll come up here and show me?" Still no one moved or said anything. When he saw this and realized no one was going to come forward and volunteer, Bostwick smiled slightly and amusingly. He stared at them and then said: "Private Lindsay!" Oh no! Dave thought. Not again! Goddamit! Not again! Why me? Why the hell does it always have to be me?

"Private Lindsay! Where are you?" Bostwick said. "Me?" Dave said, as he stepped out of formation at the rear. "Yes you," Bostwick smiled brightly and happily when he saw him. "Come over here and show me how it's done." Dave left the rear of the formation and walked over to the small wooden table where Bostwick was standing. He was raging inwardly and swearing at himself for his bad luck at being always at the wrong place at the wrong time. When he reached the table Dave stopped in front of it and stood to the right of Bostwick. He turned to the table and grabbed the Enfield. Then he faced the Company and began stripping it. The part dealing with lifting the sight, removing the bolt, snapping free the magazine, taking out the sling and flipping it around in order to open the butt, he didn't have too much trouble with. It was the same thing with cleaning it with the oil bottle, the pull-through and the four-by-two patches.

But when he came to reassemble it, however, it was a different story. Dave was slow and clumsy and could feel Bostwick standing next to him like a huge, monstrous, breathing Presence. It was a Presence that, at his agonizing slowness and clumsiness, kept on yelling: "Come on! Come on! There's a German charging you! You haven't got all day!" As Bostwick kept on yelling Dave nodded and really pressed. He desperately tried to put the parts together. But when he dropped the oil bottle, then the bolt on the floor, while Bostwick still kept on yelling "Let's go! Let's go! Move it!", it was finally too much for him and Dave suddenly turned and handed Bostwick all the parts and the rifle back unassembled.

The whole Company burst out laughing.

Bostwick smiled brightly and glitteringly at Dave and at the Company. He put the parts and the rifle down slowly on the table and then said: "Sergeant Moran!"

"Sir!" Moran said and turned and came to stand stiffly at attention next to Bostwick on his left.

"Sergeant, it appears we have a clown in this Company who seems to find it quite funny to fumble all over the place and make an absolute mess of everything."

Bostwick paused and glared at Dave who stood stiffly at attention on his right. He also glared at the Company and then turned to Moran again on his left and said: "Take this joker to Rock Point and back, Sergeant. Take him there at 130 paces per, with full combat pack and with his rifle held at High Port."

"Yes Sir!"

"Then we'll see how funny he thinks cleaning his rifle is and if he still wants to be funny. If he does, we'll send him back there again and again until he finds out what real fun is. Is that clear!"

"Yes Sir!"

"Quite clear!"

"Yes Sir!"

"All right! Move!"

CHAPTER 22

Moran stepped forward a few paces. He snapped a stiff and precise half-turn to the right and marched past Bostwick. He left the gym and the Town Hall and Dave followed him. Outside Dave crossed Main Street with him and on the east side they both began heading toward the training ground. Dave walked north on Main Street with Moran and when they were out of earshot of the Town Hall, Moran turned to him and said: "What's the matter with you! Why did you have to hand Bostwick the parts unassembled?"

"What do you think! I was pressured! That's why!"

"Come on!"

"It's true! He gave me no time!"

"Big deal!"

"It's true! And besides do you think I'll be cleaning my rifle when the Germans attack us?"

"I know that. So what!"

"It's easy for you to say. You weren't the one having to stand there and take it."

"I know that. But now look at what you've done."

"I haven't done anything."

"Sure you have. You've made him mad. And now we have to go on that forced march."

"I did the best I could."

"Well, you'll have to do a hell of a lot better than that."

"Oh sure."

"It's true. You'll have to learn how to stop fighting Bostwick and rubbing him the wrong way all the time."

The Long War

"I'm fighting him? Hell, I'm trying to stay away from him!"

"Oh no you're not. You're fighting him all the time."

"I'm telling you. I'm not."

"Oh yes you are. You may not be fighting him outwardly. But deep down you are. You hate him. And Bostwick knows that."

"I don't hate him. Not really."

"Oh no? What would you call it then?"

"I don't hate him. It's all this pressure he's putting on us I hate."

"It's the same thing, isn't it?" Moran said.

"Oh no it isn't," Dave said. "And anyway I'm trying to do the best I can."

"Well, it's not good enough."

"I know that."

"You should know enough by now and be smart enough not to provoke him like this."

"I'm sorry. But it's the best I could do."

"Well, it's not good enough. Can't you see if you want to survive you'll have to do a hell of a lot better than that?"

"I know that. And I'm trying. Believe me."

"Well, try harder."

CHAPTER 23

Dave and Moran were now coming to the training ground. They went in and headed for Dave's tent. When they reached it Moran told Dave he would wait for him outside. Dave nodded and walked into his tent. He took off his jacket and threw it on his bunk. He walked over to his foot locker and opened it. He began getting ready for his forced march and removed his field fatigues. He folded them carefully and placed them in his locker. Then he put on his combat uniform, webbing and combat boot. He reached for his big pack with the blanket roll, his respirator, bullet pouches, water canteen, map board, helmet and bayonet. Then he closed his foot locker and walked over to the circular rifle rack around the center pole of his tent.

Dave took out an old Enfield Mark 1 rifle. He fitted it with his bayonet and stepped out. Moran was waiting for him near the entrance. When Dave came out he filled his big pack with large and not-so-large stones he had found in the grass nearby. Then they both set out past the Parade Ground, around the six long rows of pale-gray Bell tents, past the lone and solitary megaphone and toward the barbed wire-topped gate in the fence at the back of the Bell tents. Dave marched crisply and briskly at 130 paces per. He held his rifle at High Port and followed Moran who was slightly in the lead. At the gate Dave shifted his rifle to the Present Arms position and they went through it. Outside the fence there were two big burly armed sentries who stood on each side of the gate.

Those two sentries stood outside of their sentry boxes and when they went through the gate, Dave looked at them briefly. He turned right with Moran and marched along the large dirt path between the barbed wire fence and the white birch and green pine forests beyond the fence. At the

The Long War

end of the fence they turned left and went on along the large dirt path that now ran alongside Lumsden Road and Terreyville. Then, as it dipped sharply and as Lumsden Road and Terreyville disappeared from view so they were just marching through the woods and then along the shore of Lake Wastassini, Dave went back to holding his rifle at High Port. By now they were definitely moving away from the town. They were proceeding along the lakeshore and had the woods of white birches and green pines on their right and the shore on their left.

They kept on marching like this for a while and when they came near a large boulder that was set in a small clearing on the right side of the dirt path, Moran turned to Dave and said: "All right. Bostwick's not going to come here and look for us. Let's stop and relax for a while."

"Oh no. Rock Point he wants. Rock Point he gets."

"Why? What are you trying to prove?"

"Nothing. Not a goddam thing."

"Why don't we stay here for a while? And then go back. I know how long it takes."

"No way. The Man said Rock Point. Rock Point he gets."

"Why? Can't you see how crazy this is?"

"It's not crazy to me."

"Sure it is. Can't you see it doesn't make any difference whether we go there or not?"

"Maybe not to you. It does to me."

"Oh no it doesn't."

"Sure it does."

"No it doesn't. Listen. Bostwick's like a force of nature and he's totally unpredictable. Can't you see it doesn't make any difference whether we go there or not?"

"Sure it does. To me it does."

"All right then. If that's what you want."

"That's what I want."

"All right then. You go on ahead."

"I will."

"I'll just stay here and you pick me up on the way back."

"I will."

CHAPTER 24

Moran stepped into the clearing and Dave went on marching crisply and briskly at 130 paces per along the lakeshore. It didn't take him long to be gone from the clearing and as he kept on with his forced march, Dave could feel the weight of his pack really pushing against his back. The straps of the pack were cutting deeply and savagely into his shoulders and he found himself sweating quite profusely. A white hazy mist was hanging low over the flat blue-gray expanse of the lake and blurring the dark outline of the rocky barren hills on the other side. A cool northern wind was also blowing from across the water. It was blustering in strong sudden gusts, raw and biting with the edge of fall in the air, and he could hear the dull steady crashing of the waves on the shore and the stark shrill-sounding cries of black crows flying high overhead.

Dave kept on marching crisply and briskly at 130 paces per. He kept on looking down at the ground in order to concentrate on his cadence and after a while thought: What are you doing? What the hell are you doing? Can't you see if you go on like this and if you keep on pushing like this, you're going to end up in the Brig or the Stockade or the Glasshouse or whatever the hell they call this place? Can't you see Moran is right? Can't you see Bostwick's a force of nature and there's no way you can outsmart or figure him out? So what the hell are you doing? Dave thought. What are you trying to prove? That you're tough? That you're strong? That you're better than him even? Is that what you're trying to do? Dave thought. Come on, now. Is that what you're trying to prove?

Dave looked up. He kept on marching crisply and briskly at 130 paces per and on watching his cadence and after a while, Rock Point loomed in the distance. Rock Point was a huge 15 feet-high moss-covered boulder.

The Long War

It was jutting into the eastern end of the lake and was two and a half miles from the training ground. Dave marched toward it and when he reached it, he made a sharp about-face and began heading back toward the training ground. Dave marched crisply and briskly and after a while, he felt the acute and savage push of his pack against his back. He was breathing heavily and knew no matter how hard he tried the style of his forced march had become by now somewhat ragged and erratic. Still Dave tried not to think about that and just kept on marching along the cool and windswept shore.

As Dave kept on marching his arms felt unbearably stiff from holding his rifle so firmly and precisely at High Port and his knees were aching from the strain of his merciless and relentless cadence. At the clearing Dave picked up Moran and they began heading back toward the training ground. Moran took the lead again and they followed the dirt path that led to the fence. Soon it began climbing and then they left the lake on their right and entered the woods of white birches and green pines. A little later Lumsden Road and Terreyville came into view on their left and when they reached the fence, they turned right and followed it until they got to the gate. At the gate they went into the training ground and marched past the six long rows of Bell tents, the lone and solitary megaphone and toward the main gate.

At the main gate they went through it, crossed Lumsden Road and got on the west side of Main Street. They headed south, with Moran still in the lead and a little to the right of Dave, and when they reached the Town Hall, Dave saw Bostwick was waiting for them. He was standing at the entrance of the Town Hall and, with his scrappy wedge cap, impeccably-starched fatigues and black shiny combat boots, he looked every inch the soldier, the fighter, the tough and hard-nosed NCO of Regimental posters and Army propaganda. At the moment his legs were planted firmly on the ground and there was a big grin on his face.

CHAPTER 25

Bostwick was watching them and waited until they both came and snapped stiffly to attention in front of him. Then he turned to Dave and said: "There you are. How was your little march?"

"It was something, Sergeant Major."

"Did you enjoy it?"

"It was not bad."

"That's good," Bostwick grinned and eyed Dave before he turned to Moran on his right. "How about it, Sergeant? How did he do?"

"He did very well, Sir."

"Did he give you any trouble?"

"No, Sir."

"Did he go all the way to Rock Point and back?"

"Yes, Sir."

"Did you personally go with him to Rock Point and back?"

"Yes, Sir."

"All the way?"

"Yes, Sir."

"And how was his form?"

"Good."

"And his cadence?"

"Oh, very good."

"Do you think from now on he'll pay more attention to the Enfield and how you clean and assemble it?"

"I think so."

"Do you think from now on he'll be less inclined to clown around?"

77

The Long War

"I don't think after this march he'll be too inclined to clown around, Sir."

"That's good," Bostwick grinned and eyed Moran before he turned to Dave again. "But I must say you look a little pale and drawn. I hope I wasn't too hard on you."

"You weren't, Sergeant Major."

"I hope you're not feeling too tired and I didn't wear you out."

"You didn't, Sergeant Major."

"I must say though, looking at you, it must have been some march."

"It was, Sergeant Major."

"I'm sure it must have been one you wouldn't like to do again."

"I wouldn't, Sergeant Major."

"That's good," Bostwick grinned and still eyed Dave and then Moran before he turned to Dave again. "Tell me something. I'm curious. Why are you in the Army?"

"I enlisted, Sir."

"Why did you enlist?"

"I didn't like what Hitler was doing."

"What are you going to do about it?"

"First I'm going to learn how to fight. And then I'm going to beat the hell out of him."

"Are you now," Bostwick grinned and still eyed Dave and then Moran before he turned to Dave again. "Tell me something else. Do you like soldiering?"

"Yes, Sir."

"And do you like the Army?"

"Yes, Sir."

"Why?"

"It's home."

"I thought you were going to say because of me."

"That too."

"I'm sure."

"It's true."

"What else?"

"It's the place where I want to be right now."

"Is it, really?"

"It is."

"That's interesting."

"It's true."

"Do you know why I say it's interesting?"

"No. Why?"

"I don't think it's true at all," Bostwick grinned and still eyed Dave, but with eyes that were suddenly very dark and threatening. "I think what you're telling me right now is all lies and complete nonsense!"

"Oh no, Sir."

"Of course it's all lies and complete nonsense!"

"Oh no, Sir."

"Of course it is! And do you know why?"

"Why?"

"Because, you, I know you. I've been keeping an eye on you. And you're not at all what you seem to be."

"What do you mean?"

"You know very well what I mean."

"I don't understand."

"Sure you do. And you're not at all like the other soldiers in the Company."

"I don't understand."

"Let me make it plain for you. You're one of those soldiers who never tells your officers or NCOs how they feel and what they want. You only tell them what they want to hear. You're also very good at telling them the reasons why you want to do things. But they're never the real reasons why you want to do them."

"I'm not like that."

"Sure you are!"

"Believe me. I'm not."

"Sure you are! And I've known that for a long time. So be careful. Don't mess with me, Private. Or else you're not going to like it!"

"I don't do that."

"Sure you do! And I'm telling you, Private, in this Company we don't need any sneaky or tricky or overly intelligent soldiers. All we need are tough, hard, mean ones. So you better learn to become one of those, Private, and soldier properly. Or else I'm going to tear you apart and break you bone by bone! Do you understand!"

"Yes, Sir. I understand."

"Good," Bostwick grinned and eyed Dave with savage and glittering eyes before he went on. "I hope you do. Because what we really need in this Company are not liars, cheaters, complainers, but killers! Tough, hard, mean characters!" his voice exploded suddenly and brutally. "I mean, look at the Platoon Sergeant here," he turned and gave Moran a savage and glittering look, as he stood stiffly at attention and stared fixedly at the ground in front of him, before he took in Dave again and went on. "Barely any sweat on his uniform! Not a hair out of place! Hard! Lean! Mean!

The Long War

The very picture of a soldier! That's the kind of soldier we want! Do you understand me, Private!"

"Yes, Sir."

"Do you!"

"Yes, Sir."

"All right then," Bostwick said and eased a little. He gave Moran another savage and glittering look, as he still stood stiffly at attention and still stared fixedly at the ground in front of him, before he turned to Dave again. "Now, then. Since you look so pale and drawn and since I wouldn't want to tucker you out, go on. Take the rest of the afternoon off. The Platoon Sergeant and I will go back in since, unlike some people I know, our day isn't done yet and we have a lot of work to do. Is that clear!"

"Yes! Sir!"

"Quite clear!"

"Yes! Sir!"

"All right! Move it!"

CHAPTER 26

Dave made a swift half-turn to the right and when Bostwick and Moran left him and walked into the Town Hall, he crossed Main Street to the east side. He began marching back toward the training ground still at 130 paces per and still with his rifle held at High Port. When Dave reached it he stepped in and headed for his tent. It didn't take him long to get there and when he went in, Dave threw his rifle on his bunk. He went and sat there and tried to catch his breath. Dave just sat for quite a while and then got up and went outside in order to empty his big pack of the large and not-so-large stones Moran had put in. When his big pack was empty he walked back in and put the old Enfield Mark 1 rifle back in the circular rifle rack.

Then Dave put his bayonet and gear in his foot locker and put on a clean pair of fatigues. Finally he walked over to the shower tent where he washed and showered before he put on his clean pair of fatigues again. Once he was dressed Dave left the shower tent and walked back to his tent where he went and lay down on his bunk and began thinking about Bostwick again. There was no doubt, Dave told himself, Bostwick was a force of nature and totally unpredictable. Moran had been right about that. And if he wanted to survive him and do well he better change his attitude. He better learn to roll with the punches and not fight him and resent him so much. Otherwise, if he went on like this, he would end up losing to him and would put himself in an absolutely intolerable situation.

Not only that, Dave told himself, but in a fight with Bostwick he just couldn't win. There was no way he could win. No. In order to survive him and do well there was only one thing he could do. This was to stay away from him and make sure he didn't get in his way. With this in mind Dave thought long and hard about what he was going to do and when he had come up with a plan, he decided to put it in action. This plan of Dave's was quite simple really. He was going to try to become the perfect soldier. This meant no matter how he felt or what he wanted to do, Dave was going to try, by soldiering as well as he could, not to be noticed. He was going to make sure, though, he didn't do too much to stand out nor too little to be obvious.

So the rest of that afternoon, and in the days and weeks that followed, Dave put his plan in action and stuck to it. Then, as the days and weeks went by and as nothing happened, Dave thought maybe he had found the ideal way to deal with the situation. As a matter of fact he had just about made up his mind on that and come to that conclusion when there occurred an incident on Friday, December 1, 1939, which made a sheer and total mockery of his plan and showed exactly where he stood with Bostwick and the Company. This incident occurred at a time, no doubt about it, when the Company was going through a lot of changes. They were said to be going to Valcartier. They were said to be going to Camp Borden. They were supposed to be heading to Western Canada. They were also supposed to be heading to the Far East even.

But in all this there was one thing for sure. There were all kinds of rumors flying around. On top of that, although they were coming near the end of their Basic Training, maybe out of a perverse and sardonic, if not pig-headed, sense of humor, their Platoon Sergeants were working them longer and harder than ever and making sure they were constantly polishing and reviewing what they had already done. Then in early November, with the oncoming of winter, private contractors were hired and a whole army of civilian carpenters, plumbers and electricians invaded the training ground. Once they were there, in a little less than a week, they built 10 wooden barracks callled H-Blocks to replace the pale-gray Bell tents they were living in. While those barracks were being built the whole Company along with the rest of the Regiment was put in the City Arena.

With the completion of those barracks Dave moved in with the rest of the Big Ten to the second one. They took up the entire south-west corner near the door. And it was a little over three weeks later, right at the beginning of December, when there occurred that incident which, more than any other, so clearly and starkly underlined Dave's position with Bostwick and the Company. This incident occurred on a cold, crisp, clear, late Friday afternoon. At that time the Company had gone to the gym in the Town Hall where their Platoon Sergeant, Norm Moran, had given them a demonstration in hand-to-hand combat. Like everything else Moran did this demonstration had been tight, clean and precise. Although, when you thought about it, with not an ounce of commitment or energy more than was absolutely necessary.

Still it had been quite an impressive performance and Dave had stood at the back of the Company and kept on listening to Moran. And it was near the end of his lecture, when Moran was reviewing what he had showed them, that Bostwick walked in. When he stepped into the gym he came and stood with the other Platoon Sergeants in front of the men. Bostwick stood a little behind Moran and a small wooden table that was between Moran and the other Platoon Sergeants. Bostwick stood there in silence and listened to Moran reviewing what he had showed them. Then, when he had finished, Bostwick motioned for him to go back to where the other Platoon Sergeants were standing.

When Moran had joined them and stood slightly to his left, Bostwick stepped in front of the small wooden table and stopped. He stared at the men silently and penetratingly and then said: "Gentlemen. You've just been given an excellent demonstration of hand-to-hand combat by the Platoon Sergeant here." Bostwick turned and pointed somewhat wryly and grudgingly, if not totally contemptuously, to Moran before he went on. "And this demonstration, with others in bayonet fighting and weapon handling, brings us to this other lesson which is never acknowledged officially and is rarely talked about in the Regular Army. In fact it would certainly be denied if it were known. But it's the key nevertheless to everything you have learned so far in the Fusiliers and has to do with what we have insisted on constantly ever since you started your Basic Training.

"In other words, it deals with that powerful and all-important word: *IMPROVISE*." Bostwick paused. He looked sharply and penetratingly at the men and then went on. "In the First World War, gentlemen, what made the Fusiliers such an outstanding Assault Unit was their ability to search for, find and take whatever would work for them and give them an edge. In other words, their ability to improvise. And, in connection with that ability, it meant they used enemy machine guns, pistols, knives, grenades, ammunition, helmets, camouflage capes and boots even; anything, in short, that was going to make them win no matter how unorthodox, peculiar or outlandish it may have seemed. And to the question some of you, more delicate and sensitive souls, may ask: 'What if, in the process, you're mistaken for the enemy and shot?'

"My answer to that is simple: *'TOUGH! THE HELL WITH IT! YOU HAD NO BUSINESS BEING THERE IN THE FIRST PLACE!'*" Bostwick paused again. He looked sharply and penetratingly at the men and then went on. "Now, once you've done that, gentlemen, the moment you've

The Long War

tried everything and fought to survive, if all else fails, there's only one more thing you can do to try and get you out of that fix. That's knife-fighting. That's right, gentlemen. Knife-fighting. And why this, you may ask? Why this specific move? Because, gentlemen, when you've met your enemy and shot at him and taken him on hand-to-hand and exhausted all means to bring him down, there's still only one classical, reliable and surefire way you can do it. Only one. And that's knife-fighting.

"So, knowing this, gentlemen, and realizing how important it is for you to have this kind of weaponry in your arsenal, I would suggest you go to any hardware store and get yourself a really good knife like this one for instance," Bostwick said and took out a dull black knife in a black leather scabbard that had been stuck at the back of his belt. For a few moments he held the bare knife in front of him in his right hand for the men to see before he lowered it and then went on again. "Okay. That, gentlemen, is a Matt knife. Or, for the more particular and fussy ones among you, a Sykes-Fairburn knife. It's as strong, tough and dependable a weapon as you'll find and for our purposes ideal. This is what I would recommend you buy, gentlemen. Take the 10 or 12-inch double-edged model since it's the one I feel is best suited for the work we have to do.

"And it's the one with which I will now proceed, gentlemen, to show you how to fight."

CHAPTER 27

Bostwick now paused and stared at the Company. Then he began pacing back and forth in front of the men and held the bare knife in his right hand. After a while he put it back in the black leather scabbard and held the scabbard in his right hand. He swung it right and left and a little later, he came and stopped in front of the men. He just stood there and then said: "All right, gentlemen. Now that we have come to the key, the ultimate, the most important lesson, I believe, we have to teach you in the Fusiliers, who'll come and fight me? That's right. Who'll come and fight me?" No one spoke or moved. As a matter of fact the Company was so still and the silence so deep you could almost hear the men breathe in the gym.

When he saw this Bostwick grinned and a bright mocking gleam showed in his eyes. He began pacing back and forth in front of the Company again and after a while, he came and stopped in front of the men. He stared at them and then said: "All right. Who'll come and fight me?" No one spoke or moved. "Go on, gentlemen," Bostwick said. "I'm sure many of you would like to take me on. Who'll come and fight me?" Again no one spoke or moved. "Go on," Bostwick said. "Who'll come and fight me?" Still no one spoke or moved. "Okay, then," Bostwick told them. "I guess I'll just have to choose the lucky one." Bostwick grinned and stared at them all. Then, after standing there and eyeing them, he said: "Private O'Hara." Once more no one spoke or moved.

"Private O'Hara!" Bostwick said. "Where are you?" "Here," Red said, as he fell out of rank near the front. "Get over here," Bostwick motioned with his right hand when he saw him. "Come and stand in front of the Company." Red left the formation. He walked up to Bostwick and came and stopped next to him on his right. For a moment Bostwick stared at Red.

The Long War

Then, as he started to give him the scabbarded knife, Bostwick suddenly withdrew it from him. He grinned at him and removed the black leather scabbard. He threw it on the small wooden table and gave Red the bare knife. As he gave him the knife he said: "Go ahead. Attack me."

Red looked at the knife and then at Bostwick.

"I don't want to attack you, Sergeant Major."

A nervous laughter ran through the Company.

Bostwick glared at the men. Then he turned and said to Red: "Try. I'm sure you can."

Red looked at the knife, then at Bostwick, and began moving in on him. From the way he started it was quite obvious Red didn't really want to do this and his heart wasn't in it. As Red made a half-hearted stabbing move, Bostwick neatly sidestepped it to the left and slapped him hard in the face.

A murmur went up from the Company.

"Go on," Bostwick said. "Attack me. I'm pretty sure you can."

Red looked at the knife once more, then at Bostwick, and began moving in on him again. As Red made another half-hearted stabbing move, Bostwick neatly sidestepped it to the right this time and slapped him hard in the face.

Another murmur went up from the Company.

"Go on!" Bostwick suddenly yelled at Red. "Attack me! Goddam you! Attack me!"

Red swallowed hard and his eyes suddenly flashed fiercely and savagely. But he checked himself and went in with another half-hearted stabbing move. As he went in with that move Bostwick neatly sidestepped it to the left again and slapped him really hard in the face. As he hit Red, Bostwick staggered him and brought blood to his nose.

A loud murmur went up from the Company.

"Sergeant Major," Dave heard himself say, as he stepped out of formation at the rear. Goddamit! What are you doing? he thought. What the hell are you doing? God! Don't you learn? Don't you ever learn? "Why don't you try me? I think I'm more your size."

Bostwick swung around: "Who said that?"

His face broke into a huge sudden grin when he saw it was Dave and he said: "Ah, the Master of Spare Parts, the Lord of Rock Point, the Enfield Specialist himself. I must say it's nice. It's very nice to have such a keen and discriminating critic of your work."

Dave didn't say anything.

"I must say it's especially nice since, as the appointed Company Comedian or, should I say, street-wise Lawyer, we're dealing here with someone who has an opinion but no knowledge, mind you, on everyone and everything. And it's especially nice since, on top of that, we're dealing with someone who makes sure he delivers very little, if anything at all, as if part of a plan, a shrewd and calculated plan it would seem, to be smart while thinking, as a result, he's better, oh so much better than he actually is."

Again Dave didn't say anything.

"Well, well. I must say. This is interesting. Oh yes indeed. Very interesting."

Once again Dave didn't say anything.

Bostwick now stepped forward and walked over to where Dave was standing at the rear. He fixed Dave with cold and icy eyes, that were also, at that moment, not entirely without a certain gleam of mockery and amusement, and said: "So you'd like to try me, hey?"

"Sure."

"You think that would even the odds a little?"

"I think so."

"Not to mention, you'd really love that and would want that, wouldn't you?"

"Sure."

"Because, let's face it, this is something you've been wanting to do for quite some time now, haven't you?"

Once more Dave didn't say anything and Bostwick grinned. He turned and pointed to the boxing ring in a corner near the entrance on his right and said: "Or, maybe, you'd like to put on gloves and try me in the ring instead?"

"If you want to."

"Or, maybe, you'd like to try me without gloves, bareknuckled and with no holds barred?"

"I don't mind."

"In a fight that would be fair and square until the best man wins?"

"Sure."

"A fight, as a matter of fact, that would go on to the finish and we can have right here? Right now?"

"Sure."

"Well, why not," Bostwick grinned. "Let's do that, then. Let's fight without gloves and find out how good you are."

CHAPTER 28

"FIGHT! FIGHT! MAKE ROOM! MAKE WAY! BIG FIGHT COMING UP!"

No sooner had those words been shouted by a member of the Company than as if by magic officers, NCOs and soldiers came rushing out. They came from the offices to the right of the black iron passageway overlooking the gym, from the passageway itself, down the steel spiral staircases and through the two huge oaken doors of the gym that were wide-open. When those officers, NCOs and soldiers came rushing into the gym, Dave left his spot at the rear of the formation with Bostwick and walked up to the small wooden table in order to take off his tunic, shirt and T-shirt.

When Dave stripped to the waist with Bostwick and turned to look at him, his heart sank and he saw what kind of a fight he had let himself in for. As he stood next to Dave, Bostwick looked as if he was made of cast iron. He had wide shoulders, huge biceps and a narrow waist. Not only that but his big compact body showed an absolutely stunning and spectacular muscle tone. Although slim and muscular too, and burned to an incredibly sharp and lean definition by all those tough weeks of training, Dave looked positively puny and scrawny by comparison. On the basis of their two builds, and even though both of them weighed about 180 pounds, Dave certainly didn't look like much of a risk nor a big threat to Bostwick. Dave tried not to think about this, however, and moved with Bostwick to the center of the circle the Company had now formed around them.

On the right side of the circle the Big Ten, led by Gennaro, Higgins and most of the long-suffering soldiers from the Company, were cheering for Dave. On the left side of it officers, NCOs and a small number of soldiers, led by Bostwick's best friend, Al Bates, the tall, bald and heavily-stubbled Quartermaster Sergeant, were cheering for Bostwick. Then, when Captain Neal Anderson, their tall, lean and wiry Chaplain who had come running into the gym and who was now standing in the center of the circle between them, raised his right arm and then brought it down, the fight was on. When it began Bostwick glanced at his friends. He winked at them and gave them a look that said: "Don't worry. This isn't going to take long." Then he swung out happily and rushed to meet Dave.

Dave was taller than Bostwick by a couple of inches and had a greater reach advantage. When the fight began he started circling Bostwick and then faked a tremendous left. As he faked the punch Dave hit Bostwick hard with two straight rights. An angry welt appeared on Bostwick's forehead. He grinned. He shook his head and moved in on Dave. Bostwick didn't have time to stop grinning when Dave hit him hard with two more straight rights. Bostwick shook his head again and moved in on Dave. Dave danced away from him and only showed him a side profile as he stayed out of range. Then he stopped, faked a right and came in with a thunderous left to the jaw. Bostwick shook his head again and kept on moving in on Dave. They kept on moving and circling like this and as the fight went on, it settled into a definite pattern.

Bostwick would rush in and swing with wild roundhouse rights and lefts. Most of them missed. Some bounced off Dave's chest and ribs. A few grazed his jaw. Dave had faster handspeed and better footwork and was able to stick and run before suddenly jumping in with savage and furious combinations. He threw booming rights and lefts, deadly uppercuts, fierce hooks and bolo punches. At times he swung Bostwick around with his right hand and kept him off-balance. Every once in a while Dave also stood his ground and faced Bostwick. He watched his hands and beat him to the punch whenever he'd rear to throw. Then he'd step back and dance away from him. But mostly, in order to stay in the fight and not give ground, Dave had to remain within punching range and mix with Bostwick.

Dave kept on moving and punching with him and after a while thought: Man. What am I going to do? What the hell am I going to do? I've hit him with just about everything but the ring post, the stool and the water bucket and the goddam guy is still standing. What am I going to do? What the hell can I do? Fighting Bostwick is like punching a gong or hitting a bronze statue or a brick wall. He doesn't feel any pain. He doesn't show any emotion. And he sure doesn't seem to have any fatigue.

What am I going to do? Dave thought. How do I fight him? How do I stop him? And, what's even more important, what can I do at this stage I haven't done already to nail him and try and bring him down? My God. What? By now Dave's jaw and chest were beginning to hurt. His hands were sore. He could hardly breathe from the fiery pain in his ribs. And he could also feel a burning shakiness in his legs.

Still Dave kept on punching and moving. At times he jumped in and at others he scrambled back. But mostly he made sure he stayed out of range and gave Bostwick nothing but profiles and angles. This long into the fight Dave knew from mixing with Bostwick that because of his slow handspeed and poor footwork he could definitely be rushed and bullied. So Dave kept on firing and mixing with him and racked his brains to try and find a solution to the fight. He knew if he didn't find one soon it would be all over. As a matter of fact he was growing absolutely frantic and desperate about finding one when suddenly, when he least expected it, he found what he was looking for. The solution, when Dave found it, was surprisingly simple. Maybe it was because of Bostwick's frustration or impatience or rage. But whatever it was, as they kept on moving and punching, Bostwick suddenly reared back and kicked Dave viciously.

Bostwick hit Dave in the right leg and sent him sprawling on the floor and feeling a burning and searing pain in his leg. When he kicked Dave, Neal Anderson, their Chaplain, jumped in between them and said: "Hey! Hey! None of this. This is a clean fight. A fair fight. Keep it that way." As the Chaplain said this the voice of Al Bates, the loud and noisy leader of Bostwick's supporters, could be heard in the background saying: "Aw. Don't bother. Let them fight. Let them go on." When he got kicked Dave got up and scrambled out of range. Dave kept on moving and circling and a little later, when Bostwick rushed in, swung wildly and tried to kick him, he leaned back and stepped to the side. Dave slipped both the punch and the kick. Bostwick tried again. He missed. Bostwick tried a third time.

By that time Dave was watching him very closely and when Bostwick reared back to try to punch and kick him, Dave jumped in at the same time and hit him with a tremendous kick in the crotch. Bostwick yelled. He bent in two to protect himself and Dave sprang on him and hit him with a hard chopping blow in the neck. Bostwick looked up from this blow more by reflex than anything else and Dave hit him with another tremendous kick in the crotch. Bostwick went down sprawling. Dave rushed to kick him in the ribs and suddenly found Slav jumping between him and Bostwick with his arms outstretched and saying: "All right. It's all right. I think you've proven your point." "Yes. Good fight. Boys.

Good fight," Chaplain Anderson also jumped in and looked at them both as he stood between them. "Naw. Let them fight. Let them go on to the finish," Al Bates, at the head of Bostwick's supporters, said from the sidelines.

"No! No! This fight is over," Chaplain Anderson said. "It's a draw. I repeat. IT'S A DRAW!"

CHAPTER 29

Suddenly the fight was over. It had gone on for a long time. As a matter of fact it had gone on for a little over an hour. But now, with Slav and the Chaplain standing between him and Bostwick, Dave knew the fight was over. He was completely worn out and exhausted and when the Company that had formed into a full circle around him and Bostwick suddenly broke up, he and Bostwick were immediately surrounded by their supporters. They were cheered and Dave was mobbed and pounded and slapped in the back. When the fight had started Red had gone to the small wooden table to put the knife back in its black leather scabbard and had then wiped the blood from his nose with his handkerchief.

Now Red, the Big Ten and Dave's other supporters told Dave what an incredible fight he had fought and how great he himself had been. Almost at the same time the Chaplain called for order and told the Company that after such a long and extraordinary fight their training for he day was over and they could all go back to their own barracks. Once the Chaplain had spoken Dave began making his way through his supporters and headed toward the small wooden table where his T-shirt, shirt and tunic were. He began dressing and when he turned from the table, he saw the Chaplain and Bostwick were coming toward him. After all the tremendous punches he had given Bostwick, Dave was surprised to see him still standing, even if somewhat white-faced and slightly-bent.

By now both of them were nearing him and when they came up to him, the Chaplain asked Bostwick to shake hands with him. At first Bostwick didn't want to. He only did it when, in a sharp and commanding voice, the Chaplain ordered him to. But, although he did it, there was a dark glittering gleam in his eyes and a look on his face that was as implacable as it was chilling. While he was doing it, as the Chaplain was briefly surrounded by soldiers from the Company who congratulated him on his refereeing, Bostwick told Dave in a voice so low it could only be heard by the two of them: "Don't you worry, kid. This is only the beginning. You wait. You just wait. I'll get back to you on this." Dave tried to ignore those words and watched as Bostwick finally left with the Chaplain.

Then, when he was about to turn back toward the table and speak to Red, Dave suddenly saw Norm Moran, their Platoon Sergeant, coming toward him. In no time Moran reached him and told him their Commanding Officer, Colonel Thomas C. Cantwell, wanted to see him in front of his office on the passageway. Now what, Dave thought. I've just finished fighting one man and the CO wants to see me. What does he want from me? What does everybody want from me? My God. What do they all want from me? Dave left the small wooden table where he was standing and began walking stiffly and painfully toward one of the steel spiral staircases that led to the passageway. The staircase was at the end of the gym on the right side. When he reached it Dave began walking up the steps until he came to the passageway.

CHAPTER 30

The Colonel was waiting for Dave near the middle of the passageway. He was a tall, lean, wiry officer in his early forties. He had neat, well-trimmed, dark-brown hair and cold, icy, blue eyes. When he reached him, Dave snapped to attention and the Colonel told him to stand at ease. He stared at Dave for a moment and then said: "If I asked you to come here, it's because I want to talk to you about a couple of things."

Dave nodded and looked at the Colonel.

"First I want to tell you how much I enjoyed your fight. It was quite something."

"Thank you, Sir."

"I always enjoy a good fight. And it was a very good one."

"I'm glad you enjoyed it, Sir."

"I certainly did. And you fought really well."

"Thank you, Sir."

"I appreciated the fact you fought within your limits."

"Thank you, Sir."

"You fought defensively and used Bostwick's weaknesses. That was smart."

"I tried, Sir."

"I know you did. That's why you kept your head and made Bostwick lose his."

"I did the best I could, Sir."

"I know that. And I have to give it to you. You can punch. My God, how you can punch! Where did you learn?"

"A couple of friends of mine taught me, Sir."

"They must have been good."

Training

"They were."

"Who were they?"

"One was a colored fighter who came here from the States. The other was a full-blooded Mohawk Indian who learned it on the reserve."

"Well, they must have been very good. Because you certainly can punch."

"Thank you, Sir."

"It's true. You really snap them from the shoulder the way it should be done. You don't throw them the way Bostwick was doing."

Again Dave nodded and looked at the Colonel.

The Colonel now stared sharply and penetratingly at him and a slight smile came into his eyes.

"The reason I can say this to you is this: Did you know I myself was a boxer once?"

"No, Sir. I didn't know."

"I was. An amateur. I fought 24 fights and had 14 knockouts."

"You must have been very good then."

"I was. Like you, if I may say so, I was a pretty good puncher."

"You must have been. Fourteen knockouts. That's pretty impressive."

"It was. But then I had to give it up. Career demands and all that."

Once more Dave nodded and looked at the Colonel.

The Colonel stared sharply and penetratingly at him again and another slight smile came into his eyes.

"That's why, you see, I enjoyed the fight. And, anyway, a fight like this is very good for the men. It gives them a chance to let off steam and get away from the toughness of training. That's why I have nothing against it. It's very good for them."

"I'm glad you think so, Sir."

"I do. But tell me. Strictly between you and me. Do you think you beat Bostwick?"

For a moment Dave looked at the Colonel and then said: "Well, Sir. It's like the Chaplain said. It was a draw. I think it was a draw."

The Colonel smiled.

"I don't think so. I think you beat him."

"No, Sir."

"Oh yes. I think you beat him fair and square."

"No, Sir."

"I think so. I think by the time the fight was stopped you had won by decision by a very wide margin."

"I don't think so, Sir."

"I do. But I'll tell you something else. By the time the fight was stopped you were getting pretty exhausted and Bostwick was getting a lot stronger. I think had the fight gone on much longer he would have caught up with you and beaten you. That's what I think."

"You may be right, Sir."

"I know I'm right. That doesn't take away from your performance, however. Nor from having done what we're teaching you in the Fusiliers."

"I tried my best, Sir."

"I know you did. In this fight you sized up the situation and adapted to it and improvised. That's how it should be done."

"It's the only thing I could do, Sir."

"I know that. But that was smart. Very smart. And that's why I say to you: 'Well done. Very well done indeed.'"

"Thank you, Sir."

"Anyway, that's the first thing I wanted to tell you. Now, for the second one."

The Colonel paused and stared sharply and penetratingly at Dave again. But this time there was no warmth or friendliness in his eyes.

"For the time being this second thing I'm going to tell you must remain strictly between you and me. The reason for that is that outside of a few officers and NCOs you'll be the only one to know. Do you understand?"

"Yes, Sir."

"You might say I'm doing this for you as a favor for the way you fought."

"Thank you, Sir."

"All right then. Save your energies. We're moving out."

"We're what?"

"We're moving out."

"When?"

"Soon."

"How soon?"

"Very soon."

"Where?"

"You'll know soon enough."

Dave stood on the passageway and looked at the Colonel.

"That's why I want you to save your energies and not get involved in any further complications. Do you understand?"

"I understand."

"I know you're keen and eager. But I don't want any more stunts and crazy moves from you. Is that clear?"

"Yes, Sir."
"All right. That's all I wanted to tell you. You may go."
"Yes, Sir."

CHAPTER 31

Dave stepped back two paces and turned. He began walking toward the steel spiral staircase and in no time reached it. Dave walked down to the gym and the rest of that day, and the next day, Saturday, he saw how right the Colonel had been. On Saturday morning Dave went to Terreyville with Red and the Big Ten in order to buy himself a Matt knife. They were on sale at the hardware store. As a matter of fact, since they were on sale, Higgins bought two and Red, three! Then they went back to the training ground and the rest of that day and in the days that followed, Dave saw how truthful the Colonel had been. They were definitely moving out. The signs were all there.

For one thing the Colonel was now seen quite often in the training ground in the company of COs and NCOs from various Companies. For another all kinds of officers and NCOs they had rarely come in contact with at the Town Hall were now seen running in and out of the compound. On top of that their training, which up to now had been extremely hard and demanding, suddenly became quite slack and uncoordinated as if their officers and NCOs were distracted and had other things on their minds. Also several inspections were scheduled at the City Arena for medical checkups, booster shots and dental examinations. This was the clincher. It was the one telltale sign that told everyone, if they didn't know it already, they were moving out.

In the circumstances no one was very surprised when, the following Wednesday evening, December 6, 1939, they were ordered to pack up and be ready to move out by 8.00 a.m. the next morning. That morning they were woken up at 6.00 a.m. They were made to shave, shower and dress. Then, after an early breakfast, they were lined up with their duffel bags

Training

on the Parade Ground. By now, near 8.00 o'clock, a light granular snow had begun falling and was covering the training ground and the city of Terreyville beyond. It gave the training ground and the city of Terreyville a white wintry look that was quite joyful and cheerful since it was early December and fairly close to the Christmas holidays. At precisely 8.00 a.m., as ordered, they were led out of the compound. They were marched south on Main Street toward the train station.

While they were being led to the station the street was lined up with people who had come out to see them leave. Like the time when they had first come to Terreyville some of the people were grinning at them. Others were waving. A few were giving them the V-for-Victory sign. Not many of the Fusiliers, however, grinned or waved back or gave the people the V-for-Victory sign. They were marched south on Main Street and near the station, they were stopped and made to stand at ease. Then, under a low overcast sky, they were taken across the railroad tracks and put on the train that had come for them. At 10.00 o'clock sharp, when they were on board, a whistle blew, the engine shuddered and they were on their way. Dave was with his Company in a wagon near the middle of the train. He was sitting on the right side of the aisle, next to the window, and Red was sitting beside him.

When they began pulling out Dave looked at the station and houses and buildings of Terreyville on his left. Then he turned and waved at some of the people who had come out to watch them leave and who were standing on the right side of the tracks. At times Dave gave those people the V-for-Victory sign. At others he sat there and looked at them. Dave did this for a while and when he turned away from the window, he saw Bostwick. Bostwick was sitting in one of the swungover seats facing him from across the aisle. There was a big brazen grin on his face and he was staring at Dave as if he wanted to get him involved in a game of stares. At first Dave wasn't sure if this was the case. But after watching him from the corner of his eyes there could be no mistake. This was definitely what Bostwick wanted.

Well, the hell with him, Dave thought. He wasn't going to get involved in such a game nor play along with him. He had already been involved with him far too much, thank you very much, and wasn't about to get involved again, if he could help it. Oh, no. He'd try to avoid that and concentrate on staying away from him. That was the smart thing to do. In fact it was the only thing to do. Dave looked out of the window again. By then they had left Terreyville behind and were making their way across the vast snowy countryside. They were moving past desolate and empty fields, woods, hills and valleys. The valleys were dotted here and there with stark isolated farmhouses, gray half-frozen ponds and stiff lonely trees. The whole landscape, however, in the clean, light, fluffy snow that was falling, looked far more inviting and fascinating than it actually was, and Dave sat by the window and looked at it.

They kept on passing several fields, woods, hills and valleys and after a while, Dave turned and looked at Bostwick again. Bostwick was still sitting in his swungover seat across the aisle. He was still staring at Dave and there was still that big brazen grin on his face. Only by now there was something truly mad and insane about it as if he knew a huge and fantastic secret about Dave and as if this was amusing him enormously somehow. In fact his stare was so fierce and penetrating it chilled Dave to the bone and he wondered what this secret was and what it could be. But then he decided not to go on with this. After all, with someone as strange, peculiar and unpredictable as Bostwick, who could tell what he was thinking. Indeed who could tell how he was thinking and if, in fact, he was thinking at all. Dave turned away from him and looked out of the window again.

By now they were heading east slowly as if they were proceeding on a strict and pre-planned timetable. The next day, when the light granular snow began turning into a cold drizzling rain, and on Saturday, when it also rained, after they had stopped in Toronto, Ottawa and Montreal to give priority to civilian trains on the line, they still kept on heading east. And it was only around 10.00 o'clock on Saturday evening, when the cold drizzling rain had stopped and turned into a raw blustering wind, that Bostwick, flanked by the Platoon Sergeants, came into their wagon and told the Company where they were going. They were going to England. Their Regiment, as *the* Elite Assault Unit, had been assigned to the 1st Canadian Division. Their immediate destination was Halifax. And the ship they were going to take was the *Empress Of Britain*.

Bostwick then had the Platoon Sergeants give the men white boarding passes that were stamped in black with the name and number of the deck, compartments and berths of the ship they were going to take. As the men got their passes and knew where they were going, this seemed to lift their spirits. The kind of surly sullen gloom that had hung over them as a result of their incredibly long and boring journey seemed to disappear at once. Almost immediately they began talking wildly and excitedly about where they were going and when he saw this, Bostwick went and sat back in his swungover seat facing Dave. There was still a big brazen grin on his face and he was still staring at Dave as if he wanted to get him involved in a game of stares. When he saw this Dave turned away from Bostwick again and looked out of the window.

Training

Now, late in the evening, it was getting dark out. In fact it was so dark Dave couldn't see anything except his own reflection in the window. The raw blustering wind that had followed the cold drizzling rain had turned quite harsh and biting and was really blowing outside. Every once in a while it would rise in great gusts and come and pound at the window. Dave leaned against the window for a moment and felt its coldness on his right cheek. He closed his eyes and after a while, lulled by the steady clanging and hammering of the wheels of the train, fell asleep. Dave slept soundly until, some time later, he heard an officer come into their wagon and tell everyone to pull their blinds down. At that moment, with Red fast asleep beside him, Dave felt the officer come, reach over him and pull his own blind down.

Then the officer was gone and, a little later, Dave heard the iron wheels of the train begin to grind down and screech against the rails. The train began to slow down more and more and, some time later, lurched a couple of times as it came and ground to a stop. When the train stopped Dave opened his eyes and looked at his watch. He saw it was now close to 2.00 o'clock in the morning and that they had finally reached Halifax.

CHAPTER 32

When the train stopped their officers and NCOs lined them up and took them off by Companies. The train had brought them to the port and almost alongside of what looked like four or five big ocean liners. Those liners were looming ahead of them in the darkness. There were no lights in the port and in the city except for the dim lights of a few trucks standing at a fair distance from one another on the docks. Once they were standing outside the train in the cold raw blustery night, their officers and NCOs began leading them toward one of the dark looming liners. As they got close to it Dave saw there was a gangplank leading up to two huge open doors. At the foot of the gangplank Bostwick began taking the Company toward those doors.

Inside the ship Bostwick led them forward and topside until they reached the proper deck, compartments and berths to which they had been assigned. Their Company was lucky since it had been assigned to the Forward Troop Deck. This was the A Deck and it stood right next to where the Company officers were quartered. Dave was even luckier since he had been put with Red in the same cabin. Their cabin was right in the middle of the cabins assigned to the Company. It was on the starboard side and when he reached it, Dave went in with Red. Since it was in the Forward Troop Deck the cabin was quite spacious and luxurious. It had two wide bunks on each side of it, a riveted small round table and chairs that stood in the middle of it, a bathroom and shower on the right side and a large metal cupboard on the left side.

It was a very spacious and luxurious cabin for them to have and when Red saw its size and roominess, its huge porthole and wall-to-wall carpet, its smart furniture and comfortable bunks, he turned to Dave and said:

Training

"Oh man! I'm telling you! Joining the Army is the best thing I could have done!"

"Really?"

"You're damn right!"

"I'm glad."

"It's true. I mean, look at this place!"

"What about it?"

"I mean, this place looks like a goddam State Room!"

"It's not a bad place."

"Not a bad place? This place's a goddam Palace!"

"It's not bad."

"That's for sure! And I'm telling you. Being with you has been very good for me."

"It has?"

"You're damn right! First you brought me to the Ritz in Montreal. Then you gave me money to gamble and win some money. And now this."

"Well, don't get too excited. They haven't stripped this ship down yet. But they will."

"I don't care about that. By then I'll be in England."

"That's true. But that's what they'll do. You can be sure they'll turn it into another troop ship."

"Well, I don't care about that."

"That's good."

"But, I have to tell you, I'm damn glad we're finally off the train and into this ship."

"Me too."

"And now for my little surprise. Let me show you what I got."

CHAPTER 33

Red left Dave and walked over to his duffel bag near the door. He bent down and opened it. He took out two bottles of liquor and walked back to Dave. One was a bottle of Seagram's Whiskey which he kept. The other was a bottle of Gordon's Dry Gin which he gave to Dave. At the sight of those two bottles Dave's eyes widened and he said: "Where did you get those?"

"I got them from a guy on the train."

"He even had a bottle of Gordon's Dry Gin?"

"He did. As a matter of fact he had all kinds of bottles."

"Isn't that something."

"You're telling me. He wanted to trade for them."

"How about that."

"So I took a bottle of Gordon's Dry Gin. Since you told me it's the only kind of gin you like."

"It is."

"And I took a bottle of whiskey for me. Since us Irishmen like whiskey."

"That's good."

"You bet."

"What did you give him in return?"

"Two Matt knives."

"Two Matt knives! That's way too much for two bottles of liquor."

"Maybe. But I wanted the liquor."

"You should have offered him one Matt knife. That would have been more than enough."

"Maybe. But I didn't want to take the chance."

"Well, you got taken."

"I don't care about that. I wanted the liquor. You know. For a dark and stormy night when the weather turns cold and the old bones ache."

"I know what you mean. And, to tell you the truth, it'll be one way of forgetting about Bostwick."

"What about him?"

"Well, now I've fought him to a draw," Dave said, "he's not going to forget it. And he really has it in for me."

"Ah, forget about Bostwick," Red said. "Everyone knows he's crazy and gives people hell all the time. But that's also the good thing about him. He might give you hell one minute but then, once it's finished, he forgets all about it and lets it go. He doesn't bear any grudges."

"Not this time. This time he's not going to let it go."

"How do you know?"

"I know."

"Why not?"

"Do you know what he told me after I finished fighting him. He said: *'Don't you worry, kid. This is only the beginning. You wait. You just wait. I'll get back to you on this.'*"

"So?"

"So that's why he's not going to let it go."

"Sure he will."

"No he won't."

"Sure he will. Listen. It was a fight. A fair fight."

"So?"

"So Bostwick's not a stupid man. He's not going to look for trouble."

"I guarantee you he will. For this he will."

"I bet you he won't. And even if he does. It won't matter."

"Oh no?"

"No. Because, if it comes down to that, you won't have to worry. I'll stand right by you. And I'll take him on."

"Like you did at the knife-fight?"

"Hey! Don't get me mad. That was different."

"What was different?"

"What do you think? Do you think Bostwick would fight anyone with a bare knife if he thought he couldn't win? Believe me, Bostwick never does anything he hasn't figured out before."

"So?"

"So I wouldn't play his stupid game and give him the satisfaction."

"At least you could have tried."

"Yes. I could have tried. But I didn't. And that's that."

"That's what I mean."

"That's what I mean too. But, if it ever comes down to Bostwick looking for you, don't you worry. I'll be right there. With you."

"That's good to know."

"You're goddam right it's good to know. But now let's forget about Bostwick and the fight and concentrate on the comforts of this journey."

"That's not such a bad idea."

"For sure it's not such a bad idea," Red said. "As a matter of fact, speaking of those comforts, I think I'll go and lie down in my bunk and see how the rich live."

"Why not?" Dave said. "What else is there to do?"

"That's it."

"And anyway we might as well do this. I don't think we'll get too many other chances to do this."

"I agree."

CHAPTER 34

Red left Dave and walked back to his duffel bag. He bent down and put his liquor bottle back in it. Dave went and put his own liquor bottle in his duffel bag which was next to Red's. Then, after they had both put their bags in the large metal cupboard on the left side of the cabin, Red went and lay down on his wide bunk on the left side. Dave went and lay down on his own bunk on the right side. He put out the light. He lay there with his hands clasped behind his head and stared at the darkness. Dave kept on staring at the darkness and after a while he closed his eyes. But he couldn't sleep. Their ship was taking on troops, supplies and equipment and this seemed to be going on all night long.

A little after 4.00 o'clock in the morning Dave got up and went to the bathroom. Then he walked over to the porthole and looked down at the dock. In the darkness he could hardly see it and looked at it for a while before he turned and went back to his bunk where he fell asleep. Dave slept late and around 2.30 in the afternoon, they finally sailed from Halifax. At that time Dave had gone with Red to the Promenade Deck so they could stand against the starboard railing. The railing was quite crowded and Dave stood there with Red and watched as the *Empress Of Britain* began leaving Halifax. It was a cold raw gray day and there was a slight mist hanging low over the water. In no time their lines were cast off and tugboats began moving their ocean liner away from the pier.

Then the tugboats dropped back and they turned slowly to starboard and began leaving the port. They slowly left Halifax behind and the Clock Tower of the Citadel stood bleakly and forlornly in the distance. It rose darkly and stiffly above the low-lying skyline and as they kept on moving further and further away from the port, they began passing the outforts and getting into the deep calm waters of the Atlantic. They kept on getting deeper and deeper into those waters and as they sailed away from Halifax, the trip to England took eight days. When they left the port behind the weather turned crisp and clear and it stayed like this for most of the way except for the few times when there were patches of mist and fog. Throughout their journey they were escorted by Canadian and British destroyers and other British warships such as a huge aircraft carrier, a battleship, a battle cruiser and a cruiser.

Those ships kept on escorting the zigzagging convoy and moving up and down its path. Sometimes they crossed it and at other times they flanked it. But they were always on the lookout for enemy surface ships and for deadly submarines. As those warships kept on with their escort there was an air of tension and unreality about the convoy. And nowhere was this air of tension and unreality greater than in Dave's ship, the *Empress Of Britain*. In fact it was so great, in order to keep the men busy, Bostwick and the Platoon Sergeants used the time for training, lectures and exercises. But there was a strained artificiality about all this. It was as if they were doing those things because they had to do them but did not really believe in them. Then, as if to add to all this tension and unreality, there was the fact they were eating in one of the luxurious cabin-class dining-rooms.

They were eating under crystal chandeliers and on tables set with fresh linen and gleaming silverware. They were eating all kinds of seven-course meals such as *Saumon Sauté, Boeuf Bourguignon, Rosbif à l'Américaine, Coq au Vin* and *Canard à l'Orange*. Not only that but those truly incredible meals were served by white-jacketed waiters who had white napkins on their arms. On top of that there were ship's concerts being held both in French and English. Also there was the undeniable fact of the boredom of the trip itself and of being confined, no matter how you looked at it, to a restricted area. All of those things made the journey quite strange and unusual. As a matter of fact, when he wasn't busy with the half-hearted and uninspiring training, lectures and exercises Bostwick and the Platoon Sergeants were giving them, Dave spent his time watching Red gamble and win some money from the Big Ten.

Dave also tried to read the novels of a well-known and very famous British author he had found in the small steel book rack at the head of his bunk. Still, even though he tried to read them, it was Dave's inability to do so and really get interested in them that led him on Sunday evening, a week after they had left Halifax, and while Red had gone to a ship's concert with the Big Ten, to take out his bottle of Gordon's Dry Gin from his duffel bag and begin drinking it. Dave had gotten a glass from the bathroom and

Training

had gone and sat in one of the chairs next to the riveted small round table. Then he opened his bottle and poured himself a drink. Dave took a large sip and frowned. Not only had Red been taken by that soldier who had wanted two of his Matt knives. But he had been taken very badly. The gin had been watered down and had lost a great deal of its edge.

Still Dave just sat in his chair and drank his watered down gin straight. When Dave had drunk almost a third of his bottle and reached that line beyond which he knew, if he went on with his watered down gin, he would be sick, he went on anyway and kept on drinking. By now Dave was drinking quite slowly. He was doing it more out of boredom and sheer stubbornness than anything else. His head was quite clear. His reflexes were good. He could also see things with that crystal clarity that came from drinking so much it seemed to make him sober instead of drunk, but in a kind of a sickly and delicate way. So Dave kept on sitting at his table and drinking. When he had gone through almost half of his bottle and felt by then he had reached the absolute limit of what he could drink and, beyond this limit, would be really sick and have a huge and monumental hangover in the morning, if not worse, as he knew he would have anyway, he screwed the cap back on his bottle and got up far more carefully and deliberately than he would have liked.

Dave headed slowly and precariously toward the large metal cupboard where he put his bottle back in his duffel bag. Then he walked back slowly and precariously toward his bunk where he threw himself down on his back. When he threw himself down on his back the pent-up and accumulated fumes of this watered down gin he had been drinking suddenly rose up in him and swiftly and mercifully made him pass out. How long Dave stayed like this he didn't know. He just remained in a deep, restless and sluggish darkness. It was one that was heavy, draining and exhausting and after what seemed to him quite a while, it seemed to rise and fall, yank and pull, shake and move so he opened his eyes and found himself staring at the figure of Red.

Red was bending over him. He was shaking him up and down and saying: "Come on! Come on! Wake up! We're here!"

"Where?"

"We're going up the Clyde. We're almost there."

"Where?"

"Greenock."

"Where's that?"

"Scotland."

"Scotland?"

"That's right. That's where we're landing."

The Long War

"In Scotland?"
"That's right. Come on. Let's go."
"How do you know that?"
"I've already been out looking. Come on. Let's go have a look."

BOOK THREE

ALDERSHOT

CHAPTER 35

Dave sat up and swung out of his bunk carefully. He put his feet down on the floor and as he stood up, he began walking slowly and precariously toward the bathroom. When he got there Dave turned on the water and splashed cold water on his face. He felt his eyelids were thick and heavy against his eyes and his mouth tasted of chalk. He could also feel his head pounding savagely and could hear his heart throbbing dully. He shook his head trying to clear the cobwebs and then shaved and combed his hair. His skin felt sore and brittle under the razor and his hair hurt under the comb. Then he slowly left the bathroom and went with Red to stand next to the crowded railing on the Promenade Deck.

As soon as he walked out on the Promenade Deck Dave was hit by the brisk chilly wind. He felt his stomach come up on him and had to fight hard not to throw up. He took deep long breaths and when his head cleared somewhat and his stomach settled down a little, he looked around to see what was going on. At that moment they were coming up the Clyde. Although there was a low-lying mist on the water they could see the snow-covered hills of the Clydeside. Seagulls were swirling above the water and around the ships and they were escorted by British destroyers. Even though it was only 6.30 a.m. it seemed thousands were standing in their houses and in buildings and lining the narrow channel. They were hanging out of windows and staring from doors and shouting and cheering and waving flags and bunting at them.

As soon as they got close to Greenock the British destroyers fell back and disappeared into the low-lying mist. They themselves kept on sailing closer to Greenock and when they anchored in the channel, a tremendous roar went up from the shore as people realized they were Canadian troops.

When they had anchored, barges came alongside the ship and began unloading them to the shore and to the Central Station. The unloading went on without a stop. By 8.00 a.m. their Regiment was put on one of the many troop trains leaving the station at regular half-hour intervals. Dave was with the Company in one of the wagons in the middle of the train. He was sitting on the left side of the aisle next to the window. Red was sitting beside him. Then, as they began pulling out of the station, Dave watched the people who were still shouting and cheering and waving flags and bunting at them.

Then they left Greenock behind and picked up speed and began heading south. The weather that up to now had been crisp and cold, with a hint of snow in the air, started turning dark and overcast and soon after they had left Greenock behind, a light drizzling rain began to fall. As the rain began to fall they went through many small towns and villages. They also went by many small streams and woods. But the whole countryside with its many fields and streams and rolling grasslands was far more crowded with small towns and villages than it would be in Canada. They kept on heading south and by early afternoon when they reached the Midlands, they sped by various industrial towns and rows after rows of narrow, grimy and dingy houses. They went by many small towns, fields and villages again and late in the afternoon, the weather cleared.

The sun broke out and beyond Farnborough, the train lost speed and slowed down as Aldershot suddenly sprang into view. A town of about 35,000, it rose starkly and sharply under the sunny coppery skies of England. Its church spires, old buildings, narrow streets and timber-fronted shops gave it that classic and striking look of the huge garrison town and the shock of its stark and sudden presence under those sunny coppery skies spoke of an old and everlasting England; an England of Agincourt, the Armada and the Battle of Blenheim; one of Nelson, Cromwell and Wellington; one of early Conquerors, mad Kings and wild Adventurers. It was quite an extraordinary town to look at and as the train reached its outskirts, they drove through its streets and avenues until they came and stopped at the train station.

At the station they were taken off by their officers and NCOs and led to covered Bedford trucks lined up outside. Dave was put with the Big Ten in one of the trucks in the middle of the convoy. When the truck was full the flap was closed. Not long after the truck left with the rest of the convoy and began moving away from the station. In the darkness Dave guessed from the way the truck had made a left turn after a while, and was then driving straight, they must be heading in a southwesterly direction. They kept on driving in that direction and some time later, the road seemed to be going down a little as they turned left, slowed down and came to a stop. Then, when the flap of the truck was opened by one of the officers and when they were taken off, Dave stood beside the truck and couldn't get over it.

The Aldershot training center rose brutally, gigantically and spectacularly in front of him. It towered over him with the same kind of raw and savage quality he had seen and felt in the training ground in Terreyville. Yet in the case of Aldershot this quality was a thousand times more powerful and overpowering than it had been in Terreyville. The training center was huge and could take in, Dave guessed, about 15,000 soldiers. This meant it was definitely the biggest training center in England, if not in the world. In the clear coppery late-afternoon sunlight it towered colossally and monumentally over him with its Main Building, its other Administrative Buildings, its rows upon rows of barracks, its massive Parade Squares and its tall soaring flagpoles flying flags from all over the world.

This was the military center where soldiers from every corner of the globe had trained, from Anzacs to Gurkhas to Burmese Rifles to Punjab Regulars to Hong Kong Grenadiers. And this was the place, Dave knew, where they were going to train as well. Their truck had stopped at the first row of barracks at the beginning of the center. It had stopped at the northwestern boundary where the first three rows of barracks on that side of the center were served by a massive Parade Ground in front of those three rows. On the northwestern side of the Parade Ground there were seven flagpoles and three of those flagpoles were flying the Union Jack, the Red Ensign and the Regimental Colors. Then, in front of those flagpoles, there was a lone and mournful megaphone.

Their truck had stopped at the third barrack. When they had been taken off they were led by Bostwick into the barrack and told to take a bunk in the two long rows of double bunks. Dave took the third lower bunk to the left side of the door as you came in. The Big Ten chose bunks around him. Once they had taken a bunk Bostwick led them to their mess hall barrack. This barrack was right in the middle of the barracks on the northwestern side of the center. When they reached it they had a leisurely dinner of tea, sausages, mashed potatoes, gravy and bread. They also had peaches and biscuits for dessert. After the meal Bostwick brought them back to their own barrack and told them to settle in and familiarize themselves with their surroundings. He himself had to go with the other officers and NCOs to a meeting that had been called in the Regimental barrack near the end of the first row.

The Long War

    Bostwick left and Dave and the Big Ten began putting their gear in their foot lockers and fixing their bunks. This didn't take too long and when they had settled in, they gathered in the middle of the barrack before Lights Out and began talking about what they had seen, felt and lived through today.

CHAPTER 36

Red was the first one to begin talking about these things and said: "Well, all I can say, I'm damn glad we're finally in England."

"So am I," Gennaro said. "It's about time we started getting into some action for a change."

"You're not kidding," Higgins said.

"We're due for it," Lang said.

"That's the good thing about the British," Slav said. "Here they really make you feel the war."

"That's for sure," Mitchell said.

"And how," Addams said.

"I agree," Delorme said.

"Mind you, this place looks a little grim," Red said and eyed them all as he spoke. "But anything to beat Hitler, right?"

"You bet," Gennaro said.

"That's for sure we'll beat him," Addams said.

"And we'll have some fun doing it too," Higgins said.

"You're damn right," Gennaro said.

"See the world and beat the Germans, right?" Red said.

"That's the ticket," Gennaro said.

Up to now Dave had stood a little apart from Red and the Big Ten and had not said anything. But as they kept on going and talking like this, he moved closer and looked at them. A wild and savage grin came on his face and he said: "You guys. You make me laugh. You really make me laugh. Do you know that?"

"What do you mean?" Red said as he turned and looked at Dave.

"You think it's going to be so easy. You think it's going to be fun and games, don't you?"

"Nobody said that."

"Sure you did. You think we're just going to walk in there and the Germans are going to fold. Is that what you think?"

"Hey! Nobody thinks the Germans are going to fold."

"Sure you do."

"Oh no. Nobody thinks that."

"Sure you do. But don't you know the Germans are united right now as they've never been before and they're tough and motivated?"

"So?"

"So let me tell you something," Dave said. "There were over ten million dead in the First World War. And, I guarantee you, by the time we're through with this one there's going to be a hell of a lot more."

"So what!" Red said. "I won't be one of them!"

"That's right. You're never going to die, right?"

"You're goddam right! Let's get this straight! Nobody's going to kill this kid!"

"I'm sure."

"It's true! And I'm telling you we're going to beat the hell out of the Germans!"

"I'm sure."

"You're goddam right we will!"

"Oh sure. Because we're such tough and mean soldiers, right?"

"No! Because they overreached themselves!"

"Ha! That really makes me laugh. All that stuff about the Germans overreaching themselves. Can't you see it doesn't make any difference?"

"Why not?"

"Do you know what the life expectancy of an infantryman in a combat zone is?"

"No. What?"

"Seven days. That's how long he's expected to live."

"So?"

"So by the time this war's over none of us are going to be alive."

"Speak for yourself. I'm going to be around."

"Oh no you're not. None of us are going to be around."

"Sure I am. And anyway, if you felt like this, why did you join?"

"Maybe I didn't want to be around."

"Oh sure."

"It's true. And that's why you make me laugh. You think the Army and training and fighting Hitler is so wonderful."

"I don't."

"Sure you do. But I don't. I know better."

"That's where you're wrong. I don't think it's wonderful at all. But I'm going to do it just the same."

"I can see that. I can sure see that."

CHAPTER 37

Dave now turned abruptly from Red and the Big Ten and began walking away from them. He headed swiftly toward his bunk and when he reached it, he threw himself down on it and stared straight ahead. He kept on staring straight ahead until Lights Out and when he woke up the next morning, he washed, shaved and had an early breakfast. At precisely 8.00 a.m., he was taken with the Company to the Parade Ground where they were lined up facing the southern end of the center. As they were lined up Dave was surprised to see a Regiment standing to the left of their own Regiment. This Regiment had its own CO and its Companies' COs and NCOs standing in front of it. It was the same thing for their Regiment.

When the two Regiments were lined up a tall, lean and stern-faced Brigadier who stood in front of both now stepped forward and introduced himself. His name was Howard K. Mason and he was the Director of Military Operations at Aldershot. Mason welcomed them to the United Kingdom and told them how proud he was to have them there. He told them how grateful he was for the Dominion of Canada to have produced such fine-looking and sorely-needed soldiers. As a matter of fact he was convinced they were going to play quite an important part in the coming hostilities. The Brigadier kept on talking like this and Dave thought this was probably the usual standard speech he gave to all the soldiers coming in to Aldershot.

Then, after telling the men how happy he was to have them here and what a great contribution he felt they were going to make to the war effort, the Brigadier thanked them and stepped back a little. He turned and left the center with the two Regimental COs, and Cecil Emmett Williams, their Company Captain, now stepped forward and studied them. Captain

Williams was a tall, broad-shouldered, narrow-hipped officer who was in his early thirties. He stood about six feet two and had a stiff handlebar mustache that curved up sharply at both ends. He wore a neat impeccably-pressed uniform and snappy brightly-polished combat boots that made him look the very picture of the smart and professional officer. After he had stepped forward and studied them, he said: "Gentlemen. As the Brigadier said: 'Welcome. Welcome to Aldershot and to the one great big party we'll give the Hun very shortly.'

"The Regiment you see lined up on your left is the 51st Midlands Regiment and their CO is Colonel John R. Randall. The reason the Regiment is lined up on your left is we thought we'd make your training more interesting and competitive. To that end we thought we'd have the Regiment do a kind of combined-unit training with you while we're in Aldershot. In this way you'll be able to compare yourselves with your fellow British soldiers and they'll be able to do the same with you. This combined-unit training will last as long as the two Regiments are in Aldershot and will take place as often as it can be arranged. For the time being though, and in order to familiarize ourselves with our new surroundings, let's get going on our own and let's begin our training now, shall we?"

Captain Williams turned and began leading the men south and away from the center. He marched them past the huge Parade Grounds and the soldiers who were training there. In that cold gray woolly mid-December morning they moved out of the center and Aldershot and some time later Farnham. They moved past small villages and brooks and rolling hills and wastelands until they reached a place called Frensham. They rested a bit in Frensham and then turned and began heading back to Aldershot. They were being led by Williams and when they got close to Aldershot, it began snowing heavily. They kept on heading toward the center and when they got into it, they were brought back to the Parade Ground. On that ground they were put through various close-order drills and physical exercises and in the afternoon, they were taken on another march in the direction of Farnborough.

In this way their stay in Aldershot began and, all things considered, turned out to be quite interesting and unusual. For one thing it proved to be the coldest winter England had ever had in over 50 years. It snowed quite a lot and although the temperatures were not as low as those in Canada, the cold icy wind blowing was so damp and chilly it made the weather seem much colder than anything they had seen back home. For another the old World War One barracks they were living in were totally inadequate for this kind of winter. The buildings were always drafty and icy. The single

The Long War

windows were always frosting over and letting in cold air. Not only that but the open fireplaces and unreliable coal-burning stoves they had were simply not able to cope with the fierceness of such temperatures.

Also they had been sent to Aldershot for Advanced Training as opposed to Basic Training, or Collective Training as opposed to Individual Training, or, to be even more precise, Training by Company, Battalion and Brigade. However, given the harsh and severe conditions of the winter, it didn't prove possible to carry out Collective Training much before the spring. Instead they fell back to Individual Training and ended up doing pretty much the kind of Basic Training they had done in Terreyville. This time, though, they did it in combined-unit training with the 51st Midlands Regiment. The training for B Company of the 51st Midlands was given by their Company CO, Captain Clive Purcell Dunston, and by their Company Sergeant Major, James "Jocko" Thompson.

Captain Dunston was a small, bony, blond-haired officer. He had a pink, cheerful, ruddy face and weighed around 120 pounds. He was in his mid or late twenties and was about five feet four or five. Sergeant Major "Jocko" Thompson was a tall, big-boned, leathery-faced NCO who was in his early forties. He was a tough Sergeant Major and was also quite good and knowledgeable when it came to training. Both of them were in charge of training for B Company of the 51st Midlands and worked closely with Captain Williams and Bostwick who did the same thing for their own Company. They worked together all winter and when spring finally came around, they began doing Collective Training. Both Regiments began training by Companies, Battalions and Brigades and getting involved in modest-sized to fairly-large operations, exercises and maneuvers.

The weather, which, during the winter, had been exceedingly cold and fierce, now turned extremely mild and beautiful. It became very warm and sunny, although their barracks always seemed to be damp and chilly. With the beginning of Collective Training their combined-unit training with the 51st Midlands began to get more intense and the two Regiments trained together as often as they could. Now that spring was here the Company should have been glad to get out of its cold and drafty barracks and exercise in the warm and sunny countryside. Yet throughout the spring there was a great deal of tension and unhappiness within the Company and this tension and unhappiness got worse as the spring went on. You could sense and feel it in almost every soldier of the Company and the reasons for it weren't hard to find.

You only had to look at the fact whenever they trained together the 51st Midlands seemed to be much better than the Fusiliers. This was true of the close-order drills they took on the Parade Ground where, despite the Regiment's best efforts, the 51st Midlands looked much more smooth and polished. This was true of the long marches they took together where, in the field, the 51st Midlands seemed to have a lot more toughness and endurance. And this was especially true in the case of fairly-large maneuvers where, in open country, the 51st Midlands proved to be far more successful and accomplished. There were all of these things and as time went on, one man caused more tension and unhappiness in the Company than anyone else. This man was their Captain, Cecil Emmett Williams.

Ever since they had landed in England Captain Williams had become a changed man. Although he had been born in Vancouver from parents who had worked in the fishing industry, now that he was in England, Captain Williams seemed to want to become more British than the British themselves. His speech became sharp and clipped in the manner of British officers and he began using all kinds of words like "tallyho", "cheerio" and "old chap". Always a stickler for spit and polish he now became driven by the idea. Buttons had to shine. Uniforms had to be spotless. Boots had to be polished. But it was in the area of physical fitness that his obsession to become more British than the British reached its greatest height. In fact it became so intense and severe it showed itself in his taking out the Company to the countryside whenever he could for short, medium and long marches.

And it was on one of those long marches, a "Williams' Special" as he called it, that there occurred this incident which turned out to be so startling and, in so many ways, unexpected.

CHAPTER 38

This incident occurred, as a matter of fact, toward the middle of June. It occurred around 11.00 o'clock on a Wednesday morning, June 12, 1940. That bright and sunny morning Williams took out the Company in combined-unit training with B Company of the 51st Midlands. There was a nice cool breeze blowing and Williams led the men out of the center and in a southerly direction. He led them on a long 30-mile full-pack marathon march to Milland and back. It was understood there would be short periods of rest to be given to the men every five miles or so. However the Company, which had already been taken on two other long marches during the past week, didn't really enjoy the prospect of going on another long march again.

As the men came out of the center and began heading toward the countryside, there was a great deal of grumbling and complaining among them. Williams, though, at the head of both Companies didn't see this. He led the two Companies sharply and briskly past several villages, rolling hills, woods, brooks and wastelands until they reached the small bleak village of Milland. At the village Williams ordered the men to lie down and rest since it was at the half-way point of the march. When Williams ordered the men to lie down and rest, Red sat down on the right side of the road and stared fixedly and pointedly at him. Throughout the march Red had been staying at the front of the Company and grumbling and muttering to himself. Now, as he kept on staring fixedly and pointedly at Williams, he suddenly stood up and said: "Ah. The hell with this!"

Red turned his back on the Company. He began leaving Milland and heading for Aldershot again. Dave, who was sitting about 100 feet from him in the middle of the Company, stood up when he saw Red leave and said: "Hey! What are you doing?" "Ah. The hell with this!" Red said and glared at him as he went by. "The man wants us to march. I'll march!" Red marched past the Company and Dave now tagged along behind him about 100 feet. The rest of the Company got up and began following Red and Dave. B Company of the 51st Midlands also got up and began following them. Both Companies filed out of Milland and hit the countryside again. They marched past several villages, rolling hills, woods, brooks and wastelands and all the time Red was in the lead.

Dave was about 100 feet behind him and at about the same distance behind Dave were the two Companies. As they kept on marching like this Dave looked at Red and thought: Look at him go. Oh man, look at him go. He's something else, that little Irishman. He sure is something else. Who could have guessed he'd have such staying power? Go on, my man! Dave thought. Go on! Show Williams what you think of him and his stupid marches! Dave tightened his pace and kept on following Red. He was still about 100 feet behind him and the two Companies were still about 100 feet behind Dave.

CHAPTER 39

Dave kept on marching and on following Red and after a while heard Bostwick's hard driving voice behind him say: "Come on! Come on! Let's move it!" Then someone from their Company broke into the harsh staccato rhythm of their Regimental Song. This was *The Fusiliers' Song* and he was soon joined by everyone from the Company:

> *One, two, three, four*
> *Pull up your socks. Bring on the war*
> *Left, right, left, right*
> *Bang! Bang! One real big fight*
>
> *One, two, three, four*
> *Load up your gun. Let's go for more*
> *Left, right, left, right*
> *Forward! Onward! All day, all night*
>
> *One, two, three, four*
> *Rack up the dice. Roll up the score*
> *Left, right, left, right*
> *Boom! Boom! Right out of sight*
>
> *Man. Oh man. It's such a great war*
> *Yeah. Yeah. Such a great war*
> *Just made for us, the Westmount Fusiliers*
> *Oh yeah! The bad mean Fusiliers*

No sooner had that song broken out from their Company than someone from B Company of the 51st Midlands launched into their somewhat longer, fuller and more rhythmic song. As he did Jocko Thompson was heard saying to the men of his Company in his gruff and gravelly voice: "Steady, lads! Steady!" The song the soldier launched into was *The 51st Midlands' Song* and he was joined almost at once by everyone from his Company:

> *When the wee thunder of the drums rolls*
> *Over copses and grassy knolls*
> *The sun is rising over the men on the line*
> *Yea! Yea! On Britain's Thin Red Line*
>
> *From Malaysia, Africa and India*
> *Fighting Warlords, Sheiks and Maharajahs*
> *We're the Kingdom's pride and joy on the march*
> *For the Empire's Glory ever so willing to grasp*
>
> *So tremble, ye bandits and sorry scrappers*
> *'Tis a bad thing to rile us, ornery fighters*
> *Spread far and wide all over the globe*
> *Wherever there's a line for the Union Jack to hold*
>
> *For we're Britain's best and finest, the Island's*
> *Young warriors from the bold fearless Midlands*
> *A rough hardy breed scorning mercy, pity or sorrow*
> *True rankers, all, with naught a care for the morrow*

As the two songs rose loudly and roughly across the countryside and tried to drown and deafen one another, Red kept on leading the two Companies. Dave was following him and the two Companies brought up the rear. Things stood like this until Frensham where they began to change. Just past the village a big tall raw-boned Private from the 51st Midlands suddenly broke out of rank and began gaining on Dave and on Red. By that time Red's combat uniform was black with sweat and he was grunting and breathing heavily. As he heard the men of the 51st Midlands begin to shout and cheer wildly for that Private, Red turned.

When he saw the Private was gaining on Dave and on himself Red yelled suddenly: "Come on, Dave! Do something! Give me a hand!"

CHAPTER 40

Dave, who had reluctantly stepped up his pace when he had seen that Private break out of the 51st Midlands' rank, now picked it up even more and found out how strong the man was. Even with his accelerated pace Dave saw the man was steadily gaining on him. After a while Dave passed Red and a little later, the man pulled dead even with him. Dave turned and looked at him. Although the man looked somewhat like Jocko Thompson, his bony angular face had such a cruel and brutal look, such a mean and stupid expression, such a raw and fiery determination to overtake him and Red and take on the lead, Dave suddenly flew into the same kind of wild and savage rage he had felt that time, when he had first stood with Red and the Big Ten in their barrack before Lights Out, in Aldershot, and thought: Screw you! Screw you, you bastard!

Dave now clenched his jaw, narrowed his eyes and really poured it on. He marched swiftly and steadily and increased the pace even with the same kind of power and drive he had seen earlier in Red. This effort made him begin to pull away from the Private. At first it was just a little, then quite a bit, and he kept on marching with his knees high, jaw clenched, eyes narrowed, and headed straight for Aldershot. Behind him Dave could hear the two Companies cheering, yelling and screaming wildly. Each one was cheering for his own man and some time later when he turned and looked back, Dave could see Williams at the head of the two Companies. He was grinning broadly and happily at the excitement and rivalry he had created and a little behind him Dunston's face was crimson and purple with rage at the thought of having been caught so badly unprepared.

By this time Dave was beginning to feel the strain and exhaustion of this marching with full combat pack and full combat uniform. Near

Aldershot

Runfold he could hear the 51st Midlands cheering, yelling and screaming more wildly than ever and didn't have to look back to know the Private was gaining on him again. When they marched through Runfold and began to get close to Aldershot, the men in his Company began to yell: "The Line! The Line! To the Line!" They were referring to the imaginary line that ran between the front of the second barrack and their own third barrack. The 51st Midlands understood this well since they too had their own imaginary line that ran between their barrack and another one next to theirs further down in the first row of barracks. Dave stepped up the pace yet still felt the Private was gaining on him.

As Aldershot came into view and as they got into the center, the Private pulled dead even with him. Dave turned and looked at him again. His bony angular face still had the same cruel and brutal look, the same mean and stupid expression, the same raw and fiery determination to overtake him and take on the lead. As Dave saw this again another wild and savage rage suddenly leapt into him for the man himself and for all he stood for and, his heart bursting, his chest heaving, his knees aching, he began running toward the line. After a while Dave could feel himself begin to pull away from the Private and heard him cry and groan inwardly as he tried to keep up. Suddenly Dave threw his hands up, leaned forward and came barreling through the line, half a length in front of the Private.

By now Dave was running so hard he was propelled past the middle of their barrack. Then he slowed down and turned and came wearily back to the line. As he stopped there he was bent in two and his heart was nearly bursting from the strain and exhaustion of his last burst of speed. When he stopped near Red at the line, he and Red were immediately surrounded by the soldiers of the Company and pounded and slapped on the back and told what a great march it had been. Dave nodded and just stood there. He was still bent in two and the sweat was pouring off his face. He only looked up when Captain Dunston and the Private from the 51st Midlands broke through the soldiers who were surrounding him and briefly and hurriedly congratulated him on the march.

Dave nodded again and when they left, he stayed bent in two and tried to catch his breath. He had such a stitch in his left side he could hardly breathe and when he was able to straighten up a bit, he looked up and saw the Colonel and his Second in Command, Major Philip Caldwell. Both of them were walking swiftly and briskly toward him. Major Caldwell was a tall, trim and blond-haired officer who was in his late thirties. He was a soldier who always had a smart look, sharp manners and a crisp bearing. As a matter of fact, from a distance, he looked very much like the Colonel. Right now both were coming toward him. The Major stood slightly behind the Colonel and to his right. When they reached him the Colonel looked at Dave and said: "Ah, Lindsay. I see you're still in the middle of things."

Dave nodded. But he didn't say anything.

"I was just coming out of Regimental Headquarters and saw your last burst of speed," the Colonel said. "I must say it was quite impressive."

Again Dave nodded. But he didn't say anything.

The Colonel now moved close to Dave and said in a voice so low no one else could hear: "But don't get yourself involved in any further incident. Don't try to play the hero and take on anybody. We're moving out."

Dave looked at the Colonel. But this time he didn't ask where nor when.

The Colonel smiled slightly when he saw this.

Then the Colonel and the Major turned and began walking away. Dave stood at the line and watched them leave. He didn't move from the line and when they were both gone, he tried to get his wind back and breathe a little easier.

BOOK FOUR

BREST

CHAPTER 41

Dave stood at the line and when the stitch in his left side began to go away, he left with the Company to go to the mess hall to eat. In the afternoon he went with the men to the gym in one of the Administrative Buildings so he could listen to lectures by Moran on tactics and weaponry. Those lectures went on for most of the afternoon and around 9.00 o'clock in the evening, Bostwick came into their barrack and told them the news. As part of the 1st Canadian Infantry Brigade under Brigadier Armand A. Smith they were going with the 51st Midlands Regiment to France. They were going to Brest and would reassemble near Le Mans in order to be able to attack the flank of any German Army coming that way.

When the men heard the news they turned to each other and cheered wildly and enthusiastically. After all the Regiment had been training non-stop for over 10 months in Terreyville and in Aldershot and the men were now really eager to get into some fighting. To be sure there had been other calls like this before. In the middle of April, when Hitler had launched his invasion of Norway, they had been taken to the Scottish port of Dunfermline in order to go and take part in a frontal assault of the town of Trondheim. But this operation had been canceled. Then, when Hitler had launched his long-awaited attack in the West, they had been sent to the port of Dover so they could go and take position alongside the British Army on the Franco-Belgian border. This operation had also been canceled. By May 15 Holland had surrendered. And on May 28 Belgium had also surrendered.

The British papers had been full of those stories and had been using terms like "fierce fighting", "savage struggle" and "stubborn resistance." Now that the men knew where they were going they began to get ready and the next evening, the Regiment was taken by rail to Plymouth where it was loaded aboard a transport. The name of the transport was *Excalibur* and it was going to take them to France. Then, around 2.00 o'clock in the morning, they sailed in total darkness from their West Pier in Plymouth and began heading for Brest. Late at night like this there was a nice cool breeze in the channel and the stars shone high and clear in the sky overhead. There was also the smell of salty spray in the air and they sailed on slowly and steadily toward France.

Dave stood fully-loaded near the railing on the starboard side with the Big Ten. He guessed they were sailing slowly and steadily like this since they were scheduled to arrive in Brest in the morning. Dave stood at the railing and talked with the Big Ten. As he did he watched the calm glassy sea and the bright sparkling stars overhead. After a while, instead of going down to the berth that had been assigned to him in one of the cargo holds, Dave put his combat pack against one of the bulwarks near the railing. He sat down on the deck and leaned against it and went to sleep. Since there was a nice cool breeze blowing and since there wasn't too much swell in the channel, Dave slept well and when he woke up in the morning, he saw the sun was shining on the calm shimmering sea. There was no longer any breeze blowing, however, and Dave knew it was going to be quite a hot and stifling day.

There was no sign of France yet. They kept on sailing in those calm and shimmering waters and near 10.00 o'clock, a line began rising on the horizon. It was pale-brown at first and then a deep golden-brown. After a while, when that line had risen enough out of the water and hardened, it turned into the city of Brest itself with its ramparts, piers, bridges, castle, museum, buildings and churches gleaming in the sunlight. That morning planes were buzzing over the city and a huge column of black smoke was rising high over it from the south and clouding the sunlight. They kept on getting closer and closer to it and when they finally docked at the huge rampart called Jetée de l'Ouest, they were taken off the *Excalibur* and marched toward the Gare SNCF.

Now, in the city itself, there was a faint smell of raw burning cordite and the streets had a bleak and dusty look about them. A black pall of smoke was drifting to the west over some of the buildings and there was a lot of broken glass and rubble in a few of the streets. Once they had left the port area behind they got onto the Rue du Château and headed toward the Gare SNCF. Near the Gare the streets were full of trucks and cars and people and soldiers and officers and at the Gare itself, they were marched in and taken to the area where the trains were leaving.

This area, like the surrounding streets outside, was also full of people and soldiers and officers. Williams was there as well as some officers from the Fusiliers. Dunston was also there with some officers of the 51st Midlands and part of that Regiment itself.

As he waited to get in one of the trains with the Big Ten, Dave found out from one of the soldiers from the 51st Midlands they had docked in Brest just before them. They had been taken there by the transport *Stella Maris*. Soldiers from that Regiment and the Fusiliers stood around and waited to get on board the various trains. Officers and NCOs from Movement Control were running back and forth over the area and talking and pointing and arguing. Then, after more talking and pointing and arguing between the Movement Control officers and NCOs and their own officers and NCOs, they were put on one of the trains. When they were on board Dave saw Dunston and some of the officers of the 51st Midlands were with them. But they had few of their own officers and some of their own soldiers were mixed with those of the 51st Midlands.

The train they were put on had two flatbed cars with 40 mm Bofors guns on them. One was near the front of the long wooden wagons and the other near the end. They themselves were put on a wagon a little over the middle of the train. Then, when the train was full, there was a lurch followed by another lurch and they were on their way. They slowly came out of the station and began heading east toward Le Mans. In no time they left Brest behind and began going by small villages like Landerneau, Laroche and Lampau. Those villages were surrounded by rugged craggy brown fields and were made up of solid stony farmhouses and cottages. The railway ran alongside Route Nationale 12. It ran to the left of it and was on a high embankment. They kept on heading east and when they got to Morlaix, Dave began noticing the refugees on the Route Nationale.

There were quite a few of them and all of them were heading toward Brest. They were heading there in big cars that were driven by chauffeurs or in smaller and less expensive ones with mattresses on top of them. They were going there in horse-drawn carriages, on bicycles and on foot. Some of the less expensive cars and horse-drawn carriages were filled with furniture and other belongings. Some of the people on foot were pushing wheelbarrows. Others carried whatever they could in suitcases or in a white sheet tied in a bundle and swung over their shoulders. There were also children everywhere: in expensive and less expensive cars; in horse-drawn carriages; on foot with their parents; and sometimes alone and wandering about.

In order to get a better look at the refugees Dave lowered the window and half-leaned out of it. He had unslung his rifle and put it next to the window against the seat on the right side. He looked at the refugees for a while and as he was half-leaning out of the window, he suddenly heard the cry: "Messerschmitts!"

CHAPTER 42

One moment Dave was half-leaning out of the window and looking at the refugees. Next he suddenly heard the cry: "Messerschmitts!" Then, as in a kind of frozen timelessness, a V of planes surged over them. It boomed past and was gone as it turned west and went back. This happened so fast Dave didn't have time to react. One moment the planes were over them. Next they were gone. Yet, although those planes were over them and then gone, for Dave it seemed as if time froze and he could see everything in huge slow motion: the V of planes surging out of nowhere, diving on them and then climbing out of range; the hard metallic rows of stitches spitting out of their two 20 mm cannons and their two machine guns; the bullets hitting and raking their wagon; officers, NCOs and soldiers staggering, spinning and being smashed against seats and windows.

For a moment everything was quiet. Then Dave heard the screams. Horrible, terrifying, hair-raising screams. Then he saw the blood everywhere in shattered faces, ripped chests, torn limbs, crushed seats and spattered windows. When he saw this Dave broke out of his momentary spell. He leaned back in and said: "The Big Ten. All you guys. Is everybody all right?" "Yeah. Sure," choked and sick voices said here and there. "Jesus Christ! I don't believe it!" Red, who had been sitting behind Dave, said as he looked around. "The Big Ten. All you guys," Dave said. "Stay close to the windows and lean out of them if there's another strafing run. That way you have a much better chance of survival." "Yeah. Sure," the same choked and sick voices said here and there. "You," Dave turned and motioned to Red. "Come and help me look at this mess."

Red nodded and they both left their seats and went into the aisle. The first officer they saw was on the left side of the aisle near the wagon doors.

He sat opposite the window from where Dave had been half-leaning out. He was lying sprawled against his wooden seat. He had been shot right through the throat and his whole chest was wet and soggy with the blood that was still gurgling out of his throat. Dave glanced at him briefly and moved on down the aisle with Red past officers, NCOs and soldiers with blown off faces, riddled chests and torn limbs. Those twin 20 mm cannons had really done the job and badly maimed the people they had hit. Most of the people that had been hit seemed to have been killed instantly. The few that had been wounded were being helped and taken care of by a Medic and a Stretcher Bearer from the 51st Midlands.

In the middle of the wagon Dave nodded and moved past the Medic and the Stretcher Bearer with Red. He went on with Red toward the end of the wagon and when he got there, Dave stopped suddenly and stared. On the left side of the aisle stood Williams and Dunston and a small group of officers from the Fusiliers and the 51st Midlands. Williams was facing Dunston and they were lying in a circle as if they had been gathering there to look at maps and talk about the coming operations. But all of them were dead. They were piled up against the smashed swungover seat and it looked as if they had been in the middle of their talk when they had been hit by the attacking planes. There were bits of brains and skins and limbs all over the place and the maps they had been using were lying messily among them and were covered with blood and broken glass.

Of the eight officers that were there two had had their faces blown off and were unrecognizable. The other six had been very badly hit but were recognizable. As for Williams and Dunston, though, they were the least badly hit of the eight. Williams had been shot through the chest and was lying at the head of the circle. He had a stunned and astonished look on his face as if he couldn't quite believe being more British than the British, spit and polish and physical fitness wouldn't prevail against twin 20 mm cannons. As a matter of fact he had a sullen and resentful look on his face as if he couldn't quite believe what had happened to him and as if, really, it couldn't happen. As for Dunston, who was lying at the opposite end of the circle from Williams, he had been shot neatly through the heart.

Dunston was slumping a little forward and looked smaller in death than he had actually looked in life. He seemed to be slipping into the floor and looked as if he was somewhat ill at ease and embarrassed at finding himself in such a position. At the sight of Williams, Dunston and those other officers of the Fusiliers and the 51st Midlands, Dave stood and stared. All the officers in the wagon had been killed. When they had left Brest a few of them had been sitting on each side of the aisle. But most of them had ended up being bunched with Williams and Dunston near the end of the wagon. Dave shook his head and came to leave the wagon with Red when he suddenly heard muffled grunts and groans from underneath the pile of officers who were lying with Williams.

Dave stopped and told Red to come and help him move those officers out of the way. In a little while he was astonished to find Bostwick lying underneath the smashed swungover seat where the dead officers were piled up. Williams was lying on top of him and Bostwick was covered with broken glass and wooden splinters. Dave and Red dragged him out into the aisle and when they had brought him there, Dave saw his right leg was covered with blood. Dave bent closer to him and said: "My God, Sergeant Major! What happened to you?"

"Stupid jokers," Bostwick grunted and brushed the broken glass and wooden splinters from him. "Standing together like a bunch of school kids."

"You're wounded in the leg. Let me have a look."

"Ah, it's nothing."

"No, no. Let me have a look."

Bostwick sighed and lay there as Dave bent over his wounded leg and looked at it. After a moment Dave looked up from his leg and said: "It doesn't look too bad. It looks like a flesh wound from a bullet splinter. But you've bled a lot."

"Ah, it's nothing."

"No, no. Let me make a tourniquet to stop the bleeding. And let me bandage the wound."

CHAPTER 43

With the help of Red, Dave went and picked up a sling from the rifle of a dead soldier who was lying not far from Williams' circle of officers. When he had the sling Dave came back and made a tourniquet above the wound on Bostwick's leg. Then he reached in his right leg pocket for a heavy-pressure bandage. With the bandage Dave dressed Bostwick's wound tightly and cleanly. When he was finished Dave turned to Bostwick and said: "Well. How is it?" "It's okay," Bostwick said and grunted a little as he stood up stiffly with the help of Dave. When he was up Bostwick sent Red to help the Medic and the Stretcher Bearer from the 51st Midlands. Both of them watched Red go and when he had almost reached them in the middle of the wagon, the cry suddenly went up again: "Messerschmitts!"

"Oh my God!" Dave said. "Here we go again," Bostwick said. Both of them froze in the middle of the aisle. They stood there while just about everyone else threw themselves on the windows. Then they heard, but didn't see, the planes dive in on them, boom past and climb away. But the V was wide this time. The two planes on each side of the V fired on both sides of the train. One fired on the refugees on the Route Nationale; the other on the field on the other side. The other plane, however, was right on top of them. It came straight down on the wagon and Dave took a deep breath and stood there with Bostwick. He watched as the two racing spitting lines of bullets sawed right through their wagon and churned through the seats past both of them. As the plane fired, the bullets killed and wounded a few more NCOs and soldiers.

It missed most of them, however, since they had all thrown themselves on the windows and were half-leaning out of them. There was a silence followed by the same kind of screams Dave had heard before: horrible, terrifying, hair-raising. Red, the Medic and the Stretcher Bearer from the 51st Midlands began rushing back and forth across the wagon and trying to help those who were wounded while just about everyone else stayed close to the windows. Dave blinked and swallowed hard. Then he turned to Bostwick and said: "Oh man! We've got to get out of here!"

"I'm with you on that."

"This place is a death trap."

"It sure is."

"Why aren't our Bofors guns firing? What's the matter with those guys?"

"Maybe they don't know how to operate them."

"That's all we need."

"That's for sure."

"And what about the goddam French!" Dave burst out. "What's the big idea of sending us to the line in those wooden wagons. Man! Those 20 mm cannons are cutting through them like through butter!"

"That's the French for you," Bostwick said.

"Yeah. The good old SNCF! Couldn't they have used better and stronger wagons?"

"Well, we were just going to a quiet assembly area. Remember?"

"Yeah. It's some quiet area, all right!"

"At least that's what the British said."

"That's right! The sonofabitches! And what about the RAF? Where's the goddam RAF?"

"Hell. They're probably still practicing loops and landings back in England."

"You're not kidding!"

"It's an interesting war, hey, kid?"

"You're telling me!"

CHAPTER 44

They were still talking about this when there was a sudden jolt that nearly sent everyone sprawling on the floor. They heard the screech of iron wheels locking and grinding on the rails and the train slammed to a shuddering stop. When it did Dave, who had grabbed Bostwick to prevent him from going down on the floor, yelled: "Out! Out! Everybody out!" With these words everybody rushed from the windows and ran for the doors. Both of them followed. They ran for the door on the left side of the wagon. This was the door on the side away from the Route Nationale and on the side of the field. At the door Bostwick turned and looked at Dave.

Their eyes met and at that precise moment the look in Bostwick's eyes said: "Wait. Wait." As Dave could see the look in Bostwick's eyes he could hear again, but not see, another V of planes diving in on them. He could also hear the noise of their diving growing bigger and bigger until it seemed to be roaring inside of him. At that moment the look in Bostwick's eyes suddenly said: "Now!" When he saw this Dave jumped clear out of the wagon with Bostwick. Dave's heart leapt into his throat, however, when he saw the plane on the outside of the V spring out of nowhere over the train and grow huge. Its twin 20 mm cannons were firing point-blank at the soldiers and people in the field. Dave and Bostwick dropped in a free fall between the two spitting slashing rows of bullets and hit the pale green-grass embankment.

Dave reached out and grabbed Bostwick to stop him from rolling to the bottom of it. He pulled him underneath the wagon with him and saw Bostwick's wounded leg leave a wide bloody trail on the grass. Then, as they both lay underneath the wagon, they looked at this V of planes also climbing and turning west. At the top of the turn the plane on the left side of the V dipped its wings. Then the planes were gone and they both lay underneath the wagon. They were both breathing hard and looking at the sky for other planes. Dave and Bostwick lay underneath the wagon for a while and then the train whistle blew. When it did Dave scrambled out from underneath the wagon with Bostwick and helped him get back on the train. The Big Ten also got back on the train and some of them helped soldiers from their Company and the 51st Midlands bring in the few dead and wounded NCOs and soldiers from the field.

When everyone was on board Dave leaned out of his wagon door and waved with his left hand to the conductor who was also leaning out of his engine. The conductor nodded and stepped back into his engine. There was a lurch followed by another lurch and they were on their way again. As soon as they were on their way Dave made sure Bostwick sat in the last seat of their wagon near the door on the left side. Since there was quite a bit of blood seeping through the heavy-pressure bandage on his right leg Dave sent Red to get another one from the Medic of the 51st Midlands. When Red came back with it Dave tightened Bostwick's tourniquet and dressed his wound tightly and cleanly again. When Dave was finished Bostwick insisted on getting up. Dave helped him on his feet.

Then, when Bostwick was standing stiffly near the door, Dave turned to him and said: "Listen. We've got to do something. We just can't go on like this." "You're goddam right we've got to do something," Bostwick said. "What do you want me to do?" Dave asked. "First, you go look for an officer," Bostwick said. "Then, when you find one, bring him to me." "You got it," Dave said. Dave turned and left their wagon. He began heading toward the front of the train and walked fast. He was almost running and kept on looking at the NCOs and soldiers on both sides of the aisle and saying: "Any officers? Any officers here?" But there weren't any that weren't wounded and able to move. There were just scared and frightened NCOs and soldiers. Dave kept on heading toward the front of the train and when he reached the first flatbed car, he stopped and stood there.

In the rear right-hand corner was Dabrowski. He was lying peculiarly on his right side. His face was unnaturally white and his chest was neatly riddled with bullets. The Bofors gunner was slumped over the anti-aircraft gun and the three Lewis machine gunners were also lying oddly on the floor. Dave looked at them for a moment and then went on to the front of the train. As he worked his way there it was the same thing. There were scared and frightened NCOs and soldiers. But there were no officers who were not wounded and able to move. As soon as he reached the front of the train Dave turned and began working his way back. In no time he went through his own wagon and made for the rear. When he reached the second flatbed car Dave saw the Bofors gunner was also slumped over his gun and the three Lewis machine gunners were also lying oddly on the floor. Dave made his way to the rear and came back.

Dave moved past the long wooden wagons and when he got to their own wagon, he walked up to Bostwick and said: "There are no officers. They're all either dead or too badly wounded to move."

"There isn't one?"

"No."

"Not even one?"

"No."

"Jesus Christ!"

"My feelings exactly."

Bostwick scratched his chin and then said: "All right. But you're sure you looked and there's no one we can talk to?"

"I'm sure."

"Absolutely no one?"

"No one."

"Well, that's great."

"I'm sorry."

"Don't be sorry."

"I just wish things were different."

"So do I."

Bostwick scratched his chin again and then said: "What about the people on the flatbed cars? Why wasn't anybody firing?"

"All the people there were killed. That's why."

Bostwick scratched his chin once more and then said: "This changes things. This changes things a great deal."

Dave didn't say anything and Bostwick said: "In that case I guess we'll have to turn the train around ourselves."

"I'm with you."

"Good."

"How do we do this?"

CHAPTER 45

Bostwick told Dave: "Go and get me one of the maps from over there." He pointed to the maps lying messily among Williams, Dunston and the other dead officers. Dave left Bostwick and walked over to the pile of officers who were lying in a circle against the smashed swungover seat on the left side of the aisle. He picked one lying not far from Williams on his right. He swept the blood and broken glass from it and went back to Bostwick. Bostwick took the map and spread it out to have a look. He studied it and then said to Dave: "We have to find a town with a switching yard so we can turn the train around."

"Rennes has a switching yard."

"No. That's too dangerous."

"Why?"

"Rennes is a pretty big town and an important rail center. If the Germans are on bombing runs and looking for targets, they might easily hit the town and we'll never get out of there."

"Where then?"

"According this map there's a small switching yard in Clermont. This is a town about five miles from Rennes and a little east of Montfort. That's the place where we must do it."

"If the Germans bomb Rennes, they might bomb Clermont too. No?"

"They might. But again they might not. They might be so busy at Rennes they'll forget about Clermont. That's why we must do it there."

"Clermont it is then."

"You bet."

"How to we do this?"

"Take Red and Higgins with you. Go to the engine and tell the conductor to turn the train around and go back to Brest."

"That's it?"

"You got it.

"I'm on my way."

"Okay. But hurry. Those Messersschmitts have a range of about 400 miles and the closer we get to Le Mans, the more we're in range of them."

"Don't worry. I don't think I want to run into them again."

"Me neither."

CHAPTER 46

Dave left Bostwick and picked up Red and Higgins. He walked through their own wagon and headed for the front of the train. At the first flatbed car Dave stopped with them and pointed to the riddled body of Dabrowski. "You see this?" he said. "This is for real. This isn't maneuvers. So stay sharp." Dave bent down and picked up a fully-loaded 9 mm Parabellum Luger with a brown leather belt and brown holster from one of the dead machine gunners. Dave strapped on the belt and put the Luger in the holster. Then he headed for the front of the train again and when he got to the tender, he climbed in with Red and Higgins. At the other end Dave climbed out with them and jumped into the engine to the astonishment of the conductor and the stoker.

The conductor was a small portly man with a neat pencil-thin mustache. He wore a blue cloth cap and blue overalls. The stoker, who was standing a little behind him, was a tall lean man who was bald and who also wore blue overalls. As they jumped in the conductor turned to them and said in French: "What are you doing here?"

"Monsieur, when we get to Clermont, you must turn this train around and go back to Brest," Dave said to him also in French.

"Go back to Brest," the conductor drew himself to his full height. "Never! I am a patriot!'

"I understand," Dave said in French. "But we must go back. Right now there are several killed and wounded on this train and we're only target practice for the Germans."

"My orders are to bring you to Le Mans. That is what I will do."

"I understand. But we must go back. We have no choice."

"We are Allies. I have my orders. You have yours."

"What has orders got to do with it? If we stay on this train, we run the risk of all getting killed. That's what."

"Never! I will never go back! I will bring you to Le Mans!"

"Ecoutez-moi, mon pote. Vous allez faire faire demi-tour à ce train à Clermont et retourner à Brest. Sinon je vous flambe la cervelle! C'est compris!" a voice, like the clap of doom, thundered behind them.

As one they turned and looked at Bostwick standing on top of the tender. He made quite an extraordinary figure with the Colt .38 he had in his right hand, his bloody and heavily-bandaged leg and his wild and savage grin. His face had that sallow and Asiatic look that so often came into it and that, right now, made him look more baleful and malevolent than ever. As a matter of fact it made him look positively monstrous and frightening and as if he was a wrathful, vengeful and merciless God come to lay down the law. With a wave of his Colt .38 he motioned for Red and Higgins to come and help him get down into the engine. Both of them rushed to help him and when he was down, Bostwick turned to the conductor and said: *"C'est compris?"*

"Oui. Mais . . . Mais . . ." the conductor spluttered in French.

"No buts, ifs and maybes!" Bostwick thundered at him also in French. "Or I'm going to blow your goddam head off! Is that understood!"

"Yes. But I protest! I truly protest!"

"Protest all you want! You'll turn this train around at Clermont!"

"But this is wrong! This is very wrong!"

"The hell with this! You'll turn this train around at Clermont!"

CHAPTER 47

The conductor came to say something else but then shrugged and turned to his engine instead. He went back to running it and Bostwick stood next to him on his right. He grinned at him and waved the Colt .38 in his face. They headed east toward Clermont and at Bostwick's order they increased their speed. They went by several towns like Plouagat, Plestan and Montauban. There were no more strafing runs by Messerschmitts, however, and every once in a while they saw bombers quite high in the sky heading west. They kept on speeding by several towns and hamlets and around 1.00 o'clock in the afternoon, they finally reached Clermont.

Clermont was a small white town that was spread in a semi-circle on the south side of the Route Nationale. It had a small red-roofed train station on the north side of it and a switching yard, turntable and water tower a little beyond it. Its various stores, shops and bistro were on the south side and faced the station. As they reached it Bostwick made the conductor slow down and stop there. At the station Bostwick told Dave to go in and try and find out where the Germans were. He was to get that information and come back and join them again when they were ready to go back to Brest. Dave nodded and got off the engine. He stood on the platform and watched them move on and stop at the switching yard. Then he turned and walked into the station.

In the station Dave saw how crowded it was. There were people lined up at the wickets that were to the left-hand side of it or looking at the train schedule that was on the wall to the left of the main entrance door. There were people also sitting on the wooden benches that ran along the walls and on others that stood in the middle of the station itself. But all of them had a tense, anxious and desperate look on their faces. Dave turned away from them and in the small glassed-in corner office, that was to the left of the wickets and had a view of the platform, the railroad tracks, the switching yard, the turntable, the water tower and the station itself, he found the man he was looking for. The man was tall and well-built and wore a black cap and uniform. He had a pleasant and friendly face and was sitting at a narrow desk.

Right now he was talking on the phone and Dave waited until he was finished. Then he opened the glass-topped wooden door of the office and walked in. As he did the man got up from behind his narrow desk and came over to where Dave was standing. When the man reached him Dave asked him in French: "Are you the stationmaster?"

"I am."

"Would you know where the Germans are?"

"I have no idea. As you know these are pretty confused and difficult times."

"I know."

"Right now no one seems to know anything."

"That's too bad."

"It is."

"Tell me. What kind of activities have you had?"

"We've seen some bombers heading west. And quite a few fighter planes also heading in that direction. That's it."

"Do you know if any of them bombed railway stations or railroad tracks in this area?"

"None that I know of."

"That's good."

"Yes."

"How would I know where the Germans are then?"

"I don't know. You should try calling other stations perhaps."

"Could I?"

"Of course. You are from the train heading for Le Mans, are you not?"

"I am."

"Why don't you try calling there?"

"Can I?"

"Certainly."

The stationmaster turned and led Dave to the narrow desk. He pointed to the phone on the desk and gave him the number for the Le Mans Station.

Brest

Dave nodded and dialed the number. In no time a man's voice came on at the other end of the line and Dave said: *"Içi Clermont.* Am I speaking to the stationmaster at Le Mans?"

"You are."

"Are the Germans at Le Mans?"

"No. They are not."

"Everything is quiet then."

"Not really. There are sounds of bombing and artillery in the distance. Quite a lot of it as a matter of fact."

"But the Germans are not there."

"No. Not yet."

"Thank you."

Dave hung up and turned to the stationmaster who was looking at him: "There are no Germans in Le Mans."

"That's good."

"But he says there are lots of sounds of bombing and artillery in the distance."

"That's bad."

"How do I find out where the Germans are?"

"Why don't you try calling at a further station?"

"Where?"

"Why don't you try calling Courtalain? That's about 32 kilometers from Le Mans."

"Do you have the number of that station?"

"Of course."

The stationmaster reached for a small black book on his desk. He opened it and stopped at a page near the beginning. He looked at it and gave Dave the number.

Again Dave nodded and dialed the number. After a moment a clipped and very precise voice came on the line: "Yes?"

"Içi Morlaix. Are you the stationmaster?"

"I am."

"Are the Germans in Courtalain?"

"No."

"How is it in your sector?"

"It is very quiet."

"There is no bombing and no artillery fire?"

"None whatsoever. It is a very quiet day."

"That's good. *Keine bange, mein freund. Wir werden bald wieder aufeinander treffen."*

The Long War

Dave hung up and turned to the stationmaster who was still looking at him: "The Germans are in Courtalain."

"I gathered that."

"That's why we can't go on to Le Mans. We have to turn back."

"I understand."

"And besides, with those wooden wagons, we have no chance against their planes."

"I understand. But, with so many soldiers needed everywhere, these were the only wagons we could spare."

"It's all right."

"I am sorry. I wish we could have done more."

"Don't be sorry. It's not your fault."

"I know. But I feel bad about it."

"Don't. It's just the way it is."

"I know."

"But will you help us get back to Brest?"

"Of course. Do not worry."

CHAPTER 48

Dave thanked the stationmaster and left his office. He walked out of the station and on the platform, he stopped and looked at their train in the switching yard. The conductor and stoker were uncoupling the engine. Dave looked at them both and then turned left and walked past the station. Then he turned left again and left the platform. He crossed the Route Nationale which was lined with a long steady stream of refugees who were heading west and walked over to the white bistro which was slightly to the left of the station. The Bistro Clermont, as it was called from the red letters painted over its front door, was quite crowded for an early Friday afternoon.

It was full of middle-aged and elderly town people and farmers who were sitting at the outside tables and at most of the tables and chairs inside the bistro. The moment Dave walked in a sudden silence fell only to be broken when he began heading for a spot at the bar. This spot was next to the cash facing the front door. Two elderly gentlemen who were sitting next to it moved a little to the right to make room for him. When they moved the patron headed toward Dave from behind the counter. He was a tall, dark-haired and deeply-tanned man in his early fifties. He had a full imposing figure and was wearing a white shirt open at the collar, black pants and a large white apron tied around his waist. As soon as he reached Dave the patron said: "Monsieur?"

"Would you have any gin?" Dave asked in French. "By all means," the patron said and looked at Dave when he spoke French. "What would you like?" the patron asked. "Would you have any gin and bitter lemon?" Dave said. "I am sorry. We only have gin and tonic water," the patron said. "Gin and tonic water will be fine,." Dave said. The patron turned and began mixing his drink. When it was ready he turned and put it down on the counter in front of Dave. Although the patron was handsome and looked the picture of health, he had deep creases around his eyes and there was a tense and anguished look about his face. It was a look that strained his features and gave his face an expression of sorrow and sadness. As he put Dave's drink down on the counter he said: *"C'est une sale affaire, cette guerre."*

"It certainly is," Dave said as he reached for his drink and took a sip. With the ice the patron had put in it, it tasted wonderfully cool and refreshing in the hot sunny afternoon.

"You are going back?" the patron pointed to their train they could see in the switching yard through the bistro window.

"I'm afraid so," Dave said and took another sip of his drink before he put it down.

"Why?"

"We can't stay here. The Germans are in Courtalain."

"Why not stay here and fight them."

"We can't."

"Why not? We can help you."

"We can't. There's too many of them and not enough of us."

"That is too bad."

"It is."

"In that case why did you come?"

"That's what I'd like to know. I think the people who sent us here underestimated the Germans."

"Ah, les Boches. They are always so much better than everybody else."

"They're not. They're just better prepared. That's all."

"They always are."

"That's true. But we'll catch up to them. Don't worry."

"Yes. But before you do there will be a great deal of sadness and tragedy."

"There will be."

"There always is with *les Boches*."

"That's true," Dave said. "And for that I'm truly sorry."

"Believe me I know what I am talking about," the patron said. "I was at *Verdun* in the First World War. Perhaps you heard of it?"

"I heard of it."

"We won of course. But before we did there was so much blood and destruction and death."

"I know."

"Well, I wish you luck. I wish things go well with you."

"Thank you."

"I also wish things go well with the *Alliés*. Please remember. Do not forget us."

"Don't worry. We won't. And you can be sure of one thing. Whatever *les Boches* will do to you, we'll do to them a thousand times over."

"I hope so."

"Don't you worry. We will."

"Let us hope so."

CHAPTER 49

Dave finished his drink. When he came to pay the patron raised a hand and said: *"Aujourd'hui c'est la maison qui paie. Pour les Alliés."* Dave thanked him and the patron turned and made him another gin and tonic. Dave thanked him again and took a sip of his new drink. He then turned and stepped out of the bistro with his glass. He looked around and saw there was still a long steady stream of refugees on the Route Nationale. The engine had now been switched and was being coupled to what had been the rear of the train. The terrace was still full of middle-aged and elderly town people and farmers and as he looked around, Dave saw a young man who was sitting at one of the outside tables.

This young man was sitting alone and as he looked at him, Dave thought: This is strange. Very strange. How come I didn't notice him when I came into the bistro? And, what's even more strange, how come he's sitting where he is? I think I better go over and check him out. This young man Dave wanted to check was sitting at a table near the front of the terrace. He was having a glass of white wine and was sitting with his back turned to the bistro. He was facing the Route Nationale and as Dave came over and stopped near him, he saw he was tall, dark-haired and strongly-built. He seemed to be in his early twenties and was wearing a well-cut dark suit, a clean white shirt and a dark tie. He had a long, bony, angular face and a thick strand of his jet-black hair was falling over his wide forehead. He also had a sharp nose, gaunt cheeks and dark eyes set deeply in their sockets.

Right now, as he was sitting on the terrace and facing the Route Nationale, the somewhat severe and conservative clothes he was wearing and his clear-cut youth made him really stand out over the middle-aged and elderly town people and farmers who were also sitting there. From time to time, as he was drinking his wine, he was looking at the train and at the refugees on the Route Nationale. And yet, as Dave stood slightly behind him and looked at him, there was something odd and peculiar about him. Something Dave couldn't quite figure out. For one thing he was the only young man in the place. For another he simply sat there quietly and drank his wine. He seemed totally indifferent to what was going on and his face showed none of the strain and anguish that was in everyone else's.

As a matter of fact, compared with the others, he looked positively serene and relaxed. It was this fact more than anything else that drew Dave to him. As he stood near him and looked at him Dave took a sip of his drink and walked over to his table. When he got there he stopped in front of him and asked in French: "May I sit down?"

"By all means," the young man said in French, with a slight accent that was hard to trace, and pointed to the chair facing him.

Dave nodded and sat down. He took another sip of his drink and when he put his glass down, he said: "It's a pretty nice day, isn't it?"

"It certainly is," the young man said and took a sip of his own drink before he also put it down.

"It's quite a spectacle, isn't it?" Dave half-turned and pointed to the refugees on the Route Nationale and to their own train across the railroad tracks.

"It is," the young man nodded and followed Dave's hand as he pointed to the refugees on the Route Nationale and to his own train across the railroad tracks.

"Are you from here?"
"No."
"Where are you from?"
"Hamburg."
"That's a long way from here."
"It is."
"What did you do there?"
"My family used to own a printing company."
"And?"
"I was a printer."
"That's a nice job."
"It is."
"And now?"
"Now I'm here."
"For a long time?"
"Long enough."

The Long War

"How did you get here?"
"That's a long story."
"How?"
"Through Austria, Holland and Belgium."
"And now you're in France."
"That's it."
"That's a long journey."
"It certainly is."
"Are you Jewish?"
"I am."
"What's your name?"
"Meyer. Nicholas Meyer."

Dave told him his name and then asked: "What are you going to do now?"

"I'm just going to sit here and wait."
"For what?"
"For the Germans to get here."
"And then what?"
"Then it'll be all over."
"You're going to give up?"
"You can't beat the Germans. You can't run away from them."
"Come on. Why should you give them the satisfaction?"
"Why not? What should I do?"
"You should try fighting them."
"With what?"
"It doesn't matter with what. Have you tried everything? Have you tried going to another country for instance?"
"Sure."
"And?"
"Nobody wants the Jews! Nobody!"
"Oh. Come on!"
"It's true! There is no place for the Jews to go to!"
"Have you tried my own country?"
"What country is that?"
"Canada."
"Sure."
"Really?"
"Of course. I have relatives there. In Toronto."
"And?"
"What do you mean? Your country is even worse than all the others!"

"Come on!"

"It's true!" Meyer said and his dark eyes flashed with anger for the first time since they had spoken. "The Germans treat the Jews badly and cruelly. Many other countries do the same. But you treat them nicely and politely. That makes it even worse. Since the results are the same."

"Now wait a minute," Dave said.

"It's true!" Meyer went on as his dark eyes still flashed with anger. "When we apply to your country it's always the same thing. You change the rules all the time. You change the amount of money needed to get in. You change the classifications. Don't tell me about your country!"

"I grant you my country isn't all that great at times," Dave said. "And it sure hasn't done a whole hell of a lot for me. But is that a reason for you to give up?"

"Maybe not. But it's my reason."

"Nobody has it all. Nobody."

"I know that."

"Why do you want to do that then? Why do you want to quit?"

"Who says I want to quit."

"That's what you're doing."

"Maybe. But that's my decision."

"Sure. But a lot of people in your situation wouldn't do that."

"So what."

"Try and tell that to Judah Halevi."

"You know Judah Halevi?"

"No. I don't know him. And try and tell that to Moses Hess."

"You know Moses Hess?"

"No. I don't know him. And try and tell that to Theodor Herzl."

"You know Theodor Herzl?"

"No. I don't know any of these people, you sonofabitch!" Dave said as an odd and peculiar gleam came into his eyes and as he switched to English. "But I'll be goddamned if I'm going to let a big strong guy like you sit on the sidelines and do nothing while the going is still good! No way!"

"What are you going to do?" Meyer sneered as he also switched to a slightly-accented English.

"I'm going to draft you into the Canadian Army," Dave went on as an odd and peculiar gleam still showed in his eyes. "After all you already tried to get in. And you have relatives in Toronto. That'll do."

"I refuse!" Meyer snarled. "I'm a Pacifist! I don't believe in war!"

"Piss on that noise!"

"I won't do it!"

"The hell you won't!"

"I won't do it!"

"Piss on that noise!" Dave burst out and reached for his holster. He took out the Luger and pointed it at him. "This gun says you'll do it! This gun says I've just drafted you in the Canadian Army!"

"I won't do it!" Meyer snarled.

"Oh you'll do it!" Dave snapped and pointed the Luger at him.

"You think I'm afraid of you!" Meyer sneered. "You think I'm worried about you! I've met plenty of people who were a lot tougher than you!"

"I'm sure you have," Dave grinned and still pointed the Luger at him as he took off the safety catch. "But you'll do it. Or I'm going to blow your brains out."

"Go ahead."

"I will. After all you're from Hamburg. And you've been to all kinds of countries."

"So?"

"So you speak several languages. And you don't look Jewish to me. You see what I'm getting at."

"No. What are you getting at?"

"You think I'm stupid? You think I don't know what's going on here?"

"What are you talking about?"

"You think I don't know what kind of game you're playing?"

"What game?"

"You're just sitting here with your back turned to the bistro. And you're watching our train and the refugees on the Route Nationale."

"So?"

"So maybe you're a spy. Maybe you're a fifth-columnist."

"This is sick."

"Maybe. But that's why I'll do it."

"Oh, for God's sake!"

"It's true."

"Oh, come on!"

"It's true. *Vielleicht. Das ist möglich.*"

"Was für ein idiot!"

"Maybe. But that's why I'll do it."

CHAPTER 50

Dave pointed the Luger at Meyer's face now and as they stared at each other, there was such a fierce and savage light in Dave's eyes Meyer looked carefully and intently at him. Then, as Dave motioned with his Luger for Meyer to get up and begin walking ahead of him toward their train, Meyer sighed suddenly and got up. He left his table and the terrace with Dave. He crossed the Route Nationale with him and slowly began walking toward their train. Meyer walked slightly ahead of Dave and headed for their train which was now lined up on the westbound tracks and pointed toward Brest.

Dave followed him and had the Luger pointed straight at his back. They walked slowly toward their train and when they reached the engine, Bostwick leaned out of the cab and said: "Well? What's going on?"

"I brought you back a recruit," Dave said and pointed with his Luger at Meyer as he gave Bostwick his name. "After all the men we lost today, I thought we could use him."

"We sure could."

"Mind you he's a Jewish Pacifist. He wanted to sit on the sidelines and wait for the Germans."

"Oh. One of those."

"That's right. But he has relatives in Toronto. So I've drafted him in the Regiment."

"That's okay. We could always use a big strong recruit like him."

"That's what I thought. And besides I told him I'll be goddamned if I was going to let someone like him sit on the sidelines and do nothing while the going is still good."

"Good point."

"Anyway. That's what I told him."

"That's good. I couldn't have put it better."

Bostwick now leaned a little bit more out of the cab and asked: "What about the Germans? Did you find out where they are?"

"I did."

"Where are they?"

"In Courtalain."

"Where the hell is that?"

"Twenty miles past Le Mans."

"Twenty miles!"

"That's it."

"Christ! It's a good thing we turned this train around."

"You're telling me."

"Otherwise we'd have driven right into them."

"That's what I think."

"But how do you know this?"

"When I called Le Mans the stationmaster told me they weren't there. But he said there were lots of sounds of bombing and artillery in the distance. But when I called Courtalain the man there spoke French with a foreign accent and said everything was quiet in his sector. That's how I knew."

"Good. That's very good."

Bostwick paused and scratched his chin. Then he looked down at Dave and said: "All right. Then we have to get the hell out of here."

"You bet."

"Okay. Where's Moran?"

"I don't know. I haven't seen him on the train."

"Okay. Then I'm naming you acting Platoon Sergeant. You got that?"

Dave nodded.

"Good. Now you go back and put people on the flatbed cars. I want you to be in charge of the first flatbed car. I want you to back me up in the engine. Put Slav in charge of the second flatbed car. If people ask you questions, tell them you've got your orders. Make it vague. I don't think in the circumstances too many people will ask you questions."

"I understand."

"Then you post guards on the wagon doors. We're going back to Brest and if this train ever stops anywhere, people will want to get on it. Also post lookouts throughout the train to warn us of oncoming Messerschmitts. Then you take Red with you and find a uniform for our

Pacifist friend. I don't think you'll have too much trouble finding one. As for me I'll stay here with Higgins and when you're ready, you wave at me from the first flatbed car. Then we're on our way. You got that?"

"I got it."

"Okay. Move."

CHAPTER 51

Dave turned and began walking with Red who had jumped down from the cab of the engine. They walked alongside the train with Meyer until they had moved past the tender and gotten into a wagon again. Once in that wagon Dave headed for the middle of the train where he picked up the Big Ten. He walked back with them to the first flatbed car where he put Gennaro on the Bofors gun. He put Red, Lang and himself on the Lewis machine-guns. Meyer would be the lookout. Then, after telling Red to help Meyer find a uniform and shoot him if he tried to escape, he went on to the second flatbed car with the rest of the Big Ten. On that car he put Slav on the Bofors gun and Delorme, Mitchell and Addams on the Lewis machine-guns.

Then Dave ran back and forth across the train and posted sentries from the Company and from the 51st Midlands on the doors of the wagons and lookouts for possible oncoming Messerschmitts. When all of these things had been done and when he had had the people on the flatbed cars pick up the dead soldiers from those cars and bring them into the wagons, Dave went back to the first flatbed car. Meyer was now standing there with Red, Lang and Gennaro. He had on a uniform that didn't look at all bad on him. As a matter of fact, all things considered, it looked pretty good. Now that all of Bostwick's orders had been carried out and Meyer had on a uniform, Dave jumped down from the flatbed car and waved his hand at the engine. Bostwick leaned out of the cab and waved back.

There was a lurch followed by another lurch. Dave jumped back on the flatbed car and they were on their way.

CHAPTER 52

They moved out of Clermont slowly and began heading west. As they cleared it they started picking up speed and went through Montfort, Montauban and Caulnes and began making their 100-mile run back to Brest. As they headed west Dave stood in the first flatbed car and kept his eyes open. He felt an odd and ever-increasing tension as he held one of the heavy Lewis machine guns in his hands and hoped the lookouts on the train would be sharp and would let them know in time if they saw Messerschmitts. After a while they saw a few bombers in the distance. They were also heading west. But that was all. They themselves just kept on speeding toward Brest and went by small towns, villages and hamlets and near Plestan, the cry suddenly went up: "Messerschmitts!"

As one they looked up and stared at the back of the train. In the distance a V of Messerschmitts was diving down and coming straight for them. From afar they showed as three black dots getting bigger and bigger. As soon as the cry went up the two Bofors guns began firing and were joined by the Lewis machine-gunners on the platforms. Their sudden concentrated fire had an effect since the V scattered out of the line of fire. The plane on the right side of the V went wide and fired alongside the field while the lead plane and the one on the left side of the V sped wide and ended up firing on part of the Route Nationale and on the field on the side of it. As the two planes on the left side of the V went by their flatbed car Gennaro on the Bofors gun swiveled to the right and fired right at them. Dave and the other Lewis machine-gunners did the same thing.

The planes flew through their concentrated fire and turned left. They began climbing and heading south. As they kept on climbing and heading south Gennaro on the Bofors gun yelled: "Man oh man! Did you see that? Hey, did you see that? The bastards aren't coming back!"

"You're goddam right they're not coming back!" Red also yelled.

"Man! This is fun!" Gennaro swiveled the Bofors gun back and forth and also cranked it up and down. "I wonder why the other guys didn't fire at them like us?"

"Maybe they weren't prepared," Red said.

"Maybe," Dave said. "But don't get too carried away. It's still a long way to Brest."

"I don't care," Red said. "I just love firing at those bastards."

"Me too," Lang said.

"So do I," Dave said. "But stay sharp. We have a long way to go yet."

"The hell with them!" Gennaro yelled. "Let the bastards come! I'm ready for them!"

"Me too!" Red also yelled.

"You bet!" Lang joined in.

"Sure," Dave said. "But let's stay sharp and alert. Let's not get carried away."

CHAPTER 53

They looked wildly and excitedly at Dave and in the front right-hand corner of the flatbed car Meyer watched them all. But he didn't say anything. They kept on heading west and going through places like St. Brieuc, Guingamp and Plouaret. They sped past brown rugged craggy fields and solid stony farmhouses and cottages and near Plouigneau, the cry suddenly went up again: "Messerschmitts!" Once more they looked up and stared at the back of the train. As before another V of planes began diving and making for them. The two Bofors guns opened up and the Lewis machine-gunners joined them. But this time it was different. The V didn't scatter. It simply changed its angle of attack.

The plane on the right side of the V went wide and tried to fire at the train from a crossover angle. The lead plane swerved 50 degrees to the left to avoid attacking head on and joined the plane on the left side of the V in also firing at an angle. Some of the wagons were hit. But they weren't hit for long since the V had to roar by at an angle in order to avoid getting hit. Once again, as the lead plane and the one on the left side of the V roared by them, Gennaro on the Bofors gun and Dave and the other Lewis machine-gunners on the platform swiveled right and opened up. Once again the two planes flew through their concentrated fire.

As they flew on Gennaro yelled: "Oh man! I don't get it! I just don't get it!"

"What don't you get?" Dave asked.

"Those two planes flew right through our fire and didn't get hit," Gennaro said. "What the hell's going on?"

"That's because we're all firing straight at them," Dave said.

The Long War

"I'm leading them," Gennaro said. "And yet they're not getting hit. How come?"

"We're not leading them enough," Dave said.

"Man! I just want to hit one!" Gennaro said.

"Me too!" Red said.

"That's all I want," Gennaro said.

"Lead them enough and you will," Dave said.

"It sure would be nice to shoot one down," Lang said.

"You're not kidding," Red said.

"All right then," Dave said. "If any more planes come, let's try and lead them. And let's see what happens."

CHAPTER 54

They nodded and turned from Dave. They stared at the back of the train again and searched the sky for planes. As they searched the sky Meyer in the front right-hand corner of the platform watched them and still didn't say anything. They kept on heading west and were really speeding now. They went by small villages like Morlaix, Lampau and Laroche and the whole countryside was racing past them. Then near Landerneau, as they came barreling toward Brest, the cry went up again: "Messerschmitts!" As one the two Bofors guns and the Lewis machine-gunners opened up. Another V of planes was coming down real fast. It was diving from quite high and heading for the train.

It was growing bigger and bigger until, under their concentrated fire, it scattered at the last moment and roared past them. The plane on the right side of the V went wide of the train and ended up firing at the field on the side. The lead plane and the plane on the left side of the V swerved violently to the left side of the train and ended up firing on the field beside the Route Nationale. As those two planes roared past them, quite low by now and huge in their strafing run, Gennaro on the Bofors gun and Dave and the other Lewis machine-gunners on the platform swiveled right and let loose on them. The two planes flew through their concentrated fire and when they came to pull up and climb, the last one on the left side of the V began leaving a black trail of smoke.

The smoke grew blacker and thicker and the plane suddenly began to come down fast and smashed into a building. A huge black and orange ball of fire mushroomed in the sky. The ball of fire spewed grayish metal parts and flashing sparks of ammunition. Then it settled into a thick black column of smoke and Red cried: "Oh my God! The plane hit a school!"

The Long War

"Tough," Dave said as they sped by and then were gone from the school where the plane had hit. There was a large yard in front of the school. Some children and a few men and women who had been in the yard were now running toward the huge black column of smoke coming out of the building.

"The plane hit a school!" Red cried.

"That's too bad," Dave said.

"Holy shit!" Gennaro said.

"My God!" Lang said.

"The pilot didn't have time to pull out of his dive," Meyer now spoke for the first time since he had been with them.

"Good!" Dave said.

"He hit a school!" Red cried.

"So what!" Dave said.

"The place was full of kids! He went down right on top of them!"

"Tough!"

"But Jesus Christ!" Gennaro said.

"I know. I know," Dave said.

"Oh man," Red said.

"I know. I know," Dave said. "Stay sharp. You just stay sharp. You see what happens when it's the real thing and not some goddam maneuver. Keep your eyes open. We're not in Brest yet."

CHAPTER 55

They kept on speeding and barreling toward Brest and Red, Lang and Gennaro stood on the platform and stared at the back of the train. It was now late in the afternoon and they stood with Dave and searched the sky for planes. There were none, however, and around 5.00 o'clock, the city began to rise in the distance and its churches, buildings, museum, castle, bridges, piers and ramparts gleamed in the afternoon sunlight. By then they were really racing for it and after a while they reached its outskirts, outlying streets and avenues and soon the Gare SNCF began coming into view. They made for it and when they reached it, they slowed down and came and stopped alongside one of its platforms.

As soon as they stopped Dave jumped off the first flatbed car with Red, Gennaro, Lang and Meyer. He saw Bostwick come down the engine with Higgins and begin talking with an officer from Movement Control. The officer took off at a flying run. He came back quickly with a couple of officers from the Medical Corps and they rushed into the first wagon. While this was going on Dave walked along the platform with Red, Gennaro, Lang, Meyer, the rest of the Big Ten and other soldiers from the Fusiliers and the 51st Midlands who had now joined them. He picked up Bostwick and Higgins at the head of the train. He began walking with them along the concourse and when he reached the entrance of the Gare, Dave stepped out. Outside he crossed the street and when he began marching toward the Rue du Château and the port, he suddenly heard: "You! Hey! You! Stop! I said: Stop!"

Dave turned to see who it was who had called out to him. It was a fat wheezing British Colonel. He was running clumsily and awkwardly and had a few soldiers with him who had their rifles drawn. He was running toward him and past all the people, officers, soldiers, cars and trucks in the street. As he was running his face was very red and purple and he was holding on to a clipboard with his left hand. In a little while he came and stopped in front of Dave on the other side of the street and the soldiers he had with him stood a little behind him with their rifles drawn. Dave also stopped and saluted the Colonel. The Colonel returned his salute and said: "You! What do you think you're doing!"

"We're going toward the port, Sir."

"You can't do that! You're under arrest!"

"Why, Sir?"

"You were supposed to go to an assembly area near Le Mans! You turned the train around without authorization!"

"We had to, Sir."

"I don't care!"

"It's true, Sir."

"I don't care!"

"But Sir—"

At that moment a small dusty military vehicle pulled up where they were all standing and a tall, slim and blond-haired officer got out. He was wearing dusty perspex goggles and a khaki shirt, pants and combat boots which were also dusty. On the left sleeve of his khaki shirt stood the triangular red, black and gold patch of his Regiment, the Wiltshire Grenadiers Guards. This was a black-rimmed golden eagle on a field of red and on the tabs of his shirt Dave saw the three pips and crown of a Brigadier. As he got out of the military vehicle he said: "What's going on?"

"Sir, I'm from Movement Control," the Colonel said and half-turned and saluted him. "These soldiers were supposed to go to an assembly area near Le Mans. They turned their train around without authorization. I'm putting them under arrest."

"I know where you're from," the Brigadier snapped and looked at the Colonel as he returned his salute. Then he turned to Dave. "What's your story?"

"Sir, what the Colonel said is true," Dave said and also exchanged salutes with the Brigadier. "We were supposed to go to an assembly area near Le Mans. But the wagons we were in were made of wood and we ended up as target practice for the Germans. We were strafed several times and there were quite a few officers, NCOs and soldiers killed and wounded. That's why we came back."

"Sir, they turned the train around without authorization."

"Keep quiet!" the Brigadier turned to the Colonel. He looked at Dave again. "Is that true? Did you turn the train around without proper authorization?"

"It's not true, Sir. We did try to get authorization."

"Did you?"

"We did, Sir. But there wasn't any officer available. The whole operation was very confused and chaotic."

"What do you mean?"

"Well, Sir, most of the officers on our train were in our wagon. A great many of them were standing around together. On the first strafing run all of them were killed. Most of the other officers on our train were also killed or badly wounded. We tried to find an able-bodied officer but there just wasn't one."

"Are you telling me the truth?"

"I am, Sir. And besides the Germans were in Courtalain only 20 miles from Le Mans. If we had gone on we would have driven right into them."

"They were that close?"

"Yes, Sir."

"And that's exactly what happened?"

"Yes, Sir."

"That's right. That's exactly what happened," Bostwick said. He now stepped forward from the Big Ten and from the other soldiers from the Fusiliers and the 51st Midlands and came and stopped in front of the Brigadier. He exchanged salutes with him and, with his bloody bandaged leg, sooty crumpled uniform and fierce Asiatic look, he made quite a figure as the Brigadier stared at him. "I gave the order to look for an able-bodied officer. When we couldn't find one I gave the order to turn the train around," Bostwick said and went on and told the Brigadier what had happened. "I'm the one who gave the order."

"Do you have any witnesses to that?" the Brigadier asked.

"Of course," Bostwick said. "Everyone who was in our wagon."

"Good. I'll have to check up on this," the Brigadier said and turned to his driver in the military vehicle. He told him to make sure before they left to take Dave and Bostwick's names, their tag numbers and the name of their Regiment. "This will definitely have to be taken up with the higher authorities."

"I understand," Bostwick said as Dave nodded.

"But Sir," the Colonel said. "This is highly irregular. This is not authorized by Movement Control."

"You already told me."

"Sir. These people should be arrested."

The Long War

"I know. You told me.
"Sir. I protest!"
"Keep quiet!"
"Sir—"

"What's the matter with you! Don't you have anything better to do than to play policeman?"

"But Sir—"

"Keep quiet! Or I'll find something else for you to do!"

"But Sir—"

"That's enough! Leave!"

CHAPTER 56

The fat wheezing Colonel stepped back and saluted the Brigadier again. Then, as the Brigadier returned his salute, he turned and began leaving slowly with the few soldiers he had with him. Those soldiers now slung their rifles over their shoulders and the Colonel looked back at them a couple of times. The few soldiers he had with him trailed behind him and when the Colonel had crossed the street and gone back into the Gare with them, the Brigadier turned to Dave and Bostwick again and said: "You understand I'll have to check up on this." Dave and Bostwick nodded and he went on: "All right. If what you told me is true and if you ever need me, my name is Haworth. Brigadier Alan Haworth.

"I'm with the 52nd Division. And I agree with you. The situation is very confused and chaotic. So you better hurry to the port. I was just coming from there and saw a destroyer getting ready to leave from the Jetée de l'Ouest. The *Rumillys* I think it was. If you hurry I think you might be able to catch it." Dave and Bostwick nodded and exchanged salutes with the Brigadier. They gave his driver their names, tag numbers and the name of their Regiment. Then they left them and began moving toward the port with the soldiers who had joined them from the train. Dave and Bostwick soon got on the Rue du Château and moved toward the port and now, late in the afternoon, the city looked pretty much the way it had looked when they had first come in.

There was still a faint smell of raw burning cordite hanging over it and it still had a bleak and dusty look. There was a lot of broken glass and rubble in a few of the streets and a black pall of smoke, that was now turning grayish, was still drifting west over it. Dave, Bostwick, the Big Ten and the soldiers who had joined them from the train, marched down

The Long War

the Rue du Château and when they got to the port area, they made for the Jetée de l'Ouest. They reached it not long after and saw the Brigadier had been right. There was a destroyer crowded with soldiers getting ready to leave. The gangplank had already been taken off and some of the sailors on the destroyer and workers in the port were getting ready to cast off the lines.

When they got close to it they saw the Brigadier had been right about something else. The name of the destroyer was indeed the *Rumillys*. As soon as they reached it Dave and Bostwick bent down toward the starboard deck. They exchanged salutes with a young Lieutenant and Dave said: "May we come on board?"

"You can't," the Lieutenant said.

"What?" Dave put a hand to his ear and jumped on board with Bostwick, the Big Ten and the soldiers who had come with him.

"Damnit, man," the Lieutenant turned to Dave after they had all jumped on board. "Can't you see there's no room?"

"There's enough."

"There's no room. I tell you."

"There's enough. We've just come from the Le Mans area and the Germans are almost there. If you don't mind, I'd rather be here rather than a prisoner of the Germans."

The Lieutenant shrugged and turned to the bridge. The Captain was standing there with another young Lieutenant who was watching them through binoculars. The Lieutenant who was with Dave signaled with his hands everything was okay. The Captain on the bridge spoke to the Lieutenant with binoculars. The Lieutenant with binoculars signaled in turn for the workers in the port to cast off the lines and for some of the sailors on the destroyer to bring them in. In a little while the lines were brought in and they began sailing away from the Jetée de l'Ouest and from Brest itself. They slowly pulled away from the port and in the distance Brest looked pale and wan in the late afternoon sunlight. In fact it looked as if the light was barely shining on its piers, ramparts and dockyard.

It was now close to 6.00 o'clock and the city sparkled briefly in the evening sunlight before it slowly began receding and fading away on the horizon. They kept on sailing away from it and when they were about half a mile from it and only the spires of its churches, tall buildings and the castle still showed on the horizon, Red, who was standing behind Dave on the starboard side, suddenly said: "Hey. What's that?"

Dave turned to Red: "What?"

Red pointed astern at a black dot over the horizon: "That."

Dave looked at this black dot growing bigger and bigger and coming from Brest. It was now racing over the water and he said: "My God! It's a bomber!"

"Are you sure?"

"Of course I'm sure!"

"Maybe it's a fighter."

"No! No! It's a bomber!"

"Are you sure?"

"You're damn right I'm sure! It's a Heinkel 111!"

CHAPTER 57

At Dave's mention of a Heinkel 111, and when soldiers from their Company and the 51st Midlands turned and looked astern, the 3.5, 4.5 and anti-aircraft guns on the destroyer opened up. Dave watched as the pale-gray and dark-green Heinkel lined itself up astern of the destroyer and came on. Its glass-enclosed cockpit and smooth stubby camouflage-painted fuselage gleamed in the sunlight. It kept on getting bigger and bigger and a dark squat 550-pound high-explosive bomb with jutting tail fins came out of its bomb bay and screamed down on them. The destroyer steered hard to port and the bomb hit the water 50 yards off starboard. A huge fountain of water went up in the air before it settled down in the sea again.

When it did Dave said: "My God! That was close!" "You're telling me!" Gennaro said behind him. "Hey! Look! Look!" Red said and pointed astern again. "There's another one!" As one Dave and the soldiers of the Company and the 51st Midlands turned and looked astern. Sure enough there was another Heinkel heading straight for them. This one was a little higher than the first one, though, and also lined itself astern. All the guns on the destroyer stopped firing at the first one and swung to this second Heinkel and began firing at it. Like the first time Dave watched as this second Heinkel kept on coming and coming. After a while it seemed glued to their ship and another dark squat 550-pound high-explosive bomb with jutting tail fins came screaming out of its bomb bay and racing for the ship.

The destroyer made a hard wrenching turn to starboard. The bomb hit so close to the ship on the port side a huge fountain of water went up in the air and sprayed it. The ship itself rose out of the water and then settled down hard in it. When it did Dave said: "My God! Those guys sure can aim!" "Not really," Red said. "They missed." "Sure!" Dave said. "But not by much!" "It doesn't matter," Red said. "They missed." "Sure," Dave said. "But that was too close." Nothing more was said on this and the destroyer kept on firing at the second Heinkel. It pulled up and turned south like the first one and began heading back toward Brest. Everyone on deck kept on watching the second Heinkel. When it was gone and the destroyer had stopped firing, they stood on deck and the wild and excited enthusiasm they had had in the morning at the thought of going to Brest was gone.

It had given way to a deeply brooding and resentful unhappiness. They had wanted to fight and beat the Germans so badly. Well, they had fought them all right. They had fought them all day long. Only it was they who had been beaten. And they had been beaten very badly. Even if the beating had been done by the German *Luftwaffe*. So they stood on deck and thought about that and watched as they sailed away from Brest and as it disappeared on the horizon. By that time the clear glassy sea was beginning to darken and take on the iridescent, mauve and blue-gray colors of evening. They kept on heading across the Channel and Dave stood on the starboard railing with the Big Ten and some members of the Company and the 51st Midlands and watched the white frothy wake of the destroyer.

Dave just stood there and kept on watching the wake of the ship and it wasn't until 3.00 o'clock in the morning on Saturday, June 15, 1940, on a clear, star-lit and moon-lit night, before they reached Plymouth and docked at the West Pier. In Plymouth they were taken back to Aldershot by train and in the next few days quite a few things happened. To begin with Brigadier Alan Haworth was true to his word. He investigated and cleared Dave and Bostwick of the charge of having turned their train around at Clermont without authorization. Apparently what clinched it for them, besides Brigadier Haworth's investigation, was the fact General Alan Brooke, the Commander of the second British Expeditionary Force in that area, or the BEF as it was called, had also given the order for the various trains to be turned around.

Then, with Bostwick's help, Dave was able to get Nicholas Meyer enlisted in the Regiment. Colonel Cantwell, besides being a tough, no-nonsense, hard-driving Commanding Officer, was also a practical man. In Cecil Emmett Williams he had lost a Company CO. He had also lost a great many men in that unsuccessful expedition to Brest and when Dave and Bostwick went to see him about Meyer, the thought of getting such a big strong sturdy recruit appealed to him. It appealed to him a great deal more, as a matter of fact, when he found out Meyer had relatives in

Toronto and when he further found out, upon investigation, those relatives of his had done a great deal to try and get him into the country. So red tape was overcome. Papers were processed. And Meyer was swiftly and officially enlisted in the Fusiliers.

Then, since the 1st Canadian Division was the only fully-equipped Division left in England after the disasters of Dunkirk, the Battle of France, which ended on June 17, 1940 when the French asked the Germans for an armistice, and their own unsuccessful expedition to Brest, they were taken out of Aldershot on Sunday, June 23, 1940. They were rushed around southern and eastern England. Day and night they were driven around in Bedford trucks in an effort, Dave thought, to boost morale and impress the population. With the real possibility of an invasion by the Germans they were driven around in convoys and after a while, they were deployed through Surrey, Sussex and around the southern outskirts of London.

In early July the German *Luftwaffe* came out and began hammering the southern ports and coastal installations of England before moving on to the city of London. The Division stayed in Surrey, Sussex and around the southern outskirts of London. It stayed there through most of the summer and through the beginning of the Battle of Britain and in the fall, they moved into permanent defensive positions behind Worthing, Brighton, Newhaven, Waring and Seaford.

BOOK FIVE

ENGLAND

CHAPTER 58

When they moved into their permanent defensive positions soldiers, engineers and signalmen began stringing barbed wire, digging trenches and blocking roads with concrete and steel barriers. They built pillboxes, laid mines and ran lines and cables. They worked extremely hard and there was a great deal of activity in their sector to try and get ready to defend the beaches. Their Regiment was handling the Waring area and the frontage of the Division was a little over 15 miles. Their own Company was covering a section of the beaches in front of Waring. It also extended a little to the east of it and was close to Seaford. In their section, close to the beaches, they organized patrols, dug deep trenches, set up machine-gun posts and laid mines.

Their Command Post was right in front of Waring. It was in a large tent in front of a small ridge and was on the south side of the highway. This was their assigned area and when they had settled there, they worked as hard as they could to try and make it secure. They succeeded in doing this and were doing pretty well until there occurred an incident, on November 7, 1940, which showed under what strain they were and how difficult and dangerous it was to try and secure such an area. This incident occurred on a Thursday night around 3.00 o'clock in the morning. That night Dave had drawn night patrol with Higgins. Since their area was a restricted one, as were all the southern ports and beaches, it had been a quiet night. Dave was doing the northeastern side of the perimeter and Higgins the northwestern side.

Now, in early November, it was a damp cold chilly night. As a matter of fact it was the kind of moonless night that was almost sinister in its deep silence and total blackout. At that hour its spectral stillness and eerie noiselessness was only broken by the dull steady rolling of the waves on the gravel beach that was mined and lying beyond in the darkness. By then Dave had begun the third hour of his patrol. It would last until 6.00 a.m., and he had just started on its eastern leg again when he stopped suddenly. In the darkness, beyond what he could see, there was a faint scraping as if against the gravel. The faint scraping seemed to be erratic. It would go on for a few seconds and stop. Then it would pick up again. Sometimes it would go on quickly for a few seconds; sometimes slowly for a few more. But there was definitely movement in the darkness.

When he saw this Dave cut across from his patrol and headed swiftly southeast toward the beaches. He held the Thompson machine-gun in his right hand and ran in a half-crouch past a space between two deep trenches until he got to a two-men machine-gun post. As he got there Dave bent down and whispered: "Do you guys hear any movement out there?"

"You're goddam right," Gennaro also whispered and held on to his Vickers machine-gun over the sandbags. "Me and Red have been picking up movement out there for the last few minutes."

"Do you have any idea what it is?"

"No idea. I thought at first it might be landing troops. But there's not enough noise for that."

"I agree.

"Besides the Channel's just too rough at this time of the year for that."

"That's true."

"Maybe it's a spy or an enemy agent," Red whispered, next to Gennaro, on his right.

"Maybe," Dave also whispered.

"Or maybe it's just a cat or some kind of animal," Red whispered.

"I don't think so. The noise's too deep for that," Dave said.

"I agree," Gennaro said.

"Listen—" Dave said.

As they stopped talking the noise began again. They listened to it for a few moments and it seemed to be right in front of them. It seemed to be just beyond the darkness and heading eastward. As they listened to it Red said: "Maybe we shine a spotlight and see what's out there."

"Are you crazy?" Dave said. "We do that and all the sonofabitches in this sector are going to start firing."

"I'm with you on that one," Gennaro said.

"What do we do then?" Red asked.

"Just stay sharp," Dave said to Red and Gennaro. "I'm going to try and track this noise and see what's out there."

CHAPTER 59

Red and Gennaro nodded and Dave crouched next to their machine-gun post and listened to the noise. As he crouched down Dave saw it kept on heading eastward. After a while, though, something new came into it. It slowed down considerably and became erratic. Before long it turned and began heading northward toward the coastal highway and then the eastern end of Waring. When he saw this Dave stood up and left the machine-gun post. He still held the Thompson in his right hand and ran in a half-crouch. He moved swiftly past a space between two deep trenches and headed for the coastal highway. As he ran there Dave could see the noise was heading slowly northward in long erratic bursts.

Dave followed the noise at a distance and then ran across the coastal highway and into Waring. Waring was a small town of about 10,000 people. All its houses, churches and shops were huddled close to the highway and faced the beach. It was a town Dave had gotten to know well from the guard duties and patrolling he had done in it. When he reached it Dave ran on Burham Street, which was the last street in Waring on the east side. In the darkness he heard the slow erratic noise ahead of him and at Sutton, the first cross street, he took it and then Slindon. Slindon ran parallel to Burham and at Merston, the next cross street, he ran back to Burham and waited at the corner. Come on. Come on, Dave thought. That's it. Come on. You come to me. Dave stayed at the corner of Burham and Merston until the noise was almost on top of him. Then he stepped out and said in a challenging voice: "Halt! Who goes there?"

Almost at once the noise stopped and Dave said: "Step forward friend, or whoever's out there, and identify yourself." Dave's words were greeted with total silence. When he took the safety catch off the Thompson,

The Long War

however, a thin querulous voice beyond him in the darkness said: "All right. All right. What's this all about?" "Advance friend and be recognized," Dave said. At that moment Dave heard but didn't see movement right in front of him. As he took out his flashlight and shone it toward the spot where the movement was coming from, it took in a slim stringy boy of about twenty. The boy was of average height and had a mop of long dark hair falling over his face. He was wearing dark-blue pants and a dark-blue windbreaker.

The boy stepped out of a narrow alleyway on Burham Street, close to the corner of Merston, and came and stopped near Dave. As he came and stopped there he walked somewhat unsteadily and his breath smelled of liquor. Dave watched him closely and when the boy stopped near him, he said: "Who are you?"

"Me? I live here."

"That's not what I asked."

"What do you want?"

"I asked you who you were."

"My name's Freddie."

"Freddie who?"

"Freddie Birkwell."

"What were you doing on the beach?"

"I was walking."

"Don't you know this is a restricted area?"

"Sure."

"What where you doing there?"

"I was coming back home from Newhaven."

"Through the beach?"

"That's right. Can't a man do that?"

"Sure. But not this late. And not through a restricted area."

"Well, that's what I was doing."

"What were you doing in Newhaven?"

"I was seeing my girlfriend."

"This late?"

"Sure."

"What's her name?"

"Louise."

"Louise who?"

"Louise Marsden."

"What where you doing going through the beach? Why didn't you come back before dark and through the coastal highway?"

"Oh, for Chrissakes! I was just having fun."

England

"Were you? Really?"

"Sure. I was just having a few drinks with her. Then we had quite a few more. And then I thought it might be a good idea if I came back through the beach. Especially since I know this area like the palm of my hand."

"Don't you know how crazy this is?" Dave said. "You could have been shot and killed."

"Well, I wasn't," the boy snapped. "I'm alive, aren't I?"

"Sure. But this area is also mined. You could have been blown up."

"Oh, don't worry about the mines."

"What do you mean?"

"Oh, for Chrissakes! I live here! I know where they are."

"You do?"

"Of course. What's the matter with you? Can't a man have any fun? Can't a man let loose every once in a while?"

"Sure."

"For Chrissakes! I work every day in a stinking factory doing 12-hour shifts and sometimes I go three or four weeks without getting a day off. Why can't I have some fun every once in a while? Why can't I have a few drinks?"

"Nobody says you can't."

"Well, that's what I did."

"Where's the factory you work for?"

"In Staines."

"What do you do there?"

"Oh, we make anti-aircraft mountings."

"I see. And you live around here?"

"Sure. On Burham Street. Just a few blocks from here."

"What's your mother's name?"

"Rosie."

"Okay," Dave said and stepped a little closer to the boy and looked at him in the light of his flashlight. "I'm taking you back to one of our posts to run an identification check. If you clear it, we'll let you go. But you can consider yourself damn lucky. The next time things might not go so well for you. You might get shot at and killed or, even worse, blown up. You think about that."

CHAPTER 60

Dave pointed with his Thompson for the boy to begin walking ahead of him. The boy nodded and they began walking back down Burham Street until they reached the coastal highway. They crossed the highway and marched through a space between two deep trenches. They headed for the beach and moved toward the machine-gun post manned by Red and Gennaro at the southeastern end of it. At the post Dave made Red place a call on the field phone to the Command Post. He made him ask for a military vehicle in order to go and run an identification check on the boy. Not long after the vehicle arrived and its dim blue headlights were the only thing you could see in the blackout.

Dave made the boy sit in front of the vehicle with Lang who was driving. Slav had also been brought in to replace Dave on patrol. Dave went with him and showed him the perimeters of the patrol. Then he came back and left with Lang in order to go to Burham Street to check out the boy. In the dim blue headlights of the vehicle they could hardly see the gravel of the beach, the coastal highway and then Burham Street itself. They drove on that street for a while and when they got to the address the boy had given them, Dave stepped out of the vehicle with him and knocked on the door of a house near the end of the street. In a moment a short, squat, sleepy-eyed and ruddy-faced woman opened the door and confirmed that her name was Rosie, that she was Freddie's mother, that he had a girlfriend named Louise and that he had indeed gone to Newhaven to spend the evening with her.

Then, after they had done a routine check of their papers which confirmed everything that had been said so far, Dave left with Lang. They got back into the vehicle and made a U-turn. They drove through Waring

England

and headed for the coastal highway. They made for their Command Post on the south side of the highway and when they reached it, Lang slowed down and stopped at the entrance. He turned off the ignition and stayed in the vehicle. Dave stepped out and walked into the Command Post. Inside he found their Platoon Sergeant, Norm Moran. He was sitting in a canvas chair and his legs were stretched out in front of him and folded. He was manning the switchboard on the left side of the entrance and when Dave came in, he turned to him and said: "I hear there was a little excitement in your sector tonight."

"You're not kidding," Dave said and reached for a canvas chair next to him on his left and sat down. He also stretched out his legs in front of him and folded them as he faced the switchboard.

"How did it turn out?"

"The guy checked out."

"Who was he?"

"Oh, he was just a kid who had quite a few drinks and wandered into our sector. That's all."

"He wasn't afraid to step on one of the mines?"

"No. He said he knew where they were."

"Really?"

"Really."

"Crazy kid."

"You said it."

"But it sure says a hell of a lot about the security of our sector, doesn't it?"

"Well, we got the guy, didn't we?"

"Sure. But it's a good thing it was you that checked him out and that you're here. I have a couple of very interesting things to tell you."

"Oh yes?" Dave said.

"Sure," Moran said.

"What?"

"To begin with. We're moving back to Aldershot."

"That's good."

"And you got a 7-day pass."

"Are you serious?"

"Dead serious. One man per Platoon got one."

"Hey. That's all right."

"It sure is. In fact I heard every man in the Regiment is going to get one."

"How about that."

"It's something else, isn't it?"

The Long War

"It sure is."

"Anyway. That's what I heard."

"I tell you. I could sure use one."

"I thought you could."

Dave didn't say anything else on that and Moran said: "You can stay here for the rest of your patrol and man the switchboard. There's coffee in the pot and some sandwiches." He turned and pointed to the right corner of the tent past the switchboard where a coffee pot and some sandwiches were standing on a table. "It's pretty quiet so take it easy. In the morning I'll pick you up and drive you back to Aldershot where you can get your pass from Bostwick."

"Thanks. I really appreciate it."

"No sweat. Right now I have to go. I have to check on some positions with Lang."

"Okay. Thanks."

CHAPTER 61

Moran unfolded his stretched out legs and got up slowly. He moved toward the tent entrance and once he was outside, Dave heard him speak to Lang. He got into the military vehicle with him and in a little while they drove away. Dave sat in his canvas chair and listened to them drive away. His feet were still stretched out in front of him and he suddenly felt very tired from all he had been doing tonight. Now he had gotten a 7-day pass and was glad he was going to be able to get away from Waring and from the patrolling, checking and guarding of all those beaches he had been doing for so long. He had grown tired of doing that and was glad he was going to be able to get away from Waring and do something else for a change.

In the morning, a little after 6.00 o'clock, Moran picked Dave up and drove him to Aldershot in one of the military vehicles. Back in his barrack Dave got out of his combat gear, washed and shaved. He took out all his money and put on a clean uniform. When he was dressed Dave left his barrack and went to pick up his 7-day pass from Bostwick in the Orderly Room. The Orderly Room was in the Company barrack next to the one serving as Regimental Headquarters and when he got there, Dave picked up his pass from Bostwick. Then he left and caught a ride from one of the garrison truck drivers to the Aldershot Station. Aldershot wasn't far from London. It was only about 35 miles away and Dave just got to the station in time to take the next train there.

Almost immediately the train left the station and they began heading northeast. They went through places like Farnborough, Brookwood, Woking, Byfleet and Weybridge and when they pulled in at the Waterloo Station, Dave walked out and just couldn't get over it. Now, a little after 9.00 o'clock in the morning, it was a clear cool sunny early November morning. There were quite a few people rushing in or leaving the station and all around him London was hustling and bustling with a kind of drive and energy that had none of the despair and pessimism he might have come to expect from such a war-torn and bomb-scarred city under the Blitz. On the contrary there was a strong and defiant look in the faces of the people and they were walking around briskly as if they wanted to get on with their lives and as if everything was all right.

Most of the people Dave saw seemed to be like that and as he took the underground subway and drove around, he realized what a great city London was. With its St. Paul's Cathedral, Westminster Abbey and Westminster Cathedral; its Buckingham Palace, Big Ben Clock and Houses of Parliament Buildings; its Tower of London, numerous bridges and Thames River; its many train stations, universities, art galleries, monuments and museums; its extremely beautiful and well-kept parks; its vastly different and wonderful areas such as Piccadilly Circus, Trafalgar Square, Hyde Park, Leicester Square and Shaftesbury Avenue; its rich aristocratic districts such as Mayfair, Kensington and Belgravia; its more modest middle-class ones such as Paddington, the Strand and Soho; its poor working-class ones such as Wapping, Stepney, the Isle of Dogs, West Ham and East Ham; with all of those famous areas, spectacular parks, monuments and buildings London, then, was a truly gigantic and extraordinary city.

In fact it was the biggest city in Europe and there was about it a huge imperial splendor that made you see right away why this was one of the great cities of the world. It was all there in its historic churches, buildings, monuments, parks and districts. It was all there surrounding him and Dave spent all morning and the better part of the afternoon getting the feel of this extraordinary city. Then, around 4.00 o'clock, Dave went to the Beaver Club across Cockspur Street where he had a few drinks before going to have a good Indian meal in Soho. After the meal he went to see a movie on Leicester Square. This was a war movie and it went on so long about War, Life, Death, Anguish and Suffering it ended up being boring rather than a good war movie.

When the movie was over, a little after 9.00 o'clock, Dave left the theater and began walking toward Piccadilly Circus. There was a nice, cool breeze blowing and Dave walked slowly and leisurely. He wanted to enjoy the lovely, moon-lit, star-filled evening and when he had almost reached Piccadilly Circus, the air-raid sirens suddenly went on. When they came on Dave rushed in the blackout with quite a few other people toward the entrance to the Piccadilly Circus Station. As he reached it Dave hurried with these people down the long staircase that led to the subway platform underground. Once Dave got there he was struck by all the activity he found on the platform. There were people who were talking, standing, sitting and sleeping there. Along the whole length of the platform there was a stale, closed-in and lived-in smell.

There were also quite a few people who, beyond a white line that separated them from the people who were talking, standing, sitting and sleeping there, were waiting to take a train east. As soon as he made it to the platform Dave walked about 150 feet to the right of it. When he stopped Dave heard the first dull crump of the bombs. It sounded quite distant. But the sound was persistent and after a while it seemed to be getting closer and closer to where he was standing. Then Dave heard a low whistling screaming sound as if the bombs were falling right on top of him. The sound was followed by a series of quick-spreading and muffled explosions. Dave listened to those explosions for a while and when they had faded and when the platform had stopped shaking a little, he turned and saw her.

The girl wasn't standing far from him. She was alone and stood near the entrance of the platform. She was quite beautiful and was a tall, slender, blue-eyed blonde. She was in her early twenties and was wearing the dark navy-blue cap and uniform of a WAAF — the Women's Auxiliary Air Force. Right now she was facing him on the platform and when another stick of bombs fell nearby and when the lights on the platform flickered, there was such a look of pain and anguish in her face Dave began walking toward her. When another stick of bombs fell nearby and when the lights on the platform flickered again, that look of pain and anguish deepened in her face and she looked down at the platform. Dave kept on walking toward her and when a third stick of bombs fell nearby, he reached her and put his right arm around her.

Dave held her gently and said: "Okay. It's okay." As he said this the girl put her head down hard against his chest and they stood like this as more bombs fell and as the station platform shook a little and some dust fell from the ceiling. They stayed like this throughout the raid. The girl kept her head down hard against his chest and Dave felt all the extraordinary pain and anguish in her. Then, when they heard the muffled sound of the sirens going on again and giving the all-clear signal and when the trains began running once more, the girl took his hand and began leading him to the platform for the trains going west. All this time neither of them spoke and when a train came by, they got on it and began heading west. The train was full of passengers who looked tired and drawn from the bombing and eager to go home.

After a while, when they reached Paddington Station, they got out and began heading south and then northeast in the blackout. They didn't speak and the girl held his hand. She kept on heading northeast with him and some time later they reached a small narrow street and turned right on it. They went on for a little while on the north side of that street and finally came to what looked like a drab three-story gray-bricked building. As they neared the building the girl slowed down and walked up the short stony steps leading to the front door. She went in with Dave and climbed a long wooden spiral staircase until they reached the third floor. On the third floor the girl turned to a door on her right and took out a key. She opened it and motioned for him to go in.

CHAPTER 62

Dave stepped into the apartment and saw it was in complete darkness. Moonlight was pouring in through a large bay window at the end of the apartment and he could make out, as he came in, a short narrow hallway, a small kitchen to the left of the hallway, a bathroom and a clothes' closet to the right of the hallway and then a huge single room with the large bay window at the end of the room. The bay window had been crisscrossed with black tape. The blackout curtains hadn't been pulled in and through the bay window Dave could see a red and orange glow on the horizon. This was in the East End where the German *Luftwaffe* had been busy bombing tonight.

Once Dave had come in the girl also stepped in and locked the door behind her. As they both came out of the short hallway into the huge single room, Dave took in the room swiftly. There was, to begin with, a large double bed against the bay window and then a chair and a dresser on each side of the bed. Once they were in the room the girl took off her cap and threw it on the chair on the left side of the bed. Then she loosened her long silky blonde hair and came and stood in front of him in the middle of the room. As she stood there she looked up at him and said: "Do you like me? Do you really like me?" "Of course," Dave said. "I wouldn't have brought you here if you didn't," the girl said. "I know that," Dave said. "I mean it," the girl said. "I know that too," Dave said.

The girl then moved to the left side of the bed and began undressing. She put her clothes on the chair on the left side of the bed. Dave also began undressing and put his own clothes on the chair on the right side. When both of them had undressed they walked to the center of the room. They stood there and faced each other at the foot of the bed. Dave put his hands on the girl's shoulders and looked at her. Then he ran his hands against her back and felt its incredible smoothness and loveliness. The girl ran her hands softly over his chest and then put them around his waist. At the same time she raised her head and kissed him. Her mouth felt very warm and soft and moist and they held each other tightly. As they did a wild frenzied need rose in Dave and he knew she was feeling the same way.

The girl then led him to the right side of the large double bed. She lay down and Dave slid in next to her on her left side. They began kissing wildly, hungrily and passionately and after a while the girl tightened her arms around him. Dave moved in on her and as he began making love to her, the air-raid sirens suddenly went on again. When they did he wondered briefly whether he should keep on making love to her. He wondered if it was smart to do this in front of a large bay window which could shatter at any time if bombs fell nearby. He hesitated for a moment and it was this hesitation which seemed to excite her. When she sensed this the girl kept on kissing him and tightening her arms around him. She kept on making love to him wildly, feverishly and excitedly. Indeed their lovemaking had such a drive and intensity to it it was close to madness and desperation.

It was as if the girl didn't care what happened and what real danger they were now becoming exposed to. As a matter of fact it was as if, for her, this act, this deed, this action, was far more important than anything else that might be happening around her. By then Dave could hear the heavy droning of planes overhead. Anti-aircraft guns were beginning to fire loudly nearby. The sky was becoming crisscrossed with the beams of searchlights. Then he heard the loud whistling screaming sounds of bombs coming down and exploding not that far away so the apartment shook and rattled a great deal. And yet it was precisely at that moment, when the bombs fell so close by, that the girl's need and hunger for him seemed to be at its most intense. It was as if, in the act of loving, giving and sharing, this was more important to her than possible death, destruction and annihilation.

And it was precisely at that moment, when he felt this so deeply and strongly within her, that Dave suddenly gave himself over to her and let himself be carried away by the sheer power and intensity of her feelings. As a result Dave kept on making love to her and increased its intensity, even, so that no matter how many planes flew overhead, how many guns were firing and how many bombs were falling, he became completely oblivious to all that. As a matter of fact he made love to her with a care and concern, a need and yearning, a gentleness and tenderness, he didn't even know he had in him and that stayed within him long after the bombs had stopped falling, the planes had left and the all-clear sirens had sounded.

England

Indeed, in that brief and sudden moment when the air-raid sirens had gone on, something had happened between him and this girl that had gone far beyond need, hunger and passion and had brought them as close as two people can ever be brought together and taken them to the very core and center of themselves, of the world and of the universe even.

It was a feeling, as a matter of fact, that was so powerful and overwhelming it stayed with them long after they had stopped making love and long after they had just lain next to each other and held hands in the darkness.

CHAPTER 63

For a long time both of them didn't say anything. They just lay next to each other in the darkness and then the girl turned to Dave and said: "I want to thank you for staying with me."

"No. I'm the one who wants to thank you."

"You have no idea how good I feel."

"It's the same thing here."

"It's been a very long time since I've felt like this."

"Me too."

"Back there, on the platform at Piccadilly Circus, I felt you understood me and were concerned about me. That's why I brought you back here and made love with you."

"I understand."

"Do you?"

"I think so."

"I don't think you do."

"Oh no?"

"No."

"Why not?"

"You see, it's not the only reason I brought you back here."

"It's not?"

"No."

"Why did you bring me here then?"

"For many reasons."

"What reasons?"

"Oh, many."

"Why?"

"Well, among other things, because I've been feeling very bad about myself."

"You have?"

"Oh yes. For a very long time now."

"Really?"

"Oh yes."

"Why?"

"It's a long story."

"Do you want to talk about it?"

"Sure."

"If you don't want to talk about it, it's okay."

"No. It's all right."

"You're sure?"

"I'm sure."

Dave didn't say anything and the girl said: "You see, it all goes back to early July this year."

"What about early July?"

"My fiancé was killed in the Battle of Britain."

"I'm sorry."

"It's all right. After all people do get killed in a war."

"That's true. But I'm really sorry it was your fiancé."

"It's all right."

"I really am."

"It's all right."

"Was your fiancé an airman?"

"He was."

"I'm truly sorry."

"It's all right. Those things happen."

"I know. I just wish they hadn't happened to you."

"So do I. Although, to tell you the truth, that's not the reason why I've been feeling so bad about myself."

"It's not?"

"No."

"What's the reason then?"

The girl moved a little closer to Dave and as she looked at him, she said: "To understand that you have to go back quite a way before the war started."

"Okay. Do you want to talk about it?"

"Sure."

"If you don't want to talk about it, it's okay."

"No. I don't mind. You see, my father was a well-known barrister and we lived in Mayfair. We had quite a large house there on Hill Street. Our neighbor was also a well-known barrister and he had a son, Tom. We were always together and it was understood when we grew up, I would marry him."

"Go on."

"Well, Tom was always lively and full of mischief. And I always got along well with him. Then the war came along and Tom decided to drop his law studies and go into the RAF. I decided to become a WAAF. You see, my father had died shortly before the war and my mother had sold our house in Mayfair and moved to Oxford."

"I see."

"Anyway, by then I was posted to Croydon as a Plotter and was doing Interception Work. Oh, I know I'm not supposed to talk about my work and say where I'm posted. But I don't care. I really don't care. I just have to tell you what happened."

"Don't worry."

"I don't care if you tell anybody."

"Don't worry. I won't."

"In any case that's what I did. Tom joined the RAF. And then I made the biggest mistake of my life."

"What mistake?"

"Well, you see, by then Tom and I hadn't slept together. He wanted to. But I didn't. I wanted to wait until we got married. A pretty silly idea, wasn't it?"

"Not really."

"Oh yes it was. You see, Tom didn't want to marry while the war was on. He said it was too risky. He wanted to wait until the war was over. You can imagine how long we would have to wait."

"I can imagine."

"Anyway, the war went on. Then, one morning in early July while I was on duty at Croydon, I could hear his voice as they were doing escort duty for a convoy near Calais. As I could hear his voice they were suddenly jumped by some Messerschmitts while Heinkels attacked the convoy. I could hear a lot of yelling and screaming from the pilots of all those English and German planes and then I heard Tom's voice yelling 'I'm hit! I'm hit!' and then the voices of other pilots from his Squadron screaming 'Go on! Go on! Bale out! Jump!' But he never did. He went straight down and crashed into the Channel."

"My God!"

"It's a pretty story, isn't it?"

"I'm sorry. I'm so sorry."

"It's all right. Those things happen."

"I know. But I'm sorry. You have no idea how sorry I am."

The girl then moved very close to Dave and said: "Then guess what happened?"

"I don't know."

"I was given a few days off."

"Then what?"

"Guess?"

"I don't know. What?"

"Then I went to an officers' club in London that evening. The club was called the Trafalgar and I picked up a handsome American flyer who was a fighter pilot in the RAF. He was tall, slim, blond and blue-eyed like Tom and I brought him back here and made love to him and did things with him I never thought I would do. Then I let him go. I knew the evening didn't mean anything to him and that for him I was just another girl. Also it was quite obvious this was all he was looking for. What he really wanted, I knew, and what he was really looking for all the time, were brand-new girls. That was all he was really interested in. So much for me!"

Dave didn't say anything and the girl went on: "After that you can't imagine how I felt. It got so bad after a while I even thought of killing myself."

"Listen. Don't be so hard on yourself. You were just going through a bad time. That's all."

"I know. But it was terrible."

"I can imagine."

"I felt I had let Tom down. I felt I had let myself down. I even felt life wasn't worth living."

"That's not true. You were just going through a bad time."

"I know. But, you see, I couldn't help seeing the terrible irony of the whole situation. I wanted to wait until I was married before making love to Tom. What happened? Tom died unloved since I'm pretty sure, despite all his bluster and bravado, he never made love to any girl before he died. I never got to make love to the man I truly loved. And I ended up giving myself to a man who didn't really care for me."

"Those things happen."

"They certainly do."

"Maybe there's a purpose to all this."

"If there is I certainly would like to know what it is."

"I know it's not easy to take. But what else can you do?"

"I know."

The Long War

"I think the best thing to do is to try not to think about all this and go on."

"That's true."

"I think that's the best thing."

"I agree. Although, to tell you the truth, it's not so easy."

"I know that."

"That's why, you see, I brought you here. When you came to me on the platform and put your arm around me and said 'Okay. It's okay.', I felt you understood me and were concerned about me."

"That's true."

"You see, I know from your uniform you're a Canadian soldier and probably in London on leave. I know I might not see you again or that you might want to see me and might not be able to. But I felt that, at least for tonight, you might really care for me."

Dave nodded and the girl went on: "Anyway, that's what I felt."

"I'm glad you felt that way."

"That's why, you see, I want to thank you. You've made me feel very good and happy and taken away the terrible things I've been feeling for so long now."

"I'm glad."

"It's true."

"You've made me feel very good and happy too."

"I did?"

"Sure."

"You mean that?"

"You bet."

"Well, I'm glad."

"So am I."

CHAPTER 64

The girl then moved a little closer to Dave and kissed him softly. Finally she lay back in bed and Dave held her in his arms. After a while she fell asleep and Dave himself only fell asleep around 3.00 o'clock in the morning. He slept deeply and soundly and when he woke up, it was close to 11.00 a.m. He looked out of the large bay window and saw it was a dull, gray and overcast day. Dave turned from the window and looked around the apartment. As he looked at it he saw two things about it. One was in daylight the large bay window over the bed made it look bigger and roomier than it had looked last night. The other was the bleak, faded and off-white walls made it look dingier and drearier than when he had first seen it in the darkness.

There was also a note on the pillow next to Dave. He picked it up and read it. He found out the girl's name was Barbara Bradford and she had been in London on leave. She thanked him for the night they had spent together and told him not to worry. They had made love at a time when it was quite safe for them to do so. She told him she had now gone back to Croydon where she was going to be on duty for three weeks. She asked him to close the door behind him when he left and make sure it was locked. Dave read the note twice and then got up and got dressed. He went to a dresser on the right side of the bed and took a pen on top of it. On the note Dave also thanked Barbara and told her his name. He gave her the name of his Regiment and told her where he could be reached.

When Dave had finished writing he put the note on the pillow with the pen on top of it. He then walked over to the bathroom where he washed, combed his hair and shaved with a small razor he found in the medicine cabinet above the sink. When he was all spruced up he left the apartment

The Long War

and closed the door behind him. He made sure it was locked and walked down the long wooden spiral staircase that led to the ground floor. Outside Dave found the small narrow street he was on was called Southwick. He headed southeast on it and saw at the corner of Sussex Gardens a whole block of houses was down. Those houses were not far away from where Barbara lived and Dave saw how dangerous it had been for both of them last night. If the bombs had just fallen a few hundred yards to the left, it would have been her apartment that would have been smashed.

No wonder it had shaken and rattled so badly when the bombs had hit. That morning the northeast corner of Southwick Street and Sussex Gardens had been cordoned off. There was an ambulance standing nearby and firemen and volunteers were poking and searching through the huge still-smoking pile of brick and plaster rubble. There was an acrid burning dusty smell in the air. Dave looked at that block of smashed houses for a moment and then headed southwest on Sussex Gardens until he turned north on Spring Street and proceeded toward Paddington Station. At the station Dave took the subway going east and got off at Tottenham Court Road Station. From there Dave went and had a good meal in Soho and afterward walked leisurely to Cockspur Street and to the Beaver Club where he had a few drinks.

Not long after Dave left the Beaver Club and went to Bond Street where he bought an expensive suit, a couple of shirts and ties, shoes, socks and a $150.00 raincoat. In Bond Street Dave changed into some of the new clothes he had bought and put his boots and clean uniform in a shopping bag. Then Dave left Bond Street and went to Eccleston Square where he rented a luxury room at the Regent Hotel. The room was huge and on the seventh floor of the hotel. It had a large double bed, a plush desk and big armchairs, a magnificent bathroom and was covered with thick and lavish carpets. On top of that the hotel also had a deep and spacious bomb shelter in the basement and an expensive and first-rate restaurant downstairs. Dave spent most of his time ordering and drinking Gordon's Dry Gin in his room or going to eat at the hotel restaurant downstairs.

If there was an air raid, which seemed to be every night, he stayed in the deep and spacious bomb shelter until the all-clear signal was given. Then Dave went back to his room and slept late before getting up and taking luxurious baths in his magnificent bathroom. When he wasn't out sighseeing he stayed in bed drinking and reading cheap trashy novels he had bought in a small bookstore on Charing Cross Road. This made for quite a pleasant and luxurious life. Indeed it was one you could get used to easily. But it was also one that was extremely costly and expensive. As a matter of fact, by the time his 7-day pass was over and he had to go back to

Aldershot, Dave found out, once he had settled his hotel bill, he had gone through most of the money he had had ever since Vancouver and only had about $100.00 dollars left.

Still, Dave thought, $100.00 dollars was a lot better than nothing. There had been plenty of times in his life when he had had a lot less. So, when Thursday morning came around and it was time for him to go back to Aldershot, Dave changed into his clean uniform and put on his boots. He put the new clothes he had bought in the shopping bag and left the bag in his hotel room. Then Dave went downstairs and settled his bill. Once he had paid he left the Regent hotel and went to the Waterloo station where he took the 6.00 a.m. train back to Aldershot.

CHAPTER 65

On the way to the station Dave found the streets were fairly deserted. That early in the morning the air was cool and crisp and the streets had a bright and shiny look to them. Once he reached the station Dave was just in time to take his train back to Aldershot. Not long after the train left the station and began heading southwest. It went through the same places they had gone through before. Only, this time, it went through them in reverse order. They drove through Weybridge, Byfleet, Woking, Brookwood, Farnborough and when they finally reached Aldershot, Dave took a taxi to the center itself. At the center Dave checked in at the Company Orderly Room and then walked back to his barrack.

It was now close to 7.30 a.m. and when he came in, Dave saw there seemed to be something wrong with the Big Ten. As soon as they saw him they rushed over and gathered around him. They asked him about London and joked about all the girls he must have met. Yet, as they stood around, there was a strange and peculiar tension in all of them. And this seemed to be especially true of Red. They all talked and joked with him for a while and then, as if on a pre-arranged signal, moved away. Red stayed with Dave and as they stood near his bunk, Dave turned to him and said: "All right. What's wrong?"

"There's nothing wrong."

"Come on. You guys all look like pallbearers."

"There's nothing wrong."

"Sure there is. What?"

"It's Meyer."

"What about Meyer?"

"He's gone."

"What do you mean he's gone?"
"He's AWOL."
"He's AWOL!"
"That's right."
"Since when?"
"Monday."
"Since Monday!"
"That's right."
"And you guys have been carrying him all this time?"
"That's right."
"Oh man! Are you crazy?"
"I know. Believe me it didn't happen the way you think."
"Oh no?" Dave said. "How?"
"Well, after you went on leave," Red said, "Meyer began asking me all kinds of questions about Greenock. You know. How far was it from here? How big a port was it? What were the size of the ships leaving from there? And then on Monday morning, when the Roll Call was made, he wasn't there."
"How come he wasn't reported then?"
"That's just it. Moran was pretty busy that morning and he did the Roll Call real quick."
"So?"
"So when I didn't see Meyer I thought maybe he was still in the barrack. And I called him Present."
"Moran didn't notice the difference?"
"No. As I said he was pretty busy."
"Oh man! This is bad. Very bad."
"I know. It just happened that way."
"What about the other days? Who carried him Present?"
"Gennaro did it on Tuesday."
"And yesterday?"
"Higgins did it."
"And Moran didn't notice the difference?"
"He did on Tuesday. But he didn't seem to know what to do about it. And he let it go."
"Oh man! I don't believe this! I just don't believe it!"
"I don't believe it either. As a matter of fact I'm still surprised at the way it happened myself."
"What the hell were you guys thinking? Are you crazy!"
"I know. I know. Maybe Moran's too close to us. Maybe if he was more of a sonofabitch none of this would have happened."

"What about Norris?" Dave asked and referred to their tall, spindly, ruddy-faced and blond-haired Platoon Lieutenant, Jack Norris. "Didn't he notice anything?"

"Ah, you know the Lieutenant never notices anything," Red said.

"What about Bostwick? Didn't he notice anything?"

"That's just it. Bostwick's been away on a 3-day pass since Monday."

"Since Monday!"

"That's right. That's why this thing has been going on for as long as it has."

"Oh man! What a screw-up! What an unbelievable screw-up!"

"I know. That's why I was anxious for you to come back. I thought maybe you might be able to help us with this thing."

Dave nodded and stood next to his bunk for a moment. He thought about what Red had told him and then turned to him again and said: "Okay. There's only one thing we can do."

"What?"

"We have to go and see Bostwick."

"Oh no! Not that!"

"Why not?"

"If we go and see him he'll kill us!"

"We have to."

"Oh no!"

"We have to see him."

"If we do that he'll bust us for having carried Meyer. And he'll bust Moran for having let us carry him."

"Maybe not."

"For sure he will."

"Maybe not."

"For sure he will."

"What else can we do?"

"Why don't we stop carrying Meyer instead?"

"No. I don't want that."

"Why not? That way it gets Moran off the hook and also gets us off the hook."

"No. I want to try and get Meyer back."

"Why? Just because you want to have Meyer in the Company doesn't mean you have to make us all suffer for it."

"Hey! I didn't start this thing."

"I know that."

"All right then."

"Why don't we stop carrying Meyer then?"

"No. We'll go and see Bostwick at lunch time."
"Why? Why don't we stop carrying Meyer instead?"
"No. We'll go and see Bostwick. That's what we'll do."

CHAPTER 66

Dave moved away from Red and went to his foot locker. He opened it and took out a pair of field fatigues. He put them on and rushed with Red and the Big Ten to the Parade Ground. Moran took the 8.00 a.m. Roll Call and Lang carried Meyer Present. Moran looked a little tense at the Roll Call but didn't say anything. After the Roll Call he began working them out and made them do light marching drills and physical exercises as if he wanted to give them a break from all the hard policing and patrolling they had done in the Waring area for the last six weeks. This workout lasted until noon and around 12.30 p.m., after a quick lunch, Dave and Red left the mess hall and walked over to the Orderly Room in order to talk to Bostwick.

The Company Clerk, Tom Taylor, was busy typing some forms. He was a tall, lean and bespectacled soldier and when Dave and Red came in, they asked to see Bostwick. Before Taylor could answer Bostwick's head popped out of his office. His office was to the right of the office of their new Company CO, Major Ross Wilson. Major Wilson was a somewhat short, flabby and pink-cheeked officer who in civilian life had been a lawyer in Orillia, Ontario. It was rumored he had joined the Regiment out of a deep sense of loyalty to his country and because of his strong belief in the dignity and nobility of soldiering. When Bostwick saw Dave and Red he motioned for them to come into his office. Dave and Red went in and closed the door behind them.

Bostwick went and sat behind his large wooden desk. Dave and Red stood on the other side of the desk and as they stared at him, Bostwick turned to Dave and said: "What can I do for you?"

"We'd like to talk to you for a minute, Sergeant Major."

England

Bostwick leaned back in his chair and stared at nothing in particular. He looked quite hungover and feverish. His huge sallow clean-shaven head was deeply-tanned and wrinkled. He ran his hand over it quite a few times and leaned forward on his desk and stared at Dave. When he did there were deep creases in the corner of his eyes and he said: "Why is it that whenever I see you two characters I smell trouble?"

"There's no trouble, Sergeant Major."

"Oh no?"

"No. We'd just like to talk to you."

"Go ahead. Talk."

"It's about Meyer."

"Ah. Meyer."

"That's right. Meyer."

"What about him?"

"He's AWOL."

"He's what!"

"He's AWOL."

Dave went on and told Bostwick what had happened. He told him how it had happened, when and what Meyer had asked Red about Greenock.

"Jesus Christ!" Bostwick said, when Dave had finished. "What a mess! What an incredible mess!"

"I'm sorry. That's why we came to talk to you about it."

Bostwick rubbed his big unshaven cheeks. He winced as he did this and stared at Dave again and said: "What do you want me to do about it?"

"I thought you might be able to help us."

"How?"

"By trying to get Meyer back."

Bostwick got up slowly from his desk and began pacing back and forth behind it. He kept on pacing back and forth and when he sat down again, he looked up at them both and said: "Let me just say this. It's a pretty goddam sad day when a man can't even leave his Company for a few days without having everyone around him screw up and make an absolute mess of everything."

Dave and Red stood in front of Bostwick and didn't say anything. As they stood there Bostwick turned to Dave again and said: "All right. What would you like me to do?"

"We'd like you to give us a chance to find Meyer."

"The man has been AWOL for four days. How are you going to find him?"

"I know him, Sergeant Major. I know how he thinks."

"What has this got to do with it?"
"I'm pretty sure I know where I'm going to find him."
"Where?"
"In Greenock."
"After all this time?"
"That's right."
"Maybe he's gone."
"I don't think so."
"How do you know?"
"I know."
"How?"
"It's a feeling I have."
"It may be a feeling you have. But after all this time he may very well be gone."
"I know that."
"The man is AWOL. Why not make it simple and bust him?"
"Oh no. Meyer's a good man."
"Sure. The man's a pacifist who's now become a deserter. Who knows? Maybe someday he'll even make it into a soldier?"
"With all due respect, Sergeant Major. I don't think you understand him."
"And you do?"
"I think so. You see, Meyer comes from a culture and tradition where people tend to analyze things and look at every side of every question. I think that's all it is."
"That's it."
"That's right. Meyer probably thought too much about being here. He felt guilty about how it came about and the fact he left so many of his own people on the Continent. He probably got very frustrated and confused thinking about this and left on an impulse. I think that's all it is."
"Meyer's a pacifist, a misfit and a trouble-maker."
"Oh no, Sir. Meyer's a good man."
"I doubt that."
"Believe me, Sir. It's true."
"All right then," Bostwick said. "What do you want me to do about it?"
"I thought maybe you'd let us have a military vehicle," Dave said, "so we could go to Greenock and look for him."
"Sure. With gas rationed and England divided in various military zones, it'll be so easy."
"It won't be easy. But it can be done."

England

"I don't think so. Every time you gas up or come to a checkpoint, they'll stop you and check your papers. And even if I give you an ordnance slip for you to go to Greenock to check on military supplies, they'll call here and want to confirm this with Major Wilson."

"How then?"

"I don't know. Something simple. Something easy."

"How?"

"I don't know. A way for you to be able to get around in Greenock, for example, or anywhere else for that matter without being bothered."

"Like?"

"A 7-day pass. That's it! I'll give you both a 7-day pass!"

"A 7-day pass!"

"That's it! A 7-day pass! That way you'll be able to look for him all you want and bring him back here if you find him."

"You want to give us both a 7-day pass?"

"That's it!" Bostwick said. "But that's as far as I can go."

"I just came back from a 7-day pass," Dave said. "Won't Major Wilson find this peculiar?"

"The hell with Major Wilson! He may be in charge of this Company. But I run it."

"Won't he find this peculiar though? The fact I got two 7-day passes in a row?"

"How should I know! Maybe I gave you another one to recover from the fatigue you feel from the first one."

"And he won't find this peculiar?"

"Who cares! He looks pooped enough and frazzled enough himself, maybe I'll give him a 7-day pass too!"

"And he won't find this peculiar?"

"The hell with Major Wilson! He hasn't got a clue as to what's going on. I just give him a bunch of passes and he signs them. That's the way it is."

"And he won't find this peculiar."

"Hell. He won't even know about it."

"I must say, Sergeant Major. I find this amazing. Pretty amazing."

"Listen. Do you want the two passes or not? Or do you want me to change my mind?"

"No. No. I'll take them."

"Good. I'll even give you one for our pacifist friend. In case you find him."

"I appreciate that."

"Now you both go back to your barrack and get Sergeant Moran. Send him here so we can straighten out this mess."

"Right away, Sergeant Major."

"Also, as far as you're both concerned, Meyer was here until today when he got a 7-day pass. You got that?"

"Yes, Sir. We got it."

"All right. Now you both get the hell out of my office before I change my mind!"

CHAPTER 67

Dave and Red didn't stay in Bostwick's office very long. They stayed there long enough for him to open the top drawer on the right side of his desk and take out three 7-day passes which he gave to Dave. Then they both left the office and began walking back toward their own barrack. When they reached it Dave went in and looked for Moran. He found him near the front door. He was standing at the entrance and talking to a couple of soldiers from their Platoon. Dave walked over to him and told him Bostwick wanted to see him in his office. Moran nodded and left at once. Dave watched him go and then went to his bunk. He got out of his fatigues and changed into a clean uniform.

Once Dave was dressed he picked up Red who had also put on a clean uniform and got a ride to the Aldershot Station from a couple of soldiers from their own Company. Those two soldiers were driving a jeep and gave them a lift. At the station Dave and Red took the 2.00 p.m. train to London. When they reached the Waterloo Station they grabbed a taxi and drove to King's Cross Station where they boarded the 4.00 p.m. train to Greenock. They got on this train around 3.45 p.m. and at 4.00 p.m. sharp, they began leaving King's Cross Station and heading north toward Greenock. In no time they left London behind and hit the countryside. They began picking up speed and went by many rolling hills, brooks, forests, small towns, villages and hamlets. They also went through much bigger towns such as Watford, Hemel Hempstead, Linslade, Bletchley and Wolverton.

In that cold crisp late afternoon those towns were washed in a clear pristine sunlight. It made them stand out ever so starkly and powerfully against the autumn landscape and gave them a timeless and everlasting look of peace, beauty and tranquility. It was a look that truly matched their

The Long War

surroundings but was a far cry from the grimness, bleakness and ugliness of war found in London. The further they sped north, as a matter of fact, the less they seemed to find any signs of it. It was so true it wasn't until they went through Rugby and had gone beyond it, for a while, before they came upon the war again so brutally. By then it was around 7.00 o'clock in the evening, on Thursday, November 14, 1940. Darkness had just fallen across the landscape and a bright full moon was shining high in the sky.

At that time Dave was sitting in his seat on the left side of the aisle next to the window. Red was sitting next to him. Dave was not looking at anyone or anything in particular when, suddenly, he sat up straight and said to Red: "Listen." "What?" Red said. "Just listen," Dave said. Both of them now sat up and listened. They bent a little forward and after a moment they could hear it. It was a hum. It was a low hum and after a while it swelled and became a roar as wave after wave of planes suddenly flew over them. When this happened many flares went up in the sky and were immediately followed by the screaming whistle of falling bombs, the eerie noises of incendiary baskets coming down and the huge detonations of parachuted land mines. At that moment the ground shook with rolling crackling quick-spreading explosions and the whole sky in the distance was lit up bright-red.

They were now about a mile from the town being bombed. As their train kept on speeding and heading toward it bombs now began falling all around them and machine-gun fire was heard overhead. Dave saw, when their train came into the marshaling yards of that town and when the wheels of the train began grinding and screeching against the rails, that the town was Coventry. This was one of England's most important industrial towns. In fact, after London, it was probably the most important industrial town in England. By now the whole center of the town was lit up and burning, and the Cathedral was looming darkly and eerily over the flames. When their train suddenly ground to a stop in the marshaling yards, not that far from the station, railwaymen were running alongside the tracks and yelling: "Get out! Get out!"

They were pointing across the tracks to what looked like factory buildings and telling them to go to the shelters there. Dave and Red ran to the door on the right side of their wagon. They jumped down and ran across the yards to a long four-story building on a street called Stoney Road. When they got to the building Dave and Red barreled down the staircase that led to the shelter in the basement and went and sat down on a wooden bench at the far end of it against the wall. After a short while the door of the shelter was closed and they sat inside in the dim light of two bulbs hanging, one at each end of the ceiling. As they sat there Dave could hear wave after wave of planes coming over and bombing the town. At times the explosions rocked and shook the shelter. In fact some of the explosions were so close Dave could hear the grinding and creaking of the building's masonry.

The lights flickered on and off and some dust and plaster fell from the ceiling. Every time this happened a group of small children who were sitting near the door of the shelter began crying and screaming loudly. An old man who was sitting not far from Dave and Red shook uncontrollably. Another man who was somewhere in the middle of the shelter kept on saying over and over: "Oh God. Oh my God." While the bombing raid went on there could be no doubt in anybody's mind this was indeed a big one. They could hear the steady drone of planes flying low overhead, the whistling screaming sounds of falling bombs, the eerie sinister noises of incendiary baskets coming down and the crashing shattering roar of explosions all around. Some of the explosions seemed far from them. Some seemed right on top of them.

After a while the door of the shelter was opened and some more people were let in. These were people who had been bombed out of their homes or who could not get back to them. In no time the shelter was packed and there were people who were standing up against the walls or sitting down on the floor or squeezing down against the people already sitting on the benches. Not long after some of the railwaymen also came running into the shelter. When they saw it was full they closed the door behind them. Once they had closed the door they stood near it and everyone else stood where they were in the damp musty smell of the basement. Dave kept on sitting next to Red and wave after wave of planes kept on coming over. After a while their droning was so steady it seemed to become a normal thing so the quick-hitting fast-spreading ever-expanding explosions all around him almost had a lulling effect.

Dave kept on sitting next to Red and the hours went by. The planes kept on coming and he almost seemed to be asleep in their noises and in the noises of the explosions. After quite a while, though, he sat up straighter and noticed something he hadn't noticed before. It was quiet. Very quiet. There didn't seem to be any more planes around. When Dave realized this it seemed everyone else in the shelter also realized it. You could feel a collective sigh of relief as well as a tension and a certain nervousness as to what it might mean and what they might find outside. The sirens hadn't sounded so far and Dave guessed they must have been bombed out. Still no one made a move to leave the shelter. After a while, though, when the quiet persisted some of the railwaymen opened the shelter door and went out to see what was going on.

In a little while they came back and told everyone what they already knew. The raid was over. With another collective sigh of relief everyone now began moving and filing out of the shelter. Since Dave had been sitting with Red on the bench against the wall at the back of the shelter, he was one of the last to leave. Dave walked slowly with Red and glanced at his watch. He noticed in the light of the bulb near the front of the shelter, and not far from the staircase leading to the shelter door, it was close to 7.00 a.m. That meant the raid had gone on for almost 12 hours! In the circumstances it must make it the biggest raid against England and probably the biggest raid of the war so far! Dave followed the long line of people ahead of him with Red. He walked up the staircase and when he came out of the shelter door, he stood there and gasped.

The sky was blood-red. A grayish pall of smoke hung everywhere and there was a burning, acrid and dusty smell in the air. Their train was still standing in the marshaling yards and seemed to have miraculously escaped being hit. But beyond the station, to the north, the whole center of Coventry had been bombed and flattened to the ground. The Cathedral had been smashed and only the outer shell of some of its walls was still left standing. There were fires everywhere. Water works and gas mains were ruptured. Power lines were down. Tram rails had been bent and were sticking out in weird and jagged shapes. Many streets were filled with huge craters from parachuted land mines. Quite a few houses were bombed out. Some of them looked as if they had been cut in two by a giant meat cleaver.

One half of the house was lying in rubble while the other half stood cleanly with the various floors intact and the furniture showing on those floors. A great many of them no longer had any roofs. As he stood there and looked at this Dave thought he had never seen such destruction before. Then he turned from the bombed out, smoking, burning center of Coventry. He began crossing Stoney Road with Red and walking toward the marshaling yards where their train was. At that moment a military vehicle roared into Stoney Road from the south and came and skidded to a stop near them. When it stopped the big burly Military Policeman who was sitting next to the driver pointed to Dave and said: "You! Hey! You!" "Me?" Dave said. "Yes. You," the Military Policeman said. "And you too," he added and pointed to Red. "Come with me. We have a big emergency and we need you. In fact we have all kinds of emergencies. Come on. Get in."

For a moment Dave thought of telling the Military Policeman they were on leave on a 7-day pass and wanted to get back to their train so they could go to Greenock. But he knew it wouldn't do any good. Not

England

in those circumstances. For sure it wouldn't do any good. Instead Dave stepped forward with Red and got into the back of the military vehicle. The military vehicle made a sharp U-turn on Stoney Road and drove past and behind the Coventry Station before it turned right on Michaelmas Road and right on Warwick Road. As it got on Warwick Road it began heading north and toward the center of Coventry.

CHAPTER 68

The driver drove as fast as he could and as they headed toward the center of Coventry, Dave saw all the buildings on Warwick Road had been badly bombed and damaged. They kept on heading north and when they got near New Union Street, Dave also saw two fire trucks on the left side of the street near two buildings that had been badly hit and were lying in a pile of rubble. In the first of those buildings, which seemed to be a three-story house, the third floor had caved in and was lying in shambles. There was a fire ladder on top of the third floor and several firemen and volunteers were moving and searching through the rubble. Next to this building, to the right side of it, was the remnant of a church also lying in a pile of rubble.

Part of the left wall of the church and part of the steeple, also on the left side, were left standing and several other firemen and volunteers were digging through the rubble. An iron sign lying half-bent in the street said: *St. Matthew's Church*. The church, Dave found out later, belonged to the Church of England, and when they reached it the driver of the Military vehicle slammed on the brakes. He came and stopped near a tall, well-built and gray-haired man who was dressed in dusty, grimy and dark-blue overalls and who was wearing a helmet. The man was standing in the middle of the street and watching and directing the firemen and volunteers who were standing over the rubble and working on the site. As soon as they stopped next to this man the Military Policeman who was sitting next to the driver said: "Here we are, Warden. I think we found you the kind of volunteers you're looking for."

"Good," the Warden said to the Military Policeman and took in Dave and Red. "You're quite right. Thanks." Dave got off the military vehicle with Red and the Warden led them both to the site and explained what was going on. *St. Matthew's Church* had been a gabled high-beamed high-ceilinged graystone church with a ground floor and two basement floors. It must have taken a direct hit as well as several other hits since it was in a direct bombing run with the Cathedral and since all the buildings in the area had been flattened out. They had been hearing cries underneath the rubble near the middle of the site. Those cries had been slightly to the right of it and they had been digging frantically and trying to get to the people.

But two huge beams had fallen near the spot where they had been hearing cries and, with the stones, plaster and other rubble that had fallen there, they had had to dig the hole at an angle underneath the beams. The digging had been slow and difficult and they now needed two fresh people like them who were both slim enough and strong enough to be lowered down through the hole in order to try and bring the people out. When the Warden had finished telling them what he needed Dave stared at him and said: "You've got to be kidding, Warden. We can't do that."

"Sure you can, lad."

"No. We can't. We're not trained for that."

"It doesn't matter. One of you is small enough to be the lead man on the rope. The other is strong enough to be his catcher. That's what I need."

"It's not fair. We were just going out on a 7-day pass."

"I understand. But you're all I have."

CHAPTER 69

The Warden then led them to the hole that had been dug. When they got to that hole Dave looked at it and it seemed pretty small to him. In fact it looked extremely small and with barely enough room for him and Red to squeeze through at an angle. At the hole Dave bent down and could hear faint and far-off cries from below. Dave listened for a moment and straightened up. He sighed and told the Warden they would do it. The Warden nodded and the firemen and volunteers, who had come over and who were taking in his conversation with the Warden, now grinned and patted him and Red on the back. Most of them were either too big or too out of shape to be lowered into the hole themselves.

Now that Dave and Red had decided to go down into the hole the firemen and volunteers got busy and a strong fireman's rope was tied in several turns around their waists. The firemen and volunteers made sure they left about six feet of slack between Dave and Red and another six feet in front of Red since he was the lead man on the rope. The rope they used was very thick. It was made of hemp and could easily carry several people. They made sure a double length held both Dave and Red. Then, when Dave and Red were tied properly, they worked out the signals. One pull on the rope would mean to lower it. Two pulls, to lift it up. Three pulls, to stop it dead. After they had made a final check on Dave and Red and after they had grabbed the long end of the rope in order to be able to give them slack and lower them into the hole, Dave turned to Red.

Dave nodded and Red walked over to the hole. He began squeezing and sliding down in it feet first at an angle and was soon followed by Dave. Then, when Dave was finally able to squeeze clear of the hole, he suddenly found himself suspended in darkness. Red's weight below him was putting pressure on the rope and on his waist. The pressure was pretty strong and as soon as he was dangling in the air underneath the rubble, Dave was hit by the damp sweet sickening smell that seemed to come from below. As they were both being let down slowly by the firemen and volunteers they were swinging slightly in the air. They were also hearing faint cries from below and Dave asked Red if he could see anything. Red said he couldn't. Dave nodded. He pulled three times on the rope and said: "A flashlight. I need a flashlight." "What?" a faint voice came from above. "A torch," Dave said in a loud voice which echoed weirdly in the darkness. "I need a torch."

Nothing was said for a moment and then Dave felt alongside his head a long industrial flashlight being lowered on a thin rope. Dave grabbed the flashlight. He pulled on the thin rope so it could be let go and tied it around his waist. Then Dave put on the flashlight in the darkness and what he took in really stunned him. In the powerful beam of the flashlight Dave saw the staircase on the right side of the church leading to the two basement floors had been smashed and was lying in a heap at the bottom of the church. There was a huge round gaping hole in the middle of the floor of the first basement and the second basement was full of rubble and crushed bodies and bits of bodies. Near the huge round gaping hole in the floor of the first basement, to the right of it, was a large semi-circular part of the floor that was cracked and bent ominously.

On that part of the floor a woman was lying on her right side and moaning. Next to her, on her right, a little dark-haired girl with a cut on the right side of her forehead was crouching and tugging at her. She was crying loudly and hysterically and saying: "Mummy! Mummy!" Dave looked down at her and at Red who was swinging below him and said: "Let's go for the woman first." Red nodded and Dave pulled down on the rope once. There was some slack on the rope, then some more, and still Red was about six feet from the floor and five feet away from the woman. Again Dave pulled down on the rope. It was lowered three more feet and stopped. Once more Dave pulled on it and when the rope didn't move, Red tried to swing out and reach for the woman. But he was still too high and too far away.

Red tried hard a few times and said: "It's no use. I can't do it." "Try to get to her in a trapeze style," Dave said. "Swing down with your hands and I'll grab and hold your legs." Red nodded. He suddenly dove down and his legs came up and were grabbed by Dave. Dave let go of the long industrial flashlight and let it hang below his feet in order to give them some light. Then they both began swinging more and more on the rope. The little girl watched them from the corner of the cracked and ominously bent piece of the floor and kept on crying loudly and hysterically. As Dave and Red kept on swinging more and more on the rope Red suddenly lunged at the woman and grabbed her legs. As he did the swing of the rope stopped for a moment and he yelled: "I got her! I got her!"

Then, as the rope began moving again and as the woman began sliding slowly off the floor, Red suddenly grabbed her strongly by the waist and lifted her cleanly. In no time they began swinging into space again and Dave felt the acute and breath-taking pressure of the woman's body on the rope. The pressure was almost unbearable around his waist and the flashlight swinging below his feet was giving weird, moving and flashing shapes to the darkness. "What do I do with her!" Red yelled. "I'm going to let go of your feet," Dave said. "Swing yourself up. And bring her to me." "Okay," Red said. At that moment Dave let go of Red's legs. Red was bent in two and after a few tries he swung the woman on his shoulder. When he did Dave lifted the rope below him and Red toward him.

Dave's waist felt as if it was being cut in two by the pull and when the woman on Red's shoulder came up to him, Red grabbed the rope above Dave and helped him grab the woman's left arm and her waist while still holding on to the rope. Red helped him hold her strongly and then Dave slowly let Red down from the slack of the rope he had pulled up. As soon as Red was down Dave pulled twice on the rope. Almost at once the rope began being raised. As it was being raised Dave heard the rubble creak and groan above him and some dust fell on his head. Dave also felt the woman soft, warm and greasy on him and when they finally got near the hole, Dave raised the woman's arms to go into it. Then he pushed up her body until he heard the firemen and volunteers say: "Easy, lad. Easy. We have her."

As they said this the firemen and volunteers began taking her out through the hole and she was soon gone. Dave pulled on the rope once and they began lowering him and Red down into the darkness again. By that time Dave was feeling tired. In fact he was feeling more tired than he could ever remember. Still he let the firemen and volunteers lower them once more and when they were about three feet away from the cracked and ominously bent floor, he said: "Okay. Now let's get the little girl."

CHAPTER 70

Red nodded and swung on the rope. He kept on swinging more and more and when he got close to the little girl, he said: "Okay. Come and catch me." The little girl stayed crouched near the corner of the cracked floor and kept on crying loudly and hysterically. When he saw this Red suddenly swung over in a trapeze style. Dave grabbed his feet again and the long industrial flashlight swung between them. It kept on giving weird, moving and flashing shapes to the darkness and Red said: "Come on. Come and catch me." The little girl didn't move and kept on crying loudly and hysterically and Red said: "Come on. Don't you want to see your mummy?"

The little girl still didn't move and Red said: "Come on. Come and catch me and we'll go and see your mummy. Then we'll go and have an ice cream cone. Wouldn't you like that? Hey. Wouldn't that be nice?" At those words the little girl looked at Red doubtfully and tearfully. But she began moving slowly and hesitantly toward the edge of the floor. Red watched her intently and said: "That's it! That's it! Come toward me!" The little girl kept on moving slowly and hesitantly toward the edge of the floor and Red watched her. Then he swung toward her and suddenly grabbed her with both hands. He lifted her cleanly off the floor and yelled: "I got her! I got her!" As he lifted her Dave felt another acute and breath-taking pressure around his waist.

Dave let go of Red's legs and Red swung himself up with the little girl. At that moment Dave lifted him until Red was able to grab the rope above him and help him grab the little girl's left arm and hold her strongly by the waist while still holding on to the rope. Then Dave let Red down again from the slack of the rope he had pulled up. Once Red was fully down Dave pulled twice on the rope. Almost at once the rope began being raised. When they got near the hole Dave put the little girl's arms through it and pushed up her body. She was quickly lifted through the hole and Dave heard the firemen and volunteers say: "That's it. That's it. We have her." As soon as the little girl was gone Dave heard them say: "Anybody else down there?" "No," Dave said. "There are no other survivors. Bring us up."

As soon as Dave said this the rope began being raised again and Dave pushed and twisted his way through the hole at an angle until he was suddenly grabbed from under the arms and pulled clear out of it. When Dave was out of the hole the firemen and volunteers kept on raising the rope until Red was also pulled out. By that time Dave was so exhausted he stood bent in two near the hole. He took deep long breaths and Red came and stood next to him and did the same thing. Dave kept on taking deep long breaths even though there was a burning, acrid and dusty smell in the air. After a while the firemen and volunteers began untying the rope from his and Red's waists and when they were free, Dave left the hole and began walking slowly with Red across the site.

Dave headed for the side of the street where the Warden was standing with a volunteer Medic who was working on the cut on the right side of the little girl's forehead. When he got to the curb Dave stopped next to the little girl and said: "Are you all right?" The little girl smiled shyly at him and said: "Yes. Thank you." "Good," Dave said. "I'll just go and see my mummy first," the little girl said. "And then we'll go and have our ice cream cone. Is that all right?" "Sure," Dave said. As he spoke to the little girl Dave looked down the street and saw her mother being laid out in the middle of it with several other bodies in a neat row. Dave turned and his eyes met the Warden's. When they did the warden lowered his head and said in a low voice: "I'm sorry. There was nothing we could do."

Dave nodded and slowly rubbed his forehead two or three times. When he took his hand away he saw his face was sooty, grimy and dusty and his uniform was covered with blood from the little girl's mother. By that time the volunteer Medic had finished working on the cut on the little girl's forehead. She left them and began running happily and excitedly toward her mother. She was saying "Mummy! Mummy!" and when she got close to her, it suddenly happened. One moment the little girl was running happily and excitedly down the street and saying "Mummy! Mummy!" The next a long dark sleek Junkers 88 leapt over the ruins and roared down the street with its machine guns blazing. As the Junkers 88 roared down the street the little girl spun around. Her small white dress suddenly showed a huge red circle in front of it and she slowly fell down at the feet of her mother.

At the same time Dave jumped into the middle of the street and began running toward her. When he reached her he picked her up and spun around. He looked at the sky toward the fast-fleeing and fast-disappearing Junkers 88 and yelled: "Bastards! You lousy stinking bastards!" At that precise moment, when Dave took a few steps in the street with the little girl in his arms, he looked up and saw Meyer. Meyer was coming down the fireman's ladder from the next building. He was also holding a little girl in his arms and when he reached the bottom of the ladder, he turned and saw Dave. In a flash their eyes met and there was such a look of rage, hatred and contempt in Dave's eyes Meyer lowered his head and understood. He understood it all.

Then, as he looked up and stared at Dave, Meyer left the ladder and came and stood next to him. At that moment Dave turned and they both left. They went and put the two little girls next to the little girl's mother in the street. Then they straightened up. They stood there and stared at the little girls, at the little girl's mother and at the other bodies lined up in the street. They stared at those bodies for a while and then they heard the Warden say in a soft low voice behind them: "It's all right, lads. I understand. I quite understand. But we have an awful lot of work to do. Come on. Let's go." Both of them turned slowly. They looked up at the Warden and then left and followed him with Red down the street.

CHAPTER 71

Dave did not have to go far with Red and Meyer. The Warden brought them to another house on Warwick Road. The house was to the right of *St. Matthew's Church*. It stood about 500 feet from it and had also been flattened. There were faint cries coming from underneath the rubble and firemen and volunteers were also working on that site. In this case Dave, Red and Meyer were needed along with the others to help dig through the rubble and try and get the people out. The Warden directed the operation. The three of them joined the firemen and volunteers and it took quite a while to be able to do that. They were lucky. An old couple and a little girl were brought out.

They had been hiding underneath the staircase on the right side of the house. The staircase led to the basement and was the only part of the house that had been spared. All the others who had gone to the basement had been crushed in the rubble. It took about three hours to get the old couple and the little girl out. Then the Warden took them to another flattened house further down the street and for the next three days and nights, covered with soot, dust and grime, they worked without a break and without eating and sleeping even in the center of Coventry and on the outskirts. They worked on bombed out houses, shops and buildings. They put out fires, dug through the rubble and pulled people out. All around them everything was down: beautiful shops with names like Boots, Flinns, Marks and Woolworth's; public buildings, civic centers and hospitals; factories like the Alvis Works, the B.L. Works and the Talbot Motor Works.

Coventry had been very heavily bombed. The center had been completely flattened and it was only on the morning of the fourth day, after they had worked with the firemen and volunteers wherever they were

England

needed, that Dave, Red and Meyer were able to go back to Aldershot. At that time the firemen gave them a lift back in one of the fire trucks that had come from London to help. The fire truck was now going back and, since they had helped the firemen so much, the driver went out of his way to drop them at Aldershot before going back to London. That morning, on the way to Aldershot, they sat at the back of the truck, totally drained and exhausted, and kept on looking at the floor. They stayed like this throughout the whole drive and when the driver reached their destination and dropped them at the center, they thanked him and headed for the Orderly Room.

By then it was close to 11.00 a.m. It was a cold crisp clear Monday morning and when they came into the Orderly Room, with dirty hair, red-rimmed eyes and haggard faces, they looked for Bostwick. They saw the office door of Major Ross Wilson, their new Company CO, was closed and the Company Clerk, Tom Taylor, was out on a morning break. Bostwick was in his office, however, and when he heard them come in, he literally sprang out of it and said: "Why you lousy sonofabitches—"

Bostwick stopped suddenly when he saw the dusty, grimy and exhausted look on their faces and said: "What the hell happened?"

"We were in Coventry," Dave said as the three of them stood facing him in front of his office.

"What the hell were you doing in Coventry?" Bostwick asked.

"Our train was coming through there when the Germans started bombing the town," Dave said. "We were forced to stop there and had to spend the night in a shelter."

"I hear it was quite a raid."

"It was."

"There were over 1000 dead," Red said. "I think it was the biggest raid against England."

"So I hear," Bostwick said and turned to him.

"They had almost 500 planes over," Red said. "It was quite something."

"It must have been."

"I can't believe how long the Germans bombed the town," Red said.

"So I hear," Bostwick said and turned away from Red and looked at Dave. "What happened?"

"Well, the next morning when we came out," Dave said, "everything was down. We spent the next three days and nights digging people out of the rubble, clearing the streets and putting out fires. There was so much to do we didn't even have time to eat or sleep."

"Nice people, hey. The Germans."

The Long War

"You're not kidding."

"What about you?" Bostwick turned to Meyer. "Where the hell were you?"

"I was in Coventry too," Meyer said.

"What the hell were you doing there?"

"Well, you know how I got into the Regiment."

"Yes. I know."

"Well, I kept on wondering if I had done the right thing. Or if I shouldn't have stayed on the Continent and taken my chances."

"Some chances."

"I know. But at least, there, I would have been with my own people."

"That's true."

"Anyway that's how I felt."

"That's why you did what you did?" Bostwick said.

"That's right," Meyer said. "I got all confused and decided to go to London to try and think this out. I was only planning to stay there one day and then come back. But in London I got even more confused and decided to go to Greenock to try and get away from all this."

"Go on."

"Well, I took the 3.00 p.m. train to Greenock. And Coventry happened to be the transfer point."

"So?"

"So I was waiting in the station when the planes came over. That's how I got caught."

"That's some story."

"You're telling me."

CHAPTER 72

At that moment the door of the office next to Bostwick's opened and Major Wilson came out. That morning he had a deeply preoccupied look on his face, as if he was weighed down by the heavy responsibilities he had been given, and was wearing a brand-new and impeccably-pressed uniform that, on his somewhat short and flabby frame, looked overly tight, ill-fitting and uncomfortable. When he saw the three dusty, sooty and grimy figures standing in front of Bostwick he frowned and said: "My God, Sergeant Major! Can't you run this place properly? Look at these men. They're a disgrace!"

No one said anything.

Bostwick now turned to the Major and said in a tight strained voice: "These men just came from Coventry. They've spent the first three days and nights of their hard-earned 7-day passes helping the people there. As a matter of fact they haven't had a chance to eat or sleep yet."

"These men were at Coventry?"

"That's right."

"Why didn't you tell me that?"

"I didn't know it until now."

"My God. These men are heroes!"

Bostwick's eyebrows quivered but he didn't say anything.

"All right. In that case I tell you what I'm going to do," Major Wilson said. "I want you to cancel their present 7-day passes and issue three new ones as of today. These men are real heroes and deserve a well-earned rest."

Bostwick nodded but his eyebrows still quivered.

The Long War

"Good," Major Wilson said and suddenly beamed at Dave, Red and Meyer before he turned to Bostwick again. "Now. Do you have anything for me, Sergeant Major?"

"Nothing, Major."

"Good. I have to see the Colonel. I'll see you later."

Bostwick nodded again and the Major left.

Bostwick watched him leave stonily and then turned to Dave, Red and Meyer who stood in front of him. "All right. Come into my office and give me your passes. I'll give you three new ones."

They all followed Bostwick into his office. They didn't say anything and after a while Bostwick turned to them: "All right. Come into my office and give me your passes. I'll give you three new ones."

Dave, Red and Meyer followed Bostwick into his office. They stopped in front of his large wooden desk and he went and sat down behind it. He took their old passes and gave them new ones. Then he motioned for them to go and when they had left his office, he suddenly sprang from his chair and came and stopped in front of them in the Orderly Room.

As he stopped there he turned to Meyer and said: "Now you listen to me, you sonofabitch! You're damn lucky to be in this Company and to have such good friends who are willing to go to bat for you and bail you out! But if you ever pull this stunt again I'll bust you! So help me God! I'll bust you so bad you won't even know what hit you! As a matter of fact I'll bust you so bad you'll wish you had never been born and had never gotten into this Regiment! Do you hear me!"

Meyer nodded and swallowed hard.

"Now get out! All of you get out! Before you make me sick!"

CHAPTER 73

Meyer quickly left the Orderly Room. He stepped out of it with Dave and Red and they moved toward their own barrack in order to get ready for their 7-day leave. As soon as they reached it they went in, showered, shaved and combed their hair. Then they changed into clean uniforms and took a taxi to the Aldershot Station. At the station they got on the 1.00 p.m. train to London and when they arrived at the Waterloo Station, they went and found lodgings in a nice rooming house on Cornwall Road. This rooming house wasn't far from the station and after they had spent most of the day sleeping, they got up and went to have a good evening meal in Soho. After the meal they headed to a pub in the Strand to have a few drinks and finally came back to their rooming house.

The next day, and in the days that followed, they spent their leave sightseeing, eating good meals, having some drinks at the Beaver Club and going to movies. They had quite a good time doing this and even picked up a few girls and went sightseeing with them. In fact the three of them hit it off so well Dave gave both Red and Meyer $20.00 each so they could have fun and enjoy their leave. This money, and the money it cost him for his week's lodging at the rooming house and the other money he spent in London and on the girls they picked up, took care of his remaining $100.00. But Dave didn't mind. After all what was money if not to be spent? Dave even went to see if Barbara was home and found out from her landlady she had indeed gone to Croydon and would be away for three weeks.

So Dave hung around with Red and Meyer and their leave went by pretty quickly. They had a really good time together and when they got back to Aldershot and to the center, a very strange period began for them, the Big Ten, the Company and the Regiment as a whole. Indeed, for the next 21 months, from late November 1940 to early August 1942, the Regiment trained and trained and trained and then trained again. They went on long route marches. They were involved in endless military exercises up and down Sussex, Surrey and Kent. They did cliff climbing in the quarries of those areas. They practiced assault landings on the South Coast. They took part in artillery shoots at Lark Hill and Salisbury Plain.

They were involved in all of these things and, during that time, passed on going to North Africa with the 51st Midlands Regiment in late December 1940. They passed on going to Greece in April 1941. They also passed on Spitsbergen in August of the same year. They didn't go on commando raids in Norway and in the Lofoten Islands in March and December of 1941. They didn't take part in commando raids in Bruneval and St. Nazaire in February and March of 1942. They didn't get involved in any of those things and it was during that long, endless and difficult time of training Dave wrote the Blues that was going to become the Blues of the Regiment and of the 1st Division as a whole. Dave wrote that Blues during those 21 months of training in the field. He worked at it and polished it. He cut it and improved it while they were between military exercises.

Dave thought the words and wrote the music and when he was finally able to launch it, they had gone on another military exercise with a British Unit, the 3rd Royal Grenadiers Regiment. This military exercise took place in early August 1942. At that time they had carried out some tactical maneuvers on the South Downs in Sussex with them. The exercise had gone on for over 10 days and they were now bivouacked with them near a place called Denton. This place was a few miles behind Waring where they had done all that checking and patrolling in late 1940. And it was there Dave launched his Blues. Dave launched it, as a matter of fact, on Friday evening, August 14, 1942. At that time, around 8.00 p.m., the Company was standing down for the night and resting quietly in a hollow of the rolling countryside.

The 3rd Royal Grenadiers Regiment was also standing down on their left flank. To the left of their hollow was a small wood where their 3/4-ton Platoon Truck was parked. The 3rd Royal Grenadiers Regiment was beyond this small wood. To their right stood some tall trees. In the clear, cool and sunlit evening their treetops were washed in a pale shimmering sunlight. As he sat on the grass with the Big Ten Dave thought it was a long time since he had seen such a magnificent evening. At that moment it was spreading before them and turning into a spectacular sunset that was reaching, sweeping and overrunning the South Downs. As Dave sat with the Big Ten and watched this magnificent and extraordinary evening slowly settling down all around them into a kind of pristine, dazzling and smoldering splendor, the talk, among some of them, turned to what they would like to do once the war was over.

Gennaro was the first one to speak and said: "Well, I'd sure like to become a millionaire."

"Why?" Dave asked.

"So that I could spend money. I love spending money."

Everyone laughed.

"What about you?" Dave turned to Red. "What would you like to do?"

"Me? I'd like to travel," Red said. "You know. See Europe on two tanks and two howitzers a day."

Everyone laughed again.

"What about you?" Dave turned to Lang. "What would you like to do?"

"Me?" Lang said. "I'd like to write a couple of books."

So this is what Lang wanted to do later on, Dave thought.

"What kinds of books?" Gennaro asked.

"Oh, a book on *The Philosophy Of History*," Lang said. "The other on *The History Of Philosophy*."

"Samey same, isn't it?" Red said.

"Not really," Lang said. "You see, the first one deals with the various movements in history and how one should always go in the opposite direction from where everyone else is going in order to keep a fair and decent balance in the overall historical development. The other deals with the growth and evolution of philosophy and how one should always try to go beyond one's culture, knowledge and limitations in order to be as far-reaching and all-embracing as possible."

"Wow!" Red said. "That's quite something!"

"You said it," Addams said.

"I'm sorry," Lang said. "But that's what I'd like to do."

"That's all right," Dave said and turned to Slav. "What about you? What would you like to do?"

"Oh, I'd like to stay where I am in Estevan," Slav said.

"Where's Estevan?"

"Near the Souris River. In Saskatchewan."

"What would you do there?"

"Oh, I'd farm, hunt and fish."

"I see."

"Maybe you should come and see me down there."

"Maybe I will," Dave said and turned from Slav and looked at Delorme. "What about you? What would you like to do?"

"In my case I think I'd like to look at *The Peoples' Question*," Delorme said.

"Why?"

"Lenin and Stalin couldn't crack it. I think I'd really like to get a go at it."

"I myself looked at it."

"Did you?"

"Sure. Lenin wanted to handle it peacefully. Stalin, brutally. It's quite interesting."

"You're telling me."

"Boy! That stuff's way too deep for me," Red said.

"Don't worry," Delorme said. "It's not going to kill you."

"That's for sure," Addams said.

"I agree," Mitchell said.

"What about you?" Higgins asked and turned to Dave. "What would you like to do."

"Me?" Dave said and also turned to Higgins. "I already told you."

"What?"

"I'd like to become an undertaker."

"Why?"

"In that line, you're never out of work."

Everyone laughed once more.

"Oh man," Gennaro said. "Another guy who'd like to make money."

"You bet," Dave said. "But what I'd really like to do right now has nothing to do with making money."

"Oh no?" Gennaro said.

"No," Dave said.

"What would you like to do?" Higgins asked.

"I'd like to have a guitar so I could play a Blues I just wrote," Dave said.

"You wrote a Blues?" Higgins said.

"Sure."

"Really?"

"I did."

"When?"

"Oh, during the time we've been training and going out on maneuvers," Dave said.

"I have a guitar," Red said.

"You do?" Dave said.

"Sure," Red said.

"Where did you get it?"

"I bought it from a soldier from the 3rd Royal Grenadiers when we were in Aldershot with them."

"How about that?"

"Isn't it something?"

"It sure is."

"Hell, the guy wanted money so bad he even threw in a harmonica."

"Where is this guitar?" Dave asked.

"Right here in the 3/4-ton Platoon Truck," Red said. "I'll go and get it. Then you can play for us."

CHAPTER 74

Dave nodded and Red got up and began heading toward the left of the hollow. He made for the small wood and moved toward their 3/4-ton Platoon Truck. When Red reached it he opened the tail gate and went in. In a little while he came out and began heading back toward them. He was holding the five-string guitar in his right hand and the harmonica in his left hand. When he reached Dave, Red bent and handed him the guitar. He gave the harmonica to Gennaro who asked to see it. Gennaro looked at it briefly and put it in the left breast pocket of his tunic. Red sat down on the right side of Dave and the rest of the Big Ten also came and sat down in a semi-circle around Dave.

When Dave got the five-string guitar from Red he stared at it for a moment and ran his right hand softly over it. He began strumming it and playing a few chords. Then he stopped and tuned it. Finally he began playing it again and running the chords higher and higher into an ever-increasing progression. Then he brought them down lower and lower into a thin filigree and let the Blues float almost on a flat straight line before he palmed the strings dead and said softly: *"The Guardhouse Blues."* As he said this Dave suddenly launched into it and began singing: *"Came to Merry Old England to get me a war / 'Stead found me pulled to graveyard guard duties / What's a man to do when there ain't no war / 'Cept standing around in the freezing boonies / Up and down the dark lonesome coast / Stringing wire, patrolling and checking ID's / All the time making sure you're at your post / Man oh man, this is giving me the willies."*

And, as Dave began getting deeper and deeper into the *Guardhouse Blues*, the Big Ten who were sitting down around him whooped and clapped their hands and yelled: "Yeah!" "Yeah!" "Go to it, my man!"

"Oh yeah!" "Go to it!" And as they whooped and clapped their hands and yelled Dave took the *Guardhouse Blues* higher and higher into such a level of fierceness, excitement and frenzy everything became, at the same time, order, precision and beauty, passion, rage and exhilaration, wildness, recklessness and ecstacy. He took them to a rare and not-too-often-given moment when, out of he struggle, pain and misery of life, everything became clear, obvious and amazingly simple, so that, in that magical and unexpected moment, confusion gave way to understanding, frustration to accomplishment, despair to optimism, anguish to serenity and hatred to love.

Then, as Dave went on and finished the *Guardhouse Blues*, he switched to other Blues. He began playing the *Working Man Blues*, the *Flop House Blues*, the *Lonesome Road Blues*, the *Boxcar Blues* and the *Thousand Miles Blues*. He even slipped into *Joual* and began singing *Le Bus Blues: "Quand j'en ai eu assez / De niaiser et d'faire le party / Quand j'voulais pu d'ma blonde / Et d'ces maudits mensonges / J'ai pris l'bus pour Détroit / Et j'ai flyé tout droit / Afin d'l'oublier / Et d'pu jamais y penser . . ."* And as Dave sang this Blues Gennaro whipped out Red's harmonica and began joining him and driving him and taking him up and up and up. As Gennaro drove him like this Dave realized with a shock how good he was with the harmonica and how well he himself was able to sing and play the guitar even though he hadn't been able to do that for over three years.

At the same time Slav suddenly jumped up in front of him and, bent to the knees, arms on his waist, legs kicking out, began dancing a Cossack dance. Slav danced it perfectly and stayed right on top of the beat. He pushed the rhythm even and brought to the dance such a stunning swiftness, grace and ease, in such a big man, it was truly an amazing thing to see. In fact, in its power, precision and beauty, this dance went all the way back to his grandfather in Warsaw and, beyond that, to his great grandfather in Kiev and, beyond that even, to his ancestors in the Wild Lands. And, as Slav danced, Dave kept on playing those Blues with power, precision and beauty. The Big Ten clapped their hands, whooped, sang and cheered. Slav moved, circled and kept on dancing in front of Dave and Gennaro stood right by him and pushed him and drove him.

Dave played all those Blues that way and when he was getting ready to take them to an even greater level of fierceness, excitement and frenzy, he suddenly heard Higgins say: "Hey! Someone's coming!" Sure enough, when Dave looked up from his guitar, he saw someone was coming down the hollow of the countryside. The figure coming down toward them was on their left flank. He was some way beyond the small wood where their

3/4-ton Platoon Truck was parked and as he got closer, Red said: "My God! It's Baldwin!" Captain Lawrence Baldwin was the tall, stringy, slightly austere and ascetic CO of B Company of the 3rd Royal Grenadiers Regiment. Baldwin had been assigned to work closely with their own CO, Major Wilson, on this military exercise they had been carrying out on the South Downs.

As a matter of fact all the officers of the 3rd Royal Grenadiers Regiment had been assigned to work closely with their own officers in the same way, for instance, their officers had worked with the officers of the 51st Midlands Regiment in the past. Baldwin was now coming toward them and heading for the small wood where their 3/4-ton Platoon Truck was parked. As soon as they saw him, in the fading yet still extremely clear light of evening, Dave and Gennaro suddenly stopped playing and gave their guitar and harmonica to Red. Red immediately took off at a flying run in order to go and put the guitar and harmonica back in their 3/4-ton Platoon Truck. Dave sat in the grass and watched Red as he ran in a crouch to their 3/4-ton Platoon Truck, put the guitar and harmonica in it, and ran back and came and sat down next to him.

In a while Baldwin reached the small wood, passed their 3/4-ton Platoon Truck and finally came and stopped in front of them. As he stopped he motioned with his right hand for them to stay where they were and said: "Ah, gentlemen. I see you were having quite a party."

"Not really, Sir," Dave said and looked up at him from where he was sitting. "We were just doing a little bit of singing."

"It sounded a great deal more than a little bit of singing to me."

"It wasn't, Sir," Red said and also looked up at Baldwin while he took in Dave. "We were just doing a little bit of harmony singing."

"Oh come, come now. I heard the guitar and the harmonica and you were doing a great deal more than just singing."

Everyone looked up at Baldwin and didn't say anything.

"You were playing, I believe, what the Americans call Blues."

Again everone looked up at Baldwin and didn't say anything.

"I must say you played them quite well. They were — what's the word? Oh yes. Quite raunchy."

"Yes, Sir. Quite raunchy," Dave said.

"They were, as a matter of fact, exceedingly down and dirty."

"Yes, Sir. Exceedingly down and dirty."

"The real mean and low-down thing, as it were."

"Yes, Sir. Just that."

"But now so much for those Blues and for all that singing," Baldwin said. "I believe it's time for you to stop."

Once more everyone looked up at Baldwin and didn't say anything.

"You see, gentlemen, you are going on a long-awaited and long-overdue action. Indeed, you are finally going to get a chance to tangle with Jerry in a big way."

Everyone stared at Baldwin and couldn't quite believe what they had heard.

"When?" Dave asked.

"Soon," Baldwin said.

"How soon?"

"Very soon."

"But how soon?"

"Very soon."

For a moment no one said anything and thought about what Baldwin had just said.

"That's why, gentlemen, you better stop playing all this music and get some rest. I don't think you'll get much of it from now on."

CHAPTER 75

Baldwin then stepped back and began walking away from them. He headed toward the small wood where their 3/4-ton Platoon Truck was parked and Dave watched him move in that direction. When Baldwin reached their 3/4-ton Platoon Truck and walked past it, Dave got up with the rest of the Big Ten and began heading back toward their position for the night. In the fading yet still extremely clear light of evening, close to 9.00 p.m., Dave walked slowly behind the Big Ten. Near the small wood where their Platoon Truck was parked, Dave stopped and took out a white sheet of paper folded in four from his left breast pocket. Dave spread out the sheet of paper. He held it in his hands and read what was written on it in block letters:

THE GUARDHOUSE BLUES

Came to Merry Old England to get me a war
'Stead found me pulled to graveyard guard duties
What's a man to do when there ain't no war
'Cept standing around in the freezing boonies

Up and down the dark lonesome coast
Stringing wire, patrolling and checking ID's
All the time making sure you're at your post
Man oh man, this is giving me the willies

England

For a soldier just wanting to come out and fight
And looking for this to really get in stride
Somehow all this standing around just ain't right
I mean, where's all the ranking drive and pride

In pulling guardhouse duties all over England
When all you want to do is come out and fight
In Merry Old England, yeah, Merry Old England
Where they just won't let you have that fight

Can't a man in them tough and funny times
Ever have what he wants and asks for
Without having to reach for it so fine
He turns out all bruised and so badly sore

In this sure funny and very strange war
There's no doubt a man just can't be a man
Unless he's willing to make it such a silly war
He ends up working hard at nothing for The Man

I mean, it's enough to give you a real bad case of the Blues
Having to pull graveyard guard duties all over England
I mean, I got some real bad low-down Guardhouse Blues
Oh yeah, pulling them graveyard guard duties all over England

Well, I must say it's a pretty damn good Blues, Dave thought as he looked at the white sheet of paper he was holding. In fact I must say it's really a great one. And I'm damn glad I was able to play and sing it. At least it's one thing I've been able to do in my life without other people or things coming into it and getting in the way. And it's a good thing I was able to do it now, Dave thought. Because I don't think I'll have much time to do it from now on. If Baldwin, who is never given to overstatement, says we're going to tangle with Jerry in a big way, then that's what we're going to do. And if that's what we're going to do, then I don't think we'll have much time for anything else. That's what I think. Oh yes indeed. That's what I think. Dave looked up from the white sheet of paper he was holding. He folded it in four again and put it back in his left breast pocket.

Then Dave walked back toward their position on the edge of the small wood. He checked with Norris and Moran and set up the various watches for the night. Finally, since he wasn't on any of those watches, Dave spread his groundsheet, lay down on it and went to sleep under the stars. He slept quite well and when he woke up early the next morning, he saw how right Baldwin had been. Bedford trucks had come to take them back to Aldershot. There were quite a few of them and later on that morning, when they were back in garrison, Dave saw something really big must be going on. They were given light Parade drills and their officers were nowhere to be seen. They had gone to their Company Headquarters where they were having a long meeting. Late in the afternoon when they finally saw them, and in the next couple of days, they had a busy and preoccupied look on their faces.

Then on Tuesday afternoon, August 18, 1942, they were taken by covered Bedford trucks to Portsmouth and put aboard the *Princess Louise*. This was a channel vessel that had been turned into an Infantry Assault Ship. All afternoon, while they were on board the *Princess Louise*, trucks full of soldiers, ammunition and equipment kept on coming into the port. The soldiers were put on the various Assault Ships and the ammunition and the equipment were loaded on those ships as well. Then, around 9.30 in the evening, they sailed from the port and cleared the Solent. They made for the Channel and as soon as they had left Portsmouth behind, Bostwick came on the troop deck with Major Wilson, the Platoon officers and Sergeants and they were told where they were going.

They were going for a surprise raid at Dieppe on the French coast. What they were going to do there was to make an unopposed landing at dawn, occupy some buildings on the west side of the harbor and attack a German Naval Headquarters building on the pier. They were also to try and get the German Naval Code Book and assault small crafts and E-Boats they might find in the harbor itself. Other Regiments would be involved in the attack on the main beach and on the flanks in order to secure the headlands on both sides of the town. On top of that a Tank Regiment would give them fire support and British Commandos would neutralize the coastal batteries. All of this would take place in the morning and they would sail back to England in early afternoon. For this operation the Regiment had been attached for support purposes to the 4th Infantry Brigade of the 2nd Canadian Division.

Their first two Companies, A and B, would be going in for the attack on the main beach on the eastern sector, the Red Beach, behind the Essex Scottish. Their three other Companies would be lying in reserve off the main beach with Les Fusiliers Mont-Royal Regiment and The Royal Marine Commandos. The Royal Hamilton Light Infantry Regiment would be in charge of the western sector, the White Beach, and would handle the attack in this sector. The whole operation would be backed by squadrons of light Boston bombers and fighters and some Flying Fortresses. It would

England

also involve seven Fleet-Class destroyers, escort vessels, beach support crafts and naval motor launches. They would be facing at Dieppe a Defense Force of about 3000 men and this Defense Force was expected to give them little trouble.

It was made up of the 302nd Infantry Division, which was considered quite a low-grade Division, the 571st Regiment, which was guarding the eastern and western headlands of the town, and the 10th Panzer Division, which was believed to be in Amiens 60 miles away. However, as Major Wilson outlined the operation to them and went over the details, Dave began feeling very uneasy. This operation was, in fact, almost exactly like one they had nearly done in early July. That one had been canceled at the last minute due to bad weather. In that one, like the present one, about 6000 men had been involved. But, since it had been canceled and since the men had been returned to their various camps, Dave wondered how smart it was to put on the same operation twice and if the Germans would be waiting for them. Dave tried not to think about that and went over the maps and photographs that were passed around.

Dave memorized his own part in the operation and, once he had checked his gear, put his combat pack against the bulwark and lay down on the troop deck against it. Around him the Big Ten did the same thing. As he got ready to settle down for the trip across Dave saw what a beautiful evening it was. When they had first sailed from Portsmouth it had been in a warm and brilliant sunlight. Now, as darkness fell across the Channel, the sky was clear and the stars were high and bright overhead. The sea was smooth and there was only the slightest of breezes blowing. The *Princess Louise* sailed on to get into formation with the other ships and head for their pre-arranged course toward the French coast. After a while it slipped through a sprawling and floating mine field swept by trawlers up ahead and went on.

By that time a white and grayish haze had settled over the Channel. The sea was smooth and some time later the moon came out. When he saw this Dave leaned against his combat pack. He closed his eyes and tried to get some sleep. He felt a cool and pleasant breeze against his face but couldn't do it. In the darkness, once he opened his eyes again and got used to it, Dave could vaguely make out the shadows of various ships all around and was too wound up to be able to sleep. So he lay there on the troop deck and didn't move and around 1.00 o'clock in the morning, a buzzer sounded and they were ordered to their Landing Crafts. In no time they got into theirs and were swung over the ship in davit cables and slowly lowered into the sea.

Then they were cut loose and began heading away from the *Princess Louise* which had now stopped and dropped anchor. It seemed to Dave they kept on circling in the darkness for quite a while before they were able to get into formation and head for the Assault Fleet. By then they were about 10 miles from the French coast. After a while their Landing Craft linked up with other Landing Crafts and formed into two columns of three boats each. Those boats carried their two Assault Companies, A and B, and their boat was the first one on the right side of the formation. Then, when they were properly formed, they turned and began making for the rest of the Assault Fleet. They headed for the French coast and in their craft nobody spoke. In a way it was the same thing as when the *Princess Louise* had sailed to their drop off point in strict radio silence.

Dave looked briefly at his watch and, for the run in, could practically see all their Landing Crafts. The stars were sparkling in the night sky. The sea was a shimmering silver. And their boats were leaving a white phosphorescent wake as they plowed through the waters. So far Dave saw everything had gone on without a hitch. And he knew, if they kept on like this, they were right on target for their scheduled landing at Red Beach.

CHAPTER 76

They kept on heading toward Red Beach and when they were seven or eight miles from Dieppe, things began to change. Suddenly, around 4.00 o'clock in the morning, tracer bullets flashed in the night on their port side. The tracer bullets showed as white and light blue dots against the darkness and the savage hammering of automatic guns was heard. When the firing began everyone kept their heads down behind the steel bulwarks of their Landing Craft as more tracer bullets swept across ahead of them. Some of those tracers bounced off their steel plates and some seemed to come from other directions as well. Then they saw a big flash and heard the boom of gunfire as they spotted one of their destroyers racing from the starboard side.

The destroyer was rushing toward the area where those tracers were coming from and firing a dozen rounds in that direction. As it rushed past them their whole formation slowed down and the close pattern of the two attack columns suddenly broke up. Everyone began drifting around out of formation and it took quite a while before they were able to regroup and look for the Assault Fleet of the Essex Scottish in order to get in behind it. By that time Dave was becoming extremely uneasy since it was getting light and since they still hadn't linked up with the Assault Fleet. Their whole plan was based on landing before daylight in order to have the element of surprise. If they came in after daylight the element of surprise would be gone and the Germans would be waiting for them.

Just then they heard the dull throbbing of bombers flying high overhead and beginning to bomb the Dieppe area as German anti-aircraft guns began firing at them from Dieppe itself. At the same time searchlights began crisscrossing the sky and aiming toward the area where the bombers were making their run. In no time the whole area in front of Dieppe became a spectacular sight of crisscrossing searchlights, racing tracer bullets, gunfire, colored lights, flashes and bomb bursts whose quick-spreading and deafening noises rolled out into the Channel. By then they were a couple of miles from the shore. From the red navigational light at the end of the long stone pier Dave could see they had drifted a mile off course from their beach. As a result they began heading west in order to line themselves up behind the Assault Fleet of the Essex Scottish which they could now see in the growing light.

The Fleet was ahead of them on their right and as they began heading for it, they couldn't quite link up. They cut in behind a column of crafts heading for the beach and found they were in the middle of a formation of Calgary tanks also going in to Red Beach. They moved in behind this column of tanks and at precisely 5.20 a.m. saw the first Landing Crafts carrying the Essex Scottish touch down on Red Beach. At the same time, just ahead of them, several squadrons of cannon-firing Hurricanes flew over the beach. Quite a few of the planes had their wheels down in order to slow their speed and improve their aim in firing at their targets on the beach, the Promenade and the houses fronting the sea. It was now daylight and Dave saw the Calgary tanks which were supposed to land on the beach at the same time as the Essex Scottish in order to give them fire support were late.

They were still heading there and were about 10 minutes late. In the circumstances the Air Force began laying smoke over the beach and over the headlands while out at sea the seven destroyers were firing hundred of shells into the buildings along the front of the town. As their formation was heading for the beach several fountains of water began bursting around their Landing Crafts and quite a few German guns seemed to be firing directly at them from the main beach. At this point a wave of white grayish smoke swept over the beach and blanketed everything. When it thinned out Dave saw some tanks had landed. The Calgary Regiment was using heavily-armored 40-ton Churchill tanks with new six-pounder guns. At that moment one of them had made it to the middle of the beach before it was hit by artillery.

When it was hit it began burning slowly. Its black billowing smoke began rising in the clear early-morning light as two others made it to the sea wall. They disappeared around the eastern end of it and got on the Promenade. By now it was their turn to go in. Their Landing Craft headed for the beach and when it came in, the ramp went down. Dave jumped out with the Big Ten and took in everything swiftly: the beach obstacles in front of him; beyond those obstacles the tank burning slowly on the pebble and shingle beach slightly to his left; beyond the tank the sea wall about 60 yards from the beach; on his right the tobacco factory burning fiercely; further away on his right the huge, sprawling and partially-demolished Casino; and between the tobacco factory and the Casino the running and crouching figures of soldiers from the Royal Hamilton Light Infantry Regiment who were landing on their right on the western end of the beach.

Dave took in all this swiftly and when he came barreling out of the Landing Craft behind the Big Ten, three soldiers from the 3rd Section of his Platoon suddenly jumped in front of him as they hit the beach and ran past the beach obstacles. When they hit the beach machine gun fire, which was raking it and which seemed to be everywhere, suddenly cut them down. Dave heard them scream and go down in front of him. They had been hit at the waist and their blood shockingly splashed the beach as they went sprawling down on it. As he saw this Dave cut sharply to the right past them and ran in a crouch at an angle toward the sea wall. Small arms and machine gun bullets splashed around him. Pebble and shingle fragments flew everywhere and he heard deep within himself the sounds of his pounding heart and the gasps of his straining breath as he closed in on and then slammed into the sea wall.

No sooner had Dave hit the wall than a soldier slammed into it behind him and said: "What's going on?" "Who knows," Dave said. "I've got to find out," the soldier said. In a moment, before Dave could do anything about it, he raised himself carefully to look over the sea wall only to moan softly and slide down slowly next to him. Dave looked at him and saw he had a neat bullet hole through his forehead. A small soldier, with a helmet so big it seemed to come down over his ears, also stared at the dead soldier. This small soldier was crouching ahead of Dave and said: "We've got to do something. We've really got to do something." Then, without warning, he suddenly pulled a little away from the wall and began running alongside it. He headed east only to be cut down swiftly by machine gun fire. Three other soldiers to the right of Dave also pulled away from the wall to run east and were cut down.

At that moment another wave of white grayish smoke swept over the beach. When it cleared Dave saw three other tanks had landed on it. The first one was spinning and skidding and slowly came up the beach. Its six-pounder gun was firing and near the sea wall it turned left and headed east alongside it. At the eastern end of the wall it turned right and disappeared on the Promenade. When it did a small group of soldiers near the end of the eastern sea wall jumped up and ran behind it until they too disappeared on the Promenade. The other two tanks which were coming up were now close to the burning tank. They were on each side of it and their treads were spinning and skidding. On the pebble and shingle beach the tanks didn't seem to be able to get good traction and suddenly both of them threw a track and stopped, close to and a little behind the burning tank.

With their tracks off the tanks stood on the beach and kept on firing to give support to the soldiers until they too were hit by artillery fire. When they were hit they began burning slowly and their black billowing smoke began mingling with the somewhat thinning smoke of the first burning tank. At the wall Dave watched those tanks burn on the beach and the noise around him was absolutely incredible. Small arm, machine-gun and artillery fire was going on everywhere and through gaps in the black billowing smoke Dave could see the Big Ten. They were crouching, running in and out of the burning tanks and firing their rifles and machine guns. There were also other soldiers crouching behind the tanks and firing since the Churchills were so heavily-armored they were able to shelter them against most of the artillery coming down on the beach.

Dave stayed at the wall and watched those burning tanks. After a while, when the smoke began to thin out, he saw Bostwick was looking for him. Bostwick was behind the first burning tank and when he saw him, he waved frantically with his right hand for Dave to come and join him.

CHAPTER 77

At the wall Dave watched Bostwick wave at him. But he couldn't go and join him. He was about 70 yards from the first burning tank and at an angle from it. He knew in this incredibly heavy fire he wouldn't be able to go five feet before being shot. Dave motioned with his right hand he was too far and couldn't do it. Bostwick then pointed to the wall behind the burning tank. At this point Dave would only be 30 yards from the tank. But the Germans knew that too. And by now they were sweeping that area with murderous fire and turning it into a real killing ground. Three soldiers who were facing the burning tank, however, were willing to try it. They were talking among themselves and pointing to it.

Then, when another wave of white grayish smoke swept over the beach, they suddenly sprang up and began running toward it. The wave of white grayish smoke hovered over the beach and blanketed everything for a while. When it lifted Dave saw the three soldiers that had sprung up from the wall were now lying on the beach halfway to the burning tank and their bodies were riddled with bullets. By that time, with the wave of smoke thinning out and clearing the beach, Dave turned and saw a Landing Craft coming toward them. The Landing Craft was heading for a spot on the beach right in front of the three burning tanks. It was coming in either to take the men out of the burning tanks and bring them back to England or to possibly land them somewhere else on the beach.

When it came to a stop its ramp went down and several soldiers from behind the three burning tanks made a run for it. When they bolted Bostwick, who stood behind the first burning tank, waved frantically at Dave to come and join him. Then he began running slowly backward and still motioning to Dave. As he was running backward he was suddenly hit on the left shoulder and spun around. A thin sudden streak of blood flew out of his shoulder. His helmet also flew off and he was grabbed from behind by Slav. He was rushed into the Landing Craft and was followed by the rest of the Big Ten and other soldiers who came barreling in behind them. The ramp of the Landing Craft went up and it slipped back out. It turned slowly and began heading out into the Channel past huge fountains of water bursting around it.

Then it was gone and they were alone on the beach. And, as another soldier came and slammed into the wall behind him, Dave saw his face below his helmet was grim, square-jawed and dead-set. Dave looked at him for a moment and then heard the mortars. He had heard them before of course. They had been coming down on them savagely all morning. But now on the western side of the wall, on his right, Dave saw one go long on the pebble and shingle beach. Another one went short on the Promenade. A third one landed right on top of the wall. Almost at the same time Dave saw one go long right behind him. Then he heard another one go short on the Promenade. He didn't hear the third one go off right behind him. When the mortar landed several fragments tore into his back.

One fragment especially hit him deep to the right side of his back near his shoulder blade. When this fragment hit him Dave screamed and dropped his rifle. He shuddered and found himself going down on his knees. His neck was bent and his head, with his helmet on, rested against the wall. For a moment everything went out of him. Then it came back on again. Dave stood against the wall. He was breathless and moaning and a strange feeling came over him. He felt alone with himself and oblivious of everyone and everything. Also every time he took a breath it seemed to cut deeply inside of him and hurt him. As a result Dave only took small breaths and tried to remain very small within himself and not breathe too much. After a while those small breaths began to have a burning and corroding edge to them and Dave used all his concentration to breathe as slowly and evenly as possible.

By now Dave felt faint and light-headed and seemed to be in a numb, semi-conscious, weirdly-detached state. In the circumstances Dave simply stood close to the wall on his knees. His head, with his helmet on, rested against it and he completely lost track of time and of everything around him. In the silence within himself that wasn't really a silence Dave could hear the noises of small arm, machine-gun and artillery fire. With the smarting of his eyes he could feel the waves of smoke sweeping over the beach from time to time. From the jumping, rushing and pounding around him he could feel the presence of soldiers slamming in and out of the sea wall. The warmth on his shoulders told him it was a bright and sunny day with a very nice light breeze.

Dave could sense and feel these things. But he could sense and feel them in an oddly muted and far-off way and after a while, it suddenly grew quiet on the beach and there was no more firing. By then Dave opened his eyes and saw a young German Captain with a Platoon of German soldiers behind him. The young Captain had his gun drawn and the soldiers were holding their rifles in front of them. They were coming from the western end of the harbor and had turned west along the sea wall. They were looking around carefully and moving along the sea wall. Dave waited until they were quite close and almost alongside of him. When the young Captain was only a few feet away Dave pushed himself from the wall. He grinned and cocked his right hand at him in the form of a pistol. He pulled the imaginary trigger with his finger and fell face down on the pebble and shingle beach.

BOOK SIX

ACROSS THE CHANNEL

CHAPTER 78

Dave didn't stay on the pebble and shingle beach very long. After a while he felt himself being roughly picked up by two German soldiers and put face down on a stretcher. When those two soldiers picked him up Dave screamed from the pain in his back. The two German soldiers dropped him on the ground and Dave heard the young German Captain rush back and bawl them out. As soon as the Captain had finished the two soldiers picked him up again and carried him along the sea wall. They headed east and turned south at the harbor where they went on toward the town of Dieppe itself. By then Dave found himself in shock and was only vaguely aware of what was going on around him.

Dave was slowly going in and out of himself all the time and some time later found he was lying on his stretcher on the grass in front of a large building in the town. All kinds of badly-wounded and not-so-badly-wounded officers, NCOs and soldiers were lying on the grass in front of that building. Some were screaming. Others were moaning. Most were lying on the grass and waiting to be looked at. German doctors and orderlies were moving among them and checking them out. After a while it was Dave's turn to be looked at. The German doctor bent over him and raised the back of his tunic and his shirt. He checked his back slowly and intently and put some bandages on it which he fastened tightly. Then he lowered the back of his tunic and his shirt and wrote something on a tag which he put around his right ankle.

Then the doctor was gone and a little later Dave's stretcher was lifted again. This time he was carried gently to an ambulance parked in the street in front of the grass where the officers, NCOs and soldiers were lying. The ambulance Dave was taken to was quite big. It was set up to take five stretchers carrying wounded on each side of it. Dave's stretcher was on the left side. It was the fourth one from the floor and when it was full, the Germans closed the doors. The ambulance left and they turned right on a narrow street. They turned right on another narrow street and after a while turned left and drove along a straight road that seemed to be heading south. The ambulance picked up speed and Dave moaned and groaned as they bounced along the road. He was still slowly going in and out of himself and took small breaths in order to try and remain very small within himself.

Dave tried to breathe as little as possible and looked at the sunlight streaming through the two square windows and playing on the walls of the ambulance. He tried to concentrate on this and quite some time later became aware the ambulance was slowing down, turning left and coming to a stop. The doors of the ambulance were opened and his stretcher was taken out by two German orderlies. They took it through the wide entrance door of a hospital and up a long winding marble staircase. At the top of the staircase they took it through another wide entrance door to the left of the staircase and not far from it. They carried it down a long narrow hallway until they came to a large disinfectant-smelling room to the left of the hallway. The room was bathed in a white, bluish, silvery glare and there was a cold, hard, steel table right in the middle of it.

Three doctors wearing surgical gloves, white masks and white smocks were standing around it and waiting for the German orderlies to slide Dave off his stretcher and onto the cold, hard, steel table on his stomach. As soon as he was on the table one of the masked doctor removed his tunic, shirt and undershirt and another one put a rubber mask on Dave's face. Almost immediately Dave found himself breathing deeply and raspingly through the mask and after a while the white, bluish, silvery glare of the room began growing bigger and bigger so it seemed to be all around him, in him, and the only thing in the room. By then Dave felt things were being done to his back. He felt an odd rubbery sensation as if a large scissor was cutting deeply into his back. Then this sensation gave way to another odd rubbery one as if someone was massaging it.

Not long after Dave had the numbing and weirdly-detached impression of feeling a thousand pinpricks. Those pinpricks were followed by a throbbing rubbery itching which, in turn, gave way to a deep and soundless darkness. This darkness went on for quite a long time and when Dave woke up and opened his eyes, he found himself lying in a bed on the floor at the top of the long winding marble staircase. The sun was pouring through the wide entrance door below and when he looked at his watch, he saw it was close to 10.00 o'clock in the morning. Dave was wearing pale-blue cloth pajamas and his upper body was wrapped tightly in white bandages. He rose slowly on his elbows and took in everything around him: the long winding marble staircase that ran all the way down to the ground floor on both sides of the entrance; the doctors, nurses, patients, German officers, NCOs and soldiers that kept coming in and out of doors on that floor; the long row of beds that also ran around the staircase on the second floor; the big round cement column with steel pegs that was not that far from the staircase and that was hung with wooden crutches, white doctors' coats, caps, masks, stethoscopes, pale-green surgical cotton tops and slacks and, at the bottom of it, white sneakers.

Dave also saw his uniform and boots were lying on top of a small locker at the foot of his bed. His bed was the third from the top of the staircase and the boy on his left had his face and arms wrapped up in white bandages. The boy in the first bed was lying still and, from the way the white and blue cloth blankets were lying on him, seemed to be missing a leg. The big round cement column was right after this boy and the boy on his right was lying in bed and also looking around. In his case, with the white and blue blankets lying over him, it was hard to tell what was wrong with him. The boy was small and wiry and had thick wavy red hair. His face was heavily freckled and he had clear piercing blue eyes that were looking around and taking in everything going on.

It was this fact, more than anything else, and the realization he looked a great deal like Red, that made Dave raise himself even more and turn to the right toward him.

CHAPTER 79

Dave leaned toward the boy and said: "Where am I?"

"You're at the *Hôpital Sacré Coeur*."

"Where?"

"In Rouen."

"They brought us to Rouen?"

"That's right. The hospitals are full. I understand they put the first bunch of soldiers at the *Hôpital Charles Nicolle*; then at the *Hôtel Dieu*; and now here at the *Hôpital Sacré Coeur*."

"How do you know this?"

"I heard one of the French doctors talk to one of the nurses."

"Do you speak French?"

"Not really. Just a little bit."

Dave raised himself even more and looked at the boy again: "I know you're going to think this is crazy. What day is it?"

"It's Thursday morning."

Dave nodded and the boy said: "I saw them bring you in yesterday afternoon. They took you straight to the Operating Room and you must have been under ever since."

"What about you? When did they bring you in?"

"Some time before you. But they operated on me later than you in the afternoon and when I came to in the evening, you were still under."

"What's wrong with you?"

"I got shot right through the left thigh," the boy said and pushed the white and blue blankets away from him. He opened his pale-blue pajamas and showed him the cast that ran from his upper thigh to just below his knee.

Across The Channel

Dave looked at the cast and told the boy what kind of wounds he had. Then, as the boy closed his pajamas and put the white and blue blankets back over him, Dave said: "What outfit are you in?"

"The Westmount Fusiliers."

"Are you kidding!"

"No."

"That's incredible! That's the outfit I'm with!"

"Go on."

"It's true! I'm with B Company."

"I'm with A Company."

"How about that."

"I must tell you," the boy said, "we took tremendous casualties."

"So did we," Dave said.

"That was some Operation."

"That's for sure."

"The people who put this on should be shot."

"And how!"

"They said it was going to be a piece of cake. Hell, that was some piece of cake, all right!"

"You're telling me!"

"It's amazing some of us even survived."

"You're not kidding. But tell me. What's your name?"

"Billy Smith."

Dave gave Billy his name and then said: "Listen. When you came in, did you notice what was on the other side of the wide entrance door down below?"

"Sure."

"What's on the other side?"

"There's just a courtyard with a semi-circular driveway."

"Is there a gate leading to this courtyard?"

"There is."

"Is this gate guarded?"

"I don't know."

"What do you mean you don't know?"

"Well, when we were coming to the entrance, one of the soldiers in the ambulance started to yell and piss blood all over the place. So I didn't really notice."

"But there's a courtyard with a semi-circular driveway leading to the wide entrance door below?"

"There is."

"That's good."

"Why are you asking me all this?"

Dave leaned a little bit more toward the boy and said: "I'm going to break out from here."

"Are you serious?"

"I am."

"When?"

"Now."

"Right now!"

"That's it."

"Are you crazy! You won't make it past the entrance door."

"Sure I will. Now's the best time to do it."

"Why?"

"Look at it this way. Right now everything's disorganized. This hospital is filled with wounded soldiers. I'll just walk through the front door."

"How? They won't let you walk out in your pajamas."

"You see the big cement column near the staircase?"

"Sure."

"You see what's hanging on it?"

"Sure. Crutches, doctors' coats, masks and all that stuff. So what?"

"I'm going to dress like a doctor and walk out. That's how."

"But you're wounded and just got operated on. You might not be strong enough."

"That's what they think. That's why I'm going to do it."

"What if you don't have the strength?"

"Don't worry. I'll have the strength."

"What if you don't?"

"Don't worry. I will. And I'll even take you with me."

"Oh no! Not me! My leg hurts like hell! And I don't think I can stand on it."

"Sure you can."

"No I can't! If you want to do it, then you'll have to do it on your own."

"You're sure?"

"I'm sure."

"Now is the time to do it. We won't get another chance like that."

"I know that. But if you want to do it, then you'll have to do it on your own."

"Well okay, then. In that case, I'll see you, Billy."

"Sure. See you."

CHAPTER 80

Dave sat up in bed and pulled his blankets aside. He swung over to the left side of the bed and put his feet down on the floor. Then he stood up and headed for the big cement column. He walked quite stiffly and carefully and when he reached it, he grabbed a white doctor's coat, a pale-green top and and pale-green slacks, and bent down to pick up a pair of white sneakers. When he bent down to pick up the sneakers he felt a sharp stabbing pain on the right side of his back near his shoulder blade and numbing burning pinpricks in his back. Dave straightened up slowly. He tried to walk steadily and carefully and when he got back to his bed, he found he was completely out of breath.

Dave got in under the two blankets and changed slowly into doctor's clothes. When he had gotten into those clothes Dave got out of bed again and put the blankets over his pale-blue pajamas. Then he turned and gave the thumbs up sign to Billy. Billy returned the sign and Dave turned from him. He left his bed and began heading toward the staircase. Dave walked stiffly and carefully and when he reached it, he found he was was sweating profusely. The distance from his bed to the staircase was only about 80 feet and yet when he got there, he found he was breathing heavily and there were dark spots dancing before his eyes. At the top of the staircase Dave stopped and stood there. Oh man, he thought. This is bad. This is very bad. I don't feel well. I don't feel well at all. What the hell am I thinking of in trying to get out of this place when I've just been operated on. Am I crazy? Or out of my mind? Or what?

Dave turned and began walking back slowly toward his bed. By now he was feeling so dizzy he kept his eyes on the floor in order not to pass out and fall down. He walked stiffly and carefully and when he had almost reached it, he looked up and saw the German doctor. He was wearing a white coat over his military uniform and was standing at the foot of his bed. His arms were folded over his chest and he was staring at Dave. He was a tall trim man in his early fifties and had close-cropped gray hair. When Dave saw him he smiled slightly at him and began heading in his direction. He walked stiffly and carefully and when he got close to him, he saw the twin silver flashes and three silver runes of an SS Captain on the black collar of his uniform.

Dave walked all the way back to him and when he reached him, the SS doctor fixed him with a cold hard stare and said in a surprisingly good English: "Ah. *Mein herr.* You weren't trying to escape by any chance, weren't you?"

"Me? Escape? Of course not."

"What were you doing?"

"I was just taking a walk."

"Dressed as a doctor?"

"I was feeling a little chilly."

"In August?"

"That's right."

"How interesting."

"It's probably the operation that made me feel like that."

"Probably."

"That's why I put on those clothes."

"I see."

"But I'm feeling much better now."

"Are you, now."

"I am."

"That's good."

"I really am. That little walk did me a lot of good."

"I'm glad to hear that. Because, to tell you the truth, you don't look too well."

"I don't?"

"No. You don't," the SS doctor said and reached out and rubbed his right hand behind Dave's back. When he pulled it out it was smeared with blood. "I think that little walk of yours was quite a bit more than what you bargained for."

"You may be right."

"And it was also quite silly."

"You may be right there too."

"Of course I'm right," the SS doctor said and suddenly turned and barked in German: "Orderlies!"

At that moment two tall thin-faced orderlies rushed out of the wide entrance door leading to the Operating Room.

"Get a stretcher and bring this soldier to the Operating Room!"

CHAPTER 81

The two orderlies rushed back behind the wide entrance door. In a moment they came out with a long rubber-wheeled steel stretcher and put Dave face down on it. Once Dave was on the stretcher they began taking him to the large disinfectant-smelling room where he had been before. The SS doctor followed them and when they got to that room, he made a short call on the wall phone to the right of the entrance. By then the two orderlies had slid Dave onto the cold, hard, steel table right in the middle of it and not long after, two other doctors in white coats also came into the room and took their places on both sides of the SS doctor. The three of them put on a white mask and white surgical gloves.

Then the SS doctor looked at the doctor on his right and that doctor reached out and put a rubber mask on Dave's face. Soon Dave found himself breathing deeply and raspingly into the mask and was filled with the white, bluish, silvery glare in the room and that seemed, once more, to be all around him, in him, and the only thing in the room. Like the last time Dave felt an odd rubbery sensation as if a large scissor was cutting deeply into his back; then as if someone was massaging it; and finally a thousand pinpricks which turned, after a while, into a throbbing rubbery itching that gave way to a deep and soundless darkness. The darkness went on for a long time and when Dave woke up and opened his eyes, he saw the sun was shining through the wide entrance door below, but in a deep, blazing and smoldering way.

By now Dave was feeling so sick and exhausted that, after he had turned to his right and found out from Billy it was almost 6.00 o'clock in the evening, he lay in bed and thought about his situation. He was sick. He was wounded. It was no time for him to try and escape and do things

Across The Channel

that were way beyond his strength. No. What he had to do right now was stay in bed and get his strength back. This was what he had to do. So Dave did that. He lay in bed and did whatever the SS doctor ordered. However, as he let his shrapnel wounds heal, he noticed one thing. Ever since his attempted escape the Germans had posted two armed sentries at the top of the staircase. They were stationed on each side of it. Still this didn't bother Dave and he kept on lying in bed and taking care of his wounds.

During that time Dave became a model patient. With the help of Lise, a tall slim blonde nurse who was drawn to him and who helped him get an idea of the layout of Rouen, he was able to fake the seriousness of his wounds and stretch his stay at the hospital to a full six weeks. By then Dave was pretty strong and healthy and wasn't that unhappy when he and several other patients, including Billy whose left thigh had now completely healed, were ordered to leave the hospital for a prisoners of war camp in Germany. Thirty of them were ordered to do so and Dave found out from Lise they were going to be taken there from the Gare Rive Gauche. These were the German orders and on Thursday, October 1, 1942, they were carried out. A little after 1.00 o'clock that afternoon, after a long leisurely lunch in the hospital dining room on the second floor, they were taken down the long winding marble staircase to the courtyard outside.

They had put on their uniforms and combat boots and outside in the courtyard, right in front of the entrance, three Wehrmacht trucks with their tarpaulins down had come to take them to the train station. It was a bright clear sunny day and when they stepped out in the courtyard, they were lined in three groups of ten. Each group was put in one of the trucks with four German soldiers. Two of the soldiers sat next to the tailgate and two of them in the cab of the truck. However, in Dave's truck a German Lieutenant sat next to the tailgate with a soldier. When Dave was put in the first truck with Billy he whispered to him what he wanted him to do. Billy nodded and Dave made sure he sat on the left side of the truck next to the tailgate. He had to sit next to the Lieutenant and face Billy and the soldier on the other side.

The tailgate tarpaulin was rolled up and left open and there were two motorcycles with sidecars escorting the convoy. One would ride at the front of it and the other would be at the back. A Lieutenant rode in each sidecar and a soldier drove each motorcycle. Then, when the three groups were put in the trucks, they started and were on their way. The convoy drove out of the semi-circular driveway and through the front entrance gate that had two armed sentries inside of it and two others outside. Then they turned right on the Rue St-André and drove a short while before they slowed down and got on the Boulevard de la Marne. They headed west on the boulevard until they reached the Place Cauchoise. Past the Place Cauchoise they headed south on the Boulevard des Belges and when they slowed down in the traffic near the Rue Anatole France and nearly came to a stop, Dave looked at Billy.

Billy nodded and Dave suddenly jumped up and rushed for the tailgate. When he jumped up Billy also leapt in front of the German soldier who sat next to him. He made as if to grab Dave and said: "Hey! What are you doing! What the hell are you doing!" Almost at the same time Dave rushed for the tailgate and struggled to get away from the Lieutenant who had also sprung up and was trying to stop him. Both of them struggled and wrestled until Dave accidentally hit him hard across the face. This staggered the Lieutenant and Dave jumped clear from the tailgate and began running across the Boulevard des Belges. He ran into the Rue Anatole France and wanted to get away from the motorcycle escort leading the convoy. There were shouts and rifle shots. Dave came barreling down the Rue Anatole France and turned right on the Rue de Fontenelle.

Dave ran south toward the Quai du Havre and the River Seine. His heart was pounding and he was gasping. He wanted to get to the Port area and lose himself in the Gare Routière. He rushed past the stunned and startled looks of passersby and onlookers. He ran in and out of wood-burning cars called gazogènes, vélo-taxis, horse-drawn carts and bicycles. He kept on going and was about half-way down the Rue de Fontenelle when the motorcycle escort leading the convoy came barreling up that Rue, having turned left on it from the Quai du Havre. When Dave saw the escort he turned back and began running north on the Rue de Fontenelle. He heard the shouts *"Halt! Halt!"* and felt a couple of pistol shots whistle past his head. By then he was aware of the motorcycle escort gaining on him until it was almost behind him.

As Dave turned and ran backward a little the motorcycle was almost right on top of him and followed him. Then the Lieutenant in the sidecar jumped out and waved at him with his Luger. He marched angrily toward him and yelled: *"Hände hoch! Hände hoch!"* Dave looked at him and slowly put up his hands.

CHAPTER 82

The Lieutenant watched Dave carefully and motioned with his Luger for him to begin walking north on the Rue de Fontenelle. Dave turned and began walking ahead of him and then turned once more and headed west on the Rue Anatole France. The Lieutenant marched behind him and the motorcycle escort brought up the rear. Dave walked with his hands up and when they reached the Boulevard des Belges, he saw the three trucks had come and stopped by the curb past the Rue Anatole France. The German soldiers were out of the trucks and guarding the prisoners with their rifles. A small crowd had gathered on the pavement and was watching the trucks.

The young Lieutenant Dave had hit hard when trying to escape was standing with a soldier. He had his handkerchief out and was wiping blood from a cut on his left upper lip. Dave crossed the Avenue des Belges and was followed by the Lieutenant and the motorcycle escort. He made for the pavement where the three trucks had stopped. As soon as he reached it the young Lieutenant he had hit hard in the face suddenly whipped out his Luger and rushed him. He began hitting Dave with his pistol and kicking him and was joined by the soldier who had been with him and by another soldier. When this happened the Lieutenant who had brought Dave back and a couple of other soldiers jumped in and managed to stop the beating. They made Dave sit down on the curb with his hands on top of his head and the Lieutenant who had brought him back ran into a café to make a phone call.

The Lieutenant was gone for a while and when he came back, they didn't have to wait long before they saw a big black Renault gazogène burst into the Boulevard des Belges and come and screech to a stop not far from where Dave was sitting. The rear doors of the gazogène flew open and two big muscular men rushed out. They had huge clean-shaven heads and massive bull necks and wore black leather jackets and black pants. One was slightly taller than the other and they rushed to the young Lieutenant Dave had hit hard in the face and to the Lieutenant who had made the phone call. They talked with both of them for a while and then grabbed Dave and rushed him into the car. They slammed the doors shut and the thin scrawny driver who also wore a black leather jacket and black pants made a sharp U-turn.

The car began speeding up the Boulevard des Belges and in no time they turned right on a side street and headed east toward the center of Rouen. They kept on speeding east and drove past the Cathédrale. Then they turned right on what Dave could see was the Rue de la République before they turned left on the Avenue Aristide Briand and kept on heading east. Soon they left Rouen behind and drove by medium-sized farms, forests and meadow lands. In the distance they saw a castle, an abbey, then a manor house glinting in the sunlight. After a while they picked up speed and drove past small and not-so-small towns like Pont St. Pierre, Les Andelys, Tourny, Ambleville and Aincourt. They drove swiftly and steadily and past Meulan, Paris began looming in the distance.

They kept on heading toward it and around 5.00 o'clock in the afternoon, they reached it through Poissy. They drove east through the Porte de Neuilly and in the bright, clear and sunny afternoon, Dave saw how harsh, grim and forbidding Paris looked. Up ahead he could see the Eiffel Tower. It had a black, white and red Swastika flying from its mast. The Swastika was also flying from hotels, public buildings and apartment houses occupied by the Germans. All the wide streets, boulevards and avenues looked empty. There were no buses and taxis. There were a few wood-burning gazogènes, some German army trucks, horse-drawn carts and vélo-taxis. There were a great many bicycles, however. But in a big, sprawling and modern city like Paris those bicycles made the streets, boulevards and avenues look bleak and empty.

There were also quite a few white, wooden, military signs. The Germans had put them up in large numbers at the corners of the most important streets, boulevards and avenues. They kept on heading east and went by the Arc de Triomphe. Then they turned right and came and stopped in front of a tall, imposing, five-story building at 74 Avenue Foch. The building had two huge round columns at the entrance and a massive wooden front door. Two enormous Swastika banners hung from the top of the columns on each side of the entrance. On both sides of the front door, and at the bottom of the fairly short stone staircase that led to the entrance, stood two black, white and red sentry boxes. Each one was manned by a tall, black-helmeted, black-uniformed SS sentry.

When they reached the building and stopped at the entrance, the rear doors of the gazogène flew open. The two big muscular men grabbed Dave and rushed him up the entrance staircase and into the building. They made for the reception desk and the slightly taller man spoke to the SS Captain on duty. The SS Captain nodded and reached for a clipboard. He looked at it and picked up the phone on his desk. He spoke into it and then put it down. He pointed to an elevator that stood to the right of the tall winding marble staircase behind the reception desk on both sides. The slightly taller man nodded and grabbed Dave with the other big man. They both walked with him into the elevator and pressed the third floor button.

They started to rise slowly and when they reached that floor, they got out with Dave and stopped at a desk to the left of the elevator. A tall, slender, pale-blond, blue-eyed, young SS Lieutenant sat there. He was going through some lists and when he saw them, he got up and motioned for them to follow him. He led them down a long thickly-carpeted hallway until he came to a door in the middle of it on the right. There was a buzzer to the right side of the door and the SS Lieutenant pressed it. In a moment there was a soft click and the SS Lieutenant opened the door and motioned for them to go in. The two big men went in with Dave and they all found themselves in a gigantic office. Once they were in that office the SS Lieutenant closed the door behind them.

He motioned for the two big men to stay near the door and led Dave to a single wooden chair that stood about 10 feet away from an enormous Louis XVI mahogany desk. When they reached the chair the SS Lieutenant motioned for Dave to sit down on it. As he did the SS Lieutenant moved swiftly behind it. He reached for a pair of handcuffs in the right pocket of his tunic and handcuffed Dave's hands behind the chair. Then he walked toward the two big men and gave the slightly taller one the handcuff keys which he put in the left pocket of his leather jacket. The SS Lieutenant then opened the office door and left softly and noiselessly with them.

CHAPTER 83

Dave waited until the SS Lieutenant and the two big men were gone and then looked around. The office he sat in was indeed truly gigantic. It was about 60 feet long and 30 feet wide. It had a shiny hardwood floor and a thick red Persian carpet right in the middle of it. There were large gilt-edged mirrors on the side and rear walls. There was also a sumptuous Louis XVI sofa and two armchairs on the left-hand side of it. A large map of Paris with red, white and blue pins stood on an easel on the right-hand side. The enormous Louis XVI mahogany desk stood in front of tall French windows and faced the room. And behind the mahogany desk stood a huge and massive officer who was sitting down and working.

The officer had barely looked up when Dave had come in. He was a man in his early forties and had a large, ramrod-stiff, Prussian head. He had closely-trimmed, neat, dark-brown hair parted sharply on the side and big, clean-shaven, pink cheeks. He also had a strong, square jaw and a huge, bull neck. Right now he was wearing an immaculate uniform that had the silver leaves and silver pips of a full SS Colonel. He was presently working on a large number of white legal-size files. Some of them had a red stripe running diagonally across them and all the files stood in one big pile on the left side of the desk as well as in one small pile that had only red stripes running diagonally across them. This pile stood on the right side of the desk and between those two piles there was a single white file lying right in the middle of it.

The Colonel was working in silence and the only noise you heard in the office was the steady ticking of a small golden Louis XVI clock on the right-hand side of the desk. He kept on working in silence and Dave saw behind him the sun was turning into a deep smoldering gold on top of

Across The Channel

the buildings on the other side of the Avenue Foch. As Dave was looking at the sunlight the Colonel looked up from the file he was working on and said to him in German: "My name is Kruger." Dave nodded and the Colonel went back to his file. He kept on working and a little after 6.00 o'clock, a buzzer sounded discreetly on his desk. The Colonel pressed on a button underneath it on the right-hand side and the door opened. A tall, slim and blond-haired man who wore a white suit, a white shirt open at the collar and white shoes came in.

The man in the white suit was with the two big men who had brought Dave to the Colonel's office. The man nodded at the Colonel and motioned for the two big men to go and stand at the back of the office. Then the man closed the door behind him and walked over to the desk where the Colonel was working. When he reached it the Colonel looked up at him and said in French: *"Bonsoir, Gilbert."* *"Bonsoir, Otto,"* the man said. *"C'est le jeune soldat Canadien qui a giflé un de nos officiers,"* the Colonel said. *"Ah, c'est celui que l'on a fait venir de Rouen,"* the man said. The Colonel nodded and he reached for the single white file lying in the middle of the desk. He gave it to the man and the man looked at it for a while. Then he put it down and walked over to where Dave was sitting.

The man stopped in front of him and said in a rough but passable English: "My name is Gilbert Montreuil. People call me *'Le Beau Gilles.'* Do you know why?"

"No. Why?"

"I have a nice sympathetic face. The kind that makes people trust you."

Dave didn't say anything and the man said: "Many people have trusted me so far. And many others will too."

Dave didn't say anything and the man said: "I'm sure many have wished by now they hadn't and I'm sure many others will feel the same too. But that's their problem."

Dave still didn't say anything and the man said: "I also work for the Police Militaire Allemande. And I do not like people who work against Germany. Do you understand?"

Dave nodded.

"I understand you hit a German officer."

"I didn't mean to hit him. I was trying to escape and hit him accidentally."

"Ah. You hit him accidentally."

"That's right. I was trying to get out of the truck taking us to the train station. And, in struggling with him, I accidentally hit him in the face."

The Long War

"How? Like this?" Montreuil said and suddenly stepped in and hit Dave with the hardest right he had ever seen. The punch exploded in Dave's face and made stars and black dots dance in front of his eyes. With the punch his chair tipped over backward and Dave found himself lying on his back on the carpet.

As soon as his chair hit the carpet the two big men rushed up and grabbed him by the shoulders. They set him straight on his chair again and Montreuil stood in front of him and smiled.

"Or. Like this," he said and stepped in and hit Dave with another incredibly hard right. Once again it exploded in his face and made stars and black dots dance in front of his eyes. Once more his chair tipped over and the two big men rushed up. They grabbed him by the shoulders and set him straight on it again.

Dave swallowed hard and tasted the blood on his tongue. It came from a cut on his left upper lip and when he saw this, Montreuil stood in front of him and smiled.

"Or. Was it like this?" he said and suddenly stepped in and slapped Dave so hard and fast with the palm of his hands his head swung back and forth before Montreuil stopped abruptly and stepped back. When he did Dave's head hung low over his chest and he was breathing heavily.

"Or, perhaps. Like this?" Montreuil said and stepped in and hit him with a hard-knuckled right to the chest. With this punch Dave bent in two and grunted as his breath went out of him and as he gasped and tried to get his wind back. Easy, easy, Dave thought. You take it easy. This is no ordinary situation. And this is no ordinary man from the Police Militaire Allemande, either. This man likes to hurt and kill people. So you better make sure you handle him carefully, he thought. Very carefully. Or else you're not going to make it out of here.

Dave forced himself to raise his head and look at Montreuil.

"Now, look at you. You don't look so good anymore and you have a cut," Montreuil said and stepped in and grabbed Dave's left upper lip with his thumb and forefinger. He squeezed the cut so hard it made blood squirt on Dave's tunic before he let it go.

"There. Isn't that better?" Montreuil said as he stepped back a little and looked at him. "There's no more blood on the cut."

Dave forced himself to raise his head again and look at Montreuil.

"Tell me. How do you feel now?" Montreuil said and stepped in again and grabbed his chin with his right hand. "Do you think you'd still like to hit a German officer?"

Dave shook his head and looked at Montreuil.

"I didn't think so," Montreuil said as he stepped back and let go of his chin. "However, remember. If you ever do, you'll make me very angry. Do you understand?"

Dave nodded.

"I must say, though. You don't look quite as fresh and relaxed as when I first saw you. What do you think, Otto?"

The SS Colonel looked up from the file he was working on and smiled.

"That's why I think it's time for us to have a nice little chat. I think it's time we found out who you really are."

CHAPTER 84

Montreuil then turned and looked at the two big men who stood at the back of the office. He motioned for them to come and pick Dave up and remove his handcuffs. The two big men rushed up to Dave and the slightly taller one took the keys from the left pocket of his leather jacket. He took off Dave's handcuffs and both of them grabbed him under his arms. Montreuil nodded slightly at the Colonel and the Colonel reached for the button underneath the right-hand side of his desk. A soft click was heard at the door of the office and Montreuil left with Dave and the two big men. Outside he led them to a small elevator with a black iron-grilled door on the left side and at the opposite end of the long hallway where the young SS Lieutenant was sitting.

They went in and Montreuil pressed a button on the right side. They began going down slowly and stopped three floors below the ground floor. Montreuil opened the door and began leading them down a long damp poorly-lit corridor. Near the middle of it he slowed down and stopped at a huge steel door on the right. The steel door had a large peephole in the middle of it and there was a buzzer to the right of it. Montreuil rang the buzzer and the peephole opened. Then it closed and the door opened with a loud jarring clang. Dave was taken through it and the door closed with the same loud jarring clang. Inside Dave found himself in what looked like a huge room. It was very dark and he couldn't see anything except a spotlight shining on a single wooden chair that was not far from the door and facing it.

To the right of the spotlight Dave caught a glimpse of a white enamel bathtub filled with water and, to the left of it, of a large ice box. Two men were moving in and out of the spotlight. Both of them were tall and thin and the slightly taller one of the two had a long scar on the right side of his face. Both of them were bald and were dressed in a white shirt open at the collar and black pants with large black suspenders. The sleeves of their shirts were rolled up and they were wearing black rubber gloves and bringing large blocks of ice to the bathtub. Outside of those men, of the spotlight shining on the chair, of the white enamel bathtub, and of the ice box, Dave couldn't see anything. But even in the darkness the room looked huge and sinister and had a damp and chilly feel to it.

In fact, as Dave looked at it, it made him think of a dungeon. Then, once they were in the room, Montreuil motioned for the two big men to bring Dave to the single wooden chair. The two big men brought Dave to that chair and disappeared in the darkness beyond. As they did the tall thin men came and stood on the edge of the spotlight on both sides of it. Montreuil waited until they were there. Then he stepped past them into the light of the spotlight and stopped in front of Dave. He stared at him and then said: "So. You hit a German officer."

"I told you. It was an accident."

"Ah yes. An accident."

"That's right."

"What's the matter with you! You think we're a bunch of idiots!"

"I don't think that."

"Sure you do!"

"No. I don't."

"Sure you do! So you listen to me, you miserable little shit! This is not a nice and pleasant little chat with Colonel Kruger we're having right now! This is the Police Militaire Allemande you're talking to! This is the Gestapo! Do you understand!"

Dave nodded and Montreuil went on: "So you listen to me real good! You think we're not on to you and don't know what's going on!"

"What are you talking about?"

"Who do you work for!"

"I told you. I was just trying to escape."

"You lie!"

"It's true."

"It's not! Stand up!"

Dave stood up and Montreuil grabbed him and shook him violently and savagely by his tunic: "Come on! Who do you work for!"

"How many times do I have to tell you. I was just trying to escape."

"You lie!"

"I don't."

"Sure you do! Who's your contact! I want the name of your contact!"

"There is no contact. And anyway that's all I have to tell you."

"It's not!"

"Sure it is. My name is David Lindsay. I'm a Private. And my serial number is D25640."

"And my name is Gilbert Montreuil. I'm with the Police Militaire Allemande. For *GrossParis*!"

"It's true. That's all the Geneva Convention requires me to tell you."

"Piss on the Geneva Convention!"

"It's true. That's all I have to tell you."

"No it isn't! Who's your contact!"

"There is no contact. And anyway what do you want me to tell you?"

"His name! Just his name! Not some stupid story you want me to hear!"

Montreuil now let go violently and savagely of Dave's tunic. He stood facing him and glaring at him and Dave said: "I told you the truth. Listen. I just had bad shrapnel wounds. I stayed at the *Hôpital Sacré Coeur* for six weeks. And then, when they took us by trucks to the train station to go to a prisoners of war camp in Germany, I tried to escape. That's all."

"Ah! You think the Police Militaire Allemande and the Gestapo are that stupid! I read your file! The kind of shrapnel wounds you had usually take three weeks to heal! You took six weeks! There had to be a reason!"

"What reason?"

"You think we don't know French hospitals are the perfect breeding ground for terrorists, communists and other enemies of the German Reich! All those silly French doctors and nurses who dream of working and fighting against us! In your case it took six weeks for your wounds to heal! That means you really stretched your time and wanted to stay at the hospital for as long as possible! Why!"

"Ah, come on now."

"It's true! You think we don't know what we're talking about!"

"In this case you don't."

"Sure we do! You stayed at the hospital this long because you had a contact or made a contact there!"

"It's not true. Why can't you accept the simple fact I just wanted to escape."

"There is no such thing as a simple fact!"

"I can see that."

"It's true! Nothing is as simple as you make it out to be!"

"I'm telling you. I told you the truth."

"No you didn't!"

"Oh yes I did."

"No you didn't! And we're going to make you talk, you miserable little shit! We're really going to make you talk!"

CHAPTER 85

Dave didn't say anything and Montreuil suddenly yelled: "Who's your contact!" Dave didn't say anything and Montreuil yelled: "Come on! Who's your contact!" Dave still didn't say anything and Montreuil grabbed him. He spun him around and the tall thin men held him as they rushed him toward the white enamel bathtub. Montreuil savagely plunged Dave's face into the bathtub and Dave nearly passed out from the coldness of the water. Large blocks of ice came floating up and burned themselves against his face. Dave could feel his lungs begin to swell and expand and couldn't breathe and fought as hard as he could to take his head out of the water. But Montreuil and the tall thin men held him and when they finally let him come up for air, water was pouring out of his nostrils, mouth and ears.

Oh God, Dave thought. Please help me make it through this. Oh please help me make it through this... Montreuil was still yelling and screaming and asking for the name of his contact. When Dave didn't answer he savagely plunged Dave's face under water again. By then Dave's lungs were beginning to swell and expand to the breaking point and he was beginning to pass out and lose consciousness. He was still vaguely aware of pushing and fighting and trying to come up for air and of Montreuil and the tall thin men holding him and pushing him under water. But Dave was now becoming aware of these things from a remote and detached point of view, as if he was watching this from outside of himself, and after a while he became aware of being savagely pulled in and out of the water, of being taken to the single wooden chair, of brandy being poured down his throat; of being slapped around by Montreuil and of being splashed with cold water.

Then Dave lost consciousness and became aware of nothing. How long he remained unconscious he couldn't tell but when he came to, he didn't know where he was. He was lying in complete darkness. But he noticed one thing right away. There was a foul and nauseating smell all around him and after a while he found out what it was. He was lying next to an iron pail full of stool and urine. Dave was sprawled on the cold damp stone floor of a narrow cell and got up shakily and went and threw himself down on the cot on the left side of the cell. The cot was at the back of the cell and he stretched his legs on it and rested his back against the back wall.

Dave felt sharp stabbing pains in his back near his right shoulder blade and his lungs were so raw and sore he could hardly breathe. He also had a dull throbbing headache and lay on the cot and didn't move. After a while Dave could hear muffled screams and moans coming from the dungeon but he was so sore all over he closed his eyes and soon feel asleep. He slept a deep and exhausted sleep and was surprised when he heard a loud jarring clang and when his cell door opened. The two big men who had brought him here from Rouen rushed in and grabbed him from under his arms. The slightly taller one made Dave put his hands out and put back the handcuffs on him. When he did Dave saw from the light that fell on his watch from the long damp poorly-lit corridor it was close to 8.00 o'clock in the morning.

Then, once Dave was handcuffed, the two big men left the cell with him and took him back to the dungeon. The door was open and once he was in, the slightly taller one closed it behind him. They made him sit on the same wooden chair he had sat on before and then each stood on each side of it as the two tall thin men Dave had seen yesterday stepped into the spotlight. The slightly taller one was carrying a small stand with a shaving bowl, a shaving brush and a white towel. When he reached Dave he put the stand down next to the wooden chair. Then he took the shaving brush and began lathering Dave's face. Finally he began shaving him and combing his hair while the other man straightened out his tie, dusted off his uniform and cleaned his boots.

When Dave was spruced up the two big men took him again and led him out of the dungeon and toward the small elevator with the black iron-grilled door. As soon as they reached it they pressed on the ground floor button and began going up slowly. At the ground floor they got out and led him along the long thickly-carpeted hallway past the reception desk and past the massive wooden front door until they were out of the building. Outside, on the fairly short stone staircase, Montreuil was waiting for them. In the cool clear sunlight of an early October morning he looked unnaturally pale and drawn. His eyes were red-rimmed and bloodshot and his white shirt and white suit were slightly soiled and wrinkled. When he saw Dave he stepped closer to him and said: "Well, well. Look at you. Don't you make a handsome figure."

Montreuil smiled at Dave and grabbed his left upper lip with his thumb and forefinger. He squeezed it but not as hard as the last time. Montreuil smiled again and said: "It's too bad you're leaving. I was beginning to be quite fond of you. I even recommended you be shot at Mont Valérien as an example of what happens when an enlisted man hits a German officer." He smiled once more. "But the High Command decided against it. They want something better for you. Much Better. I hope you'll enjoy where you're going." Montreuil smiled at Dave one more time and led him to the big black Renault gazogène waiting for him. It was driven by the same thin scrawny driver who had taken him to Paris and when they reached it, the two big men opened the rear doors and shoved Dave in.

They themselves then got in on each side of Dave and the slightly taller one was on his right. They slammed the doors shut and Montreuil waved at Dave as the car left. They began moving away from Montreuil and drove west a few hundred feet before they made a sharp U-turn and began heading east on the Avenue Foch. They hurried past the Arc de Triomphe and got on the Avenue de Friedland. After a short while they turned left and began heading north until they reached the Boulevard de Courcelles and turned right on it. They drove east on the Boulevard de Courcelles and then along the Boulevard des Batignoles past the Place Clichy. They proceeded along the Boulevard Clichy, with the gleaming white Basilica of Sacré Coeur rising in the distance, and the Boulevard de la Chapelle, and, past the Rue de Flandre, came and stopped at the Gare de l'Est.

As soon as they stopped at the Gare the rear doors of the car flew open and the two big men stepped out. They both grabbed Dave under his arms and rushed him into the Gare. Inside it was full of people, German officers, NCOs and soldiers getting off incoming trains. When Dave saw those German officers, NCOs and soldiers he guessed they must be part of German Divisions coming in from the East in order to rest and be brought back to strength. Most of the officers, NCOs and soldiers looked quite young although there were a few tough and hardened faces among them. When they were inside the Gare the two big men rushed Dave past the people, officers, NCOs and soldiers and led him to a platform in the middle of it where an outbound train was standing by and ready to leave.

A huge muscular soldier was standing on the platform alongside the train. He was from the Wehrmacht and had his rifle slung over his right shoulder. He was looking around at the crowd and wearing a uniform that looked much too small for him. He must have been in his early twenties and had a long straight nose, cold blue eyes, a massive square jaw and a thick lower lip that made his face underneath his helmet look harsh and cruel. He also had big strong hands and powerful bulging muscles that stood out over his ill-fitting uniform. Right now he had taken off his helmet and was brushing back his thick close-cropped jet-black hair. When the soldier saw them come toward him he put his helmet back on and stood slowly at attention.

In no time the two big men reached him with Dave and the slightly taller one said: "Are you the guard waiting for the prisoner from Rouen?" "I am," the soldier said. "May I see your authorization papers for this prisoner?" the man asked. "Of course," the soldier said. He took out some papers from the right pocket of his tunic and handed them over to him. The man looked at them for a moment and then handed him the keys for the handcuffs on Dave's hands. The soldier took them and put them in the right pocket of his tunic. As he did he looked at Dave's handcuffs and the man said: "By order of Colonel Kruger. Gestapo. *GrossParis*. This man is a very dangerous prisoner." The soldier nodded and the man left with the other big man.

The soldier waited until they were gone. Then he turned and motioned for Dave to begin walking ahead of him and get in the wagon alongside them.

CHAPTER 86

The wagon the soldier wanted Dave to climb in was just before the tender of the locomotive. Dave climbed in it and saw it was quite crowded. When he came in the soldier motioned for him to sit in the first row on the right side. He himself would sit in the left row. Dave went and sat in that row and close to 10.00 o'clock in the morning there was a shrill whistle. This whistle was followed by another whistle and they were on their way. They slowly left the platform and came out of the Gare De L'Est in a long wide right turn. In no time they began leaving the center of Paris and the northern suburbs. In the cool clear sunny early October morning they picked up speed and soon started going by the Pantin Freight Station and small towns like Bobigny, Meaux, Charly and Chateau-Thierry.

In the bright and dazzling sunlight they kept on speeding and heading east past many towns, villages, fields and valleys and as he sat next to the huge muscular soldier, Dave saw what a strange and unexpected journey this was turning out to be. For one thing the soldier soon took a big loaf of bread and a large piece of cheese from his combat pack and began eating. He also took out his canteen and began drinking schnapps from it. He seemed to be eating and drinking all the time and enjoying seeing Dave look at him as he ate and drank. For another he was watching Dave closely and seemed to want him to try to escape. Also Dave was handcuffed which was in clear and flagrant violation of the Geneva Convention. Finally Dave was keenly aware of the people on the train who were looking at him. Most of them were staring at him with a great deal of indifference; some with a certain sympathy; a few with downright hostility.

The first day they went through towns like Chalons-Marne, Vitry-Le-François, Brusson, Sermaize-Les-Bains and Chardogne. On a couple of occasions they had to switch to sidings in order to let military trains go by and close to 9.00 o'clock in the evening, they pulled in the Gare Centrale SNCF in Strasbourg. In the Gare the soldier spoke to the Military Police and a *kubelwagen* came for them. They left the station and got on the Place de la Gare. They drove on the Boulevard de Metz and on the Rue Sainte Marguerite until they reached the Gendarmerie where they spent the night. The next morning another *kubelwagen* came for them and took them back to the Gare. At 10.00 o'clock sharp they left the station and crossed the frontier at Kehl.

At the frontier there were gates, Swastika flags, machine gun towers, spotlights and barbed wire. The frontier post was heavily guarded and when they left it behind, they picked up speed and began going through Kehl and towns and villages like Offenburg, Haslach, St. Georgen, Villengen and Rottweil. By now they were making pretty good time and Dave noticed how the landscape in Germany was pretty much like the one in France. It had the same kind of gently-rolling hills, lush valleys, neat vineyards, well-kept fields and large forests. And yet, although the landscape was pretty much the same, there was a difference. In France the landscape had had a peaceful and serene quality about it, as if it hadn't been touched by the war at all. In Germany, on the other hand, the landcape had a harshness and grimness about it that made you feel right away you were at war and involved in a deadly struggle.

Not only that but as they kept on moving and heading east the harshness and grimness of the landcape seemed to increase so it made the whole country look even more bleak and forbidding. All day long they kept on heading east and going through towns and villages such as Oberndorf, Sulz, Nordstetten, Horth, Motzingen and Herrenberg. Around 5.00 oclock in the afternoon darkness fell and a little later, they came and stopped briefly at Stuttgart. Then they were on their way again and still kept on heading east. Their blinds were pulled down for the blackout. In fact they had been pulled down throughout the whole journey, as soon as darkness had fallen, and around 9.00 o'clock in the evening they pulled in Nuremberg. At the station the soldier spoke to the Military Police again and another *kubelwagen* came for them.

This time they were taken to the downtown Headquarters of the Military Police where they spent the night. The next morning another *kubelwagen* came and they were driven to the station. At 10.00 o'clock sharp they were on their way again and slowly pulled out of the station. They left Nuremberg behind and in a little while picked up speed and began going through various towns and villages such as Rothenback, Lauf, Hersbruch, Hohenstadt, Velden, Ranna and Pegnitz. Beyond Hohenstadt they were no

The Long War

longer moving and heading east, strictly speaking, but northeast. Berlin lay in that direction and for the first time Dave saw tanks on the road. There was also a great deal of military traffic and he even saw a Regiment march past a long, stark, low-lying wood. There were also some people in his wagon who were looking at him with contempt and hostility.

It was another cool, clear and sunny morning and they made a few more switches to sidings to let military trains go by. But mostly they kept on heading northeast and around 7.30 in the evening, they pulled into Leipzig. At the station they got off and the soldier immediately led Dave to a much shorter train waiting to leave alongside one of the middle platforms. The blinds on that train were down and at 8.00 o'clock sharp they were on their way again. They began sliding past the platform and came out of the station. In no time they left Leipzig behind and Dave saw they were now moving in the opposite direction from where they had come. They were now generally heading southeast and, through a slight tear in one of the blinds, Dave saw they were going through towns like Naunhof, Grethen and Otterwisch. The train kept on moving and heading southeast and around 9.00 o'clock in the evening, a Railway Official came into their wagon and said: "Colditz. Colditz next."

When he said this the soldier got up and motioned for Dave to do the same. Dave just froze and thought: No! No! It can't be! It just can't be! Colditz was the one place he had always been afraid of in case he ever got caught and was made prisoner. In the First World War it had been absolutely escape-proof and in this war it had been used to keep all the hard-nosed and tough-minded prisoners from trying to escape. And this was the place where the soldier wanted Dave to stand up so they could leave the train.

CHAPTER 87

At the station the soldier made Dave get off first. Then they walked along the platform and stepped inside. In the station there was an old gray-haired soldier who had his rifle slung over his right shoulder and who was waiting for them. He was of average height and stockily-built. He was holding his helmet in his right hand and when he saw Dave and the huge muscular soldier, he put it back on and walked over to them. He asked the soldier if he was bringing the prisoner from Rouen. The soldier nodded. The old soldier asked the younger one to show him his papers for the prisoner. The younger one did. The old soldier took those papers and told the young one where he could go to find accommodations for the night.

The young soldier then took off Dave's handcuffs and the old one unslung his rifle and motioned with it for Dave to leave the station and begin walking ahead of him. Dave nodded and left the station. Outside they turned left and got on a road to the right of it. Dave marched ahead of the old soldier and this soldier led him along the road through the village. Half way through the village the old soldier took him over a bridge on the Mulde river. As Dave got on that bridge a Wehrmacht truck drove by and threw some light on a small iron sign to the right of it. It showed the bridge was called Adolf Hitler. On the other side of the bridge the old soldier marched him through the rest of the village and toward the Colditz castle. In the distance the castle towered gigantically and monumentally over them and dwarfed the village and the countryside.

Its huge and massive structure was shockingly lit in the pitch-black and star-filled Saxon night. In fact, as they got closer to it along a steep cobbled road, it seemed to Dave it stood at least 250 feet over the river and rose over the blacked-out countryside with an incredibly monstrous and sinister presence. In the blackout the stars above it showed big and clear and the night was nice, crisp and cool. As they kept on marching the steep cobbled road rose quite a bit and it didn't take long before they came to a gate with a small well-lit Security Post to the left of it. There was a sentry box to the right of the gate and inside the Post there was a counter with a telephone and several clipboards on it. Two armed sentries were guarding the gate. One was in front of the Security Post and the other in front of the sentry box.

When they reached the gate the armed sentry guarding the Post stepped forward and spoke to the old soldier. The old soldier handed him the papers he had taken from the young soldier and the sentry left them and went into the Post. Inside he looked at those papers and at one of the clipboards on the counter. Then he made a telephone call from the Post. In no time he was nodding on the phone and then hung up and came out. He motioned for the sentry in front of the sentry box to lift the gate. He gave the papers back to the old soldier and motioned for them to go on. The old soldier pointed with his rifle for Dave to move on and they both walked past the gate and across a wide moat bridge until they came to a clock tower archway. Just beyond the clock tower archway was a second gate with an armed sentry.

At that gate the old soldier again showed his papers and again the sentry lifted the gate and let them go on. By now they were into a large garrison courtyard that was brightly-lit with floodlights. There was an armed sentry that seemed to stand in the middle of it and they moved west across the couryard for about 40 yards until they came to a third gate with an armed sentry. At this gate the old soldier again showed his papers. The sentry checked them and they were let through. They walked beyond another archway which seemed to take in some German soldiers' quarters on one side and solitary cells on the other. Past this archway they walked another 30 yards toward another gate on the right. There was an armed sentry at this gate and he also checked their papers.

Then this sentry rang a buzzer and two huge oaken doors swung open behind him. Dave and the old soldier walked past those two doors and when they clanged shut, they found themselves in the prisoners' courtyard. The courtyard was fairly large. It must have been about 40 yards long by 30 yards wide and was cobbled and surrounded on all side by tall buildings five or six stories high. As a matter of fact the roofs of those buildings must have been about 90 feet from the ground. When they came into the yard the old soldier motioned for Dave to walk to a door almost at the other end of the yard on the right. The door was at a right angle from the gate and when they went in, Dave saw they were in the camp's office.

Across The Channel

There was a waiting room with a few chairs and an armed guard stood next to a tall wooden door.

As soon as they stepped in the waiting room the door opened and a tall thin frail Corporal motioned for Dave and the old soldier to come in. Dave nodded and walked into the camp's office with the old soldier. Inside they found themselves in a large plain room with a faded rug on the dark hardwood floor. There was a desk in front of the rear wall, some filing cabinets to the left of the desk and a small table with a radio to the right of it. There was also a wooden chair in front of the desk and a somewhat bigger and better one behind it. A tall bony graying German Captain was sitting behind the desk. The Corporal went and stood to the right of it and a big husky soldier stood on the other side.

The old soldier closed the door of the office and then stepped to the desk where he gave the Captain the papers he had taken from the young soldier. The Captain took them and looked at them briefly. Then he put them in the top drawer on the right side of his desk as the old soldier went and stood near the closed door of the office. Finally the Captain opened a tall pale-brown file on his desk. The Captain looked at it for a few moments and then began speaking to Dave in German. When he spoke the German was translated carefully into English by the Corporal and the Captain said: "Ah. *Herr* Lindsay. My name is Carl Dietrich. I am one of the Senior Security Officers at Colditz. I see you've finally made it to our castle. I trust you will also not leave it until the end of the war."

Dave didn't say anything and Dietrich said: "I see from your file you've made two escape attempts: one from a hospital in Rouen; and another one from an Army truck as you were being taken away from that city. That's why you've been sent here as an inveterate and incorrigible escaper. I can assure you that for you those days are over."

Again Dave didn't say anything and Dietrich said: "You see, *Herr* Lindsay, we treat our prisoners fairly at Colditz. If you obey the rules and do not give us any trouble, we will be proper and correct with you. On the other hand, should you try to escape or should you try to become wild and undisciplined, we will deal with you quite severely. This I can assure you."

Once again Dave didn't say anything and Dietrich said: "I also want you to know the German Reich doesn't take kindly to an enlisted man striking one of its officers. I further want you to know we will certainly not tolerate this kind of behavior in the future. So take my advice and take this as a warning. A very strong warning. You've been extremely lucky this time. You might not be so lucky next time. Then you might be handed over to the Gestapo and the outcome might not be so happy for you. Am I making myself clear?"

Dave nodded and Dietrich closed the file. He turned and said to the big husky soldier who was standing to the left side of the desk: "All right. Take him to his cell."

CHAPTER 88

The big husky soldier unslung his rifle and pointed with it for Dave to leave the office. Dave nodded and stepped out. Outside the soldier marched him about 15 yards to an archway door at a right angle from the camp's office. When they reached that door he motioned for Dave to go in and walk up a narrow spiral staircase until they reached the third floor. On that floor he made Dave turn right and head down a long corridor. They walked past a group of cells that were obviously occupied since Dave heard noises inside of them until they stopped at a door in the middle of the corridor. That door was on the left side of it and, in that part of the corridor, everything was quiet.

At the door the big husky soldier opened it and Dave went in. The soldier locked it behind him and Dave stood in his cell and looked around. The cell he was in was fairly small and was probably like a great many other cells in the castle. It had a narrow bed on the left side of it, as you entered, a square metal trunk at the foot of the bed and a small wooden table and a chair on the opposite wall from the bed. The cell also had a narrow window with bars and when Dave walked over to the window and looked down, he saw the courtyard was 60 feet below and brilliantly lit with floodlights and patrolled by an armed sentry. Another one stood near the two huge oaken doors he had come through in order to get into the courtyard. It was now close to 10.30 in the evening and an ominous and sinister quiet hung over the courtyard and gave the castle an even more formidable and impregnable look.

Dave stood at the window and looked down at the courtyard. Then he left and began walking toward the middle of the cell when he stopped suddenly and stared at the door. There were faint erratic scratches coming from it. Dave listened intently for a few seconds and then rushed and flattened himself against the wall. He stood to the right of the door and after a while there were more faint erratic scratches and the door opened. A man came in who was wearing the high-collared tunic of a Polish officer and who seemed to be in his early thirties. The three stars on the high collar of his tunic meant he was a Captain and, except for his age, Dave thought he was staring at himself.

The Polish officer who came in was his own height. He was tall, slim and muscular like him. In his case, though, he didn't have quite the same sharp well-defined wiriness and swift powerful stance. His body, when you looked closely at it, was a little bit more lean, gaunt and bony. When the Polish Captain came in he was carrying lock-picking tools in his right hand. The moment he saw Dave he put his finger to his lips and motioned with his right hand for him to wait. Then he turned and locked the door from the inside before he put those tools in the right pocket of his tunic. By now Dave had gone and stood in the the middle of the cell. He was facing the Polish Captain and when the Captain turned from the door, Dave saluted him. The Captain returned his salute and then said to Dave: *"Anglicy?"*

"No. Canadian."

"Ah. Canadian. I also speak English."

"That's good."

"Je parle aussi Français. Si vous préférez."

"Non. Parler Anglais me va très bien."

"Ich kann auch Deutsch sprechen. Wenn sie mochten."

"Das kann ich auch. Aber bleiben wir beim English."

"All right. We'll stick to English then."

Dave didn't say anything and the Captain said: "First I must ask you. Do you really speak French and German that well?"

"Pretty well."

"That's wonderful."

"Not really. It's just I like languages."

"So do I. But I must say you're a man of many talents."

"It seems to me you're the one with many talents."

"Oh these," the Captain said and patted the tools in the right pocket of his tunic. "It's nothing."

"Still, I'm impressed."

"Oh, it's nothing. You see, the Germans are using cruciform locks in the castle and we can open all of them. In fact there isn't any lock in the castle, cruciform or otherwise, we can't open."

"Do the Germans know this?"

"Of course. But there isn't a thing they can do about it."

"How come?"

"First, they can't check the locks all the time. Second, they can't know who can and cannot open all the locks."

"I see."

"As a matter of fact, when you'll have a little bit more time, maybe I'll be able to interest you in the fine art of lock picking?"

"Maybe."

Both of them didn't say anything and then the Polish Captain smiled at Dave and put out his hand: "By the way my name is Jan Mieteck. Eighteenth Uhlans."

Dave shook his hand and told him his name and the name of his Regiment.

"I was with the Pomorze Army at the battle of Krojanty. There wasn't much we could do."

"I was with the 2nd Canadian Division at Dieppe. It was pretty much the same thing."

"And now you're a prisoner at Colditz."

"That's it."

"A legendary one, I might add. Your reputation, I must tell you, has preceded your arrival here."

"It has?"

"Certainly. Everyone here knows about your two escape attempts and about your striking an officer on your second try. I must say it's pretty exciting stuff."

"It didn't quite happen the way you think."

"Maybe not. But it's still pretty exciting stuff."

"How do you know all this?"

"My dear fellow, there isn't anything that happens to the prisoners of Colditz we don't know about. We regularly break into the camp's office and read the Commandant's files. We sometimes read them before he has time to read them himself!"

"That's pretty neat."

"It certainly is."

"I must tell you, though. It didn't really happen like that."

"Oh no? How?"

"This way," Dave said and went on and told Mieteck what had really happened on his two escape attempts.

"There. You see. That's the Germans for you," Mieteck said, when Dave had finished telling him what had happened. "They always see or want to see things in black and white. That's why they use such brutality with other people. And that's why they'll also lose the war."

"I'm not so sure about that."

"They will. But they really are an amazing people."

"Why?"

"Well, let's look at your case. They're putting you in a block of empty cells between the British and Polish officers. That way they think they'll punish you and that the British and Polish officers will also be punished by having an enlisted man among them."

"Is that what they think?"

"Oh, absolutely. They're strange that way."

"To tell you the truth I don't really care about what they think."

"May I ask why?"

"Sure. You see, even though I studied German and liked the language, I never felt particularly close to it nor to the people. But, on the other hand, by being with Polish people I'll feel I'm among friends and people I can trust. That's the difference."

Mieteck stared at Dave and then said: "You like Polish people?"

"Sure. I really feel at ease with them."

"Do you know any?"

"A few. You see, in Vancouver I met a Polish merchant seaman and some of his Polish friends. They told me all about Poland and its history and made me read about it. In a way Poland's history reminds me of the history of my own country."

"In what way?"

"Same impossible country. Same impossible dream."

"I see," Mieteck said and stopped suddenly and stood facing Dave. Although it was quite cool and damp in the cell he broke into a heavy sweat and seemed to stagger for a moment. All the color drained from his face and Dave stepped closer to him and grabbed him by both arms. He held Mieteck briefly and when Mieteck pulled away, he smiled at Dave again and said: "My God. I must say I really felt weak and dizzy for a moment."

"Are you all right?"

"Certainly. I just felt faint for a moment. That's all."

"Are you all right now?"

"Of course. Don't worry. It must be living on 1200 grams a day that did it."

"Do you want to sit down?"

"No."

"Or lie down on the bed?"

"No. No. I'm fine."

"All right, then."

"It's true. Living day after day on so few calories is bound to get to you after a while."

"I'm sure."

"So, please. Don't bother about me. I'll be fine."

By now the color had come back to Mieteck's face. He wiped some sweat from his forehead and finally looked much better. He became intense and serious again and looked once more like the real professional soldier and disciplined officer he was. He smiled at Dave again and said: "Anyway, on behalf of the Polish officers and enlisted men of Colditz, welcome. Welcome to our Bad Boys' Club. May you live up to your extraordinary and legendary reputation."

"I'll try."

Mieteck now fixed Dave with his clear and deep-brown eyes and said: "And now, on a somewhat more serious and important matter, when you go for your Personnel Interview tomorrow morning after *Appell*, make sure you mention you're a carpenter by trade."

"Why? I don't know anything about carpentry."

"It doesn't matter. The Germans don't know that."

"Why do you want me to say I'm a carpenter?"

"I'm a carpenter. And I'd like you to work with me as my assistant."

"Do you really need an assistant?"

"I do. The one I had has just been transferred to Laufen."

"Why don't you ask for one of your own people then?"

"I can't. The Germans simply won't allow two people of the same nationality to work together."

"You mean your assistant wasn't Polish?"

"No. He was French."

"Why me?"

"Let's just say I like what I saw and heard about you."

"I don't get it. Why do you work as a carpenter? I thought officers weren't supposed to work."

"They're not."

"Why do you work as a carpenter then?"

"What do you think? Maybe I like to go to all kinds of places in the castle where no other Allied officer is allowed to go."

"I see. In order to check out the place. Right?"

"Now you understand."

"But what if I have to work on my own? Then the Germans will know I'm not a carpenter."

"Don't worry. It's not going to happen."
"You're sure?"
"Of course I'm sure."
"How do you know?"
"I know. And you'll always work with me as my assistant."
"I see."
"And anyway. I'll teach you. It's not that complicated."
"Well. Okay then."
"Good. But remember. Tomorrow, at the interview, make sure you make the Germans feel you just want to be a prisoner and not work as a carpenter or at any other job. Otherwise they might get suspicious and not give it to you."
"Don't worry. I'll make sure I get it."
"Good. I'll see you tomorrow then."

CHAPTER 89

Mieteck now turned and walked over to the door. He took out his lock-picking tools and opened it from the inside. He walked out and locked it from the outside. In a moment Dave heard him walk to the right of the corridor toward the Polish quarters. His footsteps quickly died away and Dave went and lay down on his bed. He soon fell sound asleep and was only awakened around 7.00 o'clock in the morning to the shouts of: *"Aufstehen!" "Aufstehen!"* Not long after Dave's cell was opened and he was taken down to the courtyard and to the canteen in order to have his breakfast. The canteen was to the left of the camp's office. The breakfast he had was made up of a cup of ersatz coffee, two slices of bread and a small amount of margarine.

At 8.30 there was an *Appell* in the courtyard and a little after 9.00 o'clock, Dave was marched into the camp's office for his Personnel Interview. The interview turned out pretty much as Mietieck had told him. Once again Carl Dietrich, the tall bony graying Security Officer, sat behind the desk and the same tall thin frail Corporal who had been with him last night did the translation into English. They told him there were presently over 300 British, Dutch, French and Polish officers at Colditz as well as several orderlies and enlisted men and warned him about trying to escape. They also asked for his name, rank and serial number. But mostly the interview was about his various duties as a prisoner and about what he could expect of the Germans while he was their guest. Then, when they got around to what he had been doing in civilian life, Dave told them he had been a carpenter.

They nodded at this but when Dave told them he just wanted to be a prisoner and not work, they told him stiffly and in no uncertain terms they

The Long War

were the ones who decided what prisoners did in Colditz. They didn't like enlisted men telling them what they wanted to do and told him he would be assigned to work as a carpenter for a Polish Captain. Then Dave was swiftly led out of the camp's office and into the courtyard and later on in the morning, he was taken to the tool shop in order to begin his work as a carpenter. Mieteck was waiting for him inside the shop. The shop wasn't far from the courtyard. It was in a room at the back of the parcels' office and was slightly to the left of the entrance gate to the courtyard. When they were alone Mieteck motioned for Dave to get closer to the large wooden table where he was working. When Dave stepped close to it Mieteck began giving him a crash course in carpentry.

Mieteck showed Dave how to hold the hammer by the end of the handle so its weight would do the work for him. He taught him how to use the square for everything and the plumb line in order to make long straight lines. He showed him how to use the saw and how to take long easy strides downward in order to cut the wood swiftly and cleanly. He told him how the chalk line worked as the plumb line and taught him how to use it as such. Mieteck made carpentry seem not all that difficult and after they had had lunch, they went on their first job together. This job was in the French quarters. Their quarters were at a right angle from the Polish quarters and Mieteck took him to the officers' day room where some of the hinges on one of the latticed windows were broken. They worked on those hinges and then went to the Commandant's office in order to repair a chair and one of his desk drawers.

Then, in the days and weeks that followed, they went on various jobs in the Chapel, the canteen, the theater, the sick ward, the guard house, the kitchen, the dentist's room, the parcels' office and quite a few other places. They went all over the castle to do those jobs and as he worked as Mieteck's assistant and looked around extremely carefully, Dave came to one conclusion. There was simply no way you could escape from Colditz. You could possibly have done it in 1940 when the officers and guards weren't that well trained and organized. Some had done it then and up to this year. But this was now late 1942. The outside walls were seven feet thick. The inner courtyard was 250 feet above the river level. The cell where he was living was another 60 feet on top of that. There were almost as many guards as there were prisoners.

Not only that but there was a lot of barbed wire being strung everywhere. Sound detectors were being installed. There were more searchlights being put on the walls and battlements. The officers and guards were being rotated all the time so they couldn't get too familiar with them. Then, as if this wasn't enough, by early November the weather turned quite cold and blustery. In the middle of the month it began snowing and the cold and blustery weather really settled in. It snowed on most days and it was snowing on that Friday evening, November 20, 1942, when Dave heard some scratching at his door. It was around 10.00 p.m. and just after *Appell*. At that time Dave was lying in bed and when he heard the scratching, he turned and saw the door of his cell open and Mieteck walk in.

CHAPTER 90

That evening Mieteck looked quite pale and tense and asked Dave to get up and come with him. Dave stood up and got dressed. Then he left his cell with Mieteck and headed for the Polish quarters. There were Polish lookouts along the corridor and when they reached the Polish day room, Mieteck opened the door and motioned for Dave to go in. Dave stepped in and saw most of the Polish officers, orderlies and enlisted men were standing in a semi-circle in the middle of the day room. Once Dave was in Mieteck also stepped in and closed the door behind him. Then he came with Dave and stopped in front of the semi-circle of Polish officers, orderlies and enlisted men.

Dave was on the right side of Mieteck and as they came and stopped in front of the men, Mieteck turned to him and said: "If I brought you here this evening it is because of your love and appreciation of Poland. As a result of this love and appreciation I have the honor of offering you a chance to escape from Colditz and to carry in your heart on behalf of all my fellow officers, orderlies and enlisted men the White Polish Eagle and to make it rise, soar and fly into freedom."

Dave stared at Mieteck and couldn't believe what he heard.

"Are you serious?"

"Very serious."

"Why?"

"Let's just say this escape is a split-second and sharply-timed operation that will require a great deal of speed and physical exertion. In the circumstances I believe you are the man to do it."

"How am I going to do this?"

"By walking through the front gate."

"Just like that."

"That's it."

"How is that possible?"

"It's simple. I have spoken to the British Escape Officer and he will coordinate the escape with us."

"How?"

"We will use a room under the stage which the British used for one of their own who escaped to Switzerland earlier this year. We discovered this room almost at the same time as they did and the British will keep it open for us while you make your escape."

"Do the Germans know about this room?"

"They don't."

"I see. And where does this room lead?"

"It leads to an enclosed bridge passing over the main gate of the prisoners' courtyard and to the attic of the guardhouse. Then there is a stone spiral staircase that leads to the guardhouse entrance and goes by the officers' mess on the first floor and the guards' quarters on the ground floor. Past those quarters you'll step out on the outer courtyard and be on your way. That's how we'll do it."

"Why me? Why don't you do it?"

"I'll explain later. For now let's just say I think you're the man to do it."

"And how will I do this?" Dave asked.

"It's simple," Mieteck said. "You see, every Monday evening whenever he's is on duty, Captain Richard Reinhardt leaves the castle after the *Appell* and his shift is over at 10.00 p.m. to go to town. He's an officer who's also a bachelor. He likes all kinds of girls whether they're easy or not and is open to bribes. At the same time as he leaves to go to town, however, there are two sentries who take turns coming on to a post near the parapet. Also there is another one coming on at that time to a post near the inner courtyard gate. But that one is too far away to see properly anyone coming out of the guardhouse entrance." Mieteck paused and looked at Dave. "Do you follow me so far?"

Dave nodded and Mieteck went on: "All right. Now the two sentries who come on at 10.00 p.m. are called Hans and Fritz. Hans is just an average and ordinary sentry who doesn't care about anything and puts in his time until his shift is over at 6.00 a.m. But Fritz is different. He's a very sharp and conscientious sentry who checks out everything and does his work far too well for our own good. Now on the present rotation either sentry is usually relieved five or six minutes early which means they probably do the same thing themselves when they go on shift. So if Hans

The Long War

is on shift we'll make the move. You'll step out of the guardhouse and start walking toward the three gates that lead out of the Castle." Mieteck paused again and looked at Dave. "Are you still with me?"

Dave nodded and Mieteck went on: "All right. At 10.00 p.m. sharp Captain Reinhardt usually stops and talks with the relieving officer in the guardhouse for five or six minutes also. That means, with the five or six minutes it will take at the last Moat Bridge gate to discover who the real Reinhardt is and for the alarm to be given, you'll have about a 15-minute start for your escape. That's why it will call for a great deal of speed and physical exertion."

Dave nodded and Mieteck went on: "Now. To come back to your question as to why I myself don't make this escape. You see, for a long time now I haven't been feeling well. I have been feeling tired and exhausted all the time and have had those sweaty dizzy spells like the one I had when I first met you. At first I thought it was nothing and was only caused by the poor food we're eating. But in the past few weeks it got so bad and I have felt so sick and weak I had myself examined by three doctors here. All of them agree. I have leukemia. This is an advanced disease of the blood cells and they tell me it's not going to get better, but worse. Much worse. That's why I'm not going to be able to make this escape. I had planned it and figured it out some time ago when I was strong enough to do it. Now that I can't, I want you to do it."

"Why me?" Dave said. "Why don't you offer it to one of your fellow officers?"

"I would if that was possible," Mieteck said. "It's not."

"Why not?"

"With all due respects, none of them is as qualified as you are to do it."

"I'm afraid I don't follow."

"Let me explain. You're the same height and build as me. In fact you almost look like me. You also speak flawless French and German. None of them have those qualifications."

"Surely those aren't the only qualifications needed for this escape."

"Unfortunately they are. At least for this one."

"Why do you need those particular qualifications?"

"Have you ever looked at Richard Reinhardt? He's the same height and build as you and me. If we're going to use him as the model for the escape, we're going to need someone who looks like him. That means you and me."

"You have other people who look like you and me."

"True. But none of them can speak flawless French and German."

"Why is that so important for this escape?"

"You see, the papers are already made for Reinhardt and the cover story. They say the bearer is a Frenchman working for the Germans. The man who carries those papers has to be able to act out those stories."

"And that's me."

"That's right. Especially since all the clothing has also been made and since it'll fit you perfectly."

"Why don't you wait a while," Dave said. "And make new papers and new clothing."

"I would do that if I could," Mieteck said. "I can't."

"Why not?"

"I can't. You see, there's a great deal of urgency to this escape. We used to be 80 officers of all ranks here. Now we're down to 20 and those remaining are mostly below the rank of Captain. There are rumors we will soon be sent to Lübeck to join our fellow officers in that camp. That's why we have to move fast."

"So I'm the one chosen for this escape."

"That's right."

"I see."

"But remember one thing."

"What?"

Mieteck now stepped a little closer to Dave and said: "This is quite an honor you're given. When you escape you have to remember you're doing it for Poland. That means you have to do it at all cost. Even if it means to the death. Do you understand?"

"I understand."

"Remember. This escape has been planned for weeks and months and is very important to us. With the way things are going none of us may outlive the war or even have a country to go back to when it's over. That's why it's important you escape to freedom and you do it for us and for Poland."

"I understand."

"You see, when you live Poland lives. When you're free Poland is free. Do you follow me?"

"I do."

"All right then. Do I take it you're willing to accept the honor and responsibility of escaping for Poland?"

"I am."

"Good. In that case we'll do it next Monday evening if Reinhardt is on the evening shift and if the conditions for it are right."

BOOK SEVEN

ESCAPE

CHAPTER 91

Mieteck then turned and walked to the door of the day room with Dave. He motioned for Dave to step out with him and closed the door behind them. He walked back down the corridor with Dave until they reached his cell. He opened the door and told Dave to be in the Polish day room in the morning after *Appell*. He would go over the plan in detail with him. Dave nodded and Mieteck locked his cell door from the outside. In a moment Dave heard his footsteps fade along the corridor and went to bed. Dave didn't sleep well and when he woke up the next day, he found himself quite busy. In the day room Mieteck carefully went over the plan with him and gave him his two cover stories. He also gave him his two sets of papers and made him try on the clothes.

In the day room Dave also met the two other Polish officers who were closely connected with the plan. They were Stefan Bronski and Michael Novack. Both of them helped him memorize his cover stories and study his papers. He spent the weekend with them and with Mieteck. Then, on Monday evening, he was told by one of the British officers who was helping to coordinate the escape Reinhardt was definitely on the evening shift. The escape was on. It had started snowing quite heavily in the morning and by evening, the snow hadn't let up at all. Around 9.30, after the *Appell*, Dave left with Mieteck, Bronski and Novack and all four of them headed for the fourth floor of the theater building. In the theater they made for the stage and for an escape hatch that stood right in the middle of it. The escape hatch led to a room underneath the stage and this room in turn led to the attic over the Guardhouse.

The civilian clothes Dave would wear, his German uniform and various other articles had been put in that room for him a little earlier.

Dave went down the escape hatch on a bed-sheet rope. He was followed by Mieteck who was helped by Bronski and Novack. Once he was in that room Dave put on his civilian clothes and folded his dark-brown leather winter boots, cap and scarf and tied them tightly around his chest. On top of his civilian clothes Dave put on his German uniform, with its military boots, cap, greatcoat, belt and holster. When he was dressed Novack fitted him with the black wig and fake black mustache that would make him look like Reinhardt. Then he added a few make-up touches to his face and to his eyebrows. Finally, when he was ready, Dave looked up at the escape hatch.

One of the British officers stood next to it. One finger would mean it was Hans who was the sentry on duty on the parapet; two fingers, Fritz. At 9.52 p.m. the officer looked through the escape hatch and flashed one finger. Dave nodded and turned and thanked Bronski and Novack. Then he moved with Mieteck across the room to the door separating the bridge passage from the Guardhouse. Mieteck took out his lock picking tools and opened the door. They walked across the enclosed bridge that passed over the main gate of the prisoners' courtyard and at the far end of the bridge they came to another door. This was the door that led to the attic, the stone spiral staircase and the guardhouse entrance. Mieteck opened that door and Dave turned and suddenly held Mieteck tightly in his arms.

Mieteck felt very thin, bony and frail and when he pulled away from him, Dave looked at him and said: "Thanks. Thanks for everything." "It's nothing," Mieteck said. "No. It's a lot. You mean a lot to me," Dave said. Mieteck smiled and Dave said: *"Niech Zyja Polska!"* "Yes. Long live Poland!" Mieteck also said in Polish. Dave held Mieteck tightly in his arms again and then stepped through the door and stood there while Mieteck closed it behind him. Dave waited a full minute and then moved quickly to the stone spiral staircase. He began walking down and before he got to the first floor, he stopped. The door of the officers' mess was wide open and a bright yellow light spilled onto the staircase. There were laughing and talking voices inside and the song *Lily Marlene* was playing on a wireless. An officer's voice came close to the door. The officer was singing *"Lily Marlene, wie ich sie liebe!"* to the music playing and when he got close to the door, he suddenly slammed it shut.

Dave took a deep breath and walked swiftly past it. He headed for the ground floor and when he reached it, the door to the Guardhouse was slightly open. Dave stopped once more and then moved swiftly past it. As he did he saw a pair of boots through the partly open door. In no time Dave was at the Guardhouse entrance. He took another deep breath and stepped into the courtyard. By now it was snowing wildly and heavily. The snow

Escape

was blowing in great gusts and swirling everywhere. It was completely blanketing the courtyard and when he stepped out, Dave saw how Mieteck had been right. The guard at the prisoners' entrance gate was too far to see him. As for Hans he was exactly as Mieteck had told him. He was sloppy and careless and didn't check him closely. He came slowly to attention near the parapet and saluted him indifferently.

Dave returned the salute and marched toward the first gate. In the arclights that bathed the courtyard in a cold harsh metallic light Dave kept on marching firmly and steadily and when he reached the first archway gate, the guard snapped to attention and gave him a smart salute. Dave returned the salute and the guard swiftly opened the gate for him. By then Dave's cap, uniform and boots were covered with snow and he kept on marching across the garrison courtyard toward the Clock Tower gate. When he reached it the guard also opened it swiftly and saluted him. Dave returned the salute and began heading for the Moat Bridge gate. This was the third and final gate and when he reached it, the guard near the Security Post stepped out and saluted him. Dave returned the salute and handed him his officer's passbook, Colditz identification papers and overnight pass.

The guard nodded and went into the small well-lit Security Post. He checked those papers against one of the clipboards lying on the counter. Twice he looked at Dave through one of the windows of the Post before he looked down at the clipboard again. By now it was snowing so wildly and heavily you could hardly see anything and finally the guard came out and walked over to him. He handed him his papers and said: "It's quite a night to go out into town." "Ah, you know. The girls," Dave said. "Can't keep them waiting." "Yes. There is always that," the guard smiled and motioned for the other guard to lift up the gate for him. In a moment the gate was lifted and Dave marched down the steep sloping roadway that led out of Colditz.

Dave marched firmly and steadily and when the road had dropped down quite a bit and was out of sight of the last Colditz gate, he took off at a flying run and made for the bottom of the roadway.

CHAPTER 92

As soon as Dave reached the bottom of the roadway he turned right and ran into the wood that was on the right side of the castle. In that now blinding and swirling snowstorm Dave ran and skidded and stumbled through the undergrowth and headed south and then westward in a big sweep in the direction of the river Mulde. After 20 minutes Dave heard the faint muted barking of German shepherds in the distance. As he did Dave kept on moving and picked up the pace. He kept on running and skidding and stumbling in the deep snow and after a while, he crossed fields and roads. With roads Dave had to be careful in order not to be seen and to avoid traffic. In fact on three occasions when he he was about to cross them, he saw lights.

This was unusual in the blackout and Dave went to ground. On the first two occasions he saw an Army motorcyclist speeding down in the darkness. The third time he saw two motorcyclists who were coming from opposite directions stop and talk to each other before they left and went on their way. Dave waited and made sure they were gone before he crossed the road and kept on moving southwestward until he finally reached the river Mulde. A deep slope ran down to the river. There was a narrow road running alongside its bank and a high-level railway bridge crossing it. By that time it was so bitterly cold and snowing so wildly and heavily Dave's eyelids felt frozen and he could hardly see anything. In this blizzard the visibility was almost down to zero. Dave went to ground near the river and looked at the bridge on his left.

In this weather it was hard to tell whether it was guarded by sentries or not. After he had looked at it for a while Dave began backtracking in a wide circle and crossed the railway line quite a distance from the bridge.

Then he kept on moving southwestward parallel to the river until he came to an arched double-spanned road bridge further downstream. Near the bridge Dave lay down in the field and watched it. It was deserted. The road that ran alongside the river and the one that crossed the bridge were also deserted. The snow kept on blowing and swirling all around and as he watched the bridge, Dave saw it wasn't very long. There didn't seem to be any tire tracks or footsteps in the snow and just past it on the other side there was a bend in the road. There were also bushes and trees on both sides of the road leading to it and out of it.

Dave watched the bridge for a while and then took a deep breath. He jumped up and began running and skidding and stumbling through the sloping field until he got to the bushes and trees near the entrance to it. Dave hid behind those bushes and trees and then took another deep breath. He jumped up again and began running across the bridge. There was quite a lot of snow on the bridge. There was over a foot of it and Dave gave up trying to run on the side and ran right in the middle of it. Although the bridge was short he was sweating and breathing heavily and when he had almost reached the other side, he suddenly heard the noises of motors beyond the bend in the road. When he heard the noises Dave stepped up his pace wildly and desperately. Dave ran as hard as he could and on the other side, he threw himself headlong into the bushes and trees on the left side of the road.

No sooner had Dave skidded down past those bushes and trees that a Staff car and two Army trucks full of soldiers leapt out of the darkness and got on the bridge before they disappeared on the other side. Dave lay at the bottom of those bushes and trees. He was wet and frozen. He was also out of breath and covered with snow. When he was able to get his breath back Dave got up and began heading southwestward again on a compass bearing. He was still walking across various fields in deep snow that sometimes reached up to his waist and when dawn came, he finally came within sight of the town of Penig.

CHAPTER 93

When Dave first saw Penig he was still some distance from it. He was walking in a field that led to a road running south and going through the town about half a mile away. There was a snow-covered thicket in a small wood close to the road where he was heading and when he reached that thicket, Dave stepped in and spruced himself up. He shaved with a small razor that Mieteck had given him and combed his hair. He washed his face thoroughly and removed the last traces of make-up from his face and from his eyebrows. Then he took off his black wig, fake black mustache, cap, greatcoat, military uniform and black boots. He buried the black wig, fake black mustache and military clothes in the snow and put on the dark-brown leather winter boots, cap and scarf he had with him.

Then Dave took out a small mirror and looked at himself. With the cap he was wearing, his brown winter jacket and scarf, thin brown sweater with a shirt and tie to match, brown winter pants and dark-brown leather boots, he looked like any ordinary German or foreign worker. Dave looked at himself once more to make sure everything was all right and then stepped out of the thicket. He got on the road that led south toward Penig and when he reached the town, he saw it wasn't much. Penig was just a small, bleak, industrial town. It was drab, shabby, dingy and looked as if it had seen much better days. It had a tram line, some coalyards, a few factories and a bridge that crossed a small river. It also had in the town proper houses close to the street and that for the most part, with their broken window-panes, peeling paint and rusty ironwork, looked rundown and neglected.

Dave followed the tram line over the bridge and into the town itself. He headed for the railway station at the other end of it and by the time he reached it, around 7.00 a.m., he was completely covered with snow as were most of the people who were at the station. Since a few of them had already been to the wicket to enquire about the Munich train via Zwickau, Dave asked one of them. It turned out the Munich train had been due to get to Penig at 10.00 a.m. But on account of the blizzard there was a two-hour delay and it would only get there at noon. Now that he knew its arrival Dave left the station and kept on walking on the road that led out of town. In no time Dave found himself in the country again and on the right side of the road, not far from the town, he saw a group of three barns. In the blizzard they looked deserted and Dave left the road and made for the first one.

There was a door at the back of it and it wasn't locked. Dave opened it and went in. Inside he saw it was used to keep a couple of old tractors and ploughs as well as other rundown agricultural equipment. The hayloft was full of hay though. Dave closed the door behind him and climbed on a ladder in the middle of the barn that led to the hayloft. In the hayloft Dave found a spot on the right side of it and at the back that gave him a good view of the road and of the surroundings through some cracks in the boards. Dave sat in the hayloft and leaned his back against the wall. He reached for a small plastic bag in the right pocket of his winter jacket and opened the bag. He took out one of the chocolate bars. He began eating the first half of it and put the second half back in the plastic bag.

Then Dave sat and rested. Around 11.30 a.m. he got up and brushed the hay from his clothes. He climbed down the ladder and headed for the back door. Dave opened it and stepped out. He began walking back toward Penig and saw by now the blizzard had become worse than ever. There was a cold icy wind blowing and the snow was rising and swirling everywhere in huge sudden gusts. In no time Dave was again covered with snow and when he got back to Penig, it didn't take him long to reach the railway station. There were quite a few people waiting on the platform and all of them were also covered with snow. Dave walked inside the station and asked the woman at the wicket for a third-class ticket to Munich. The woman handed him one and Dave paid for it and walked out to wait for his train to Zwickau.

A little past noon the train for Zwickau arrived and stopped at the station. Dave got onto it and shortly after they left and began heading south. Dave stood close to a group of workmen who had gotten in and who seemed to hang around together. He stood in the corridor and looked out of the window at the snow blowing outside and hitting the window and partially covering it with frost. The journey to Zwickau was extremely slow and when they came to it around 4.00 p.m., Dave saw it looked almost exactly like Penig. The only difference was it was a bigger town. But, like Penig, the town looked drab, shabby, dingy and it had a real look of poverty and hardship about it that was reflected in the faces of the people, the houses and buildings. At the station Dave checked and found the overnight train for Munich was leaving at 8.00 p.m.

Dave left the station and began walking along the main street. He followed the tram line and saw by now the blizzard had stopped raging and given way to an incredibly savage and penetrating cold. As he walked along the tram line Dave slapped his sides from time to time and when he saw a movie theater on the right side of the road, he headed for it and went in. The theater wasn't big. It looked as if it could seat about 300 people and had a glass front with two doors leading in. Inside there was a cashier's booth that stood between the two doors and faced the lobby. Dave stepped to the cashier's booth and bought a ticket. Then he made for the left door leading inside and saw in the darkness there were men's and ladies' rooms at the back on his side. There were also several rows of seats leading to the screen and one aisle on each side of the seats.

Dave headed for the left aisle and went and sat down at the first seat in one of the back rows. There was a fair number of people in the theater. Most of them seemed to be from the Army, Navy and Air Force. There were also some civilians and a few workers. Some of the soldiers, sailors and airmen were slumped in their seats and had their combat packs or duffel bags in the seat next to them. A few of the civilians and workers also had suitcases in the seat next to them. But most of the people in the theater were dozing and paying little or no attention to what was being shown on the screen. There was no heating in the theater and Dave sat in his seat and rubbed his sides. He was shivering and tried to get interested in what the newsreels were showing.

They were going on about the mighty and glorious German Army in Africa and about what was happening on the Leningrad, Stalingrad and Balkan fronts. After a while there was a very long, boring and theatrical movie about Frederick The Great and when it was close to 7.00 p.m., Dave decided to change seat. The one he was sitting in was broken and sloping a little to the left. So he got up and went and sat on the first seat on the right side in the same row. This seat was far more comfortable and after he had been sitting in it for a while, Dave turned and saw something that made his hair stand on end. A couple of rows back, in the first seat, there was an old and faded brown leather suitcase. It was just lying there and didn't seem to belong to anyone.

Oh man, Dave thought. I don't believe this. I just don't believe this. To whom does this suitcase belong? To some member of the Military or to a civilian or workman? But, if that's the case, how come no one is sitting near it at the back? How come no one in the theater is looking at it as if it belongs to him? Could it belong, maybe, to someone who's been in the theater and who's so tired and exhausted he's left without it and doesn't even realize he's done that? Or could it have been placed there, he thought, to be used as a trap? Is someone, in fact, watching to see who's going to take it? Hey listen, he thought. Get yourself together. Start thinking clearly. It's no use going on like this. The suitcase being there can only mean one of an infinite number of possibilities and it's silly going on like this and driving yourself crazy. Either you take it or you don't. That's it.

Dave kept on looking at the suitcase and after a while, he suddenly got up. He left his seat and when he came near it, he reached for it and quickly grabbed it.

CHAPTER 94

Dave walked swiftly with the suitcase to the back of the theater and turned right in the darkness. He headed for the left side of it where the men's room was. When he reached it Dave opened the door and went in. The men's room wasn't big. It had two narrow wooden stalls and one urine-streaked urinal. That was all. Dave went into the first stall. That stall faced the entrance door to the men's room and he closed the door behind him and sat on the toilet bowl. As he sat on the bowl Dave opened the suitcase and couldn't believe his eyes. Inside there was a large thick brown woolen sweater, a large pale-blue flannel pajama, a couple of shirts and three big pairs of white woolen socks.

Dave stared at those things and took off his brown winter jacket and scarf and hung them on the hook at the back of the door of the stall. Then he reached for and put on the large thick brown woolen sweater over his other thin brown sweater. As soon as Dave put on the large thick brown sweater he could feel a surge of warmth coming over him. This sent his confidence soaring and for the first time he began thinking he might be able to escape after all and go all the way. Dave sat on the toilet bowl for a while and let his body take in the heat and warmth his new sweater was now giving him. Then he closed the suitcase and put it down. He stood up and reached for his brown winter jacket and scarf. He put them on and a few moments later left the men's room with the suitcase.

Dave headed toward the left exit door and when he reached it, he stopped briefly and then stepped into the lobby. A small group of tall well-built young Werhmacht soldiers were standing around the cashier's booth and talking to the cashier and Dave left the theater and turned left. He walked back along the tram line until he reached the railway station.

Escape

At the station he went in and bought the *Volkischer Beobachter*. Then he got on the overnight train for Munich and at precisely 8.00 p.m., the train left and began heading south. It was quite stuffy inside and crowded with Army, Navy, Air Force officers, NCOs and soldiers. There were also quite a few civilians, workmen, down-at-the-heels seedy-looking businessmen and Government officials. Dave spent the whole night in the corridor next to a couple of tired and sleepy workmen.

It was extremely hot on the train and Dave opened his newspaper and tried to read it in the pale night light. He was trying to stay awake and alert and when morning finally came, he saw they were slowing down and coming into the outskirts of Munich. In town the train slowed down even more and moved through the outlying districts before it came and stopped in the Haupt Bahnhof Railway Station. As soon as it stopped there Dave got up and filed out with the other passengers. He walked along the disembarkation platform and when he reached the middle of the main concourse, he walked over to the wickets where he bought a second-class ticket for Rottweil. It was now a little after 8.00 o'clock in the morning and the station, which didn't seem to have been touched by the war so far, was full of officers of all ranks, NCOs, soldiers, Government officials, businessmen, civilians and workmen.

Now that he had his ticket for Rottweil Dave left the concourse and went to a stall in the men's room where he had the second half of the chocolate bar he had started to eat earlier. Then he left the men's room and went to an underground bomb-proof waiting-room for the use of passengers who had to wait for more than half an hour for a train. In this underground bomb-proof waiting-room Dave was able to rest for a while and pretend to read the *Volkischer Beobachter*. Then, when there was a routine Paper Control, he got through it easily. At 10.00 a.m. Dave left the waiting-room and went to take the train for Ulm. In order to go to Rottweil Dave had to take this train. There was a short 10-minute wait and a change there for a train to Tuttlingen. In Tuttlingen there was a longer wait and a change for the train to Rottweil.

Once he got on the train for Ulm Dave didn't have to wait long. Soon they were on their way and began heading out of the station. In a little while they cleared Munich and the train picked up speed. They kept on going west this time through the hilly countryside, deeply buried in snow and filled with deep dark stiff forests, and kept on moving through towns and villages like Olching, Hattenhofen, Augsburg, Jettingen and Offingen. There were quite a few people on the train and it was stuffy. Dave stood by one of the windows and saw it was an incredibly cold, gray and overcast day. He kept on standing there and not long after they had passed through

The Long War

Günsberg, around 1.00 o'clock in the afternoon, their train slowed down and came into Ulm.

In Ulm Dave had to leave his train to take another one on a parallel track. This one was lined up and waiting alongside the platform of the station. Dave walked across the track to his new train and went and sat in one of the middle wagons. He sat on the first seat on the right side near the door. It was stuffy in the wagon and Dave got up and lowered the window all the way down on his side. Then he sat down again and breathed in the cold clean fresh air. After a while Dave closed his eyes and kept on breathing the the cold clean fresh air and when he opened them, he looked out of the window and suddenly saw a Gestapo Inspector. The Inspector was a tall, strongly-built and muscular man. He was in his early thirties and was wearing the ever-present and ever-familiar black leather hat and black leather coat.

There was a tough hard look on his face and from the way he was walking briskly toward his wagon Dave thought he was checking the middle of the train while a couple of other Inspectors were probably doing the front and rear of it. When the Inspector reached his wagon he climbed in and came and stopped in front of Dave. He fixed his cold chilly eyes on him and said: *"Ausweis, bitte?"*

"Natürelich," Dave said and took out his old French leather wallet and handed him his identification papers.

"Ihren namen?"

"Louis Durand."

"Sie Sind Auslander?"

"Jawohl."

"Where do you come from?"

"Leipzig."

"And where are you going?"

"Rottweil."

"What are you doing there?"

"I'm a construction worker for the Reich. I work for the Todt Organization."

"Doing what?"

"I'm a fortification worker. I specialize in pouring concrete."

"So close to the frontier?"

"Is Rottweil close to the frontier?"

"Rottweil is 48 kilometers from the frontier. That's close enough."

"I didn't know that. I'm just going there to work for the Todt Organization."

Escape

"I didn't know the Todt Organization used foreign workers so close to the frontier."

"That's where they're sending me."

"I must say I find this strange."

"Well, that's where they're sending me."

"All right. Show me your hands."

"I beg your pardon?"

"You heard me."

Dave put out his hands and turned them on both sides a few times for the Inspector to look at them.

"Those hands look like the hands of a classical pianist. Not a construction worker."

"Well, I'm a concrete specialist."

"I doubt that. If you want to see real worker's hands, look at these."

The Inspector showed Dave his hands and they were big, strong and calloused.

"I must say those are quite impressive hands."

"That's why I don't believe you're a construction worker."

"You don't have to believe me. Just call the Todt Organization."

"Don't you worry. I will."

CHAPTER 95

At that moment there was a commotion on the platform. There were yells of *"Halt! Halt! Stehen bleiben oder schiesse!"* Then a tall slim blond man in his early twenties, with curly hair and a long hook nose, ran past their window. People scattered right and left as a tall flabby Gestapo Inspector with a gun in his hand ran after him and was followed by a short overweight one also with a gun. The first Gestapo Inspector wanted to lower his gun and shoot at the man. But there were too many people on the platform and the man was starting to gain on them. The Inspector who was with Dave leaned out of the window and looked at what was happening. As he looked he suddenly said: *"Ach, schiesse!"*

Then he stepped back from the window and threw Dave's identification papers on the seat. He bolted out of the wagon and took out his gun. He also began running after the man and gained on the two Inspectors. In a short while he passed them both and near the end of the platform threw himself on the man and tackled him to the floor. Almost at once he was joined by the other two Inspectors and all three of them got tangled with the man in a writhing struggling kicking mass as a shot rang out and as all four of them kept on fighting and shoving and kicking on the floor. At the same time a whistle blew. Dave's train began moving slowly and they pulled out of the station. Dave looked out of the window and watched the station glide by. Then he turned from the window and sat still.

Dave was breathing hard and wiped the dryness from his mouth. After a while he got up and closed the window. Then he picked up his Identification Papers from the seat next to him and put them in the right pocket of his jacket. He sat down again and stood still and looked at the countryside going by and at the woods, fields and valleys deeply buried in snow. Their train kept on moving southwest and going through towns and villages like Blaustein, Hutten, Munderkingen, Ertingen and Muhlheim and around 5.00 o'clock in the afternoon, they reached Tuttlingen. In Tuttlingen there was a fairly long wait for the train to Rottweil. But Dave had no intention of taking that train. Rottweil was 30 miles from the frontier. Tuttlingen however was only 15 miles.

With this in mind Dave walked along the station platform and told the Railway Official at the gate he was going into town for a while and would be back in time to take his train to Rottweil. Then Dave left the station and walked out of Tuttlingen. He began heading west for Switzerland and moved quickly along a road that led in that direction. After a while though he saw he was completely lost. There were no road signs around Tuttlingen and it was pretty hard for Dave to get his bearings. He kept on walking and finally saw the road he was taking wasn't the right one. It was taking him due south instead of westward past an area of camouflaged factories and gun emplacements. When he saw that Dave tried to take a short cut across the countryside to another road which he knew was heading westward.

But this was really no better. This road took him over hilly country quite a way from where he wanted to go. Dave kept on looking for the right road and it wasn't until early evening before he found it. Once he was on the right road Dave walked on it for several miles and when it was close to midnight, he couldn't go on anymore. By then he made for the woods in order to find a place to hide for the night. Soon he found what he was looking for in a depression among the snow-laden pine trees. Those trees stood not far from a clearing near the road and the depression was covered with quite a few broken branches. Dave made himself a shelter with those branches and settled down for the night. Dave had his suitcase to rest on and the snow to camouflage his shelter and soon dozed off.

Dave slept fitfully throughout the night and when he opened his eyes in the morning, he saw it was going to be another incredibly cold, gray and overcast day. Dawn was slowly breaking over the countryside and as he stood in his shelter, Dave was paralyzed by the cold. The large thick brown sweater he had found in the movie theater in Zwickau wasn't enough to keep him warm. Dave rubbed his hands and feet and slapped his sides. Then he got up and spruced himself up. He shaved with his small razor and combed his hair. He also swept himself clean of the snow that had blown on him during the night and ate a whole chocolate bar from his small plastic bag. Then he left his shelter and stepped out of the woods. He got on the nearby road and began walking westward again.

Dave walked along that road and then along other roads heading southwest. Most of the time he tried to keep off them and move through

The Long War

woods and fields. But eventually the countryside became more open and rolling and he was forced onto the roads again. Dave held on to his suitcase and went through several villages scattered through the open and rolling countryside. In one he had to return the friendly *"Heil Hitler!"* of a soldier who was walking down the main street. In another he had to walk through a bunch of children who were coming out of school and running and laughing and playing among themselves. In a third he felt the cold hard stares of a couple of old men who were standing in front of a tobacco shop and looking at him as he moved past them and out of the village.

Dave kept on going and after a while the countryside became wooded and hilly again. As it did Dave got off the roads and disappeared into the trees. He kept on heading westward in a day so cold and icy he was beginning to feel numb and at times confused. To make sure he made no mistake he moved by compass bearing and frequently checked the small escape map sown inside his winter jacket. By evening he finally reached Singen and the frontier road that ran east and west. The frontier road was five miles west of Singen and was passing within half a mile of the Swiss frontier. Dave kept on heading westward through the woods and when he was close to the frontier, he suddenly hid behind a tree and stood still. Not far from him in the woods was a woodman's hut! Dave watched it for a while and then ran to the door. It was locked.

Dave walked quickly to the back and couldn't believe his eyes. Three of the planks were loose. Dave bent down and quickly removed them. He sneaked in and put the planks back together. In the hut Dave was immediately hit by the surprising warmth that was there and put his suitcase down on the wall next to the window near the door. Then he lay down against it and waited.

CHAPTER 96

Dave waited all evening. He closed his eyes and rested against his suitcase. Then, close to 2.00 o'clock in the morning, he stepped close to the window and looked out. A thick light fluffy snow was now falling and blanketing the woods. Dave moved away from the window and opened his suitcase. He reached for and put on a big pair of white woolen socks over his boots. Then he closed it and opened his small plastic bag. He ate his third and last chocolate bar and finally moved to the rear of the woodman's hut with his suitcase. Dave removed the three loose planks at the back and stepped out. He put the planks back on and not far from the hut buried his suitcase in the snow.

Then Dave left the hut and set out for the frontier. He moved westward and after a short while, he crossed some railway lines and got into the edge of another wood. By now he was very close to the frontier road and even heard and saw a motorcyclist on that road. Dave moved left in that wood and walked for about 100 yards before he hid behind a tree and stood still. About 15 yards ahead of him stood a sentry box. The sentry was out of his box and rubbing his hands. Now Dave knew exactly where he was. From where he stood Dave could see fields and hedges and a wooded hill to the left of those fields and hedges. The top of that hill was his goal. The end of the wood was his target. There was no blackout in Switzerland and Dave could see the faintest haze beyond the hill. Now Dave backtracked for about 70 yards and got close to the road again.

Near the road Dave bent low and began running. He crossed the road and headed for his target. He came out of the wood and ran close to it through snowy hedges, ditches, fields and meadows. He heard his heart pounding loudly and savagely and hoped there was no barbed wire. In this

The Long War

thick light fluffy snow he could hardly see anything and kept on going and running and when he reached halfway, he slipped into the wood and stopped. His heart was still pounding loudly and savagely and he stood bent in two. Then, when he was able to pause and catch his breath, he slipped out of the wood again and went on. Dave still stayed close to the wood and ran in a sweeping curve. First he ran toward his right and then toward his left before he straightened up and headed for the top of the hill. The top of the hill was his target.

Dave kept on running and moving through snowy hedges, ditches, fields and meadows and when he had almost reached the top of the hill, he suddenly heard: *"Halt! Wer da!"* Dave froze and saw the guard through the trees on his left. He was covered with snow and stepped out from behind a pine tree into the open. He was holding his rifle in both hands and had it pointed at him.

It's not right, Dave thought. It's just not right. To have worked so hard and to have come so far to end up like this. It's just not right.

The guard now moved further into the open and came toward Dave. As he did Dave suddenly saw the outline of his Tyrolean-style cap and the crosses on the snow-flecked gleaming buttons of his uniform. The guard was a Swiss guard.

Dave had finally made it into Switzerland!

CHAPTER 97

The guard stopped close to Dave and said: *"Wer sind sie?"* *"Ich bin ein Kanadier,"* Dave said. *"Was machen sie hier?"* the guard said. *"Ich bin ein entlaufender straeffling,"* Dave said. *"Ich moëchte zur Schweiz fliehen."* *"Jawohl,"* the guard said. *"Kommen sie mit mir."* The guard then turned and stepped into the trees again. He headed south and Dave followed him. As they were walking alongside the edge of those trees the guard looked to his left and said: *"Alles in ordnung. Nur ein Kanadicher flüchtling."* When the guard said this Dave turned and saw another guard through the trees. He was holding his rifle in his hands and stood about 15 feet from the first guard. The guard nodded and the first guard went on through the trees with Dave until they reached the top of the hill.

Then they went down on the other side and got on a snowy road that led to a small village called Ramsen. Near the village the lamp posts were lit on both sides of the road and in Ramsen the guard took Dave to the Commander of the Guard Post. The Commander gave Dave a stiff cognac and a hot bowl of soup and sent him to bed. Early in the morning Dave was taken by a border guard to Schaffhausen for interrogation. At 10.00 a.m. he was taken by the same border guard and put on a train for Berne. The guard got on the train with Dave and went with him to Berne in order to take him to the British Legation. By rail the distance from Schaffhausen to Berne was a little over 90 miles and as they began heading southwest, they went through quite a few towns and villages such as Neuhausen, Jestetten, Rupperswill, Waldshut, Brugg, Aarau and Olten.

Along the way, on a day that was turning out to be clear, cold and sunny, Dave was amazed to see how clean and prosperous Switzerland looked. From the jagged towering mountains all around to the trim snow-clad hills, steep-walled dark-wooded valleys, placid peaceful countryside, small well-kept meadows and pleasantly-rolling gently-sloping plain of the Mittelland, every town and village looked extremely neat and spotless. In fact in all those towns and villages they went through there was an astonishing look of affluence and prosperity that was quite different from anything Dave had seen in France and Germany. In France, while most of the countryside had been quite nice and untouched by the war, all the cities and towns had looked scarred and battered. In Germany it had been worse. There all the cities and towns as well as the countryside had been the very picture of bleakness, grimness and gloominess.

In Switzerland, on the other hand, there was only this astonishing look of affluence and prosperity that seemed to be everywhere, and this seemed to be especially true of Berne when they reached it around 2.00 o'clock in the afternoon. With its many churches, palaces and museums, its various flags hanging everywhere, its string of high-level bridges connecting the Old Town and the New, its arcades over the sidewalks, its quaint square towers and ornate fountains, it looked like the richest and wealthiest city Dave had seen so far in Switzerland and one that had done quite well and really profited from the war. As soon as they pulled into the Bahnhof Dave was led by the border guard to a diplomatic car waiting for them outside. They got in and the car left and took them to the British Legation on the Aarbergergasse near the Wainsenhausplatz.

The British Legation was located in a large three-story graystone building and when they reached it, the border guard showed his papers to one of the Royal Marines who let them in through the front gate. They drove up the small half-circular driveway and came and stopped at the front entrance. They got out and again the border guard showed his papers to one of the Royal Marines at the door. They were let in and inside the lobby, the border guard spoke to the soldier on duty at the front desk. The soldier signed his papers and the border guard turned and left. When he was gone the soldier at the desk motioned for Dave to go and sit in one of the tall leather chairs facing the front desk and the two circular staircases that went up on each side of the front desk.

Dave went and sat in one of those chairs and the soldier picked up the phone on his desk. He dialed a number and spoke into the receiver for a while. Then the soldier put down the phone and not long after, a tall, slim and impeccably-dressed man in his late twenties came down the right circular staircase. The man had extremely well-groomed pale-brown hair, clear pale-brown eyes and was wearing an expensive light-brown suit with shirt, tie and shoes to match. As soon as he reached the lobby, he came and shook hands with Dave and told him to follow him. The man then turned and headed for the right circular staircase. He walked up the staircase and when he came to the second floor, he turned left and walked to a door not far from the staircase and to the left side of it.

When they reached that door he opened it and motioned for Dave to go in. Dave stepped in and found himself in a large conference room with French windows giving out on the Aarbergergasse. There was a long shiny boardroom table with big leather chairs around it and on the wall facing the windows stood the pictures of famous British politicians and diplomats. Once they were inside the conference room the man closed the door and turned to Dave. He motioned for him to go and sit in one of the big leather chairs near the head of the table on the right side while he himself went and sat at the head of it. Then he turned to Dave again and said: "Welcome. Welcome to Switzerland. My name is Christopher Bowden. You can call me Chris."

"Good," Dave said and told Bowden his name.

"I'm the Junior Secretary of the Legation and I'll be handling your case."

"Shouldn't a Military Attaché be doing that?"

"Normally that's the case. But our Military Attaché has been recalled to other duties."

"I see."

"The new one hasn't arrived yet so I've inherited your case."

Dave nodded and Bowden said: "Before we go any further, however, I believe congratulations are in order. You've broken out of Colditz and made a home run. That's an extraordinary achievement."

"I was lucky."

"No. No. Anyone breaking out of Colditz isn't lucky."

"It wasn't as extraordinary as you think."

"Not extraordinary? My dear fellow you broke out after having been there only seven weeks. I call that extraordinary."

"I had help."

"I'm sure you did."

"You can't imagine how much."

"I don't doubt it."

"So what's the next step?"

"The next step is to get you out of here and safely back to England."

"How are you going to do this?"

"By taking you through France to Gibraltar. And then on to England."

"When?"

"These things take time. Usually two to three months."

"Two to three months!"
"That's right. But in your case I believe you're lucky."
"Why?"
"You'll see."
"No. Why?"
"Before we talk about this there's someone I'd like you to meet."
"Who?"
"You'll see."
"No. Who?"
"You wait. You just wait for me here."

CHAPTER 98

Bowden stood up and told Dave he'd be back shortly. Then he left the conference room and Dave sat in his big leather chair and looked at the sunlight coming through the windows and shining on the long boardroom table and on the pictures of famous British politicians and diplomats. In a short while the door opened and Bowden came in with a girl who appeared to Dave to be about 18 years old. She was tall and slender and had pale-brown hair and clear-blue eyes. She was wearing a white blouse, a light-blue skirt and light-blue shoes. She looked somewhat shy and reserved and although she had a nicely-rounded back and fully-rounded legs, she looked quite frail and fragile.

When Bowden came in with the girl Dave stood up. Bowden walked over with her and introduced her as Jeanne. He told Dave she was one of the best guide the British had to help Allied soldiers get back to England. Dave shook hands with her and Bowden told Dave he'd see him in a little while. He left the conference room and Dave stood facing the girl at the head of the table. The girl then motioned for him to sit down in his chair again and sat down herself at the head of the table. As she did the girl smiled at Dave and said in an English that had a light French accent to it: "Well, David. That was quite an extraordinary thing you did."

"It wasn't all that extraordinary."

"It was. Escaping from Colditz is always an extraordinary feat."

"I had help," Dave said and went on and told her how his escape had come about and how Jan Mieteck and the Poles had helped him.

"Why, that's wonderful," Jeanne said when he had finished. "To have people help you like this."

"It is."

"And now you would like to get back to England."
"I would."
"It won't be easy."
"I know that."
"Actually it will be pretty risky."
"I know that too."
"To try and go back now, as a matter of fact, will be extremely dangerous."
"Why?"
"Well, with the Allies landing in North Africa, the Germans have taken over the south of France. The whole country is crawling with them. And the frontier posts are more guarded than ever.
"What do you propose then?"
"I don't know yet. But no matter what it will be, it will be extremely dangerous."
"Why?"
"I'll have to take you across France to Bayonne. And from there into Spain."
"That's a very long journey."
"It is."
"It's almost 440 miles. Why don't you take me south to Perpignan? It's a much shorter route."
"I would do that if I could. But I don't have any organization there."
"I see."
"And besides I understand the frontier post at La Jonquera is heavily guarded and extremely difficult to get through."
"But, if you take me East-West, we'll have to go through many large towns and that'll also be very dangerous."
"That's true."
"We're bound to run into quite a few paper controls."
"I agree."
"Why run the risk?"
"Well, we'll be traveling at night. And I'm very familiar with that route."
"So that's how you propose to take me."
"That's right."
"If you take me."
"That's it."
"Will you?"
"I don't know yet."
"Seriously. Will you?"
"I'll see."

CHAPTER 99

Jeanne then stood up and shook hands with Dave who also got up. She left the conference room and Dave sat down again and looked at the light coming through the windows. He didn't have to look at it for long before the door opened and Bowden came in again. He walked over to where Dave was sitting and took the same chair he had used before at the head of the table. Then he turned to Dave and said: "Well. What did you think of her?"

"I don't know."

"What do you mean, you don't know?"

"Exactly that. I don't know."

"Why? You didn't like her?"

"Oh, for God's sake, man! The girl is about 18!"

"Come on."

"It's true! And she looks so frail and fragile I don't think she could work her way out of a paper bag!"

"Oh, come on."

"It's true! And this is the girl you want me to follow across France?"

"It's not like that at all. You're misreading all this."

"Oh yes? Listen. She wants to take me the long way across France so we can go through all these major towns and have all those paper controls! How about that for being smart."

"She can do it."

"Oh, sure."

"I'm telling you. She can."

"What if she can't?"

"She can do it. Listen. This girl is simply the best guide there is."

"I don't care if she's the greatest guide in the world. It still looks pretty risky to me."

"Not really, old man. I'm telling you this girl is good. And she'll take you to Spain."

"She's only 18 years old for God's sake!"

"That's where you're wrong. She's 24 years old."

"Eighteen years old! Twenty-four years old! What's the difference!"

"The difference is she'll take you to Spain."

"I'm not so sure."

"Oh yes she will."

"Well, I don't have any confidence in her."

"Why not?"

"Why should I?"

"Listen. Do you know how long it takes to get out of Switzerland? I said two to three months. Well, I downplayed it for you. Actually it takes up to a year."

"So?"

"So count yourself lucky she agreed to take you."

"I'm not asking her to take me."

"I know that."

"If she doesn't want to take me that's fine with me."

"She'll take you. And besides. Do you think we would send you out with her if we thought she couldn't do it?"

"That's what I'm wondering."

"Don't. If we tell you she can do it, she can."

"I hope so."

"Take my word for it. She can."

CHAPTER 100

Bowden stood up again and motioned for Dave to follow him. Dave also got up and they left the conference room. They turned right and walked down the hallway until they came to a door near the end of it on the right. Bowden opened it and they stepped inside of what looked like a small office. There was a chair, a desk and a somewhat bigger chair facing the desk. As they came in Bowden told Dave to get rid of his escape clothes and put on the clothes on the chair facing the desk. Dave nodded and got out of his escape clothes. He put on a pair of underwear, heavy woolen socks, a flannel shirt and tie, pale-gray corduroy pants, a large woolen sweater, a gray scarf, a navy-blue winter jacket, a navy-blue woolen cap and thick black winter boots.

When Dave was dressed Bowden left the Legation with him and took him in an unmarked diplomatic car to a small tailor shop on the Brunngasse to have his picture taken in a shirt, tie and suit jacket. Then Bowden took him to the small room they had rented for him in a pension on the Speichergasse. This room was not far from the British Legation and the Lorrainebrücke. It was on the third floor of a three-story gray-stone building and had a spectacular view of the Alps. In his room Bowden gave Dave en envelope with Swiss Francs for him to use while he was in Berne. He told him to report to the Legation every morning around 11.00 o'clock and to wait for the call for his escape. In the present circumstances the call might not come that quickly. Finally Bowden left and now that it was a little after 4.00 o'clock in the afternoon, Dave stepped out of his room and went for a walk on the Speichergasse.

In a tobacco shop not far from his pension Dave walked in and bought a postcard with a view of the snow-covered sun-swept Alps. Then he went and sat in a small café next to the tobacco shop where he ordered a cold beer and wrote to Mieteck in the back of the postcard:

> I'm taking a holiday in Switzerland. The country is beautiful. The air is wonderful. I'm truly enjoying the magnificent view of the Alps and the spectacular sight of all those eagles that are flying so high in the distance, especially one that's red, white and free.

Dave signed the postcard, Your brother Tadeusz, and addressed it to: Jan Mieteck, c/o Oflag IV C, Colditz, Saxony. After a while he left the café and went and mailed it at a Post Office nearby.

Once he had mailed the postcard Dave kept on walking on the Speichergasse and when he came back to his pension, he went up to his room where he lay down and went to sleep. In the morning Dave went to the same small café he had gone the day before and had a wonderful breakfast of *Kässchnitte mit Ei und Schinken*. This was a meal of melted cheese on bread with a fried egg on top and cooked ham on the side. He had a hot steaming mug of coffee with the meal and after the meal went to the Legation to report. Then he left the Legation and went for a walk as he settled down to wait for the call for his escape. He didn't have to wait long. As a matter of fact the call came pretty quickly. It came 10 days later on Monday, December 7, 1942. That morning Dave went to the Legation and was told by Bowden the escape was on. He was to to report to him at 6.00 o'clock in the afternoon.

Dave left the Legation and went back to his pension to rest. At 6.00 o'clock sharp he reported to Bowden who took him in the same unmarked diplomatic car they had taken before to the Bahnhof. At the station they got on the 7.00 o'clock train for Geneva. This was a slow train that stopped at Lausanne and at many other places like Mühleberg, Galmiz, Murten, Avenches, Moudon, Céligny and Bellevue. All evening long they kept on heading southwest and a little after midnight, when they reached the Gare de Cornavin in Geneva, Bowden took a taxi and brought Dave to the Hotel Servais on the Rue du Rhône. He had reserved a room for them on the 5th floor and in that room they waited until a little after 1.30 in the morning. At that time there was a discreet knock at the door and Jeanne came in with a slight dark-haired man who had a dark narrow mustache.

The man was in his early twenties and wore a dark leather jacket and black corduroy pants. Jeanne herself was wearing a dark-blue winter jacket and dark-blue slacks and she introduced the man as François. Then she shook hands with Bowden and talked with him for while. Finally, when it was close to 2.00 o'clock in the morning, she turned to Dave and told him to get ready. Dave stood up and put on his scarf, winter jacket and cap. He thanked Bowden for everything he had done for him and left with Jeanne and François. They took the elevator to the lobby and outside a four-door black Renault was waiting for them. A big man with a hat sat at the wheel and Jeanne got in front with him. Dave and François sat at the back and they left the hotel and began driving east on the Rue du Rhône.

In no time they crossed the Rue des Eaux Vives and kept on driving east and began leaving Geneva behind. In the clear, cold and star-filled night they kept on driving east and on heading toward the French border. At this hour all the Rues and Boulevards were deserted and roughly five miles out of Geneva the driver killed his lights and came and stopped near the French border. They now stood a little to the east of Voiron. This was a small village on the French side of the border. As soon as they stopped Jeanne quickly got out of the car with François and Dave. François told them not to talk and follow him. They left the road and went down a fairly steep embankment. They walked through a sloping field and through a sloping wood and when they stopped in a clearing near the middle of it, François turned and whispered to them to wait here while he went ahead to see if everything was all right.

There was a clear moon shining through the trees and at the end of the wood Dave could see another sloping field and the thin silver of a stream showing. The silver stream was the border. Beyond the stream there was another sloping field and another sloping wood and Dave could hear the faint barking of German shepherds in the distance. He could also hear the stiff and steady blowing of the wind through the trees and after a while Jeanne looked at her watch. She was staring at the trees at the end of the clearing and some time later there was a faint rustling through the wood and François came into the clearing. Jeanne and Dave stepped up to him and Jeanne said in French: "What's wrong? What's taking you so long?" "It's the Germans," François said. "They've changed the timing and pattern of the patrols and I have to make sure they've gone to the other side of the wood before we cross. You wait here. I'll come to get you when it's time."

François then turned and walked out of the clearing again. Dave watched him disappear through the trees and thought: I knew it! I just knew it! This whole operation is run on a shoestring and no one really knows what the hell's going on. Why me? he thought. Why the hell do these things always have to happen to me? What have I done to always end up in these incredibly silly and stupid situations? By now Jeanne was looking at her watch again. She was also staring at the trees and then François suddenly reappeared in the clearing. "Come! Come!" he said. "Quickly!" François then turned and left the clearing. He now moved fast and ran in a crouch through the trees. Jeanne and Dave followed him and they came out of the wood and ran down the slope of the field toward the stream.

The stream was only about 10 yards wide and they ran into it and splashed across. In the middle of it the water rose above Dave's knees. It was unbelievably cold and icy and as they ran and splashed across it, a thick heavy-set man in a dark winter jacket and dark slacks ran out of the wood on the French side and waved for them to hurry up and move into the wood. The first one to make it was François. He was followed by Jeanne and then Dave. When they were into the trees they ran with the thick heavy-set man up the slope of the wood until they came to a tall hedge by the side of a road that ran east and west through the trees. Near an opening in the hedge the thick heavy-set man put a finger to his lips and disappeared through the opening.

In no time the man was back and told them to get on the road and stay in the shadow of the trees on the other side. François nodded and got on the road. He was followed by Jeanne and Dave and the thick heavy-set man brought up the rear. They walked swiftly westward and could still hear German shepherds barking in the distance. The trees on both sides of the road were quite tall and the wind was blowing stiffly and steadily through them. In a little while they reached the small village of Voiron and François stepped up to the first house of the village on the right. He knocked softly on the front door. The door opened and they all went in.

CHAPTER 101

Inside the house a big broad-shouldered woman greeted them and led them to the kitchen. She made them sit around the table and served them some red wine, bread and a bowl of hot lentil soup. After the meal she led Dave to a small narrow room on the second floor where he was to spend the night. She closed the door behind him and Dave lay down in bed and immediately fell asleep. When he woke up in the morning he looked at his watch and saw it was close to 11.00 o'clock. Dave walked downstairs to the kitchen and found Jeanne sitting there with the big broad-shouldered woman and the thick heavy-set man. François was gone. When Dave came in the woman served him a good breakfast of coffee, bread, ham and eggs.

After the breakfast the thick heavy-set man got up from the table and took Dave and Jeanne to a Renault gazogène parked outside. They left the house and began heading for the town of La Roche. This was a small town about 10 miles from Voiron. When they reached it the man dropped them at the Régina Hotel. It was another cold, clear and sunny day and when they stepped out of the car, the owner of the hotel was waiting for them inside the lobby. He was a big burly man and as soon as they walked in, he nodded. Then he turned and they followed him up the half-circular staircase until they came to a room on the third floor on the right of the staircase. The man motioned for them to go in and locked the door behind them. Inside, on the bed, were the room keys, a large manila envelope and a big brown leather suitcase.

Once they were in the room Jeanne reached for the large manila envelope and opened it. She turned to Dave and gave him a passport, an *Ausweis*, a wedding ring, various other papers, some French Francs, an old

French leather wallet and told him their cover story. They were a married couple named Pierre and Louise Dumont. They were both teaching at a Lycée in Lyons and were traveling across France to go to the wedding of her sister Anne in Bayonne. They had both taken a week off and had first driven to La Roche to visit some friends before going on to the wedding. The clothes they were to wear to Bayonne were in the suitcase on the bed and they were to get out of the clothes they now had on. They were to put on those new clothes and put their old ones in the suitcase. There was also a razor and a comb in the bathroom for Dave to spruce himself up before they left.

Dave nodded and reached for the suitcase. He opened it and took out his and Jeanne's clothes. Dave's clothes were made up of a black winter coat, a scarf, a gray suit, a tie, a white shirt, gray socks, black shoes and black winter boots. Jeanne was wearing a navy-blue winter coat, a scarf, a navy-blue suit, a gray sweater, a white blouse and navy-blue winter boots. When Dave had given Jeanne her new clothes she went and put them on in the bathroom. Dave put on his new clothes in the room itself. Once they were dressed he put their old clothes in the suitcase and closed it. Finally Dave went to the bathroom to wash, shave and spruce up. Then they both sat in the room and when it was 2.30 in the afternoon, Jeanne stood up and told Dave it was time to go. They both left their room and Jeanne locked it behind them. They began walking down the half-circular staircase and in the lobby, Jeanne gave the keys to the owner.

The owner took them and they left the hotel and began walking to the railway station. At the station Jeanne bought two tickets for Chambéry. She walked with Dave to the embarkation platform and at 3.00 o'clock, their train pulled out of La Roche and began heading for Chambéry where they arrived at 5.00 o'clock in the afternoon. At 6.00 o'clock they boarded the train for Lyons and began their long journey across France. Throughout the evening and the night they headed west and went by large towns like Clermont-Ferrand, La Miouze, Brive-La-Gaillarde, Libourne and Bordeaux. They also went through smaller towns, villages and hamlets with strange names like Lepin, Givors, Andrézieux, Merlines, Périgeux, Ambarès, Dax, Sanbusse and Bénesse.

There were dangerous train changes at Chambéry, Lyons, Clermont-Ferrand and Bordeaux. There were also tough paper controls in those towns and more routine ones on the trains between those towns. All evening long and throughout the night they kept on heading west and as he sat next to Jeanne, Dave thought this was definitely the most extraordinary journey he had ever taken. For one thing the danger on the various trains they took was far greater than he could possibly have imagined. The Germans were pouring troops in southern France and the stations and trains were crawling with Gestapo Inspectors, Police Militaires, officers and soldiers. In the major towns the paper controls were very strict and it was extremely dangerous to wait in stations for train changes.

For another the people on the trains didn't look very happy. A third of them looked really angry and eager to take on the Germans. Another third looked extremely sullen and resentful at their having moved south. And a third looked truly stunned and amazed by what had happened and quite worried and anxious as to what it might mean. Then there was Jeanne herself. As they kept on heading west across France and as the danger on the trains became very great, it seemed to bring out the best in her and she became absolutely fearless. During the evening and the night she seemed to be able to size up every situation and deal with it. At Chambéry she faced the young Gestapo Inspector and was a happy bubbling sparkling newlywed who was excited to be going to the wedding of her sister.

At Lyons she was a sober married older sister who was properly respectful of the law and who remarkably matched the mood of the grim and gloomy Gestapo Inspector who was checking their papers. In Clermont-Ferrand she was all flirt with a much younger and better-looking man and joked, laughed and teasingly flashed her gold wedding ring at him. At Bordeaux she was all business with the tough older Inspector and looked extremely busy and impatient to get to Bayonne and to the wedding itself. Jeanne was all of those people. And she played those roles with such precision and perfection it stunned Dave and made him feel it was out of all proportion with the frail and fragile girl he had met at the British Legation. At the Legation the girl had been shy and reserved. On those trains she was quite something else.

On her way across France with him Jeanne faced all those Gestapo Inspectors with such a fearlessness and confidence it gave her a complete mastery over them. This mastery of hers, in fact, was so absolute and complete it was an amazing thing to see. As a result Dave sat back and watched her. As a matter of fact Dave was so amazed by what he saw he tried to fit in with the various roles she was playing and to reinforce them and support them by going along with them and by playing, himself, whatever role he felt was required of him. And this absolute fearlessness and confidence of Jeanne was still with her when they finally came into Bayonne around 9.00 o'clock in the morning.

BOOK EIGHT

OVER THE PYRENEES

CHAPTER 102

In Bayonne the station was full of Germans. They were on the platform, on the concourse and at the ticket barriers where they were standing with several Gestapo Inspectors and doing a tight paper control. As they came out of the platform and onto the concourse Dave froze. When she saw this Jeanne put her arm through his and began walking swiftly and briskly toward the ticket barriers. She made for a young and pale-blond Gestapo Inspector and when they reached his barrier, she smiled at him and said: "We're going to a wedding. Do you like weddings?" "Sure," the Inspector said. "It's too bad you're working," Jeanne smiled. "You could have come with us." "Why not," the Inspector said and waved them through as his eyes narrowed on an elderly couple with long hooked noses and kinky hair coming up behind them.

Jeanne and Dave hurried out of the station and headed for the Pont St. Esprit and then the Pont Mayou. Past the Pont Mayou they got on the Rue Victor Hugo and then the Rue D'Espagne. There were German patrols in the streets and past the Rue de Luc they came to a large three-story white-stucco house. This house was on the west side of the Rue D'Espagne and when they reached it, Jeanne stepped to the front door and rang the bell. The door opened and they went in. A tall dark-haired woman greeted them and led them down a long hallway to two rooms on the right side of it. They were to change clothes in those rooms and she gave each a new passport and a new cover story. Dave went into the first room and put on white woolen underwear and socks, a pale-brown flannel shirt, workman's corduroy pants, a large woolen sweater, big brown winter boots, a pale-brown scarf, a pale-brown winter jacket and a beret.

When he came out Dave saw Jeanne had also put on a pale-brown winter jacket, a pale-brown scarf, brown corduroy slacks and brown winter boots. She was talking with the tall dark-haired woman and when he stepped out, Jeanne turned to him and fixed his beret to be worn flat on the head like a Basque since they were now in Basque country. Then she led him to the hallway entrance where two bicycles stood. One was for a woman, the other for a man. At the entrance Jeanne thanked the woman. Then she took out the woman's bicycle and stepped out. Dave took the other bicycle and outside they got on their bicycles and began heading south on the Rue D'Espagne. In a little while the spire of the Cathédrale Cloître disappeared in the distance and they turned right at the Avenue Pampelune and began heading southwest toward St. Jean De Luz.

Now, close to 11.00 o'clock, it was a cool crisp cloudy day and in no time they left Bayonne behind and kept on heading southwest toward St. Jean De Luz. They bicycled at a steady pace and Dave saw there was a great deal of military traffic on the road. They came upon a couple of Staff cars, some motorcyclists and quite a few Wehrmacht trucks. Most of the traffic was heading north toward Bayonne but a Staff car and some motorcyclists and Wehrmacht trucks were also moving southwest toward St. Jean De Luz. All were speeding and most of the Wehrmacht trucks were full of soldiers. Dave and Jeanne kept on bicycling and going through the small villages of Anglet, Bidart and Ghétary and when they finally reached St. Jean De Luz around noon, they went and left their bicycles in a bicycle rack next to the railway station.

St. Jean De Luz was also full of Germans. There were quite a few around the station and Dave saw a Staff car, a few motorcycles and some Wehrmacht trucks parked there. In St. Jean De Luz Dave felt tense and nervous. The beret he had on and the clothes he was wearing did not strike him as being right. As a matter of fact he felt he didn't look like a Basque and wasn't moving like one either. But they didn't stay in St. Jean De Luz long. As soon as they reached the station and put their bicycles in a rack next to it, Jeanne led him away from it and in a fairly short time they began leaving St. Jean De Luz behind. They walked up a dusty and stony road that was quite hilly at times and heading southwest. By now Dave saw they must be quite close to the Spanish frontier since he could see the Pyrenees looming ahead of them in the distance.

They kept on walking at a fast and steady pace and after a while they saw an old and rusty truck coming down the road toward them. As the truck neared them it slowed down and the old Basque driving it shook his head and pointed up the road. Jeanne looked intently at the old Basque and then said to Dave: "There's something wrong! Quick! Let's get off the road!"

CHAPTER 103

Dave and Jeanne scrambled off the road. They ran down the slope on the right side until they came to a big boulder about 15 feet from it. As they came and crouched behind the boulder Jeanne said to Dave: "You stay here. I'll be right back." Then Jeanne was gone and ran to his right until she disappeared past some boulders. When she was gone Dave stayed behind the big boulder and watched the road. After a while Jeanne ran back and dropped down next to him. "All right," she said to him. "You follow me when I tell you." Then Jeanne turned and watched the road. After a while she gave Dave a slap on the shoulder and they both scrambled up the slope and ran across the road in a half crouch.

They both dropped down on the other side and Jeanne ran fast. She moved away from the road and then parallel to it. When they were quite a way from the spot where Dave had hidden and waited for Jeanne they came to two big boulders lying together in a slight depression in the field. They stopped and dropped down behind those two boulders. Once they were down Dave turned and looked at the road through a small crack between the boulders. There was a low white mist hanging over the field. In fact the mist was higher and thicker behind them than toward the road where there was hardly any. And right in front of them, about 500 yards away, there was a big roadblock. There were German troops and three motorcyclists manning the roadblock. Behind it, and parked on the right side of the road, stood two empty Wehrmacht trucks with their tarpaulins rolled up.

Besides the three motorcyclists Dave could see there was a Captain, a young Lieutenant and two Sections manning the roadblock. The Captain was holding his binoculars and staring straight at them. Then he swung

Over the Pyrenees

his binoculars to the right and to the left before turning and talking to the young Lieutenant who was with him. That accounted for the officers and soldiers in the first truck. But where were the officers and soldiers of the second truck? As Dave was thinking about this he felt a slight tap on his shoulder. He turned and Jeanne motioned for him to follow her. Then Jeanne was on the move again. She left those two boulders with Dave and dropped away from them in a half crouch. She backed away quickly from the road until they disappeared into the low white mist and were a fair distance from it.

Then Jeanne turned left and began moving parallel to the road. By this time she was really moving and ran in a half crouch and scrambled across the rocky barren field covered at times with a chest-high mist. Dave was right behind her and they kept on running and scrambling like this for a while. Finally, when they came near a big boulder in the field, Jeanne suddenly stopped and dropped down behind it. Dave dropped down right behind her and saw what she was looking at. About 100 yards to their left a young German Captain suddenly surged out of the mist and held his pistol in his right hand. He had with him a Section of German soldiers who were holding their rifles in front of them and who stood a little behind him on his right and another Section was on his left. A young German Lieutenant was leading that Section and when that double patrol had moved past them and disappeared into the mist, Jeanne waited for a while and then began moving again.

But now Jeanne really ran and scrambled. At first she moved away from the road and then parallel to it. Some time later, when they seemed to be out of the mist and quite a distance from the double patrol and the roadblock, she began making for the road again. She moved swiftly and carefully and when they got close to it, she lay down in a depression in the field with Dave and watched it. The road seemed to be empty. They watched it for a while and when they were about to get up and run across it, they suddenly saw a large cloud of dust rising above it. The cloud of dust was speeding north and they saw it was a motorcyclist and a Wehrmacht truck probably going to St. Jean De Luz. Jeanne waited until they were gone and then stood up with Dave and ran across the road. On the other side she moved away from it and when they had gone quite a distance, she turned left and headed west.

Jeanne walked swiftly and briskly and made sure she was keeping to a southwesterly direction. As they kept on heading in that direction Dave could see they must be close to the frontier since the Pyrenees were now rising massively and gigantically in front of him. The rocky barren field they were in was always dropping slightly and they seemed to be in a large valley. They kept on walking and heading past rocks and boulders and after a while came to a scratched and wooden sign that said: Urrugne. Past that sign they began going by scattered farmhouses and Dave saw Jeanne was making sure they were staying away from the farmhouses. She was moving back slightly toward the road until they came to the last farmhouse in the village.

That farmhouse was isolated and quite a way from the other farmhouses. It was also closer to the road and in the distance, Dave could see the road and the farmhouses on the other side of it. Jeanne kept on heading for that farmhouse and when they reached it, she dropped down behind a big boulder with Dave and watched it.

CHAPTER 104

Jeanne watched the farmhouse for a while and then picked up a small pebble and threw it at the window on the left side of the front door. In a moment the door opened and a tall red-haired woman came out. She smiled when she saw Jeanne and Dave stand up from behind their big boulder. Then she turned and motioned for them to come in. They both began moving toward the farmhouse and when they came in, the woman closed the door behind them and led them to the kitchen to the right of the front door. In the kitchen the woman told them to take off their coats and scarves and served them a big glass a milk and two chopped eggs sandwiches. Then, after the meal, she left the kitchen with Dave and brought him to a large and comfortable room upstairs.

In that room the woman told Dave to lie down and get some rest before they began their long journey across the Pyrenees. Finally she left and Dave lay down on the bed and soon fell asleep. He slept deeply and soundly and when the woman shook him gently and woke him up, it was dark outside. It was a little after 5.00 o'clock in the afternoon and when Dave came down to the kitchen with her, he saw a tall muscular dark-haired man who was in his early fifties sitting at the table with Jeanne. The man wore a thick black mustache and had a quick flashing smile. As Dave came into the kitchen with the woman, Jeanne introduced him as Raoul and told Dave he was their Basque guide who was going to take them across the Pyrenees and into Spain. Raoul then got up from the table and shook hands with Dave and the woman served everyone a hot bowl of vegetable soup with delicious pieces of beef in it. To go with the soup the woman gave them some cheese, bread, butter and a big mug of hot scalding coffee.

Once the meal was over Raoul got up from the table and motioned for Jeanne and Dave to get ready to leave. Both of them grabbed their winter jackets and scarves and Raoul did the same. Then he put on a big backpack while Jeanne put on a smaller one. Finally Raoul gave Dave a big strong walking stick and headed for the front door. He left the farmhouse and was followed by Jeanne and Dave. Outside they moved away from it and headed west. Raoul was in the lead. Jeanne was behind him and Dave brought up the rear. They walked in silence and in a single file. After a while they turned left and began heading south toward the road which they could see as a gleaming silver strip in the distance. They kept on making for the road and when they reached it, Raoul went to ground with them and watched it. There was no one on the road.

Raoul watched it for a while and then suddenly sprang up and ran up the slope. Raoul crossed the road with Jeanne and Dave and barreled down the slope on the other side. He kept on moving away from the road and headed south and after a while, he turned right and began moving west toward the hills. By this time, a little after 7.00 oclock in the evening, the sky was beginning to clear and the hills loomed in dark-blue, amber and lavender folds ahead of them before dissolving into the orange-slashed and violet-crested darkness of the Pyrenees beyond. There was a cool crisp dry wind blowing and a faint hint of snow in the air. As they kept on walking the moon came out and Dave could see the stars high and clear overhead. Some time later they found themselves in the hills and Dave stepped up his pace and fell right in behind Jeanne.

By then Raoul was walking at a steady pace and Jeanne and Dave were right behind him. Now that they were in the hills there was a huge silence all around them and this silence was only broken up by sharp sudden gusts of wind. They were now climbing and as Dave kept on walking behind Jeanne, he noticed this thing about Raoul he hadn't seen before. Although Raoul kept on walking at a steady pace it seemed to Dave the more they climbed, the faster his pace became. As a result Dave really had to scramble to keep up with him and Jeanne and when they finally left the hills behind and found themselves in the mountains a couple of hours later, the swift steady pace he had kept up was completely gone and Dave found himself gasping and stumbling after them.

In the darkness Dave could hardly see Jeanne's back ahead of him. He kept on gasping and stumbling after her and after a while he noticed this other thing about Raoul. Not only was he increasing his pace but now that they were in the mountains, he seemed to really be in a hurry for some reason. By now the climb which at first hadn't been so bad was quite steep and difficult. As they kept on going up in the mountains, which in this area rose to over 7,000 feet, Dave found himself truly pushing and straining to keep up with them. As they climbed the air really began to thin out and Dave found himself gasping and reaching deep within himself in order to breathe. By then he was no longer able to keep up with Jeanne and Raoul and kept on sliding and skidding and falling behind them all the time.

Every once in a while Jeanne would come back to him and say: "Come on, David. You can do it. I know you can do it." Dave tightened his jaw, gritted his teeth and kept on climbing. At times he was helped by Jeanne. Most of the time, though, he was not and skidded and scrambled after her. It went on hour after hour like this and the climbing now became so extremely steep and difficult Dave had to help himself with his walking stick. By this time Dave was barely able to hang on and was staggering along and when he finally reached the end of his strength and was no longer able to go on anymore, the climbing suddenly began leveling a little and then more and more.

They had reached the top of the Pyrenees.

CHAPTER 105

When they slowed down and then stopped on top of the Pyrenees, Dave was so exhausted he was bent in two and had a big stitch on each side of his ribs. He was gasping and heaving and after he had been able to catch his breath and straighten up a little, Raoul walked over to him. *"Como esta?"* he asked and grinned at him. *"Muy bien,"* Dave said. *"Valor. Valor,"* Raoul said and slapped him on the back. He slipped out of his big backpack and put it down. He took out his bota and began drinking deeply and thirstily from it. He drank for a while and when he stopped, Jeanne put down her own backpack and opened it. She gave Dave some bread and cheese and made him drink water from her canteen. She herself only drank water.

Dave ate the bread and cheese and drank the water Jeanne gave him and when he was finished, he turned and looked around. By now Dave knew they had been in the mountains for several hours and that it must be some time after midnight. The night was crisp, clear and cold and the stars were so big overhead he felt he could reach out and touch them. From where they stood it was as if they were on top of the world and they could now see a distinct glow from the Spanish side of the frontier. Behind them the coast of France lay completely dark, gloomy and impenetrable. They were quite a way from the coast and from St. Jean De Luz. The strong beams of the lighthouse at Fuenterrabia were swinging wildly across the hills and making weird and peculiar shadows in the valleys.

From their height the blinking lights of Spain were clear in the distance. Below they could see the frontier town of Irun at the mouth of the Bidassoa. Further in the distance they could even see the lights of San Sebastian along the coast. From where they stood this made for quite a spectacular sight and Dave stayed there with Jeanne and Raoul and took it all in. Then Raoul put on his big backpack again and Jeanne reached for hers and did the same. When they were ready Raoul looked at them and said: *"Anda. Anda. Vamonos."* He began walking again and they began going down. Since they were coming down Dave thought this part would be easier than when they had been climbing. But it didn't turn out that way. For one thing, since their coming down was quite steep, it was hard to get a good grip on branches and trees. For another, since the night was crisp, clear and cold, the rocks and pebbles were wet and slippery and it was almost impossible to get a good footing.

So Dave kept on coming down and skidding and scrambling after Jeanne and after a while, they suddenly ran into a snowstorm. At first it was just a light white fluffy snowstorm. But then it turned into a deep, heavy and blinding one. As this happened Dave kept on sliding and skidding and trying to keep up with Jeanne and some time later, it got so bad Raoul stopped ahead of them and crouched down. He wet his right thumb and moved it this way and that. He also checked a few stones with his hand and tapped the ground with his feet. Then he straightened up and they were on their way again. Dave kept on climbing down and trying to stay as close as he could to Jeanne. He kept on sliding and skidding behind her and suddenly slipped on a large flat stone and went sprawling down about 40 feet. When he did he slammed into a tall slender tree and lay on the ground as his big walking stick went clattering down in the darkness.

For a moment Dave didn't move and then felt two strong hands lifting him up. As they did he found himself standing next to Jeanne and Raoul and Jeanne said: "Are you all right?" "Sure," Dave said. Jeanne brushed the snow from him and they were on their way again. Raoul took the lead once more. Jeanne followed him and Dave brought up the rear. He kept on sliding and skidding after her and after a while, just as suddenly as they had run into it, they were out of the snowstorm. As they came out of the storm they found themselves climbing down in a crisp, clear and cold night. By this time they were in a deep narrow valley and had to be extremely careful in working their way down since the stones and pebbles were wet and slippery. As they kept on coming down the lights they had seen from the Spanish side of the frontier began disappearing and after a while, they could see the faint gray metallic gleam of a road far below.

From time to time they could see a car driving along that road and its headlights would shine briefly in the valley and in the Bidassoa river that ran alongside it. There was also a railway that ran alongside the road and stood between it and the Bidassoa. It stood on an embankment that was slightly lower than the road and every once in a while they could see the red glow of a locomotive disappearing down its tracks. Dave kept on working his way down in the crisp, clear and cold air and when he had come down quite a bit, he suddenly heard the noise. It was the strangest noise he had ever heard. At first it was distant and had a low humming tone to it. Then, as he kept on coming down more and more and staying close to Jeanne, he saw what it was. It was the deep raging roar of the Bidassoa rushing past them toward the sea at Irun.

Through the trees, as they kept on coming down and getting close to it, Dave could see the white boiling water rushing and smashing and twisting through the rocks in the darkness. The river seemed to be running fast and when they got close to it, Raoul held up his hand as he crouched down behind some trees and looked around. Not that far from where they were, to their right across the river, stood a brightly-lit frontier post. There were two sentries patrolling on both sides of it and alongside the road. Raoul looked at the frontier post and at the sentries for a while and then turned to them. He put a finger to his lips and motioned for them to stay where they were. Then he slowly backed off from where he was and began moving through the trees to his left. When he was about 50 feet from where they stood he began climbing down until he stood in the trees close to the Bidassoa.

CHAPTER 106

In the trees Raoul looked at the Bidassoa for a while. Then he took off his trousers and folded them. He held them in his right hand and after a moment ran in a crouch out of the trees and down the sloping field. He headed for the river and in no time slipped into the fast-running water and tested the footing. Then he waded into the waist-high water and swiftly crossed the river. On the other side he rushed up and hid in a clump of trees near the end of the sloping field. As soon as Raoul was hiding in those trees Jeanne began moving with Dave to the same spot where Raoul had stood before. In that spot Jeanne told Dave to take off his trousers and tie them around his neck. She did the same thing and motioned for Dave to follow her into the river.

Dave hesitated and Jeanne took his left hand and began running with him to the river. Once they reached it Dave found the water unbearably cold, icy and fast-flowing. Jeanne waded into it and led him across the smooth slippery stones until they were across the river and had run to the same clump of trees where Raoul was hiding. When they dropped down beside him Jeanne told Dave to put his trousers back on as Raoul had done and as she herself would do. Dave did what she told him and they rested in the wet sloping field. Then Raoul began climbing and taking them to the embankment leading to the railway line. This didn't take long and after Raoul had watched the line for a moment, he suddenly took them over it until they went to ground near the road and hid behind a big boulder.

As they hid behind the big boulder Dave saw Raoul was watching the brightly-lit frontier post to their right. One of the sentries was quite far from them. The other one was about 200 feet away. Raoul waited until the closer one turned from the end of his patrol and began walking back toward the frontier post. As soon as that sentry had his back turned to him Raoul suddenly stood up and ran in a crouch across the road and up the sloping field until he disappeared into the trees. Now it was Dave's turn. Jeanne gave him a small slap on the back and Dave also stood up and barreled across the road and climbed and scrambled up the field until he made it into the trees. Then it was Jeanne's turn. When she came to get up and follow them, however, they heard a noise coming from the left side of the road and Jeanne went to ground behind the big boulder.

Almost at the same time an Army truck came down the road and passed them. It slowed down and stopped in front of the frontier post. Two *carabineros* in their smart green uniforms and black cocked hat dropped down from the truck and walked into the post. Then the truck left and disappeared down the road. From where he was hiding with Raoul, Dave could see Jeanne was watching the road again. She was waiting for the sentry closer to her to finish another patrol and begin walking back toward the frontier post again. When the sentry began his walk back Jeanne stood up in a flash. She barreled across the road and climbed and ran up to where they were hiding. Once they were all together Raoul gave Jeanne a chance to catch her breath and then turned and began leading them again. He climbed through the trees with them and after a while they were no longer climbing.

They were coming down and the darkness now began to fade as dawn began breaking around them. They kept on coming down through the trees and some time later found themselves in a valley and on the other side of the mountains. As they did Jeanne fell back and moved closer to Dave. She walked alongside him and then half turned and pointed behind her: "Look." Dave turned and stared at what she was pointing at. Behind them in the distance loomed an incredible sight. Spain, in that glorious, magnificent and extraordinary dawn, was rising in all its splendor. The gold, orange and amber folds of its valleys shone in the sunlight and the beauty of its landscape warmed, soothed and surrounded them in the fresh early light. By now they were moving through clean fields and hearing the clear tinkling of sheep bells.

After a while they found themselves in a large valley and could see in the distance the red-tiled roof of a white-stucco farmhouse. It rose above the low-lying, pale-white, golden-silver mist and glinted in the sunlight. They kept on moving toward that farmhouse and when they got quite close to it, Raoul dropped down behind a big boulder with them and watched it.

CHAPTER 107

There was no noise around the farmhouse and after a while Raoul let out a low long whistle. In a moment the front door opened and a big dark-haired woman came out. She also let out a low long whistle and Raoul stood up from behind the big boulder with Jeanne and Dave. As they all stood up the woman grinned at Raoul and said to him: *"Hola guapo."* Raoul also grinned at her and said: *"Hola preciosa."* Then they both walked toward each other and embraced. When the woman pulled away from Raoul she turned to Jeanne and Dave and motioned for them to follow her and Raoul into the farmhouse. Once inside the woman led them to the kitchen to the right of the front door and made them thick delicious tortillas. She served them with butter and big slices of bread and also brought out hot steaming mugs of coffee.

After the meal the woman got up from across the table from Dave and told him to follow her upstairs. Dave stood up and when he came to leave, he turned to Raoul who had also gotten up and who was standing next to him on his right. As he looked at Raoul, Dave turned to the woman and said to her in Spanish: *"Hablas Vasco?"* *"Si. Hablo Vasco,"* the woman said. "Tell Raoul how grateful I am for what he has done for me and that I will never forget it," Dave said. The woman turned to Raoul and translated this in rapid-fire Basque. When she was finished Raoul also spoke in rapid-fire Basque and the woman turned to Dave and said: "He says he's very happy and that he would do this with you anytime." Dave said: "Tell him I'm honored. Tell him he's like a brother to me. *Dile eso a el.*" Again the woman told this to Raoul and Raoul spoke to her in Basque.

The woman turned to Dave and said: "He says he's also honored. And that he feels the same way." "Ask him why he is doing this," Dave said.

The woman spoke with Raoul and then said to Dave: "He says he's a Basque. And that Basques do not like to be told what to do." Dave laughed and said: "Tell him I'm a Basque too." The woman told this to Raoul and he broke out into a big happy grin and stepped forward and embraced Dave tightly. Then Dave pulled away from him and left with the woman to go upstairs. He nodded at Jeanne as he left and when they were upstairs, the woman led him to a big and spacious room with large open windows and told him to lie down and rest. Then the woman left and Dave got undressed and slipped underneath the thick comfortable quilt.

In the clean cool fresh air of the Pyrenees he quickly fell asleep and when he woke up, it was dark outside and close to 7.00 o'clock in the evening. Dave got dressed and walked downstairs to the kitchen where he found the woman. Again she gave him a hot steaming mug of coffee and served him a thick delicious tortilla with butter and big slices of bread. After the meal the woman took him to the bathroom next to the kitchen. She told him she had put various toilet articles near the sink for him to wash his face, comb his hair and shave. Dave stepped into the bathroom and spruced up and when he came out, he heard a car drive up outside. In a moment the front door opened and Jeanne came in. She seemed to be in a hurry and after she had talked with the woman for a little while, she motioned for Dave to leave the farmhouse.

Dave thanked the woman for what she had done for him and when he stepped out of the front door, he saw in the light spilling outside that the car parked at the door was a black shiny four-door Vauxhall and that it had diplomatic plates. There was a tall, slim driver in a black cap and uniform at the wheel and the back door of the car was open. Jeanne went in at the back and was followed by Dave. When Dave had closed the door they pulled away from the farmhouse and began driving southwest until they reached a road about half a mile away. They turned left on that road and kept on driving west on it. In the darkness the driver drove carefully and steadily and after a while Dave could see in the flash of the headlights they were going through places like Rentaria, San Sebastian and Zarauz.

They kept on driving west and went through other places like Zumaya, Alzola, Eibar, Amorebieta and Galdacano and when it was close to 11.00 o'clock in the evening, they came to Bilbao where they spent the night at the British Consulate. Early in the morning they left again with the same driver and the same Vauxhall and headed south. They began driving through cities, towns and villages like Murguia, Artaza, Encio, Rubena, Burgos, Lerma and Aranda. They kept on heading south and going through places like El Molar, San Agustin and Fuente Del Fresno and when it was close to 3.00 o'clock in the afternoon, they made it to

Madrid. In Madrid they stopped at the British Embassy where they were given British passports and a new cover story. They spent the night at the Embassy and early the next morning they were on the road again and still heading south.

This time, though, they were driven by an older, stockier driver in a long wide-bodied black Wolseley and went through cities, towns and villages like Getafe, Aranjuez, Ocaña, Manzanares and Valdepeñas. They kept on heading south and going through places like Bailen, Jaen, Granada, Santafe, Malaga, Torremolinos, Fuengirola, Marbella, San Pedro, Estepona and San Roque. And, as they kept on driving through those cities, towns and villages, Dave thought their long journey across Spain was turning out to be even more extraordinary than the one they had taken across France. Again this had to do with Jeanne. When they had gotten into Spain she had become yet another person. In Switzerland she had been shy and reserved. In France she had been absolutely daring and fearless. In Spain she had become quiet and withdrawn.

In her dealings with the Military Attaché at Bilbao and with the Senior Secretary of the Embassy in Madrid she had been polite and courteous. As a matter of fact she had been so polite and courteous her manner had been almost diplomatic. Also, as soon as they had gotten into Spain and come under the protection of the British, it was as if she had given herself over to that protection and had withdrawn deeply within herself. From Bilbao onward, when they had driven south on their long journey across Spain, she had sat on his left on the back seat of the Vauxhall and then of the Wolsely and her eyes had been half-closed and her hands had rested in her lap. She hadn't said anything and her silence had been truly startling. She had never once looked up. She had never once looked out.

Jeanne had just sat like this and hadn't said anything, and she was still sitting like this when they finally reached the town of La Linea a little after 3.00 o'clock in the afternoon and were only two miles from the frontier.

BOOK NINE

FREEDOM

CHAPTER 108

Jeanne looked up for the first time, since they had begun their long journey across Spain, outside of La Linea. She told the driver to pull up on the side of the road and as soon as they had stopped, she told Dave to get out of the car and then stepped out herself. When they stood on the side of the road they could see the huge and massive Rock of Gibraltar in the distance. It was rising into the sky and was lush-green at the top and deep-purple and dark-brown at the base. From its airfield a Lancaster was taking off toward the Atlantic and glinting in the sunlight. Dave and Jeanne watched it climb in the clear blue sky and then looked at the long lines of battleships riding at anchor in the harbor.

Then Jeanne stepped back into the car and got into the back seat. She folded back the armrest and pushed hard at the bottom of the seat. The seat suddenly popped up and showed a hidden compartment. The compartment was the width of the car and was three feet deep and about four feet across. It had holes to breathe at the bottom and at each end of it. It was made of wood and when Jeanne had slipped out of the back seat, she told Dave to get in and not to worry. He would be able to breathe and would not be in there long. Dave climbed in and stretched in the hidden compartment. When he was in Jeanne snapped it shut and Dave felt her slip in and sit on top of the seat as the armrest came down. Then Dave heard the rear door of the car close and they were on their way. They began heading south toward Gibraltar and now that he was hidden safely underneath the back seat, Dave felt the road they were taking was quite rough and bumpy.

In the darkness Dave was sweating a great deal and could hardly breathe. He just lay still and it seemed to him they drove for five or ten minutes before the car slowed down and stopped. As soon as they stopped

Dave heard vague Spanish voices. After a moment he saw it was the voices of their driver and of a Spanish Customs Official. At one point he even heard Jeanne speak in poor Spanish to the Customs Official. He heard the man open the doors and the trunk of the car and walk around it a couple of times. Then there was a low hum and they were on their way again. They still headed south and after a little while the road seemed to become harder and more level. Dave guessed they must be leaving the Spanish road and crossing the British lines. They kept on moving south and a short while later the car slowed down, turned left and came to a stop.

A few moments later Dave heard the left door open. He felt Jeanne slip out of the back seat and then get back in. Right after that he felt the armrest come up and there was a heavy push at the bottom of the back seat. Suddenly it popped up and cool crisp clean air rushed in. Dave looked up and found himself staring at the happy and smiling face of Jeanne. He had made it to freedom! Dave climbed out of the hidden compartment and stepped out of the car. He found himself in a courtyard and in front of what looked like a large five-story white-walled building. It had white stone steps that led to a big black wrought-iron front door and to the right of the building was a tall white pole flying the Union Jack. There was also a thick white stone wall surrounding the building and armed sentries were guarding the big black wrought-iron front gate and the grounds.

Through the front gate Dave could see the deep blue waters of the Algeciras Bay and as soon as he stepped out of the car, Jeanne congratulated him on having made it to Gibraltar. Dave thanked her for all she had done for him and then a tall, slim and gray-haired soldier came out of the front door with a young, thin and sandy-haired Captain. The Captain hung slightly behind the soldier, on his right, and both stopped on the steps. The soldier was wearing a scarlet-rimmed cap and a khaki shirt and pants. The shoulder tabs on his shirt had the Pip and Crossed Swords of a Lieutenant-General and when they saw him, Dave and Jeanne left the car and walked over to where he was standing. Once they reached him and stopped, Dave saluted the General and the Captain smartly and they returned his salute. Then the General shook hands with Jeanne and said: "Jeanne, my dear. How are you?"

"Fine, Sir."

"I trust you didn't have too much trouble getting here."

"No, Sir. No trouble."

"Good," the General said and turned to Dave and also shook hands with him. As he shook hands he said: "My name is Sir Neville Nicholson. I'm Assistant Governor of Gibraltar and I've been asked by the Governor to welcome you to Gibraltar."

"Thank you, Sir."

"I trust you had a pleasant journey."

"Yes, Sir. Very pleasant."

"It's always pleasant traveling with Jeanne."

"That's true, Sir."

"So how does it feel to be a free man?"

"It feels wonderful, Sir."

"I've also been asked by the Governor to congratulate you on your escape and especially on the spectacular manner in which it was done."

"It's nothing, Sir. I had a lot of help."

"That's true. But it's remarkable just the same."

Dave didn't say anything and the Governor said to Jeanne: "And that goes for you too, my dear."

Jeanne blushed slightly and the General pointed to the front door and said: "Shall we go in?"

Jeanne shook her head and said: "I'm sorry. I have to leave with the driver and go back to Spain. I have to be in Madrid by tonight."

"That's too bad. I would have liked you to stay with us for a while."

"So do I. Maybe the next time."

"Of course."

Everyone now fell silent. Dave and Jeanne turned to each other and Jeanne shook hands with Dave and said: "Well, David. Goodbye. I wish you luck."

"Goodbye."

Jeanne left him and the General and walked down the steps toward the car. Dave watched her go and when she had almost reached it, he suddenly ran down the steps toward her and said: "Wait. Don't go like this."

Jeanne turned as Dave came up to her and he said: "I don't want you to go like this. I don't want you to leave."

Jeanne didn't say anything and Dave said: "Please, take me with you. I'm good with languages. I'm good at what you do. We'll work well together."

"Oh, David."

"It's true. I can pass for a Frenchman. I can pass for all kinds of people. Let me stay with you."

"I would if I could. But I can't."

"Why not? Can't you see I'm offering you my life."

"I know that."

"I don't care about the risk. I'm not afraid to die. I just want to work for you."

"The answer is no."

"Why not?"

"It's not what you have to do."

"How do you know?"

"I know."

"What must I do then?"

"I don't know. But I believe it's something that will truly amaze you."

"Oh, come on."

"It's true. I believe you'll do something very great in your life."

"How can you talk like that?"

"It's true."

"What if you're wrong and I belong with you?"

"Believe me. I'm not."

"What if you are?"

"Don't be foolish," Jeanne said and her voice rose suddenly and her eyes hardened. "If I thought for a moment you belonged with me I would have asked you already." Her voice then went back down to normal and she said: "But you don't. You don't belong with me."

"Where do I belong then?"

"To England."

"England?"

"That's right. So go back there and do what you have to do."

"What's that?"

"Fight. You go back there and fight."

CHAPTER 109

Jeanne then reached out and kissed Dave softly on the cheek. She got into the rear seat of the car and closed the door behind her. She waved at him through the rear window and spoke to the driver. They began moving away from the courtyard and in no time Jeanne's car reached the big black wrought-iron front gate and went through it. Then it turned right and was gone and Dave left the bottom steps and began walking toward Sir Neville Nicholson and the young Captain. At the top of the steps they all turned and moved toward the Governor's Residence. Inside the Captain took Dave to a large and spacious room on the fifth floor that had a magnificent and spectacular view of Algeciras Bay.

There was a soldier's uniform on the bed and boots on the floor and Dave got out of his civilian clothes and put on the uniform. He spent the rest of the day taking it easy and the next evening Sir Neville Nicholson gave him a lavish formal party. The 57th Highland Grenadiers Regiment who were guarding the Governor's Residence gave him a more informal one the following evening. Then the Captain who had been with Sir Neville took him sightseeing all day on Monday. Yet throughout those two parties and while he was sightseeing on Monday, Dave's mind wasn't really on this. He was thinking of Jeanne and of all they had done together. He could still see her as she had been in Switzerland, then in France and finally in Spain. There was one thing about her. One thing that could not be denied. This second Joan of France didn't have anything to envy of the first one. That was for sure.

Dave kept on thinking about Jeanne and was glad when he sailed for England the following Tuesday morning aboard the destroyer *H.M.S. Valour*. Dave sailed for England at 6.00 a.m. on a bright, cool and sunny day. The journey took six days. It had been scheduled to take three. They had been expected to get to England by leaving Gibraltar and following the coast of Portugal, France and then sailing through the St. George's Channel and the Irish Sea. But on the second day something happened which made the journey far more deadly and dangerous than they had expected and completely changed their schedule. That morning around 10.00 a.m., on a cool, crisp and cloudy day, Dave had been invited by the Exec, Ian Stuart, to come to the bridge to see how a destroyer worked. Dave had taken him up on the offer and gone there to watch the officers and seamen.

Dave hadn't been there long when the soundman suddenly reported to the Captain he was getting Asdic impulses and that an enemy ship was tracking them and trying to get perfect target value. Almost at the same time a seaman who was standing to the left of the Captain and scanning the heavy gray-green sea with his binoculars yelled: "Torpedoes on port! I repeat! Torpedoes on port!" "Full rudder starboard!" the Captain yelled and the helmsman began frantically to twist the helm to starboard. "What's the range and bearing!" the Captain yelled. "Eighteen hundred meters and bearing two three five," the seaman said. "A perfect fan shot," Stuart told Dave as his eyes were glued to port. Dave watched with fascination as the two long gray silver torpedoes kept on coming faster and faster toward the ship.

Even though the helmsman was twisting the helm frantically the destroyer was turning agonizingly slowly and ponderously and Dave watched with horror as the two torpedoes kept on getting bigger and bigger. In no time at all the outside torpedo raced past and just off the bow of the ship. But the inside torpedo was coming broadside and Dave watched it as it kept on getting bigger and bigger. When it was about to hit them at midship Dave closed his eyes and waited. However nothing happened and when he opened his eyes, Dave saw that the torpedo was now racing starboard past the ship. "What happened?" Dave asked. "The torpedo has undershot us," Stuart said. "It serves that Captain right for not setting them to run at the proper depth," the Captain said. "Now the party begins."

CHAPTER 110

By now the destroyer had slowly and agonizingly turned to starboard and the Captain pointed ahead of him. "Do you see the launching spot?" he asked Stuart. "I see it," Stuart said and looked at a white bubbly swell that was clearly visible half a mile away on the heavy gray-green sea where the launch had been made. The Captain gave orders for depth charges and the destroyer raced toward the spot where the launch had been made. As soon as it reached it a 24-canister spread was dropped astern. Almost immediately huge explosions rocked the sea and sent gigantic fountains of water up in the air. The Captain waited a little and then swung the ship hard to port. He turned and came back in a figure eight and dropped a 20-canister spread this time.

Once more huge explosions rocked the sea and gigantic fountains of water shot up in the air. The Captain let the ship continue on its course for a little while before he swung it hard to starboard again and came back and dropped some more depth charges. Again and again the Captain dropped depth charges in the area where the launch had been made. He crossed it and crisscrossed it endlessly and tried to blanket it in a square pattern. Then, after more than an hour, he came and stopped 1,000 meters from where the launch had been made. By then the soundman was reporting the Asdic impulses he had been getting had faded and stopped altogether. As a result the Captain stopped the destroyer in the water and waited. From the talk he was having with Stuart and the other officers and seamen on the bridge Dave gathered what had happened was quite extraordinary.

U-boats didn't normally attack destroyers. And from the Asdic impulses the soundman had been getting, this definitely looked as if they had been attacked by a U-Boat. As a rule U-Boats worked in Wolf-packs of 20 to 40 boats. They usually stayed quite deep in the Atlantic in an area called the Black Pit where they were beyond the range of all planes and bombers. That was where they worked and attacked convoys. But they rarely attacked destroyers and only if they themselves were attacked by them. However this was December 1942 and another one of those months when Allied ships were being sunk in record numbers. As the Captain talked with Stuart and the other officers and seamen Dave gathered he was wondering if the U-Boats had changed tactics or if they had been attacked by a renegade Captain.

Just to be on the safe side, for the next three hours or so, the Captain began racing the destroyer again and stopping and dropping depth charges in an erratic and irregular pattern all over the launching area. Then, when there was no trace of the U-Boat and when the officers and seamen felt he had probably gotten away by lying deep at the bottom of the sea with his motors turned off and by simply letting himself drift away in the current, the Captain decided to move on and leave the area. As a result the Captain ordered full speed ahead and they left the launching area. Dave knew from his conversations with Stuart the *Valour* could far outgun and outrace any U-Boat. It was with this in mind the Captain decided to make for the deep waters of the Atlantic and sail for England by way of the Azores.

That way they would be less likely to run into any U-boats and if they did, they would have plenty of room to maneuver. Also at the speed they would maintain there would be little possibility of any U-Boat being able to keep up with them and attack them. This was why the Captain now ordered them to proceed full speed ahead on a westerly course and then swung them north on the third day and sailed them toward England. When they had left Gibraltar the weather had been cool, crisp and sunny. There had been an edge of fall in the air rather than winter. Now, by the second day, the weather had already turned quite cold and chilly and there had been a low cloud ceiling. By the third day, when Stuart told Dave they had now gone past the Azores and turned and begun heading north toward England, the weather became positively frigid and there was no mistaking this was winter.

Huge, gray-green and gray-white waves 40 to 60 feet high rose in the Atlantic and gale winds blew and smashed white breakers over those waves. The visibility dropped quickly to less than a mile and after a while all you could see were those huge, gray-green and gray-white waves rising, falling and crashing over the bow of the *Valour* as it rode heavily through them. On and on they went through the wild and stormy sea and on the fifth day, when they were coming into the St. George's Channel, the wind dropped slightly and the sea became calmer somewhat. The visibility was still less than a mile, however, and it was unbearably cold and windy. They kept on heading north and toward the Irish Sea and on the sixth day, they sighted land.

That cold gray cloudy Sunday morning, with a cold icy wind blowing in from the Irish Sea, a thin gray line appeared on the horizon. Then, around 10.00 a.m., it grew and grew until the city of Liverpool suddenly loomed in the distance. As it rose out of the water its three monumental buildings, the Royal Liver Building, the Cunard Building and the Dock Board Offices Building, as well as its gigantic cranes, rising and hanging over the huge and sprawling docks, towered over it.

They had finally reached England.

CHAPTER 111

As soon as they sighted Liverpool the Captain took the *Valour* inside the harbor and came and dropped anchor at the Sandon Docks. When the *Valour* was properly secured Dave left it and was picked up by a young Lieutenant who was driving a military car. The Lieutenant took him to the Mill Street barracks of the Liverpool 41st Infantry Division and Dave spent the day in those barracks. Around 11.30 in the evening the Lieutenant came and took him to the Lime Street Railway Station. He put Dave aboard the overnight train for London and told him another Lieutenant would pick him up in the morning at King's Cross Station. Dave nodded and at 12.30 sharp his train left the station and began heading for London.

Dave had been given a first-class ticket and settled comfortably in his padded leather seat. It was quite crowded on the train and after a while he closed his eyes and fell asleep. Dave slept soundly through most of the night and was only vaguely aware of the train stopping at various stations as they headed slowly toward London. He just lay back in his padded leather seat and slept and when he finally opened his eyes, he saw it was close to 8.00 o'clock in the morning and they were now coming into King's Cross Station. As they slowed down more and more and then stopped at one of the disembarkation platforms, Dave was picked up by another young Lieutenant. This Lieutenant took him to another military car parked outside. Dave got in with him and they quickly left the station.

In that clear, cool and crisp Monday morning the Lieutenant first got on Pancras Road and then on Euston Road. He headed west on Euston Road before he turned left and headed south on Upper Woburn Place, on Woburn Place and then on Southhampton Row. He turned right on New Oxford Place and left on Monmouth Street. He drove south on Monmouth

Street and then on St. Martin's Lane and when they reached Trafalgar Square, he turned left on Northumberland Avenue and came and stopped in front of a tall, sturdy, graystone building. As they stopped Dave knew where the Lieutenant had taken him. The Lieutenant had taken him to the War Office. When they stopped in front of that building the Lieutenant gave Dave a red pass to get into it and told him he was expected.

Dave took the pass and got out of the car. He began walking toward the building and showed his pass to the two armed sentries who were guarding the sandbagged entrance. Dave walked past them and rang a buzzer on the right side of the front door. In no time a small gray-haired porter opened it. Dave gave him his red pass and the porter brought him to the large entrance hall where he turned him over to a young Lieutenant near the front desk. The Lieutenant checked Dave's name on a clipboard on the front desk and then picked up the desk phone. He spoke on it for a while and then led Dave to an elevator on the right side of the entrance hall. He took him to the fifth floor and stepped out with him past the armed sentry who stood next to the elevator.

Then the Lieutenant walked with him to the left of a long hallway until they came to the desk of a young Captain on the right side of the hallway. The desk stood next to a large leather-padded door and when they reached it, the Lieutenant handed him over to the Captain. He left and the Captain pressed on a buzzer underneath his desk. In a moment the large leather-padded door opened and the Captain motioned for Dave to go in. Dave stepped in through the door and it closed softly behind him. When it closed Dave found himself in a spacious and sumptuous office. At the other end, and facing the door, was a massive mahogany desk with two phones on the left side of it. One of the phone was black; the other, red. Behind the desk, and the huge mahogany chair that went with it, were heavy dark-red damask curtains.

The curtains were closed and on each side of the desk stood bronze floor lamps of a modern flaring-out design. To the right of the desk there was a tall narrow grandfather's clock and on both sides of the desk itself stood two superbly mounted pistols: a Mauser on the left side of it; and a Luger on the right side. There was another huge mahogany chair facing the desk and the middle of the hardwood floor was covered by a thick Persian rug. There was an officer sitting at the massive mahogany desk and he was one of the most handsome men Dave had ever seen. He was tall and slender. He had thick well-combed gray hair parted neatly on the side and a trim gray-white mustache. He had a smooth deeply-tanned face and wore a superbly-tailored uniform made even more impressive by the impeccably-polished Sam Browne belt he wore.

This officer also had on his tunic the red tabs and Crossed Swords of a Major General. Presently he was reading a file and there was a triangular name plate right in the middle of his desk that said: General James S. Wynford. As soon as Dave had come into the office he had saluted the General and the General had returned his salute. Then he had motioned for Dave to take the chair facing him while he kept on reading the file. The General kept on reading it for a while and then put it down and began debriefing Dave. The debriefing was one of the most precise and thorough Dave had ever gone through. It was very comprehensive and dealt with specific and detailed questions about the possibilities of other escapes from Colditz; the morale of Allied prisoners in the castle; the capabilities of the French underground; the movements of troops he had seen in the various countries he had been in; the strength, morale and outlook of those countries; and any other observations he felt might be of some importance.

Dave tried to answer all those questions as fully as he could and while he talked, the General wrote a great deal in the file he had been reading. All in all the debriefing took a little over two hours and when it was finally finished, the General closed the file and said: "Now. Please stand at attention." Dave got up and snapped to attention as the General opened the right drawer of his huge mahogany desk. He took out a shiny medal from a small black velvet box and rose and came to pin it above the left breast pocket of Dave's tunic. When he did he said: "By order of his Majesty, George VI. For your outstanding courage and bravery at Dieppe. For your bold and fearless attempts at escaping in Rouen. For your magnificent daring and resourcefulness in doing it at Colditz. We are pleased to award you the Military Medal and offer you our most sincere and earnest congratulations."

The General then shook hands with Dave and motioned for him to sit down again as he, himself, went and sat behind his huge mohagony desk once more. Dave did as ordered and as the General went and sat down behind his own desk, he leaned a little forward on it and said: "I must say getting out of Colditz in less than two months is quite extraordinary."

Dave didn't say anything and the General said: "Not only that but you made it to Switzerland in five days. That makes it a truly spectacular escape."

"Thank you, Sir. But I had help."

"I know that. Still, it's quite a feat."

"Not really. I was lucky too. You need a lot of luck to be able to do something like that."

"I quite agree. One only has to look at that business with the *Valour* to know that."

"That's true."

"You certainly had a lot of luck there."

"I certainly did, Sir."

"From what I read in your file it must have been quite something."

"It certainly was, Sir."

"So I understand. But I must say, talking about all these things, a thought suddenly occurs to me. Would you be interested in working for the French underground?"

"I already asked."

"You did?"

"Yes."

"And?"

"It didn't work."

"Who did you ask?"

"Jeanne."

"Ah. The girl who brought you to Gibraltar and who runs *La Ligne Interallié*."

"That's the one."

"And?"

"She didn't want to take me."

"Why?"

"She said this wasn't what I had to do."

"Really."

"That's right. She said I didn't belong with her."

"That's interesting."

Again Dave didn't say anything and the General said: "From what I hear she's quite demanding."

"She certainly is."

"I also hear she's quite extraordinary."

"That she is too."

"Since you like her so much, would you like to work for us then?"

"No, Sir."

"Even if it was in the French underground?"

"No, Sir. If I was to work there, it would be for her. No one else."

"You're sure?"

"Yes, Sir."

CHAPTER 112

The General sat back in his chair for a few moments and when he leaned forward on his desk again, a smile came on his face and he said: "Now then. For the really good news."

Dave looked at the General and the General said: "You're getting a three weeks' leave."

"That's good."

"And then you're going back to Canada."

"To Canada!"

"That's right."

"Why?"

"My dear boy. You've become very valuable. You're going back there on a speaking tour."

"On a speaking tour!"

"That's right. To sell War Bonds."

"General, you've got to be kidding!"

"I'm not."

"General, I don't want to sell War Bonds!"

"Why not?"

"I just don't want to."

"What's wrong with selling War Bonds?"

"General, there's nothing wrong with it. It's just I don't want to do it."

The General leaned a little bit more forward on his desk and said: "May I ask why?"

"General Wynford, all the time I was escaping from Colditz and trying to make it to Switzerland, I only had one thing in mind. I wanted to get back to my Regiment and to my Company. That's why I escaped. Not to sell War Bonds."

"My dear boy, we can't personalize the war. All of us have to do what we're told."

"I understand that. But I don't want to sell War Bonds."

"All right then. What would you like to do?"

"General Wynford, I trust you. I know you can help me. And what I want to do right now is to go back to my Regiment and to my Company. That's what I want to do."

"I'm afraid that's not possible."

"Why not?"

"As I said, you're too valuable. We've already released details of your escape to various London and Allied newspapers. I'm afraid you've become far too important."

"I don't want to become important."

"I understand that. Sometimes, though, we don't have any choice in these matters."

"Why can't you return me to my Regiment and to my Company?"

"My dear boy, a person like you the Army wants to use and promote. Not return to your Regiment as a simple soldier."

"Why not?"

"It just isn't done."

"I know you can do it if you want to."

"I can't. Not as a simple soldier."

"Is there any other way then?"

"Maybe."

"What other way?"

"As an officer maybe."

"As an officer? But I can't!"

"Why not?"

"General, I'm not very comfortable with officers."

"There you are."

"Forgive me, General. I don't mean to offend you. It's just that from where I come from I just don't see myself as an officer."

"I understand."

"You see, all my life I've been uncomfortable with any kind of authority. And I don't see myself changing now."

"It's quite all right. You don't have to explain."

"I do. Believe me it has nothing to do with you personally."

"I know that."

The Long War

"Tell me, though. How could you return me to my Regiment as an officer?"

"There is a group of Canadian officers we're planning to train. Maybe you could be included as a candidate among them."

"Do you think I could?"

"Maybe. Although, as I understand it, the group is almost set and there's little time left before they begin their training."

"If I was. Would you then return me to my Regiment and to my Company?"

"I would try."

"Would you really?"

"I would if I could. Although there is little chance of that."

"But would you?"

"Yes."

"May I have your word as an officer on that?"

"Of course."

"All right then. In that case I would like to become part of the group you've just mentioned."

"Are you sure?"

"Yes, Sir."

"Very sure?"

"Yes, Sir."

"All right then. You come and see me tomorrow morning at 9.00 o'clock. I'll see what I can do."

"Thank you, Sir."

CHAPTER 113

Dave stood up and saluted the General. The General returned his salute. Dave then turned and headed for the door. Outside the Captain at the desk asked Dave to wait for a moment and went into the General's office. He didn't stay there long and when he came out, he was holding a large pale-brown manila envelope in his hand. He gave it to Dave and asked him to check its content. Dave opened it and found a red pass which he would need to get into the building tomorrow. He also found $100.00 dollars in Canadian currency as an advance on his back pay and the address of a boarding house on King Street where the War Office was putting him up. The Captain asked Dave to sign for those things and walked with him down the long hallway to the elevator.

The Captain rode down the elevator with him and handed him over to the small gray-haired porter who led him out of the War Office. Outside Dave turned right on Northumberland Avenue and headed west. He went by Trafalgar Square and got on Cockspur Street where he made for the Beaver Club. When he reached it Dave walked in and ordered a beer. There were quite a few soldiers from the 2nd Canadian Division in the club but none from his own Regiment. Dave drank his beer alone and then left the Beaver Club and went to Soho where he had a Chinese meal. After the meal Dave walked over to Leicester Square where he went to see a first-run war movie. The movie turned out to be as long and boring as the one he had seen in 1940 and when it was over, he walked over to the Durham hotel which wasn't far from his boarding house on King Street.

In the nice cool dark bar of the hotel Dave spent the rest of the afternoon and part of the evening drinking gin and bitter lemon. Then he left the hotel and walked over to his boarding house. At the boarding

The Long War

house he spent the rest of the evening also drinking gin and bitter lemon from a bottle of gin and a bottle of bitter lemon he had bought from the bartender at the Durham. Dave went to bed late and spent a restless and sleepless night and when he woke up early in the morning, he washed, shaved and combed his hair. Then, around 8.30, he set out for the War Office. It was a clear cool sunny day and Dave headed northeast on King Street and then south on St. James's Square. After a while he got on Pall Mall and then on Cockspur Street. He walked by Trafalgar Square and got on Northumberland Avenue.

Dave walked northeast on Northumberland Avenue and when he reached the War Office, he showed his red pass to the two armed sentries at the sandbagged entrance. Then he walked past them and and rang the front door buzzer. Almost immediately the door opened and Dave found himself facing the same porter he had met the day before. Dave gave him his red pass and the porter led him to the large entrance hall where he went through the same security procedures he had been through the day before. He was handed to another Lieutenant who brought him to the desk of the Captain he had met yesterday on the fifth floor. This Captain was going through some papers and when he saw Dave, he said: "Ah. Lindsay. Go in. The General's expecting you." Dave nodded and the Captain pressed on a buzzer underneath his desk. The large leather-padded door opened softly and Dave stepped into General Wynford's office.

Inside Dave found the General talking on the black phone and saluted him. The General returned his salute and motioned for him to come and sit in the huge mahogany chair facing him. Dave came and sat in that chair and when the General had finished talking and hung up, he leaned forward on his desk and said: "My dear boy. I believe congratulations are in order once more."

Dave didn't say anything and the General said: "You're a very lucky young man. But you've cost me a great deal of trouble."

Again Dave didn't say anything and the General said: "I must say my efforts on your behalf were quite intense. But the end result is, I believe, quite worth it."

Dave looked at the General and he went on: "Now. Here is the good news. Given the truly remarkable reputation of your Regiment, your outstanding bravery at Dieppe, and the spectacular initiative you've shown in your escape from Colditz, it has been decided to cut through red tape and admit you as a candidate in the group we're going to train for the Canadian Army."

"Thank you, Sir."

"Don't thank me. You've earned it."

"I appreciate it, Sir."

"Don't mention it."

"Well, I truly appreciate it, Sir."

Both of them didn't say anything for a moment and then the General said: "Now let me give you an idea of what having been admitted as a candidate officer means."

General Wynford leaned a little bit more on his desk and said: "That means you'll be undertaking a shortened version of the training we give to our regular officers at Camberley and Quetta. The duration of the course will be three months. The first month will be spent in the classroom learning tactics, strategy and grand strategy. The next two months will be spent in the field with British units learning how to become an officer."

Dave nodded and the General went on: "Now, during the first month, you'll be doing map reading, field sketching and military topography. You'll also be doing organization, administration and transport studies as well as large-scale tactical exercises without troops. Finally you'll be studying military law, engineering and history."

"What about the other two months?"

"If you go through the first month successfully, you'll be assigned to a British unit in the field and learn how to become an officer."

"And where will this course and training take place?"

"I'm afraid I can't tell you that at the present time."

"I see."

"However, you'll know that in due time."

"I appreciate that, Sir."

"It's no trouble. I've recommended you believing you'll do as well as a candidate officer as you've done in escaping from Colditz."

"I'll try, Sir."

"I'm sure you will."

"Believe me. I'll give it my very best."

"I know you will."

"I truly will."

"I know that. But now, if you want to make sure you join that group of officers we're going to train, I think you better leave for the assembly area."

"Of course. Where is it?"

"In Aldershot. Go there and ask for Captain Alex Bolton. He's in charge of the group."

"I will."

"He's already been called and knows you're coming."

"Good."

"He's also been told your file and admission papers will be sent to him shortly."

"Okay."

"Now, if you leave presently and head for the Waterloo Station, I believe you'll be able to make the 10.00 o'clock train."

"I'll do that."

"Also drop me a note at the War Office from time to time."

"I will, Sir."

"I'd like to know how you are doing."

"I certainly will, Sir."

"Good luck."

"Thank you, Sir."

CHAPTER 114

Dave now stood up and saluted General Wynford. The General returned his salute and Dave left his office. He stopped by the Captain's desk and told him he had to catch a train for Aldershot. The captain got up and walked with him to the elevator. He rode down with Dave to the large entrance hall and let him out of the War Office. Outside Dave crossed Northumberland Avenue and hailed a taxi. He told the driver to take him to the Waterloo Station and the driver left immediately. He headed west on Northumberland Avenue before he turned left and drove south on Whitehall, then on Parliament Street and finally got on Bridge Street. He crossed Westminster Bridge, turned left on York Road and then came and stopped at the station.

Dave went in and saw the train for Aldershot was getting ready to leave. He just had time to buy his ticket and rush to take it before it began pulling out. In that clear cool sunny morning it picked up speed and began heading southwest. Dave stood in the corridor and kept on looking out. They went through familiar places like Lambeth, Wandsworth, Weybridge, Woking, Brookwood and Farnborough and a little over an hour later, they reached the town of Aldershot. Outside the station Dave hailed a taxi and they began heading for the training center. When they reached it Dave paid the driver and went into the Main Administrative Building. In that building he found Captain Alex Bolton and his group were located on the northwestern side of the center. They were located in the first four barracks of the second row and Captain Bolton himself was in the first barrack.

Dave left the Main Administrative Building and walked toward that barrack. When he reached it he went in and told the clerk in the Orderly

Room he wanted to see Captain Bolton. Before the clerk could turn and go into the Captain's office to the right of the Orderly Room, the door opened and Captain Bolton stepped out. He was a tall, lean, dark-haired officer and had a strong, clear-cut, bony face. When he saw Dave he smiled at him and said: "David Lindsay?" Dave nodded and saluted him. Bolton returned his salute and said: "General Wynford has called me about you. I must say you have quite a reputation. You're also very lucky. The group's getting ready to leave and you came in just in time." Bolton then motioned for Dave to go into his office and Dave stepped in ahead of him. Bolton closed the door behind him and motioned for Dave to go and sit in a chair in front of his desk.

Bolton then came and sat behind his desk. He leaned a little forward on it and began explaining to Dave what the group was all about. The group Dave had joined, he told him, was a pilot project of both the Canadian and British Army. It was made up of about 150 hand-picked men and was presently known as the Bolton Group. This was the name it would have until its real name could be disclosed and it was actually made up of 78 officers, 63 non-commissioned officers and 12 candidate officers. In the coming weeks all the men in the group would be trained by the British to become officers in the Canadian Army. The men in the group who were already officers would have their skills sharpened. The NCOs and candidate officers would be brought up to the level of officers and would be expected to succeed since they had been chosen for their outstanding skills and leadership abilities.

If the project went well there would be other groups like this in the future. Given the fact there was a really critical shortage of young officers in the Canadian Army, as well as in the other Allied Armies for that matter, it was important for the group to do well. For the time being, since the group was leaving so shortly for its training destination, Bolton told Dave to take it easy and get acquainted with the men. His clerk would now take him to his assigned bunk and Bolton wished him luck in his training as an officer. From what he had heard of his reputation he had no doubt Dave would succeed. Bolton then got up and walked Dave to the door of his office. He opened it and asked his clerk to take Dave to his assigned bunk. The clerk nodded. He left the Orderly Room with Dave and led him to the third barrack where Dave was given the third bunk on the left side of the aisle near the door.

Then the clerk left and Dave turned to the men around him and began talking with them. The men wanted to know what Regiment he was from and he told them. They also wanted to know what he had done and he told them about Dieppe, Colditz and his escape. Dave then asked about his own Regiment and found they were still stationed at Aldershot. However they were not there right now since they had gone to Scotland for winter training. Dave also asked the men where they came from and what they had done. They told him and as they talked, the day went by quickly. Dave went to bed late and when he woke up in the morning, he saw Bedford trucks had come for them. It was a cool gray cloudy morning and after an early breakfast, they were put on those trucks and taken to the train station.

At the station a military troop train had come for them. It was quite a long train and it was made up of four wagons for them and of several covered flatbed wagons carrying war supplies. Officers and NCOs from Movement Control put them aboard the train and Dave ended up sitting in the middle of the first wagon. He took up a seat next to the window on the left side of the aisle and a little after 8.00 o'clock in the morning, they left and pulled out of Aldershot. In no time they moved beyond Farnborough and picked up speed as they began heading north. Once they had moved past Farnborough Dave saw how they were going through many small towns, fields and villages. In that late December morning the whole countryside had a bleak, dreary and deserted look and after a while, he realized they were not heading strictly north but rather northwest.

Dave leaned back in his seat and listened to the steady hammering of the wheels on the tracks. He kept on looking out of the window and by early afternoon, they began coming into the Midlands. They sped by one industrial town after another and then they were out of the Midlands and into the countryside once more. By now they were passing many small towns and villages again. They sped by some streams, woods, empty fields, and rolling grasslands, and a little after 8.00 o'clock in the evening, as the train began losing speed, Dave knew where they were going. They were heading for Greenock and for the Central Station. The train kept on slowing down and when they reached the station, they came and stopped at one of the disembarkation platforms.

In the station they were taken off the train and put into another long line of Bedford trucks parked outside. Once they had been put into those trucks they left the station and got onto Terrace Road. They then got on Dalrymple Street and finally Container Way and were taken to the massive barracks of the 73rd Infantry Division on Haig Street near Clarence Street. They spent the night in those barracks and the next day were taken to the huge Army Depot near the Port Terminal. In this Depot they were outfitted for Overseas Duty. It took quite a while for the men to get their equipment and when they had their full gear, they were taken back to the massive barracks on Haig Street. They spent the rest of the day there and the next morning were taken by Bedford trucks to the Port area. In the port area they were put on tenders and taken to the transport ship *H.M.S Glendeboye.*

When they were on board the *Glendeboye*, since it was Christmas, the men were served a big dinner of turkey, vegetables, cranberry sauce, tea and plum pudding. They stayed anchored in the Clyde Channel all day long while the ship took on supplies and equipment and the next morning, they lifted anchor and set out on their journey. Quite early that morning tugboats had turned the *Glendeboye* around and a little after 8.00 o'clock, they began slipping down the Channel. It was another cool gray cloudy day. As a matter of fact it was cold rather than cool and there was a strong hint of snow in the air. They slowly moved down the Channel and got into the Firth of Clyde. They sailed south in the Firth of Clyde until they got into the North Channel and kept on heading south. By then the weather had turned cold and blustery and there was an icy sleeting snow falling.

Once they had left Greenock and the Firth of Clyde behind visibility soon dropped to less than a mile. They kept on heading south and late that afternoon they sailed by the Isle of Man. It was only a dark blur and was barely visible on the port side. They kept on heading south in the Irish Sea and then through the St. George's Channel and the next day when they hit the open sea, they still kept on sailing south. They were actually proceeding south by southwest and the sea was dark-green and metal-gray. It was also heavy and choppy but not stormy. In that dark-green and heavy sea the *Glendeboye* was sailing slowly at 10 to 12 knots and on the third day, the weather began to change. From being cold and frigid, it began to soften a little. The visibility was still poor and less than a mile. But now there were banks of fogs lying over the ocean. The wind had dropped down considerably and the sea was not so heavy.

They were now sailing strictly south and on the fourth day, they changed course and began heading east. As they changed course the weather lifted. The skies cleared. The sea became much more calm and glassy. From a distance a pale, dark-blue, lavender color began creeping into it. They kept on heading east and on the fifth day, they still proceeded on that course. But now they were sailing in a zigzagging and irregular pattern and on the sixth day, Captain Bolton gathered everyone around him on deck and finally told the men where they were going.

They were going to Algiers.

BOOK TEN

NORTH AFRICA

CHAPTER 115

The news the men were going to Algiers made them very happy. They had been on a long journey and Algiers seemed a good place to go to. Captain Bolton told them from now on they would be known by their proper name: The Algiers Group. Those who successfully completed the first month of the course would be assigned to fighting units of the British 1st Army in Tunisia. That made the men really keen and eager to get on with their training and two days later, around 10.00 a.m., they caught their first sight of Algiers. In the distance the city looked incredibly beautiful. It was startlingly white and lying in a semi-circle of clear-green hills. That Tuesday morning it rose out of the pale-blue lavender sea and burst into a flight of clear pristine whiteness toward the deep blue sky.

In the distance it gleamed and shimmered in the sunlight and spread before them in a dazzling and glittering display of never-ending whiteness and beauty. When they reached the harbor, however, and were taken off the *Glendeboye*, the city didn't look quite so white and beautiful. In the harbor, and not far from the Central Station, they were put in a long line of open Bedford trucks. Then, when they were on board, they left and began heading south on the Boulevard de la République. But, by the time they had passed the Central Station, they saw how the city's whiteness seemed faded and tarnished and how its beauty also seemed run-down and worn-out. The city was also full of soldiers. The Allies had only recently landed in North Africa and their landing had not made everyone happy.

There was a tense atmosphere in the city and a lot of the French, English and American soldiers had a grim and sullen look on their faces.

The Long War

There was a lot of military traffic on the Boulevard de la République and when they reached the wide palm-lined Boulevard Laferrière, they drove around it in a semi-circle until they came and stopped in front of a large white five-story building. This building stood not far from the University of Algiers and was on the southwest side of the Boulevard. On top of that it was not far from the Boulevard Camille Saint-Saëns and the Boulevard Baudin. As a matter of fact it stood roughly at an equal distance between the Town Hall to the north of the city and the Agha Station to the south. When they were taken off the trucks they were led inside the building where they were welcomed in the large reception area by a young British Captain.

The Captain told them this building was named the Lycée De La Rochefoucauld and that under the Vichy Government it had been a Lycée for French students. With the landing in North Africa it had been taken over by the British Army and would now be used for the training of groups like the Algiers Group. The Captain then invited them to follow him and gave them a tour of the building. On the first floor he took them to the gym. The gym stood opposite the front door and had a door near each end of it. It was used for lectures for large groups and also had a stage to the right of it. The messhall was found to the right of the front door. To the left of it you had a large bulletin board and then the Administrative area. On both sides of the gym were staircases that led to the second and third floors where the classrooms were located. The staircases then went on to the fourth and fifth floors where the dormitories were found.

At this point the Captain brought them back to the reception area and told them to pick up their gear and go and choose a bunk in one of the dormitories. They would have the rest of the day free and would begin their training in the morning. The Captain left and Dave picked up his gear and went and chose a bunk on the fifth-floor dormitory. He chose the third bunk at the northwest corner. His bunk was right next to windows on that side of the city and in the distance he could see the Fort L'Empereur, the Librairie Nationale and the Government Building. Once Dave had taken out his things and put them in his foot locker, he went downstairs and spent the rest of the day talking with the men, and the next morning they began their training in earnest.

Several instructors began lecturing them on tactics, strategy and grand strategy. There were also sand table exercises, seminars and special lectures by specialists on technical subjects. At the end of each week there were several papers to be written on subjects that had been taught. As main lecturer they drew Colonel Alec Dawson. Colonel Dawson, a tall, slim, gray-haired officer in his late forties, was a world authority on military history, tactics, strategy and grand strategy. He had written several books on those subjects and his opinions carried a great deal of weight within the British Army. As a matter of fact he was so highly regarded he had been made a Special Adviser to Churchill. And it was while talking to him it had been suggested to Dawson he come to Algiers to oversee the group in its first month of training.

Dawson had agreed on the condition he only do this once and because he wanted the Algiers Group to succeed. He was a very tough and demanding lecturer and always insisted the papers he requested be submitted on time and be written in precise and flawless English. Colonel Dawson had a truly amazing and extraordinary knowledge of military history. There wasn't a period he hadn't studied nor covered in depth. In the following weeks he took them from the Sumerian times right up to the present. He covered with them the Greek, Roman and Byzantine periods. He covered the Medieval Wars, the 17th and 18th Centuries, and the French Revolution. He also went over the First World War and the Second World War so far.

Dawson spoke at length and powerfully about the great military figures like Alexander the Great, Caesar and Napoleon. But he also went on about lesser known but equally good ones such as Belisarius, Narses and Turenne. He was a fierce supporter of the indirect approach to battles and campaigns. He knew exactly what had worked with them, what had gone wrong and what could have been done for the ones that had gone wrong to succeed. In teaching them those subjects Colonel Dawson had very definite ideas about modern warfare. He felt modern Armies, and especially the British Army, would have to learn to attack in strength and defend in depth. He believed, however, the focus should always be on attack. Battles were not won by retreating but by attacking.

But, whether in attack or in defence, modern tactics, which is what most of them would be involved in, could be summed up in three words: concentration, command and control. An officer must learn that and train his men to live hard, move light and fight ferociously. He must also teach them to develop enormous powers of endurance. This is what made great soldiers and what made even greater Armies. In lectures, seminars and sand table exercises Dawson relentlessly drove home those points. He was absolutely insistent on that. And, during those four weeks, Dave sat at the back of the classroom and listened to Colonel Dawson and to the other lecturers. He wrote the papers. He joined in the sand table exercises. And he took part in the seminars.

Dave did all of those things fully and conscientiously and on Friday, January 29, 1943, around 4.00 o'clock in the afternoon, it led to an incident which, even though it was quite surprising and unexpected, went a long way in deciding what kind of future he was going to have with the Canadian Army.

CHAPTER 116

That afternoon Colonel Dawson had been lecturing them for the last time. They were using a third-floor classroom on the northern side of the Lycée. It was the end of their month-long training and Dawson was reviewing what they had learned so far about military history, tactics, strategy and grand strategy. Dave was sitting at the back of the classroom and as he was listening to what Dawson was saying, the back door suddenly opened and an officer came in. The officer stepped in so quickly and unexpectedly Dave didn't get a good look at him. He only knew it was an officer from the tabs on the open-necked khaki shirt he was wearing and from the smart and impeccable cut of his uniform.

When the officer came in Dave turned slightly to try and get a good look at him and then went back listening to Colonel Dawson. Once Dawson had finished his lecture he turned from the blackboard and thanked them for the hard work they had done for him. He told them from now on until 8.00 o'clock on Monday morning everyone was on leave. They would be told on Monday about the results of their month-long training and about their assignments. Dawson then wished them well and left the classroom. The men followed him and as Dave turned to leave, he finally got a good look at the officer who was standing behind him. The officer was tall, slim and blond-haired and on the tabs of his open-necked khaki shirt he wore the Crossed Swords of a Major-General. Dave suddenly looked closely at him and as he walked up to him, he stopped and saluted him smartly. The General returned his salute and Dave said: "General Haworth?"

"That's me."

"I'm sorry. I didn't recognize you."

"It's quite all right."

"I see you've become a Major-General. May I offer you my congratulations?"

"By all means."

"And may I also thank you for clearing us in turning the train around at Clermont."

"Certainly."

"I must say that British Colonel in Brest was quite angry."

"I know he was. I don't suppose we'll see many more like him before the end of the war."

"I don't suppose so."

"He was quite something, though, wasn't he?"

"He certainly was."

"He's probably still playing policeman somewhere."

"Probably. Still I want to thank you for clearing us."

"Think nothing of it. Anyway General Alan Brooke had already issued orders for the trains to turn around."

"We didn't know that."

"I know you didn't."

"Believe me. Your efforts were most appreciated."

The General nodded and Dave said: "What brings you to Algiers?"

"Oh, 8th Army business."

Dave looked at the General and he said: "We're always on the lookout for promising young officers. And when we heard about the Algiers Group I was asked to look into it while I was in London on business."

Dave nodded and the General went on: "While I was there I asked General Wynford about the group. Among other things he mentioned this very interesting candidate officer who had been at Dieppe, had escaped from Colditz and made it to London in record time. When he mentioned your name I became curious and wondered if you were the same soldier I had met at Brest. I had your file pulled and sure enough you were."

"I see."

"So on my way back to the 8th Army I was asked to spend a few days here to go over the files with Colonel Dawson and assess everyone in the group."

Dave nodded again and the General went on: "I gather your escape from Colditz was quite spectacular. And I understand your telegram to the Poles made them very happy."

"They received it then."

"Oh yes. They received it."

"I'm glad."

North Africa

"As a matter of fact, given their circumstances, I'm told it meant a lot to them."

"That's good."

"And especially to their leader. What's his name?"

"Jan Mieteck."

"That's the one."

"How do you know that?"

"A young British officer who escaped after you from Colditz told General Wynford."

"I see."

"I don't suppose they have much to look forward to. Having someone escape on their behalf like this helped them a great deal."

Dave didn't say anything and the General said: "Anyway. That's what I heard."

"I did my best."

"Of course."

"How is Mieteck?"

The General frowned and said: "Don't you know? Didn't they tell you?"

"Tell me what?"

"He died."

"When?"

"Late December."

Dave looked down and when he looked up, the General said: "Was he a good friend of yours?"

"He was."

"I'm sorry."

"So am I."

"I thought you knew. I thought they had told you."

"They didn't."

"I'm truly sorry."

"It's all right."

"I wished I had known. I wished they had told me."

"It's all right. It's just he did a lot for me."

"I'm sure."

"There's no way I could repay him for all he did."

"I understand."

"He was a very great man."

"I don't doubt it."

Dave looked down again and when he looked up, the General said: "I'm truly sorry about your friend's death."

395

"It's all right."

"But I must deal with the business at hand. And I must ask you. Do you always listen to a lecture from the back of the classroom?"

"Always."

"Why?"

"It's better from there."

"Why?"

"Let's just say you don't get bothered as much."

"And you don't like to be bothered?"

"Not if I can help it."

"Why not?"

"Let's just say listening to a lecture is not one of my favorite occupation."

"Why?"

"It just isn't."

"You don't like Colonel Dawson?"

"Sure I do."

"You were lucky to get him."

"I know that."

"He's one of the best military thinkers there is."

"I know that."

"What's the problem then?"

"Let's just say doing military studies is not what I like."

"What do you like?"

"Combat. Field operations."

"That's what you want?"

"Yes."

"And that's what you'd like to get as soon as possible?"

"That's right."

"Very well then. Let me see what I can do for you."

CHAPTER 117

The General then stepped back and Dave saluted him. The General returned his salute and Dave watched him turn and leave by the back door. Dave also left by that door and slowly took the staircase on the left side of the building leading to his bunk on the fifth-floor dormitory. When he reached his bunk Dave sat on it and stared at the empty dormitory. Finally he got up and went to the window behind his bunk. In the distance he could see the late afternoon North African sunlight glinting on the windows of the Fort L'Empereur, the Librairie Nationale and the Government Building. Dave stood at the window and looked at that late afternoon North-African sunlight for a long time and then left the dormitory.

Dave walked downstairs and at the entrance, he left the Lycée and stepped on the Boulevard Laferrière. Then he crossed it and began heading north on the Rue de la Lyre toward the casbah. Now, late in the afternoon, the sun was turning into a deep smoldering gold all over the city and there was a cool stiff breeze blowing. Quite a few soldiers were on the Boulevard and in some of the sidewalk cafés, Dave saw NCOs and officers from the Algiers Group wave at him to come in. Dave walked on and in the casbah, he stepped into a small dusty dirty bar called Café Joumine. The café was crowded with Arabs drinking strong sweet-smelling coffee and Dave went and sat at the back where he ordered a cheap bottle of retsina wine. All evening long Dave drank this wine and ate some couscous and for the rest of the weekend, he spent his time alone at that bar.

Dave sat at the back of the Café Joumine and drank cheap retsina wine and around 9.00 o'clock the following Monday morning, after he'd shaven and taken a long cold shower to get rid of the hangover he was feeling from having drunk so much of that sweet sugary wine, he walked

The Long War

downstairs to the reception room to see where he had been assigned. The list for the assignments had been pinned on the bulletin board. The names of the members of the Algiers Group had been listed alphabetically with their ranks and new assignments. Dave stepped close to the board and after he had gone down the list three times, he saw his name wasn't on it. There it is, he thought. You see what happens when you tell the truth to people. Nothing happens. That's what happens.

I shouldn't have told General Haworth how I felt and the kind of assignment I wanted, he thought. I should have told him what he wanted to hear. That's what counts. That's what works. Let's face it. People don't want to hear the truth. They only want to hear what they want to hear. Dave stepped back from the bulletin board. He left it and walked into the deserted messhall to the right of the entrance door. In the messhall he had a tasteless breakfast of tea, some eggs and two toasts. Dave was finishing his breakfast when a short slender Corporal, who was holding a clipboard in his right hand, walked in. When he saw Dave was the only soldier in the messhall, he walked over to him and said: "Are you David Linsday?"

"I am."

"Good."

"What's this all about?"

The Corporal looked at his clipboard and then looked at Dave: "Let me ask you something. Are you connected with General Haworth?"

"Why do you ask?"

"You've been given a very unusual assignment."

"Really?"

"Oh yes."

"Where?"

"Can't tell you that. Top secret."

"Tell me something at least."

"What?"

"Have I passed the course?"

"Of course."

"With what rank?"

"Lieutenant."

"How come my name isn't on the list?"

"That's just it. Your assignment's very unusual."

CHAPTER 118

Dave didn't say anything and the short slender Corporal motioned for him to follow him. They left the messhall and in front of the Administrative area, the Corporal told him to go to the dormitory to get his gear and that he'd be picked up at the front door in half an hour. The Corporal then saluted him and after he had returned the salute, Dave left and took the left staircase to his bunk on the fifth floor. Once on that floor he quickly packed his duffel bag and half an hour later walked down to the Administrative area where the Corporal told him a jeep was waiting for him outside the front door. The jeep was driven by a tall slim Private whose name, the Corporal told him, was John Haskins. Haskins would take him to his assignment.

Dave thanked the Corporal and when he stepped out of the Lycée, Haskins got out of the jeep and helped him put his duffel bag in the back seat. Then they both got in and left the Boulevard Laferrière. They turned right on the Boulevard Baudin. They headed south and took the Rue Sadi-Carnot toward the Maison-Blanche Airport. They kept on heading south and then southeast and soon left Algiers behind. The day was gray and overcast and there was a cold icy wind blowing. They kept on heading southeast on twisting and winding roads through the Atlas Mountains and went through small towns and villages with names like Harrach, Lakdaria, Bouira, Bordj-Bou-Arreridj, Sétif and El Eulma, and they stopped and spent the night in Constantine in a small rundown house near a tank park used by the 6th Armored Division.

Early the next morning they were on the road again. The day was even more gray and overcast than the day before and they still kept on heading southeast. From the way Haskins was driving Dave guessed he was taking him to the front in Tunisia. The front was roughly 400 miles from Algiers and they drove through small towns and villages with names like El Khroub, Guelma, Souk-Arras, Jendouba, Bou Salem and Béja. After Béja they were no longer heading southeast, strictly speaking, but north, and when they reached the small bleak village of El Daram, Haskins came and stopped in front of a dirty rundown café called El Amir.

Haskins pointed to it and said: "You go in."

"Then what?"

"Someone else will pick you up. I'm going back to Algiers."

CHAPTER 119

Dave got out of the jeep and picked up his duffel bag. He thanked Haskins and walked into the café. Inside there were only two old Arabs. They were sitting to the right of the front door and drinking strong black coffee. The owner stood at the bar at the back and was leaning on the counter. To the right of the bar was a door with a bead curtain. When Dave came in a tall slim brown-haired soldier in pale-brown camouflage stood behind the bead curtain and motioned for Dave to follow him. Dave nodded and walked through the bead curtain. He followed the soldier down a short hallway and turned left toward a door at the back of the café. Once they were outside the soldier told him to follow him and then turned and began walking quickly away from the café and the village.

The soldier led him down a narrow winding trail and soon they found themselves in a long sloping valley. The soldier walked ahead of Dave swiftly and briskly and in the valley the cold chilly wind blowing from the mountains was extremely sharp and biting. They kept on going down this valley and heading north and after a while found themselves in other hills and valleys and still kept on heading north. The soldier who was leading him never talked or looked back and late in the afternoon Dave found himself in a long sloping hill strewn with big boulders. They walked down this hill and began climbing another. By now they must have walked ten miles and Dave found himself very tired and out of breath. He was beginning to wonder if they would ever reach their destination when, near the top of that hill, a soldier stepped out from behind a big boulder and Dave stared at him and couldn't get over it.

The soldier who stood in front of him was none other than Jocko Thompson! When Dave came close to him, he suddenly stood at attention and saluted him. Jocko returned his salute and Dave said: "My God, Sir! What are you doing here?"

"Couldn't stand all that training in England, laddie."

"Needed to see a little bit more action?"

"Certainly did."

"I see you're wearing the three pips of a Captain."

"That I am."

"You must have done well then."

"Not that bad, laddie."

"Congratulations."

"Thank you."

"I'm glad for you."

"Thank you. I see you've also done well."

"Oh, that."

"You've made Lieutenant. That's very good."

"I did my best."

"I know that. But come. Come. Let's go and meet the Colonel."

CHAPTER 120

Jocko then stepped aside and motioned for Dave to go behind the big boulder. The tall slim brown-haired soldier who had brought Dave to Jocko had already gone behind it. Dave nodded and when he turned right and stepped behind it, he saw that well-camouflaged soldiers were hiding behind other big boulders further up the slope and watching the hill. The big boulder that Dave had stepped behind stood in front of a dark opening in the hill and could be moved back to completely hide that opening. At the back of the boulder Dave found himself staring at that dark opening. It led to a platform elevator and Dave got on this platform with Jocko. When he did Jocko pressed on a red button on a switch hanging on a black rubber cable on the side of the platform.

They began going down slowly until they came to a stop, Dave guessed, 60 feet below. Dave stepped out of the platform with Jocko and found himself on a dark slope that had narrow-gauge rails leading to and stopping at the platform. Jocko began walking down that dark slope with Dave until they came to a huge black tarpaulin strung across it. There was a slit in the middle of the tarpaulin and when Jocko stepped through it with him, Dave found himself in the middle of a well-lit iron mine. The narrow-gauge rails kept on going to the end of the shaft in the darkness. On the left side of the shaft were large sections covered with plywood and wooden doors with glass panes. Those sections had been made into offices, signal and supply areas while on the right side were two sections with strong steel doors on them and then other open sections to store weapons and ammunitions.

Near the end of the shaft, to the left of it, was a section leading to sleeping quarters and another section, to the right of it, also leading to sleeping quarters as well as to the messhall. Lights were strung on various wires and connected to a generator next to the last section for ammunitions on the right side of the rails. Once they were in the mine Jocko brought Dave to the Colonel's office. His name was Mike Campbell, Jocko told Dave, and his office was the first one on the left side of the mine. He was a big strong burly officer with a bristling mustache and at the moment he was sitting at his desk and reading some papers. When Jocko knocked on his door the Colonel looked up from the papers he was reading and got up. He came around his desk and stood in front of it as Jocko brought Dave into the office. The Colonel smiled at Dave and said: "Ah. David Lindsay."

"That's me," Dave said and saluted the Colonel who returned his salute.

"Welcome to Commando No. 34."

"Thank you, Sir."

"General Haworth must like you a great deal to have put you on attachment here."

"I believe he does, Sir."

"So do I."

"Thank you, Sir."

"I understand you also like combat and field operations."

"I do."

"Well, you'll get plenty of those here."

"I hope so, Sir."

"As a matter of fact we're going out on a little party tonight."

"Are you?"

"We certainly are. Are you interested?"

"Of course."

"Good. You leave with us at midnight then."

CHAPTER 121

The Colonel then turned and went back to sit at his desk. He began reading his papers again and Dave left and stepped out of his office with Jocko. They walked down the mine shaft and Jocko introduced him to various officers, NCOs and Privates. When those introductions were over Jocko brought him to his sleeping quarters to the left side of the mine shaft. In those quarters he told Dave to put his bag at the foot of the double bunk he would be sharing with the tall slim brown-haired soldier in pale-brown camouflage who had brought him here. The name of this soldier, Dave found out from Jocko, was Tom Porter and he was also a Lieutenant. Jocko told Dave to take the upper bunk and put his gear in one of the two lockers at the foot of his bunk.

Dave went to his locker and emptied his duffel bag. He also put his duffel bag in the locker and put on one of the two dark-brown camouflaged uniforms lying on his bunk. Then Jocko brought him to the messhall on the other side of the rails where he had bully-beef, hardtack and a hot cup of tea. After that Jocko told him to go back to his bunk and that he'd come to get him when it was time to go on the raid. Dave nodded and went back to his upper bunk. He lay down and soon fell asleep and a little after 11.00 o'clock at night, he was wakened by Jocko who told him it was time to go. Dave stepped down from his bunk and went with Jocko to one of the sections for ammunitions and another one for weapons where he was issued a pistol, a Thompson machine gun, some grenades and ammunition. Then he lined up with the other commandos and they began leaving the iron mine.

Two hundred commandos were going on this raid. This was almost half the men of Commando No. 34 and when they stepped outside, they split into two parallel columns and began walking down the hill. They moved away from the mine on a cold clear moon-lit night and at the bottom of the hill, they walked behind and around the small deserted village of Djerna. Then they began climbing another hill and headed northeast deep into Tunisia. They walked swiftly and in silence and an hour later a heavy torrential rain began to fall. It swept in huge blowing gusts across the hills and valleys and turned the trails they were using into deep mud that rose sometimes up to their knees. Still they kept on walking and heading northeast and a couple of hours later they suddenly found themselves out of that heavy torrential rain and still heading northeast.

They walked on steadily and silently and an hour later went to ground in a deep valley. Ahead of the columns Dave could see the heads of a few soldiers silhouetted against the skyline and then they all stood up and began moving again. But they were moving slowly and Dave found from Tom Porter they had run into a French outpost holding the line in this valley. One of the French Lieutenants was now taking them through a minefield and a little while later they found themselves in a No Man's Land patrolled a great deal by the Italians and Germans. They kept on pushing through the night and when dawn came, they stood down and hid behind big boulders and wet shrubs. With the coming of dawn Dave heard a Storch Fieseler plane flying high over the hills and valleys and then fell into a deep and exhausted sleep.

When Dave woke up again it was dark. There was a cold stiff wind blowing from the mountains and after he had eaten some more bully beef, hardtack and drunk some hot tea, they were on the move again. By now the two columns had split up. The first column led by Colonel Campbell, Dave found out, was going to Cap Serrat on the Mediterranean in order to embark on landing crafts and land behind Italian lines. They were going to carry out hit-and-run raids in the rear of Italian outposts before reembarking and coming back to join them. Their own column led by Jocko and Tom Porter was going to go down the various hills and valleys of the Mateur Valley in order to look for a large fuel and ammunition dump that, their Arab friends had told them, had supposedly been put up by the Italians recently. If they found that dump, they were to blow it up and move on.

In no time Dave's column found itself going up and down various hills and valleys and looking for that dump. They were searching northeastward and eastward and after a while the column split into five sections of 20 men each in order to increase the range of their search. Each section would cover a hill or a valley and around two o'clock in the morning, when nothing had been found, the five sections came together again and kept on pushing eastward. By then Tom Porter came to Dave with Jocko. He handed him a four-power night scope and said: "Here. Take the point. Let's see if you can bring us luck." Dave took the scope and as he moved to the point, he roamed over the hills and valleys with it. This sniper's scope, with its extremely sharp optics, its post and sidebar reticle that left the top of the field of vision wide open, was ideal for moving around and searching.

Dave kept on leading the column and on roaming through various hills and valleys and around three o'clock in the morning, when they were coming into a new hill, he stopped the column and kept on ranging with his scope over it. He swung the scope to the right and to the left and was about to move it to the right again, when he stopped abruptly. Dave swung it back to the center of the hill and as he magnified the distance, he grinned suddenly. Bingo! There is was. In the cross hairs the lines outlining the bottom of the hill were quite different from the lines of hill itself. The lines, in the high resolution of the magnification, had a clearness and sharpness not found in the lines of the hill. But if he was looking at the dump, where were the soldiers guarding it? Dave swung his scope to the left and to the right and after a while, he grinned again.

On both sides, near the bottom of the hill, he could see the silhouettes of two Italian soldiers. They wore the high plumed helmets of *carabenieri* and now, so late at night, they were both holding on to their rifles carelessly and looking sleepy. Dave turned and handed the scope to Tom Porter who was standing behind him. He pointed to both sides of the hill, at the bottom, and Porter lowered the scope. He looked where Dave had pointed and after a moment, he handed the scope back to Dave and nodded.

CHAPTER 122

Porter turned and spoke to two commandos behind him. In no time both got up ran in a crouch past Dave and Porter. They scrambled to the bottom of the hill and after a while were lost from view. Dave was watching the sentry posts and not long after, he saw both commandos rise from those posts and hold their right thumbs up. Dave turned to Porter and Jocko and talked to them briefly. Then he too got up and scrambled down to the bottom of the hill. At the bottom Dave came by those posts. Both commandos were behind them and watching him with their rifles. They had put on the plumed helmets of the Italian sentries and those sentries were lying on the floor of those posts.

Dave told the commandos to cover him and went on. He slid down until he was at the bottom of the hill and near the camouflage netting. At that point the two sides of the hill formed into a large V and the camouflage netting had been carefully spread out so that it covered both sides of it. At the bottom Dave slowly lifted the netting and went in. Inside he found himself on a wooden floor and when he looked around, he couldn't get over it. The dump was much bigger than it looked from the outside. To his right were rows upon rows of oil drums. To his left were crates after crates of weapons and ammunition stacked up high. There were narrow alleyways between the rows upon rows of oil drums, weapons and ammunition. As Dave hid behind the oil drums he suddenly heard firing in the distance.

In the mountains the sounds carried sharply and clearly and Dave left the dump and came out of the camouflage netting. He moved past the commandos who were watching him and ran in a crouch up the hill until he dropped down in a fold about one hundred feet from the netting. The whole column had stopped and gone to ground behind that fold.

When Dave reached it he turned to Porter and Jocko and talked with them briefly. Then he said: "Okay. When I come out of the dump you send four commandos with dynamite and short fuses to place them on the boxes of weapons and ammunitions. When they come out and get back here with the two commandos from the posts we'll blow up the dump. Is that understood?"

Porter and Jocko nodded and a commando handed Dave two big bags of dynamite, a coil of wire, some black industrial tape and a pair of pliers. Dave took those things and got up and ran in a crouch down the hill again. At the bottom Dave lifted the netting again and went in. Inside he swiftly stepped to the oil drums and took the dynamite out of the bags. He wedged and braced two large blocks of dynamite against the barrels, made sure they were tightly taped and secured, set them properly with wires, and when he came to move out of the netting, he heard the firing again in the distance. It was sustained and heavy and when he heard the firing, Dave looked and saw a sentry coming down the alleyway toward where he was standing. Dave took out his Matt knife from one of the right pockets of his pants and grabbed the two dynamite bags with his other hand.

Dave moved swiftly away, around another alleyway to the left, and the sentry came out where he had been standing and looked quickly to the right and to the left. Then the sentry turned and walked back down the alleyway from where he had come from. Dave moved back to where he had been standing and at the other end, the sentry stopped and spoke to another sentry. They both listened to the firing for a while and then moved on to the left to go and talk with a third sentry further down on the other side of the oil drums. When the sentries moved away Dave began paying out the wires until he was out of the netting and moving up the hill. Dave kept on paying out the wires and when he reached the fold, he dropped down behind it. Then Dave tied the two wires properly onto the plunger and looked down at the dump.

When Dave had come out of the netting he had seen four shadowy figures run toward it and go in. Now, as Dave had his hands on the plunger and was watching the dump, he felt his heart pounding within him and was sweating. Dave kept on watching the dump and soon saw one shadowy figure come out. Then he saw two more. Finally the last one also came out with the two commandos from the posts. They scrambled up the hill until they dropped down in the fold behind him. As soon as they were there Dave pushed down hard on the plunger. There was a huge shattering roar and an enormous black and orange column of smoke rose in the sky. As this happened far-off machine-gun fire was heard over the roar and there were the faint yells and screams of: *"Attaco! Attaco! Siamo attacati!"*

The Long War

Then there was just the noise of exploding ammunition and of far-off firing beyond the exploding ammunition, and the only thing you saw was that huge black and orange column of smoke rising in the sky and turning after a while into a thick black column of smoke. As soon as the dump had been blown Jocko tapped Dave on the shoulder and he and Porter and the rest of the commandos pulled back and began moving away from the dump. They marched swiftly away from the hill and lost themselves in the folds of other hills and valleys. It was now close to 4.00 o'clock in the morning and Dave took the point again and kept on leading the column southwestward.

They kept on marching through hills and valleys and near 5.00 o'clock in the morning, when it began to grow light, Dave made the men stand down for the day in the fold of a hill. However he made sure, when they stood down, they spread camouflage netting over themselves in order not to be seen from the air.

CHAPTER 123

Sure enough, not long after, Dave heard two Fieseler Storchs flying high over the hills and valleys. Dave listened to them for a while and then quickly fell asleep against a big boulder. When he woke up again it was dark and Dave had a hot cup of tea and some bully beef. Then the column was up and moving again. A stiff cold wind was blowing from the mountains and Porter took the point this time and led the column. They could now hear quite a few columns of Italians and Germans roaming the hills and valleys and Porter kept on switching them from hills and valleys in order to avoid running into them. He kept on leading them southwestward and near the ruined and abandoned village of Jalta they met Mike Campbell's column coming back from Cap Serrat and their successful raid behind Italian lines.

The two columns linked up and kept on heading southwestward and around 6.00 o'clock in the morning, when it began to grow light, they reached the small deserted village of Djerna again and began walking up the long hill leading to their hideaway in the mine. When they came inside the mine Dave headed for his bunk where he changed into his other clean camouflaged battle-dress. Then he left his bunk and walked over to the messhall in order to meet Porter and Jocko. Once they met they all went and sat at the back of it and had some tea and biscuits. While they sat there they were joined by other commandos and they talked about how well the raids had gone. Then they left to go to their bunks and get some sleep and the next day, the Colonel called the officers in his office and worked out their respective assignments for the next raid.

They were moving out the next evening to go and carry out another raid behind the Italian lines. That evening they left as soon as it was dark, and in the days and weeks that followed the patrols and raids all fell into the same pattern. The Colonel and Jocko would lead a column each and Dave and Porter would do the same. Sometimes all four columns would be out raiding, sometimes only two. Some of those raids would be behind Italian and German lines, some of them would only be probing patrols to try and find out where the enemy was and how strong he was. Most of the time, though, there was one or two columns out probing and looking for the enemy. At that time the Germans were pouring troops in Tunisia. They had replaced a soft and inefficient General, Walther Nehring, by a tough and competent one, Jurgen von Arnim.

By then the Germans knew the British were weak in Tunisia and tried everything to prevent their linkup from the south with the 8th US Army. In order to do that they first attacked at Bou Arada, then south at Robaa, and then at Ousseltia. Their main goal was to prevent the linkup between the British and American Armies and to destroy the Allies' landing in North Africa. Facing them and trying to hold them off was the British 1st Army. But calling the British 1st Army an Army was really an exaggeration. That Army was only made up of the 78th Division, a Brigade of the Guards, some commandos and paratroopers, and was supported by the 6th Armored Division. It was holding a long line that stretched from the Mediterranean and went south through the mountains and valleys to about 35 miles west of Tunis.

This was the Army fighting the Germans and Italians in Tunisia and the mission of the Commandos No. 34 was to throw in hit-and-run raids and patrols in their sector to keep the enemy off balance and give the impression they had much bigger forces than they actually had. As a result the Commandos always had a patrol or two out and were probing and looking for the enemy. Their favorite way to do this was to go to Cap Serrat and get in landing crafts to land behind enemy lines to carry out their hit-and-run raids. Then they would get back into their crafts and sail up the coast in order to move back into the hills and valleys and lose themselves in their hideaway. As the days and weeks went on the Commandos increased their raids and patrols and the Germans and Italians slowly began giving ground.

There were still severe clashes and ambushes in the hills and mountains, but it was obvious the British were strengthening themselves from the north and the Americans were coming from the south. Dave kept on going on patrols with the Colonel, Jocko and Porter and by the beginning of April it became quite clear the Allies were going to win in North Africa. The Americans had recovered from the disaster of the Kasserine Pass and the British fought two brilliant battles at Thala to prevent a German breakthrough. By the end of April the Germans found themselves cornered in the northeast corner of Tunisia and the British armor and infantry were driving hard toward Tunis while the Americans were storming down the Mateur Valley toward Bizerte.

During that month Dave kept on going on raids with the Colonel, Jocko and Porter. And it was early on a Friday morning, on April 30, 1943, when he had come back from a long raid near Damla where he had discovered an enemy supply dump and blown it up, that Dave received an information from the Colonel that was going to have such deep and profound repercussions in his life.

CHAPTER 124

That morning, after he had come back from his successful raid on Damla, Dave was called in the Colonel's office. Jocko and Porter were already there and when Dave came in, all three turned to him. The Colonel put down on his desk a dispatch he had been reading and looked at Dave. There was a big grin on his face and he said: "My dear boy, congratulations on your raid in Damla."

"Thank you, Sir."

"It appears you've become quite an expert at blowing up dumps."

"So it appears."

"I also believe you found your target fairly easily."

"I did, Sir."

"Our Arab friends were reliable then."

"Very reliable."

"When you win your friends always become very reliable."

"I agree, Sir."

"And now, I believe far greater congratulations are in order."

Dave looked at the Colonel and the Colonel said: "My dear boy, you've been reassigned."

"Where."

"To England."

"With whom?"

"The Westmount Fusiliers."

"Are you serious?"

"I am."

"As what?"

"Commanding Officer of B Company."

North Africa

"I don't believe it."

"You better believe it. With the rank of Captain."

Dave looked at the Colonel again and the Colonel said: "I'm very happy for you."

"I must say I often thought of going back to my Company."

"I'm sure you did."

"But I didn't think it was possible."

"Well, it is."

"And certainly not as Commanding Officer."

"Well, you are."

"I see."

"I must say, though, it couldn't happen to a better man."

"Thank you, Sir."

"I believe you'll do well there."

"I hope so."

"You will. You're a born leader of men."

"Thank you, Sir."

"It's true. You've done very well here. And I believe you'll do as well with your old Regiment."

"I hope you're right, Sir."

"I am. Not too many officers want to go on attachment with us. But you did and performed splendidly."

"Thank you, Sir."

"We were quite lucky to have you."

"I feel the same way about the Commandos, Sir."

"I'm glad you do."

"I certainly do, Sir."

"I must say I'm quite proud to have had you under my command."

"Thank you, Sir."

"I want you to know there will always be a place for you here, should you wish to come back."

"I appreciate that, Sir."

The Colonel then fell silent and Dave said: "What will you do now, Sir?"

"Me?"

"No. The Commandos."

"Oh, I suppose we'll go somewhere else where we can battle the enemy."

"I see."

"The fighting here in Tunisia is pretty much over. I'm sure the Army will find another trouble spot for us."

The Long War

"I'm sure."

"You see, my boy. The Commandos are troublemakers in the same way, for instance, your old Regiment puts out fires. That's what we do in this war. That's our specialty."

"I see."

"That's why a unit like ours will always be used by the Army in the same way, for example, as your old Regiment will be."

"I'm sure."

The Colonel fell silent again and then said: "At any rate, I must offer you my congratulations once more on your promotion to Captain."

"Thank you, Sir."

"We'll be missing you around here."

"I'll be missing you too."

"Your orders are to leave tomorrow morning for Algiers."

Dave nodded and the Colonel said: "Porter will take you to El Daram."

"Good."

"A driver will pick you up there and bring you back to Algiers."

Dave nodded again and the Colonel said. "In Algiers you're to go back to the Lycée De La Rochefoucauld. New orders will be given to you and you'll be told when to sail for England and report to your Regiment."

"I understand."

"That's it. Good luck."

"Thank you, Sir."

CHAPTER 125

Dave left the Colonel's office and went back to his bunk in order to pack his duffel bag and get ready to leave for Algiers. When he was finished he went to sleep briefly and then spent the rest of the day saying goodby to the Commandos. Dave had made many friends there and tried to speak to as many as he could. He also said his goodby to Jocko and Porter and in the morning, he left early with Porter to begin walking the 10 miles back to El Daram. Now, at the beginning of May, there was a nice soft breeze blowing and on the way there, they had to go up and down several hills and valley. That early in the morning the air was fresh and the cool clean smell of spring was in the air.

When they reached El Daram Dave saw a jeep was parked in front of the café El Amir. A frail young Corporal was driving the jeep and when they reached it, Dave shook hands with Porter and thanked him. Porter left and Dave put his duffel bag in the back of the jeep. He stepped in and the Corporal made a U-turn and began driving south toward Béja. Now that the campaign in Tunisia was almost over the drive was quite pleasant and enjoyable and at Béja, the Corporal turned west and began heading toward Algiers. The Corporal's name, Dave found out, was Jim Irwin and as he sat next to him and looked out, Dave saw the mountains, hills and valleys were beginning to turn green. They kept on heading west and drove through the same small towns and villages he had gone through before and when they reached Constantine, they stopped and spent the night in another small rundown house near a tank park used by the 6th Armored Division.

In the morning they were on the road again and driving through other small towns and villages and when they reached Algiers in the early evening, they came and stopped in front of the Lycée De La Rochefoucauld. As he got out of the jeep Dave thanked Irwin. Then he took his duffel bag and walked into the Lycée. Inside Dave headed for the Administrative Area and spoke to the same short slender Corporal who had looked for him earlier to tell him about his assignment to the Commandos. The Corporal's name, Dave found out, was Peter Duncan. Duncan told Dave to report to the Administrative Area on Monday morning and that he would be given orders as to when he would sail for England. For the time being, though, he was free to do as he pleased. Then Duncan took Dave to the fifth floor and gave him a bunk facing the west side of the city.

Dave thanked Duncan and when he left, he put his duffel bag on top of his foot locker. Then he walked out of the dormitory. He went and spent the rest of the evening at the Café Joumine and on Monday morning, he reported to a tall slim Major in the Administrative Area. The Major's name was John Douglas and he told Dave he would sail at 6.00 o'clock on Tuesday morning on the transport ship *H.M.S. Argyll*. The *Argyll* was bringing back some officers and war materiel to England. He would sail along with those officers. Dave thanked the Major and at 5.00 a.m. the following morning, he boarded the *Argyll* with the other officers and was given a cabin on the top deck. Then, right on the stroke of 6.00 a.m., they sailed from one of the piers facing the Palais du Gouvernement.

The journey to England took nine days and during that time Dave stayed mostly in his cabin and did not bother much with the other officers. Dave opened his duffel bag and spent most of his time drinking the rest of his stale bottle of gin with water. When it was finished Dave stayed mostly by himself in his cabin. But that early Tuesday morning, when they sailed, he went and stood on deck and saw the sun was shining brightly and warmly. Then, as they pulled away from the pier and began heading west in the Mediterranean, Algiers rose before him startlingly and dazzlingly white against the semi-circle of clear-green hills. In the distance it looked stunningly and incredibly beautiful and seemed to burst in the sky in a flight of white pristine splendor.

There was a light cool breeze blowing over the water and when they left Algiers behind, they kept on sailing westward in the Mediterranean until, on the third day, they reached the Strait of Gibraltar. They went through the Strait and kept on heading west until, near the Azores, they turned north and began heading toward England. Now, in early May, their Captain took them into such a far westerly course because the Allies had once again, in the last few months, lost a considerable number of ships to U-Boats. The sea was still full of Wolf-packs and he made sure they sailed in an irregular and zigzagging pattern when they went by the coasts of

Portugal and France. Then they were past those coasts and every day the sun shone clearly and brightly. The sea was smooth and calm and in this kind of weather, the *Argyll* sailed at about 14 knots.

This made for a fairly smooth and uneventful journey and on the seventh day they reached the Celtic Sea. The next day they came into the St. George's Channel and the day after they sailed into the Irish Sea. That early Tuesday morning the weather was sunny and mild. The sea was a pale clear-green and around 10.00 o'clock in the morning, a thin dark line began appearing on the horizon. As they sailed closer to it, it grew and grew until it hardened and turned into the city of Liverpool itself. The same three huge buildings, the Royal Liver Building, the Cunard Building and the Dock Board Offices Building, rose over it and several gigantic cranes towered over its massive and sprawling docks.

Dave had reached England once again.

CHAPTER 126

When they sighted land the Captain took the *Argyll* inside the harbor and came and dropped anchor at the Nelson Docks. Once the ship was properly secured Dave walked down the gangplank with the other officers and was picked up by a young Lieutenant who was driving a jeep. The Lieutenant left the Nelson Docks with Dave and drove him to the Mill Street barracks of the Liverpool 41st Infantry Division. Dave spent the rest of the day in those barracks and around 11.00 o'clock in the evening, the Lieutenant came and took him to the Lime Street Railway Station. In the station Dave boarded the overnight train for London. He had been given a first-class ticket and told he would be picked up by another young Lieutenant at King's Cross Station.

At 12.30 sharp Dave's train left and began heading for London. As they pulled out of the station Dave closed his eyes and quickly fell asleep. The two months he had fought in Tunisia had left him pretty tired and he slept deeply and soundly. He didn't move from his comfortable thickly-padded leather seat and by the time he opened his eyes, he saw it was getting light outside. It was now close to 8.00 o'clock in the morning and when they came into King's Cross Station, he saw the young Lieutenant who had come to pick him up. He was waiting for him on the platform and when the train finally stopped, Dave got off and walked over to him. The Lieutenant exchanged salutes with him and led him to a jeep parked outside. They left the station and got on King's Cross Road.

They headed south and got on Farringdon Road, Farringdon Street and New Bridge Street. They drove across the Blackfriars Bridge and turned right on Stamford Street. They got on York Road and then came and stopped at the Waterloo Station. At the station Dave was just in time to get his ticket and get on the train leaving for Aldershot. As soon as Dave boarded it, it left the station and began going through the same towns and villages he had gone through before. It was a bright, cool, sunny day and Dave sat in his seat on the left side of the aisle and looked at the rolling countryside and at those towns and villages. It didn't take him long to reach Aldershot and when he got there, Dave left the train and took a taxi to the center. When he reached it Dave stepped out and paid the driver.

Then Dave walked over to the Administrative Building and found the Regiment was back from training once again in Scotland. As a matter of fact it was using the same barracks it had stayed in when they had first come to England. The Regimental barrack was still further down the first row of barracks. Dave left the Administrative Building and walked over to that barrack. The walk there wasn't long and when he reached it, he went in and asked the big husky Corporal at the entrance desk to see the Colonel. The Corporal asked for his name and got up from his desk. He walked toward a closed door to the right of the barrack and knocked on it. Then he went in and came out a few moments later. He motioned for Dave to go in and Dave headed for that door and thanked the Corporal.

When Dave went in Colonel Cantwell stood up from behind his big wooden desk. He was still the same tall, lean, wiry officer Dave remembered and also had the same cold icy blue eyes. As Dave went in the Colonel said: "Ah. Lindsay. Come in. Come in." At the same time he motioned for him to close the door behind him and come and sit in the chair in front of his desk. Dave did what the Colonel asked and after they had exchanged salutes, the Colonel sat down behind his desk again and said: "My dear David. May I call you David?"

"Of course, Sir."

"Still in the forefront of things, I see."

"Yes, sir."

"How was your journey?"

"Very pleasant, Sir."

"I'm damn glad you're here now. We can certainly use you."

"Thank you, Sir."

"I must say yours is quite an impressive record. First your fight with Bostwick; then your race against the 51st Midlands; then Dieppe; next your escape; and now North Africa. It's quite something."

"I did my best, Sir."

"It's more than that. Very few men have a record like that."

"Thank you, Sir."

"Believe me. Very few men have ever gone on attachment with the Commandos and done so well. It's quite remarkable."

"If you say so, Sir."

"I certainly do. And it seems you've become a Demolition Expert."

"So it appears."

"My dear David, you have no idea of the extraordinary recommendation Colonel Campbell gave you."

"I believe Colonel Campbell was overly partial to me."

"No, no, my dear David. Things like that are earned. They are not given."

"I did my best, Sir."

"You certainly did. And may I offer you my congratulations, by the way, on your promotion to Captain."

"By all means."

"I tell you. B Company can certainly use someone like you."

"Thank you, Sir."

"Believe me. You couldn't have come at a better time."

Dave didn't say anything for a moment and the Colonel said: "I tell you. I'm very glad to have you."

"I'm glad to be here."

"Good."

"But may I ask, Sir, what happened to my predecessor?"

"Major Wilson?"

"Yes."

"He's been reassigned to the Advocate General's office."

"May I ask why?"

"Certainly."

CHAPTER 127

The Colonel leaned back in his chair and when he leaned forward again and put his elbows on his desk, his eyes were no longer cold and icy but tired and weary. He looked at Dave for a moment and then said: "Let's just say Major Wilson is a fine man. He loves soldiering in the ideal. But I'm afraid he's not quite as comfortable with the practical and hands-on aspects of it."

Dave didn't say anything and the Colonel said: "Do you know anything about exercise *Spartan*?"

"No."

"This was an exercise that took place this March and was designed to study the problems that would arise from an advance from an established bridgehead."

Dave nodded and the Colonel went on: "The exercise lasted two weeks and was opposing two Canadian Corps and one British Corps against a so-called "German" Army of two Corps."

Dave nodded again and the Colonel went on: "Anyway, at one point, General McNaughton ran his Second Corps against the First Canadian Corps' lines of communications. This was our own Corps and for a while everything became pretty confused. As a matter of fact things got so bad Major Wilson just couldn't get B Company moving. Sergeant Major Bostwick had to intervene and it was he who got the Company going again."

"I see."

"Then, when we went to Scotland for a refresher course in assault landing, Wilson became very nervous. He was always overreacting or underreacting."

The Long War

Dave nodded once again and the Colonel said: "Finally, when we held specific tactical exercises at Aldershot recently, he passed out twice from high blood-pressure flareups. That's why we had to replace him."

Dave nodded once more and the Colonel said: "Major Wilson is a lawyer. He's very good with legal matters. That's why he'll do well in the Advocate General's office. But not as a Company Commander."

"I see."

"But I must tell you. B Company has had a strange history since the war began."

"What do you mean?"

"Well, the first CO, Captain Cecil Emmett Williams, changed completely once he came to England."

"How?"

"He became more British than the British and wasn't very efficient."

"I see."

"Next, Major Wilson proved to be a nice man. But not fit for battle-field command."

Dave looked at the Colonel and the Colonel said: "That's why, you see, I was so anxious for you to get here."

"Why?"

"Well, with your reputation, I'm hoping you'll take charge. And do something with that Company."

"I'll try."

"Good."

"But may I ask how I came to be chosen?"

A smile suddenly crossed the Colonel's face and he leaned even more forward on his desk. He looked at Dave for a moment and then said: "Your choice came as a result of one of the most extraordinary situation I have ever seen."

"What do you mean?"

"Well, I had gone to Headly Court to discuss the manpower requirement of the Regiment with General McNaughton. While I was there I mentioned I needed a new CO for B Company."

"Go on."

"While I was with him two other Generals happened to be there: General Wynford to discuss the political-military situation; and General Haworth on behalf of General Montgomery. When I mentioned I needed a new CO for B Company both of them looked up."

"And?"

"General Wynford said he knew a young candidate officer in Algiers who wanted to be back with B Company and gave your name. General

North Africa

Haworth mentioned he knew you from Brest and Algiers and that it was he who had assigned you to the Commandos No. 34."

"So?"

"So when I mentioned I also knew you from your memorable fight with Bostwick and your winning run against the 51st Midlands, everyone was in agreement and you were chosen."

"I see."

"It's a small world, isn't it?"

"It certainly is."

The Colonel didn't say anything for a moment and when he looked at Dave again, his eyes became serious and thoughtful. He leaned a little bit more forward on his desk and said: "Let me explain what's happening around here."

Dave didn't say anything and the Colonel said: "Something really big is going on."

"What do you mean?"

"There's an intense debate going on in the Army right now as to whether it should be kept intact or split up to fight the enemy."

"Who's involved?"

"General McNaughton who wants to keep the Army intact and the CGS Ken Stuart and Defence Minister Ralston who want to split it up."

"How do you feel about that?"

"General McNaughton is a fine soldier who truly built this Army. But I must say there's something to be said for the other side of the argument as well."

"Such as?"

"Well, this Army is super-trained. In fact it's been training for more than four years. I think it's time for part of it or all of it to fight the enemy."

"Well, there's been Spitsbergen and Dieppe."

"True. But these were isolated operations."

"The soldiers at Dieppe wouldn't think so."

"True. But that doesn't change my point."

"No. It doesn't."

"Let me put it another way. You and I are both boxers. I think this Army is like a fighter who has trained 500 rounds in the gym but has never gotten in the ring to fight an opponent."

"I see."

"That's why I believe something really big is about to break out. I don't think we would have been sent to Scotland for a refresher course in assault landing if nothing was going to happen."

425

The Long War

"I agree."

"That's the reason I want you to take over the Company right away. Do a few tactical exercises and get to know it as well as you can. I don't think we'll be staying here long."

"Okay."

"The Company knows you're coming. You can settle in the officer's barrack to the right of this one. And then get going."

"All right."

"No one was made Acting CO since I knew you were coming. In fact Bostwick has been running the Company in the same way he was running it under Major Wilson. But I want someone with greater technical and strategical skills."

"Sure."

"Bostwick is all right on tactical matters. But I want an officer to better fine-tune it and bring it to a greater operational level."

"I understand."

"Well, that's it, David."

"Yes, Sir."

"Get going."

"Right away, Sir."

CHAPTER 128

Dave got up and saluted the Colonel. The Colonel returned his salute and Dave left him. He walked out of the Regimental barrack and went to the officers' barrack to the right of it where he took over Major Wilson's living quarters. The Major had had a small room in that barrack and Dave opened his duffel bag and put his things in the small wooden locker at the foot of his bed. Then he left and walked over to B Company's Orderly room where he had his office. The Orderly Room was in a barrack to the left of the Regimental barrack and when he walked in, the Company Clerk, Tom Taylor, didn't seem overly surprised to see him. As for Bostwick, he was quite proper and cooperative. Although, in his case, he seemed stunned to see Dave promoted CO of the Company and was making an enormous effort to be pleasant and accommodating.

Once Dave was in his office he called in Bostwick and then Taylor and told them what he wanted from them. Then he took over the Company and in the days and weeks that followed began training it and getting acquainted with it. Dave ran Section, Platoon and full-Company exercises, and in a few instances, with Captain Tom Clark of A Company, carried out a two-Company Assault Training Program. All these exercises were designed for him to get the feel of the Company and it didn't take him long to see how right the Colonel had been. The Company was super-trained. It was doing all these things well but in an easy-going and overly-confident way that was highly questionable. It was one thing to carry out infantry assaults in training and look good and confident. It was quite another to do them under the guns of a real enemy when it might mean instant death.

There was also another matter. When Dave had been on assignment in North Africa with the Commandos, if you had asked each and everyone of them the question: "Are you willing to die for the 34?" The answer would have been: "Yes!" That was what made them such a great unit. There was a powerful, cohesive strength about them that tolerated no dissension. In the Canadian Army, Dave found out for himself and from discussions with other Company COs and high-ranking officers, whenever you made a decision it was often discussed endlessly by the other ranks and you had to show them why it was the right decision. This was fine it you had time to do it. But it you didn't, as was the case right now, it made for an Army of stubborn, undisciplined and overcritical soldiers. Worse than that, however, it produced immature soldiers who thought they were much better than they actually were.

Still Dave tried to overlook that weakness in the Company and kept on training it and on Thursday, June 24, 1943, the order came for them to get ready to move. That early morning, after breakfast, a long line of Bedford trucks came to take them to the Aldershot Station. The men packed their gear, filed out and were put aboard the trucks. Then the trucks left and took them to the Aldershot Station where a long train was waiting for them. In no time the men were put on board and the train left the station. It began heading north and going through the grassy rolling countryside and many small towns and villages. They kept on heading north and by early afternoon reached the Midlands. They went through various industrial towns and then were into the open countryside again and moving past many woods, fields and streams.

By early evening, when the train slowed down while still keeping on heading north, Dave knew where it was taking them. The train was taking them to Greenock and not long after, when it began slowing even more, it came and stopped at the Central Station. Outside they were put aboard other Bedford trucks and taken to the massive barracks of the 73rd Infantry Division on Haig Street where they spent the night. In the morning they were taken to the huge Army Depot near the Port Terminal where they were issued tropical kits. Then they spent the rest of the day and the weekend in the barracks of the 73rd. Finally on Monday morning they were taken to the port and by tenders to the troop transport *H.M.S. Glengyle* in the Clyde channel. The channel was full of troop transports and tenders and escort ships and from the huge stores of equipment that were in the port and being tactically loaded, Dave knew this was no isolated operation but something big.

The *Glengyle* stayed in the channel all day. In early evening it lifted anchor with the rest of the troop transports and began slipping away. It had been a bright, warm and sunny day and Dave stood at the railing of the *Glengyle* and looked at the civilians, soldiers and women walking on the riverside and swimming at the beaches. A young blonde girl was running laughingly from her tall and slender boyfriend and as he caught up with her, he put his arms around her and kissed her. Some children stood on the riverside when the *Glengyle* slipped past and looked at the troops. A few old men and women waved at them. Then the *Glengyle* was gone from the last lingering sunlight and moving with the rest of the transports into the gathering darkness of the open sea.

They were sailing slowly down the Clyde and into the North Channel and from the way they were heading, Dave guessed they were sailing around the northern coast of Ireland and into the Atlantic Ocean. They were sailing at 12 knots with a large escort of destroyers and corvettes and the next day, they kept on heading on a westerly course. The day was once again bright, warm and sunny and they maintained that course all day. On the third day they turned left and began sailing on a southerly course toward the Azores. The weather was still nice and mild and on the fourth day, Thursday, July 1, 1943, the Colonel gathered the Company around him on the upper deck and told the men where they were going.

They were heading for Sicily.

BOOK ELEVEN

SICILY

CHAPTER 129

When the Colonel told the Company where they were going, wild and excited cheers broke out among the men. Although the Regiment had taken a terrible beating at Dieppe most of the men still wanted to get at the Germans and fight them very badly. The Colonel told the men they would be landing on the eastern coast of Sicily as part of the British 8th Army under General Montgomery. They would belong to the 30th Corps of Lieutenant-General Oliver Leese. As the 1st Canadian Division they would be led by Major-General Guy Simonds and their Regiment would be going in on the right sector of the beach in the Pachino peninsula. This sector was called Roger Beach and they would land in this sector as part of the 1st Infantry Brigade.

The British and Canadians would move up the eastern side of the island, the Colonel went on. The American 7th Army, under General George S. Patton, would land at Gela and would move up on the western side. The code name for this operation was *Husky* and it would involve 180,000 Allied soldiers as well as 230,000 Italians and 40,000 Germans. Twenty-six thousand Canadians would take part in it. The Colonel talked about the operation at great length and when he was finished, large maps and photographs of the area were taken out. The plaster model of the Pachino peninsula was lifted out of its wooden box and placed on a table where it could be studied. Dave made sure his Company went over the photographs carefully and knew the Pachino peninsula well.

Dave also gave detailed briefings to his men about their part in the coming operation and on Sunday, July 4, 1943, as they passed through the Straits of Gilbraltar, the heavy bombing of Sicily began by the Northwest African Air Force. Throughout their journey the weather had been nice and mild. But now that they had sailed into the Mediterranean, the sun became searing hot and the sea was a flat and iridescent blue-green. They stayed close to the coast of North Africa and sailed on past Oran, Algiers, Philippeville and Bone. Then they met other convoys and as they headed for their assembly area south of Malta, Dave looked around him and couldn't get over it. There were hundreds and hundreds of ships, from aircraft carriers, battleships, cruisers and monitors, to destroyers and corvettes, not to mention troopships, tank-landing crafts and torpedo boats, while, overhead, fighter planes flew back and forth across the clear blue sky.

They kept on sailing east and went around Cap Bon. Then they went down toward Tripoli and swung back on July 9, 1943 toward Malta in order to launch their assault. So far the sea had been calm and flat. But that morning one of those freak Mediterranean wind blew up. This was the *Sirocco* and as the wind began blowing to gale force, the *Glengyle* rose and fell in the heavy sea. It kept on sailing toward Malta and as they passed it in the early evening sunlight, they headed for the Pachino area. By then the sea was getting so heavy and stormy Dave wondered if the operation would go on. Still they kept on sailing northeast toward the Pachino peninsula and at 1.00 a.m. on Saturday, July 10, 1943, on a clear and starlit night, the ship's loudspeaker system suddenly came alive with the voice of an officer calling groups by serial numbers to transfer to their boat stations.

Dave took the Company to the three assault landing crafts assigned to them. They were slung on davits over the rolling sea and when the crafts were lowered and hit the water, they smashed into the side of the *Glengyle* with a screeching and jarring sound. Then they were taken out by the swell before coming and smashing into the ship with another screeching and jarring sound. Finally they were swept into the rolling and stormy sea and began sailing in the darkness and looking for other assault landing crafts. By this time the wind had died down. But the sea was still rough and heavy. The three crafts rose and fell in the water and when they had linked up with six other crafts, they turned away from the ships and began their run-in toward Roger beach.

CHAPTER 130

Their assault landing crafts headed toward the beach. They were sailing at about seven knots and Dave's craft was the first one in the column on the right. Ahead of them Pachino was in flames three miles inland. The Northwest African Air Force had fire-bombed the town in order to give them direction. As they closed the distance toward the beach Dave could see huge fountains of water rising here and there all around them. Six-inch Italian guns were firing on incoming crafts and behind them the navy opened fire on coastal targets. A monitor moved up and opened fire with her two 15-inch guns. Dave could feel the blast sweep over the ocean and as they sailed toward the beach, he could see the stark black outline of the town standing against the burning fires.

From the shore there was the constant shattering roar of exploding shells and Dave couldn't hear anything except the swooshing booming noise of their own naval guns firing. The darkness was beginning to thin out and as the sky slowly started to grow pink and orange, they came within sight of the beach. Red, green and white tracers were coming from three concrete pillboxes to the right of the beach. The medium and heavy machine guns of those pillboxes were raking it and the water in front of them. Then their assault landing crafts hit the beach and the men jumped into waist-deep water. Rifle and machine gun bullets were kicking and spurting all around them. The men waded through the water and rushed for the beach. When they reached it they threw themselves on the sand and began returning fire. Red, Gennaro and Higgins quickly crawled to the barbed wire and began cutting it.

Soon they breached it and the men began moving through it and spreading themselves on both sides. Dave who was behind Slav on the right side made sure the Company made it safely beyond the wire. Past it the beach was rising gently and there were some ridges leading to the pillboxes. Dave kept some riflemen and Bren-gunners firing at the pillboxes and sent the 1st and 2nd Platoons to outflank them. The fire from those pillboxes was pretty intense and the men had to crawl alongside the first ridge out of sight of them. When they reached their flanks they rose and jumped into the next ridge. They kept on jumping from ridge to ridge until they were close to the pillboxes. While they were doing this there was some wild and erratic fire from Italian riflemen who seemed to be on the flanks of those pillboxes.

Nobody was hurt, though, and when the men had reached the last ridge, they suddenly stood up and rushed the pillboxes. They ran right against them and threw satchel charges through the firing slits. Then they threw themselves on the ground as sharp rocking explosions shook those pillboxes and as a thick black acrid smoke came pouring out of the firing slits. There were yells and screams and the heavy iron doors of those pillboxes grated open. Bleeding and wounded men came staggering out with their hands up and one Italian Captain who was bleeding from the nose and ears kept on yelling: *"Io sono un facista! Io sono un facista!"* When he reached for his Beretta he was shot down. The others were sent roughly to the beach and Dave ordered some of his riflemen and Bren-gunners to go and deal with the Italian riflemen who had been firing on them.

This didn't take too long. When Dave's riflemen and Bren-gunners moved in on them most of the Italian soldiers stood up and surrendered. A few tried to fight it out and were shot. Some tried to run away. But most of them gave up and surrendered.

The fight for Roger beach was over.

CHAPTER 131

Once the beach had been secured Dave left it and led his Company toward its next objective. He took it back to the narrow dusty road heading north. By this time the sun was sizzling hot and there was a white flowery dust rising everywhere along the narrow road. Behind them, on the beach, tanks, guns, Bren-gun carriers and trucks were coming out of landing crafts and lining up for their long move inland. Dave kept on leading the Company north on the narrow dusty road and when they reached Pachino, he stopped for a moment and couldn't get over the destruction done to the town. It had been fire-bombed mercilessly all night in order to guide the invasion in and everything was down. Whole blocks of houses had been smashed wide open and spilled into the streets. Broken telephone poles and electrical wires lay on top of the rubble.

A white grayish acrid smoke hung over the whole town and some of the buildings were riddled with machine-gun bullets from the short sharp fight that had gone on a little earlier before the Italians had given in. As they kept on heading north through the town there were huge slogans painted in red on some of the walls of the smashed buildings: VINCEREMO! CREDERE! UBBIDIRE! COMBATTERE! EVVIVA IL DUCE! German and Italian soldiers, old men and women, a few young children, and many cats and dogs lay dead in the streets. At one of the crossroads they ran into a group of old women who were dressed in black and who were moaning and crying hysterically. Outside a demolished wine shop an old man was sitting in the rubble and mumbling and shaking convulsively. Further down the street a young pregnant woman was holding on to a bloody rag doll and singing and dancing crazily.

Everywhere in town there was the dusty stinking choking smell of death. Dave led the Company through the bombed-out and rubble-strewn streets and when they left the town behind, they could see the hangars of the Pachino airfield. This was their next objective and in the distance Dave could hear a lot of firing and saw that some of the Italians were using light mortars. Dave took the Company off the road and walked on the right side of it past furrowed green and brown fields until he reached the rear of a Company attacking in front of him. As he made his Company go to ground he saw a tall slim young Captain running toward him in a half-crouch. The Captain soon reached Dave's position and dropped down next to him. As he did he extended his hand and said: "Tom Needham, A Company, Hastings and Prince Edward Regiment."

Dave told the young Captain who he was and the name of his Regiment.

The Captain nodded and Dave said: "What's going on?"

"Well, Captain, this was supposed to be your objective. We were supposed to come in behind you in support."

"That's what I understood."

"But, since you were busy mopping up at the beach, the General decided to bring us up."

"So. What's the situation here?"

"Well, this is the funny thing. Most Italians are giving up. But we run into some hard pockets of resistance."

"And this is the situation here?"

"That's right. The Italians have several pillboxes and machine-gun nests covering the hangars of the airfield. We can't outflank them since we don't have enough men to do it. So we have to attack them head-on and it's long and tedious work."

"Why don't we bring up our artillery."

"Can't do that. The artillery's not ready yet."

"I have to tell you. I'm not too crazy about frontal assaults."

"Neither am I. But the General wants us to hurry up and get on the objective."

Dave nodded and took up his binoculars. He studied the attacking Hastings in front of him and the fire lines the Italians were using. It was well-spread and concentrated and they did use mortars. Dave studied the unfolding of our own attack and the Italian response and then put down his binoculars and turned to the Captain.

"Here is what I suggest," he said and went on and explained to the Captain the plan he had in mind. "What do you think?"

"It's not a bad idea."

"All right. Let's do it then."

CHAPTER 132

Dave began backing up his Company from the airfield. When he was out of range of the firing and the mortars he turned right and began taking the Company east. Then he turned right and began moving toward the right flank of the pillboxes and machine-gun nests covering the hangars of the airfield. Once he started making this move he could see a young Italian Lieutenant and a Captain who stood behind one of the machine-gun nests talking and pointing wildly toward the Company. Dave spread the Company in an arrow formation with the Ist Platoon on the point and the 2nd and 3rd Platoons on the flank. He took them to the far end of the pillboxes and machine-gun nests on the right flank in order to outflank them and even take them from the rear, if necessary.

When he closed in on the Italians Dave sent his Bren-gunners and riflemen into action. There were quite a few furrows in the burnt green and brown fields and as they crept closer to the Italians and began firing, Dave could see most of them were firing 6.5 mm Breda Modello machine-guns and using light Brixia mortars. They were not putting down their mortar fire accurately, though, and seemed confused by this two-company assault now going in. Now that they had enough men for a proper flanking attack, Needham, of the Hastings, shortened his angle of attack and left Dave to deal with the pillboxes and machine-gun nests on the right flank. By shortening his angle of attack he could increase his density of fire and keep the Italians pinned down with his own Bren-gunners and riflemen. The idea for this attack was for Dave to deal with the pillboxes and machine-gun nests on the right flank and for Needham to keep the Italians pinned down in the center and on the left flank.

Then Dave would swing to the center in order to envelop it with Needham and finally both of them would deal with the left flank. By now Dave's 3rd Platoon had reached the pillboxes on the right and were rushing them and throwing in satchel charges. As for the machine-gun nests the men were overcoming them with grenade, machine-gun and rifle fire. The 2nd Platoon was also outflanking pillboxes and machine-gun nests on the left. The 1st Platoon kept a steady rate of fire and made sure the Italians stayed where they where. To Dave's surprise none of them turned and ran. They just stayed in their pillboxes and machine-gun nests and returned fire. At one point some of them ran out of their positions to meet Dave's men. A wild hand-to-hand combat followed. But mostly they stood their grounds and had to be taken out with grenade, machine-gun and rifle fire.

Finally, when the pillboxes and machine-gun nests were cleaned on the right flank, Dave's men turned to the center and linked up with the Hastings. At this point the Fusiliers and the Hastings intensified their rate of fire and the depth of their attack. Everyone was firing and Bren-guns, Thompson submachine-guns, pistols, and rifles were used. Grenades were launched, bayonets were drawn and quite a few satchel charges were thrown. The two Companies began moving together and when they started rushing the center pillboxes and machine-gun nests, the young Italian Lieutenant and Captain Dave had seen earlier suddenly stood up and yelled: *"Basta! Basta! Mi arrendo!"* They put up their hands and as they stood there, most of the Italians also stood up and surrendered. Those who didn't and fought on were shot down.

Dave's men and the Hastings then moved up to the surrendering Italians and made them throw down their arms. They sent them down to the beach and Dave's Company then began moving toward the hangars near the airfield while the Hastings stood at their rear in support. The three hangars were near the runways and when Dave's 1st Platoon opened the huge sliding iron door of the first hangar, the men went in and couldn't believe what they saw. Despite the fiery oppressive heat outside, the temperature inside the iron corrugated-roofed hangar was damp and cool. They put on the light and saw several sharp-looking brand-new Messerschmitts and Macchis M.C. 200s. They were neatly lined up and smelled of clean fresh paint. But there were no airmen or mechanics anywhere. Dave's men checked the other two hangars and also found sharp-looking brand-new Messerschmitts and Macchis M.C. 200s.

The planes looked as if they had been flown in and left in those hangars. But there were no Italian airmen or mechanics to be found. Dave's men left those hangars and checked the runways. They saw they had been thoroughly ploughed up and were not usable at the moment. The airfield was completely deserted and Dave got in touch with Colonel Cantwell on his # 18 wireless set and reported the airfield was in our hands.

B Company had secured its objectives.

CHAPTER 133

The original plan for B Company had been that, once it had secured its objectives, it would stand down and the Hastings would go through them. But now, since things were going so well, as Dave spoke to Colonel Cantwell on the wireless, it was agreed he would keep on going and that the Hastings would come up behind him in support. So Dave left the airfield and led the Company across more burnt green and brown fields. A few miles from the coast they had to silence a battery that was firing every once in a while at the beach. Then Dave kept on moving the Company north across those fields, that were now rising and falling in small barren hills, as they stretched north across the peninsula.

There were dingy and low-lying farmhouses in some of those fields and most of them had bleak and dreary vineyards. Dave stayed fairly close to the road and by sundown he was almost ten miles from the beach. B Company settled down for the night in a small and gloomy vineyard, and the next morning Dave led them to the narrow and dusty road and took them north again. They finally had their artillery and whenever the Italians tried to fight them at bridges and roadblocks, they used it and saw them surrender in large numbers. Now, on this second day of the invasion, the road was jammed with Italian prisoners being taken to the beach and truck, artillery and tank convoys going north. They went through several villages and hamlets and in each of those villages and hamlets it was always the same thing.

The old people lined the streets with young girls and children. The old people were dressed in black and smiled at them with bad teeth. Every once in a while an old man would wave at them and say: "*Mussolini kaput!*" The young girls and children ran alongside them and cheered and threw flowers. Sometimes some of the young children stopped running abruptly and snapped sudden child-like salutes. All along the streets they heard the cries: *"Sigarétte!" "Cioccolate!" "Biscòtti!"* But they couldn't stop. They had to go on. The British, with two Corps under the leadership of Lieutenant-Generals Oliver Leese and Miles C. Dempsey, were attacking on the eastern side of the island while the American 7th Army, under General George S. Patton, was doing the same thing on the western side.

In the circumstances General Guy Simonds was driving the 1st Canadian Infantry Division hard and after they had stopped and rested briefly in Modica, they were on the move again and heading north through the mountains to Vizzini. In Modica Brigadier Howard D. Graham came to see the Regiment and Colonel Cantwell introduced him to Dave. The Brigadier was a tall and fairly slender officer with the smooth and civilized manners of a diplomat. He was in his mid- thirties and spent two hours with Dave explaining what he wanted and expected of the Regiment in Sicily. Then, after their brief rest, the Regiment was on the move again and for 20 miles they traveled along a narrow twisting road that wound up through the mountains.

There were sheer drops along the side of the road and they went through a narrow climbing pass through the mountains and through the bleak and barren towns of Giarratana and Monterosso before coming down into the long sweeping valley leading to Vizzini. In Vizzini they were ordered to advance north and then west and near Grammichele, they finally ran into the Germans. They were fighting with the Italians and the Germans they ran into were from the *Herman Göering* Division. There was an intense tank-and-infantry battle in Grammichele and then they kept on going as the Germans used their sharp and disciplined method of retreat. They dug in quickly into new positions and set up machine-guns and heavy mortars. They always had a few tanks and guns to support the infantry and the 88s they used were absolutely deadly.

They were also using snipers and Dave had to remove his epaulets and hide his binoculars and Browning 9 mm Automatic underneath his bush shirt. Saluting became strictly forbidden. The Germans were also laying down mines and cratering the roads and it was becoming much more difficult to deal with them as Dave kept on heading north and was then ordered to go over the hills in the east before he came down on Valguarnera. There was a sharp savage fight in Valguarnera, with the Hastings on his right flank and supporting him, and then they went through it and kept on heading north until, on Tuesday evening, July 20, 1943, 10 days after the landing and about 60 miles from Pachino, they came within sight of one of the cliff-top towns guarding the entrance to the Agira valley.

The name of the town was: Assoro.

CHAPTER 134

That evening the Company had come with tanks and guns over burnt and blackened fields to the hills and cliffs leading to the four-mile ridge that stood between the cliff-top towns of Leonforte and Assoro. That ridge guarded the entrance to the Agira valley and they had come and stopped in a field two miles from the Dittaino Railway Station. As they stopped in that field it was understood the 2nd Brigade would attack Leonforte while the 1st Brigade would take on Assoro. The German 15th Panzer Grenadiers were defending both towns with infantry, tanks and guns. They also had machine-gun nests all over the hills and cliffs leading to the steep winding roads around those hills and the roads themselves were well registered by their mortars and artillery.

It was just before twilight and as the men in Dave's Company could see Assoro gleaming in a last lingering sunlight in the distance, they could also see the Hastings standing down slightly ahead of them on their right flank. Dave made his Company go to ground in order to look over the town and then saw Captain Tom Needham, of the Hastings' A Company, run toward him in a low crouch. Needham dropped next to him and said: "Good evening, Captain."

"Good evening."

"I"m afraid I have some bad news for you."

"What news?"

Dave looked at Needham and he said: "Our own Lieutenant-Colonel has been killed."

"What!"

"Lieutenant-Colonel Sutcliffe has been killed."

"When?"

Sicily

"Earlier this afternoon."

"What happened?"

"He was checking this area and was killed by an 88."

"Those guns don't miss."

"They sure don't."

"Was there anybody else killed?"

"Yes. The Intelligence Officer."

"Not a pretty picture."

"No."

"Who's replacing him?"

"Major John Tweedsmuir."

"I see."

Dave didn't say anything for a moment and then Needham said: "As a matter of fact, the Major saw your Company coming."

"I see."

"He has spoken to Brigadier Graham and would like you to help us launch an attack on Assoro."

"Has Brigadier Graham agreed to this?"

"Indeed."

"How about Colonel Cantwell?"

"I believe the Brigadier has also spoken to him."

"And he's agreed?"

"Yes."

"What kind of an attack?"

"Well, we can't launch it through the roads. They're all well registered and it would be suicide."

"I agree."

"So, part of the reconnaissance we did today, was to find another way."

"Did you?"

"Yes."

"What way?"

"You see, the Germans are defending the ridge and the hills leading to the roads. But on the eastern flank of the town there's a 2000-feet cliff. That's where we'll attack."

"Up that cliff!"

"That's right. The Germans don't think it's possible to scale it."

"Can it be done?"

"It can. Our reconnaissance says so."

Again Dave didn't say anything and then Needham said: "That's why the Major would like you to join us."

"Why our Company?"

"The Major knows your Company. He's seen you in action. That's why."

"Who's going?"

"Your Company. And our own A Company."

"That's it?"

"That's it."

"How are we going to do this?"

"Our Company will go up on the eastern face of the cliff. You'll go up on the western face."

"How?"

"Loaded with Bren guns, rifles and ammunition."

"It's not much."

"It's not."

"Why so little?"

"That's all we'll be able to carry."

"I see."

"How are your men?"

"Okay."

"Can they do this kind of thing?"

"Yes."

"Good."

"When do we leave?"

"In an hour. We start this attack in an hour."

CHAPTER 135

At 9.00 o'clock in the evening the Divisional Artillery began laying down a four-hour irregular barrage on Highway 121 east of Leonforte and taking in a junction where a side road led to Assoro. Half an hour later, when darkness had fallen, the Hastings and Dave's Company set off in a single-file two-mile-long column toward the town of Assoro. One mile from the Dittaino Railway Station they turned east and then headed north-east across the hills and fields that stretched roughly and endlessly ahead of them. There was a bright moonlight and they marched up and down ridges, ravines and boulder-strewn narrow streams. They walked carefully and at times could hear the voices of Germans in the darkness.

They kept on heading north-east and when they finally reached their 2000-feet cliff, Dave stopped and stared at it. In the moonlight the cliff loomed starkly and darkly in front of him. What made it amazing, however, was that there was a huge ravine leading to the base of it. You could only get there through some narrow goat paths and after they had slowly gone down to the bottom of the ravine, it was now close to 4.00 o'clock in the morning. At the base of the cliff, the Hastings went to the east side of it and Dave's Company to the west side. Dave was leading his Company and when he saw the Hastings begin climbing the cliff, he reached for a few vines above him and also began climbing. The cliff, it turned out, as he began scaling it, was made of narrow vineyard terraces indenting it from bottom to top.

Dave reached for vines and stepped on rocks and even though he was lightly-armed and lightly-loaded, he found the climb was slow and exhausting. It seemed to him they were climbing straight-up and Dave stared in front of him and did not look down for fear of finding out how high he stood. He kept on climbing and pulling himself upward and after a while, he saw the darkness was beginning to thin out. Dave tried not to think about this and kept on climbing and after 40 tense, nerve-racking and exhausting minutes, he finally reached the top of the cliff and looked around. To his right was a machine-gun post well dug-in and with sandbags all around it. The machine-gun seemed to be an MG 42 on a tripod and there were two Germans manning the gun. Dave was behind them and to their left. Red and Gennaro were also slightly behind them and to their left.

Dave looked at Red and motioned toward the machine-gun post. Red nodded and in a moment he was over the top of the cliff with Gennaro and running toward the machine-gun post. Not long after there were the two figures of Red and Gennaro and of the two Germans standing starkly against the thinning darkness and then there were only the figures of Red and Gennaro as Red motioned for Dave to come over the top and join them. At the same time Dave thought he heard firing from the eastern side of the cliff. Then there was silence and Dave went over the top with Slav and ran to the machine-gun post. The two Germans lay slumped in a corner. As Dave ran in with Slav he told Red and Gennaro to take the two bodies and hide them behind a large boulder not far from the machine-gun post. Then Dave stepped in behind the MG 42 with Slav on his right and looked around.

By now the two Companies had come over the top and were digging narrow foxholes all along the crest of the cliff. There was a ruined Norman castle at the eastern end of it. Behind the castle, slightly to the right of it, and across the road, stood a bombed-out church. The Hastings were digging in behind the ruined Norman castle and they had brought a big # 22 wireless set which they carefully put down next to a tripod-mounted artillery periscope. This periscope was in an observation post that stood slightly to the left of the ruined Norman castle and that had been overrun a little earlier. The periscope was in the observation post and the post was dug in behind a low stone wall. The periscope rose just above the wall and gave a complete view of the surrounding area and of the road leading from Leonforte to Agira. This road ran between the town and the bombed-out church on one side and the ruined Norman castle on the other.

The town of Assoro was to the right of Dave and on the other side of the road. As Dave looked around it was quiet on the cliff, and the sun now came out and began shining hotly and blisteringly on the men. Dave stood in the machine-gun post with Slav and pointed the MG 42 at the town. He watched the road and nothing moved on it since the Germans didn't know they were on the cliff.

CHAPTER 136

Dave stood in the machine-gun post with Slav and kept on watching the road and around 6.00 o'clock in the morning, some doors opened in the houses in Assoro and Germans came out. They were Panzer Grenadiers and they headed toward three Wehrmacht trucks parked in front of the houses. The trucks were parked on the wrong side of the road and pointed east, and most of the Germans got into them. Two of the Germans, however, came out of a house near the western end of the town and closer to the machine-gun post. They were talking and laughing and when they reached the road, they began crossing it and heading for the post. At this point the road was two hundred yards from the houses and another two hundred yards to the post.

When the two soldiers left the house and began crossing the road, Dave could feel Slav's left hand on his shoulder tightening. The two soldiers made it to the middle of the road and then the tallest of the two froze and pointed wildly at the crest of the cliff. He began turning sharply in order to run back toward the house with the other soldier and yelled: *"Alarm! Alarm! Feidenen!"* Dave had been tracking them both with the MG 42 and when they began turning back, he fired a short burst. Both of them went down in the middle of the road and didn't move. When Dave began firing both Companies let loose along the crest. The three trucks parked on the wrong side of the road began leaving and Dave led the first one and fired a long sustained burst at the motor. The truck suddenly blew up and sent green, blue and orange sparks and pieces of metal flying all over the road.

Some of the Germans jumped off the trucks and began returning fire. A few of them were on fire and as they ran and screamed, they threw themselves down on the dirt road and tried to roll over. But they just lay there on the road and burned in a black grayish smoke. Dave then sprayed the three trucks with 7.92 mm bullets and saw most of the Germans jerk and lay still while a few others jumped down and began returning fire. Almost at the same time a convoy of eight trucks appeared at the eastern end of the road. On that side the road rose slightly to the houses in Assoro, and the trucks were also full of Germans. Surprisingly this convoy didn't stop or turn around at the sight of the three burning trucks. It kept on coming and Dave held his fire until the eight and last one was in view. Then he began firing at that one until it began burning and blocked the road to the other seven.

Germans were also jumping down from that truck and returning fire and Dave swung the MG 42 back and sprayed all the trucks. The two Companies were also firing at those trucks and there was screaming and yelling and quite a few Germans were lying still in the street. Most of the trucks were set on fire and as Dave and the two Companies kept on firing at them, he suddenly heard a mortar that went long behind him and dropped into the fields below the cliff. A few more rounds went wide in front of him and to the left side of the road. By that time the Germans had moved into the houses across the road and were firing at them from there. Dave looked at the first box of ammunition on his right that was nearly empty and held his fire unless he could aim at a point-blank target. Then he heard the swish and woosh of a shell as it exploded down the road near the ruined Norman castle.

Dave turned and saw a German battery that was in Leonforte had swung around and was now firing at them. Two more rounds came crashing on the road near the ruined Norman castle and raised huge fountains of dirt. To the left of the ruined castle Dave saw a tall and lean soldier was crouched over the radio and giving out target ranges and coordinates. Soon some of our 25-pounder field guns began opening up and the gun from Leonforte stopped firing. There was constant firing and mortaring, however, on the part of the Germans and not long after they brought in their heavier mortar, the much-feared *Nebelwerfer*. This multi-barreled mortar wasn't very accurate but it was deadly with flying shrapnel. In no time the shells began landing with terrifying noises all over the ruined castle and the Hastings' A Company was blanketed in a pale blue-black gray smoke.

By now the two Companies along the cliff were holding their fire unless they could also aim at point-blank targets. The sun had risen high in the sky and was absolutely unbearable. It was hurting Dave's face, hands and arms and by 4.00 o'clock in the afternoon, he saw the Germans were

Sicily

assembling in the houses at the eastern end of Assoro. Those houses were slightly to the left of the bombed-out church and were the closest way to cross the road and get at the ruined castle. They were also partly sheltered by the burnt-out wrecks of the Wehrmacht trucks. At a command from one of the soldiers they came out running and tried to cross the road. Dave, at the MG 42 with Slav helping him with the ammunition belts, steadily fired on the houses, through the wrecks of the trucks on the road, and on the road itself and stopped the Germans from getting to the ruined castle.

With a range of almost 4,000 yards and a rate of fire of 1,500 rounds per minute, the MG 42 was a deadly weapon and mowed down anyone who tried to cross. After two attempts, and several dead near the houses and across the road, the Germans ran back into the houses again and Dave stopped firing. He was hurting from the burning sun and from the lack of sleep and as he looked to the right at his Company, he saw Tom Needham. He was running in a half-crouch and coming toward him in the machine-gun post.

CHAPTER 137

Dave watched Tom Needham run toward him. He asked Slav to move over to the crest to make room for him and when Needham reached him, he dropped down next to him in the machine-gun post and looked at him. He was wearing his helmet and his forehead and the left side of his face were caked with blood. When Needham dropped down next to Dave he glanced briefly at the five boxes of ammunition around the MG 42 and said: "Good afternoon, Captain."

"Good afternoon, Tom."

"Pretty busy afternoon so far."

"Yes."

"Wonderful weapon this MG 42."

"It is."

"And you certainly know how to use it."

"I'm trying."

Needham wiped some more blood coming from the left side of his forehead and Dave said: "What happened to you?"

"Nothing."

"How did you get hurt?"

"Just a shrapnel wound from their *Nebelwerfer*."

"They do make a lot of damage, don't they?"

"They do."

"It's a good thing they're not accurate."

"It is."

"Are you okay, though?"

"I am."

"What do you have?"

"A scalp wound."

"It looks to me like you've bled a lot."

"I did."

"Those scalp wounds always bleed a lot."

"I know."

"But you're okay?"

"Yes."

Dave didn't say anything for a moment and then Needham said: "How's your Company?"

"Not bad."

"Not too many casualties?"

"Not so far."

"Can you hold on?"

"That depends."

"On what?"

"We're out of food, Tom. And we're very low on ammunition."

"It's the same for our Company, Captain."

"In this heat we need water. And we need food."

"True."

"Also, if the Germans send tanks up the road, that's it."

"I agree."

"As a matter of fact, I wonder why they haven't done it before?"

"Our artillery's keeping them busy."

"Let's hope."

Needham wiped some more blood from his forehead and said: "Listen. The Major has sent me to talk to you."

Dave nodded and Needham went on: "Our situation here is critical. As you said. We need food, water and ammunition."

Dave didn't say anything and Needham went on: "We have to send someone down to Brigade Headquarters to get those things. And we have to do it now."

"In broad daylight!"

"That's right."

"That's suicidal."

"It's true."

"Listen, if the Germans are ringing the base of the cliff around Assoro as I believe they are, whoever is going to be sent down there hasn't got a chance."

"I know that."

"They'll shoot him as he comes down the cliff."

"That's a risk we have to take."

"Why not do it when it's dark?"

"We can't."

"Why not?"

"It won't give us enough time to bring the supplies here for tomorrow."

"I'm sure we can hang on for another day."

"Not really."

"Why not?"

"Look at your ammunition for the MG 42. You've used three boxes already and only have two left."

"That's still a lot of ammunition."

"But not enough to hang on for another day."

"What do you propose then?"

Needham wiped some more blood from his forehead and said: "We have to send a party down now. We would do it. But we've been taking the brunt of the German attacks and have a lot of casualties. Major Tweedsmuir would do it but he's too busy holding the right flank of our position. I, myself, would also do it, but I'm very dizzy from my scalp wound right now and don't think I can make it. That's why we're hoping someone from your Company will do it."

Dave sighed deeply and said: "As I said. It's suicidal."

"I agree."

"Only a miracle will allow a party to be able to go down there in broad daylight."

"We have to try, Captain."

"I know that."

"It's our only chance."

"You're telling me."

"So?"

"So it's just that my men aren't in much better shape than yours."

"True. But they haven't borne the brunt of the German attacks and haven't suffered quite as many casualties."

"I agree."

"So?"

Again Dave sighed deeply and said: "Okay. I'll do it."

Needham nodded and Dave said: "I'll take two men with me and try to be back by daylight."

"Good."

"I'll leave now and hope I make it."

"You will."

Dave didn't say anything for a long moment and then said: "You know. This whole operation is based on a miracle."

Needham looked at him and said: "I know, Captain. I know."

CHAPTER 138

Tom Needham then left the machine-gun post to go back to his Company and Dave motioned for Slav to come over. He told him they were leaving to try to reach Brigade Headquarters and to tell Red he was also coming with them. Slav was to tell Bostwick he would be manning the MG 42 with Gennaro and to let the Platoon Officers and Sergeants know of the change. In no time Slav was gone to let everyone know and soon after Bostwick arrived with Gennaro to take over the machine-gun post. Slav and Red were with them and Dave told them he would go down first and would be followed by Slav and Red. Then Dave left the machine-gun post and ran to a thinly-dug foxhole near the crest.

From that foxhole Dave ran over to the crest and went over it. Slav and Red were behind him and they began going down the 2000-feet cliff. Dave hung on to vines and groped for rocks and if the climb upward had been completely nerve-racking and exhausting, the climb downward proved even worse. As he slowly and painfully made his way down the cliff Dave felt extremely naked and vulnerable and kept on expecting a German bullet to slam right through his back. Also when he had been climbing upward he could always see the vines he was going to grab and the rocks he was going to step on, but on the way down he couldn't see anything and felt himself hanging in a void and groping for everything. It was now close to 6.00 o'clock in the evening and as he looked sideways to his left and down, he could see the hills and fields of the Assoro valley below bathed in the splendor of a hazy, smoky and smoldering sunlight.

The hills and fields seemed far away and Dave went back staring at the vines and rocks in front of him. Now, late in the afternoon, the hot broiling sun hurt his face, arms and legs and he kept on slowly and painfully making his way down from ledge to ledge and small terrace to small terrace. He tried to think of nothing but the next ledge to grope for and step on and finally, one hour and twenty minutes later, Dave reached the bottom of the huge ravine below. The climb down had taken twice as long as when they had gone up. Soon Slav and Red joined him and they began walking up one of the narrow goat paths that led out of the huge ravine at the base of the cliff. Dave took the lead and told Red to follow him. Slav would bring up the rear. They kept on walking up this goat path and then found themselves in the hills and fields that led to Brigade Headquarters.

In daylight the terrain looked quite different than at night. The hills and fields were strewn with huge boulders and there were quite a few small dry riverbeds. Dave was covered by Red and Slav covered Red while bringing up the rear. They moved from big boulder to big boulder and marched up and down ridges, ravines and narrow streams. At 9.00 o'clock the darkness came on and they stepped up their pace and marched faster. They did this for over an hour and as they were coming down a small ridge, Dave suddenly froze and went to ground. Red and Slav behind him did the same. Not far from them in the darkness, and possibly in the next ridge, Dave heard three clear German voices. The first one was saying: *"Gehst du werklich mit dem Mädchen aus?"* *"Klar,"* the second voice said. *"Komicher kerl!"* the third voice said. Then the voices faded and Dave moved away from that ridge with Red and Slav and from those voices.

Dave kept on heading south-west with Red and Slav and around 11.00 o'clock at night, as they were coming down a long steep hill, he suddenly heard the click of rifles being bolted and found himself with Red and Slav surrounded by several Canadian infantrymen.

The one in the lead was tall and wiry and when he came close to Dave, he said: "Halt. Who goes there?"

"Captain David Lindsay. B Company. The Westmount Fusiliers."

"Oh yes? Prove it to me."

"What do you want to know?"

"Who's the Prime Minister of Canada?"

"Mackenzie King."

"Who's in charge of this operation."

"General Guy Simonds."

"You're from the Fusiliers, did you say?"

"That's right."

"What's your motto?"

"Perpetua fidelitas. Nullus passus retro."

"What does that mean?"
"Loyalty always. Not a step back."
"Really?"
"Really."
"Well, well."
"Do you want me to tell it to you in another language?"
"You don't have to, Captain."
"Good."
"I'm sorry. But we have to check."
"It's all right. Now take me to Brigadier Graham."

CHAPTER 139

The infantryman in the lead turned and began marching Dave, Red and Slav down the long steep hill toward the Brigade Headquarters. There were several other infantrymen with him and they surrounded Dave as well as Red and Slav. They walked in silence in the bright star-lit moonlight and went up and down quite a few hills before they reached the Brigade Headquarters. The headquarters was located in a low-slung stone farmhouse in the fold of a hill and when they reached it, the lead infantryman told Dave to wait at the door with Red and Slav and went into the farmhouse. He wasn't gone long before he came back and told Dave to follow him. Red and Slav were to stay at the door.

The infantryman then went back into the farmhouse with Dave. They walked into a big stony room to the right of the door. That room had a long wooden table in the middle of it, with some maps, a big teapot and five metal cups on it, and there were a few large wooden chairs against the walls facing both ends of the table. There was also an Everest pack down on the floor next to one of the chairs against the front wall and the room they were in was obviously the dining-room. As they came in Brigadier Graham was standing at the table and looking at one of the maps with a Lieutenant-Colonel. Brigadier Graham still looked like the same tall and fairly slender officer Dave remembered and still had the same smooth and civilized manners. The Lieutenant-Colonel next to him, on his left, was short, stocky and well-built. He was also in his late thirties.

When Dave came into the big dining-room with the infantryman, the Brigadier turned to him with the Lieutenant-Colonel. There were deep creases around his eyes and, as the infantryman left the room, he said: "Ah, David. Glad to see you."

The Long War

"Thank you, Sir."

The Brigadier then introduced the officer standing next to him as Lieutenant-Colonel Ralph Crowe of the Royal Canadian Regiment and said: "What's going on in Assoro?"

"We're holding, Sir."

"Were you able to get up there before the Germans found out?"

"Yes, Sir."

"I tell you. I've been really anxious about this one."

"I can imagine, Sir."

"What about casualties?"

"We have quite a few of them, Sir."

"In both Companies?"

"In John Tweedsmuir's Company mostly."

"That's not good."

"It's not."

The Brigadier didn't say anything for a moment and then said: "Now. What brings you here?"

"Major Tweedsmuir sent me

"Why?"

"Our situation is critical."

"How critical?"

"Very critical."

"In what way?"

"We have no food and we're almost out of ammunition."

"So you need to be resupplied."

"That's it."

"When?"

"By tomorrow morning."

"You were sent down to tell me this?"

"Yes, Sir."

"And who will lead the resupply party back to Assoro?"

"I will, Sir"

"With your two men?"

"Yes, Sir"

Brigadier Graham now moved closer to Dave and looked at him for a moment. Then he said: "In that case you'll need a strong supply group to go with you."

Dave nodded.

Lieutenant-Colonel Crowe now also stepped forward.

"I can arrange that."

Brigadier Graham turned to the Lieutenant-Colonel.

Sicily

"Can you, Ralph?"

The Lieutenant-Colonel looked at the Brigadier.

"Of course."

The Lieutenant-Colonel turned to Dave.

"When do you need this supply group?"

Dave stared at him.

"As soon as possible."

"You got it."

The Lieutenant-Colonel left the farmhouse and as Dave watched him go, he rubbed his eyes. The Brigadier made Dave sit in one of the large chairs facing the table near the front wall and said: "You look tired, David."

"I'm fine, Sir."

"Are you okay?"

"Sure?"

The Brigadier then reached into the Everest pack on the floor near the front wall and took out a canteen. He handed it to Dave and said: "Here. Have a drink."

"Thank you, Sir," Dave picked up the canteen and took a big gulp.

"I was saving it for a special occasion," the Brigadier said. "This is a special occasion."

"Thank you, Sir."

"It's rum. It'll do you good."

Dave took another big gulp from the canteen and when he handed it back to the Brigadier, the Brigadier said: "Have you eaten anything recently?"

"Not really."

"I'm afraid I haven't much to offer you," the Brigadier said and reached into the Everest pack again. He took out a compo pack and handed it to Dave. "Here. Eat. And have some tea from the pot on the table. Use one of the metal cups."

The Brigadier then left the farmhouse to go and make sure Dave's men were also being properly taken care of. When he was gone Dave began eating some bully beef, sardines and cheese, and poured himself a cup of lukewarm tea. He quickly finished eating and drinking and as he sat quietly in his chair, the Brigadier came back again. He was walking slowly and stiffly and when he saw Dave was through eating, he said: "Ralph Crowe is lining up two Companies for you. One stripped down and carrying 60 pounds of food and ammunition in Everest packs and bandoliers. The other fully-armed and protecting the supply Company. They should be ready to leave shortly."

The Long War

Dave nodded and the Brigadier said: "Is there anything else I can do for you?"

Dave looked at the Brigadier and said: "You've got to send tanks and soldiers up the road from Leonforte. We need a support group soon."

"I understand."

"So far we've been very lucky."

The Brigadier looked at Dave and Dave said: "We've captured an artillery periscope and a soldier from the Hastings has been able to pinpoint artillery targets."

"A tall and lean soldier?"

"That's right."

"That's Major Bert Kennedy."

"Who is he?"

"He's John Tweedsmuir's Second in Command."

"Well, he's very good."

"I agree."

"In fact, he seems flawless in artillery communications."

"He is."

"We also overran a machine-gun post with an MG 42."

"That's very good."

"I tell you, Sir. That gun is what's really kept us going."

"It's a pretty formidable weapon."

"It is. But we won't be able to count on it for much longer."

"Why not?"

"We're running out of ammunition for it."

"Don't worry. I've arranged for the 48th Highlanders to attack up the road."

"Good."

"We'll also give you full artillery support."

"That's nice."

The Brigadier didn't say anything for a moment and then said: "By the way, I'm recommending you for the Military Cross."

"Thank you, Sir."

"I'm also recommending Major Tweedsmuir for the Distinguished Service Order."

Dave nodded and the Brigadier said: "What you've done, and are doing here, is absolutely magnificent. I can't tell you how General Simonds and I appreciate it. It brings great credit to you, to Major Tweedsmuir and to the Regiments involved. It also makes me very proud and I thank you both for your efforts."

Dave nodded again and the Brigadier said: "Well. Shall we go out? The two Companies should be ready by now for you to lead them back to Assoro."

CHAPTER 140

Dave left the farmhouse with the Brigadier and outside he saw Red and Slav had just finished eating compo rations. They were sitting on boulders to the left of the door of the farmhouse and handing their compo packs to a soldier. When Dave came out he nodded at them and looked around. It was a clear bright moon-lit evening and the stars were high in the sky. Even though it was dark the air was heavy and oppressive and Dave saw Lieutenant-Colonel Crowe was talking to two Companies some distance to the right of the farmhouse. Dave was standing slightly to the left of the door of the farmhouse and the Brigadier was a few feet behind him to his right. Red and Slav were sitting on boulders against the wall of the farmhouse.

In a moment Lieutenant-Colonel Crowe came over and told them the two Companies were ready and would assemble slightly past the farmhouse. Soon the two Companies began to move. They were lined up in two single files with the supply Company on the left and the fully-armed Company on the right. As they began moving to their assembly point the first soldier of the supply Company, a short and wiry man who was built pretty much like Red, stopped by Dave and said: "Are you the officer who's going to lead us to Assoro?" "Yes," Dave said. "Good," the soldier said. He gave Dave a slight tap on the shoulder and moved on. Then the soldier behind him did the same thing and as the supply Company moved to its assembly point, all the soldiers in the line gave Dave a slight tap on the shoulder before moving on.

Behind Dave the Brigadier watched the men do this and smiled slightly. When the two Companies had fully assembled, Dave nodded at the Brigadier and moved to their head with Red and Slav behind him. He

Sicily

told the two Companies to maintain strict silence and to march carefully. They were to move in two single files and follow him. Then Dave began leading them out of the farmhouse. In no time they were going up and down long steep hills and ridges and ravines. They kept on walking around big boulders and down past small dry riverbeds and narrow streams. Now, on the way back to Assoro, and heading northeast, it seemed to Dave they were moving uphill all the way and that the air was heavier and more oppressive than ever. They could hear clear German voices in some of the hills and at the crest of a ridge, they came upon a machine-gun post where they found fresh bread and a few unopened bottles of red wine.

Dave kept on leading the twin columns northeast and on picking up the pace and quite some time later, the 2000-feet cliff of Assoro began looming starkly and darkly in the distance. Dave kept on closing on it and at the ravine, he began leading the men down a narrow goat path to the base of the cliff. By then it was almost 4.30 in the morning and there was only about half an hour of darkness left. Dave told the men to stack up the supplies against the base of the cliff and then clear it before it became light and they risked being caught. The men unloaded quickly and then left and Dave turned to the cliff with Red and Slav. Slav would climb behind him and Red would climb to the right of both of them. Then Dave reached for some vines above him and began the climb upward again. Dave moved up slowly from ledge to ledge and terrace to terrace and kept on groping for vines above him and stones to step on.

The climb upward was agonizingly slow and painful and after a while, the darkness began to thin out. Dave stared at the vines and rocks in front of him and kept on climbing and some time later, he couldn't remember feeling so exhausted. Dave had felt very tired fighting Bostwick and then taking the little girl and her mother out of that bombed-out church, but this exhaustion was greater than anything he had ever felt before. Dave kept on groping and lifting himself upward and then he just couldn't do it anymore and stopped. It was quite clear now and Dave stayed hanging on to upward vines and closed his eyes since he couldn't feel himself anymore. He didn't seem to know where he was and seemed to be outside of himself. He could feel the warmth of the sun beginning to burn on his back, arms and legs, and breathed deeply.

Dave felt he was in a strange dark place outside of all reality and could no longer feel his hands and feet. He breathed deeply and heavily and as he was wondering if he shouldn't let go, he suddenly felt the strong right hand of Slav in his back. Slav was grabbing him by his shirt and pushing him upward and Dave began moving slowly and numbly again. Slav kept on lifting and pushing him upward and after a while Dave began coming

The Long War

back into himself and feeling his hands and legs. Then he got his second wind and, on his own, began reaching for upward vines and stepping on rocks. In a little while he was climbing steadily again, although ever so slowly and painfully, and could see Red on his right. Red was grinning at him and flashing the thumbs up sign.

Dave smiled tiredly at him and kept on climbing and some time later, he finally reached the crest and went over it.

CHAPTER 141

Dave rolled into a thinly-dug foxhole and then slowly got up and ran to the machine-gun post. Bostwick told him Captain Tom Needham had seen him coming and had organized a resupply party for the Hastings. Bostwick had done the same thing for the Fusiliers and soldiers from both Companies had already gone down in order to grab and bring up the supplies. Dave nodded and Bostwick left the post with Gennaro in order to go and join the resupply party for the Fusiliers. Dave went and stood behind the MG 42 again and was soon joined by Slav who stayed on his right side. Dave held on to the machine-gun and slowly closed his eyes. After a while he opened them again and smiled tiredly at Slav.

Dave kept on holding the MG 42 and not long after heard: "Germans coming up the road from Leonforte!" Dave swung the MG 42 around and saw a Company of German Panzer Grenadiers was indeed coming up the road. The Germans were on both sides of it and as they came up a slight rise leading to Assoro, Dave began firing at them. At the same time Germans broke out of the houses in Assoro and tried to cross the road in order to get at the crest and the ruined castle. When they came running out of the houses everyone on the crest began firing at them and Dave kept on firing long sweeping bursts down the road toward Leonforte and then swung around to do the same thing across the road in Assoro. At the same time he looked toward the tall and lean Major crouched over the radio and signaled with his hand for him to call in artillery targets.

The Major nodded and went back to his radio as Dave kept on firing on both sides of the road. The distance from the slight rise in the road from Leonforte to the machine-gun post was about 300 yards and even though Dave kept on firing long sustained bursts and sweeping the road, some of the Germans were able to come dangerously close. This was because Dave also had to swing around and fire down the road in Asssoro in order to keep that part of the road clear. Soon some of the Germans from the road from Leonforte would be within grenade throwing distance and when he saw this, Dave kept the MG 42 firing down that road and swept both sides of it. Still some of the Germans kept on coming and just when it looked as if they might be able to close in and break into their positions, Dave heard the huge express train rush of shells from our 25-pounder field guns smashing on the Leonforte road, near their positions, and further down on the road in front of Assoro.

That stopped the attack on the road from Leonforte cold and Dave dealt with the few remaining Germans who were coming too close by mowing them down. At the same time the shells that had crashed on the road in front of Assoro had also stopped that part of the attack and the Germans had turned and run back into the houses. Almost at the same time a red flare went up into the sky and, after a barrage from our mortars and 25-pounder field guns, Dave heard firing down the road leading to Leonforte. Just then he also turned and saw Bostwick signaling from a thinly-dug foxhole the resupply was complete all along the crest. Dave nodded and looked at the boxes of ammunition next to the machine-gun. He was down to half a box and Dave now swung the MG 42 toward the houses and began firing wildly and savagely until he had exhausted all his ammunition.

Then Dave ran with Slav to a thinly-dug foxhole where he picked up a rifle. Dave looked down the crest and signaled with his hand to the tall and lean Major at the radio for the Hastings to cover them. The Major nodded and Dave jumped over the foxhole and yelled: "Let's finish it!" Dave then ran across the road with the rest of the Company toward the houses in Assoro. Everyone was yelling and firing and near the houses, they blew the doors and windows open with grenades. Then they rushed in and fired at anything that moved. The Company dealt with the houses in Assoro one by one. Anyone coming out had to have his hands up or was shot down. There were yells and shouts and screams inside the houses and you heard: *"Komen sie!" "Idioten! "Bastards!" "Mörder!" "Smutzig hunden!"* There was also hand-to-hand combat inside and outside some of the houses.

A few Germans ran out and faced the company with their rifles and bayonets. They were shot down. Others also ran out and fired at the men. They were also cut down. In some cases, when the rifles of the Germans jammed or ran out of ammunition and when they took out their bayonets, the men stopped shooting and also took out their own. All morning long the fighting went on closely, brutally and savagely. No quarters were given, but slowly, surely and steadily the Company cleared Assoro. If it couldn't be done with rifles and bayonets, it was done with Bren guns and grenades. If the Germans fought too stubbornly in some of the houses, they blew the inside with satchel charges. On a few occasions when the soldiers on both sides ran out of ammunition or couldn't use their bayonets, they fought with rifle butts or with their fists.

In the early part of the attack the Hastings had given B Company covering fire and then they went on the attack themselves at the eastern end of the road. They also began clearing the houses one by one and by noon had succeeded with the Company in cleaning the town. By then the few Germans who were left had jumped out of the houses at the back and begun running down the road to Agira. Then, when the two Companies had finished clearing the Germans from Assoro, they saw the 48th Highlanders coming up from the western side of the road. This was the road from Leonforte and they, themselves, had cleared that part of the road. Dave was just coming out of one of the houses in the center of Assoro. The 48th Highlanders were coming up the road and the Hastings and B Company were standing in the middle of it.

Suddenly, when the three Regiments appeared on the road, there was a great deal of cheering, yelling and waving and the soldiers rushed to greet, embrace and slap each other on the back. From where he stood in front of a house in the center of town, Dave let out a deep sigh and lowered his rifle.

The battle of Assoro was over.

CHAPTER 142

The soldiers from the three Regiments stood in the middle of the road and whooped and yelled and cheered. Some of them had organized an escort party and were taking the Germans who had been taken prisoners down the road to Leonforte. The Chaplain and Medics were moving around and taking care of the dead and wounded. The soldiers and officers, however, were walking around and shaking hands and greeting each other. Dave left the house where he stood and went and mixed with the soldiers and officers on the road for a while. Then he left and walked toward the crest and when he stood to the right of the tripod-mounted artillery periscope, he suddenly saw Captain Tom Needham.

Needham was coming from the observation post toward him on the crest. The left side of his face was slightly swollen and heavily caked with blood. He was covered with dust and walking very slowly and when Dave saw him, Needham smiled and walked over to him. They embraced tightly and when they pulled away, he said: "Well, Captain. A few busy days?"

"That's right, Tom."
"But we did it."
"Yes. We did."
"I always knew we would."
"I can't say I did."
"I guess the miracle held after all."
"It did."
"But how do you feel, Captain?"
"I'm fine, Tom."
"Good."
"And you?"

Sicily

"Never better."

"Let me see your wound."

Needham took off his helmet and Dave saw a pressure pack had been stuck to the left side of his head. The pack was bloody and glued to his scalp and Dave said: "You better get this looked after."

"I will."

"I'm not kidding. This could get serious."

"Don't worry. One of the Medics will look after me."

"When?"

"Soon. He'll take me to one of our dressing stations."

"Good. You wouldn't want an infection."

"I know."

Both of them didn't say anything for a moment and then Needham said: "Come. Major Tweedsmuir wants to see you."

CHAPTER 143

Needham turned and began walking back toward the observation post. Dave followed him and when they reached it, Dave saw there were a few officers and some soldiers who stood inside of it. Needham went in with Dave and tapped the shoulder of a tall and slender officer who was presently looking through the periscope. This officer now stepped back from it and as he turned to Needham, Needham pointed to Dave behind him and said: "Major Tweedsmuir. This is Captain David Lindsay of the Westmount Fusiliers."

"Ah, Captain Lindsay," the Major said as he reached out and shook hands with Dave. "May I offer you my congratulations for the magnificent way in which you and your Company fought with us.""

"The feeling is mutual, Sir."

"We certainly gave the Germans a good drubbing, didn't we?"

"We certainly did, Sir."

"Major Kennedy thinks highly of you," the Major said and turned to Major Kennedy who stood next to him on his left.

"I certainly do," Major Kennedy said as he moved forward and also shook hands with Dave. "Your trip to Brigade Headquarters and back was quite a feat."

"You would have done the same, Sir."

"Still it's quite a feat."

"So was your target-calling, Sir."

"Oh, you liked that, didn't you?"

"I did, indeed!"

Sicily

Both Major Tweedsmuir and Major Kennedy smiled and then Major Tweedsmuir said: "Would you like to have a look through the periscope?"

"Sure," Dave said and both Majors stepped back a little and motioned for Dave to come and have a look.

Dave walked up to the periscope and as he looked through it, he just stood there and couldn't get over it. Around him for over 50 miles he could see the green and yellow Sicilian mountains, the green-brown valleys, the narrow dusty roads, the sun-burnt farmlands, bleak vineyards and spare olive groves. And quite far to the east he could see the stately, majestic, blue-gray shape of Mount Etna. The volcano rose and towered over Sicily and its white furrowed crest was crowned by a thin pale white smoke rising slowly and swirlingly into the sky. It was quite a sight to behold and when Dave stepped back from the periscope, Major Tweedsmuir said: "Not a bad view, isn't it?"

"I'll say."

"This periscope gives us a perfect fix on German positions."

"That's good."

"Believe me, it's a great tool for calling artillery strikes on them."

"I like that."

"I like that too."

"I hope you use it well and we hit them hard."

"We will. Major Kennedy will see to that."

"Good."

"I say. Let them be on the receiving end of it for a change. Don't you think?"

"I agree."

CHAPTER 144

Dave then shook hands again with Majors John Tweedsmuir and Bert Kennedy. He left the observation post with Needham and they walked along the crest of the cliff. They walked to the right of the observation post and in a break in the low-slung wall not that far from the periscope, Needham stopped. He told Dave he was now going to see a Medic in order to have his scalp wound treated. He also shook hands with Dave and Dave watched him leave and head toward the road for a moment. Then Dave turned and sat down to the right of the break against the low-slung wall. He could feel a deadly fatigue pulsing and throbbing through him and from where he sat, he could see the valley of Assoro far below and the deep dazzling glittering sunlight that was smothering it.

Dave closed his eyes and leaned against the low-slung wall. In a little while he felt a slight tap on his shoulder and saw the big muscular figure of Slav bending over him and telling him they had to be on the move. Dave got up slowly and followed Slav. The Company had been ordered to pull out of the line and rest for a couple of days in one of the hills on the road from Leonforte. Then they were on the move again with the other Companies of the Regiment and went through towns like Nissoria, Agira and Regalbuto. The Germans by now were being pushed to the northeast corner of the island and their resistance became far more fierce and fanatical. With their supply lines becoming shorter they were able to throw in tanks, mortars and deadly fire from their 88s. The only way the Regiment could fight them was by launching tank, artillery and infantry attacks.

Then on Friday, July 26, 1943, it was announced Mussolini had resigned and in the villages and hamlets they went through, the people went wild and began yelling and dancing. Old man and women started grinning and clapping their hands and there were cries of: *"Mòrte à Mussolini!" "Mòrte al fasismo!" "Viva l'Italia!"* The Regiment kept on heading northeast through the hills of the valley of the Salso and occupied the west bank of the Simeto river. They rested there for three days and then went on toward Lentini. By then the Germans were leaving the island. They had been pushed to its northeast corner and were now busy ferrying their troops across the Straits of Messina. Under the leadership of Colonel-General Hans Hube, a tough one-armed veteran of the Russian front, they were able to move over 40,000 of their soldiers, 60,000 Italian troops and a great deal of their materiel to the mainland.

Finally, on Monday, August 16, 1943, the Americans entered Messina and the Sicilian campaign was over. Thirty-eight days and over 100 miles later, the Germans had been driven out of the island and the Regiment was resettled in Lentini. This was a camp 12 miles south of Catania and they were taken there to stand down. Lentini was not a good rest camp, however. It had too many bugs and mosquitos and quite a few soldiers got sick with dysentery, sand-fly fever or malaria. When Colonel Cantwell saw that he arranged to have the Regiment taken three miles southwest of Catania to the small hamlet of Liri. This was in the hills where it was cool at night and where there were not so many bugs and mosquitos. The Colonel, himself, had his headquarters in a small dingy farmhouse in one of those hills.

A few days after they had settled there, the beaches were cleared of mines and Dave could swim daily in the cool waters of the Mediterranean. After the dust and searing heat of the last 38 days, it was quite a relief for him to be able to swim in those cool waters and to let the water wash over his body and get rid of all the fatigue he had been feeling ever since the battle of Assoro. During that time Dave slept as late as he could. He watched sports meets. And he put the Company through a little training. But mostly he rested. He swam and relaxed and as the days went on, he found it a very nice life.

In fact it was one you could get used to easily and as Dave began settling in it and enjoying it, he was told by Slav, on Wednesday afternoon, September 1, 1943, Colonel Cantwell wanted to see him at his headquarters in Liri. Slav took him there by jeep and the Colonel gave him the news.

They were going to the mainland.

BOOK TWELVE

ITALY

CHAPTER 145

After his meeting with the Colonel, Slav drove Dave back to his quarters near the beach, and the next morning a long line of Bedford trucks came to Liri and picked up the Regiment. They headed north and at Mili Marina, the men were taken off and led to some of the hills nearby. Brigadier Howard Penhale, of the 3rd Infantry Brigade, came to those hills with Colonel Cantwell and told the men where they were going. They were going to sail across the Straits of Messina and land at Reggio. The landing would take place near dawn tomorrow morning and they would then head north toward the Calabrian mountains.The operation they would be involved in, Brigadier Penhale told them, was called *Baytown* and they would be led by General Montgomery

It would be launched by the 13th Corps on a two-Division front. The 1st Canadian Division would be on the right and the British 5th Division on the left. The Canadian Division would land on a good beach north of Reggio. The British 5th Division would land opposite Messina between Reggio and San Giovanni. The Canadian sector was code-named Fox and split into two beaches — Amber beach to the north and Green beach to the south. The Fusiliers would land at Amber beach, as the leading Regiment in the landing, Brigadier Penhale explained, and then push inland as fast as it could in support of the 3rd Infantry Brigade who would be leading the attack.

Brigadier Penhale, with the help of Colonel Cantwell, then went on and outlined the whole operation in detail to the Regiment. Finally both of them left and Dave helped his men go over their own specific assignments and those of their Sections and Platoons. The men also checked their gear and equipment. Then they lay down and rested in the hills and around 1.00

o'clock in the morning, an officer came and went from group to group. He told the men to get ready to go to the beach and follow the guide who would take them there along a well-marked white-taped path. The men from the Company got up and began walking fully-loaded toward the beach where the landing crafts had come to take them. On the beach the men walked up the metal ramps and stepped into the landing crafts.

A short while later those crafts pulled up their ramps and began slipping away. Once they had left the beach they began circling until a dozen others had joined them and then they sailed in the direction of San Giovanni. A strong current was running through the Straits and they cut across it at an angle in order to get themselves into the proper launching position. In the distance Reggio rose starkly across the seven-mile Straits and behind it the hills and mountains of Calabria loomed even more darkly. It was a beautiful moon-lit night. There was a slight haze over the narrows. But the sea was calm. The air was cool. And the stars were high in the sky overhead. They kept on sailing toward Reggio and after a while, all the landing crafts had linked up and they moved into four assault columns.

They kept on heading for Reggio and at 3.30 in the morning, the guns from Messina to Mili Marina began firing. They could feel the huge express-train rush of shells sweeping past them overhead and heading for the mainland. Four hundred guns were firing from Sicily and at midway point in the narrows, red tracer shells from a heavy anti-aircraft gun began racing across the Straits toward the beach north of Reggio where they were going to land. Their landing crafts followed the tracers and warships of the Royal Navy now sailed into the Straits and also began firing. At the same time the blue beams of six searchlights suddenly went up in the sky from the shores of Sicily and through the roaring of the guns, the tracers, the searchlights, the smell of cordite and the sea haze, they kept on closing the distance and heading toward Reggio There was hardly any firing from the mainland. Here and there you saw firing from the hills and the beaches. But those flashes were quickly smothered by our own guns.

Then there was no firing except from our own guns and warships targeting the mainland. By now the distance to the shore was less than two miles. The landing crafts cut slightly to the right and headed for Reggio. They were closing the distance fast and, in this beautiful moon-lit night, were right on target to land at Amber beach.

CHAPTER 146

The landing crafts kept on heading for Reggio and less than a mile from the beach you could see it clearly in the distance. Dawn was slowly breaking and there were thick columns of smoke rising from the town and sweeping over the beach. Through the thick black drifting smoke you could see many seafront buildings had been hit and were burning. The beach itself had been smashed by our artillery. Several buildings inside Reggio had also been hit and huge explosions and detonations could be heard as the noise swept and traveled over the water. Then the distance to the beach was less than a quarter of mile and Dave's Company got ready, as their landing craft began making its final run for the beach. In a short while there was a bump, the ramp went down and the men came barreling out.

    They began running up the beach and there was no barbed wire and very little firing. The little firing there was stopped as soon as Dave put his Bren-gunners in action. The Italians firing surrendered almost immediately and Dave led his Company up one of the beach roads. To his left he saw a British battalion that had been landed in the wrong sector and was now moving north in a long file toward San Giovanni. Almost behind him engineers were landing in order to carry out demolitions and blow away any obstacles or obstructions that might block the beach exits for the guns, tanks and transports waiting to come in. Dave kept on leading his Company up one of the beach roads and over the bridge that took them to the center of Reggio. So far no one was firing at them and the lone *carabiniere* they met told them the Germans had gone away in a great hurry the day before.

    Past the bridge they finally got into Reggio and Dave saw the town was in complete shambles. The destruction was worse than what he had seen in Pachino. Telephone lines were cut and lying all over the place. Streets after streets were strewn with blocks of concrete, bricks and rubble. Buildings were roofless. Shops had been blown open. Windows were shattered. Trees were torn off. Dave led the Company through smoke-filled and rubble-strewn streets and when he reached the main square of Reggio, he saw a few Italian officers standing in front of the steps of the city hall and waiting for them to arrive. The leading officer was a Colonel who was in his early fifties and he was standing with two Majors, three Captains and a Lieutenant. The Lieutenant was carrying a white flag and the Colonel was sharply dressed in the infantry uniform of the 211th Coastal Division.

The Colonel was short and flabby and had thick dark hair and a thick dark mustache. Even though it was early September he was wearing tight-fitting black leather gloves and his black leather boots were impeccably shined. He was standing in front of the other Italian officers and when Dave came into the main square and walked over to him, he said: *"Parlare Italiano?"*

"Si."

"Bene. Io sono Colonello Luigi Morandini e sono in carrica di Reggio."

Dave nodded and the Colonel said: *"Mi piage di andare a sorrento e affitare uno ufficio."*

"Io sono un ufficiale."

"No. I mean an officer of my rank or above."

"I'm afraid I'll have to do."

"I'm afraid you do not understand. I wish to surrender to your Colonel or General."

"I wish I could accommodate you, Colonel. But they're a little busy right now."

"And who are you?"

"I told you. I'm an officer."

"But what is your rank?"

"Captain."

"No. That will not do. I wish to surrender to someone of my own rank."

"Listen, Colonel. Either you surrender right now or I'll have my men shoot up your town and take you all prisoners. It's as you wish."

"This is not proper. In the Great War my father fought on your side and received the Military Medal."

"So?"

"So, as a former ally, I should be entitled to certain courtesies."

Italy

"You're not an ally now. You're just an enemy officer to me."

"You think I liked fighting under Mussolini?"

"I know. You stood by him for over 20 years and now you suddenly hate him."

"I fought for him. But I did not approve of him."

"Well, you're not fighting now."

"Of course not. This fight is pointless."

"Well, since you're not fighting, I request you surrender."

"Of course. But to the proper authorities."

"Enough! That's enough of this nonsense! Either you hand me your pistol now or I'll have my men take it forcibly from you!"

"All right! But I protest!"

"Protest all you will!"

"This is not the proper way to handle an officer of superior rank!"

"Colonel! Your pistol!"

"All right! But I protest!"

CHAPTER 147

The Colonel handed his pistol angrily to Dave. Then he formally surrendered the town to him and was sent down with an escort to the beach with the other officers. Once he was gone Dave went through Reggio with the Company and led them north through the hills. Italian coastal troops were surrendering everywhere. First they surrendered by Platoons and then by Companies and Battalions and were sent down to the beach without escort to be taken away. Dave kept on leading the Company through the hills and never slowed until, around 2.00 o'clock in the morning, they finally stopped near Straorini. This was a village five miles from Reggio and they spent the night there.

In the morning they were off again and moved into the mountains toward San Stefano and Gambarie and Delianova. Then, on Wednesday, September 8, 1943, in the late afternoon, as they were making their way toward Delianova, the news came over the wireless of the Italian surrender. When the people of Delianova found out they went wild with joy and yelled and clapped and cheered. Wine bottles were taken out and there was mad singing and dancing and celebrating in the streets. Those celebrations lasted far into the night and Dave's Company was offered a great deal of wine and drawn into some of those celebrations. Then, in the morning, Bedford trucks came for them and for the next two weeks they began carrying out their long 400-mile advance across southern Italy. It was a strange thing. The Germans kept on falling back and were always a day or two ahead of them.

The Company moved on through demolitions in roads and at bridges. It kept on driving through the mountains and Dave saw how magnificent the country looked. It had great valleys and thick pine forests and massive

Italy

mountains and the air was crisp and clear. It reminded him of his own country and of being out west near the Rockies. They kept on heading north through the mountains and when they reached Cittanova, they swung east and went through Locri. Then they sped north to Catanzaro and went through places like Cotrone and Rotondella before they came out of a broad valley, on Saturday, September 18, 1943, and reached Potenza. In Potenza they were given a 10-day rest and then they were on the move again. They were now in autumn and as the weather became cold, damp and chilly, they began having sweeping torrential rain that turned the roads they used into a sea of mud.

Still, the pressure was on to keep on moving, and General Chris Vokes, who had temporarily replaced General Simonds who had become ill, ordered them out of Potenza. Soon the Division moved east to Gravina, then north through Spinazzzola, Canosa, to the hard black asphalt road across the Foggia plains. From there the Division turned west into the rough tough pine-clad Abruzzi hills and during the next two and a half months, from late September to early December, the Division went through places like Motta Montecorvino, Monte Miano, Volturara, Gambatesa, Jelsi, Campobasso, Baranello, Montagano, San Stefano, Guardiaregia, Vinchiaturo, Torella and Molise.

CHAPTER 148

The Germans, as they fell back, used the Biferno, Sangro and Moro rivers as natural defensive positions and there were fierce and fiery artillery duels on both sides of those rivers. It was now raining a lot and, when the skies cleared, the Division was supported by the Kittyhawks, Spitfires and Boston bombers of the Desert Air Force. It also had the full backing of as many as nine Field Artillery Regiments and the infantry was attacking with squadrons of tanks from the Calgary, Three Rivers and Ontario Regiments. The Germans were trying to stall the Canadians' drive across Italy and waiting for the onset of winter and the closing down of the few serviceable roads leading north. Even though they had little air support, they used their Mark IV and Tiger tanks well and their artillery and mortar fire were as deadly and devastating as ever.

The Division was facing the 90th Panzer Grenadier Division. This was a Division that based its defensive tactics on strong tank and infantry counterattacks. It was a tough and fearless Division and at no time would it give ground without a fierce and bloody struggle. In early December the Division and the Regiment began their three-week campaign for the Moro river and valley. There were brutal and savage battles for San Vito, San Leonardo, Roatti, Berardi and the Gully, and on December 15, 1943, the 90th German Panzer Grenadier Division, a very tough but rigid and inflexible Division, was replaced by the 1st German Parachute Division. This Division, that was wearing *Luftwaffe* blue and yellow pipings, was the best defensive Division of the German Army in Italy.

By then, and true to its reputation as the Firemen's Brigade, the Regiment was assigned to the 2nd Infantry Brigade, under Brigadier Bert Hoffmeister, in order to take pressure off the Loyal Edmonton Regiment since they had been involved in heavy fighting ever since they had landed in Italy. The Regiment and Dave's Company went through them along the coast road that was called Highway No.16 until, around noon, on Monday, December 20, 1943, they came to a small town of about 11,000 people that stood on a cliff 200 feet above the sea. To the east of that town you found the pale blue waters of the Adriatic. To the west there were rich and rolling farmlands that led to the snow-capped Appennine mountains in the distance. The town seemed to be a mile long and most of its buildings appeared to be two to four story high.

As Dave made his Company go to ground in a field about two miles from it and looked at it though his binoculars, he saw it had a couple of main streets, one of which, the Corso Vittorio Emmanuele, they were supposed to go through in order to reach the other end of town, a large square stony castle to the east of it, and a tall and imposing white church whose stately dome he could see ahead of him in the distance. The Regiment and Dave's Company were assigned to go through the town on the eastern side. This was the coastal side and Dave's Company would attack on the eastern side of the Corso Vittorio Emmanuele while Tom Clark's A Company would attack on the western side.

The Loyal Edmonton Regiment would follow behind Dave's Company and move to its right flank on the coastal and port side. The Seaforths were scheduled to go through the town on the the western side. Both main streets were full of rubble and fallen wires and Canadian and German artillery were shelling its approaches so that the town itself was blanketed in a thin film of white smoke and dust. This thin film of white smoke and dust hung over it and there didn't seem to be any people around. Also both main streets had, in quite a few places, collapsed buildings and as he spotted a still-standing sign by the side of the road, Dave saw the name of the town on the sign read: Ortona.

CHAPTER 149

The field where Dave had made the Company go to ground led to a deep narrow ridge. That ridge was about 3000 yards long and brought them to the first buildings of the town. One of the Field Artillery Regiments lay down a creeping barrage and Dave made his men walk in the ridge behind this barrage until they reached the edge of those buildings. Near those buildings the men hid behind the ridge while Dave looked at the town once again through his binoculars. From the end of the ridge to the first building was a distance of about 12 yards. When you crossed that distance you would hit a brick wall that was the side of the building. This brick wall led to a small staircase and low passageway that ran from the side of the building to its main wall on the Corso Vittorio Emmanuele.

This small staircase and low passageway led to a semi-basement entrance at the front of the building. The distance, however, was on open ground and even though Dave couldn't see anything, he knew the parachutists were out there and waiting for them. After a short pause three soldiers volunteered to try and cross it. The three stood poised at the edge of the ridge and then bolted for the brick wall. Before they had gone five yards rifle, machine-gun and sniper fire opened up on them and the three of them lay on the ground. A few soldiers rushed to grab them and bring them back to the ridge. They too came under heavy fire and some of them were also injured. From his position behind the ridge Dave saw the fire seemed to come from the top of the buildings across the Corso Vittorio Emmanuele and from the buildings themselves.

Two of the soldiers had been shot through the head and Dave knew the parachutists were using snipers. The German snipers were using Mauser Kar 98K rifles and at 500 meters their firing was deadly. Two other soldiers volunteered to bolt across that distance and slam against the brick wall. Both of them were shot dead within a few yards of the ridge. When he saw that Dave ordered one of his rifleman with a PIAT to fire at the wall of the building in order to breach it near the bottom. One shot didn't do it. But a second shot from another rifleman with a PIAT made a hole big enough for a couple of men to go through it. Once the wall was breached Dave had his two-inch mortarman fire smoke shells at the buildings across the Corso Vittorio Emmanuele in order to blanket the area. Then he bolted himself with a couple of soldiers toward the hole in the wall.

CHAPTER 150

As soon as Dave began running toward that hole with the other two soldiers he could hear the hammering of machine-guns and the cracks of rifle shots through the smoke. Dave kept on going and near the hole he reached out and threw a grenade inside. Then he flattened himself on the side of the hole before going in and spraying the inside with his Thompson machine-gun. As he was firing Dave found himself in what looked like the ground floor of the building with the other soldiers. In a moment Dave stopped firing and motioned for them to spread out and stay away from the hole. They seemed to be in the living-room of the building and could hear faint voices from the second floor.

The voices were low and guttural and appeared to be German. Dave moved close to the large living-room doors and slowly opened them. He now stepped in what looked the hallway entrance and carefully checked the rest of the first floor. There was a kitchen next to the living-room, then, at the back, on the right, a staircase leading to the second floor and the basement, and a parlor and a bathroom also on the right side. At a signal from Dave the three of them took out grenades. Then they rushed up the staircase and threw them on the second floor before running in and spraying the floor with bullets. Three Germans were in the hallway leading to what looked like four bedrooms and they died instantly under the hail of grenades and bullets. Next the three of them moved carefully and burst open the doors of those rooms and fired at whatever might be moving inside of them. Two more parachutists were killed inside of those rooms.

But one of the soldier who fired at one of the parachutists while standing in front of a window was shot through the throat and fell down on the floor. He was bleeding profusely and after a while, stopped moving. Dave, who had knelt next to him and looked to see if he could help him, now moved away from him. He made sure he stayed away from the windows and, with the other soldier, took the staircase at the back, on the right, and checked the second floor. Near the windows giving out on the Corso Vittorio Emmanuele they found rifles and belts of ammunition. In one of the windows there was even an MG 42. Dave told the soldier to watch the second and ground floors while he, himself, would go down to the basement to see if it was clear of Germans. The soldier nodded and Dave went down the staircase carefully to the ground floor before he opened the basement door softly. Then he threw down a grenade and, after it had gone off, rushed down to the basement. Dave ran down around it and sprayed it with bullets from his Thompson machine-gun.

After a while Dave stopped since he saw there were no parachutists there and that it only contained a small apartment at the semi-basement front entrance of the building. This apartment had a small door that led to a furnace room at the back of it, on the left side of the building. Past that furnace room you found a storage room and on the right side of the basement there was a small wine cellar, a coal bin, and then the staircase at the back. Dave stayed in the basement for a moment and leaned against the furnace room wall. Then he pulled himself away from the wall and slowly walked back up to the living-room where he moved near the hole in the wall and looked out. It was now close to 3.00 o'clock in the afternoon and the sky was gray and overcast.

A light drizzle had begun to fall and through the hole in the wall, Dave could see Slav in the ridge. He motioned for him to go and tell their two-inch mortarman to fire more smoke shells on the buildings on the Corso Vittorio Emmanuele and to make sure other soldiers were ready to come and join him. Slav nodded and quickly left the ridge.

CHAPTER 151

Slav was back in no time and not long after smoke shells began landing on the buildings across the Corso Vittorio Emmanuele and near Dave's building. The open ground between the ridge and their own building became covered with a thick grayish smoke and as soon as the open ground was blanketed with that smoke, soldiers from Dave's Company began barreling out of the ridge and making for the hole in the wall. In a short time several soldiers had slammed past it. There were quite a few yells and screams as many others were shot through the smoke and lay on the ground wounded or dying. Almost at the same time Sherman tanks from the C Squadron of the Three Rivers Regiment began shooting at the buildings across from them on the Corso Vittorio Emmanuele with their 75 mm guns.

When the tanks began firing at those buildings soldiers from Tom Clark's A Company began running through a small ditch that led at a right angle from the ditch where Dave's Company had gone to ground to a *pensione* facing Dave's building across the Corso. This *pensione* was behind slit trenches manned by parachutists who were waiting for the Fusiliers' attack. After a while there was a great deal of fire coming from that *pensione* and from the Three Rivers tanks who were still hammering the buildings across the Corso. Through all this shooting, firing and dark grayish smoke blanketing the whole area, soldiers from Dave's Company kept on barreling through the hole in the wall and spreading out throughout the building.

In no time the building was full and the thick grayish smoke covering the open ground soon began to thin out. By now it was close to 4.00 o'clock in the afternoon and darkness was coming on. Dave talked with some soldiers of the Company and a few of them wanted to leave the house and try to make it to the small staircase and low passegeway that ran around the building into the Corso. The passageway was about four feet deep and those soldiers felt they could slip into it and make it past the building into the next building. Dave agreed to let them try and around 4.30 in the afternoon two of them decided to do it. By then the tanks from the C Squadron of the Three Rivers Regiment were still firing and hammering at the buildings across the Corso. But, with the oncoming darkness, they were getting ready to withdraw and hull down for the night on the outskirts of Ortona.

While some of them were still firing, however, the two soldiers who had decided to do it bolted out of the hole and began making a run for it. As soon as they were out of the hole Dave heard the hammering of machine-guns and cracks of rifle fire and a soldier who looked quickly out of the hole told him they were lying alongside the building. Three more soldiers now stepped to the hole. After a moment they bolted out and began making for the small staircase. They were firing their Thompson machine-guns and they too were hit by machine-gun and rifle fire. All three lay not far from the other two soldiers and one of them managed to crawl back and slip into the hole. He had been hit in the chest and legs and was bleeding a great deal. Some of the soldiers tried to stop the bleeding while a few others gathered around Dave and talked on how they could get to the small staircase.

They were still talking about this when a huge towering six-foot-five Major came barreling through the hole and headed straight for Dave. The Major's name was Jim Stone and he was in charge of D Company of the Loyal Edmontons. In fact, he had met Dave and the other Company COs of the Regiment when, along with the Loyal Edmontons, they had been given their present assignments. Right now, since he was so close to the action, he was actually running the Loyal Edmontons instead of Lieutenant-Colonel Jim Jefferson whose headquarters was further to the rear. When the Major reached Dave, he grinned broadly at him and said:
"Hey, Davie! How is it going?"
"Very well, Major."
"Good."
"What are you doing here?"
"Just checking to see how you were doing."
"I'm doing fine."
"Your men are in good shape?"
"Yes, Sir."
"And you had no problem getting through the ridge?"

The Long War

"No, Sir."

"That's good."

"What about you, Major? How are you doing?"

"Oh, we're slowly coming into Ortona through a ridge on your right flank."

"Good."

"Mind you, it's hard work. But we're getting there on the port side."

"Glad to hear it."

"What about you, Davie? What's your progress in Ortona so far?"

"Twelve yards."

The Major laughed.

"This town looks like it's going to be a tough nut to crack, hey?"

"You're not kidding."

"At least you're into one of the buildings."

"That's true."

The Major didn't say anything for a moment and Dave said: "Why are the Germans bringing in so many parachutists in Ortona?"

"They want to defend it."

"Why?"

"If they lose it, the road is open to Pescara."

"And?"

"If they lose Pescara, we have a very good lateral road leading to Avezanno and then on to Rome. That's why."

Dave nodded and then said: "As you mentioned. This town's going to be a tough nut to crack."

"You bet."

"Those parachutists are not like the soldiers of the 90th Panzer Division."

"They sure aren't."

"They're smart. Instead of having by-the-book tank-and-infantry attacks, they just yield ground slowly and make you pay for every inch you take."

"That's it."

"It's going to be very hard taking them on."

"Very."

"And very bloody."

"That too."

"Can we do it with the units we have?"

"Sure."

"How?"

"House by house. Street by street."

"That's going to take time."
"Maybe. Maybe not."
"Why not?
"We've got tanks. We've got artillery. We'll do it."
"I hope you're right."
"Don't worry. We will."

CHAPTER 152

Major Stone then slapped Dave in the back and barreled out of the hole in the same way he had come. Dave watched him go and spent the rest of the afternoon and evening in making sure the men in the house were spread out properly. He had decided to stay in that house for the night and in the morning, he launched his attack around 8.00 o'clock. He had been in touch by wireless with the Colonel and he sent him the same tanks Dave had had the day before. These were the tanks of the C Squadron of the Three Rivers Regiment and they had orders to take on the buildings on the Corso Vittorio Emmanuele and give his Company close support. Around 8.00 o'clock Dave could hear the Shermans rumble down the road to Ortona and, on the outskirts of the town, begin firing at the buildings and on the Corso itself.

The tanks had sappers with them and they were trying to clear the road of teller mines. When those tanks were right by his building, Dave, who had gone to the basement of the house, softly opened the semi-basement front door. Dave slipped out of the door and made sure he stayed down below the four-feet passageway that ran all around the house. Still, as soon as he slipped out of the semi-basement door, there was machine-gun fire and rifle shots pretty close to him. Dave kept his head down and crawled past the short stony staircase that led to the front door until he reached the end of the passageway giving out on the next building. That building also had a similar passageway and there were six feet of open ground between the two buildings.

Already there were two soldiers lying down in the passageway behind him and on the Corso Dave could hear two Shermans firing at buildings on the other side. Those two Shermans seemed to be right in front of him

Italy

and in front of the six feet of open ground before the next building. Dave waited a moment and then jumped up over the four-feet passageway as he heard several machine-guns and rifles open up. The two soldiers who had been lying down behind him also followed him and Dave jumped and landed hard into the narrow concrete floor of the next passageway. He hugged the wall of the passageway and suddenly heard a huge SWISH-BOOM! as a parachutist with a *Panzerfaust* fired at him from one of the upper floors of a building across the Corso.

Dave threw himself as far as he could to the end of the passageway and there was a shattering explosion near the semi-basement door. Stones, pieces of metal and broken glass flew everywhere and when the dust settled, Dave saw there was a big hole in the wall near the semi-basement door. The two soldiers behind him were buried in rubble and didn't move. Dave slowly turned and, still hugging the wall, crawled back until he lay in front of the entrance to the hole. Then he turned and bolted through it as more machine-gun and rifle fire was heard behind him. Inside the hole Dave lay down against the wall on the left side and looked around. He was in what seemed another small basement apartment and two German parachutists lay dead some feet from him on his left.

There was a thick dust lying in the air and one of the parachutists was wearing perspex goggles. They were around his neck and Dave moved over to him and took them. He put them around his own neck and turned as another soldier came barreling through the hole followed by a hail of machine-gun and rifle fire. This soldier lay down against the wall on the right side of the hole and Dave pointed with his finger to the ceiling to let him know there were Germans on the ground floor. You could hear the muffled tones of their low guttural voices and after Dave had rested a little, he motioned with his finger for the soldier to follow him and that they were going upstairs. Dave then got up and walked slowly with the soldier past the rear door of the apartment, the furnace room, the storage room, and to the staircase at the back, on the other side of the building.

This staircase led to the ground floor and when they reached it, Dave nodded at him as both of them took out grenades. Then they rushed to the ground floor and threw them. They ran down the staircase and then rushed up again and fired their Thompson machine-guns. Dave briefly caught sight of three German parachutists racing up the staircase and heading for the second floor. Davè paused on the ground floor with the soldier and before he could run up to the second floor with him, there was a tremendous explosion that rocked the building as the second floor was blown apart by one of our tanks' 75 mm gun and as you could hear Germans scream and moan through the blast. Some of the floor crashed through the ceiling at the front end of the building and, from where Dave and the soldier were standing near the staircase, at the back, there was so much dust in the air Dave had to put on his goggle in order to see.

The smell of cordite, stone and plaster was everywhere and Dave and the soldier went back down to the basement. They lay down near the hole and Dave slipped past it with the soldier behind him and crawled toward the end of the passageway. They no sooner had made it than another tremendous explosion shook the ground and the building in front of them crashed down in a heap of stone, plaster and rubble. In the Corso our Shermans were still firing and some of our self-propelled and anti-tank guns were now in action. Dave lay in the passageway with the soldier behind him and after a while, another dirty and dusty soldier crawled beside him. This soldier told Dave one of our tanks had blown the second story of the house when he had seen parachutists there and that the Germans had blown up the next building in order to slow down our advance.

However, there was a hole in the rubble, the soldier told Dave, slightly at a right angle from this passageway, and it probably led through the third building. Dave nodded and, after telling the two soldiers to follow him, waited until it seemed more Shermans were right alongside them and the six-feet of open space leading to the next building. Then he bolted up, jumped the passageway and made for that hole in the rubble of the third building. That hole was, indeed, slightly at a right angle from the passageway and when he reached it, Dave threw himself headlong into it. Bullets were racing all around him and when Dave threw himself into that hole, he fell cleanly about 10 feet before he landed hard in what looked like the basement. There was the smell of crushed flesh, cordite and spilled wine all around and as soon as Dave had landed, he was followed by the other two soldiers.

Only the area where Dave had landed with the two soldiers seemed intact from the blast. This was a spot near the furnace room and most of the basement was filled with rubble except for a narrow passageway that ran from the furnace room through the coal bin. This passageway looked big enough for a man to squeeze through it and after Dave had slipped in it and followed it, he was amazed to see it led to another hole on the other side of the building. This hole, this time, was at a left angle from the passageway of the next building. The other two soldiers had followed Dave and near the hole there was enough room for the three of them to stand inside the rubble. All of them caught their breath and as he looked at his watch, Dave saw it was almost noon.

The sky was again gray and overcast. A steady drizzle was falling and, with all the dust hanging low over the city, it was so dark it could have been evening or close to midnight.

CHAPTER 153

Dave watched the next building and when two more Shermans came rumbling on the Corso and firing at targets on either side, he suddenly jumped up and ran at a left angle until he threw himself down in the passageway. As he ran the ground around him was stitched with machine-gun and rifle bullets. Then, as he crawled to the end of the passageway, the two soldiers who had been with him dove in the passageway behind him. By now an MG 42 was firing just above the passageway and the wall of the house behind them was pockmarked with rifle fire. Dave hugged the wall and made sure he kept his head down and suddenly the ground under him shook with another tremendous explosion.

Almost at the same time there was a huge explosion to the left of the semi-basement front door and stones, pieces of plaster and broken glass flew everywhere. Dave lay still as this rubble flew past him and as some of it hit him. Then, when he moved, he turned and saw he had been cut on the right side of his head near his helmet and was bleeding. The wound wasn't serious, however, and after he had wiped some of the blood away with his hand, he turned again and saw the other two soldiers were moving and signaling to him they were okay. The soldier behind him had slight scratches to his face while the third soldier had a bloody right hand and was rubbing his left shoulder. The MG 42 kept on firing and Dave crawled back slowly and pointed to the two soldiers the huge hole in the left side of the semi-basement door.

The two soldiers nodded and all three waited until they heard two more Shermans lumber slowly past them and also fire at targets further down the street. Then, when the tanks were alongside of them, the three of them turned and crawled swiftly through the hole. There was more machine-gun and rifle fire and when they were inside, Dave lay against the wall on the left side of the hole while the two soldiers did the same on the other side. The two tremendous explosions had come, Dave saw, from a German 88 and a *Panzerfaust*. The blast from the 88 had sliced open the left wall of the apartment and the one from the *Panzerfaust* had made the hole near the semi-basement front door quite big. There was rubble everywhere and a thick black dust filled the basement so that even with his perspex goggles, Dave could hardly see anything. He caught his breath for a moment and then motioned for the two soldiers to follow him.

Dave got up and moved carefully to the staircase, on the right, leading to the ground floor. The two soldiers followed him and on the ground floor, Dave saw two dead parachutists near the spot, at the front of the building, where the shell had gone into the basement. Dave then pointed to the staircase leading to the second floor and took out some grenades. The two soldiers did the same and, at a nod from him, all of them rushed up the staircase. They threw their grenades and, once they had exploded, ran in on the second floor and sprayed it with their Thompson machine guns. Three of the parachutists had run to the end of the hallway near the windows and were now turning to return fire. One of them was shot through the head through the window and the other two were shot through the chest before they could return fire. Two more who were hiding in one of the rooms on the right side of the hallway were blown up with grenades.

Dave then moved near one of the side windows and saw the next building had completely been blown up and that all floors had crashed into the basement. This left the building in large piles of rubble and beyond it, you had the beginning of large blocks of apartment houses. Dave left the window and went back down with the two soldiers to the basement. They lay down again on either side of the hole. Dave lay on the left side of it and the two soldiers on the right side and as they were lying there, there was another tremendous explosion as the second floor crashed on the ground floor and as the basement suddenly filled with dark and sooty dust. There was so much of it the air became acrid and unbreathable and you could hardly see. Through the darkness, though, you could hear the ceiling of the basement creak and groan and Dave signaled with his right hand for the soldiers to move closer to him on either side of the hole.

On the Corso some of the tanks were going back and still firing at the buildings. Our artillery and the German artillery were also raking the buildings. You heard the thump thump thump of crashing mortars and the harsh staccato of MG 42s. There was also the steady hammering of our Bren guns and the B-u-r-p B-u-r-p of Schmeissers. Rifle shots echoed everywhere. By then Dave saw a few soldiers had come into the basement

The Long War

and tried to find out from them where his Platoons and Sections were and to get a sense of what was happening. But no one seemed to know. The whole Company was fighting piecemeal. Soldiers were fighting room by room and house by house. No one could get into the street. No one could charge the next building. No one knew what the next Company or Regiment was doing. Their signalman had been killed and no one knew who was replacing him.

It was now close to 2.00 o'clock in the afternoon and was very dark and raining outside. For the next four hours all Dave could do was lie down near the hole and watch as more soldiers came into the house and as he was able to gather a Section around him. By then he had to stop operations for the night, and all he had to show so far, ever since they had come into Ortona, was the taking of four houses and a total gain of 90 yards.

CHAPTER 154

Dave set up a perimeter inside the building and then went and lay down near the hole. With the oncoming night things became a little more quiet and the whole town was filled with a thick gritty sooty dust. All the time, though, you could hear the stiff barking of machine-guns and the sharp crack of rifles. Dave stood watch near the hole and around 4.00 o'clock in the morning, the soldier lying down next to him, on his left, tapped him on the shoulder and pointed to the hole. There was some movement in front of it and then the new signalman staggered in with two other soldiers. As soon as he came in Dave got busy on the wireless and contacted the Colonel. He arranged for the Three Rivers tanks to come and back them up in the morning and then waited for the dawn.

Around 6.00 a.m. a round bloody sun rose through the low-lying haze and shone palely on the ruins of Ortona as Dave began to hear in the distance tanks coming down the road. They were firing at the roofs and windows of buildings and when they came by his house, Dave rushed out of it and ran alongside them with the soldiers he had until they could get to the various piles of rubble that used to be the next building. Once they were there Dave and the other soldiers were able to hide behind those piles of rubble and move toward the large blocks of apartment houses that were coming up next. By then the tanks were acting as artillery for them and shooting at anything that moved or fired on them. As for Dave and the soldiers who were with him they just moved from pile to pile of rubble and got closer to the first large block of apartment houses.

By 8.00 o'clock some of our self-propelled guns had been brought into action and blew a big hole in the first large block of apartment houses. That hole was near the bottom of the large block, on the side of it, and Dave and the soldiers who were with him now took out grenades and rushed the hole. They threw the grenades into it and then went in and sprayed the area inside. As they came in they found themselves in what looked like the basement garage of this large block of apartment houses and hid behind large cement columns and fired at the parachutists who were also hiding behind columns and returning fire. There was a wild scramble near the hole as everyone was yelling, screaming and firing and in the dust-filled and echoing darkness the parachutists slowly began moving away and falling back to the other side of the garage.

By now more soldiers were coming into it and slowly and steadily beginning to drive the parachutists out of the garage, on the other side, and toward the upper floors. At this time Dave had enough of them to be able to assign to individual soldiers and small groups the tasks of clearing the basement and the upper floors room by room and apartment by apartment. This took time and as the attack went on, the battle in Ortona turned into one of unbelievable savagery and ferocity. The Germans were now firing through this first block of apartments and through the holes they made in the garage and upper floor, Dave could see how the battle was going. At one point he heard huge sirens as a troop of tanks advanced in the middle of the Corso followed by some infantrymen. Those tanks tried to go over a huge pile of rubble blocking the Corso and that stood not that far from the Piazza Municipali.

But they couldn't do it. They had to retreat with the infantrymen, and the Germans drove some of their tanks into cellars. Then they blew up the buildings on top of them and used their tanks as stationary artillery. No German was allowed to surrender. Anyone who raised his hands and came running and yelling *"Kameraden! Kameraden!"* was shot. A German machine-gunner who had been blinded and was firing on sound was pulled out of his emplacement while yelling: *"I'm a good soldier! I hope my son is a good soldier!"* All over town the parachutists were firing their *Nebelwerfers*. Those much-feared six-bareled rocket mortars kept on crashing on houses and buildings and they made a sound that was like the end of the world. MG 34s, 42s, Schmeissers, Mauser Kar 98 Ks and *Panzerfausts* were in action. Whole buildings were collapsed in the streets in order to delay the advance.

Everywhere you went there was artillery, mortar and gun fire. The parachutists fought and died in place. No one surrendered. In some of the buildings they yelled and screamed at our soldiers: *"Zeigen mir! Zeigen mir! Was sie gelten!"* This kind of savage and ferocious fighting made for tough and slow going. But by early afternoon Dave and his Company had cleared the first block of apartments. An anti-tank gun blew a hole in the

Italy

second block of apartment houses and Dave went in with his Company and began clearing it slowly from the garage to the upper floors. This took a while and by the time they were finished it was early evening and very dark out. Everyone was filthy and exhausted and as Dave and some soldiers from his First Platoon were getting ready to sit down against some of the columns in the garage and rest a bit, a big, tall, strapping soldier came in with three other soldiers.

This soldier was Brigadier Bert Hoffmeister, the Commanding Officer of the 2nd Canadian Infantry Brigade. Dave had met him when the Regiment had been assigned, in mid December, to act as infantry support to the Loyal Edmontons. Brigadier Hoffmeister had discussed with Dave and other Company COs the forthcoming operations that would be undertaken by both the Regiment and the Loyal Edmontons and when he saw Dave, the Brigadier walked over to him and said: "Ah, David. How are you?"

"Fine, thank you. Sir."

"Can we talk?"

"Sure."

CHAPTER 155

Dave turned and led the Brigadier to a fairly-large self-enclosed room near the end of the garage on the right. This room was used as one of the locker rooms for the building and inside, there was a big candle on a shelf to the right of the door as you entered. Dave took out a match and lit this candle and after he had closed the door behind them and turned to the Brigadier, the Brigadier said: "How is it going?"

"No complaints, Sir."

"Good."

"What are you doing, Sir, so far in the front lines?"

"I wanted to see how you were doing."

"I'm fine."

"Are you, really?"

"Yes, Sir."

"This town of Ortona is not an easy town to take, is it?"

"It isn't."

"Do you think you can do it?"

"Yes, Sir."

"I was talking to General Vokes today. There's a lot of pressure on him to do just that."

"I can imagine."

"Do you really think you can?"

"Yes, sir."

"What's your fighting strength right now?"

"Sixty percent."

"That's not a great deal."

"That's enough."

"You're only a quarter of a mile into town."

"I know that."

"The town is a mile long. It might not be that easy."

"That's true."

"With your attrition rates, do you realize you may run out of men before you get to the end of it?"

"I won't."

"What makes you say that?"

"Believe me, Sir. I won't"

"All the Regiments are taking tremendous casualties."

"I'm aware of that."

"You won't be able to sustain those rates much longer and still be a fighting unit."

"I know that."

"Maybe it's not worth going on. What do you think?"

Dave's eyes flashed and he stepped closer to the Brigadier.

"Are you telling me to quit, Brigadier!"

"No. All I'm telling you is that your attrition rates are too high."

"Nobody quits this fight! Nobody!"

"I understand. But I'm telling you we can't keep on taking such tremendous casualties."

"The hell with casualties! Do you think the Germans don't have them!"

"I'm sure they have. But we're talking about us."

"So am I! And we're attacking! That's it!"

"At the cost of such tremendous casualties?"

"You bet we are! What the hell do you think this is! This is a little Stalingrad on the Adriatic!"

"And like Stalingrad we're taking terrible casualties."

"So what!"

"So it matters."

"In the First World War the Fusiliers had to learn how to fight in the deep mud, trenches and barbed wire of Arras, Vimy Ridge and Passchendaele! Well, in the Second World War we're learning how to fight in dark rooms, cellars and basements! We're learning it and what we're learning here will be taught to armies everywhere!"

"That's all very well. But in the meantime we're running out of men."

"Do you think that's not happening to the Germans!"

"I'm sure it is."

"You're damn right it is!

"So that's why you want to go on."

"You bet!"

"Because you think the Germans are being hit a lot harder than we are."

"You're damn right!"

"But in the meantime we run the risk of losing all strength as a fighting unit."

"We won't! And because if we quit now, Brigadier, after all the sacrifices we've made and blood we've shed, all the Regiments in this battle will lose their fighting spirit and won't be worth a damn!"

The Brigadier didn't say anything for a long moment. Then he looked at Dave and said: "I'm glad you feel that way."

Dave didn't say anything and the Brigadier said: "I feel exactly as you do."

"Do you?"

"I do. And that's what I told General Vokes."

"Good."

"But I wanted to hear it from you."

Dave nodded and the Brigadier said: "You're one of the leaders of this attack. That's why I wanted to come here and find out for myself how you felt."

"I appreciate that."

"So the battle goes on."

"Yes, Sir. The battle goes on."

CHAPTER 156

The Brigadier flashed the thumbs up sign at him and Dave nodded and opened the door. He blew out the candle and both of them left the locker room and walked back down the garage toward the hole where the Brigadier had come in with three soldiers. Near the hole the Brigadier wished him good luck and left with those soldiers. Dave watched them go for a moment and then set up a perimeter around the garage until the morning when they would go on the attack again. Dave was also in contact with the Colonel and made sure the Three Rivers tanks would be there for that attack so they could back them up as mobile artillery. Then he settled down for the night and around 6.00 o'clock in the morning, he began hearing the tanks rumbling down the Corso and heading their way.

Another low round red sun had risen and was shining palely on the jagged and smoking ruins of Ortona and when the tanks came alongside his block of apartment houses Dave rushed out and ran beside them until they reached the next block of apartment houses. At that block the tanks blew a hole at the bottom of its side wall with their 75 mm guns and Dave and some of the soldiers who were with him ran toward that hole and threw grenades in. Then they rushed in and exchanged fire in the darkness with the parachutists. Dave and the soldiers who were with him hid behind and then moved from cement to cement column as they slowly drove the parachutists out of the garage, on the other side, and to the upper floors. While this was going on German artillery was firing at our tanks outside and blowing holes in the basement.

The air was full of dust and of a burning acrid smell and, like the block before, the Fusiliers slowly and steadily cleared it of parachutists. This was slow and difficult work although, since they now knew how to do it,

The Long War

a little faster, and around 9.00 o'clock, Dave and his men had cleared that block and had moved to another block. They finished clearing that other block around noon and it was at that time, when Dave was in the basement of this second block with the Big Ten and other soldiers who had cleared it, that it led to an incident that was going to change his life so deeply and unexpectedly. By then all of them were dead tired and exhausted and most of them had laid down near holes blown by the German artillery in the garage in order to take it easy and rest for a few moments. Casualties were high. Tempers were frayed.

And it was at that time, when Dave and some members of the Big Ten and a few other soldiers were lying down near some holes at the front of the garage, that this incident happened. The hole where Dave was lying down with some members of the Big Ten and other soldiers was giving a clear view on the Corso and on the big pile of rubble that was blocking it and stood not far from the Piazza Municipali. As Dave was lying there with everyone he saw a short, muscular soldier from the Loyal Edmontons rush out from one of the blocks of apartment houses ahead of them. This soldier must have been from one of their Companies on their right flank, on the coastal and port side, and that Company must have been ahead of them.

This short, muscular soldier ran up the big pile of rubble and drove in the Red Ensign flag on top of the pile. At about the same time a tall, lean parachutist also ran up the pile with the Nazi flag and almost drove it next to the the Red Ensign flag. When both of them did this, they then turned and began fighting. No one fired from both sides as the two of them took out their bayonets and began moving on each other. Each one was trying to lunge at the other and the short, muscular soldier suddenly jumped near the parachutists and held him close to him. Then both of them fell on the top of the pile of rubble with the flags flying close to one another until another tall, lean parachutist ran up the pile and pried loose the Red Ensigh flag and threw it down next to the Nazi flag.

Then this parachutist ran down the pile and as Dave was watching him through his binoculars with some of the Big Ten and other soldiers, Gino Gennaro, who was standing next to him, on his right, said: "No. No. They can't do this." Ever since the Battle of Ortona had begun Gennaro had kept pretty much to himself and had lost a lot of weight. He was down to skin and bones and his skin was drawn tightly across his face. There was a look of wildness and ferociousness in his eyes and his black hair was dirty and unruly. As he watched what was happening on the big pile he suddenly turned and began running out of the garage through a door at the back. When Dave saw him do this he yelled: "Hey! What are you

Italy

doing!" "I can't! I can't let them do this!" Genaro yelled. "Get back! It's not even our flag!" Dave yelled. "The hell it isn't!" Gennaro yelled. "It's the one we fight and die for!"

Then he was gone out of the garage and Dave watched through his binoculars as Red and Slav slipped on either side of him. After a while Gennaro appeared from the same block of apartment houses ahead of them. He ran up the big pile of rubble and picked up the Red Ensign flag and began driving it in the same spot where it had been before. Almost at the same time the tall, lean parachutists who had thrown down the Red Ensign flag before reappeared and began running up the pile. No one from either side fired and when the parachutist was on top of the pile he tried to stop Gennaro from driving the flag in. Gennaro had already succeeded in doing this, however, and the two of them now turned and began fighting each other.

Through his binoculars Dave could see each held his bayonet. Both were lunging and slashing at one another and as both of them ran into each other, they just stood there toe to toe until both fell backward on top of their own flag and lay still on the big pile of rubble. "God! Oh, God!" Red said and rubbed his eyes. "It can't be! It just can't be!" Slav said and closed his fists tightly. Dave kept on watching through his binoculars and suddenly German 88s opened up on the pile and sent the rubble flying high in the air before it settled down again in a shower of dust and debris with no trace of Gennaro, the Loyal Edmonton soldier, the two parachutists, and the two flags. Dave watched the big pile of rubble a few moments more and when he lowered his binoculars, there was a dark and terrible light in his eyes.

"All right," Dave said. "If that's how they want to play it, that's how we're going to play it." Dave stood up and stepped back from the hole. He turned and yelled at a short and sturdy soldier who was standing a little behind him: "Get me a pioneer!" The soldier nodded and ran out of the hole while Dave stood a few feet from it and looked down and didn't say anything. Some time later the soldier who had been yelled at came in again with a tall and lean soldier who seemed to be in his early thirties. The soldier's uniform was filthy and he himself was dirty and dusty and looked totally exhausted. When he stepped through the hole Dave moved up to him and said: "Are you a pioneer?"

"Yes, Sir."

"What's your name?"

"Lawson."

"All right, Lawson. What's the fastest way we can clear those buildings?"

"I don't know, Sir. By using tanks as shelter?"
"Don't be silly, Lawson! Those streets are deadly! Think again!"
"I don't know, Sir. It's not that easy."
"Go ahead! Surprise me!"
"I think we should try to do it by staying inside the buildings."
"How?"
"That's just it, Sir. It's not that easy."
"Who said it was going to be easy! Go ahead! Tell me!"
"Maybe we can do it with Teller mines."
"How?"
"We jam a bayonet into a wall. Hang a Teller mine on it. And light a short fuse."
"That will be enough to breach the wall?"
"One mine, maybe not. Two will do it for sure."
"And we can go from wall to wall through buildings like this?"
"Yes, Sir."
"And, in this way, we can speed up clearing those buildings?"
"Yes, Sir."
"All right then. Let's do it."

CHAPTER 157

Lawson left Dave and ran through the hole. He was gone for a while and when he came back a little over an hour later, he had three Pioneers with him and quite a few Teller mines and short fuses. By then Dave had moved into the next block of apartment houses. Tanks from the Tree Rivers Regiment had blown a big hole at the bottom of the block and Dave had rushed the hole with two Sections of soldiers. They had thrown grenades through it and slowly and steadily begun clearing the garage. Then, when they had gone to the beginning of the block and reached the fourth and last floor, Dave brought Lawson to that floor with his Pioneers. On that floor Lawson jammed a bayonet in the wall and fixed the Teller mine with a short fuse.

Lawson then lit the fuse and ran quickly down the stairs with the Pioneers, Dave and the two Sections of soldiers. There was a huge shattering explosion and as soon as it was over, Dave ran up the stairs with the soldiers and threw grenades through the dust-filled smoking hole. Once those grenades had exploded Dave ran through the hole with the soldiers and sprayed the inside with his Thompson machine-gun. In this way they began clearing the fourth floor and moving from apartment house to apartment house until the fourth floor of the block was clean. Next they moved down to the lower floors until the whole block was free of Germans. Once they had finished with that block they attacked the next one with the Sherman tanks acting as mobile artillery and blowing a big hole in the basement of the next block.

This way none of them was exposed to the streets. They could move from one apartment house to another without being seen by snipers and could clear those blocks more safely and efficiently. This was still difficult and dangerous work. But it went much faster than having to rush every apartment house from the garage to the upper floors, and this technique of fighting became known as mouse-holing. Major Jim Stone had once told Dave the British had apparently had a tactical doctrine for fighting in built-up areas that included a strategy known as the "Vertical Tactic." But he, himself, had been to various British battle-drill schools and had never heard of it. Mouse-holing became a technique invented by the 1st Canadian Infantry Division at Ortona and it really speeded the process of clearing large blocks of buildings without being seen in the streets.

By evening they had cleared two more blocks of apartment houses and Dave saw Lawson had been right. One Teller mine wouldn't necessarily make a hole in a wall. This was especially true if they ran into a double wall. But two Teller mines would almost always do it. They finally stood down for the night and the next day, another bleak, pale and sunny day, Dave went on the attack again backed by the tanks of the Three Rivers Regiment. They cleaned four more blocks of apartment houses and by 3.00 o'clock of the afternoon, they were on the last block before the Piazza Municipali. The sun had suddenly broken through the pale and dusty haze hanging low over Ortona and was shining brightly and dazzlingly as the Sherman made a hole at the bottom of the side wall of the last block for them to go in.

Dave rushed the hole with some soldiers who were with him. They threw grenades in and then raced and sprayed the inside with bullets. Then they moved from square cement column to square cement column in the sun-filled darkness toward the staircase at the other end in order to clear the garage first as well as that staircase. German artillery had been busy shelling the building and making some holes in the basement and it was at that time that there occurred an incident that Dave, who was bringing up the rear and who was the last one getting ready to rush the staircase, knew was coming and had been expecting for some time. Suddenly Dave saw a parachutist bolt from one of the square cement column near the staircase toward one of the holes on that side the basement.

At that time Dave was just stepping from the column next to the one from where the parachutist had bolted. When the parachutist came to run away toward that hole Dave turned and fired at him. Dave's Thompson machine-gun jammed and when the parachutist saw that he also fired at him. The parachutist's Schmeisser also jammed and he threw it down as Dave did the same. Both of them took out their bayonets and the parachutist moved quickly toward Dave and half-circled in front of him between the two columns. When the parachutist had wanted to run toward one of the holes on that side of the basement his helmet had fallen down on the floor

Italy

and Dave saw he was blond and had clear blue eyes. He was also tall and slim and as he moved and half-circled in front of Dave, he looked closely and intently at him.

Dave also half-circled in front of him and watched his eyes. They were extremely serious and intense and as Dave also moved quickly toward him and closed the distance, with his bayonet in his right hand and his left hand out as a guard, he suddenly stepped in and drove it a few inches underneath his heart. Dave could feel his bayonet go deep into the parachutist. But although his left hand was extended as a blocking guard, the parachutist went over it and came in, unbelievably strong, as Dave tried to turn in order to only give him an angle and slip his move. But the parachutist was too strong and Dave didn't turn enough so he could feel his bayonet go through him on his right side as he was turning.

Dave could feel the bayonet go through him incredibly swiftly and burningly and then both of them stood facing each other. The parachutist was looking down. He was sweating and biting his lower lip and then both of them moved away from each other as they took out their bayonets. Both stood looking at each other for a moment. Then the parachutist staggered backward and fell down against the square cement column closest to the staircase as his bayonet and water canteen clattered on the floor. Dave stood looking at him for a moment. Then he began moving away from him and suddenly felt his legs go from under him. He dropped his bayonet and staggered back as he fell down against the square cement column from where he had stepped out.

That column was facing the one where the parachutist was lying and from the holes that the German artillery had made in the garage, sunlight was streaming in and Dave could see his strained and sweaty face. He, himself, was lying against his square cement column and could feel the blood seeping and running through his tunic. Dave tried to put a hand against his right side and press down in order to stop the bleeding. The German was lying against his own cement column and his hands were resting on either side of him. He was looking at Dave and suddenly smiled at him. Dave tried to smile back. But he was no longer able to do it. He seemed to be in a place outside of himself and looking at what was happening to him. The parachutist was looking at him and saying: *"Vater. Vater."* He tried to straighten up and move toward his canteen next to his bayonet.

At the same time Red came bolting down the staircase. His face suddenly became wild and twisted when he saw Dave lying against his column and the parachutist moving toward his canteen. In a leap Red was next to him and began hitting him in the face with the butt of his rifle

The Long War

until the parachutist no longer had a face. When he saw this Dave tried to move or speak to Red but he couldn't do either. He just saw Red's wild and twisted face that was now tear-streaked, and his mouth was wide and distored as he was running back and forth between Dave and the parachutist. Then other soldiers ran in, a stretcher was found and Dave was put on it. Before they lifted him a soldier put a pressure pack on his wound and taped it tightly. Finally they raised Dave up and began running out of the sun-filled garage with the stretcher.

They were running from one block of apartment houses through another and as they ran, Dave could feel Red's hand. He had taken his left hand and was holding it tightly. His mouth was very wide and distorted and tears were running down his dirt-caked face. Dave could feel the warmth of Red's hand in his and that was good. He was a nice boy, Red. He was a true friend. There were so many things Dave wanted to tell him. But he couldn't. It was out of his control now. He just felt the soldiers running with the stretcher and Red's hand in his and then they were out of the blocks of apartment houses in Ortona and into the bright and dazzling light of day. Dave wanted to hang on and stay with Red. But finally he just couldn't do it anymore.

You can only hang on and do what's right for so long and then you have to let go. You truly have to let go and let someone else do it for you. That's how it is. That's how it always is at the end. And that's how it was now as Dave slipped away from Red and those soldiers and found himself instead on a train making a long slow turn. The train was losing speed and coming and stopping at a small wooden railway station. The station was painted black and the people at the station were also dressed in black. Dave was standing alongside the train and there was a tall and slim blonde-haired girl walking toward him. The girl had a black veil on and was dressed in a magnificent black satin gown with a long black silky train. She was smiling and coming toward him so he could lift her veil and kiss her. But something made Dave step back a little and not kiss her. The girl kept on walking toward him and smiling.

Again Dave moved back a few steps and avoided kissing her. The girl tried a third time and again Dave stepped away from her. Then Dave found himself on the train again and they were were moving across this huge, massive, gigantic country he had come to know so well. They were heading across vast sun-filled wheat fields swaying and rippling in the wind and there was now a cool and soothing breeze blowing through the train and through him. They were moving and speeding past clear sparkling rivers, green rolling fields and valleys, endless hills and distant shores, and sun-swept snow-covered mountains. They were steadily moving and speeding across that huge, massive, gigantic country and as Dave could still feel that cool and soothing breeze blowing through the train and through him, he began easing up inside of himself and letting go a little since they were now moving and speeding across what was, for him, the one, the true, the only good country.

BOOK THIRTEEN

WAITING

CHAPTER 158

Quite some time later Dave began coming out of that huge, massive, gigantic country he had come to know so well and opened his eyes. He found himself looking at three round swaying lights above him. A freckled-faced exhausted nurse was bending over him and saying: "He's coming out of it." A haggard-looking white-masked young doctor now stepped close to him and said: "He's going to be okay." There were booming and thundering noises in the background and Dave looked at the nurse and at the doctor for a moment. Then he drifted into a deep soundless sleep and after a while, there were movements in his sleep. He felt himself being lifted up and then found himself being bumped up and down for a fairly long time.

Dave also felt an incredible weakness within him and that weakness was pulling him toward a line which he didn't want to cross. Finally Dave opened his eyes and found there was sunlight and he was in a plane. There were several wounded stacked up on both sides of the plane and nurses were moving between the stretchers in the aisle and taking care of them. Then Dave felt the plane racing down a runway and in no time they were airborne. Dave felt exhausted and soon drifted into another deep soundless sleep. Every once in a while he opened his eyes and looked at the sunlight in the plane and at the nurses moving across the aisle and helping the wounded. At one point it seemed to him the plane was losing altitude and then straightening up and touching a runway.

At the end of the runway it turned and slowly came to a stop near a hangar. Then the door of the plane was opened and more wounded were put aboard the plane. In a while the plane was full and took off again in the sunlight. It kept on gaining altitude and soon Dave closed his eyes and drifted into another deep soundless sleep. Dave wasn't feeling well. His right side where he had been stabbed seemed to be frozen in a hard core of pain around the hole where the bayonet had gone in. He was now sweating a great deal and his whole body was burning and aching. He also had a terrible headache and had a hard time breathing. Nurses seemed to be around him a great deal and some were giving him injections. Finally, after what seemed a long time, they touched down on another runway and came and stopped near a hangar.

There was a nurse with him all the time now and they took him out of the plane and put him in an ambulance. Other wounded were also put in the ambulance and then it left and seemed to speed north. Dave saw flashes of sunlight through the closed rear doors of the ambulance and also the worried look of the nurse who was with him and wiping the sweat from his face. After a while the ambulance drove in and stopped abruptly in what seemed like a circular courtyard. The doors were opened and Dave's stretcher was lifted out of the ambulance by two big orderlies dressed in white. They rushed him inside a hospital entrance to an elevator. When this elevator came, they went in and took him to one of the upper floors.

When the elevator door opened they brought him to what looked like an operating room and slipped him from his stretcher onto the operating table. A doctor quickly put an oxygen mask on him and soon Dave sank into a deep and impenetrable darkness. He could sense things being done to his wounded side and felt a kind of weakness he had never experienced before. Twice Dave found himself alongside that long train that was stopped at that black railway station with people outside the train also dressed in black. Both times the tall and slim blonde-haired girl in a magnificent black satin gown with a long black silky train came next to him. She was lifting her black veil and smiling and wanted to kiss him. Both times Dave stepped aside and didn't let her do it. Then the train was gone and Dave was left in a sweaty and exhausted darkness.

His right side was very sore and tender and the weakness he felt was so bad it seemed as if his heart was hanging on a string and might snap at any moment. Dave vaguely sensed flashes of darkness, of sunlight, of movement around him and when he finally opened his eyes, he found himself in a large hospital ward. Through the windows at the left end of the ward he could see the dome of St. Paul's Cathedral in the distance. Dave was on the fifth bed on the left side of the ward from the windows and as he looked around, he could see a nurse coming toward him. The nurse was tall and well-built. She had nice round shoulders and seemed to be in her early thirties. She also had pale-brown hair and wore a white cap and a white uniform. When Dave half-rose on his elbows and lay against his pillow, she walked over to him and said: "Ah. You're awake?"

"Yes."

"Good."

"Where am I exactly?"

"This is St. Peter's Hospital."

"Is this St. Paul's Cathedral I see through the windows?"

"It is."

"We're in the heart of London?"

"We are."

Dave didn't say anything for a moment and the nurse said: "How do you feel?"

"Not that well."

"You're a very lucky young man."

"I know."

"For a while, there, the doctors didn't think you'd make it."

"They're not the only ones."

"You had a six-inch stab wound just below the ribs."

"That bad?"

"Yes. And you bled a great deal."

"That I know."

"The bayonet used on you was also rusty."

"How do you know?"

"You developed bad blood poisoning and they had to operate on you a second time."

"How are things now?"

"You should be all right. They stopped the bleeding and took care of the blood poisoning."

"I must tell you I'm not feeling well."

"With the wound you had, you should be grateful you're alive."

"I know."

Again Dave didn't say anything for a moment. Then he said: "Tell me. How did I get here?"

"That's a long story."

"How?"

"Well, you were first operated on in a small hospital in San Vito Chietino. Then you were taken to the Foggia airfield. You were flown from the airfield to Gibraltar. Then from Gibraltar to Croydon. And finally brought to this hospital where they operated on you a second time."

"I must tell you. I feel really terrible."

"I know."

The Long War

"What do I do?"
"Just rest and take it easy."
"That's it?"
"That's it."

CHAPTER 159

The nurse left and Dave soon drifted into a sweaty and uneasy sleep. When he woke up later on in the night a nurse came and checked his pulse and blood pressure. Then she gave him some pills and in the days and weeks that followed, things went pretty well according to a routine. Every two or three days Dave was checked by doctors. They gave him some blood transfusions and took him to the operating room almost every two weeks. In that room they gave him a local anesthetic and checked his wound. Otherwise, during that time, Dave lay in bed and didn't move. He was feeling extremely weak and could hardly sit up. He was exhausted all the time and sweaty and running a small fever.

It was extremely quiet in the ward since most of the officers and soldiers there had received bad wounds. The nurses were quite devoted and checking on them constantly. Time seemed very long for Dave, however, since he couldn't really move and lay in bed sweaty and exhausted. His extreme weakness worried him as well as the fact he had a small headache all the time and was running a slight fever. This caused him to sweat and made all the bones in his body ache. Still, by the middle of February, he began to get a little stronger and was now able to sit in bed. The slight fever he always seemed to have finally left him and he stopped having a headache and sweating and having all his bones ache. The stab wound on his side was healing nicely and the only trace there was of it was a nice thin pink scar where they had operated on him.

Dave's side was just a little sore and tender now and when he began to feel stronger and better, he started to sit up in bed and then go around in a wheel chair. By the beginning of March he was able to shift from the wheel chair to walking around with a cane. His strength was beginning

The Long War

to come back and the nurses on the ward helped him walk around and rebuild his strength. In early April Dave was able to walk around the ward and the grounds of the hospital without a nurse. Then, near the end of the month, on Wednesday, April 26, 1944, on the day before he was to be discharged from the hospital and reassigned, the tall and well-built nurse, with pale-brown hair and nice round shoulders, whose name, Dave had found out, was Nell Gwyn, brought him a comfortable steel chair with a leather bottom so he could sit in it on the left side of his bed and rest when he wanted to.

Nell Gwyn brought him that chair around 9.00 o'clock in the morning, after Dave had dressed, gone to the cafeteria to have breakfast and then come back, and he sat in it. He looked at the bright sunlight sparkling and glittering on the dome of St. Paul's Cathedral and burning into a pale smoldering orange on the right side of it. Dave simply did this for a while and then a tall slim dark-haired British Major-General walked in with a Canadian Colonel and Major. The Major-General talked with Nell at the entrance of the ward for a moment. The nurse turned and pointed to Dave. The Major-General spoke to her again briefly and then left her with the Canadian Colonel and Major and walked over to where Dave was sitting. When he reached him, with the two Canadian officers hanging slightly behind him, the Major-General looked at Dave and said: "Are you Captain David Lindsay?"

"I am," Dave said as he stood up and saluted the three officers who returned his salute. "Good," the Major-General said and told Dave his name was Jeffrey Richards and that he was from the War Office. He added that the two officers who came with him were from the Canadian Corps H.Q. in Leatherhead. Then he said: "Please stand at attention." Dave did that and the Major General reached for an envelope from the inside left pocket of his tunic. He took out a sheet of paper from it and began to read: "To Captain David M. Lindsay, Commanding Officer, C Company, of the Westmount Fusiliers. His Imperial Majesty, King George VI, is pleased to award you the Military Cross. The citation reads: 'For his outstanding courage and bravery in leading his Company in an attack up a 2000-feet cliff in the town of Assoro in Sicily.

"'For his unparalleled leadership and tenacity in helping to repel several attacks by the Germans once his Company was on top of that cliff. For his extraordinary daring and determination in climbing down that cliff in order to go and get supplies and ammunitions for the Companies fighting there. And for his even greater initiative and fearlessness in carrying out the final attack and winning the town from the Germans.'" The Major-General then folded the sheet of paper he was reading and put it back in the envelope he had taken from the inside left pocket of his tunic. He put the envelope back in that pocket and took out the medal from the right pocket of his tunic. He pinned it on the left side of Dave's tunic, shook hands with him and said: "Congratulations."

"Thank you," Dave said. He saluted the Major-General again as well as the two Canadian officers who were standing with him, and they all returned his salute. Then the two Canadian officers also stepped forward, shook hands with him and congratulated him. Finally the Major-General and the two Canadian officers spoke with him for a while before the Major-General took out a folded pale-brown manila envelope from the same inside left pocket of his tunic and handed it to Dave. When he had done that he turned and left with the two Canadian officers. Dave watched them leave and then looked at his Military Cross for a moment before he opened the folded pale-brown manila envelope and looked at what was inside. In it Dave found a notification he had been granted a 21-day leave as of tomorrow with the money that was due to him from his back pay.

On top of that Dave had been given accommodation at the Durham hotel. This was the same hotel where he had gone to drink before in the nice cool dark bar at the back of the lobby. In the envelope there was also a letter from the War Office. Dave read it carefully three times and around 11.00 o'clock, the next morning, he dressed and walked downstairs where he made a phone call to General James S. Wynford. Then he signed his discharge papers and managed to get himself a ride in an ambulance heading toward Paddington Station.

CHAPTER 160

The ambulance that gave Dave a ride was bringing some of the badly wounded officers and soldiers from his ward to the Birksdale Manor in Leighton. This was in Bedford and the ambulance was bringing them there for rest and rehabilitation. When it was ready to leave, around 1.00 o'clock in the afternoon, Dave sat on the front seat with the driver, and they drove away from St. Peter's Hospital and got on Charing Cross Road. It was a bright, sunny and unusually warm late April afternoon and when they got on Charing Cross Road, they headed north until they reached Tottenham Court Road. As Dave sat next to the driver and looked out the window, he saw London looked pretty much as he remembered it: proud, battered and defiant.

There were quite a few bombed-out buildings but the people walking around did not seem to mind nor to be unduly bothered the sights. They moved around briskly and seemed intent on carrying on with their lives and acting as if everything was normal. Dave kept on looking at them and at the city for a while, and on Warren Street they turned left. They turned right on Cleveland Street and then left on Marylebone Street and drove west. Finally they turned left on the Old Marylebone Road and got on Sussex Gardens until they reached Southwick Street. The ambulance driver let Dave out at the corner of Southwick Street and Sussex Gardens. Then he was gone and Dave walked northwestward on Southwick Street past the bombed-out houses at the corner of Southwick Street and Sussex Gardens.

The sun was very hot on his shoulders and when he reached the middle of Southwick Street, he stopped and couldn't get over it. The drab three-story gray-bricked building where Barbara Bradford had lived was gone

Waiting

and so were the next two buildings. Instead there was just a flat empty lot covered by gravel. Dave stood there and looked at this lot for a while and then crossed the street and walked up the short stony steps of the house facing the lot. On the landing Dave rang the front-door bell and not long after, the door opened. A short heavy-set woman with curly gray hair and a pleasant ruddy face stood in front of him and said: "Yes?"

"Can you tell me what happened to the houses across the street?"

"Why?"

"I'm a friend of Barbara Bradford."

"You don't know?"

"No."

"That's surprising."

"I've been fighting overseas. I just came back."

"It was tragic, Captain. Very tragic."

"What happened?"

"Well, on Friday, February 18 of this year, to be exact, around 7.00 o'clock in the evening, a terrible accident happened."

Dave looked at the woman and she said: "The reason I remember the date so well is because it was such a terrible accident."

"What accident?"

"Well, a squadron of Wellington bombers were on their way from Biggin Hill to one of our aerodromes in the north."

"And?"

"As a matter of fact, they were on their way to Dyce near Aberdeen in Scotland."

"Go on."

"Well, as they were flying over us, one of the bombers lost a motor and then fell like a stone from the sky."

"That quickly?"

"Yes."

"So?"

"So it happened so suddenly no one had time to bail out. The plane just came down unbelievably quickly and hit the house where Barbara lived."

"Barbara was in it?"

"Yes. She had just come back that afternoon from her work at Croydon."

"What happened?"

"The plane hit her house head-on and there was a huge explosion."

"Did anyone survive?"

"No."

"What about the people in the other two houses?"

"No one survived."

"I see."

"We were told the plane had a full load of fuel. That's why there was such a tremendous explosion."

Dave didn't say anything for a moment and the woman said: "It was sad. Very sad."

Again Dave didn't say anything and the woman said: "We were told the plane suffered from mechanical failure."

Dave nodded and the woman went on: "When the plane hit there was this tremendous explosion followed by a huge fire."

"I see."

"It took three days for the firemen to put out the fire."

"How come the lot is flat and there's no rubble?"

"Well, there was so much fuel everywhere the firemen said it was dangerous. They had the rubble taken away and cleaned the area."

"You're sure Barbara was in the building?"

"Oh yes, Captain. She was positively identified as well as the 14 other victims."

"What did they do with the bodies?"

"There was a huge funeral at St. Justin's Church. The Archbishop of Canterbury came down and officiated himself."

"I see."

"Barbara's mother also came from Oxford. It was very sad."

"I can imagine."

"This is not a lucky street. A few years ago we had another block of houses bombed out at the corner of Sussex Gardens."

Dave stood on the landing and the woman looked closely at him: "May I ask you what was your relationship with Barbara, Captain?"

"I was a friend."

"I see."

"A very good friend."

"It's funny. She never mentioned you."

"She was discreet."

"Yes. She was."

CHAPTER 161

Dave thanked the woman for talking to him and walked down the short stony steps of her house. He crossed the street and made for the empty lot covered by gravel. Dave stepped on that lot and walked a few feet before he stopped. He stood there and looked at the houses on both sides, at the sky and at the lot itself. He could feel the sun hot and warm on his shoulders and pawed a little at the gravel with his right foot. He felt a dull throbbing pain in his right shoulder blade and a sharp stabbing twinge in his right side. Dave stood there for the longest of time and then turned and slowly left the lot. He walked northwestward on Southwick Street until he turned left and headed southwestward on Star Street. He turned right on Norfolk Place and then left on Praed Street and made for the Paddington Station.

  At the station Dave walked down the long underground staircase and took a train heading east. There were not too many people on the train and Dave sat in one of the sideways seat with his eyes half-closed. He was sweating slightly and wiping his forehead and when they finally reached the Charing Cross Station, he got up and walked out of the station. Outside, his eyes hurt for a while in the bright dazzling sunlight as Dave walked northeastward on Northumberland Avenue until he reached the War Office. When he reached it Dave took out the letter he had received and showed it to one of the armed sentries who was guarding the sandbagged entrance. The sentry nodded and Dave stepped past him and rang the front door buzzer. In no time the front door opened and Dave showed the letter to the skinny red-haired porter who had opened it.

  The porter took it and left with Dave. He brought him to the front desk in the large entrance hall where he handed the letter to a tall thin lieutenant who sat at this desk. The Lieutenant looked at it for a moment and then picked up the phone. He spoke briefly into it and then handed the letter back to Dave. Dave put it in the left pocket of his tunic and in no time a young slim Captain showed up and took Dave through the same security procedures he had gone through before when he had been at the War Office. He escorted him to a tall blond-haired Captain who sat at a desk next to Major-General James S. Wynford's office on the fifth floor. This Captain also asked to see the letter and then pressed a buzzer underneath his desk. In a moment the large leather-padded door to the right of it opened and Dave stepped past it.

It closed soundlessly behind him and Dave saw General Wynford sat at his massive mahogany desk and was on the phone. With his superbly-tailored uniform, his impeccably-polished Sam Browne belt he was wearing, his tall and slender build, his deep even tan, his thick well-combed gray hair and trim gray-white mustache, the General looked as handsome as ever. The only difference was his face and neck were now cris-crossed with slight lines of fatigue. When Dave came in, after they had exchanged salutes, the General motioned for him to come and sit in the huge mahogany chair facing his desk. Dave came and sat in this chair and when the General had finished talking on the phone, he hung up and said: "My dear David. How are you?"

"Fine, thank you. Sir."

"I must tell you I've heard some very nice things about you."

"Don't believe everything you hear, Sir."

"No, no. First you won the Military Medal. And now the Military Cross. That's quite impressive."

"Thank you."

"And I've also appreciated the kind letters you sent me."

"That was the least I could do."

"Well, that was very nice."

"It was nothing, Sir. Believe me."

"Now. What can I do for you?"

Dave reached into the left pocket of his tunic and took out the folded letter from the War Office. He handed it to him and the General looked at it for a few moments before he returned it to him.

"Ah, yes. Your letter from the War Office."

"That's it."

"What of it?"

"General, I don't want to go back home."

"My dear boy. There's nothing I can do."

"General, I believe you can help me."

Waiting

"What can I do?"

"You can help me return to my Regiment."

"My dear boy. You're a much-decorated war hero and an officer. The Army has better uses for you."

"What better uses?"

"My dear David. You're a born leader who can inspire people. That's how the Army sees you and wants to use you."

"By going back to Canada?"

"That's right. By speaking to people there and becoming a high-ranking officer."

"General, I don't want to become a high-ranking officer."

"What do you want to do?"

"I want to go back to my Regiment."

"Ah, the officer with a Field Marshal's mind who wants to remain a simple officer."

"That's right."

"Can't you see the absurdity of your reasoning?"

"What's so absurd about it?"

"No one with your talents has the right to settle for such a small role."

"General, it's not such a small role."

"Oh yes it is."

"General, I beg to differ."

"At any rate this whole discussion is pretty pointless."

"Why?"

"My dear David. Regulation 1214 forbids it."

"General, I don't care about Regulation 1214."

"You should. It has been worked out at the insistence of your Chief of Staff, your own government, and our own Chief of the Imperial General Staff."

"So?"

"So it states any Canadian officer or soldier who has been severely wounded twice must be returned home."

"General, I don't want to return to Canada."

"Why not?"

"I just don't want to."

"My dear boy. Can't you see if you persist in this, it will only end in death."

"General, that's a risk I'm willing to take."

"That's a very poor reasoning."

"Maybe."

"And a very selfish one, I might add."
"Maybe. But that's one I'm willing to take."
"Why?"
"I don't know. I just have to, Sir."
"Why?"
"I can't explain it, Sir. But I must finish what I started."
"You *will* finish what you started."
"No, Sir. I must do it on my own terms."
"Well, I'm sorry. The Regulation is quite clear."
"What does that mean?"
"It means there's nothing I can do."
"Sure there is, Sir."
"No. There isn't."
"Sure there is, Sir. I know there is."

General Wynford sighed deeply and the slight lines of fatigue now showed clearly on his face and neck.

"What do you want me to do?"
"Find a way for me to get back to my Regiment."
"Regulation 1214 states clearly you can't."
"I'm sure you can find a way around that, Sir."

General Wynford sighed deeply again and said: "There's only one man who can do that so we do not end up with a military or political problem."

"Who?"
"General Haworth."
"Where is he?"
"In London."
"What's he doing here?"
"He's working on the invasion plans for Montgomery."
"Can you give him a call?"
"I can."
"Will you?"
"I will."

CHAPTER 162

The General then told Dave he would call General Haworth to try and set up a meeting. He asked Dave to come and see him at 9.00 o'clock tomorrow morning so he could tell him how they were going to proceed. Then he picked up his black phone and told the tall blond-haired Captain outside to give Dave a red pass for the morning. When the General hung up Dave got up and saluted him. The General returned his salute and Dave turned and left the office. Outside, the tall blond-haired Captain handed him a red pass and walked down the hallway with him to the elevator. They both took it to the ground floor and walked together past the entrance hall to the front door.

 The Captain held the door open for him and Dave thanked him and stepped out. On Northumberland Avenue Dave slowly walked west toward the Charing Cross Station. The sun was very hot and warm on his shoulders and when he finally reached the station, Dave went down the long underground staircase and took a train heading west. He got out at the Green Park Station and walked west on Piccadilly until he reached the Officers' Club in the Park Lane Hotel. The club was full of officers from the 2nd and 3rd Infantry Divisions and Dave sat in a corner of the bar and had a beer. He didn't know any of them and when he finished, he left and went to have a good Chinese meal in Soho. After the meal Dave walked over to Leicester Square and went to see a first-run movie.

 This was a war movie and it turned out to be as long and boring as the last one he had seen more than two years ago. Once it was over Dave left the theater and headed toward the Durham hotel. By then, close to 10.00 o'clock in the evening, there was a nice breeze blowing and the sky was clear and full of stars. Dave walked slowly and leisurely in order to enjoy the evening and when he reached the Durham, he stopped by the front desk and picked up the key for his room. Then he went to sit in the cool dark bar at the back of the lobby and ordered a gin and bitter lemon. His right shoulder blade and right side were still hurting and Dave sat at the back of the bar and slowly drank his gin and bitter lemon. He ordered a couple more but found he couldn't really drink. His right shoulder blade and right side were hurting too much and after a while Dave left the bar and took the elevator to his room on the fifth floor.

In his room Dave undressed and lay in bed. But he found he couldn't sleep either. He was sweating a little and lay in bed and stared at the darkness as he wiped the sweat from his forehead. Dave lay awake most of the night and around 6.00 o'clock in the morning, he shaved and took a long shower. Then he dressed and took the elevator downstairs where he went and had some breakfast in the hotel's dining-room in the lobby. Dave drank some tea and ate a couple of English muffins with jam. Finally he left the Durham and got on Pall Mall. It was another bright, sunny, late April morning and Dave headed east toward Northumberland Avenue. When he got there Dave walked on the northern side of it and at the War Office, he showed his red pass to one of the two armed sentries and stepped to the front door.

Dave rang the buzzer and in no time it was opened. A tall thin porter took his pass and, at the entrance, he was put through the same security procedures as before. A tall and slender Captain escorted him to the fifth-floor desk next to Major-General James S. Wynford's office. The Captain sitting at the desk pressed a buzzer underneath it and motioned for Dave to step past the large leather-padded door to the right of the desk. The door opened and, inside, Dave found General Wynford sitting behind his massive mahogany desk and working on some papers. Dave exchanged salutes with him and the General said: "My dear boy. It's been arranged. General Hayworth will see you now." The General picked up his black phone and spoke briefly into it. In no time the leather-padded door opened and the Captain at the desk came in.

The General told him to take Dave to General Hayworth's office and, after they had exchanged salutes once more, Dave left the office with the Captain. The Captain led him down the hallway until they neared the end of it. Three doors from the end the Captain motioned for Dave to go into an office on the same side as General Wynford's office. Dave opened the door and went in. He found himself in a fairly spacious one with a big desk near the windows and a chair behind and another one facing the desk. There were two large easels on each side of the desk and on those easels were large-scale maps of the northern coast of France. Behind the desk

Waiting

and the chair facing the desk stood a long table with several magnified maps on it that showed certaim sections of the northern coast of France.

General Hayworth was sitting behind the big desk and studying one of the large-scale maps. The heavy red damask curtains behind the desk were closed and the office was lit by two high-stemmed modern-looking floor lamps on either side of the desk. When Dave came in he put down the map he was studying and looked at him. Dave exchanged salutes with him and as he stood in front of him, Dave saw, with his blond hair and tall slim build, he still looked as handsome and impressive as ever. There was a quality about him that made him look bold and daring and it was reinforced by the superb cut of the uniform he was wearing and by the sharp and intent look he was giving him. As he stood in front of him Dave also noticed something else about General Haworth. His uniform was impeccably pressed and Dave saw that on the tabs of his open-necked khaki shirt a Pip had now been added to his Crossed Swords.

This meant he had been promoted to Lieutenant-General.

CHAPTER 163

General Hayworth motioned for Dave to come and sit down in the chair facing him. Dave nodded and after he had stepped up to that chair and settled into it, the General said: "Ah, David. How are you?"

"Fine, thank you. Sir."

"Good."

"May I congratulate you, Sir, on your promotion. I see you're now a Lieutenant-General."

"You may. And the same goes for you. You won the Military Cross."

"Thank you."

"That was quite a feat you did."

"I only did my duty."

"Still. That was quite impressive."

"Thank you. Sir."

The General didn't say anything for a moment and then said: "Now. What can I do for you?"

"Did General Wynford talk to you about me?"

"He did."

"Then you know why I'm here."

"I do."

Again the General didn't say anything and then said: "Why do you want to go back to your Regiment?"

"I just have to, Sir."

"Why?"

"I have to fight this war to the end.

"You *are* fighting this war to the end."

"I must do it with my Regiment. And with my Company."

Waiting

"Why?"

"I don't know. I just have to."

"Do you understand what you're saying?"

"I do."

"If you go on like this you'll probably end up dead."

"I don't think so."

"You will."

Dave didn't say anything and the General said: "Something else bothers me about your request."

"What?"

"You're trying to force the way your career is going."

"I'm not doing that."

"Oh yes you are."

"No. I'm not."

"You certainly are. And that's never a good thing."

"How am I doing that?"

"You're trying to play a much smaller role than what you're entitled to."

"I'm not."

"Yes you are."

"How?"

"You have a fine mind and a rare sense of leadership."

"So?"

"So you don't want to make use of those gifts."

"Sure I do."

"No you don't. You persist in wanting to be a simple officer when you should try and become a high-ranking one."

"I told General Wynford. I don't want to become a high-ranking officer."

"That's just the point. You should."

"Why should I? Look at you, Sir. With General Horrocks, you're the fighting Generals of Montgomery. Well, I want to be the fighting Captain of my Company. What's wrong with that?"

"There's nothing wrong with it."

"What's the point then?"

"The point is what I'm doing has come about naturally."

"And what I want to do doesn't?"

"No. You're trying to force things."

"I'm not."

"Yes, you are. You don't let them happen naturally."

"Are you trying to tell me going along with Regulation 1214 is the way to act?"

"I am."

"I don't agree."

"I know you don't."

Dave didn't say anything and the General suddenly looked closely and intently at him. He looked at him like this for a long moment and then said: "You see, I believe there's something else in all this."

"What?"

"I believe, underneath all this, you're trying to deal with something that has nothing to do with what we're talking about."

"What do you mean?"

"I don't know. But let me tell you something about a man like you."

"What?"

"You simply cannot avoid your responsibilities and settle for a role that, for you, is way too small and insignificant."

"What does that mean?"

"It means you have to accept the responsibilities of your gifts."

"And that means?"

"Look at Pilsudski. You told me in Algiers what a great man you thought he was and how much you admired him. Well, he made himself a Field Marshal and worked hard all his life to create a modern Poland."

"What has this got to do with me?"

"It means, for people like you, you must accept the responsibilities of your gifts."

"Don't you think that's stretching it a bit?"

"Not at all. Every gifted man has to act like that."

"Well, I don't think I'm quite ready to do that."

"You should be. You have rare gifts and you should be willing to act on them."

Dave didn't say anything and the General said: "You're an officer and a much-decorated war hero. You must keep on acting that way."

"I never said I wouldn't."

"I know you didn't."

"So?"

"So leading people in battle is an art. You must always keep on doing this."

"I know that."

"As an officer you should always try to improve and have the skill and knowledge of a high-ranking officer."

"I understand."

"Look at your own Generals. Your most gifted one is so cold he is mostly feared and disliked. Your other high-ranking one is such a careerist he has had little time to learn military skills. And the one I like best thinks you must swear like a dock worker in order to be one. This is not the way to lead."

Dave nodded and the General said: "Remember. The higher you go in an Army, the more soldiers you'll have under your command."

"I know that."

"That means you must always care and be willing to die for them, if necessary."

"I think I've shown that."

"I know you have."

Dave didn't say anything and the General said: "Promise me one thing."

"What?"

"Promise me you'll do that."

"Of course."

"And promise me you'll keep on doing it more and more."

"I promise."

"It's only on these conditions I'll authorize your return to your Regiment."

"Don't worry. I will."

"If you do that, your career will still go on naturally and I believe you'll be called upon to do great things."

"I understand."

"All right. In that case you can go back to your Company. I've spoken to your Colonel and cleared it with him."

"Thank you, Sir."

"You understand by doing this you'll have to forget about your 21-day leave."

"I do, Sir."

"All right, then. You can go back. It's been cleared."

CHAPTER 164

The General then picked up the phone on the right side of his desk and spoke into it briefly. In no time the same tall blond-haired Captain who had brought Dave to General Haworth's office came in and General Haworth asked him to let Dave out of the building. The Captain nodded and Dave got up and saluted the General. The General returned his salute and Dave left with the Captain. Together they took the elevator to the ground floor and the Captain led him to the front door and held it open for him. Dave thanked him and stepped out. It was now very bright and sunny outside and Dave crossed Northumberland Avenue and hailed a taxi. They soon got on Whitehall, Parliament Street, Bridge Street before they crossed the Westminster Bridge, turned left on York Road and reached the Waterloo station.

At the station Dave rushed to one of the wickets and bought a ticket since the train for Aldershot was about to leave. It was crowded with all kinds of military personnel and civilians and as soon as Dave got on it, it began pulling out. Now that Dave knew he was going back to his Regiment he began feeling better somehow. He still had a dull throbbing pain in his right shoulder blade and a sharp stabbing twinge in his right side. But the pain was not so piercing and acute and Dave stood in the corridor, that was full of soldiers, airmen and sailors, and looked out of the small dusty window at the sunny countryside as they went through well-known and familiar places like Lambeth, Wandsworth, Weybridge, Woking, Brookwood and Farnborough before, a little over an hour later, they finally reached the town of Aldershot.

At the station Dave got off and took a taxi to the training center. When they finally reached it Dave paid the driver and walked into the Main

Waiting

Administrative Building. In that building he found out the Regiment had moved back into the same barracks they had used twice before. They were taking the place of the 41st Infantry Division from Liverpool that had been sent to Italy. Dave then left the Main Administrative Building and headed for the Regimental barrack in order to find Colonel Cantwell. This barrack was to the the right of the Fusiliers' barracks. It was near the end of the first row of barracks in the training center and when Dave reached it, he went in. Inside there was the same big husky Corporal at the entrance desk Dave had seen earlier before he had gone to Sicily.

His name, Dave now found out, was Jim Johnson, and Dave asked him to see the Colonel. Johnson nodded and got up from his desk. He walked to the closed door of the Colonel's office and knocked. This door was to the right of the barrack and then he went in. When he came out he told Dave to go in and that the Colonel would presently see him. Dave nodded and walked to the Colonel's office. He stepped in and saw the Colonel was sitting behind his desk. Dave exchanged salutes with him and the Colonel told him to close the door and come and sit in the chair facing his desk. Dave nodded. He closed the door behind him and, after he had come and sat in front of the Colonel, he saw he looked as sharp and trim as ever.

But now there was some gray in his neat, well-trimmed, dark-brown hair and his cold, icy, blue eyes were no longer so cold and icy. They were rimmed with slight wrinkles of fatigue. The Colonel waited until Dave had sat in front of him and then said: "Well, David. I must say I didn't expect seeing you here."

"I'm sure you didn't, Colonel."

"I must tell you I was a little surprised when General Hayworth called."

"I'm sure you were."

"What's the matter? Don't you want to get out of this war?"

"Of course."

"What gives then?"

"Let's just say going back home and making speeches about the war is not what I wanted."

"You want to be a line officer."

"That's right."

"That's not a very smart choice."

"Maybe. But that's what I want."

"Not that I object, mind you. I can sure use you."

"Good."

The Colonel didn't say anything for a moment and then said: "Tell me. How do you feel?"

The Long War

"Fine."
"Are you fully recovered from your wounds?"
"Yes, Sir."
"And you're all shipshape and ready to go?"
"Yes, Sir."
"God knows I can use you."
"That's good."
"B Company's not an easy Company to handle."
"I know that."
"In fact, you're about the only officer who's been able to do it."
"Thank you, Sir."
"And God knows it really needs some handling."
"I'm sure."
"Trust me. It does."
"Who was taking care of it last?"
"Lieutenant Jack Norris."
"What happened to him?"
"He got killed by sniper fire near the Piazza Municipali."
"When?"
"On December 28."
"The Germans sure had a lot of snipers in Ortona."
"They did."
"We were never able to get a good grip on them."
"Let's just say a citizens' Army's not very good at that."
"At least we tried."
"That we did."
"Who took care of the Company after Norris?"
"Bostwick."
"How did he do?"
"Okay."
"Bostwick always does well."
"Bostwick's Bostwick.'"

Dave didn't say anything for a moment and then said: "When did we win in Ortona?"
"On December 28."
"What happened then?"
"We went on and took Point 59."
"And after that?"
"We suspended operations."
"Why?"
"We were a spent force."

"That bad?"
"Oh yes."
"How bad?"
"All our companies were down to forty percent."
"That's pretty bad."
"It is."
"Can't fight at those rates."
"No. We still had the fighting spirit. But not the manpower."
"But we won. That's the main thing."
"We did."
"When did we come back to Aldershot?"
"We sailed out of Italy on April 10. And got here on April 20."
Dave nodded and then said: "What happens now?"
"We're here to rebuild the Division up to strength."
"Do we have the replacements for that?"
"It wasn't easy. But we do."
"Good."
"We have to make them fit with the veterans."
"That's not going to be easy."
"It's not. And we have to do it in record time."
"Why?"
"The big show is coming up and I believe we're going to be in the thick of it."
"As an elite assault Regiment?"
"That's right."
"How are we going to be used?"
"I think for the rest of the war we'll be assigned to the 2rd and 3nd Infantry Divisions. We might even be assigned to British units on some operations. On still others we might be operating with other Canadian Divisions or on our own."
"Still the Firemen's Brigade."
"That's it. That's why it's critical for you to get hold of the Company quickly and bring it to full operational strength."
"How much time do I have?"
"My guess is a month or a month and a half. Then the big show will go on."
"That's not much time."
"It's not."

CHAPTER 165

The Colonel then told Dave to get going and wished him luck with the Company. Dave thanked him and got up. He saluted him and the Colonel returned the salute. Dave turned and left the Colonel's office and when he was outside, he walked over to the officers' barrack to the right of the Regimental barrack and settled down again in what used to be Major Wilson's living quarters. This didn't take long and then he left and walked over to B Company's Orderly room. The Orderly Room was in a barrack to the left of the Regimental barrack and his office was to the right of it. When he reached it he called in his office the Company Clerk, Tom Taylor, who didn't seem too surprised at his being back and Bostwick, who, this time, seemed oddly happy at his taking over the Company again.

Dave told them what he wanted from them and then got down to train the Company and get it ready for the big show. The Colonel had been right. Although it had been difficult, Canadian Army Headquarters had brought the Regiment back to full strength again. Now that he had all the replacements he needed Dave began the complicated task of trying to make them into good and efficient soldiers. The savage fighting at Ortona had cut down the strength of the Company to just below forty percent and he began taking all those new recruits and trying to mold them into tough and smart infantry soldiers. However, the results didn't turn out quite as he had expected. That Friday afternoon, after he had seen the Colonel, Tom Taylor and Bostwick, and in the days and weeks that followed, Dave began training the Company by Sections and Platoons and in combined assault operations involving two or more Companies.

The focus was on speed, toughness and endurance and the emphasis on weaponry, tactics and flexibility. When Dave began working with those

Waiting

new recruits he saw it wouldn't be so easy to make them one with the veterans of the Regiment. Those veterans had been in Dieppe, Sicily and Italy. They had seen what war can do to soldiers and weren't interested in becoming too friendly with recruits who had no idea of what was coming. As he worked and tried to bring those recruits and veterans together Dave saw the Company and the Regiment had changed since Ortona. It had become more wary, watchful and close-mouthed. And this was especially true of the First Platoon.

Since the death of Gennaro and Jack Norris, who had been replaced by the Platoon Sergeant, Norm Moran, who had been promoted to Lieutenant in his place, it had stayed close together and did not particularly welcome any new friendships or acquaintances. As a result the veteran soldiers of the Company carried out the training program Dave had laid out for them. But they only did this with the strict minimum of effort and energy that was required. Like all Armies and soldiers who had long been in the field they brought to their training a kind of tired and resigned performance. They had been in combat. They knew what was needed and expected of them. And they had no intention of putting into their training any effort and energy that went beyond the strict minimum.

This led to Dave ending up with two distinct groups within the same Company. First you had the veterans who were making sure they were carrying out their training program properly and efficiently but with not an ounce of commitment and dedication more than was absolutely necessary. And then you had the recruits. The recruits were quite serious, eager and enthusiastic. But they didn't receive any help from the veterans. This made for two distinct groups and Dave wondered how these two groups would do as a Company when they would be thrown into action in the big show everyone knew was coming. With this in mind, and as the days and weeks went on, Dave trained and drove the men hard and made sure the new recruits were at least familiar with the weaponry they would encounter and with the tactics the Germans were most likely to use.

The new men followed his training program eagerly and enthusiastically and the veterans did their work coolly and efficiently. Still the split between the veterans and the recruits of the Company remained. But this was a problem, Dave found out, that wasn't his alone. The other Company COs in the Regiment, Tom Clark, Bob Brown and Bill Blair, also had it. Veteran soldiers and new reinforcements, it seemed, did not mix well. Also Dave had the added burden of wondering how these fresh recruits would do in battle. It was one thing to train in Aldershot. It was another to fight the Germans on the battlefield. In the face of all this Dave trained and worked

The Long War

his men harder than ever and after a while, the split that existed between the veterans and the recruits in the Company began lessening a little.

The veterans slowly began coming out of their close-mouthed aloofness and helping the new men and Dave thought if he could get a few more weeks he would be able to bring the men together. But he didn't get a few more weeks. On Friday morning, at 10.00 a.m., June 2, 1944, five weeks after the men had been training in Aldershot, Bedford trucks came for them. The men were put on board with their full gear and the trucks left Aldershot and began heading southwest. They drove down the large highway past Farnham, Alton, New Alresford, Winchester, Eastleigh until they reached the coast and the port of Southhampton. Near the coast the trucks slowed down as they ran into convoy after convoy heading for the port.

In Southampton the men were taken off the Bedford trucks. They were led to the docks and put on tenders which took them to their troop transport anchored in the Southampton waters. Their troop transport was the *H.M.S. Glengyle* and was the same transport that had taken them to their landing in Sicily. Once on board the Regiment was given quarters in one of the cargo holds and when Dave went topside in the early evening, he saw the Southampton waters were filled for miles with white-and-gray destroyers, frigates, monitors, minesweepers, assault boats, troop ships, gun boats, landing crafts and other surface vessels and that different units were still being taken by tenders to various troop transports according to pre-set loading tables. This loading of troops went on all day Saturday and on Sunday, June 4, 1944, the day dawned gray and overcast.

There was a strong wind blowing right down the Solent from the white-capped channel and the sea was rough and heavy. Even though at anchor, ships were heaving up and down in the Southampton waters and, around noon, when Dave went topside again and stood on deck, the signal was flashed to the fleet: *"Twenty-four hours postponement."* Dave left the deck and went back to the cargo hold to be with his men and, late the next morning, when he went topside once more to get a breath of fresh air, he saw the wind had begun to die down a little and that the sea had become a little less stormy. But the day was again gray and overcast and there was a pretty stiff gale blowing down the channel. The ships still kept on heaving up and down at anchor and as Dave stood on the deck and kept on looking at the Solent, he saw the Colonel also come on deck to get a breath of fresh air and tell him the news.

The invasion was on.

BOOK FOURTEEN

FRANCE

CHAPTER 166

Dave went back down the cargo hold to tell the news to his men and at 4.00 o'clock in the afternoon, the *H.M.S. Glengyle* raised anchor and began slipping down the Southampton waters. The day was gray and overcast and a strong wind was still blowing in from the channel. They sailed slowly by the Isle of Wight on the starboard side and in the distance Southampton looked flat, gray and sprawling under its balloon barrage. All around them were assault and cargo ships stretching for miles in the channel and destroyers were moving up and down through them and screening them as they were sailing toward the lanes that would take them to France. After a while England faded on the horizon and all you could see everywhere were ships heading south to France under a gray and heavy sky.

The sea was rough and the *H.M.S. Glengyle* rolled and pitched as they headed south. They kept on sailing toward France and when darkness came, Dave, who had gone up to the deck for a breath of fresh air, saw the sky had turned pitch-black. The wind was worse than ever and a cold and chilly rain was falling. Since it was such an awful night and that he could barely make out the outline of the other ships around him, Dave left the deck and went back down to the cargo hold where the men of his Company were gathered. Most of them were lying on their bunks and studying the maps and aerial photographs they had been given the day before for their assignment. Some were simply resting. Others were cleaning their weapons. But all of them had been briefed extensively when the Colonel had come in around 10.00 a.m., yesterday morning, and told them where they were going.

As part of the 3rd Canadian Division, the Colonel had told them, the Regiment was going to land on Juno Beach at Courseulles as an assault

Regiment in support of the Regina Rifles in the attack on the town. The Regiment would be on the left flank of the Regina Rifles and both Regiments would be backed by the tanks of the 1st Hussars from London, Ontario. Both Regiments would also have assault engineers in order to increase their firepower. They would attack to the east of the inlet and the Seulles river and the Royal Winnipeg Rifles were to assault the beach and sand dunes to the west of it. A Company of Canadian Scottish from Victoria would also go in as support of the Royal Winnipeg Rifles on their right flank. The time of the landing would be just before 8.00 a.m. and would be preceded by a massive bombing from medium and heavy bombers from the Royal Air Force and the United States Army Air Force.

At times more than 1,000 planes would be involved in the bombing of targets, the Colonel had told them. Once the bombing was done a huge artillery program from six Artillery Regiments would be put on before the attack would go in. The Normandy invasion, that was called operation *Overlord* and that, on the first day, would involve the landing of over 150,000 Allied ground and airborne troops, would take place in three sectors, the Colonel had explained. The Canadians would be attacking in the center. The British would be on their left. And the Americans on their right. The Canadian sector was four and a half mile wide and the Fusiliers and the Reginas would be attacking on the western side of it or on the right. They would be part of the 1st Canadian Army under General Harry Crerar and General Guy Simonds would be in charge of the 2nd Canadian Corps

The Colonel had gone on for quite a while briefing them and outlining the operation. Then he had wished them luck and left. This had been yesterday, however, and now that he was back with his men, Dave sat on his bunk and studied the maps and aerial photographs they had been given. Then he lay down and tried to sleep. But he was too tense and edgy and after a while, he just lay on his bunk with his eyes closed and tried to rest. Some time later he fell into a fitful and uneasy sleep and at 4.00 a.m., the ship loudspeaker system suddenly came alive with the voice of an officer calling groups by serial numbers to transfer to their boat stations. Dave got up and took the Company topside, fully-loaded, to the three assault landing crafts that had been assigned to them.

Each craft, that were also known as LCAs, could take in 30 men and Dave got in the first LCA with the First Platoon. The craft was slung on davits over the rolling sea and when it was lowered and hit the water, it smashed with a loud bang against the side of the *H.M.S. Glengyle* before it was taken out in the swell and began heading away from the ship. The sea was still rough and heavy and as the men stood tightly packed in their

LCA, they were drenched by the spray from it. Their assault landing craft moved away from the *H.M.S. Glengyle* and joined hundreds of other crafts bobbing in the sea and trying to get to their start line for their assault on the French coast. Since the Fusiliers were landing on the western side of the Canadian Sector with the Regina Rifles, they had the least distance to cover and by 6.00 a.m., they had finally joined the other LCAs that were part of the assault formation going in to Courseulles.

By then it was getting light and Dave could finally see the coast of France on the horizon. It rose in front of him as a thin dark strip of land against a cloudy and dark-gray sky and when it began to get lighter, the whole channel seemed to fill with a gigantic booming noise as medium and heavy bombers from the Royal Air Force and the United States Army Air Force came over and began hitting their targets. They flew across the channel in a huge stream from England and the whole coast in front of Dave burst out in racing lines of white-orange and gray-green explosions. Then the planes were gone and at 6.30 a.m., the whole fleet began firing on the coast.

The firing was massive and deafening and by that time the crafts in Dave's attack formation were about ten miles from their target. The wind had now died down considerably but the sea was still rough and heavy. The day was gray and overcast and when they got closer to the coast, Dave began seeing the church spire of Courseulles to the right of the town. The water tower was behind the town itself and on the left, he could see reinforced houses running from the railway station near the inlet down almost to the sand dunes. He could also see the Seulles river past the sand dunes and, beyond the town, green rolling fields. There were some small neat woods in those fields and he could make out narrow roads leading from the coast toward Caen and Bayeux.

The town of Courseulles was becoming clear and visible by now and at 7.30 a.m., the LCAs in Dave's attack formation lined themselves up on it and began making their run-in for the beach.

CHAPTER 167

Dave's LCA was the first in the formation heading for Courseulles. It was on the right side of it, and the formation was made up of 30 boats who were spread out in three lines of 10 boats each. When they were one mile from the beach huge water fountains began bursting all around them and they could hear mortar and machine-gun fire. Then their LCA cleared the under-water obstacles and began heading for the beach between the hedgerows. Not long after the ramp went down and the men in the LCA came barreling out. There was about 200 yards from the slightly-rising beach to the barbed wire and the sand dunes and as Dave began running toward the wire, he couldn't believe how much firing there was on the beach.

German 88s, rifles, Schmeissers, MG 34s, 42s and mortars were hitting and raking it, and all around him Dave could hear the screams of soldiers who had lost a leg, an arm, had been hit in the head or shot through the chest or legs. These soldiers screamed as they fell and lay bleeding and dying on the beach and when Dave reached the wire, he saw Slav and Meyer had made it before him. Slav and Meyer were lying down and cutting the wire and behind them tanks of the Ist Hussars were landing and firing point-blank at gun bunkers and trenches beyond the sand dunes. There was a lot of smoke and dust in the air and in no time, Slav and Meyer had made a hole through the wire. As soon as the hole had been cut Dave sent the men of the First Platoon on both side of the wire in order to get into the sand dunes and hit the trenches.

On his right flank Dave could see the men of the Regina Rifles doing the same thing. Those men had also cut a hole through the wire and were getting into their side of the trenches. Beyond the sand dunes the Germans had several lines of trenches and the men of Dave's First Platoon, now reinforced by the Second, Third and Fourth Platoons, began getting into those trenches and clearing them. They threw hand grenades and fired their machine-guns. At times they used their bayonets or the butts of their rifles. But slowly the men of B Company began clearing them. Once in a while they had to do it with bayonets or in fierce hand-to-hand combat and Dave used his riflemen and Bren-gunners to fire at any German who wanted to fight and didn't want to surrender.

The tanks of the 1st Hussars had now all landed and were moving up and down the beach. They were firing at the openings in gun bunkers and taking on machine-gun nests and gun positions beyond the town. Our own self-propelled artillery had also landed and was giving support to the Company by firing at any target they could see. In the area assaulted by Dave's Company the Germans had set up five lines of trenches. Those trenches were beyond the sand dunes and Dave had to deal with each line of trench in turn while some of the men from the Company helped the assault engineers in throwing satchel charges through the openings of various gun bunkers and blowing them up. Others were taking on the snipers and machine-gunners who seemed to be everywhere in the trenches.

This made for slow, deadly and nerve-racking work and Dave was surprised to see how well the Germans were fighting. On his part of the beach they were facing the German 716th Infantry Division. This Division was supposed to be second-rate, yet each one of its soldiers was fighting smartly, fiercely and fanatically. Dave kept on pushing and leading the Company and by 10.00 o'clock in the morning, the men had cleared the five lines of trenches in their section and were now ready to move on to the second part of their assignment. This was to take on a line of five reinforced houses which stood near the railway station by the inlet and ran into the sand dunes. By then Dave had reached the end of a trench that stood near the side of the first of those houses.

Dave looked at that side through his binoculars and then met with his assault engineers in order to work out a plan of attack. Next he sent a runner to a tank of the 1st Hussars that stood in the sand dunes with four other tanks behind it. When he reached that tank the runner told the driver what Dave wanted. The driver nodded and took a mike from his turret. He spoke into it and then closed his turret and moved forward from the sand dunes until he came close to the side of the first reinforced house. Its 75 mm gun turned a little and zeroed in on the side of that house. Then he fired and a huge gaping hole appeared at the bottom of the wall. Black smoke came out of the hole and the tank fired again.

Dave waited until the tank had fired a second time. He had split his Platoons in two flanking assault groups, and after the tank had fired twice he and his men began running toward the house.

CHAPTER 168

Dave's men ran on each side of the hole. When they got there they stopped, threw grenades and rushed in. There was wild firing inside and the throwing of more grenades as the men ran to the other side of the house. On that side the assault engineers set up demolition charges and blew a hole in the wall. As soon as they had blown a hole they could hear a tank firing twice at the bottom of the next house so they could run into it and clear it. Those houses were nothing but reinforced bunkers and the fighting inside reminded Dave of the fighting in Ortona. The only difference was that in Ortona they had had to work their way to the top of each building and then clear it.

Here they just blew a hole in the house and rushed to get to the other side. On that side they blew another hole in order to get to the next house. When they were in the next house the assault engineers blew down the house they had just left. It was as simple as that. But the fighting inside those houses was not easy. In fact, it was truly savage and brutal. It began with grenades being thrown in and was followed by wild and heavy firing. No one paused to clean them and at the end of the second one, after they had blown a hole in the wall, Dave saw a tall and muscular German soldier lying near the hole. He was sprawled on the floor and his chest was riddled with bullets. He was wearing the Iron Cross, First Class, and his face was gray and dusty. There was a thin film of blood on his lips and his pale blue eyes were moving and following him.

Dave looked at him briefly and then rushed with the men toward the hole made by a tank in the third house. In that house Dave and his men did the same thing they had done in the first two. They fought their way to the end of it and blew a whole in the wall as the tanks fired and made a hole for them to get into the next one. Then the assault engineers blew down the house they had just left. Dave's men fought their way through all five houses like this and by noon, they had worked their way into the streets that led from the inlet to the market square. Some of the tanks of the 1st Hussars were with them and in some of the streets to their right, they heard firing as the Reginas Rifles were also working their way to the market square. Some of the Germans were fighting in groups and there were snipers and isolated soldiers in the buildings and houses.

Dave's men made their way toward the market square behind the tanks and huddled close to the buildings and houses. The tanks were firing at the upper floors of those buildings and houses and zeroing in on the windows and balconies from where the fire was coming. After a while Dave's Company made it to the market square and a little later, it was joined by a Company from the Reginas Rifles. Dave's Company was on the left side of the market square and the Reginas Rifles, on the right. To the left of the square there was a big strongly-built castle. This castle was the German headquarters for the Courseulles sector. It had a large graystone staircase leading to it and a huge Swastika flag hung from the entrance staircase.

Dave's Company set out to take on this castle while the Reginas Rifle kept on moving, on the other side of the market place, in order to go through Courseulles and head inland west of the Mue River. Near the castle Dave split his Platoons. He put his First and Second Platoons on the left side of the castle entrance and his Third and Fourth Platoons on the right side. Some of the German soldiers and snipers were firing from the upper windows and when two of the tanks came and began spraying those windows, Dave and his men ran up the staircase toward the front door. They blew it open and threw grenades in. Then they raced in and began firing wildly and heavily all around the big entrance hall. They fired at retreating Germans on each side of a large staircase leading to the upper floors and at snipers on each side of the second floor landing.

When they rushed in and began firing wildly and heavily, they riddled the walls and the large furniture of the entrance hall as well as a huge painting of Adolf Hitler that hung on the wall facing the entrance. The painting crashed on a massive oaken table filled with maps showing the German positions on this coastal sector. Almost at the same time an enormous round chandelier that hung over the table also came crashing down. As this happened the men rushed both sides of the staircase and cleared the upper floors of soldiers and snipers. The snipers stood their ground and were killed in place while most of the German soldiers dropped their weapons and surrendered. Those who didn't were shot. There were

France

no German officers since they had fled just before the arrival of Dave's Company.

Once the castle had been taken Dave sent some of his men to secure the big orchard behind it. There were large steel and concrete air raid shelters in the orchard and Dave made sure there were no German snipers or soldiers hiding in those shelters. Then, when the castle and orchard were free of Germans, and when those who had surrendered had been sent back to the beach under escort, Dave led his men back to the market place in order to head to the end of it and make for the rich farmland to the south.

CHAPTER 169

When Dave led his men back to the market place there were still some Germans who were firing at them from the end of the town. The 1st Hussars tanks backing the Company drove forward and took care of them. Behind those tanks the Company moved out of Courseulles and into the farmland to the south of it. This was fairly open country and they moved from wheat field to wheat field in a countryside that was flat and only dotted with small hills and a few scattered woods. But the hills and woods gave the German gunners excellent observation to fire their deadly 88s on Dave's men and on the tanks supporting them. Dave made his tanks return the fire and kept his Company going and by 1.00 o'clock in the afternoon, the weather began to change.

Until now it had been bleak and dreary and the Norman coast had been covered with low-lying and gray-white clouds. Now the clouds thinned out and scattered and the sky became clear and blue. The sun began shining warmly and pleasantly and as it swept through the whole countryside, Dave kept his men going. By 3.00 o'clock in the afternoon they held and went through the town of Reviers. This was two miles south of Courseulles and on the main lateral road that was running east from Tailleville to Douvres and the Orne River. They also held the crossings of the Mue River, and for the rest of the afternoon Dave maintained the momentum of his attack. He kept his men going and when they captured a town or a village, they went through it and made for the next one.

But in all these towns and villages the Germans fought fiercely and fanatically. The Germans had their guns zeroed in on the roads and on the exits from mine fields and they fought in place in deep trench systems and strong gun positions. Besides firing at Dave's men and tanks they were also mortaring them mercilessly. Still Dave kept his men going and by 6.00 p.m., he had them moving south into the Mue River valley. Whenever they reached a town or village Dave didn't stop with his men to clean it. He just attacked it, went through it and kept on going to the next town of village. This seemed to throw the Germans off balance and they couldn't dig in properly and fight them. If the resistance was too fierce Dave brought up the tanks and had them fire on the trenches and gun positions

In this way Dave was able to keep his men moving and by nightfall, they were deep into the Mue River valley and on the road to Caen. They had captured the towns of Basly, Anguerny, Anisy and Colomby-sur-Thaon and near midnight, Dave made the men stop and dig in for the night on the north side of a small lateral road like the one that ran east from Tailleville to the Orne River. By then they were eight miles from the coast and Dave thought they had probably gone further inland than anyone else on D-Day.

CHAPTER 170

The men stayed in their positions for the night and at first light, Dave took the Company and began leading it south in the Mue River Valley again. He kept on taking them south until they seized Bretteville, and for the next two and a half months, as they kept on fighting and slugging it out in Normandy, Dave saw how tough the Germans were. By now they were facing the 21st Panzer Division and the 12th SS *Hitlerjugend* Division. The 12th SS was particularly deadly. It was made up of 16 to 18 years-old boys who had been trained to believe in the invincibility of German arms and in the superiority of the German race. They were smart, fast and ready to die for their Führer. They wore long knee-length camouflage smocks and were expertly led by a veteran from the Russian Front, Colonel Kurt Meyer.

Those boys were tough, hard-headed and fanatical and most of them would rather die than surrender. This made for extremely intense and heavy fighting and Dave's Regiment battled through the towns of Buron, Gruchy, Carpiquet, Villeneuve, Rots, and the Abbey of Ardennes, before entering Caen on July 9, 1944. At this point the Regiment, and the Division, were attracting a great deal of German armor in the Caen sector while the Americans were attacking toward Cherbourg in order to swing east and go for a wide sweep across Bittany. As a result, the Regiment, and the Division, kept on pushing south and fighting through Colombelles, Vaucelles, and Potigny.

In order to capture those towns the Allied launched 1,000-plane raids against German positions. They laid down huge artillery barrages and used searchlights to create artificial moonlight. They put into action armored carriers to take the infantry to their objectives. They employed rocket-firing Spitfires and Typhoons to break up German tank and infantry counter-attacks. In Vaucelles some of the American planes bombed short. When this happened, Major-General Rod Keller, the Commander of the 3rd Canadian Division, was badly hit in the arm and had to be sent back to England. He was replaced by a tall, slim, 31 years-old Brigadier named Dan Spry who was brought in from Italy and promoted to Major-General.

The Regiment, and Dave's Company, kept on going and it wasn't until Friday morning, August 18, 1944, that they entered Falaise. But they didn't stay there long. They kept on moving and went through St. Lambert-sur-Dives where General Crerar, through General Simonds, gave them orders to move east toward the Seine. The Germans were falling back and the idea was to pursue them. As a result their Regiment, with the 3rd Dvision, and Dave's Company, were sent through Vimoutiers, northeast of St. Lambert-sur-Dives, and spread out over the roads and highways that ran through the low hills and sloping farming country leading to the Seine. In no time they took Orbec, Thiberville and Bernay.

The Germans still kept on falling back and, in many instances, were simply running away. They were blowing up bridges and mining roads. But they didn't have time to dig in properly and fight. This was true even on the south side of the Risle river. The 3rd Division just kept on moving and on Thursday morning, August 31, 1944, entered Rouen from the south. As soon as it arrived there were wild and enthusiastic celebrations. But the Division didn't stay in Rouen. It went through it and moved northeast toward the Channel ports. It had been given orders to take the ports of Boulogne, Calais and Cap Gris-Nez. As the Germans moved toward Belgium they reinforced the garrisons at all three ports and the battle for those ports became fierce, savage and deadly.

Heavy bombing raids were ordered. Huge artillery barrages were laid down. Spitfires and Typhoons flew over the German positions and strafed them. Flail and flame-throwing Crocodile tanks were used. The assignment to liberate those ports turned out to be extremely harsh, brutal and bloody. The Germans fought with all the fierceness and ferociousness they were known for, and on Wednesday, September 20, 1944, the Regiment, and Dave's Company, were taken out of the line, before they could take part in the attack on Boulogne, and assigned to the 2nd Division which was in Belgium and trying to outflank Antwerp. The town itself, and the vitally-needed docks, had been taken by the British 11th Armored Division on September 4, 1944.

However, the Germans controlled both banks of the Schelde that flowed for 45 miles from Antwerp to the North Sea. They were into the northern suburbs of the town as well and the idea was to cross the Albert

The Long War

Canal and test their defenses in the suburbs. This was the assignment that was now given to the Regiment.

CHAPTER 171

As a result, on Wednesday morning, September 28, 1944, a gray and overcast day, Dave's Regiment was brought into the suburb of Merxem. They were to cross the Albert Canal there, get into Merxem proper and see how strong the German positions were. Dave's Company would be the lead Company in this action. That morning, the Company had come into Antwerp past the Cathedral and the big open-air market. Downtown Antwerp was a strange place. All the department stores and movie theaters were open. The hotels were full. The cafés were filled with people who were sitting, drinking and eating. Yet, in the suburbs like Merxem, a deadly and vicious war was going on. Dave's company had been brought near a bridge that stood to the right of a railway bridge the Allies had tried to bomb earlier.

The concrete roadway of that bridge was badly chipped from shrapnel bursts. It was about 500 feet long and its half-circular steel spans, with its many steel girders, were also chipped with shrapnel bursts. As well the banks of the canal, at both ends of the bridge, had been badly hit and large chunks of the stone walls, that ran on each side of the canal, had fallen into the 20-feet canal and were lying across it just below the surface. As Dave's Company came to the bridge the men lay flat on both sides of the road and looked at it. Dave was on the right side and was staring at it through his binoculars. Despite having been chipped with shrapnel the bridge was still intact. There were large blocks of apartment buildings facing it at the other end, on each side of the road going north through Merxem, and on both sides of that road a second-floor window from one of those apartments was open. Those windows were close to the roadway and overlooking it. There might be other windows open as well.

However, from the distance Dave was looking at the bridge, it was hard to tell. The banks had been hit badly and the piles of overturned earth and broken stones that had fallen all the way into the canal, and across it, were huge. As he was looking at the bridge through his binoculars Dave said: "I don't like it. I don't like it al all." He was lying flat with Red, Slav and Delorme on the right side of the road. They were also looking at the bridge and Dave said: "It's too quiet. Way too quiet" "I agree," Red said. "So do I," Delorme said. "That's for sure," Slav put in. "This bridge is intact. And the Germans don't leave bridges like that." Dave nodded and ordered the Company to get up and start moving across the bridge on the right side. But they were to skip from steel girder to steel girder. That way, if there was any firing, they would have some protection. The men of the Company stood up and began filing across the bridge.

At the beginning everyone skipped from girder to girder. But once they were a third of the way on the bridge three new replacements, who had only been with the Company for a couple of weeks, suddenly stepped out of the girders and began running toward the end of it. Once they were about halfway on the bridge MG 42s opened up and they went skidding down on the roadway and stayed there. "Goddamnit!" Dave said. He was still lying flat on the right side of the road near the entrance and was still looking at the bridge through his binoculars. The soldier who had gone the furthest seemed to have been shot through his right shoulder and was lying on his back and shaking convulsively. The soldier behind him seemed to have been hit in the legs and was trying to crawl back behind a girder. But every time he moved machine-gun bullets were kicking dust all around him. The third soldier was lying on the roadway and not moving. He looked as if he had been hit in the chest.

Dave looked at those soldiers, at the roadway, at the blocks of apartment buildings at the end of the bridge, and at the piles of overturned earth and broken stones. Then he turned to Red, Slav and Delorme and said: "Have the Company fire at those two open windows and at the end of the bridge. When you see me come on the bridge from the other end give me covering fire until I'm back." "What are you doing?" Red asked. "This is crazy," Slav said. "Let me go with you," Delorme said. "No. You all stay here," Dave motioned with his right hand.

Then he got up and began running in a crouch down the bank, on the right side of the bridge, that led to the canal.

CHAPTER 172

Dave could hear firing from above and when he got to the canal, he began stepping on the broken stones and rubble in it until he made it to the other bank. That bank had been churned up with overturned earth and chunks of broken stone and Dave used that rubble as cover to go up to the top of it next to the stone walL Through a hole between two broken stones Dave could see that on each side of the bridge the rubble had been used by the Germans to set up machine-gun emplacements. There were two Germans in each emplacement manning an MG 42. Alongside them, in those emplacements, were some Germans firing rifles. Behind them, through the two open windows facing the roadway, Dave could hear the savage hammering of two other MG 42s.

Dave looked at the two machine-gun emplacements and at the two open windows. He took a deep breath and left the pile of rubble behind which he was crouching. Dave ran past a break in the stone wall, across the exit road, and flattened himself on the wall underneath the open window on the right of the bridge. There was so much firing all around the Germans were just manning their MG 42s and firing their rifles. They didn't see nor heard him. Dave took out a grenade and lobbed it through the open window. Then he ran across the road to the open window on the left side of the bridge. Dave took out another grenade and lobbed it through that window. Then he ran to the machine-gun emplacement to the left side of the bridge and fired his Thompson machine-gun and threw in a grenade. Dave kept on running past that machine-gun emplacement and made for the second one on the right where he fired this Thompson machine-gun and again threw in a grenade.

Dave didn't stop and turned and ran away from the emplacements toward the right side of the bridge. By then there was screaming and moaning from the Germans who had been wounded in the houses and in the machine-gun emplacements. Dave kept on running and moving toward the right side of the bridge. Heavy fire was still coming from there toward the windows and down the left side of the roadway. Dave was breathing heavily and when he got on the bridge, he made for the first soldier who had been shot through the shoulder and who was shaking convulsively. When he reached him Dave grabbed his tunic and began dragging him across the bridge. Red, Slav and Delorme came running and helped him drag the soldier out of sight behind girders at the entrance. Dave straightened up and went back on the bridge. He ran to the soldier who had been hit in the legs and also grabbed his tunic and dragged him back to safety. That soldier left a twin trail of blood on the bridge and Dave ran back on it to get the soldier who had been shot in the chest. Dave was running hard and when he came close to this soldier, two bullets went through his groin on the right side and he went sprawling down on the roadway not far from him.

Dave watched numbly as blood began pouring out of his groin and onto his thigh and suddenly felt two strong pair of arms under his armpits as he began being dragged out of the bridge. The arms belonged to Slav and Delorme and Red was holding him by his tunic. Dave could see the blood seeping rapidly over his groin and his right leg and suddenly his sight flickered and wavered twice. Then it faded abruptly and a strong and deep darkness suddenly overwhelmed him.

BOOK FIFTEEN

OSTEND

CHAPTER 173

For a long time this strong and deep darkness hung over Dave. First it felt as if it was being pressed on and molded. Then it was quiet and undisturbed. Finally, after quite a while, it seemed as if someone was cutting right through it and Dave felt an excruciating pain that went right into his heart. As a matter of fact the pain was so bad that his heart skipped and then he felt an unbearable weakness as if he didn't have any heartbeat at all. Then he felt his heartbeat again. But it seemed to be beating through an endlessly dull and aching cutting. The cutting went on for quite some time and then Dave felt bumps in the darkness before he opened his eyes. Dave could see the tops of trees and telephone poles.

Those trees and telephone poles were racing by and Dave saw he was strapped in a jeep and they were speeding north. Dave closed his eyes and the darkness came back on. His groin was on fire and he could feel the faint ragged beating of his heart. The darkness went on for along time and in it Dave could see trees, telephone poles, a jeep and a half-circular steel-spanned bridge with iron girders. The bridge was on top of the trees and telephone poles. The jeep was below the bridge. Everything kept on moving and changing all the time. Sometimes the bridge was on top. At other times it was the trees and telephone poles. Every once in a while it was the jeep. This went on for quite a while and then the darkness seemed to stop moving as everything stood still.

Then the darkness turned hot, draining and sweaty and became agitated again. There was more excruciating pain in his heart and Dave felt more pressing and molding around his groin. Finally the darkness became still again and when he opened his eyes, Dave saw he was lying in a hospital bed. The chrome sides of the bed had been raised. Dave

The Long War

was lying under nice clean-smelling sheets and a tall white curtain had been pulled around his bed. At the foot of the bed, on the right, was a wooden chair. A nurse was sitting on it and looking at him. This nurse was tall, slim, blonde, and in her mid-twenties. She was wearing a pale-blue uniform and a white nurse's cap and apron. She had deep blue eyes and right now they were creased and wrinkled a little.

Dave was grabbing the sides of his bed and the pain in his groin was so bad he couldn't speak. All he could do was hang on to the sides and look at her. In fact the pain was so acute tears were squirting from his eyes. Dave looked at this nurse and their eyes met. She had the deepest blue eyes he had ever seen. They were clear and sunny and there was a great deal of kindness and tenderness in them. They looked at each other for a moment and Dave wanted to say so many things to her. But right now he was hurting too much and couldn't do it. All he could do was try and put up with the pain. Dave kept on looking at her and after a while she smiled.

She stood up and came and smoothed the sheets over him. All Dave could do was hang on to the sides of his bed. Then she bent, kissed him lightly on the forehead. and said: "Shush. Shush." In a moment she was gone and Dave closed his eyes and fell into a deep and restless darkness again. After a while, though, this darkness became less painful and agitated. It was quiet and untroubled and when he finally opened his eyes again, Dave saw the same nurse was sitting in the wooden chair at the foot of his bed, on the right side, and looking at him. When Dave opened his eyes, the nurse sat a little straighter on her chair and said:"How do you feel?"

"Not so good."

"Don't worry. You'll get better."

Dave nodded and said: "Where am I?"

"In St.Gertrud's Hospital."

"Where's that?"

"In Belgium."

"Where in Belgium?"

"In Ostend."

"Why there?"

"It's one of the major hospitals for Allied and German soldiers near the front."

Dave nodded again and said: "You have a slight accent. Are you German?"

"Yes."

"Where did you learn English."

"My father sent me to England to study it for two years when I was eighteen."

"Woher sind sie gekommen?"

"Hamburg."

"Was machen sie hier?"

"Das ist eine lange geschichte."

"Sage mir."

"I don't think you'd want to hear it."

"Sure. What are you doing here?"

"Well, when the Allies got here, we had a lot of wounded. Some of us stayed behind to take care of them."

"Both doctors and nurses?"

"That's right."

"That's quite amazing."

"Not really. We had to do it."

Dave didn't say anything and then said: "What's your name?"

"Nina Haegen."

"Nina. That's a nice name."

"Actually it's Bettina. But everyone calls me Nina."

"Nina it is then."

"What's your name?"

Dave told her.

Nina nodded and Dave said: "About the last time. I'm sorry."

"About what?"

"For not talking to you."

"It's all right."

"I was hurting so much I couldn't talk."

"I understand."

Dave didn't say anything for a moment and then said: "Tell me the truth, Nina. Is my manhood gone?"

Nina smiled.

"Don't worry. You have nothing to fear."

"I tell you. I'm hurting real bad."

"I know."

"None of my vital parts have been touched or damaged?"

"No."

"It feels like it."

"Don't worry. You're fine."

"How come it hurts so bad then?"

"You're lucky. The two bullets that hit you went through the fleshy part of your right thigh. You're going to be all right."

"Why do I hurt so bad then?"
"It's because of your operations."
"Operations?"
"That's right."
"There were more than one operation?"
"Yes."
"How many?"
"Two. One in Antwerp. And one here."
"Why two?"
"After the first operation, you had some infection in the groin area. They had to clean it up."
"And now I'm okay?"
"Now you're fine."

CHAPTER 174

Dave nodded and Nina stood up from her chair. She came over to his bed, bent and smoothed his sheets. In a moment she was gone and Dave lay in bed and looked at the ceiling. His groin was on fire and after a while, Nina came back again. She gave him a pill and then Dave closed his eyes and fell asleep. He slept a long time and when he woke up, the white curtain had been pulled away from around his bed. As he straightened up a little Dave saw he was lying in a large ward. There were beds on each side of the ward and his bed was the last one on the right. There was a spacious aisle between the beds and his bed was facing a bed from across the aisle. There were also two doors that stood right in the middle of the thick stone walls on each side of the ward.

The door on the right, Dave found out, led to an outside terrace. The one on the left opened on Möerdik Lane, alongside the hospital, and was used to bring in wounded officers and soldiers. Beyond the bed Dave was facing were tall wide windows and the sun was pouring through them. Dave's groin was still on fire and as he lay in bed and took in the ward, Nina came in and gave him another pill. The pain in his groin was so bad, at times, Dave's heart skipped and the pain went right into his heart. His wounds in Dieppe and Italy had been bad. But this was worse. The pain was unbearable and he was always shaking inwardly and sweating. Several nurses came around to give him different pills and he was taken a few times to one of the operating rooms on the second floor where the doctors had a good look at him.

Dave ended up staying in bed through the month of October and near the end of it, on Friday, October 27, 1944, when he wasn't feeling well, a Major-General, who was named John Murray, from the First Canadian

Army, came in with a Colonel and Major, and told him he had been awarded the Distinguished Service Order Medal. The Medal had been awarded, Major-General Murray told him, for four things: his bravery under fire in Merxem; his having taken out four German positions; his having saved two soldiers; and his having been seriously wounded while trying to save a third one. He then bent and pinned the Medal on his pajamas as Dave lay in bed and half-rose to talk to him. The Major-General congratulated him and spoke with him for a while with the Colonel and Major. Finally he left and Dave lay back down against his pillow.

Dave was breathing hard and sweating and after a while he closed his eyes and drifted to sleep. Dave spent the entire month of October lying in bed and fighting the excruciating pain he felt in his groin. The scar tissues were healing over the two entry wounds. But they were burning badly and angrily and Dave didn't feel strong and steady enough to try and get out of bed. Dave was out of breath all the time and always running a slight fever. He also felt extremely weak but by the beginning of November the pain in his groin began to leave and his slight fever finally disappeared. Although he was still quite weak Nina helped him sit in a wheelchair and took him out on the terrace on the right side of the ward. The weather was a bit cool and chilly. But it was mostly sunny and Nina made sure he was well dressed and wrapped in a blanket.

Nina would take him to the railing of the terrace and would sit with him for a while as they looked at the North Sea. At this time of the year the waves were gray-green and you could see the wind ripple across them as it swept in from the sea. Other nurses also came with officers and soldiers in wheelchairs or on crutches and sat with them on the terrace. "Sometimes a few of the nurses came out with German officers and soldiers. When they did there was usually a guard with them. After the confinement of the ward it was always nice for whoever was out to breathe clean and fresh air again. Nina took him out on the terrace as often as she could and by the middle of November, Dave began shifting from the wheelchair to a cane. He forced himself to get up and walk with a cane even though he felt quite a bit of pain when he walked and was pretty unsteady.

Dave made himself walk all over the hospital and found out the ground floor contained the elevators on each side of the entrance that led to the upper floors. It also contained the doctors and nurses' stations and, behind those stations, the ward where he was staying. This ward only took in seriously wounded officers and soldiers. The second floor was for the operating rooms and the doctors and nurses' quarters. The third floor gave access to a large rest room for the wounded and to the various specialized departments. The fourth and fifth floors were reserved for the less seriously wounded officers and soldiers. Most of the doctors and nurses had their quarters at the hospital and the German doctors and nurses were allowed to move about quite freely, even though the hospital was under Allied control. Many of them spoke English or French and most of them were taking care of the German officers and soldiers.

Dave kept on roaming around the hospital with his cane. He walked to Möerdik Lane and stood there watching the ambulances bring in the casualties. He also went out on the terrace quite a lot and sat in one of the wooden chairs and looked at the North Sea. Even though it was mid-November there were still quite a few seagulls flying over the beach. Far out on the horizon he often saw battleships and freighters. One Wednesday morning in mid-November Dave stayed on the terrace for quite a long time. It was a crisp and sunny day and the wind was blowing in from the sea. The pain in Dave's groin was almost gone. But he still felt quite unsteady on his feet. After a while, though, the crispness of the air began making his groin ache and Dave got up carefully and began walking back toward the door of the terrace.

As Dave was walking toward that door Nina came out. She was wearing no cap and her pale blonde hair was blowing in the wind. When Nina saw Dave she smiled. Dave smiled back and when he got close to her, he suddenly stumbled and nearly fell on the terrace. Nina ran to steady him and as they stood close to each other, near the terrace door, Dave took her in his arms and looked at her for a moment. He brushed his lips against hers slowly and suddenly kissed her hard. Her lips were soft and moist and then she kissed him hard too. Dave could feel her body tight and slim against his and as he pulled away from her, he said: "Good morning." "Good morning," Nina smiled.

Nina was standing close to him and Dave shifted his cane to his left hand. Then he took her hand and both of them stood close to each other and held hands in the sunlight.

CHAPTER 175

After a while Dave and Nina left the terrace and went back inside the ward. Dave walked back to his bed and lay down. He rested for a while and in the days that followed, Dave forced himself to get out of bed every morning and walk all over the hospital with his cane. His groin was no longer sore. But it was extremely tender and he still felt quite weak and unsteady. In early December the winter came. One day the weather was clear and sunny. They next it clouded over and snow started to come down and blanketed Ostend. In no time the terrace of the hospital was covered with a thick layer of snow and Dave could hear a strong gale that was blowing in from the North Sea and rattling the windows of the ward.

The hospital itself was full of badly wounded officers and soldiers from the battles of the Schelde, Walcheren Island, South Beveland and the Maas river. The German doctors and nurses were kept on and still allowed to move around freely. Dave saw Nina almost daily. She came around to give him his pills and, now that winter had settled in, often went with him to the rest room on the third floor where they sat down and talked. Nina gave Dave her address in Hamburg as well as the address of her relatives in Hoffnung and Barmstedt. Dave told her where she could find him. Ever since they had held hands in the sunlight Dave felt very close to her. Every time he saw her tall and slender figure he stood still and couldn't get over how beautiful she looked. Nina was one of those rare women who had an inner as well as an outer beauty. There was a kindness and tenderness in her that touched him and made him happy to be with her.

Whenever Dave was with her he realized his fear of losing his manhood was unfounded. In fact, his manhood was very much there, although the whole area around his groin was extremely tender and always hurt whenever it got too cold or damp. By mid-December Dave was feeling much better and let go of his cane, just as there was a scare in the hospital. The Germans had launched an offensive in the Ardennes and were hoping to make it to the sea and retake Antwerp. By the end of the month, however, the offensive failed and everything got back to normal. By then Dave was walking without a cane and although his groin was still tender and hurt every once in a while, he forced himself to walk without it.

Without the cane Dave wasn't steady but he forced himself to ignore his wounds and walk normally. As his strength slowly and steadily came back Dave's balance improved so that by the end of January 1945 he was fit and healthy again. On Tuesday, January 30, 1945, Dave placed a series of calls to the Headquarters of the First Canadian Army in Tilburg. Then at 9.00 am, on Saturday morning, February 3, 1945, a jeep driven by a tall, slim and dark-haired Private, who was named Tom Bradley and who had been sent to the Company as a replacement, came to pick him up. Dave had signed his discharge papers the day before and had told Nina in the afternoon he was leaving. Although, in her case, Dave suspected she had known for quite some time.

Now, on that clear and sunny morning, Nina came into the ward and helped him pack. The Army had provided Dave with a duffel bag and she put his newly-issued uniforms and personal things in it. Then Dave picked up the bag and she began walking out of the ward with him. Outside Nina stopped not far from the entrance. Dave put down his bag and, as he turned and looked at her, she said: "Why are you doing this?"

"Doing what?"

"Going back."

"I have to."

"You've already been wounded three times. Why must you go back?"

"Just like you stayed here. I have to."

"You might get killed. Why don't you stay here?"

"I can't, Nina."

"Sure you can."

"No I can't."

Nina looked down and tears came into her eyes.

"Haven't you had enough of war? Can't you quit?"

"Not now, Nina. Not like this."

"If you get hurt, I won't ever be able to get over it."

"I have to go, Nina. Really."

"Why don't you stay here?."

"I can't."

Nina looked at him through her tears and said: "*Meine leibe. Meine schönheit. Meine Zärtlichkeit.*"

"*Es ist okay.*"

"*Es ist nicht okay! Du hast verlassen!*"

"*Ich habe zu.*"

"*Niemals werde ich dich vergessen! Niemals!*"

"*Ich weiss.*"

Dave now stepped close to Nina and said: "Listen. It's hard for me to say these things. But I'll say them anyway."

Nina looked at him and Dave said: "I've never said that to anyone else before. But I love you. Do you understand?"

"I understand."

"I love you more than I've ever loved anyone."

"I know that."

"Do you?"

"I do."

Dave looked at her and said: "If I survive this war, I'll come looking for you in Hamburg."

"You will?"

"I will. It may take some time. But I will."

"You promise?"

"Yes. I promise."

CHAPTER 176

Dave now stepped close to Nina and took her in his arms. He held her tightly for a while and could feel her heart beating against his. Then he kissed her hard and moved away from her. He bent and picked up his duffel bag. When he straightened up Dave turned and began walking toward the jeep parked across the street and waiting for him. Dave threw his duffel bag in the back of the jeep and went around it and sat in the front seat next to Tom Bradley. In a moment Bradley pulled away from the curb and began heading east on Löewen street before he turned right and started making for the main street of Ostend. As they left the curb Dave caught a last glimpse of Nina.

    She was standing near the entrance and looked incredibly beautiful in her blue nurse's cape and with her blonde hair blowing in the wind. Dave looked at her for a moment and then turned and looked straight ahead as Bradley made it to the main street of Ostend before he turned left and began heading east out of the city. Bradley drove fast and in no time they left the city behind and went through cities and towns like Bruges, Zelzate, and Antwerp. In Antwerp they drove through Merxem over the same bridge where Dave had been wounded. The suburb itself was full of smashed houses and rubble-strewn streets, and then they headed north toward Brecht and Breda. In Breda they turned right and began heading east again just as the sky started to get dark and woolly and as a thick and fluffy snow began to fall.

    After a while the cities, towns and villages became covered with it as the weather turned cold and as the snow began coming down in huge swirling gusts. Once they reached Tilburg they drove through it and kept on heading east toward the German border. Bradly drove swiftly

The Long War

and expertly and Dave was amazed at the amount of trucks and military vehicles also moving east. By now it seemed they were passing one long convoy after another and Bradley weaved in and out of those convoys and kept on heading east past cities and towns such as S-Hertenbosch, Heesch and Cuijk. In Cuijk they turned left and kept on moving north and then northeast past Mook until they reached the town of Groesbeek near the German border. When they came to Groesbeek Dave could see the town was full of tanks, guns, armored carriers and was the assembly point for the Regiment.

They reached Groesbeek around 4.00 o'clock in the afternoon, and it had been a 140-mile ride from Ostend. The sun was beginning to set in a sharp streak of pink and orange over the stark and snowy town and Bradley told Dave the Regiment was located in barracks at the entrance of the town. As for the Colonel and his staff, they were to be found in a small office they used in the town hall, itself, off the main square. Bradley drove Dave right to the door of that town hall and told him he could go in. He, himself, would see to it his duffel bag be brought over to the Company. Dave nodded and thanked him for the drive.

Then he got out of the jeep and began walking up the short staircase that led into the town hall.

CHAPTER 177

All the windows were blacked-out with tall black curtains and, inside, Dave saw the place was full of heavily-armed soldiers. A table had been set up at the entrance for information purposes. Dave found out from the young Lieutenant who was sitting at that table that the whole Regiment had offices in the town hall. The Colonel's office was the second one on the left side of the left hallway on the ground floor. Dave thanked him and walked over to the door of that office. At the door Dave opened it and found himself in a small office where a Company Clerk was busy looking at some forms. The Company Clerk was tall, thin and bespectacled and reminded Dave of a Clerk his Company had once had, Tom Taylor. The Clerk said his name was Tim Allan and Dave told him the Colonel was expecting him.

Allan nodded and asked Dave to wait in the small office for a moment. Dave stood at the entrance and waited as Allan opened a door to the right side of the office and went into another office next to it. In a moment that door opened and a tall, lean and dark-haired Major came out. He glanced briefly at Dave before he left the small office. Then the door on the side of the office opened once more and Allan came out and motioned for Dave to go in. Dave thanked him and walked past that door to find himself in a somewhat larger office to the right of the one where he had been standing. This office was bare except for a large wooden table with trestles that was filled with large-scale maps of northeastern Holland and northwestern Germany. A small chandelier lit the room and there were a few wooden chairs next to the wall facing the blacked-out windows.

Major Philip Caldwell was standing over this table and looking at a large-scale map of northwestern Germany. Major Caldwell didn't quite look like the tall, trim and blond-haired officer Dave remembered. He now had some gray in his hair and his skin looked tightly-drawn and wrinkled. He was still tall and trim but looked a little lean and weary. The most important change, however, was in what he was wearing on the shoulder tabs of his tunic. Major Caldwell was wearing the the pips and crown of a Colonel. When Dave came in he turned from the wooden table where he was standing and and put down the large-scale map of northwestern Germany he was looking at. Dave walked up to him and saluted him. Colonel Caldwell returned his salute and Dave said. "I see you're now a Colonel?"

"I am."

"Congratulations."

"Thank you."

"What happened to Colonel Cantwell?"

"He's been promoted to Brigadier."

"Where?"

"In the 5th Armored Division."

"With what unit?"

"The 12th Canadian Infantry Brigade."

"Who's replacing you?"

"A Major named Don Strickland."

"Is that the Major I saw coming out of the office?"

"That's it."

"Where is he from?"

"The 1st Division."

"Where was he?"

"In Italy where he was wounded."

"Where?"

"In Rimini."

"Well, I must say. Things are changing."

"They certainly are."

"I'll say. "

Dave didn't say anything for a moment and then Colonel Caldwell said:"How are you, David?"

"I'm fine, Sir."

"Really?"

"I am, Sir."

"I must say I was glad when I found out you were coming back to the Regiment."

"Thank you, Sir."

"You're ready to go back fighting?"

"Yes, Sir."

"Because, I must tell you, it's not going to be a picnic."

Dave nodded and the Colonel said: "We've been assigned to the 30th British Corps."

"For what purpose?"

"For an attack on southwestern Germany."

"What's our task?"

"We're going to be part of a four-Division assault on the Reichswald forest."

"Why us?"

"The British need assault experience and know-how on the right flank of this attack."

"Why the right flank?"

"Because the 51st Highland Division, which we will be supporting, will be attacking various towns on the south side of the German border. We will be backing them up in those attacks."

"Why don't the British use their own troops?"

"They're stretched to the breaking-point right now. They have no more troops to spare."

"So we provide the experience and punch on the right flank."

"Exactly."

"That sounds risky."

"It is. To attack with so many troops on a four-mile frontage *is* risky."

Dave didn't say anything and the Colonel said: "You'll have to work fast."

"Why?"

"The attack is scheduled for five days from now. That's all the time you'll have to work with your Company."

"That's not much time."

"It's not."

"Has the Company been brought up to full strength again?"

"It has."

"It won't give me much time to work in the replacements with the veterans."

"It won't."

Dave nodded again and the Colonel said: "Are you up to it?"

"Yes, Sir. I am."

CHAPTER 178

Colonel Caldwell then motioned for Dave to get closer to the wooden table, on his left, and picked up the large-scale map of northwestern Germany he had been looking at. The Colonel showed Dave how, as part of the British 30th Corps, the Regiment would be involved in a four-Division attack on the Reichswald. This attack would be called operation *Veritable* and for the first phase of it, the British 30th Corps would have a total of seven Divisions and 200,000 men. They would be led by Lieutenant-General Brian Horrocks and would be temporarily under the command of the 1st Canadian Army. In their part of the attack the 2nd Canadian Infantry Division would be on the left flank.

The 15th Scottish Infantry Division would be to the right of the 2nd Canadian Infantry Division. It would be followed by the 53rd Welsh Infantry Division, then the 51st Highland Infantry Division and finally themselves. The Regiment would cover the right flank of the 51st Highland Infantry Division and would support their attack on various towns on the south side of the German border. They would be facing the German 84th Division and, if the weather held, and if the roads stayed hard and frozen, a savage concentrated punch through the 84th Division should get them through the forests and onto the Rhine itself. This was the briefing the Colonel gave Dave and when he was finished, Dave left the town hall and walked back along the main street to the barracks where the Regiment was located.

Once he got there Dave asked one of the soldiers where his Regiment was. Dave was told out it was located in the first barrack. Dave thanked the soldier and made for this barrack. When he came in Dave ran into both Lieutenant Moran, of the First Platoon, and Sergeant Major Bostwick.

Ostend

Moran seemed truly relieved to see him while Bostwick only grinned and said: "Welcome back." During his absence Dave learned Moran had been in charge of the Company. But, after talking to both Moran and Bostwick, it was obvious who had been in charge. Both of them showed Dave a small room at the end of the barrack. This small room was on the left side of the barrack and facing the front. The Company was run from there, and for the rest of that day and Sunday Dave asked both to introduce him to the new men.

They did and as Dave talked to them, he could hardly recognize the Company. It was now mostly made up of replacements and Dave guessed the veterans from Terreyville only amounted to a little over 30 % of it. The replacements were nice, pleasant and eager to learn. But they had had little training and there was no time to give it to them. Dave made sure they were placed alongside the veterans in each Platoons and in the next three days, Colonel Caldwell and his Second In Command, Major Strickland, often came and gave the men various briefings. For his part Dave tried to explain to the new men the German tactics and how to counter them. There was no room and no time for field exercises and by Monday morning, the weather began to change.

Up to now it had been very cold and blustery. But suddenly it became mild and the skies turned gray and overcast. It started to rain heavily and all the snow in the town melted. This pouring slanting rain went on day after day and in his briefings, Dave could see the Colonel looked tense. Still the Colonel and Major Strickland tried to meet every Company and Platoon and see to it they knew what was expected of them, and at nightfall on Wednesday, February 7, 1945, they heard the heavy droning of planes in the distance and the quick-spreading and nerve-shattering explosions of bombs as the sky glowed red in the west and as cities and towns burned. The booming, thundering and crackling explosions in the west went on for a long time and at 3.00 a.m. on Thursday morning, the men were taken out, fully-loaded, from their barracks and brought to their starting line a little in front of the town of Groesbeek.

BOOK SIXTEEN

GERMANY

CHAPTER 179

The Regiment was on the right flank of the 51st Highland Infantry Division and Dave's Company was the lead Company in the attack. The tanks of the 6th Guards of the 8th Armored Brigade were lined up in front of them and would show the way. It was still raining steadily and heavily and at exactly 5.00 o'clock in the morning, the British artillery opened fire. In a moment the German positions in the Reichwald became drowned in a sea of quick-flashing, fast-spreading, orange explosions. Not long after they fired 25-pounder base-ejections shells. Those shells released clusters of canisters which fell into the forest. As those canisters hit the ground they let out a thick white smoke which soon blanketed the whole forest and the German view of the west.

This savage and intense artillery barrage went on for over five hours and at 10.29 a.m., a line of yellow smoke shells was dropped to indicate it was the last minute before the barrage was lifted. Then the order was given for the 6th Guards tanks to move and Dave's Company began to walk behind them across the Dutch border into Germany. With this heavy slanting rain the trails had turned into mud and as Dave moved eastward with his Company into Germany, he had expected heavy machine-gun fire, mortars and artillery. Instead the Company only received fire from a few soldiers and machine-gunners. But that was all. There was only the heavy slanting rain and the huge stark forest of the Reichswald looming over them. In this rain the trails turned to deep mud and the tanks were churning up belly-deep in it.

After a while some got stuck, others moved slowly, and Dave walked past them with his Company. They were going up narrow trails and firebreaks. As they moved over a mile into the forest there was hardly any firing. Whenever there was the men in the line of fire would go to ground while others on the flank would take care of it. Dave kept on leading his men and as they moved deeper into it, the going became much slower and tougher because of all this mud and rain. Except for the slashing dripping rain it was eerily silent in the forest and by 2.00 o'clock in the afternoon, when they were almost two miles into it, Dave began hearing heavy firing on his left flank. The firing was sharp and steady and was coming from over a mile on his left flank.

Dave knew it had to do with the 51st Highland Infantry Division and made his Company stop and go to ground for a moment. Dave listened to it and saw it was increasing and getting worse. He was about to turn and send a runner to see what was going on when Higgins, who was with Addams and Mitchell, dropped down beside him on his left side and tapped him on the shoulder. Dave turned and Higgins pointed at some trees on their left flank. A short stocky soldier was running in and out of them and was holding on to his Thompson machine-gun. His helmet was camouflaged with leaves stuck into the netting and he was wearing the uniform of a British soldier. He was also bent in two and running hard toward them.

CHAPTER 180

Dave waited until this soldier was quite close to them and then motioned to Addams and Mitchell, who were standing behind Higgins, to his left, to cover him with their rifles. Soon this soldier ran into their lines and when he came up to Dave, he said: "I'm looking for Captain Lindsay."

"That's me."

"I'm Captain Jack Walsh."

"Glad to know you, Captain."

"Thank you."

"What outfit are you in?"

"The 2nd Derbyshire Yeomanry."

"What Company?"

"A Company."

"What can I do for you?"

"There's been a change of plan."

"What change?"

"My Colonel has run into your Colonel. And we need your help."

"You already have it."

"No, no. Not for the flank support."

"What for then?'

"For this attack we're making."

"The one I'm hearing on the left flank?"

"That's right."

"What can I do for you?" Dave asked.

"You have to bring your Company westward and line it up on Marburg."

"Is that the name of the place you're attacking?"

The Long War

"That's it. Actually, it's Reichswald-Marburg. Since there's another Marburg. But everyone calls it Marburg."

"Why the line-up?"

"The place is a little tougher to crack than we thought."

"Why?"

"It's the anchor position on the lateral road running from Kranenburg, Frasselt and Hekkens. And the Germans are defending it to death."

"What's the new plan?"

"Your Regiment will attack on the right flank of Marburg. We'll attack on the left."

"Why can't some of your Regiments do it."

"They're all busy fighting on the left flank of Marburg."

"Is that why we're hearing so much firing?" Dave asked.

"That's why."

"How come there's hardly any firing on this flank?"

"Remember the Air Force bombed all these towns on the left flank. I think the Germans are reinforcing there first."

"So what's the plan?"

"You'll bring your Company in line with mine in front of Marburg."

"And then?"

"We'll attack at first light tomorrow morning."

"What about the other Companies in our two Regiments?"

"We'll both attack head-on. The other Companies will try and outflank the place."

"I have to tell you, Captain. I'm not too crazy about frontal attacks."

"Neither am I, Sir. But this plan was worked out by our two Colonels."

"I'll have to confirm this with Colonel Caldwell."

"By all means, Sir. But you won't be able to do it."

"Why not?"

"We tried. And our other Regiments have tried. The wireless sets don't work here."

"Why not?"

"The atmospherics don't allow it."

"I you don't mind, Captain, I'll try anyway."

"Please do. But I was ordered to tell you to start moving right away."

"I understand," Dave said.

"Also, if I were you, I'd back down half a mile before I went and lined up on Marburg."

"Why back down?"

Germany

"That way you'll be able to avoid the snipers and machine-gun nests in front of it."

"How far do they extend ."

"About a quarter of a mile."

"Maybe we should try and take them from the rear."

"Don't. Because if you do, we won't be able to make the attack."

"I know."

"It will get dark soon in this forest. If you don't mind my saying, Captain, I think you should start moving right away."

"I will."

"That way, you'll be able to get a better look at the place."

"Don't worry. That's what I'm going to do."

CHAPTER 181

Captain Walsh left Dave and began running back in a crouch toward his Company. He weaved in and out of the trees and ran laterally toward his own position. Dave watched him go for a moment and then walked back to the middle of his Company. A new replacement named Tom Stromka was manning the wireless and Dave tried to raise the Colonel. Walsh had been right. The atmospherics in the forest made it impossible to contact him. When he saw this Dave turned the Company around and made them walk back over half a mile in the slanting rain. Then he began taking them laterally toward Marburg until they were lined up with it. Now, close to 3.00 o'clock in the afternoon, it was starting to get a little dark in the forest and Dave made the Company go to ground in their new positions and dig in for the night.

As they were doing this Dave went forward with Higgins and Addams to have a look at Marburg while there was still some light. The three of them crawled through the mud until they reached a large tree rising a little above the ground and overlooking it. By then they were a little over a quarter of a mile from it and Dave took out his binoculars and looked at it as well as the surroundings. How about that, he thought, as he swung his binoculars from side to side and took in the ground around him. No wonder Walsh said it was a tough nut to crack. In the few aerial photos we have, it looks as if it's only a few buildings. In fact there are seven buildings, then the lateral road, and seven other buildings on the other side of it. This is not something we studied too well in Algiers when we were taking military topography.

Let's face it, Dave thought, from the way this position was defined you could say that, what we are dealing with here, is elementary cartography.

Also, each one of those one-story houses has a firing slit facing the forest. That means they are reinforced bunkers and won't be easy to take on. Not only that but the floor of the forest rises steadily toward those bunkers which means that by the time we can get to them we'll have to run up a little over five feet. I'll bet, he thought, that's one thing our wonderful and esteemed Colonel in Algiers never had to deal with. Not to mention we'll have to take on snipers, riflemen and machine-gun nests. And, while we're at it, also look out for their mines, mortars and artillery.

It's easy, Dave thought, when you're in a nice and comfortable position away from the front, to look at the big picture. It's another thing when you're right in the middle of the action and trying to take on a position that's not properly defined or targeted. Then there's also the fact that, as a result of the forest always rising steadily, the road on which those bunkers are is on an embankment which will give the Germans an excellent field of fire. Not only that but we're expected to take those bunkers in a frontal assault. Oh well, he thought. A new Colonel, a new frontal assault. That's how it goes. Although, technically speaking, and in the same way as in Assoro, it's not really a frontal assault since our other Companies will try and outflank the position.

However, for us chosen ones, Dave thought, it's a frontal assault. Truly, with Dieppe, Pachino, Reggio, Assoro and now this place, we are becoming frontal assault specialists. If you ask me, that's what we're becoming. With all the bloodshed and casualties those frontal assaults imply. That's why, for once, he thought, I'm glad there's all this rain and mud and overcast weather. At least, this way, it should help a little. Especially if we want to carry out that plan that was worked out by our two tough and fearless Colonels. Well, I hope our replacements won't lose their heads and know how to fight, he thought. In an action like this there's not much room for bad judgments and mistakes.

Dave put down his binoculars. It was now getting quite dark in the forest and before total darkness came and blanketed everything, he turned and motioned for Higgins and Addams to crawl back with him until they reached their positions and settled down for the night.

CHAPTER 182

When they got back to their lines Dave checked the various positions of the Company and made sure his men were well dug-in. Then he slipped into one of the slit-trenches that had been dug for him and stood near the front of the lines. That slit-trench was facing Marburg and was a little over a quarter of a mile from it. Soon darkness came and completely blanketed the forest. It rained steadily and heavily throughout the night and around 6.30 a.m, Jack Walsh ran through their lines again and told Dave the attack would go in at 8.00 a.m. sharp. Then Walsh was gone and as Dave looked at Marburg through his binoculars, he saw it was getting light in the forest.

A pale grayish light was seeping through the trees and narrow muddy trails and in the distance, Dave could see the white low-slung houses of Marburg looming against the cloudy overcast sky. It was raining harder than ever and at times the rain came down in sudden swirling gusts that splashed against the trees and narrow muddy trails. Dave passed the word around for his men to get ready and at precisely 8.00 a.m., the 2nd Derbyshire Yeomanry launched their attack. First the British Artillery opened up and their Anti-Tank, Medium and Field guns raked Marburg and the German positions in front of it. This artillery barrage lasted a good half hour and then the 2nd Derbyshire Yeomanry jumped out of their slit-trenches and attempted to storm Marburg.

The Germans recovered pretty quickly, however, and their snipers, riflemen and machine-gunners were soon in action meeting the attack. When this happened Dave also launched his own attack on the right flank of Marburg. The moment his men began rushing from tree to tree to get to Marburg they were met with a deadly sweeping fire from the German positions in front of the houses. Dave had already anticipated that and split his Platoons to try and get into the trench lines and clear them. Once this was done his men then moved forward and went after the snipers and machine-gun nests. This took time as the men were fighting in deep, greasy and slippery mud. The only good thing with that was it helped smother some of the German shells landing in front of their positions.

Still the men kept on slugging forward and by 10.00 a.m., when it was raining harder than ever, both the Derbyshire and the Fusiliers had gained about 200 yards each. The two Regiments had covered only about 1/8 of a mile to Marburg and as each kept on pressing forward, Dave's Company was reinforced by Tom Clark's A Company while Jack Walsh's A Company was also reinforced by another Company of the Derbyshire. By then the fighting was truly vicious and brutal. It was done at close quarters and bayonets, rifles, machine-guns and grenades were used. When the two Regiments came within 100 yards of Marburg Dave heard the huge shrieking whining of 88s smashing through the trees and coming down on Marburg itself.

The Germans were also laying down a deadly mortaring fire in front of their own positions and Dave saw trying to get to Marburg through a frontal assault with his Platoons moving abreast on a single line through the trees, with Tom Clark's A Company doing the same thing right behind him, wasn't going to work. Something else was needed. Dave made his Company, and Tom Clark's Company, pull back a little from the attack and go to ground while still keeping their fire on Marburg. Then he turned to Mitchell who was standing behind him and told him to go and get him a Pioneer. In a moment Mitchell was gone and when he came back a little later, it was with a tall and lean soldier who seemed to be in his early thirties. This soldier's uniform was dripping wet and he looked haggard and exhausted. Dave looked at him for a long moment and then said: "Do I know you from somewhere?"

"Yes, Sir."

"From where?"

"Ortona, Sir."

"That's it. Your name is Lawson, isn't it?"

"That's right, Sir. Tom Lawson."

"You're the one who blew holes in the apartment houses with Teller mines, right?"

"That's me, Sir."

"All right, Lawson. I have another job for you."

Lawson looked at Dave and Dave pointed to the houses in Marburg and said: "You see those reinforced houses over there?"

The Long War

Lawson looked at the houses Dave was pointing to and said: "Yes, Sir."

"They're all one-story reinforced bunkers. Can we blow them up?"

"Of course."

"How?"

"We use satchel charges with very short fuses."

"And this will bring them down?"

"Yes, Sir."

"How?"

"First we throw the satchel charges through the firing slits. And then we run around those bunkers and blow open their front doors?"

"That's it?"

"That's it."

"If we blow down one of those bunkers. Can we work from its ruins to bring down the others?"

"Of course."

"To do it right. How many men do you need?"

"Three others."

"Do you have them?"

"Yes, Sir."

"All right. Go get them."

CHAPTER 183

Tom Lawson left to go and get the other Pioneers and Dave ran back in a crouch to A Company to speak with Tom Clark about what he wanted to do next. Then Dave ran back in a crouch to his own Company as Lawson arrived with three other Pioneers and the needed explosives. Dave told the Pioneers what he expected and then went on the attack again. This time he brought up the two Companies close together so they could rush the last house on the right flank in one swift movement. Dave was leading the Companies and when he stood up and began running toward that house, the men also stood up and followed him. Everyone was yelling and firing and this time Dave made it up the long slippery slope of the forest to the house.

    Dave was with a few soldiers and the Pioneers stood behind them. At the wall Lawson and another Pioneer threw satchel charges through the firing slit. Then the men threw themselves on the ground as there was a tremendous explosion. As soon as this explosion was over Dave was up and running again with the soldiers who were with him and with the Pioneers. They came barreling around the house, onto the muddy forest road, and to its front door. Lawson put a satchel right against the door, everyone stepped back, and there was another huge explosion that made a big hole in the door. Grenades were thrown in and when Dave rushed in with the other soldiers, he saw the house was exactly as he had expected it. The basement and ground floor had been reinforced with four feet of concrete and with some armor plating near the firing slit.

    There were German bodies everywhere and Dave watched as the Pioneers busied themselves setting up charges to bring the house down. Then Lawson flashed the thumbs-up sign at Dave. Everyone rushed out of the house and threw themselves flat on the road as the house blew apart and pieces of armor plating and chunks of concrete flew all around. A huge cloud of dust hung over where the house had been and there was firing from some of the houses across the road. At about the same time Dave could hear heavy firing from behind the house facing the one they had just blown up and behind some of the houses on the other side of the road at the other end of Marburg. Also, in the distance, he could see Jack Walsh running up to the house at the extreme end of the left flank. Walsh was with some soldiers and in a moment he disappeared against the wall of that house.

By then Dave was running with the soldiers who were with him and the Pioneers toward the second house. When they got to that house they did exactly to it what they had done to the first one. First they threw in satchel charges in the firing slit facing the forest. Then they ran around it to blast open the front door. Finally they threw grenades in and set up charges to bring this house down. Once this was done they moved on the the third house. By then Dave had quite a few soldiers with him and more Pioneers. There were screams and yells from the soldiers who were shot or wounded. Smoke was everywhere. There was now heavy firing behind the houses on the other side of the road as soldiers from Bob Brown's C Company and Bill Blair's D Company also ran around those houses and blew them apart with satchel charges.

On the left flank Walsh was doing exactly what Dave was doing. He was blowing up the houses he was attacking and German artillery was dropping on both sides of the road as well as on some of the houses. Several soldiers of Dave's and Tom Clark's Companies were lying dead near the houses and on the road and it was the same thing for quite a few men of Bob Brown's and Bill Blair's Companies. Some of the wounded were screaming and others were bleeding badly. By then it was close to noon and there were only two more houses in the center of Marburg that needed to be overrun. Those houses were on each side of the road and Dave signaled to Walsh he was going to take the one closest to him and that Walsh should go for the one on tbe other side of the road.

Walsh nodded and Dave could see him run in and out of the ruins of the last one he had blown up and firing his Thompson machine-gun. Dave, himself, was busy rushing the last one with his men and blowing it up with the Pioneers. By then everyone was tired and it took a little longer. But finally they blew it apart and once the huge cloud of dust had settled on the road, Dave noticed there were no more houses standing on either side of Marburg. Only ruins. The rain was still falling steadily and there was some isolated firing on both sides of the road from the forest. But

Germany

that was all. The Reichswald was mostly silent and men from the Fusiliers and the Derbyshire now came out of the ruins. They just walked around silently and held on to their rifles or machine-guns.

But there was no whooping. No cheering. Just plain bone-breaking fatigue. There were dead and wounded everywhere. Already the Chaplains and Medics were moving through the forest and along the road and checking them. Dave was standing in the middle of the road with Lawson and some Pioneers when he saw Walsh. He was holding on to his machine-gun and walking very slowly. His right cheek was bloody from a slight cut and when he saw Dave, he came over to him and said: "Captain."

"Captain."

"That was quite a show."

"It was."

"Never thought the Germans would fight so hard."

"They always do."

"They never seem to know when they're beaten, don't they?"

"They don't.

"I wish they did, though. Every once in a while."

"Me too."

Walsh now stepped close to Dave. He embraced him wearily and said: "Thanks."

"It's all right. Any time."

CHAPTER 184

Walsh left and Dave watched the Chaplains and Medics move through the forest and then up and down the road in order to take care of the dead and wounded. Some of the men of Bob Brown's C Company now came out from the other side of the road and began taking the Germans that had been made prisoners down the trails that led out of the forest. As he walked back and forth along the road Dave saw he had lost quite a few men. Most of them were replacements. Soon after Colonel Caldwell drove up in a mud-splattered jeep with Major-General T.G. Rennie of the 51st Highland Infantry Division. Both of them called Dave and Walsh over and congratulated them on their taking Marburg.

With its capture, General Rennie told them, they had now gained control of the lateral road from Kranenburg, Frasselt and Hekkens. As a result the 51st Highland Infantry Division would move southeastward into Germany and the Regiment would follow them and provide assault support. The Colonel then left with Major-General Rennie and the next day, the 51st Highland Infantry Division and the Regiment began their southeastward move. A little over three miles into the forest they ran into the *Siegfried Line*, with its many trenches and anti-tank ditches, and the going became a lot tougher. In order to slow down the advance the Germans used Shu-mines, self-propelled guns, mortars and artillery. The 51st Highland and the Fusiliers were now facing German parachutists and those parachutists fought fiercely and fanatically for every inch of ground.

The 51st Highland Division was then involved in the brutal and savage battles for Hekkens, Kessel, Asperden and Goch. Dave's Regiment, and his Company, provided the assault support for those battles. From February

9 to February 21, 1945, the weather during those battles was atrocious. It rained all the time except for one day of sunlight. Mud was everywhere and severely restricted access to our tanks along the forest trails. No air cover could be given. Now, for the first time since they had entered Germany, the weight and accuracy of German artillery was equal to our own. The 51st Highland Divison just kept on slugging its way eastward and Dave's Regiment followed. Then, on Wednesday, February 21, 1945, Goch was taken and a new assignment was given to Dave's Regiment.

That day General Crerar decided to make his main assault in Germany in the north. He chose to make it with General Simonds' 2nd Corps. This Corps had the 2nd and 3rd Canadian Infantry Divisions, the 4th Armored and two British Divisions, the 43rd Wessex and the 11th Armored. On his right General Horrocks' 30th Corps would guard his flank while, at the same time, taking over parts of the country alongside the Maas river. Once this decision was made Dave's Regiment stayed in Goch where it was brought up to strength again. Then on Monday morning, February 26, 1945, it was reassigned to the 2nd Canadian Infantry Division. This Division was now led by Major-General Bruce Matthews, and the Regiment was taken to new positions east of Udem for its next task.

The Regiment was going to be involved in the push through the Hochwald forest.

CHAPTER 185

In the early hours before dawn, on February 27, 1945, it had been decided by General Matthews that Dave's Regiment would go down the slopes leading to the Hochwald Forest. This operation was called *Blockbuster* and those slopes led to the *Schlieffen* defenses at the edge of the forest. The South Saskatchewan Regiment would come in behind the Fusiliers and both Regiments would be supported by tanks of the South Albertas. They would be on the right flank of the Calgary Highlanders and the Fusiliers Mont-Royal and those Regiments would also be attacking with the support of tanks from the South Albertas. Finally other Regiments would also be used on the right flank of Dave's Regiment to try and break through Point 73, the Tuschen Wald and the Balberger Wald on the right side of the forest.

That night the sky was clear, star-filled and moon-lit and at precisely 4.00 a.m., the tanks of the South Albertas and Dave's Regiment were ordered to move. The tanks began going down the slopes and Dave's Company followed behind them. The Regiment was spread out in the arrowhead formation. This meant Dave's Company was in the lead at the top of the arrowhead. Tom Clark's A Company was some distance back on the right flank. Bob Brown's C Company was also some distance back on the left. Bill Blair's D Company was in the center at the rear. The South Albertas tanks moved down the slope into open ground and Dave's men followed behind them. In a short while they could see in the clear, star-filled and moon-lit night a row of low white farmhouses, to the right, at the edge of the forest.

The tanks kept on coming down until, halfway to the row of farmhouses, the leading tank exploded in a huge red and orange ball of fire. MG 42s began firing from the farmhouses and the second tank was hit by a *panzerfaust* and burst into flames. Dave's men went to ground and 88s began hitting the open ground and the slopes behind them. The other tanks began rushing the row of farmhouses and firing at them with their 75 mm guns and their machine-guns while Dave's men suddenly got up and began running toward those farmhouses in order to overrun them. The tanks were firing at the roofs and upper windows and not long after, the men in Dave's Company got into the farmhouses and began cleaning them out. Most German parachutists in those farmhouses were from the Parachute Army Assault Unit.

They stood their ground and died at their posts, and the few that ran away were shot by our Bren Gunners. The German artillery and mortars were extremely precise and were hitting most of the farmhouses. As soon as those farmhouses had been overrun the tanks and Dave's men began moving into the forest itself covered by smoke from the tanks. By then it was daylight and Dave's men, and the Regiment, found themselves into the *Schlieffen Line*. This was a defensive line made up of a network of fortified houses and hidden machine-gun nests in the forest itself. The parachutists defending them were fighting to the death and it took all day, as well as the next, to clear it and move past them. By the time they had been able to do that, on the second day, it was close to nightfall and Dave's men had to fight off two German counter-attacks before things became quiet and they were able to settle down for the night

The weather was getting cooler and it was very dark and quiet in the forest except for the occasional firing of an MG 42 or a Bren gun. Dave's men were well dug-in, in positions that were some distance past the *Schlieffen Line* and in the morning of the third day, they came out of those positions and began moving deeper into the forest with the tanks. By now they were shelled and mortared mercilessly by the Germans. The tanks could only move slowly through the trails and Dave could hear heavy firing on both flanks of his Regiment. The Germans were shelling the trails and the tree-bursts were causing heavy casualties among his men. With every foot of ground his men were learning the hard lesson that when shells hit the trees it was better to hug them rather than to throw yourself on the ground.

If you hugged the trees you had a pretty good chance of survival. If you threw yourself on the ground, on the other hand, you ran the risk of being cut to pieces by shrapnel. The parachutists used their self-propelled guns to fire at them from the trails. There were always new fortified houses and machine-gun nests to deal with. Dave had to charge twice on each side of the trail they were using in order to prevent the parachutists from firing at the tanks. Snipers and *Panzerfaust* teams were everywhere. The shelling and mortaring was the heaviest Dave had seen since Normandy. Thick, gluey, heavy mud was slowing down the tanks. Several savage counter-attacks were launched by the parachutists and had to be stopped. Dave's men were getting killed by shrapnel, *panzerfausts* and machine-gun fire.

Schu-mines were laid on some of the trails so when you avoided them and moved past them, you would step on other mines buried beneath the trails. There were also booby-traps and trip-wires on most of those trails. The going was extremely slow and by the end of the third day, Dave's men had moved close to the first of two lateral roads that ran north-south through the forest. The first one ran about halfway through it while the second one stood near the end of it on the east side. The parachutists were well dug-in behind that first lateral road and since it was getting close to nightfall again, Dave decided to wait until daylight before assaulting it. With daylight he felt they would be better able to see the German positions and, this way, try and break through them and through the forest.

CHAPTER 186

Dave's men stayed in their positions all night and at first light, Dave couldn't believe what he saw. A light slanting snow was falling all over the forest and blanketing the Hochwald. Their slit-trenches, and all German positions, were covered with snow and hard to see. The snow was falling steadily and fluffily and the men and tanks were covered with it. With daylight the tanks began moving toward the first lateral road and then it happened. Artillery, mortars, *panzerfausts,* MG 34s, 42s, machine-gun and rifle fire started raking their positions as the tanks began firing back at German strongholds and at the parachutists. Dave's men jumped out of their own slit-trenches and ran in a crouch behind the tanks.

Everyone was firing and yelling. There were tree-bursts all around. Shrapnel was coming down on all sides. The tanks were trying to smash through the lateral road and keep on moving. Despite the snow all trails were filled with mud. Dave's men were behind the lead Sherman and were sweeping the flanks with fire. The tanks were moving slowly but managed to smash through the road and keep on going. Behind them Dave's men jumped in the German positions and fought the parachutists with machine-guns, rifles, pistols, bayonets and at times bare hands. As always the parachutists fought fiercely and to the death. By early afternoon, while the snow was falling more thickly and heavily than ever, Dave's men had left the first lateral road behind and were moving toward the second one.

By now their progress through the forest could be measured in yards. The Germans used the snowy trails and pine trees well to defend against their advance. In fact the rest of that day and the next one were spent slugging it out and trying to get to the second lateral road. For those two days the fighting was always the same. The tanks were firing at the parachutists and their positions. The German used *panzerfaust* teams to try and sneak on our tanks and blow them up. Their artillery and mortar fire was deadly. Whenever progress was made through the trails the Germans regrouped and launched counter-attacks. They came running through the pine trees and yelling and screaming and Dave's men had to shoot or fight with them at close range. There were dead and wounded everywhere and the snow where they had fought was bloody and muddy.

By the third day, Dave's men had almost made it to the second lateral road. It was still snowing heavily and fluffily and in the distance they could see a break in the pine trees where the forest ended. By now the artillery and mortar fire was more vicious and savage than ever and the lead tank had difficulty going up a slight rise in the forest trail. They were stopped about 1000 yards from the road and tree-burst and shrapnel were exploding all around them. There was an MG 42 machine-gun on each flank that was keeping the men crouching behind the tanks and Dave knew if they stayed there much longer they'd all get killed. Dave was about to lead another charge on the right side of the trail to silence the MG 42 on that flank when Higgins, who was standing behind him, suddenly stepped in front of him.

When he did Higgins turned to Dave. He grinned at him and said: "Do you remember what my old man told me?" "Sure," Dave said. "He said that, in anything, going in at the top and doing things first-class was the only way," Higgins said. "Well, he's wrong. Dead wrong. That's the way. That's the best way." Higgins then jumped down the right side of the trail and began running toward the MG 42. He was running low in the folds of the forest and as he disappeared from view with his machine-gun, Dave could hear him yell: *"Deutschen sind scheisse!" "Ich pisse uber Deutschen!"* There was wild firing in the distance and then the explosions of grenades. The firing went on for quite a while and Addams, who was now standing behind Dave, said: "The hell with this!"

In a moment Addams also jumped down the right side of the trail with his machine-gun and ran low in the folds of the forest until he, too, was lost in the falling snow. After a while there was the short, staccato sound of machine-gun fire and Dave heard Addams yell: *"Kommen sie!" "Kommen sie!" "Was furchten Ihr!" "Ihr bastarden!"* There was more wild firing and the explosions of grenades and Mitchell, who had now stepped close to Dave behind the lead tank, suddenly said: "No! Oh no!" Then he turned and jumped down the trail on the left flank with his machine-gun. He was closely followed by Mike Messina, one of the new replacements, and they, too, ran low in the folds of the forest on that side before disappearing in

Germany

the falling snow. In no time wild firing and the explosions of grenades could be heard from that flank as well.

The wild firing and explosions of grenades carried quite distinctly and Dave could hear Mitchel yell: *"Mordernen!" "Schmutzige bastarden!" "Ich werde toten alles euch!"* Tom Bradley now dropped down next to Dave and said: "Gee. I didn't know those guys spoke German." "They don't," Dave said. "Those are insults. Lang taught them." By then there was a great deal of firing on both sides of the trail and the lead tank was also firing steadily straight ahead and machine-gunning the German positions in front of them. The tank was also churning through the mud and then beginning to move and go up the trail. The other tanks behind them were also now moving and Dave ran with his men behind the lead tank.

Everyone was yelling and firing and as they crossed the second lateral road, Dave saw in the distance Higgins and Addams lying bloodily on top of two Germans. Their snow-flecked faces were turned toward the road and both of them had slight rills of blood running down their mouths. Dave turned to the other side of the road and saw Mitchell and Messina lying face down in the snow near machine-gun positions. Then the lead tank and Dave and his men burst through the tree line and made it to an open and snowy road past those trees.

They had broken through the Hochwald forest.

CHAPTER 187

When they broke through the Hochwald forest the faces of Dave's men were drawn and haggard. They walked slowly down the open and snowy road and Dave stopped on the left side of it to let some of them go by. In the distance on his right, about a mile away to the southeast, he could see a small, low-lying, snow-covered wood that was called Weston. Dave could hear steady and heavy firing coming from there and knew the Black Watch and Maisonneuve Regiments were busy attacking it and trying to clean it up. Dave's men walked past him in silence and two miles past the Hochwald, they came to a long low-slung farmhouse on the right side of the road.

There were several logs lying on both sides of it, near the entrance, and a few of the tanks now left the road and headed for it. Some of Dave's men ran behind them and when they reached the farmhouse, they went in to see if any Germans were hiding there. In a moment they came out and motioned with their rifles it was clean. There were no Germans inside. Dave headed there with his men and as he moved toward it, he noticed Bostwick a little ahead of him. Bostwick was holding on to his Thompson machine-gun and was covered with snow. He was breathing heavily and was gripping his machine-gun tightly. He was walking slowly and when he came near the entrance, he turned around suddenly and yelled: "I hate them! I hate the bastards!" Bostwick waved his machine-gun around wildly and yelled: "They fight! and fight! and fight! and never quit! The bastards never quit! Why don't they quit!"

Bostwick looked at them all wildly and stabbed at the sky savagely with his machine-gun as he yelled: "Well, no German is going to kill me! Do you hear me! None!" Dave, who had been watching Bostwick carefully, now stepped closer to him and said: "We hear you, Sergeant Major." Bostwick now turned to Dave and screamed: "I'm never going to die! Never! Do you hear me! Never!" "I hear you, Sergeant Major," Dave said. "And you! You!" Bostwick screamed as he threw down his machine-gun in the snow and took out a black matt knife from the back of his belt. "Didn't I tell you I was going to get back to you! Hey! Didn't I tell you!" "Calm yourself, Sergeant Major," Dave said as he began backing away from him a little and also threw down his machine-gun in the snow.

"Come on! Come on!" Bostwick yelled as he swung his knife back and forth in front of him and moved in on Dave. "I'm sick of you! and the Germans! and the war!" "Please, calm yourself, Sergeant Major," Dave said as he backed away from him a little more and as he could see Slav, at the back of Bostwick, step closer to him and raise his machine-gun somewhat. "Come on! Come on!" Bostwick screamed at Dave as he ran closer to him and tried to stab him. Dave stepped back to the left to avoid the move and then both of them began circling and facing each other. There was a wild insane look in Bostwick's eyes and Dave watched him carefully as they kept on circling each other.

In a moment Bostwick came in hard with a stabbing move from underneath. Dave stepped inside the move and blocked it hard with his left forearm before springing in the clear. Bostwick was watching him wildly and narrowly and he came in again with a fast stabbing move from underneath. Once more Dave stepped inside the move and blocked it hard with his left forearm before springing in the clear. By now Slav's machine-gun was leveled at the back of Bostwick and he came in with a third stabbing move. Again Dave stepped inside the move and blocked it hard with his left forearm. But this time Dave didn't spring clear from the move. He blocked it hard with his forearm and then grabbed Bostwick's left arm. Dave kept his left arm away from his body while he stepped close to Bostwick and held him tightly.

Dave could feel Bostwick's heart pounding and his body shaking and said: "It's okay, Sergeant Major. It's okay." Bostwick tried hard a few times to bring his right arm close to Dave's body to stab him. But Dave held it away from him and as they stayed close together, Dave said: "Drop the knife, Sergeant Major. Please, drop the knife." Bostwick tried a few more times half-heartedly to stab him and then dropped the knife in the snow. As Dave still held him tightly Bostwick was shaking and muttering: "Higgins, Addams, Mitchell, Messina. They've killed them. They're killing us all." Then Dave stepped away from Bostwick and as Bostwick just stood where Dave had held him and looked down, Dave turned to where Bostwick had dropped his knife in the snow. Dave was drenched in sweat and exhausted and when he bent and picked up the knife, he looked at it, looked at Bostwick, and then handed it to him.

"I believe this belong to you, Sergeant Major," Dave said. Bostwick looked at the knife, looked at Dave, and then picked it up and put it back in his belt. Then he slowly picked up his machine-gun and went and sat on a snowy log to the right of the entrance, as Slav lowered his machine-gun and as a huge sigh of relief was heard from the soldiers who had been standing around and watching them fight. Dave, himself, also picked up his machine-gun and went and sat on another log not far from Bostwick, on his left. He sat on this log with Slav and a few soldiers, and for the longest of time he looked at the snow and didn't say anything.

CHAPTER 188

After a while all the men of Dave's Company made it to the farmhouse and he got up and led them down the open and snowy road toward a small village called Mirten, about half a mile from the farmhouse. This village turned out to be deserted and Dave's men, and the rest of the Company, took it over and ended up staying there for a month while the Regiment was brought up to strength again. All the Companies were down to about 20% strength and new replacements were needed once again to rebuild the Regiment into a strong fighting force. Then on Tuesday, April 3, 1945, they were assigned to the 4th Canadian Armored Division that was led by Major-General Chris Vokes. They were to support the 4th Canadian Division on its drive to northwestern Germany and to the city of Oldenburg.

On Thursday morning, April 5, 1945, on a bright and sunny morning, the Regiment crossed the Rhine at Rees and reached the Ems River two days later. They stormed across the Ems and overran the town of Meppen in support of the Argylls and Sutherland Highlanders of Canada. Then they were on their way to Sögel and when they reached it and, some time later, Friesoythe, they were fired upon by civilians. In the face of such unmilitary actions General Vokes warned them by blowing up some houses in Sögel and then leveling Friesoythe. By now it was spring and as they kept on closing in on Oldenburg, the fighting became extremely fierce and ferocious. They were attacking across flat swampy ground and that meant the tanks could only use the roads. As a result most of the fighting had to be done by the infantry.

The Germans were using mines and demolitions to try and slow down the advance and their artillery and mortars were as deadly as ever. Then, on Tuesday, April 17, 1945, in order to be able to attack on higher and drier ground and get to Oldenburg faster, General Vokes ordered the Algonquin Regiment to cross the Küsten Canal and attack Oldenburg through the north side of it through Bad Zwischenahn. Dave's Regiment would attack from the south side of it through lower and swampier ground. By then the Regiment was fighting units of Infantry, Engineers, Marines and Parachutists and on both sides of the canal the fighting was brutal and savage. Still the Regiment kept on pushing forward and on the early morning of May 4, 1945, it finally reached Oldenburg.

In the distance, it gleamed in the sunlight and its Church spires, castles, mansions, and many round-roofed and low-lying buildings gave it an ancient and medieval look. Oldenburg was a town of about 150,000 people and Dave's Company was the first Company of the Regiment, and of the Division, to reach it. The Company came into it from the south side of the Küsten Canal and Dave carefully led his men into the town itself from the south. The men walked in a single file alongside the canal road, past the linden trees, and the town seemed to be deserted. There had been rumors for the last few days of a German surrender and as they came into Oldenburg, Dave led his men across the Bremer Bridge past a large castle, a high-steepled church, an open market and some municipal buildings until they got on a long street called the Alexanderstrasse and another one called Schulweg that led to the end of town.

Oldenburg looked as if it hadn't been bombed. A few buildings looked damaged in the center of town. But this could have been from returning bombers dropping their excess ordnance; not from any bombing. All along the town the streets were empty and deserted and near the end of it, on Schulwegstrasse, Dave, who was carrying his Thompson machine-gun and looking around carefully, saw a gray-haired unshaven old man in a filthy brown sweater and worn-out brown pants come up the road toward him. The old man was toothless and walked with a limp and when he reached Dave, he pointed down the road and said to him: *"Jung SS sind in die barrikade ausserhalb der stadt. Sie sagen das sie wollen zu nachgeben." "Danke,"* Dave said. Red was standing next to Dave and asked: "What did he say?" "He says," Dave told him, "there are young SS who want to surrender down the road."

Dave took out his binoculars with his left hand, while still holding on to his Thompson machine-gun, and looked down the road. Sure enough, just a little past the end of the town, about 200 feet away, in a depression on the left side of the road, was a group of young SS in mottled-green camouflage who were standing behind an MG 42. The MG 42 stood right against the left side of the road and on the other side, there was a small pine wood. One of the young SS, a bareheaded medium-sized trim blonde

Germany

soldier, also had his binoculars out and was looking at them. Dave put down his binoculars and said: "I don't know. I just don't know about this one." "I don't know either," Red said. Lang now came up to them and said: "What's up?"

Dave pointed to the old man who was standing in the street and said: "This old man says these young SS want to surrender." "It might be true," Lang said. "Maybe," Dave said. "But I don't trust the SS." "Let me go and talk to them," Lang said. "You never know." "All right," Dave said. "But be careful." Lang nodded and tied a white handkerchief to the top of the barrel of his rifle. He waved his rifle at them and then began walking toward them. The young SS who had been looking at them with his binoculars now climbed out of the depression where the MG 42 was. He got on the road and began walking toward Lang. He was carrying a Schmeisser in his right hand and both of them came and stopped about 100 feet from where the Company was standing.

The young SS began talking with Lang and Dave raised his binoculars again with his left hand and watched them. The young SS was nodding and talking with Lang. Then Lang turned and as he began walking back toward the Company, Dave suddenly gripped his binoculars very tightly because, as Lang began walking toward them, he saw the young SS grin and say: *"Wissen sie nicht Das SS niemals nachgeben."* What the young SS was saying was: "Don't you know the SS never surrender." Then he leveled his Schmeisser at Lang and fired a short burst into his back as Dave yelled: "No! NO!" Then Dave took off and began running after the young SS as he turned and began running back into the path the MG 42. At the same time heavy firing broke out all around as the young SS turned and saw Dave gaining on him.

When he saw this the young SS cut suddenly to the right toward the wood and Dave also cut to the right and came yelling and barreling after him. There was now the harsh staccato sound of the MG 42 firing and the sharp explosions of several grenades as Dave kept on running swiftly and savagely after him. In no time they were past the tree line and running through the wood that was mottled with sunlight. Dave was gaining on him and when they were nearly in the middle of the wood, the young SS cut to the right and began running down a trail between the trees. Dave was still yelling and screaming at him and as he was getting closer to him, the young SS ran into several fallen pine trees that were blocking the trail. When he saw this he turned suddenly and leveled his Schmeisser at Dave.

The young SS pulled the trigger but his Schemeisser jammed and as he stood there with a wild and twisted face, he began yelling *"Mutter!"*

The Long War

"Mutter!" as Dave reached him and fired and fired at him in the face until he had no face left and then at his body that was just a bloody mottled mess on the wood floor until he had emptied the magazine in his Thompson. Then Dave turned and threw his Thompson machine-gun away from him before he went and sat down on a fallen log not far from the dead young SS, on his right. It was now very quiet in the wood. The sun shone brightly on the mottled floor. The birds were singing. And there was a nice breeze blowing through the trees.

Dave sat there for a long time. He was breathing heavily and looking down at the floor of the wood. After a while he heard creaking through the trees and saw Slav coming toward him with other soldiers. Slav had his Thompson machine-gun and when he reached him, he said: "Come. Come, Captain. It's all right. It's all over."

CHAPTER 189

Dave sat in the wood for a little while more. Then he got up heavily and began walking back with Slav and the other soldiers. Dave walked slowly and when they came out of the wood, he saw all the young SS who had stood behind the MG 42 were lying sprawled around it. A few were lying face down in the grass a little distance from it. On the road itself some men of the Company had brought up a stretcher and were putting the body of Lang on it. Then they lifted the stretcher and Dave took Lang's left hand with his right hand and held it as they walked back to the outskirts of town. On the outskirts they lay the stretcher down by the curb of the road and Dave walked around it.

Dave sat down on the curb and stared at the stretcher. He sat with his arms on his knees and after a while, Moran ran up to him and handed him a message from the Colonel that had come in on the wireless. Dave nodded at Moran and looked at the message briefly. Then he folded it and put it in the right pocket of his tunic as a jeep came barreling down the road. The jeep made a sharp U-turn and came and stopped in front of them. The soldier in the jeep wore the full crowns of a Major and had on a spotless and brand-new uniform. His helmet and boots were shiny and he was of average height and a little flabby. As he came and stopped in front of them, he said: "Can anyone around here tell me where I can find Captain Lindsay?" Red swung sharply to him and said: "Who wants to know?"

The Major looked startled and said: "Me." "I'm Captain Lindsay," Dave said as he got up heavily from the curb and walked over to the jeep. "My God, Captain!" the Major said when he saw Dave walk toward him. "Am I glad to see you!" Dave nodded and the Major said: "Do you know what day it is?" Dave didn't say anything and the Major said: "It's Saturday, May 5, 1945." "So?" Dave said. "My God, Captain," the Major said. "The Germans are surrendering this afternoon at Wageningen." "So?" Dave said. "Don't you know what this means?" the Major said. "The war is over." "Good," Dave said. "No, no," the Major said. "You don't get it." "What do I not get?" Dave asked. "I work for the *Maple Leaf,*" the Major said. "They want pictures, interviews, articles. And they want a couple of war heroes to be there and add prestige, shall we say, to this historical event."

"What has this got to do with me?" Dave said. "My God, Captain," the Major said. "You're a real war hero. You won the MM, the MC and the DSO. You landed in Dieppe, escaped from Colditz and fought all through the war. The paper wanted me to find you." "What for?" Dave asked. "To accompany me to Wageningen," the Major said, "so you can be present at the surrender." "No way," Dave said. "I won't do that." "Listen, Captain," the Major said. "The orders don't come from me. I'm brand new at this job. The orders come from Colonel Johnson of the paper itself. And he got his orders from General Crerar." "And if I don't do this?" Dave said. "You don't have a choice," the Major said. "General Crerar wants a couple of much-decorated war heroes at the surrender. My assistant, Jean Watson, is working to also bring Joe Norton to Wageningen."

"Who's Joe Norton?" Dave asked. "Like you he's a much-decorated war hero," the Major said. "He won the MM, the MC and the DCM." Dave nodded and didn't say anything for a moment. Then he said: "All right. If that's what they want." Dave left the jeep for a moment and walked over to Bostwick who was standing in the middle of the street with Lieutenant Moran. Bostwick's eyes were wide and brilliant and he had that baleful, malevolent and Asiatic grin Dave had seen on him when he had first met him. "Are you all right?" Dave asked when he came close to Bostwick. "Of course, Captain," Bostwick grinned. "Are you sure?" Dave said. "Never been better, Captain," Bostwick grinned. "Good," Dave said. "Listen, you two. I have to go on some business with this Major. I'll be gone for a couple of days and I want you to take over the Company for me."

"No problem, Captain," Bostwick grinned. "The Lieutenant will run it. And I'll watch." "I mean it," Dave said. "I've just received a message from the Colonel. The Germans are surrendering and the stop line for our advance is where the MG 42 and the small wood is. Dig in there and wait for the other Companies and the Colonel to catch up with you. Do you understand?" Moran and Bostwick nodded and, as Bostwick grinned at him, Dave walked back to the Major's jeep. He got in on the passenger's side and the Major left and drove south through Oldenburg. By now a few old men and women were coming out in the streets and they drove out of the city and through Friesoythe, Sögel and Meppen. They crossed the Ems river at Lingen, drove through Nordhorn, and Dave noticed there was a lot of military traffic on the road.

Most of the traffic was heading northeast and Dave saw many German units were now being escorted by Allied soldiers. They crossed the Dutch border at Denekamp and went through Hengelo, Lochen, Zutphen, Rheden, Arnhem, Renkun until they finally reached the small town of Wageningen on the Neder River. By then it was close to 2.00 o'clock in the afternoon, and they had driven almost 115 miles on a bright and sunny day. Wageningen was full of Allied soldiers and the Major, whose name, Dave now found out, was John Maxwell, took him to the dusty lobby of a run-down and shell-torn hotel where the surrender was to take place. The Major made Dave stand at the rear of the lobby facing the entrance.

Dave stayed at the rear with several other officers and photographers, and a plain wooden table had been put in the middle of the lobby with several maps of Holland and northwestern Germany on it. The sun was pouring in through the windows of the lobby and after a while there was a stir as the Germans came in. Colonel-General Johannes Blaskowitz, ex-conqueror of Poland and present commander of the 25th German Army for Holland and northwestern Germany, now stepped in with Lieutenant-General Paul Reichelt and other German officers. Blaskowitz was wearing a dusty black leather coat and his face was gray and pasty. He was swallowing hard, blinking and looking around him. Blaskowitz came and stood near the table with General Reichelt and the other German officers and in a moment, Lieutenant-General Charles Foulkes entered, from a door to the right of where Dave was standing, with Brigadier George Kitching, Prince Bernhard of the Netherlands, other officers and the German translator.

General Foulkes took a sheet of paper from his coat pocket and began reading the terms of surrender. Several cameras flashed and clicked in the silence of the lobby. General Blaskowitz nodded as the translator told him the terms of surrender and occasionally said: *"Ja." "Ja."* Once in a while he asked for more time for the disposition of his troops but, mostly, he only said: *"Ja."* Then General Foulkes handed him the surrender document. General Blaskowitz took out his pen, bent down and signed it. Then he gave the document back to General Foulkes, saluted and left the hotel with the other German officers.

The Second World War was now officially over.

BOOK SEVENTEEN

AT THE END

CHAPTER 190

The Second World War may have been over. Peace, however, was only beginning. As soon as General Blaskowitz had signed the surrender document and left the hotel, the officers and photographers in the lobby began smiling and shaking hands. The Major took Dave out on the steps of the hotel where Lieutenant Jean Watson, his assistant, interviewed him. Jean Watson was a bright-eyed, slim, young, blonde woman, in her mid-twenties, and she asked Dave all kinds of excited questions such as: Did he have a good war? Did he kill himself a whole lot of Germans? How did he feel about winning so many medals and being a hero? Dave tried to answer her questions as best as he could and the Major then took pictures of him as well as of Joe Norton who was now brought out on the steps of the hotel.

Joe Norton was a full-blooded Mohawk Indian in his mid-thirties from the reserve at Katahnabe in southern Ontario. He was tall, strong and muscular and his thick dark hair was cut short in a crew cut. He belonged to the Algonquin Regiment and was very fond of whiskey. As soon as the Major and Jean Watson had finished interviewing and photographing them and had gone to talk to General Foulkes, he offered Dave a drink from a small silver flask he carried in his tunic. In fact he always carried two of them and as they stood on the steps of the hotel, they drank Norton's whiskey. They drank to war and peace, to their health, to the success of their Regiments and then the Major came and brought them inside the hotel. He had booked two rooms for them on the second floor for the night and told them they would be driven back to their units in the morning.

The Major had also arranged for the hotel to prepare them a meal of potatoes and salad and when they had eaten this meal, in a small dining-room to the right of the lobby, they went up to Norton's room where they spent the evening drinking Norton's whiskey and talking about Black Foot, Geronimo, and Tecumseh's attempt to set up a Confederation of Five Nations. Dave went to his room around 2.00 in the morning and when he woke up, it was a little after 9.00 o'clock. Dave went down to the lobby and found Norton had already gone. Dave had some coffee in the small dining-room and then was picked up by a tall and thin Lieutenant, who was called Don Draper, in order to be driven back to his Regiment.

They left Wageningen and drove back to Oldenburg through the same places Dave had gone through before. It was another bright and sunny day and they went through Renkum, Arnhem, Rheden, Zutphen, Lochen, Hengelo and crossed into Germany at Denekamp. This morning there was again a lot of military traffic on the road and they saw more German units being escorted by Allied soldiers. Draper drove slowly and Dave made him speed up. The war was just over and there might still be renegade soldiers and snipers wanting to fire at them. In Germany they went through Nordhorn, crossed the Ems river at Lingen, and drove through Meppen, Sögel, Friesoythe until they reached Oldenburg around 2.00 o'clock in the afternoon. Now that Germany had surrendered there were several old men, women and children in the streets and Dave found his Regiment at the stop line at the other end of town.

All the Companies were at that stop line with the Colonel and they were getting ready to move out. Their new assignment: Wilhelmshaven, a town of almost 100,000 people. They were going there to do occupations duties and oversee the huge prisoners of war cages that were going to be built for the German officers and soldiers in northwestern Germany. At 4.00 o'clock in the afternoon Bedford trucks came for them and they were taken northwestward to Wilhelmshaven itself. This was a 35-mile ride and when they reached it, Dave saw the city was pretty damaged. It lay in one of the direct bombing runs with England and many of its downtown houses and installations near the Hafen Canal had been damaged or smashed to rubble. Once they came to Wilhelmshaven they were put, on the Markstrasse, in the huge graystone barracks that had been used by the soldiers of the German 25th Army.

Those barracks were not that far from the Hauptbannhof and for the next few weeks, the Regiment was busy going up and down the autobahns and bringing large formations of Germans to the huge prisoner of war cages that were being built south of Wilhelmshaven. Those cages were being built to contain German officers in some of them and German soldiers in the others. Also, now that the war was over, a great big victory parade was organized to take place in July in Berlin. Lieutenant-General

At The End

Alan Haworth would take part in it and lead the British 1st Corps. In the meantime, though, the CAOF was created. This was the Canadian Army Of Occupation and it was made up of volunteers from the Canadian 3rd Division. It was led by Major-General Chris Vokes and its headquarters was at Bad Zwischenahn.

The Westmount Fusiliers, as the Canadian Army's elite assault unit, was stationed at Wilhelmshaven and its mission was to carry out specialized occupation duties alongside the 3rd Canadian Division for northwestern Germany. The Regiment was to patrol the autobahns and make sure there was no trouble in the huge cages being built for German officers and soldiers. Dave rode the autobahns with Bostwick and, since he spoke German and several other languages fluently, was also assigned to the Denazification Office of the Civil Affairs Bureau. This Bureau dealt with providing financial, engineering, food, labor, legal and supply services to occupied Germany.

The Denazification Office handled the investigations and background checks of suspected Nazis. This was done through interrogations and through their filling the *Denazifikations Forme No. 174*. This form had 174 questions and was made up of four equal parts: background; work history; war record; and party affiliations. The office was run by Major Ted Edwards, a tall, thin, balding lawyer, in his late thirties, from Kitchener, Ontario, and he was helped by Dave and Jim Davis, a frail, slender, blond-haired Lieutenant, in his mid-twenties, from Gaines, Manitoba. Dave's assignment in the Denazification Office was to interrogate people since his German was more fluent than the German of Major Edwards and Lieutenant Davis. Davis' job was to run the office and keep it going while Edwards studied the evidence on each person and had the final say as to whether they should be prosecuted or handed their denazification papers.

Since Dave spent so much time in the office, located on the Schillerstrasse, not far from the barracks of the Regiment, and in the jeep on the autobahns with Bostwick, he took a large single room on the Bremerstrasse, not far from the office, while Bostwick also took a single room on the Werftstrasse, close to the Regimental barracks. With his double assignment Dave spent most of his time in the office and on the autobahns and when the day was over, he went and spent his evenings at the *Bar Europa*, a large comfortable bar located on the Markstrassse, near the Hauptbannhof. Dave went to the *Bar Europa* since it was the only bar in Wilhelmshaven that had Gordon's Dry Gin. The bar had been a favorite of the officers of the German fleet and the owner seemed to have an endless supply of Gordon's Dry Gin.

Bostwick, himself, liked to hang around the *Bar Valhalla* located on the Kielerstrasse, not far from the City Hall. This was a bar Dave didn't like. He found it too small and the crowds too loud and noisy. As a result Dave spent all his evenings at the *Bar Europa*. When he got there he always sat at the same round table with four big wooden chairs at the back. This table faced the bar and the entrance and he sat alone and drank gin and bitter lemon until the curfew came on at 10.00 p.m. Then he would take a bottle with him to his single room and drink until 2.00 o'clock in the morning when he would finally fall asleep.

This went on day after day, and weeks after weeks, until it led to an incident, on Monday, August 27, 1945, that was finally going to clarify his situation with Bostwick and the Regiment.

CHAPTER 191

This incident occurred around 9.00 o'clock in the evening. At that time Dave was sitting at his usual table at the *Bar Europa* and drinking Gordon's Dry Gin. Lately the more he drank, the more he found himself cold sober in a kind of delicate and fragile way. By then Dave had drunken quite a bit and, as he looked up from his table, he saw Bostwick come in. Bostwick was with two other Company Sergeant Majors, Mike Mason of A Company and Bob Thorne of C Company. The three of them were staggering a little and went and sat at the bar where they ordered a cold pitcher of beer.

The owner, whose name was Albert Dressler, was a big burly man in his early forties. He had a thick handlebar mustache and a ruddy complexion. When he brought them the pitcher and three glasses, the three of them filled their glasses and drank them quickly and noisily. Then they filled their glasses again and as Bostwick turned from the bar and saw Dave sitting at his table at the rear, he exchanged salutes with him and said something to the other two Company Sergeant Majors. Then he got up and picked up his glass. He walked slowly and erratically toward Dave and when he reached his table, Bostwick grinned at him and said: "Ah, Captain. May I join you?"

"By all means, Sergeant Major."

Bostwick sat down heavily and, after putting his glass on the table, said: "I'm afraid I'm a bit drunk, Captain."

"I can see that, Sergeant Major."

"We had quite a run at the *Bar Valhalla* and wanted to round it out here."

The Long War

Dave didn't say anything and Bostwick said: "Fancy seeing you here, though. It's quite an honor."

"Same here."

"If I'm a bit drunk, Captain, it's because I'm celebrating my return home."

"You're leaving?"

"That's right. On the *Aquitania*."

"When?"

"Tomorrow morning."

"What are you going to do in Canada?"

Bostwick grinned.

"Enjoy the peace."

"Well, you've earned it."

"Of course."

"I must say, though. I'll miss you, Sergeant Major."

"I'll miss you too, Captain."

"Are you looking forward to going back?"

Bostwick grinned again.

"Of course. They'll be all these wonderful parades, all these great parties, and all these terrific girls."

"Somehow, from the way you say it, I don't think you'll enjoy it much, Sergeant Major."

Bostwick grinned once more.

"Ah, yes. The peace. I think it'll really be interesting."

"At least, we survived."

"Yes, Captain. We survived."

Bostwick now raised his glass and took a big sip of his beer. When he put the glass down he said: "Dieppe. Sicily. Italy. France. Germany. It was quite something."

Dave took a big sip of his gin and bitter lemon.

"I'll drink to that."

Bostwick raised his glass again and took another big sip of his beer. When he put the glass down he said: "They can't say the Canadian Army didn't do its duty, Captain."

"No. They can't, Sergeant Major."

"When it counted, we were there."

"You bet."

"When the going got really tough, the Westmount Fusiliers were there."

"We certainly were."

"That's why we're the best assault unit of the Canadian Army."

At The End

"I agree."

"And, in my opinion, the finest assault unit in the world."

"I'll buy that."

"All the boys in it were good."

"They were."

"And I did my best, Captain."

"You certainly did, Sergeant Major."

"In fact, I did pretty well, hey. For someone who was left on the porch of a church in Timmins, Ontario when he was a little boy."

Dave looked intently at Botwick.

"You were left on the porch of a church?"

"That's right."

"How come you never told me?"

"Well, you never asked."

CHAPTER 192

Bostwick then raised his glass and said: "To all the good ones. To the ones who are alive and to the ones who are dead. Good soldiers all. Fighters. Believers. Heroes. I salute you." Bostwick drank from his glass and Dave also raised his glass and took a sip of his gin. Bostwick put his glass down on the table and suddenly slid off his chair spilling beer on the table and upending one of the big wooden chairs. He just lay on the floor and as the two Company Sergeant Majors, from the bar, and a couple of middle-aged Germans, who were sitting at a table nearby, rushed to help Dave pick him up, Dave put out his right hand toward them and said to the two middle-aged Germans: "*Rühre nicht. Rühre nicht.*"

"*Warum nicht?*" the first middle-aged German asked. "This man is a friend of mine," Dave grinned. "And nobody touches a friend of mine." The two Germans shrugged and went back to their table as the two Company Sergeant Majors returned to their seats at the bar. Dave watched them all for a moment and then bent and picked up Bostwick. Dave put him over his shoulder and walked to the cash of the *Bar Europa*. He paid the owner and bought a bottle of Gordon's Dry Gin. Then Dave stepped outside on the Markstrasse near the Hauptbahnhof and put Bostwick down on the passenger seat of his jeep. Bostwick was breathing deeply and heavily and Dave walked around the jeep and put his bottle underneath the seat on the driver's side. Finally he got in and left the *Bar Europa*.

Dave drove north on the Markstrasse before turning left and then getting on the Börsenstrasse. He headed south on the Börsenstrasse and when he reached the Werftstrasse, he turned right until he came and stopped in front of a big graystone house. This house was just past a high-steepled Lutheran Church and was not far from the Peterstrasse. It was on a stretch of the Werftstrasse that had been bombed heavily and when Dave reached the big graystone house, he stopped and walked around the jeep. Dave reached for Bostwick and put him on his shoulder. He walked up the short stone staircase leading to the house and knocked on the front door. Soon a thin bespectacled gray-haired woman, who was named Frau Unger, appeared at the door and opened it to let Dave come in with Bostwick.

Dave knew the place for having picked up Bostwick at that house on a few occasions and when he stepped in, the woman walked ahead of him down a short hallway to Bostwick's room to the right of the hallway. She opened the door for him and Dave went in and lay Bostwick down on the bed. Bostwick was still breathing deeply and heavily and Frau Unger said: *"Der Feldwebel ist sehr müde."* "Yes," Dave said. "The Sergeant Major is very tired." Dave thanked Frau Unger for letting him bring Bostwick in and then left the house and walked back to his jeep. He got in and drove west on the Werfstrasse until he reached the Bremerstrasse and turned right. Dave headed north on the Bremerstrasse until he came to his own big graystone house near a park.

Dave stopped his jeep in front of that house and got out. He picked up his bottle and walked up the short stone staircase leading to the front door. Dave took out his keys and let himself into the house. His room was just past the entrance, on the right of a short hallway, and when he stepped inside, he saw the thick black curtains covering his room window were open. It was a clear star-filled moon-lit evening and when Dave came in, he saw the moonlight was coming through his window. It shone on his bed and Dave put on a small light on a table that stood, with a chair, next to a big clothes' cupboard facing the bed. This clothes' cupboard had a tall narrow mirror on each one of its two doors and those mirrors were yellowing.

Dave put down his bottle on the table and walked over to the mirrors where he looked at himself for a moment. He had always been wiry and muscular. But now he was down to skin and bones and his skin was deep-tanned and tightly-drawn over his face. Dave looked at himself in the yellowing mirrors and then turned off the light. He picked up his bottle and went and sat down on his bed. There was a small table next to his bed with a big pitcher of water and a glass and Dave sat on the bed in the moonlight and drank his gin with water. Dave drank like this until almost 2.00 o'clock in the morning. At that time he got up and went and put his tunic on the chair facing the table next to the clothes' closet. Then he came back and lay down on his bed. He was sweating and restless and when he finally fell asleep, it was close to 3.00 o'clock in the morning.

The Long War

Dave didn't sleep long. At 6.00 o'clock he was wakened up by his landlady, Frau Steiner. She was a big pleasant ruddy-faced woman, in her late fifties, and she was now walking back and forth in the kitchen and making herself breakfast. Dave stayed in bed for another hour and then went to the bathroom at the other end of the hallway, on the right, and facing the kitchen. In the bathroom there was a big pail of water in the bathtub, since there was no running water in the house, on account of the constant bombing that had taken place during the war, and Dave used some of that water to wash himself and shave. Then Dave walked back to his room and changed his uniform before leaving the house. The day was bright and sunny, with a mild warm breeze, and he got into his jeep and made a U-turn on the Bremerstrasse.

Dave drove south on the Bremerstrasse until he turned left and headed east on the Werftstrasse. He drove east for a short while until he reached Bostwick's house where he made another U-turn and came and stopped in front of it. Dave got out of his jeep and walked up to the house where he knocked on the front door. In a moment Frau Unger appeared and Dave said: *"Ist der Feldwebel in sehr zimmer?" "Nein,"* Frau Unger said. "Where is he?" Dave asked. "He's gone," Frau Unger said. "Where?" Dave said. "He said he had to take a boat home," Frau Unger said. Dave thanked Frau Unger. He walked back to his jeep and when he got in, he began driving west on the Werftstrasse.

CHAPTER 193

When he came to the Bremerstrasse Dave turned right and headed north. At the Gökerstrasse he turned left in order to get on the Bismarckstrasse. Then he drove north on the Bismarckstrasse until he reached the Hannoversche Strasse and the huge Nordhafen docks. It didn't take him long to get there and when he came to the docks, he could see the four-stack ocean liner *Aquitatania* moored at one of them. The gangplanks were down and naval sentries were guarding the liner. Dave drove to the first gangplank and stopped near it. He got out of his jeep and found out from the naval sentry some of the officers and non-commissioned officers had already gone on board.

As a matter of fact, as he was talking to the sentry, Dave could see Lieutenant Norm Moran going up the first gangplank with a Lieutenant from C Company. The *Aquitania* was due to sail at 10.00 o'clock and was taking home most of the Westmount Fusiliers as well as some soldiers from three Regiments of the 2nd Canadian Infantry Division. Those Regiments were the Royal Regiment of Canada, the Royal Hamilton Light Infantry and the Essex Scottish Regiment. The soldiers from those Regiments had remained in Germany to do occupation duties while the few soldiers from the Westmount Fusiliers who were not going home were people who, because of their skills, were considered occupation specialists. Those soldiers were still needed in the various civil administration offices. But everyone else in the Regiment was leaving.

Dave stayed near the gangplank and as he talked with the naval sentry for a while, he saw the dock was rapidly filling with wives and girlfriends and older German people who had come to see the soldiers leave. There was a feeling of loneliness and sadness on the dock and at 9.00 o'clock

The Long War

sharp, the huge door of hangar No. 14 slid open and the Westmount Fusiliers came out. They were being led by a young naval Lieutenant and some sentries and as they headed toward the gangplank where Dave was standing, Dave saw that Tom Clark's A Company was first. But there was no sign of Tom Clark. B Company then followed. The First Platoon was in the lead and when it moved closer, Dave saw some of the Big Ten. They were all talking and standing together.

Tom Bradley, who had been taken in as one of the new members, was first; next, there was Nicholas Meyer; then, Slav; and finally, Red. They were carrying their duffel bags and when they saw Dave, they straightened up and saluted him. Dave returned their salutes and as they came and stopped near the gangplank where he was standing and put down their duffel bags, Dave looked at Tom Bradley and said: "You don't want to stay here for any more wars, Tom?"

"Oh no, Captain.

"Why not?"

"I may not have seen all of this one, Captain. But what I've seen here with you was quite enough. Thank you."

"It was really something, wasn't it?"

"It sure was. Those Germans and those two forests. Boy. That was incredible."

"What are you going to do now?"

"I'm going home."

"Where's home?"

"Lawrenceville, Ontario."

"What are you going to do there?"

"I'm going to farm with my dad."

"That's it?"

"You bet. And play with my cats and dogs."

"How many cats and dogs do you have?"

"Three cats and five dogs."

"And then?"

"Then I don't know."

"Well, good luck."

Dave shook hands with him and as Bradley picked up his duffel bag and began walking up the gangplank, Dave turned to Meyer: "What about you, Nick? What are you going to do?"

"I'm going to go to Toronto and see my relatives."

"And then?"

"Then I'm going to go to Palestine and see what's going on."

"That's not a bad idea."

"As a matter of fact, could I interest you in going out there with me?"

"No. Not me."

"Why not?"

"I think I've seen enough of war."

"You could lead us out there like you did here."

"No. That'll be your job."

"You're sure?"

"I'm sure."

Dave didn't say anything and Meyer said: "I want to thank you, Captain."

"For what?"

"For what you did for me in Clermont."

"I didn't do anything."

"Sure you did. You made me fight. Instead of quit. And that I appreciate."

"It was nothing."

"No. It means a lot to me."

"I'm glad."

Dave shook hands with Meyer and as he picked up his duffel bag and also began walking up the gangplank, Dave turned to Slav: "What about you? You're also going to farm?"

"Oh yes, Captain."

"In Estevan?"

"You bet, Captain."

"You won't get bored with this?"

"Oh no. I'll also hunt and fish."

"Near the Souris River?"

"For sure."

"That's a nice way to live."

"It is. The fishing is always good on the river."

"I'm sure it is."

"It really is. Maybe you'll come and see me down there."

"Maybe I will."

Again Dave didn't say anything. Then he said: "Thank you for looking after me."

"Oh no, Captain. It's you who looked after us."

"No. It's the other way around."

"I don't think so."

"Sure it is. At any rate, I really appreciated it."

Slav nodded and Dave said: "Keep in touch."

The Long War

"I will."

Slav embraced Dave in his huge arms and as he picked his duffel bag and also went up the gangplank, Dave turned to Red. Like Dave he was only skin and bones and his face was deeply-tanned and tightly-drawn. His eyes were red and there was a cold and icy light in them. Dave looked at him and said: "So. That's the end of the line."

"You bet, Captain."

"I'm sure there's not going to be any more wars for you."

"You can say that again, Captain."

"What are you going to do now?"

"How should I know?"

"You must want to do something."

"Well, I'm not going to be a short-order cook in Vancouver. That's for sure."

"What are you going to do then?"

"I don't know. And I couldn't care less."

Dave didn't say anything and Red said: "That old man in Oldenburg. You know he set us up, don't you?"

"Red. Let it go."

"That sonofabitch really set us up!"

"Red. Turn the page."

"The bastard wanted Lang dead!"

"Red! Look at me! It's over. It's all over. Do you understand?"

"Man, the things we've seen. The things we've done. . ."

"I know. But it's over. It's all over."

Red didn't say anything for a moment but as he looked at Dave, the cold and icy light left his eyes and he suddenly looked tired. Very tired. A slight exhausted smile came on his face and he said: "Maybe you're right. Maybe it's better to turn the page."

"Trust me. It is."

"Maybe I'll go to Montreal and learn some of that *parlez-vous* for myself."

"That's not a bad idea."

"I'll live near the Regiment. That way you can get in touch with me."

"Sure."

"But if I do that. Promise me you're going to get in touch with me."

"I promise."

"You promise."

"Yes. I promise."

CHAPTER 194

Red suddenly stepped up to Dave and embraced him tightly. Then he picked up his duffel bag and walked up the gangplank. Dave stayed on the dock and watched Red get into the *Aquitania* and as he showed up at the lower railing with the other Big Ten, Dave saw the dock was now quite crowded with people. Some were kissing soldiers of the Westmount Fusiliers. A great many were running toward soldiers of the Royal Regiment of Canada, the Royal Hamilton Light Infantry and the Essex Scottish Regiment, who were now coming out of the huge shed No. 14, and embracing them. Others were waving at some of the soldiers who were already standing at the railings of the liner.

At 10.00 o'clock sharp, the gangplanks were taken out and tugboats began taking the *Aquitania* out of the Nordhafen dock. Dave stayed on the dock and watched until the *Aquitania* was out of the port and on the North Sea for its eight-day journey back to Canada. Then he walked to his jeep and left the dock. Dave drove south on the Hannoversche Strasse until he got on the Bismarckstrasse. Then he headed south on the Biskmarckstrasse until he reached the Schillerstrasse and turned left on it. Dave drove east on the Schillerstrasse until he came to the Denazification Office close to the Peterstrasse where he made a U-turn and came and stopped in front of it. At the curb Dave stepped out of his jeep and walked into the office. As usual it was full of Germans who were being interrogated by Jim Davis and who were sitting at the various desks at the entrance and busily filling the *Denazifikations Forme* No. 174.

Dave went into his office, on the right side of the entrance, and closed the door. He sat at his desk and picked up a file that had been on it for some time. Dave looked at this file for quite a while and then put it down and walked to the office of Major Ted Edwards, next to his, on his left. The door was closed and he knocked on it. "Come in," Dave heard Major Edwards say through the door. Dave opened it and saw the Major was busy reading a file and making some notes. Dave walked in and closed the door behind him. Major Edwards put the file down and as he looked at him, Dave said: "I just wanted you to know. I'm going out of town for a day or two." "Now?" the Major said. "Yes. Now," Dave said. "My God," the Major said. "We're completely swamped with work. Why don't you wait until we're less busy." "No," Dave said. "I have to go right now."

Major Edwards looked as if he was going to argue with Dave. But then he let it go. Dave had been putting in long hours at the office and he knew it wouldn't be right to refuse. As a result he reluctantly gave his approval and Dave left the office. He got into his jeep and made another U-turn. Dave turned right on the Peterstrasse and began heading south until he had left Wilhelmshaven behind. It was another bright and sunny day, with a mild breeze blowing, and Dave headed south and went through places such as Oldenburg, Oloppenburg, Lüningen, Lingen, Nordhorn and crossed into Holland at Denekamp. All along, as he headed south and then southwest, it was easy to tell where the Canadian Army had been.

In those towns and on the road, Dave went by endless smashed tanks, burnt trucks, shattered artillery pieces, wrecked planes and ruined jeeps. In Holland it was the same thing as he went through such towns as Hengelo, Apeldoorn, Zutphen, Reden, Arnhem, Nijmegen, Heesch, 'S Hertogenbosch, Bortel, Best, Eindhoven, Duizel, and until he crossed into Belgium at Grootbos. In Belgium it was almost the same thing as he drove through Antwerp, Wilrijk, Vilvoorde, and until he reached Brussels. Brussels, however, was different. A city of about 1,000,000 people, with its exotic 15th-century medieval look reflecting its Flemish, Latin and Germanic roots, it looked as if it had hardly been touched by the war. When Dave reached it around 4.00 o'clock in the afternoon, after a 280-mile ride, it was gleaming in the sunlight and showing a beauty and elegance all its own.

With its gilded City Hall, that went back all the way to the Middle Ages, its Churches, museums, parks, canals, hotels, and restaurants, it looked like a city fully caught in the whirlwind and headlong pace of daily life, and when Dave came into it from the north, he drove to the Shaarbeek district where, not that far from the Place Broukère, he turned left on the Rue Rogier and came and stopped in front of a modest, two-story, graystone house that faced a small park called Parc Edmont. Dave stepped out of his jeep and walked up the short stone staircase that led to the front door. That door had a large brass knocker on it and the number on the door was 82. Dave knocked on the door and after a short while, it opened and a frail slender man of average height, with gray hair and a thin gray mustache, stood at the entrance.

Dave looked at him and said: *"Monsieur Pierre Dumont?"*
"C'est moi."
"Vous êtes le père de Jeanne Dumont?"
"En effet."
"La fondatrice de la Ligne d'Évasion Interallié?"
"That's me."
"May I see you for a minute?"
"By all means."

CHAPTER 195

Monsieur Dumont stepped back to let Dave in. Then he closed the door and led Dave to a modest living-room to the left of the front door. There was a latticed window in the living-room giving out onto the street and the sunlight was pouring through this window and shining and gleaming on the sparse furniture. In the middle of this living-room stood a square glass dining-room table between two small sofas facing each other. There were also waist-high bookshelves on the wall facing the living-room entrance and two floor lamps, one on each side of the bookshelves. Dave saw that most of the books on the shelves dealt with history and the French language.

When they were in the living-room Monsieur Dumont motioned for Dave to sit in the sofa closest to the window while he sat on the other. Dave went and sat in that sofa and when Monsieur Dumont had settled in the other one facing him, Dave looked at him and said: "I'm with the Occupation Forces in Wilhelmshaven. We investigate all kinds of people and when I checked your daughter's file, I saw she was arrested by the Gestapo on June 20, 1944. But that's all there is in your daughter's file. Can you tell me what happened to her?"

"May I ask why you were checking on my daughter?"

"Certainly. I escaped from Colditz. And she helped me cross into Spain in order to get to England."

Monsieur Dumont looked at Dave for a moment.

"You don't know what happened to my daughter?"

"No. Sir."

"She was killed one week after she was captured, on June 27, 1944."

"Why?"

"They wanted her to talk. She didn't."

"How did Jeanne get caught in the first place."

"Sheer bad luck."

"What do you mean?"

"She was at the wrong place at the wrong time."

"What does that mean?"

"The Allies were moving in on Paris. Rol Tanguy and the communists were desperate to show they could fight the Germans. So they shot a German Colonel and his French mistress in the Montparnasse Métro Station. Jeanne was bringing a radio transmitter to Paris from the south for a courier who had gone to pieces from the strain of the previous months. When the communists shot the German Colonel the métro station was surrounded immediately and Jeanne couldn't get out. They checked every passenger and, naturally, when they found the radio transmitter, they took her to the Gestapo headquarters at 74 Avenue Foch and began questioning her."

"I'm not surprised she didn't talk."

"Me neither."

Dave looked at Monsieur Dumont and he went on: "You see, even though she was 25 at the time, my daughter looked much younger. Jeanne passed herself off as Julie Mortain, a student from Tours. Jeanne had several cover stories like that. The Gestapo didn't realize she was the leader of an escape line. But the fact she carried a transmitter worried them. And when she didn't talk, they handed her over to their best henchman."

"I have a feeling I know who that is."

"Who?"

"Gilbert Montreuil."

"How do you know that?"

"It's a long story."

"How?"

"Let's just say I had the opportunity to get to know this gentleman."

"Anyway, this Gilbert Montreuil, or *Le Beau Gilles* as he is called, absolutely wanted to find out why she was carrying a transmitter and who she was."

"The man can be very persistent."

"He certainly can. And he was. He beat her. Her plunged her under water. He took out her toenails and cut the back of her feet. And still she wouldn't talk. Finally, during the night of the 27th when she wouldn't talk, he smashed her again and again against her bed. By then she was dying and when he kept on yelling at her to find out who she was, she whispered to him: 'You want to know who I am?' 'Yes!' Montreuil yelled.

'Come closer,' Jeanne whispered. Montreuil leaned close to her ear and she whispered: 'I am *France.*' Montreuil went mad when he heard this and began punching and kicking her until she was dead."

Dave bent a little toward Monsieur Dumont and said: "How do you know this?"

"They later arrested one of Montreuil's accomplices in Senlis. He was a tall balding man with a large scar on the right side of his face. His name was Laurent Leclercq and he was present the whole time Montreuil tortured Jeanne. He confessed everything and was then shot by the FTP."

Dave looked very fixedly at Monsieur Dumont and said: "Go on."

"Anyway, after Montreuil killed Jeanne, Leclercq said it was terrible what went on in the underground chamber. Montreuil was just screaming and howling like an enraged animal. He was crying and still punching and hitting Jeanne, even though she was dead, and wouldn't let Leclercq or anyone else touch her or come near her body. Finally, around 4.00 o'clock in the morning, Montreuil arranged with some SS friends of his to take Jeanne's body to the main cellar where they sprayed it with gasoline and burnt it until there was nothing left. Then Leclercq said one of the SS took the bones and the ashes with him and buried them on the outskirts of Paris so no one could find them."

Dave was still looking very fixedly at Monsieur Dumont. There was a dark and terrible light in his eyes and he said: "I'll find him. And kill him. And his girlfriend. And his parents. And grandparents. I'll kill them all!"

"You think I didn't think about that, Monsieur, when I found out! That's all I thought about!"

"And?"

"Gilbert Montreuil *is* dead! He was killed in Soissons on August 23, 1944 by a strafing Allied plane as he was trying to escape to Germany in a truck with a group of SS."

"The bastard! The lousy stinking bastard!"

"You can say that again, Monsieur."

"How could he do that? How can anyone do that to another human being?"

"You see, that's the strange thing about Gilbert Montreuil."

"What?"

"Well, when I found out what he had done to my daughter, and that he was dead, I hated him so much I decided to kill his whole family."

"And?"

"Then I made an incredible discovery."

"What discovery?"

At The End

"Gilbert Montreuil *has* no family. He was born of a prostitute and a pimp. His mother was a drug addict and his father a violent alcoholic. They both beat him constantly. His mother died of a drug overdose. His father was stabbed to death in a quarrel with another pimp. And Montreuil was handed over from prostitute and pimp to prostitute and pimp, all of them with drug and alcohol problems."

Monsieur Dumont stopped talking and Dave just sat in the living-room. He looked down at the floor and didn't say anything for a long time. Finally, when he straightened up, Monsieur Dumont looked at him and said: "May I ask what was your relation with my daughter?"

"I wanted to fight for her. But she wouldn't let me."

"Why?"

"She just wouldn't."

"Why not?"

"She said this wasn't what I had to do."

"Jeanne very rarely made mistakes."

"I wish she had."

"Why?"

"I would have given my life to fight for her."

"You would?"

"Yes. And I would have asked her to marry me, if she'd let me."

CHAPTER 196

Monsieur Dumont nodded and Dave stood up from the sofa. He thanked him for seeing him and stepped out of the living-room. Dave left the house and slowly crossed the street. He went and sat on one of the benches facing the small park. It was now close to 5.00 o'clock in the afternoon and the sun was turning into a deep smoldering gold settling on the houses and on top of the trees surrounding the park. There were many young children running around and playing in the park and Dave sat on his bench and looked up at the sky. He was breathing heavily and angrily wiped some tears from his eyes. Dave just sat on his bench and after a while felt something touch his feet.

Dave looked down and saw that it was a small white soccer ball for children. A little dark-haired girl, in a white dress, was standing shyly in front of him and saying: "Can I have my ball?" "Of course," Dave forced a smile at her and pushed the ball toward her with his foot. The little dark-haired girl grabbed her ball and ran back to play happily and excitedly with her friends. Dave sat on his bench and watched them play for a while. Then he got up and walked back slowly toward his jeep. Dave stepped in and turned the jeep around. He drove west on the Rue Rogier until, near the Place de Bruckère, he turned right and headed north out of the Schaarbeek district. In no time Dave left Brussels behind and drove back past Vilvoorde, Mechelen, Wilrijk and Antwerp.

Dave crossed the Dutch frontier around 8.00 o'clock in the evening and kept on heading northeast through the same towns he had gone through before. He drove through Duizel, Eindhoven, Best, Bortel, 'S Hertogenbosch, Heesch, Cuijk, Nijmegen, Arnhem, Reden, Zutphen, Apeldoorn, Hengelo, and finally crossed the German frontier at Denekamp

At The End

around 11.00 p.m. Although night had fallen Dave was surprised to see how much traffic there was on the road. There were many jeeps, cars and trucks, and Dave drove through Nordhhorn, Lingen, Lüningen, Oldenburg before reaching Wilhelmshaven around 2.00 o'clock in the morning. The streets in Wilhemshaven were deserted and when Dave pulled up in front of his rooming house on the Bremerstrasse, he went in and immediately went to bed.

Dave was exhausted and after he had undressed and lain on top of his bed, he kept on staring at the darkness in his room and couldn't sleep. Dave finally fell asleep around 4.00 o'clock in the morning and when he woke up, it was almost noon. It was another bright and sunny day, with a nice soft breeze blowing, and, after he had washed and shaved, Dave got dressed and left for the office. Dave stopped by the *Bar Europa* to have a coffee and a couple of hard-boiled eggs and when he walked into his office, he saw it was full of young, middle-aged and elderly German couples. Dave dropped by Major Edwards' office to let him know he was back and then headed for his office where he closed the door behind him.

Dave went and sat at his desk and as he looked at some of the new files that had been put on it, he could hear Jim Davis through the door asking: *"Bist du, varst du, Nazi parteigenosse?"* As usual, the answers were always the same. *"Nein. Niemals war ich ein Nazi." "Ich niemals glaubte an es." "Aber ich hatte es zu tun." "Ich war nur den befehlen folge leistend."* No one had ever been a Nazi. None of them had ever believed in it. They had had to do it. Or they had been merely following orders. This was how it went. Dave listened to Davis for a while and then left his office to go and sit at a desk at the entrance with him and help him with the interrogations. Dave did this for the rest of the day and for the remainder of the week and on Friday afternoon, August 31, 1945, around 4.00 o'clock in the afternoon, he walked into the office of Major Ted Edwards and told him he was leaving.

"What!" the Major said. "I'm leaving," Dave said. "You can't do that!" the Major said. "We've far too much work!" "I'm leaving," Dave said. "I've been away for six years. That's long enough." Major Edwards tried hard to persuade Dave to stay. But he didn't succeed. The *Empress Of Australia* was leaving on Monday and taking home soldiers from three Regiments of the Canadian 3rd Infantry Division. Those Regiments were the Royal Winnipeg Rifles, the Queen's Own Rifles of Canada and the Regina Rifle Regiment. Dave had booked himself on that ocean liner since, for this journey, it was landing in Montreal instead of Halifax. On top of that, given the fact Dave had more than enough points for demobilization, there was little the Major could do.

As a result, the Major thanked Dave for the work he had done at the Denazification Office and wished him luck back home. Dave officially ended his duties at the office that Friday afternoon and paid his landlady, Frau Steiner, an additional month of rent for the room he was letting go. Dave then spent the weekend getting ready to leave and at 8.00 o'clock on Monday morning, he boarded the *Empress Of Australia*. This was one of the five liners that had come to Halifax in 1939 to take them over to England and when he came on board, Dave saw he had been assigned to the Forward Troop Deck. This was the A Deck and he had been given a private officer's cabin on the starboard side.

This cabin was spacious and luxurious and it had a big porthole, a wide bunk on the right side, a large metal cupboard past the bunk, a riveted small round table and chairs in the middle of it, a bathroom and shower on the left side, and wall-to-wall carpeting. Dave put his duffel bag in the large metal cupboard and when he walked outside to the railing, he saw the *Empress Of Australia* was moored in the same dock where the *Aquitania* had been. Soldiers from the three Regiments were still boarding the ship and at 10.00 o'clock sharp, the ship's foghorn sounded and the gangplanks were removed. Tugboats began taking the *Empress Of Australia* out of the Nordhafen dock and into the North Sea for the eight-day journey back to Canada.

CHAPTER 197

Dave stayed at the railing of the *Empress Of Australia* until Wilhelmshaven began fading in the distance. In the early morning sunlight its low-slung skyline had a burning, coppery look and then the town slowly disappeared on the horizon as the ship began getting deeper into the North Sea and heading toward the open waters of the Atlantic. Dave stayed at the railing for some time and then left and went back to his cabin. Once inside Dave opened the metal locker next to his bunk and took out a bottle of Gordon's Dry Gin from his duffel bag. To be on the safe side Dave had bought three from the owner of the *Bar Europa* as well as a large jar of pickled hard-boiled eggs.

Now Dave opened the first bottle and sat down in one of the riveted metal chairs. He began drinking his gin with water but after a while had to stop. The clear and sober feeling he used to get in a kind of delicate and fragile way was gone and his stomach tightened up and couldn't take any more gin. Dave put his bottle back in his duffel bag and went wandering through the ship. He walked on the promenade decks and went to look at some of the luxurious sitting-rooms. But he was edgy. Dave didn't know any of the officers, NCOs and soldiers on the ship and all of them seemed younger than him. Dave also borrowed a couple of British novels from the ship's library. But he couldn't get interested in reading them. He was very tense and restless and ended up spending the next couple of days in his cabin.

Some of the officers he met on board seemed eager to talk to him. However, this didn't appeal to him either. As a result Dave spent most of his time in his cabin trying to drink his gin, which he could no longer do, and eating some hard-boiled eggs. He never went to the luxurious officers' dining-rooms and didn't bother to try and meet anyone. He just sat in his cabin or stood looking out of the big porthole. At night he lay in his bunk restless and sweaty and by the third day of the journey just stayed there since he didn't feel very well. For a long time now he hadn't been able to eat anything except hard-boiled eggs and he began having incredibly severe cramps and stomach pains. Dave thought of seeing a ship's doctor but decided against it. He just lay in his bunk bent in two and holding on tightly against the pain and on the fourth day of the journey, around 3.00 o'clock in the morning, he just couldn't take it anymore and left his cabin and walked to the stern of the ship.

It was a beautiful night out. The stars shone high and clear in the sky. There was a nice cool breeze from the sea. The air smelled clean. And there was no one in the stern area. Absolutely no one. Dave leaned on the railing and looked at the huge white wake the ship was making. After a while Dave leaned even closer on the railing and thought: Go on. Do it. Why don't you do it? All the good ones are gone anyway. Do I need to name names? Jack Gabriel. Leroy Robinson. Jan Mieteck. Gianni Gennaro. Eric Lang. Jim Higgins. Bob Addams. Steve Mitchell. Mike Messina. Jeanne Dumont. Barbara Bradford. And more. So many more. That makes for quite a Roll Call, doesn't it?. Yes, Sir. Quite a Roll Call.

So, go on, Dave thought. Why don't you do it? You've got nothing to live for anyway. You know everything you love has been taken away from you. The war. You're sick. You can't stop drinking. You can't even eat. So what's the point? Why go on? A man can only carry on for so long. And then you get tired. And used up. And you can't go on anymore. Although, in your case, he thought, that's not strictly true. You've got someone. You've got Nina. And she loves you. Ah, yes. Nina, he thought. Nina needs and is entitled to someone who'll give her children, a house, a future. In other words, she needs someone normal. And I'm not normal. Never have been. And never will be. So much for having someone. And that's nothing. Oh no. There's much more.

Take the Army, for instance, Dave thought. Do you remember how you went in? You hated it and only went in to put an end to the things you're facing now. It's ironic, isn't it? The chicken sure have come home to roost, haven't they? You went in hating it and got good at it and ended up loving it. How about that for a change? You loved it because you ended up meeting people you loved and who loved you. And the reason you loved it so much was because it ended up being your home. The only thing you've ever had in this life, let's face it, you could truly say belonged to you. And let's not kid ourselves, he thought. You enjoyed the assaults, the battles,

At The End

taking care of the men. Even if it meant death. Oh yes. Even that. That was worth the price.

But now, Dave thought. The war's over. The Army's being taken away from you. Or, rather, you no longer have the strength to go on and stay with it. Every man has his limit. And you've been operating way beyond yours for quite some time now. Yes. Quite some time. And you've reached a point where you can't do it. You just can't. So what do you have? he thought. Nothing. That's what you have. The war's over. You're out of the Army. You're not well. And you're not like other people. So what are you going to go home to? he thought. Tell me. What are you going to look forward to? Dave stepped to the railing and put his right leg over it. From the stern it seemed a long way to the water. He was looking down at the huge white wake of the ship and was trembling and shaking all over.

Something inside of him was saying: "Go on! *Go on*! JUMP!" But something else, deeper, better, stronger, was also saying: "NO! NO! DON'T JUMP!" Dave just stood shaking and trembling all over, with his right leg over the railing, and then threw himself back down on the stern and began running and staggering toward his cabin.

CHAPTER 198

Dave ran along the stern until he got inside the ship and made for his cabin on the A Deck. When he reached that deck Dave ran along the passageway until he reached his cabin and went in. He closed and locked the door behind him and went and threw himself on his bunk on his back as the memories of all he had kept hidden within him and in his heart for so long came surging up and washed over him, and as he faced it all finally. *He had been seven years-old and living in a log cabin in the Charlotte Islands with his mother, Anne Decarie, a slim and dark-haired French-Canadian beauty, and his stepfather, Tom Bolton, a tall and blond-haired forest ranger, with nice manners and an easy smile, who had been very good to him.*

That morning, in early August, Dave had woken at first light when a black crow had been cawing loudly outside the cabin. Dave had gotten up and dressed in order to go out and see why the black crow was cawing so loudly. At any rate Dave liked to get up early and go wandering in the woods outside the cabin when it was fresh and cool. That morning he had crossed the dirt road since he could see the black crow perched high in a tree across it. He had just gotten through the tree line when he had turned and seen someone coming up the road. It was Bill Lindsay, his father, an American railwayman from Stirling, Minnesota, who had a strong wandering streak in him and who could be just as charming when he was sober as he was mean when he was drunk.

His father, his mother had told Dave, was drunk quite often. When Dave was born he hadn't wanted to marry her and by the time Dave was five, his mother had gotten tired of his running around with other women, his wild mood swings, his never-ending restlessness, and had left him.

At The End

She had moved out of Montreal with Dave in order to go to Vancouver to try and make a new life for herself before heading out to the Charlotte Islands where she had met and married Tom. Now his father was coming up the road and he had a gun in his hand. Dave watched him from behind some trees and his father walked straight into the log cabin. Dave heard two shots and then his father came out of the log cabin. He had a wild and crazed look in his eyes and said in an odd and cooing voice: "Davie. Davie. Where are you?"

Dave had moved back further into the tree line and his father had screamed suddenly, "Davie!", and had raised his gun and blown his brains out. Dave had moved even further into the tree line and for the next four or five days had seen people moving through the woods and calling: "David. David." Dave had kept on moving to avoid them and on the evening of the fifth day, they had found him near some trees nearly unconscious and delirious. They had flown him to Vancouver where several doctors and nurses had come to talk to him and take care of him. Dave hadn't talked to any of them. What was the use? They had talked among themselves and Dave had heard them say words like Traumatic Syndrome and Psychological Damage and after a while, they had put him in a juvenile home.

Dave hadn't spoken for three years and when, suddenly, he had begun talking again, they had placed him in a foster home. Dave had stayed there for two years and then there had been a series of other foster homes. In those homes the people had told him they loved him but what they loved, really, as a result of what had happened to him, was the Government check that came for them every month. By the time he was fifteen Dave had been to quite a few foster homes and schools. He didn't do well in school since the people there had nothing in common with him and didn't really understand him. But he had discovered reading and languages. Dave loved reading history, even when he truly didn't understand it, and learning languages. He loved the roll and flow of languages and how each one spoke to him in a different way.

Each language, Dave found out, had a beauty and greatness that made you rise above pain and suffering and gave you an understanding of the world that was truly extraordinary. But he also found out, unfortunately, that reading and languages didn't make you survive in this world. For this you needed money. And you needed people who gave you the time to study and get educated so you could make the money. Those two things, however, Dave didn't have. So he hit the road and traveled in boxcars, buses and trucks from one end of the country to the other. And it was on one of those boxcar runs he met the two people who were going to have such an influence on his life: Jack Gabriel and Leroy Robinson. Jack Gabriel was a full-blooded Mohawk Indian from the Kahnawake Reserve who told him about Tecumseh and the Indian ways and the Spirit of the Longhouse.

Leroy Robinson was a black middle-aged former middleweight fighter who taught him how to box, fight dirty and play the guitar. Together the three of them traveled back and forth across the country and survived with Leroy playing the guitar, Jack doing Indian dances and Dave collecting the money they made. It wasn't such a bad life and they were doing pretty well until that fateful day in early June when Dave was nineteen. That time they were coming into Sydney, Nova Scotia, from a boxcar run from Vancouver and had been warned by other boxcar riders there might be railway policemen in the yards since the railway companies now felt there were too many people riding boxcars. As a result they had looked carefully before jumping out of their boxcar in the yards and were walking alongside the cars before crossing the yards and heading toward the city of Sydney itself.

Leroy Robinson was in the lead. Jack Gabriel was behind him. And Dave came last. They had just begun walking alongside the cars when they suddenly heard: "Hey!" Jack and Dave who happened to be walking between two cars, and at a fair distance from Leroy since he was in the lead, suddenly disappeared between those two cars while Leroy was caught further ahead alongside one of the cars. A big muscular railway policeman with a billy stick stepped out from behind one of the cars and began walking toward Leroy. He was slapping his stick in his hand and saying: "You bum! What are you doing riding one of the boxcars?" "I wasn't riding anything, Sir," Leroy said. "Just walking along the yards." "Like hell, you were!" the railway policeman said and stepped up to Leroy and hit him hard in the arm.

"Sir, take it easy," Leroy said and stepped back a little as he rubbed his arm. "You bum! You lousy stinking bum!" the railway policeman said and stepped in and hit Leroy hard again in the arm. Leroy grinned at the policeman and as he raised his clenched fists, the policeman said: "Oh. So that's how you want to play it." He rushed Leroy and began hitting him with his stick. As he began doing this Jack, who was hiding with Dave between two cars, suddenly rushed out toward the policeman only to have another policeman step from behind a car with a rifle as Jack ran by him and shoot him in the back. By then several policemen were running from everywhere in the yards and surrounding Leroy and the policeman who had hit him and Jack who was lying face down on the ground and not moving.

At The End

When he saw this Dave got underneath one of the cars and ran back past several cars until he was far enough from the policemen to be able to race across the yards in a crouching run and disappear into the narrow streets of Sydney. Dave stayed at the home of the sister of one of the boxcar riders and the next morning when he came out, he saw the headline of one of the Sydney newspapers was: TWO BOXCAR RIDERS KILLED TRYING TO ASSAULT RAILWAY POLICEMAN. *The other papers all had similar headlines. Dave stayed in the home of that sister for two weeks and then was given enough money to take a bus back to Vancouver. When he got to that city Dave began doing odd jobs to stay alive such as delivering groceries, working in a car wash and being a night cleaner in one of the downtown buildings.*

Dave did this for three years and spent all his free time reading and learning languages. This was the only thing he liked to do until he became so tired of those low-paying and dead-end jobs he finally decided on what he was going to do from now on. Dave would travel across the country robbing banks and spending all his free time doing what he really liked to do: read and learn languages. And, since Leroy Robinson had taught him how to get into cars and start them while Jack Gabriel had taught him how to disguise himself so no one could recognize him, it had led to his taking that Ford on that Monday morning, September 11, 1939, disguising himself and walking into that bank in order to pull off that robbery. This is what had happened and all of these things came back now.

They all washed over Dave and he accepted them for what they were. He just faced them and looked at them fully and squarely and suddenly felt free as if a thousand pounds had lifted from his shoulders. All the anger, tension and uncertainty Dave had felt in the past were gone and he closed his eyes and fell into a deep and exhausted sleep.

CHAPTER 199

Dave lay on his bunk and slept. And now his body seemed so tired from all the tension and uncertainty he had felt for so long, he just slept and slept. His body seemed to crave that sleep and he stayed in his bunk and didn't move. Dave only got up occasionally to have some water and eat a few hard-boiled eggs. But mostly he slept. This went on for almost four days and at first Dave just lay bent in two and having incredible stomach cramps and pain. His face became pink and swollen and at times it seemed the riveted table and chairs were moving around in his cabin. Dave could see huge helmeted close-jawed German faces near him and hear the mad pounding and hammering of mortars, 88s, MG 34s, 42s and the wild rumble of words such as: *"Idioten!" "Bastarden!" "Mördernen!"*

Dave kept on tossing and turning in his bunk and after two or three days, the incredible stomach cramps and pains began lessening a little and then disappeared. The swelling in his face began to go down and by the fourth day he stretched in his bunk and let go. Red had taught him that in Ortona when he had held his hand. You can only hang on for so long. But then you have to let go. You have to learn to let go. Dave just stretched now in his bunk and was looking at a train making a long slow turn. The train was losing speed and coming and stopping at a small wooden railway station. The station was painted red and the people there were dressed in bright and vivid colors. They were all smiling and, alongside the train, there was a tall and slim girl walking toward him.

The girl's veil was up and she was dressed in a magnificent white satin gown with a long white silky train. Her hair was blonde and she was also smiling at him. Dave returned her smile and then found himself away from her and the people and the station and on that train he had

At The End

been looking at. They were moving across vast and sun-filled wheat fields swaying and rippling in the wind. At times the sun disappeared behind clouds and enormous shadows raced across the fields only to vanish when the sun broke out of the clouds and the fields were caught in the sunlight again. There was a nice cool breeze blowing through those vast and sun-filled fields and in the distance you could see sun-swept and snow-covered lavender mountains. They were always moving toward them and then Dave opened his eyes and found himself lying on his back in his bunk.

Dave put on the bunk light and saw it was 4.00 o'clock in the morning, on Tuesday, September 11, 1945. This was the eight and final day of their journey and Dave got up from his bunk and went into his bathroom. Dave washed and shaved and, although he felt a little weak, left his cabin and went to one of the luxurious dining-rooms for the first time since he had been on the ship. Dave felt hungry and sat at one of the deserted tables and ordered some scrambled eggs, toasts and coffee. Normally those dining-rooms would be closed at this hour. But in appreciation for what the Canadian soldiers had done overseas they were kept open all night during the whole trip. When he was served his food Dave ate slowly and carefully and then got up and left the dining-room.

Dave walked outside on the starboard side of the promenade deck in the Forward Troop Deck. This was the A Deck and Dave went and stood at the railing. It was now close to 5.00 o'clock in the morning and the waters of the St. Lawrence were turning dark-blue and silver in the first light before sunrise. The shore was beginning to come out of the darkness and streetlights glowed faintly in the pale dawn. The horizon was slashed with wild streaks of pink and orange and Dave stood at the railing and looked at the river that was now taking on those colors. He was leaning on the railing when he heard a slightly-accented English voice behind him say: "Pretty impressive, hey, Captain?" Dave turned and saw it was Pierre Delorme who exchanged salutes with him and then came and stood on his left. "I'll say," Dave said. "But how come you're on this boat?"

"Oh, I got tired of being an Occupation Translator. I felt it was time to come home."

"You too?"

"You bet."

"What are you going to do now?"

"Do you remember the books Lang wanted to write?"

"Sure."

"I think I'm going to try and write them."

"That's not a bad idea."

The Long War

"I don't necessarily agree with all he said. But I agree with a lot of it ."

"Me too."

Delorme looked at Dave and then said: "Why don't you write?"

"Are you crazy?"

"I'm dead serious. Why don't you write about what we did?"

"Do you realize what kind of life that will mean?"

"Sure. But sometimes you don't have a choice."

"I've just finished an impossible job. And now you want me to take on an even more impossible one."

"That's right. You're the man for it."

"I don't think so. And, even if I did, no one would believe it."

"It doesn't matter what people believe. It matters that you did."

"Why don't you do it? You're good with words."

"But not like you. And besides. You're the one who led us. Not me."

"What has this got to do with it?"

"Everything. A book like that has to be written by the one who knew. No one else."

Dave didn't say anything and Delorme said: "Sometimes a country produces a gifted son who can inspire others. When you have that gift, you can't say no."

"And you think that's me."

"You bet."

"Why do you want to make my life so miserable?"

"I don't. It's just something a person has to do sometimes."

"Well, I don't want to do it."

"Maybe not. But you just have to."

"Why?"

"Someone has to do it."

"Why?"

"To make us remember how good we were."

"When we were soldiers?"

"That's right."

"Fighting for a better world?"

"That's it."

"Well, I'll see."

CHAPTER 200

Dave and Delorme stayed at the railing and watched the shore of that magnificent, mysterious, majestic, much-maligned, much-ignored and much-misunderstood country slip by. After a while the sun rose and the river ignited in a clear pristine gold. Montreal was looming in the distance and the wild streaks of pink and orange on the horizon now widened and seeped into the dark-blue and silver of the St. Lawrence. They were slowly coming to the massive structure of the blue-green Jacques Cartier Bridge and as they sailed under it, Montreal now rose in front of them and loomed darkly against the orange sky. As proud, vain and imperious as ever it towered over the river, and the mountain, skyscrapers, churches and buildings gleamed in the early morning sunlight.

In the harbor ocean liners and freighters rode whitely at anchor. Further on the Victoria Bridge also gleamed in the sunlight and in the distance Dave saw a seagull soaring swiftly in the morning sky. It climbed and climbed until it seemed to hang in the sunrise, so white, stark and magnificent, before it turned swiftly and made for the greenery of St. Helen's Island on the port side of the ship. Then they were slowly sailing toward one of the downtown docks as tugboats came and began steering the ship toward one of those docks. Even that early in the morning Dave could see there were quite a few people on the dock and when they finally entered it and the lines were cast, it was almost 7.00 o'clock in the morning. By then there were quite a few other officers and soldiers standing at the railing and waving and smiling at some of the people on the dock.

Dave told Delorme he would go and get his duffel bag and they should meet here at the railing. That way they would leave together. Delorme nodded and Dave left and walked back to his cabin. Inside he opened his

The Long War

metal cupboard and took out his duffel bag. He began making for the door and then stopped and put down his bag. Dave opened it and took out the three bottles of Gordon's Dry Gin as well as the large jar of pickled hard-boiled eggs. He went to the bathroom with those bottles and the large jar and emptied the bottles in the sink. Then he put them and the large jar in the waste basket underneath the sink. Finally he walked back to his duffel bag and closed it. Then Dave left his cabin and headed back to the railing where Delorme was waiting for him with his own duffel bag.

The two of them left the promenade deck and went down the Forward Troop Deck until they got to one of the gangplanks. They walked down the gangplank until they came on the dock and began moving away from the ship. There were now quite a few young women and older people on the dock. There were also some children. The women were yelling, jumping up and down, and rushing into the arms of officers and soldiers. Some women were crying. Others were kissing the officers and soldiers madly. Others were looking at them and not saying a word. The children were tugging at their mothers' skirts and hiding shyly behind them. The older people were just shaking hands and embracing the officers and soldiers. Dave and Delorme had to walk through all these people until they were able to find a taxi on the dock to take them to downtown Montreal.

Dave and Delorme put their duffel bags in the trunk of the taxi. Then they climbed in and the taxi left. They soon got on St. Lawrence Boulevard before they turned left on Dorchester Boulevard. They drove west on the Boulevard until they came to Dominion Square and to the corner of Peel Street. At that corner Dave told the driver to stop and paid him. They got out and took their duffel bags. They put them down on the sidewalk, not far from Peel Street, and Dave turned to Delorme who stood on his right and said: "Well, it sure was a long war."

"It was."

"But we survived.

"We did."

"And now we're going to live."

"You bet."

"Another long war."

"That's it."

Dave didn't say anything for a moment and then said: "You take care of yourself."

"You too."

"Remember. *Loyalty always. Not a step back.*"

"For sure."

"But one last thing."

"What?"

"Did you finally find out how the French are being treated in the world?"

"I did."

"And?"

"Let's just say it's a little bit more complicated than I thought."

"In what way?"

"Let's just say it all goes back to *The Peoples' Question*."

"It always does."

"You're telling me."

"And?"

"I believe time and decency will solve it."

"Just like that."

"No. Not just like that. But it will."

"Even though the world may get more complicated and difficult to handle?"

"Even though that may be the case."

Dave nodded and then said: "Where are you going now?"

"Home."

"Where is home?"

"In the East End."

"I see."

"And you?"

"The other way."

Dave then stepped up to Delorme and embraced him. Delorme exchanged salutes with him again and picked up his duffel bag. He began heading eastward on Dorchester Boulevard and Dave watched him go for a while. Then he picked up his own duffel bag and began walking westward across Dominion Square into the clear, bright and dazzling light of day.